# Her Father's House

# Her Father's House

*Emma Sinclair*

PIATKUS

First published in Great Britain in 1996 by
Judy Piatkus (Publishers) Ltd of
5 Windmill Street, London W1

**The moral right of the author has been asserted**

*A catalogue record for this book is available
from the British Library*

ISBN 0-7499-0318-X

Set in 11/12 pt Times by
Create Publishing Services
Printed and bound in Great Britain by
Mackays of Chatham Plc Ltd

# Prologue

The black Citroën was making little progress along a road choked with refugees.

Inside the car, Genevieve Veryan stared out at the weary, sad and frightened families, some pushing handcarts, others carrying bundles, all, like herself and her parents, fleeing before the approaching German Army. She was ten years of age, bewildered bored and sad; bewildered because everything had happened so quickly, bored because the journey seemed endless, and sad because in their haste to leave Paris she had been forced to leave behind all her most precious things. "Essentials only, Jennie," her father had said, handing her a small suitcase to pack her clothes. "Now hurry up." That had been yesterday afternoon and now it was late-morning, their slow progress forced down to walking pace, jammed as they were between people and vehicles. Her father had said they were going on a ship to England. She had vague memories of England and a large house by the sea. The sea was the place to be on this hot June day; even with the windows lowered it was stifling inside the car. "How much longer, Papa?" she asked wearily.

"Soon, darling, soon." Auburn-haired, with pale aesthetic features, Charles Veryan lit a cigarette and eased the vehicle along in first gear, his mind racing anxiously. Would there be a ship, or boat, or anything that would float? Would they and the remaining British troops heading for St Nazaire find another Dunkirk? That miracle had been two weeks ago; could they expect a second one? Seated beside him, his French wife was quiet, too quiet. He saw how ashen-faced she was and, trying not to show his fear for her, placed a comforting hand on her arm. "It's going to be all right, darling. How are you feeling now?"

Weak and drained, Monique felt like death, but forced a smile. "I am well," she lied.

He knew she lied. Those large brown eyes concealed nothing. It was

1

incredible, he thought, that after all she had been through, Monique could still look so hauntingly beautiful. Christ! What a time to lose a baby, and after five months of pregnancy too. Had it not been for this private tragedy in a world of tragedies, his wife and daughter would have been safe in Cornwall by now. The nuns at the hospital had been marvellous, the doctor sharp.

"Monsieur Veryan, there must be no more babies. Your wife hae-morrhaged badly and there were dangerous complications. She has told me how much you want a son. Be thankful for your daughter."

Monique had been grief-stricken and he had wept silently. But there was no time now for grief. During her three weeks in hospital, Holland, Belgium and France had fallen and the Germans were marching on Paris. Yesterday he had brought her out of hospital and here they were heading for the only port left open to them.

Hearing an approaching aircraft, Jennie leaned out of the window watching curiously as it dived towards them. The car stopped. Her father shouted to her to get out. The next thing she knew he was hurling her into a ditch, the weight of his body pressing down on her as bullets thudded into the ground. Shocked and terrified, Jennie managed to turn her head and look up. The plane had circled and was diving again. She bit into her fist, choking on a scream as bullets spewed for the second time.

At last the plane veered off and flew away. For one moment there was a deathly silence then the air was shattered with screams and wails of grief. She felt her father's protective weight lifting from her and slowly stood up, her eyes rivetted on a woman in a white blouse who lay staring up at the sky. The white blouse was turning red. Even as her young eyes took in the horror, her mother was kneeling beside the woman. Monique shook her head, crossed herself then staggered along the line desperate to help, but without the means or strength. All about them people were lying on the ground, some moving slightly, others quite still. Slowly the survivors staggered to their feet, gathered their families to them once more and tried to move on. A screaming woman clutched a dead child to her. Jennie trembled at the sight, then saw her father approaching, half-carrying her protesting mother.

"There's nothing you can do, and you're too damned weak even to try."

"We must do something," cried Monique.

Charles stared about him in a state of emotional turmoil. Of course he should do something, but his first duty was to his own wife and child. The Stuker might return. They had to get to St Nazaire before the port was cut off. "Back to the car."

"Can't we take the hurt people with us, Papa?"

Charles wasn't listening to Jennie; he was staring at the Citroën in disbelief. Riddled with bullets, steam hissed from its engine and water poured from the radiator on to the road. The car was now quite useless. Trying to hide his mounting fear, he bent his tall thin frame into the car, retrieved one large and one small suitcase, placed his brown trilby back on his head and handed Jennie her own case, trying to sound light of heart. "That's it, sweetheart. Can you manage this, while I take the other?" So saying he placed a supporting arm about Monique and carried the heavy case in the other hand.

How long they walked, Jennie could no longer tell. Her legs staggered and the small case became heavier and heavier. Her mother looked so ill, she thought, and her father desperate as he half-carried her along. Suddenly she heard the plane returning. There was panic as people searched for cover where there was none. The Stuker dived, spat more bullets into the soft column of humanity, then flew off. Again the shocked silence was followed by harrowing screams.

"Bloody murdering bastards!" cried Charles, as he picked up his wife and child and all three staggered on once again. They were not going to make it, he thought grimly. Monique could not go on. Even if the Stukers didn't pick them off they would never reach St Nazaire now. He heard the sound of an army truck trying to force its way along and turned. As he did so Monique collapsed in his arms. He knelt in the road holding her tightly, almost weeping from sheer despair while Jennie placed her arms about her mother and burst into tears. The truck stopped and the driver, an English corporal, climbed out. He helped Charles with Monique, lifting her into the rear of the crowded lorry where the soldiers shuffled about making room for the English family. There was no room for suitcases. Car gone, cases gone, all that they owned, now gone, Charles Veryan lifted Jennie into the truck, thanked the troops, sank to the floor with his daughter in his arms and sighed with relief as the vehicle rumbled on.

Under air attack as they approached, St Nazaire was crowded with British troops looking for anything that would float them back to England. In this chaos, small boats in the harbour picked off men and moved away. Somehow the Veryans ended up on an old tug which took them three miles out to sea where a passenger liner, pressed into war service and now painted battleship grey, lay at anchor in the roads.

One of the soldiers with them laughed. "Blimey, looks like we're going 'ome in style."

Charles smiled at his wife and daughter. A few hours ago he could never have envisaged this marvellous moment. The air attack was over as, on a clear sunny afternoon, he and his family were helped on board the *Lancastria*. Decks, cabins, wardrooms, state rooms and holds were already filled with deeply relieved troops and civilians. Someone gave Jennie a child's life jacket, but there were none left for her parents. Seeing this, a young soldier handed Monique his, saying, "I shan't need it. I'm a strong swimmer." Monique refused to take it from him but the soldier insisted, pushing it into her arms then walking away to be lost among the crowds.

On the crowded deck Jennie leaned over the rail watching, fascinated, as more tugs ferried troops out to the liner. She turned her gaze to the open sea, thinking how calm and blue it was. Then the little boats stopped coming and it seemed the ship would leave. Nothing happened. By four o'clock her father's anxiety had turned to outright anger. "Damn it, there must be at least five thousand on board. Far more than this ship is built to take. What's the hold up? We're sitting ducks out here."

No sooner had he spoken than Jennie heard the sound she had learned brought death and terror. Dark against the blue sky, the Stuker streaked towards them in a steep dive. The bomb struck, the ship lurched. A second bomb exploded close to them, filling the deck with flame and smoke. She heard screams as men died about her, then there was fire and she was screaming also. Her father, his arm ablaze, burst through the flames, grabbed her and pulled her from the danger. She screamed again, seeing him burn. Someone threw a jacket over him to smother the fire. The vessel started to list. A voice on the tannoy gave the order to: "Abandon ship". Somehow, in all the shock and horror of that moment, soldiers helped Jennie and her parents along the crowded deck where women and children were assembled and lifeboats were being swung out. When Monique was safely in one, a soldier picked up Jennie and lowered her into anxious waiting arms. Charles refused to follow, saying that any available places should go to the seriously wounded men. Seeing how badly burned he was, the crew practically forced him in then gave the order to: "Lower away".

With the ship now listing to starboard, launching was proving difficult. In terror of the height, Jennie clung to her mother as, slowly and jerkily, the lifeboat was lowered. Suddenly it lurched, stopped, hung precariously in mid-air then snapped from its davit, hurling everyone into the sea below.

Screaming, Jennie fell through the air and hit the water so hard that it crushed the breath from her body. Then she was coughing, spluttering, lashing out desperately in a sea of flame. An arm came about her and she was dragged from the fire, but oil was everywhere. Men were jumping from the ship now; the water was cold, the thick oil impossible to swim through. People were choking on it. She heard her father's soothing voice as he swam with her towards her unconscious mother who was drifting face upwards. Then Jennie was being pushed on to the keel of the upturned lifeboat and clinging to it for dear life. A soldier appeared beside her, gasped as he hauled himself on to the boat, made certain she was secure then turned to help her father. But Charles slipped back into the water. Jennie cried out in alarm. "Don't worry," said the soldier, holding her tightly. "Yer dad's 'elping yer mum." Reaching out, he pulled Monique over the keel then helped Charles also. More men climbed on until there was no more room. The unlucky ones swam to other lifeboats or, exhausted and choking on oil-filled lungs, sank beneath the calm sea. Almost at once, Jennie vomitted up the oil she had swallowed.

All too aware now of the pain from his burns, Charles clung desperately to his wife, at the same time keeping a careful eye on Jennie. He blamed himself for their plight. In March he had arranged for Monique and Jennie to return to England. But Monique had refused to believe that France would fall and her arguments, tears and sheer obduracy had forced him to relent, telling himself that if the situation became grave there would be time enough to get his family out. How wrong he had been. If they lived through this it would owe more to chance than judgement. If they lived through this he would never allow his instinct or authority to be challenged again.

"Look! Oh, Christ, look!" Turning at the shout, Jennie stared in disbelief. The great liner had rolled over and was sinking. Across the water she could hear the sounds of men trapped and injured in the holds, men who had thought themselves homeward bound, fighting instead for their very lives as the waters rose over them. Then the *Lancastria* was gone and the only cries came from those struggling in the sea.

Shocked, and shivering with cold, Jennie leaned back against the soldier and lost all sense of time. Perhaps she slept, she wasn't sure, but a fit of coughing wracked her small frame and brought her back to the world. All about them was sea. She had never dreamed there could be so much of it. Something was happening. The people on the boat were shouting and waving. She turned her head to see a destroyer heading towards them.

# Part One

# Chapter One

Florence Veryan gazed from the window of her chauffeur-driven Phantom III Rolls-Royce, seeing not the suburbs of Plymouth but the face of her son as he lay in the hospital bed. Anguished at the memory of his pain, she reminded herself how lucky she was to have him at all after the disaster; how lucky she was to have all three of them.

At sixty-one, Florence was still a good-looking woman, her fair complexion and blue eyes enhanced by discreetly applied make-up; her grey hair curled gently beneath a small-brimmed hat which matched her sensible cream linen suit. Tearing her thoughts away from her son, she turned her attention to her grandchild and daughter-in-law sitting so tense and still beside her. Yes, she had been very lucky. Understanding their trauma, she tried to make light conversation in a desperate effort to bring mother and child back to life once more.

"It isn't far to Portlyn. Thank goodness we had a tankful of petrol. After this the Rolls will stay in the garage. Our chauffeur has been called up anyway. Philip will get an allowance for the Riley, he's a magistrate and in charge of local civil defence, but we can hardly use that for personal matters." She smiled and looked at Jennie who was seated beyond her mother at the far window. "And so we've decided to bring out the trap from the old coach house. Would you like that, Jennie darling? Pony and trap should be much more fun than a boring old car."

The child's large brown eyes flickered and a smile, the first smile in days, lifted the pale face into a radiance which tugged at Florence's heart. "We have a four-year-old pony called Kelly, a lovely little mare. Do you ride, Jennie?" The head shook solemnly from side to side. "No? Then I'll teach you." Glancing at Monique, who had sat with vacant expression since leaving the hospital, Florence wished she would say something. "They can do wonders these days. Charles will be in excellent hands."

Leaning back against soft upholstery, Jennie stared out at the tall Cornish hedgerows rushing past. She wished she could see over the top. Instead her gaze fell on the wild flowers and cow parsley that grew in abundant profusion along the verges. It had a hypnotising effect; her eyelids became heavy and soon she was drifting into half-sleep ... the half-sleep which brought back the horror yet again: explosions, searing flame, her father bursting through the flames, his body ablaze. "Papa ... Papa..."

"Genevieve". The soft voice broke into the nightmare. "Wake up, *ma chérie.*" Monique held her trembling daughter close and stroked her forehead gently.

Looking up into dark eyes set in a lovely pale face, Jennie reached out and touched her mother's hair, thinking how lank and dull it looked when it had always been a shining hazel colour. It was the oil, of course, the terrible clinging oil which no amount of washing could remove. Her own hair was just the same. She could even smell it, but then that smell had been in her nostrils for days. How many days? The destroyer had plucked them from the lifeboat then later had transferred them to another large ship which was also crowded with survivors. Dodging the wolfpacks, this other ship had finally landed them at Plymouth where, suffering from shock and exposure, they had spent three days in hospital. It was there that they discovered how serious her father's condition really was. He would need specialised treatment for a long time, the doctor had said.

Glancing at her grandmother, Jennie thought she was sleeping. Of this kind lady who smelt of scent she remembered very little. All she really did remember was the apartment in Paris where she had left her bedroom filled with old and much loved dolls, books, her paints and paint brushes, ballet shoes and the Japanese fan. Were German soldiers in the room now, destroying the things that were so precious to her? And what of her schoolfriends and the kind old concierge who had told her so many stories? Where were they? What would happen to them all?

For all that her eyes had closed, Florence was too worried to sleep. If only Monique would say something instead of sitting in that tense and silent manner. It was all such a contrast to the woman she and her husband Philip had encountered the minute word reached them. Then Monique had lain in a hospital bed, her words tumbling out quickly in a mixture of French and English as she tried to describe the horror. But for her account, they would have known nothing of the disaster since the press and the BBC had made no mention of the *Lancastria.* It seemed unbelievable that so many had perished just days after the miracle of Dunkirk, yet no word of it had reached the British people. Churchill's hand was behind it, she knew that. In this grave hour, people needed to know about miracles, not tragedies. Just why her own family had been caught up in this one was still a mystery to her. As a diplomat, Charles could not leave France until the last minute, but his wife and child had had every opportunity to return weeks ago when she had written urging them to come home. Like all the French, however, Monique could be very stubborn at times. Charles should have put his foot down, but he would often bend to his wife's strong will. This time the consequences of such weakness had been catastrophic.

"It was kind of you to bring clothes for us," Monique said suddenly. Her English was flawless, her accent still strong.

Florence smiled, relieved that the dresses fitted after such a last-minute rush around. "Yesterday at the hospital we were told that Charles was being transferred to Roehampton. I was very surprised to see him still in his bed this morning. Had he known, Philip would have come with me to say goodbye to him again. What happened?"

"Roehampton is full after Dunkirk and..." Monique's voice trailed off. On the rescue ship she had watched as a doctor had administered morphine and tried to tend the burns as best he could. The memory of what she had seen still horrified her. Now she recalled the anguish of kissing Charles goodbye that morning, of knowing his pain, of sitting by his bed holding his hand until it was time for them to part. "Today he will go to a place called East Grinstead."

"That's in Sussex." Florence turned to Monique, patted her hand comfortingly and thought it small wonder that Charles had been bowled over by this art student at that fateful party on the Left Bank. She smiled to herself, recalling the shock-waves which had run through the family when Charles, the heir to a baronetcy and a Cornish estate, had informed them that he wanted to marry a French girl from St Cloud.

"But who is she? What is her background? You know what's at stake. Can she take it on?"

Charles had been adamant that his beloved Monique could take on anything. She had no pedigree to speak of and hardly knew England but she was a natural lady, a woman of great charm, and would adapt quite easily to her future role as chatelaine of Trevellan. Nothing would stop him, nothing. He loved her and intended to marry her. After much heated argument, he had won the day.

In the event only Florence and her husband had travelled to Paris for the small wedding and, whatever her misgivings, she soon warmed to her new daughter-in-law. It was not so with Charles's sister, however. On learning that Monique Gravier had been born to a restaurant owner, orphaned in childhood, raised by a maiden aunt, and, worst of all sins, educated in a Roman Catholic convent, Laura Veryan

11

Willoughby marvelled that her parents could be so foolish as to admit a Catholic foreigner into an English Protestant family whose pedigree could be traced back to Domesday. In the twelve years since the marriage, Laura had never met Monique and never forgiven Charles for marrying her. But now that Laura was divorced and living at Trevellan once more, the two women would soon come face to face. Florence dreaded the moment.

At a turn in the road, Jennie had her first glimpse of the rugged Cornish coastline stretching away into the distance. Against a pale blue sky the sea glimmered in varying shades of turquoise, deepening to a dark blue horizon. The Rolls eased its way down through the steep and twisting lanes of Portlyn, before climbing on to the upper road once more. Looking over the stone guard-wall to the harbour below, Jennie's eyes took in the rows of slate-roofed, whitewashed cottages. Fishing boats rested on mud; fishermen mended nets on the harbour wall, beyond which a blue trawler headed out to sea. There was a flash of pink from the thrift-covered cliffs on either side of the village then the sight was gone as they headed into a wooded valley. Jennie's eyes softened. After the horror, such beauty, such peace. The car climbed uphill again and ran alongside a castellated stone wall until it turned through a large gateway. As the wheels of the Rolls crunched along a gravelled drive the girl leaned forward and gasped at the sight of the house that stood before her, the house where she had been born.

Built in 1569, Trevellan was an E-shaped Tudor manor house and had been the home of the Veryan family for nearly four hundred years. A Royalist stronghold during the Civil War, it and the Veryans had suffered greatly under Cromwell, but endured to become prosperous once more after the Restoration. Now, in the morning light, the mullioned windows of the East Front seemed like so many dark eyes against the sunwashed stone.

The Rolls came to a halt, the chauffeur climbed out and opened the door for Lady Veryan to alight. As Florence put her well-shod foot on to the path, two black labradors came racing from the house to bound around her in high excitement. She patted them fondly, saying, "See now, here's Jennie. You must both look after her." Tails still wagging, the bitches walked slowly towards the girl. Seeing Jennie's hesitancy, Florence said, "It's all right. They're very gentle. The larger one is Portia and the other is her daughter, Rosalind."

Jennie bent to Portia, smiling as the bitch nuzzled her hand then let it slide across the wide forehead and along the sleek back. Jealous of this attention, Rosalind pushed her mother aside to be fussed also. Jennie laughed with delight.

Florence felt her shoulders fall with relief. It seemed that two labradors could help her grand-daughter through the trauma of her terrible ordeal more than honeyed words, false jollity or expressions of sympathy. "Rosalind's the naughty one, I'm afraid, so keep your bedroom door shut or she'll be in there nosing into everything." With that she turned, wondering why the large oak door was open yet her butler was not there to greet them.

The panelled entrance hall was dominated by a large medieval oak chest. There were rooms to right and left, but Florence walked on, out of the sixteenth century and into the eighteenth, to a much larger hall where a cantilevered staircase soared upwards in a light Georgian interior. This had once been the courtyard of the original building and was typical of the mixed styles introduced to Trevellan over the centuries. Here she paused, staring in disbelief at the flurry of activity all about her. The floor was covered in tea chests and crates. Two estate workers were carrying a gilt-framed painting across the hallway towards the cellar stairs; from below them came the sound of hammering. Somewhere, out of Florence's vision, a man with a "fine arts" accent seemed to be supervising the proceedings. Eyes glinting with anger she retraced her steps, returned to the sixteenth century and entered what had once been the Great Hall of the house and was now the main dining room.

Following curiously, Jennie found herself in an oak-panelled room, with very large stone-mullioned windows. The great fireplace was littered with straw and old newspapers as an auburn-haired woman in a dark blue dress packed the family's crested Sèvres dinner service which now covered a long rosewood dining table. Beside her hovered the butler, looking uncertain as the woman spoke in haughty tones.

"I don't care how they do it, Keynes, that painting has got to be removed to the cellar."

"But, Madam, it is quite out of the question. The narrow passageway will simply not allow for it. It cannot be manoeuvred around the corners. It has stood on the staircase wall for many years. I fear its removal may cause the very damage you wish to avoid."

"That's absolutely correct, Keynes," Florence said in icy tones. "Laura, I thought we had agreed to forget this nonsense?"

Turning in surprise, Laura's blue eyes widened and slowly she rose to her feet. Tall and very slim, with finely chiselled features and a porcelain complexion, she smiled weakly, faint lines fanning out from the corners of her eyes. "Good heavens, you're here already. I had no idea."

Walking towards Monique who had now entered the room, she extended a cold cheek without making contact. "And so we meet at last. I am Laura." Glancing down at Jennie and thinking what a mess

13

the girl looked in the yellow frilly dress Florence had purchased for her, Laura placed a finger under the small defiant chin and lifted it slightly. "And you are Genevieve, only everyone calls you Jennie. What a shame. You favour your mother in looks, I see."

The remark was left hanging in the air as she turned to Florence and said, "I can't understand it. They can tell us August Bank Holiday is cancelled but nothing of the *Lancastria* being sunk." She gazed about the dining room and sighed. "Look at this mess. I have to apologise for the chaos, Monique, but now that we're well and truly at war, we must expect these things, I suppose."

For one dumbfounded moment, Monique just stared at her, then said thinly, "You do not yet know what chaos truly is."

Laura's smooth brow puckered slightly but she did not shift her imperious gaze from Monique's eyes. "Now that France has so shamefully divided and fallen, leaving us to stand alone, I've no doubt we soon will. But we shall see it through. Have no fear."

The brown eyes glinted dangerously. "It is said in France that England will be over-run within two weeks."

"I suppose they would say that," said Laura with infuriating calm, "but we British are made of stronger steel. Frankly, I'm more worried about the threat of schoolboys over-running us. And that is why I'm crating the paintings and storing them in the cellar."

Monique gave a harsh laugh. "By crating them you only make it easier for the Germans to ship them home. They will be most grateful."

Appalled at the way this first meeting was going, Florence raised a calming hand. "The French Army fought valiantly, Laura. What has happened is a great tragedy for France. After all that Monique and Jennie have been through, we must thank God they are safe and with us. It is surely a miracle that they are." Even as she spoke it dawned on her that Laura had achieved what the doctors could not – she had snapped Monique out of her trauma at last. The French woman was now fighting mad.

Laura sighed and waved a vague hand in the air. "Yes, well, of course you've been through a terrible ordeal, but I simply don't understand why you waited so long before leaving France in the first place." Her tone implied that Charles and Monique had brought it all upon themselves, for like her parents she knew nothing about the miscarriage.

In an effort to turn the conversation, Florence gazed about the room, saying, "Why have you removed the paintings when I had made it clear that I was against it? Really, Laura, it ill becomes you to do such a thing when you knew I wouldn't be here to stop you."

"That was why, darling," said Laura. "It had to be done. I wished to spare you distress, that's all."

14

"How bare it's all going to look, and all so unnecessary. Cornwall won't be bombed and the school doesn't move in until September. You'll leave us the paintings in the drawing room, I hope, otherwise we'll be staring at blank walls."

"The Opies and the Lely? Don't be silly, Mummy, of course not. They must all be stored out of harm's way. The Reynolds has already been removed from the Green Drawing Room. Don't worry, everything's in good hands and being taken care of by an art dealer, who knows just what to do."

Florence sighed. "Oh dear, all our ancestors relegated to the cellars. They'll spin in their graves, poor old things." She turned to Monique. "A boys' school from Kent is to be billeted on us in September."

As she listened, Jennie stared up in amazement. Not so long ago she and her parents had been fighting for their lives in a burning sea. Yet now the talk was of paintings and schoolboys. She felt like Alice, having just stumbled on the Mad Hatter's tea party. Suddenly her grandmother was looking down at her and saying, "I'm afraid you may find it all rather lonely, my dear. Still, your cousin Clive will be home next month. He's at Winchester College. I do hope you'll be good friends."

"Oh, Mummy," sighed Laura with growing impatience. "Clive is fourteen, for goodness' sake."

At this Florence gave up, and since her maid had vanished, turned on her heel and said, "Come along, Monique and Jennie. I'll show you your rooms. You must both be feeling very tired and will want to rest before luncheon. I can't imagine where Rosa is." As she led the way up the elegant blue-carpeted stairway, she felt a growing sense of doom. This was not going to be the easiest of times. Laura would always be Laura, selfish and determined to have her own way. She had been especially difficult over the matter of bedrooms.

"But you can't possibly give Clive's room to Jennie," Laura had stated when it was decided that being placed next-door to her parents would be better for the girl, who would probably have nightmares over her experience. "He'll be furious."

Florence however had put her foot down hard, banishing the unsuspecting Clive to the old nursery suite in the north wing, saying, "He'll be better off. After all, it includes a large bedroom, the school room and a small sitting room. Most boys of his age would jump at the chance of having their own suite."

"He'll hate it and feel insulted," Laura had snapped. "It's freezing up there too. Nanny always had to keep fires going even in the summer. Besides, it's so far away from everything."

"Exactly. Which is why it's quite wrong for Jennie. She would be

15

alone and frightened." There the matter had rested, and Laura had had been forced to accept defeat.

In her bedroom, Jennie's eyes drifted dismally from the William Morris wallpaper to heavy green velvet curtains and antique furniture. Only the bed was modern, with a mahogany headboard and a green satin counterpane. Walking across to the window, she gazed out through small panes on to a bright sunlit lawn then lifted her eyes beyond the trees to make out a thin ribbon of blue. At that moment, Portia and Rosalind came bounding into sight, making soft growling sounds as they played and chased each other across the freshly mown grass.

"Maman, may I go and play with the dogs?"

Monique said that she might and watched as the child ran back down the stairs, dodging boxes and workmen before chasing out through the open door and on to the drive. "She will not get lost?"

Florence shook her head. "What she needs now is to play in bright sunshine and forget."


The Ninth Baronet did not put in an appearance until just before luncheon when he greeted his daughter-in-law and grand-daughter with the same distant reserve he showed to all guests. Tall and thin, a man of sixty-four years, his grey and thinning hair, gaunt face and pale blue eyes, spoke of a once handsome and aesthetic-looking man, as Charles was now.

"Forgive me for not being here to greet you, Monique. The RAF want to place some sort of transmitter on my land and surround it with Nissen huts. The army have already wired off paths and beaches. Lethic Sands is mined, Florence. Be sure the dogs don't go near it. All nonsense, of course. All the Germans have to do is cross twenty-one miles of Channel from Calais to Dover."

They were in the large and elegant drawing room which, like the vast hall, was part of the later building. The furniture was mainly inlaid walnut or satinwood; a concert grand stood in the tall window bay; on the piano were silver-framed photographs of Veryans past and present, sprinkled liberally with a few royal visitors. The only thing now adorning the walls was a large gilt-framed mirror. Philip walked to the drinks table and poured himself a scotch and soda. "Soldiers are guarding the harbour entrance, would you believe? Would anyone care for a drink while I'm about it?"

Seated on a rose brocade sofa, Florence and Monique accepted dry sherry while Jennie was offered sparkling lemonade. She watched as the light from the window danced among the tiny bubbles, and thought

16

how stern her grandfather was. Yesterday, at the hospital, he had looked awkward and lost, as though wishing himself elsewhere. Aunt Laura didn't want them here, that much was obvious. Didn't he want them either? Was that why he seemed so angry? And didn't he care about her father? He knew he was all burned, yet hadn't asked how he was.

Taking up his favourite stance before the Adam fireplace, Philip's face was heavy with anxiety but because of his repressed nature he still could not bring himself to speak about the son he loved so deeply, hiding instead behind lighter problems. "Hope to God Laura knows what she's doing." He drained his glass and only Florence could tell, by the quickness of his drinking and the strain in his voice, what he was really going through. "I take it that this school understands they're only having the north and part of the east wings?"

Florence turned to Monique. "The Allendale School had already evacuated but it didn't work out so they're re-locating to the Headland Hotel. Of course the hotel couldn't possibly accommodate all five hundred boys and staff, so we're having the fifth and sixth-form pupils, just to sleep. Lessons and meals will be taken at the hotel. At least, that's the plan. I hope it works out all right." She relaxed back against the sofa and placed a hand to her brow in a vain effort to rub away the headache which had started earlier that day. "Philip dear, shouldn't we invite this art dealer to luncheon?"

As though awakening from deep thought, he started slightly. "What? Oh ... no ... no. Laura's arranged something. Apparently he wants to catch the late-afternoon train to London and has no time to spare." Suddenly he turned to Monique and said, "Have you heard anything from Roehampton yet?"

Monique met the bright, piercing eyes steadily. She had always found her father-in-law intimidating and knew that he wished his son had married an Englishwoman from his own background. Better still, an Englishwoman who could give his son an heir. Could this really be Charles's father? The man she had married was the perfect gentleman, kind and considerate of others, passionate too beneath that correct manner of his. People soon fell under the spell of his good looks and easy charm, she foremost among them. But now, staring into those piercing, almost accusing eyes, she asked herself if Philip's attitude was so unexpected? With the leaders of her country in disarray and, in her opinion, letting down the whole French nation which, in turn, had let down the British which, in turn, had been forced to abandon France, was it any wonder that this proud man was looking at her in such a manner? He was waiting for an answer.

"Charles was still in Plymouth when we left. He is going to East

17

Grinstead today, not Roehampton. He will have skin grafting operations down his right side and along the arm and wrist."

Skin grafts! Philip looked away and lapsed into silence. Was it really true that his son, his dear golden son, graced with good looks and a fine mind, was now so horribly mutilated that his body must be rebuilt? The anguish was made more poignant by knowing he had missed a last chance of visiting Charles. Instead, the precious moments had been spent with military personnel. God, it made him want to strike someone.

Monique was clenching and unclenching her fists without being aware of the fact. "I am told that wonders can be done these days..." How could burned flesh ever be made whole again? She looked at Philip's expression and her thoughts jumped to the young soldier who had insisted on giving her his life jacket. The English were a strange people, a Puritan people, and yet this ordinary soldier with a rough London accent had behaved with age-old chivalry to a foreign woman he had never met before. Had that chivalry cost him his life? The thought haunted her and would for the rest of her days.

Since the dining room was out of the question, luncheon was served in the small breakfast room where sunlight streamed through the windows, stabbing off knives and forks set on white damask linen. There the family sat down to fresh crab salad, with new potatoes from the kitchen garden, strawberries from their fields and cream from the dairy at Home Farm, followed by coffee, cheese and biscuits.

"Enjoy the cream while you can," said Laura, "There won't be much of it about from now on." She paused then smiled. "Ironic isn't it that the war will actually be good for this estate. I shall miss my coffee and cigarettes though. Have you seen the rations, Mummy? Goodness knows how town dwellers will cope."

Florence tensed at her daughter's seemingly heartless remarks in the wake of all that had happened. Worse was to come, however.

"What I still don't understand is why you waited so long before leaving Paris?" said Philip, glaring across the table at Monique.

In no mood to discuss the loss of her baby with anyone, much less this arrogant man, Monique murmured something about staying with Charles because he needed her.

Laura smiled thinly and gave her sister-in-law a strange, almost pitying, look. "Goodness, such loyalty. Are men worth it? I know a good many who wouldn't think twice about cheating on their wives. But you'd never dream it to look at them."

An awkward silence followed these bitter words. Everyone knew that John Willoughby had left Laura, who was not an heiress, for a woman who was.

18

"But why St Nazaire?" Philip was asking. "It's miles from Paris."

Florence sighed with exasperation. "They had no other choice, dear. It was hardly a Cook's Tour. Now enough. Poor Monique has been through a great deal and doesn't need to be questioned in this manner."

Philip grunted and pushed away his plate. "Nevertheless, you damned well should have got out when you had the chance instead of leaving everything to the last minute. If you had then Charles might have made very different arrangements for himself and would not now be lying in hospital with agonising burns."

"Philip!" exclaimed Florence in horror.

It was too much. These past days Monique had been stonily unmoved but now she began to tremble. Her mind filled with the sights and sounds of families being machine-gunned, of screaming men trapped in burning holds, of drowning men, of men dying in many different ways, and one who had given away his life jacket, probably dying also. She thought of her baby son dying before he had known life, scrambled to her feet and fled the room, to be followed by a deeply concerned Florence.

Jennie rushed after them, pausing only to look back at her grandfather and shout: "Maman came out of hospital the day before we left. She's been very ill." Leaving two shocked people sitting at the table, she ran out into the hall. Halfway up the stairs she found her mother hunched over, weeping, and being comforted by her grandmother.

Florence bent and stroked the smeared head, murmuring, "I'm so sorry, my dear. You must forgive Philip. He's been in such a state these past few days that I don't think he really knows what he's doing or saying any more. Come on. A good long sleep is what you need." Gently she raised up her daughter-in-law then turned to see Jennie staring at them with large frightened eyes. "Don't worry, darling. Mummy is very tired, that's all. I'm sure you are too. So now you're both going to have a nice long rest and, later, I'll take you to the cove."

Feeling Monique's trembling body against her own, Florence led her to the large bedroom which was always kept for Charles and his wife, drew the heavy curtains then took the young woman's hands into her own, saying, "Really, I could kill the silly man. Now rest, and leave Jennie to me." With that, she closed the door, took Jennie to her room then walked back down the stairs to deal with her husband.

Monique lay back on the four poster bed, and looked up at the ornately worked canopy. It was a miracle surely that all three of them had survived when thousands had not. How many thousands? The ship had been so full. She thought of Charles, her wonderful, darling Charles, who was now scarred for life. It was her fault. She should have gone with Jennie in March when she had been well, leaving him free to manoeuvre without the encumbrance of a wife and child. Philip was quite right and had merely said out loud what everyone was thinking. She would never forgive herself.

Poor darling Charles! Her mind journeyed back to that small apartment on the Left Bank where Maddie Veryan had thrown one of her many parties. The room had been packed with fellow students from the Ecole des Beaux Arts, when in had walked this tall, attractive Englishman with charm, eloquence and perfect manners. In Paris for a short holiday and persuaded by his cousin, Maddie, to attend her party, he had stood, a fish out of water, in correct grey suit and sober tie while Monique had quietly fallen in love with him. Her senior by four years and a junior diplomat from Whitehall, he offered the sophistication, security, protection and warmth which she had craved and never found. After their marriage, she made the transition from gauche student to young diplomat's wife with comparative ease and, blissfully happy, came to understand and accept the strange ways of the English, save for their cuisine.

Insisting that his son and heir be born at Trevellan, in accordance with family tradition, Charles had shown nothing of the disappointment he must have felt when, in this very bed, she had given birth to a girl. "She's adorable," he had said, rocking his daughter in his arms. "Like a perfect rosebud. And there will be plenty of time for sons to come along."

But in the years that followed, when they had moved between Belgium, Holland, London and Paris, Monique had suffered five miscarriages. This had taken its toll both physically and emotionally, leaving her grieving, tired and unable to stand for long hours at diplomatic receptions. In the end, she became the invisible wife, staying at home when she should have stood by Charles. She had failed him in that and failed him also by being incapable of doing what all other Veryan women had done: produce a male heir. Was she to be the only failure? Idiot! It only took one to end a dynasty. That was another thing no one would say to her face, that the Veryans felt they were paying dearly for Charles's insistence on marrying a French girl from no background when he should have married an upper-class English brood mare.

Now there was war and she would have to live with this family day in and day out. One day she would be chatelaine here. No wonder her sister-in-law disliked her so much. It was hard on Laura, first born but unable to inherit. One could almost feel sorry for the woman, but Monique did not. Turning on her side, she felt exhaustion sweeping over her once more. What did Laura or the Veryans matter? The

Germans were coming and with them horrors that the English could not know about. Perhaps it was God's will that the son she had carried was no more. This was not the time to bring another child into the world.

Jennie opened her window; the smell of grass and sea filled her nostrils. If only she could go to the cove right now with her grandmother. The sunshine beckoned and she longed to be out in it. Maman had cried, and that was alarming, as alarming as the day they had carried her into an ambulance and rushed her off to hospital. No one had yet explained what made Maman ill. Jennie wanted her to be well again, to be calm and comforting as she used to be. Feeling lost and a little frightened, Jennie walked across to a large bookcase, selected a book by Richmal Crompton and lay on her bed reading about William Brown.

Later, when Florence looked in, she found her grand-daughter sleeping soundly, her face stained with tears.

The walk to the cove was by way of a path which led through the old kitchen gardens until it reached fern-carpeted woods beyond. As it descended into the valley, the path became enclosed by verdant banks topped by trees bent inland from winter gales. Then the banks flattened, the way broadened and the cove lay ahead. Jennie could hear the sea long before she and her grandmother came upon it in the clear light of late-afternoon. The tide was well out, and the unthreatening ribbon of blue laced with white surf. Fat herring gulls waded in small rivulets which carved gulleys in the sand and seaweed-covered barnacles clung to exposed rocks. Furze-covered cliffs rose either side of the cove but only one was accessible, its track climbing from the beach up and over the hill.

Making her way down five wooden steps, Florence stood on the beach, lifted her face to the sun and listened to the cries of gulls, thankful that this dangerous rocky place remained free of wartime protection. Flinging a cashmere cardigan around her shoulders, she walked slowly along the damp, pebbly sand, watching as Jennie ran ahead with Portia and Rosalind. The bitches bounded about the girl then turned their attention to chasing seagulls before finding a piece of driftwood, gripping it with their teeth as they tugged it from each other in play.

A small crab moved away from Jennie's shadow as she reached into a rock pool to touch a pink urchin. The urchin closed lightly over her fingers. She laughed with delight, all memories of recent horrors suddenly replaced by a vague recollection of being in this place before. Thoughtfully she ran back to her grandmother. "What happened to the boat? I remember a boat."

21

Florence looked surprised. Two years was a lifetime when one was only ten. "Fancy you remembering that. You went sailing in *The Rose* with your father and grandfather that last summer when you were here. I'll take you home the other way then you can see it. Tomorrow, I think we'll start those riding lessons."

At that moment Jennie's attention was drawn to a kestrel hovering above the cliff. Fascinated, she watched it swerve across the cove then circle higher and higher, the sunlight filtering through its outstretched wings. Like a thing suspended by unseen wires, it just hung there in the sky. Her eyes darted back to the cliffs as a dark figure appeared against the light. Whoever it was held out an arm. She heard the sound of tiny bells and saw something trailing from the kestrel's legs as it swooped down towards the outstretched hand. Then it and the dark figure moved away and out of her sight.

Florence was tired. It had been quite a day and the telephone had rung constantly as worried friends wished to be reassured that Charles and his family were out of France. She had left Monique talking to Maddie who had spent most of the afternoon trying to get through from London. Maddie would be here tomorrow, and Florence thanked God for it. Monique needed her old friend right now. "Time we were leaving, my dear." Halfway up the cliff path she paused and, a shade breathless, turned to her grand-daughter. "You must never come to the cove alone, Jennie. It can be very dangerous. People have been trapped and swept away. Never ever come here alone."

Furze along the cliff edge gave a false sense of security, but where the undergrowth thinned out to rocky ground, the sheer drop was alarming and always made Florence feel a little dizzy. Then they were over the top with views of the beautiful coast outlined clearly for miles. In the distance, a bank of cloud darkened the sea and a ribbon of gold shimmered on the rain-threatened horizon. At last they were gazing down on Portlyn, nestling in a valley. Evening sun slanted across the embankment on the far side of the village, lifting shrubs that clung there to a bright clear green; it washed over the white and grey cottages and bathed the scene in a soft amber light. Gulls screamed from chimney tops, lobster pots covered the harbour wall, and a black saloon car snaked up through twisting narrow lanes until it reached the upper road. Jennie watched until it moved out of sight then followed her grandmother down to an inlet where a small stone quay formed a private mooring.

Surveying the thirty-foot gaff-rigged yacht, now covered in tarpaulin, Florence said sadly, "There she is, *The Rose*. I'm afraid she'll spend the war in Watson's Boatyard. The boathouse only holds a dinghy."

The boathouse itself was built into the cliff. Above it, standing proud of the rock, was a stone wall with a bow window which overhung the quay. Climbing a steep flight of steps, Florence reached above the lintel for the key, unlocked the door and urged Jennie into a small room which smelt dank and musty. Dried flowers cheered the stone hearth and shabby leather armchairs stood either side of it. Dominating the centre of the room was a round table covered with a baize cloth. On the stone floor were two brightly coloured rugs. Drawn at once to the view, Jennie sank on to the window seat and gazed out at the sea. "I like this house."

Florence smiled. "So do I. I can make tea in the kitchenette without ringing for Keynes or Rosa, I can read and watch the sea, just enjoy my own company. But that's our special secret, Jennie."

Jennie stared up at her curiously. "Are you frightened in the big house then?"

Frowning, Florence shook her head. "No, darling. Why? Are you?"

"No." Better to lie than to appear babyish. In truth, though, Jennie dreaded the night to come.

Florence sank down beside her on the window seat and felt a deep sense of relief. This little outing had been more than successful. The tense, frightened child of the morning had now changed beyond all belief.

Before returning home they took a last look at the yacht Sir Philip had bought in 1927. *The Rose* had been his pride and joy. Now Florence found herself wondering if he and Charles would ever sail it again. The thought of England being swallowed up in the dark and terrible shadow now sweeping all Europe, sent a cold dread through her which knotted her stomach muscles and filled her mouth with a bitter taste.

Maddie descended on them the following day, a Junoesque woman with the Veryan auburn hair, her strange flowing garments covering an unwieldy figure, her moon face crumpling into tears as she and Monique embraced warmly. Monique lapsed into French as she explained all that had happened and neither could believe that German soldiers now dominated Paris where once they had spent such happy times together. But never one to dwell on woe, Maddie produced a case filled with sketch pads, watercolour paper and tubes of paints and declared they would go out the next day and paint the glorious seascapes.

Later, the family sat in the drawing room listening to the Veryan who had broken out of the gentry mould. Maddie, they thought, was positively Bohemian and leading a life of which they disapproved. Rumours abounded of her dubious relationship with a young artist

23

called Bruce Aston, to whom she had given patronage. He lived at her Chelsea home and used her attic studio for his work. What else went on Florence hardly wished to think about, but Maddie was the daughter of Philip's dead brother and Monique's closest friend. So they must all put on a good face, forget her morals and treat her with kindness.

"Dreadful journey," she was saying. "Filthy train, crowded out with soldiers and sailors. Everyone smoking and standing in the corridors. Couldn't get to the lavatories. It was forty minutes late, so I missed the Portlyn bus and had to wait another hour."

Florence looked concerned. "Yes, I'm sorry we couldn't pick you up but..."

"Oh, don't be. I understand about the petrol rationing. Living in London, of course, it doesn't really matter but down here it's going to make an awful difference to you. Country bus services are impossible. Look, do you think I can take some dairy produce back with me? Rations are simply awful and going to get worse, I shouldn't wonder."

Laura crossed her long shapely legs and placed a cigarette in its tortoise-shell holder which she then put between her lips. As she lit the cigarette with a silver lighter and inhaled deeply, her eyes never left the ungainly woman flopping on the sofa opposite. It was as well, she thought, that because Monique had nothing to wear they had temporarily dropped the tradition of dressing for dinner, otherwise who could say what horror would adorn Maddie? And yet she seemed to attract men. Extraordinary. Or was it simply that men who had artistic ambitions just used her? As for Jennie, the child should have dined at six o'clock and been tucked up in bed by now. Monique wouldn't hear of it, of course, insisting she ate with the family, and saying she was frightened upstairs all alone. Typically French, keeping children up all hours. Monique had a lot to learn.

"And how is the gallery doing, Maddie?" asked Philip in an effort to be affable after his drumming from Florence yesterday.

Maddie leaned forward, frowning slightly as she twirled a sherry glass between her fingers. "It had been doing very well, but you can hardly expect people to fork out for paintings at a time like this. In any case, I've taken the precaution of placing my stock in the cellars, bringing up only a few each day for display purposes. Better to be safe than sorry." She gazed around at the bare walls gloomily. "I was really looking forward to seeing your collection again. Was it absolutely necessary to pack them all away?"

Deeming this remark an insult to her forward thinking, Laura snapped back at once: "What a question! Of course it was necessary."

Florence jumped in quickly. "Maddie, I do hope you'll come to us if bombing starts? I wouldn't rest if I thought you were in danger."

"Thank you, Aunt Florence, that's very kind," said Maddie. "But if it does start I shall be driving ambulances." Seeing the surprise on their faces, she smiled. "Oh, yes, I'm an auxilliary. You should see me in my government issue and tin hat."

Shuddering at the thought, Laura prayed she never would.

"In any case, I couldn't leave the gallery," Maddie went on. Thinking this sounded rather ungrateful, she added, "But if things get too awful, then I'll take you up on your kind offer." She would, of course, do no such thing. The very idea of being buried alive in Cornwall when all the excitement was in London was not to be contemplated. Lovely in summer, she told herself, but the long, boring and damp winters with nothing to do would soon drive her to the mad house. It would do the same for Monique and what she needed now was was plenty of distraction. If things remained quiet she would entice her to London and get her to help with the gallery, or induce her to start painting again. Monique was a very good landscape painter and earlier this year had sold three paintings. Last year she had sold four. It would be criminal if she just stopped and ended up doing charity work with Florence and Laura.

With this thought in mind she set off the following day with Monique and Jennie towards the cove. "I've stacks of room at my place, especially now that Bruce has been called up. He leaves next week. Pity. He was just beginning to do well after that last exhibition." Her face clouded and her voice shook a little. "I'm going to miss him dreadfully. Bloody Germans."

Monique looked thoughtful. "Maybe I shall join you later on for a few days. But you remember your promise now, you will come here if London is attacked?"

Maddie laughed, her full face reddened and freckled already by the warm sun. "I'm not sure the family would really welcome me. I'm their black sheep, remember. Thank God I'm independent of them. I do as I please and live as I please."

Having inherited her parents' wealth and property after their deaths in a car crash eight years earlier, Maddie found it little consolation for losing two people she had loved so much. More like friends than parents, they were fun, lived life to the full and surrounded themselves with well known talent from the world of art. An only child, she missed them dreadfully. Watching now as Jennie ran on ahead, Maddie whispered.

"I think you're wrong not to tell Aunt Flo about your latest miscarriage. She's very kind and you need her right now." When Monique said nothing, Maddie frowned. "Look, I know how devastating it must

25

have been and how dearly you want that son, but you must heed your doctor's advice and avoid another pregnancy, you really must."

Monique look troubled. Her whole being cried out to be a mother again. What an unfair world it was when some women were unable to carry children, some gave birth to too many and others believed in free love, used contraception and made sure they never conceived at all. Maddie made no secret of the fact that as one of the new women, she fell into the latter category. Fond of her as she was, Monique disapproved. "When I am well, and Charles also is well, which may not be for a long time yet, then I will certainly try again. I am only thirty-three. Charles must have an heir."

"And put your life at risk? That's foolhardy, Monique. Come to London and I'll take you to a clinic where you can be fitted for a diaphragm."

Shocked at such forthrightness, Monique said nothing to this, it being at odds with her strict Catholic upbringing. Yesterday she had thought the death of her son was God's will in such awful times. But that was yesterday. Today she longed to be pregnant again, doctor or no doctor, war or no war. It was different for Maddie, a Protestant and a free spirit with an independent life. She, on the other hand, needed the discipline of her faith and the security of marriage.

For the rest of the morning all three sat painting on the steps of the cove while Maddie, determined to be positive and take Monique's mind off things, chatted on about the estate, aware that her friend knew little about it. "When I was a child you could walk miles and still be on Veryan land, but now they're down to fifteen hundred acres which includes Portlyn itself and two other villages inland. It's dairy farming mostly with six hundred acres given over to cereal crops. Tenant farmers all over the place. They own a lot of property in the area and the London house too. I think you can safely say that Aunt Flo and Uncle Phil are still worth a bob or two. But it won't be like that for Charles if Uncle doesn't hand the estate over to him soon. Death duties will cripple Trevellan. The upkeep of the house itself is enormous."

Monique shrugged and shook her head. "East wing, west wing, north and south ... I still have not seen all the rooms. How many are there?"

Maddie frowned, trying to remember. "Fifty-two, I think. Not that large a place really, certainly no grand stately home, just a good old-fashioned country manor. Freezing in the winter, so be warned."

Bored with the conversation and worried that the sun was drying her watercolour too quickly, Jennie's mind drifted once more to the horror until it was driven out by the sound of noisy seagulls above her. She looked up. The kestrel was back; gulls were mobbing it. Watching as it

26

flew higher and higher to escape attack, she heard a shout from the clifftop. Placing a hand to her brow to shield her eyes from the sun she could just make out a boy with dark hair. When the kestrel flew to his outstretched hand, the seagulls dispersed. For one moment the boy stood looking down at the cove, then turned and walked out of sight.

When Maddie left, as noisily as she had arrived, the house was suddenly dull and quiet without her and Jennie noticed how withdrawn her mother had become once more. Portlyn also was quiet, lacking holiday visitors. The RAF transmitter towered over them all and Nissen huts sprang up close to it. A few lonely airmen wandered into the village, wondering what to do with their time off, and usually ended up at the Harbour Inn. One or two romances sprang up, the Cornish girls welcoming this new infusion of male blood into their isolated corner of the world, but all in all, the airmen were well behaved and the threatened invasion of drunken servicemen the villagers had feared, faded into nothing. The question on everyone's minds was, "What is the transmitter for?" But secrets were secrets and "careless talk costs lives", so the good people of Portlyn went about their daily business and kept their thoughts to themselves.

Returning from Winchester College for his summer vacation, Clive Willoughby instantly declared his displeasure at being ousted from his room. "Why? Everything I need is in it." Told that the nursery suite could be a useful flat for him, he regarded his mother with cold eyes and continued saddling up the chestnut hunter his grandfather had said he might ride. "Oh, great. Tucked away overlooking the back of the kitchens and laundry, and freezing as well. I've asked Tippett to join me next week. He'll laugh his head off when he sees where I've been put, and he'll tell the other chaps. I'll have to put him off, that's all."

"Nonsense," said Laura flatly. "Tell him you asked for the suite so that you could have somewhere to entertain your friends and play records as loudly as you like. He'll envy you. Use your brains, Clive, and stop moaning."

Tightening the girth, he made a scoffing sound. "It wouldn't have been so bad for anyone else, but damn it all . . . for Frogs!"

"I don't want to hear you speaking like that. Things are difficult enough, Clive."

"Well, I didn't start it." Hauling himself into the saddle, he eased the horse out of the stable yard, calling back to his mother: "I'm going for a ride. Has anyone any objections to that too?"

"You be careful," said Laura anxiously. "That's a powerful horse. Settle down and don't take risks. No jumping."

Trotting his mount across the estate, Clive reached open clifftop and there gave the hunter free rein, spurring the animal on, scattering alarmed Friesians before him until, all anger spent, he finally came to a halt. It was almost six o'clock, the rugged coastline crystal clear in a golden light, the fresh sea breeze welcoming after the heat of the day. And what a day, thought Clive. What a home coming. Early that morning he had said goodbye to his fellow Wykehamists and caught the train from Winchester, eager to return to his family for the summer holidays. And what had he found on arrival? Some pasty faced daughter of a French woman happily settled in his room. His room! The cheek of it! Of course, he hadn't just survived a disaster as Jennie had, otherwise he too might be spoilt a little occasionally. But who had ever rushed around saying "poor Clive"? If anything he came under criticism to such an extent that he felt clumsy and awkward, as if being aware of disapproval seemed to increase it in some way. How different it all was to Buckland Park where his father, prior to being called up, had indulged his every whim. There, he had been taught to shoot pheasant on the Gloucestershire estate, drive his father's car in the confines of the parkland and drink alchohol when he and his father were alone. At that Palladian mansion he could do no wrong, it seemed, so long as he kept out of his stepmother's way and stayed no longer than six days. Six days in each year! That was all the time his father had been able to spare for him. Now, here was this French woman and her daughter, pushing him around in his own home. He might have expected his mother to stand up to them on his behalf. It was not to be.

As if to make up for Clive's hostile attitude to Jennie, Florence spent far more time with the girl than she could truly afford, teaching her to ride, and taking her in the pony and trap to visit the farm tenants on her many duty trips. Jennie loved the farms where she soon became friendly with the women in the Land Army, helped with the milking on one disastrous occasion, and watched cheese making in the dairy of Home Farm. In spite of all this, she longed for a friend of her own age but was denied the companionship of village children, especially the rough London evacuees. "You are a Veryan," her aunt had told her time and time again. "People look up to us. Remember this and never do anything to embarrass the family."

Tippett came, the nets went up on the old dilapidated tennis court and shouts of "Fifteen, love" rang out in the hot summer air. Jennie watched the boys from a distance, hoping they would ask her to join them, but in their eyes she scarcely existed. It was after Tippett left, on a hot July day, when Monique, Philip and Florence were visiting Charles in Sussex, that things took a dangerous turn for the worse.

Having ridden Kelly, Jennie was grooming the pony when Clive walked into the stable yard and stood, hands in the pockets of his long

28

trousers, looking apprehensive. "Why is it that r
speak about your father's burns? Are they that

Jennie paused, brush in hand, as fearful me
mind. "Of course the burns must be bad. Papa w.

"What are these operations he has to keep havi

"Maman said they're called skin grafts. They t.
from one part of the body and graft it on to the bu.

"Don't!" shouted Clive, shuddering.

Shrugging, Jennie resumed her task. She was in no
the matter with Clive or tell him what she truly be
grafting would make everything perfectly normal aga

After an awkward silence he finally asked the ques
haunted him for so long. "Is it ... is it his face?"

Sensing his fear, Jennie smiled to herself. He had treate
and called her "Frog" in front of Tippett. Let him sw
moments. Let him know the taste of fear. "Oh, you mustn'
you." She stopped brushing, turned and thought how grey
looked. Before she could explain, he turned and walked aw
ing as he strode out of the stableyard Jennie now recalled
mother's words to her aunt after returning from the last vi
Grinstead.

"They put burn cases in saline baths. And in these baths the
the dressings. Well, I was always raised in the belief that you
never put water on burns. I only hope this Mr McIndoe know
he's doing. And, oh my dear, there were a couple of young pilot
ward and ... their faces, their poor burned faces ... it was horri
horrible ... poor souls."

Clive had heard those words also and was thinking of them now
wandered the grounds in solitary fear. Until this moment, no one
answered his questions about the sinking of the *Lancastria* or abou
uncle, treating them as an impertinence at best and ghoulish fasci
tion at worst. Now here was Jennie confirming that the man looked li
a monster. Appalled, he sought out his mother and found her in t
walled kitchen garden talking to Ben, the only gardener left to them

Seeing him beckoning anxiously, she crossed to where Clive stood.
"What is it? Can't you see I'm busy?"

"Is it true about Uncle Charles?"

"Is what true?"

Hesitating before finding words to describe the horrific pictures he
had conjured up in his mind, Clive murmured, "That ... that his face is
all burned away."

"What?" Laura's brow furrowed. "Of course not. Who told you
such nonsense?"

Jennie." Clive's deep sense of relief was overtaken by a sudden
[su]rge of rage. She had been toying with him, having a laugh at his
[exp]ense. "Some joke, huh?" With that he turned and stormed towards
[th]e house to take solace in his room.

Laura stood, one hand resting on the old water pump. How dare
[Je]nnie say anything so wicked to Clive? She would soon see about this
[n]onsense. Walking to the stable yard she found no sign of her niece,
[a]nd Kelly was back in her paddock. The moment's pause gave Laura
[ti]me to think. Children! This had been revenge, pure and simple. Clive
[h]ad, after all, been rather cruel to his cousin, showing none of the
[c]harm he could produce when he wished, the charm that always
[r]eminded her of John Willoughby, the charm that had destroyed her
life. What a gullible fool she had been then. Her father had gained
John's measure at once, saying, "The man's all show and no substance,
my dear. He comes from nowhere, has no background and even less
money, I dare say. What he does have is an eye for the main chance and
that, my dear Laura, is you. Get shot of him."

But she, stubborn and in love, had gone her own way, marrying John
in Portlyn's old church and hurting her parents deeply. They who had
given her everything, love, education, the coming out ball, the London
Season, the couture gowns and the Veryan good looks to wear them
well, could not, however, give her basic common sense. She and her
husband had moved into the Kensington Square house just until he
found a place of their own. He never did. Instead he lived well, left her
alone a lot, and continued running up bills all over London, knowing
his wife would meet them rather than face the humiliation of dealing
with angry creditors. On finding out the truth, her father promptly
withdrew her allowance, saying they must learn to live on John's salary
from his bank employers. Within days of this announcement, he
walked out. Now she was homeless, penniless, and relying on her
parents for everything, even Clive's school fees. One day she would
have to rely on Charles and the daughter of a French restaurant owner
instead. God, it was intolerable! And now this nonsense from Jennie.
Where was the wretched girl?

Having changed into a cool cotton dress, Jennie was playing with the
labradors on the south lawn when her aunt approached and snapped,
"I've been looking everywhere for you. What do you mean by telling
such outrageous lies?"

Startled, Jennie looked up. Silhouetted against the bright sun, her
aunt seemed a tall, dark and threatening figure. At first, she could find
no words, but slowly rose to her feet and, tilting her head, looked at
Laura with a calm, level expression. "I don't understand. I haven't told
any lies."

30

The look and measured words were proof enough to Laura that her first impressions of Jennie were correct. She was older than her years with a guile that belied those spaniel-like eyes and that enigmatic expression. Small wonder the yellow frilly dress had been such a disaster. Here was no Shirley Temple. It was the French influence of course. She had never liked the French. "Don't play the innocent with me, child. It simply will not work. What were you thinking of to say such terrible things? I want you to go to Clive right now and apologise."

Jennie would do no such thing. When her aunt left her, she ambled slowly across the lawns, through the shining rose gardens, and stood gazing at the cows grazing in the meadow beyond the ha-ha. She wished her mother would hurry back. They were all expected in time for dinner, but that was hours away. Meanwhile the pressure would be on her to humble herself before Clive who would smirk as only he could smirk. Never! Never! She must get away from the house. Her thoughts turned to the cove and she recalled her grandmother's warning. But she wouldn't be alone, she told herself. She would have the dogs with her and, if she was careful, what could possibly happen?

Calling to Portia and Rosalind, she walked through the grounds and took the woodland path she now knew so well. Running ahead, Portia sniffed into sun-dappled ferns until a startled pigeon flew up into the trees. The bitch watched it curiously, one paw lifted off the ground, then joined her daughter and Jennie as they continued on their way.

The minute she reached the steps, Jennie breathed in the fresh clean air and felt cooling sea breezes lifting her light hazel-coloured hair, free at last from oil. The sea was closer today and, as she ran along the edge of the waves, it seemed the horizon was above her. Suddenly afraid, she moved back on to the beach and hurled sticks for the labradors to chase and play with. Searching then for shells, she became engrossed until frantic barking made her look up.

Rosalind stood on distant rocks with the sea surging about her. Not far from her Portia whined and moved back and forth in growing agitation. Alarmed, Jennie suddenly realised that the tide was coming in and coming in faster than she could have dreamed possible. "Roz, you stupid girl! Come on, come now." But her cries and entreaties were useless as Rosalind just stood whining and barking.

There was nothing for it but to go out herself and help the frightened bitch before it was too late. Jumping from rock to rock and wading across a channel of water which was already up to her hips, she reached Rosalind, caught the collar and tried to lead her to safety. Panicking as waves flowed over the rock on which she was standing, the bitch pulled away from Jennie who clung to her for dear life. Neither was prepared

31

for the rush of surf which knocked both of them off their feet. Finding herself in the channel, Rosalind swam and quickly gained dry land but Jennie could not regain her balance. The sea was all around her now and terror froze her mind. She grabbed at the rock but the next wave pushed her into the channel then pulled at her feet as it swept outwards. For one brief moment she touched bottom and reached for the rock again, but another wave crashed over her head and she lost her grip.

Choking and gasping, she floundered in the water, feeling her body being tossed back and forth in the undertow. Terror and blind panic overwhelmed her and she was again lost in the oil, among shouting drowning people as, weakening quickly against the battering, she felt all strength leave her.

# Chapter Two

Slipping and tumbling down the steep cliff path, the boy reached the cove at last. Labradors at his heels, he raced across to the outcrop of rocks and on into the sea.

Jennie neither heard nor saw his approach but felt a hand grip her shoulder as an arm came about her waist, trying to raise her up. She fell again; the arm tightened then she was being hauled shoreward out of reach of the next incoming wave. Vaguely aware that she was being half-carried along, she found herself lying on the steps, coughing up sea water before bursting into shuddering tears. At last she raised her head and looked into anxious deep blue eyes set in a suntanned face that was topped by dark tousled hair.

"You should have been told about the cove. It's very dangerous. Another minute and you would have been swept away." The voice, Jennie noticed, held neither the broad Cornish tones of the villagers nor the strangely clipped accent of her own family. "Are you all right?" When she nodded, he went on, "You must be one of the London evacuees that Mrs Martin has taken in."

Realising that her arms and legs were badly grazed and bleeding, she winced, sniffed and wiped her wet face with an equally wet hand, but the tears kept flowing. "I'm from Paris. The dog got stuck on the rocks so I went to help and ..."

"Idiot! Dogs can swim." The boy removed a soaking wet shirt from his sturdy suntanned body and glanced at the labradors. Rosalind was digging furiously, sending sand flying in all directions, while Portia nuzzled at Jennie attentively. Paris, did she say, or had he misheard? "These dogs are from the big house. How did they get here on their own?"

"I brought them here." If only she could stop crying.

"Does Lady Veryan know?"

"Of course," Jennie lied. "She's my grandmother."

33

He stared at her in bemusement then slowly recalled all that his father had said about the family from France, plucked from the sea. "You were on the *Lancastria*?" he asked in awe. When she nodded he sucked in his breath as a hundred questions rushed into his mind. Instinct told him it would be cruel to ask them. "That must have been terrible." As he looked at the pathetic shivering girl slumped on the steps beside him, he thought what a tragic and ironic twist of fate it would have been to survive such a disaster only to die in this place which had claimed so many lives in the past. Strange then that another twist of fate had brought him to this lonely spot in time to save her. Suddenly remembering his manners, he said, "I'm Mark Curnow. You probably know my father. He's Sir Philip's agent, and manages the estate."

Jennie nodded, remembering the burly man who was often talking to her grandfather and spent so much time in his study. More than that, she knew little of Mr Curnow who only said "Hello" whenever he passed her in the house or grounds.

"I'm Jennie Veryan," she murmured, as the tears stopped. "Thank you for saving me, Mark. But please don't tell anyone. I'll get into terrible trouble if you do."

He smiled and thought her a grave little thing. "Don't worry. Your secret's safe with me. But don't come here again, not alone." Standing up, he gazed skywards, murmuring, "Where has she gone?"

"Who?"

"My kestrel. I was flying her to the lure, in Farthing Field, but she grew bored and headed this way." He smiled at Jennie. "Good thing she did, I suppose."

Jennie shuddered at the memory. It seemed she owed her life to a wayward bird and a boy she judged to be about two to three years her senior. "So you're the one I've seen on the clifftop? Our concierge kept a parrot but it was always in a cage."

He gave her a strange look. "Kestrels are birds of prey. They're falcons. You don't keep falcons in small cages, you keep them in a mews. They need exercise.

She stared at him curiously. "Why did you buy a kestrel?"

"I didn't. A holiday maker found her last year not far from here and brought her to our house, thinking she had been abandoned. It was the wrong thing to do, of course. The parent might have been close by. But the damage was done. She was only a fledgling and could just about fly. If I hadn't taken her on she would have died. Dad said she would die anyway since kestrel chicks are difficult to feed, but I asked Will. He's a poacher and knows everything about wild creatures. He told me what to do and how to feed her. In the wild she'd take small rodents and insects, but since she's never been taught to hunt I have to feed her. I set traps for mice. She can't eat butcher's meat. She needs guts, fur and feathers to keep healthy." As Jennie winced he went on: "I found a book about falconry in the library and learned how to man her. The first thing was training her to the lure, but she soon grows bored with that and ends up sitting on a fence just preening herself or staring at me."

He looked so perplexed that Jennie suddenly wanted to laugh. "Aren't you afraid she'll fly away?"

"Sophie?" Mark smiled. "I'm the one with the food, remember." He looked up and pointed to a speck hovering above the cliff on the far side of the cove. "There she is." He searched about for the thick leather glove he had dropped in his haste to rescue Jennie, found it and felt in the pockets of his trousers for the pieces of meat. They were still there. "I think the dogs are putting her off." He looked at the shivering girl in concern. "You'd better push off home before you catch pneumonia." With that he moved away, clutching his wet shirt.

Watching until he reached the top of the cliff once more, Jennie saw him swinging the lure and heard him call out. With tinkling bells, Sophie swooped across the cove and soared up to settle on the lure. Mark bent. When he stood up again, Sophie was perched on his fist. With his right hand he waved to Jennie and disappeared from her sight.

Wondering if she would see him again, Jennie called to Rosalind and Portia then started back along the woodland path. She had made a friend, a boy who had not only saved her life but kept a falcon and was glad to talk to her. He had said that her secret was safe with him. Suddenly, she knew that it was. At the house she took the dogs to the rear and down a flight of steps to a flagstoned corridor that led to the large kitchen. It was the best way of avoiding her aunt, but not Cook.

"Good gracious, child! What on earth has happened to you?" Mrs Hodges was kneading dough on a long wooden table, her ample frame overheated by the warmth of the Victorian black cooking range. On a day as hot as this, the large kitchen of Trevellan was no place to be. Her moist, shining face had turned quite scarlet.

Jennie paused at the doorway. Rosalind and Portia stood on either side of her, each aware that this was another forbidden area and expecting to be shooed away. "I ... I fell into some water, Mrs Hodges." Still shivering, Jennie walked swiftly towards the warm stove and stood beside it gratefully.

"Some water my eye. You fell into the sea, didn't you? Were you at the cove?" When the girl nodded, Mrs Hodges frowned and asked who had been with her.

35

"The dogs." The voice was a frightened whisper. Jennie looked down at her shoes, the only thing about her that was dry since she had left them on the steps. "Please, Mrs Hodges, don't tell anyone. There was this boy. He helped me. His father is Mr Curnow. But he isn't going to tell so, please ... Mrs Hodges?"

A long sigh escaped the woman's lips. Wiping dough-covered hands on a damp tea towel, she walked across to the child, her face shadowed with anxiety. "You must have been told to keep away from the cove. What you did was extremely dangerous. I'm vexed the army didn't wire off the place after all. You're all alike, you children. Think it can't happen to you. One of the evacuees has already been in trouble. No, they ought to have wired it off."

At fifty-one, Mrs Hodges looked ten years older. She wore no make-up, combed her grey hair into an unflattering bun, always wore a dark grey dress under her starched white apron and was overweight. But her cheerful smile had soon won Jennie's heart, and she loved teaching the girl to make pastry and cakes. Widowed and childless she had cooked for the Veryans for twenty-two years and remembered better days; days when the staff had included ladies' maids, chamber maids, parlour maids, kitchen hands, gardeners and journeymen. But those days had gone and, since the chauffeur had joined the army, they were down to Keynes, Rosa, herself, Ben and two women who came in from the village to help clean and launder. Much of the house had been shut off as a consequence.

Handing a clean white towel to Jennie to dry her face and hair, she glanced at her arms and legs and frowned. "Oh, m'dear, just look at those grazes. First thing for you is a hot bath. Go on up to Rosa. Use the servants' stairs. You'll find her in the sewing room mending sheets. Get her to run the bath, wash your hair, put out fresh clothes and get that dress washed quickly before anyone sees it. She must put iodine on those grazes. It'll sting a bit but you don't want them to turn nasty. Go on, off with you now. Your mother and grandparents should be home soon, and your aunt might start wondering where you are."

Jennie sighed with relief. "And you won't tell?"

Mrs Hodges sighed, then smiled. "If I play fair by you, you must play fair by me. I promise to say nothing if you promise never to go to the cove alone again." When Jennie gave her most solemn pledge, she smiled and said cheerfully, "So then, it's all past and forgotten. Now hurry up. You've got minutes, not hours. Then come back down and I'll give you some hot tea and a slice of cake."

As Jennie ran from the kitchen, Mrs Hodges let the dogs out then placed a towel over the dough, setting it to rise in a warm area. She knew she had done the right thing. Winning a child's trust was the best way to guarantee the safety of that child. Yet, all the same, her heart churned at the thought of what might have happened.

"A day school!" Laura's loud exclamation caused Jennie to start in surprise. Two days after her latest brush with death, she was painting alone in a corner of the rose garden. Raising her head, she saw her aunt walking into view. Since it was always good policy to stay out of her way, Jennie remained still and quiet, then heard her mother's voice, sharp, angry even.

"The Convent of Our Lady is excellent, I am told."

It was a hot, lazy afternoon when everything seemed still save for a lone Hurricane trailing a blaze of white across blue Cornish skies, its distant drone echoing the hum of bees hovering among the roses. Hardly the time for hoisting storm cones, but Laura just stared at her sister-in-law in disbelief.

"What are you talking about? Jennie's name is down for Roedean. She's to start in September."

"I have changed my mind," said Monique, sniffing one of the roses. "When Charles insisted on Roedean it was, he said, because we must move so much and Jennie's education would suffer. But now we are at war and Roedean has evacuated from Brighton. Some of the girls have gone to Canada and some many miles to the north of England. So Jennie shall go to the convent instead."

Laura sighed, recalling the letter from the school confirming that Jennie would be taking her place there in the autumn. "Keswick is in the Lake District. It is a beautiful part of England and Jennie will be very happy there. In any case, Charles will not allow his daughter to attend a Roman Catholic convent. For you to go behind his back when he is in hospital is simply not on, Monique."

"But to send her all the way to Keswick is madness when other schools are coming to Cornwall," said Monique. Having caved in on the matter of Jennie's religion, for which she was now truly sorry, she had no intention of being bullied into being parted from her daughter as well. Vaguely she recalled visiting the school with Charles many years ago, and thinking it charming, but she had put it from her mind long since, never once mentioning the subject to Jennie. "I cannot understand this English habit of packing children off to boarding schools as though they were parcels." She clipped a pink rose and placed it in the flower basket. "After all that Jennie has been through, I will not allow it."

"I think," said Laura quietly, "you will find you may have to allow it. After all, you have no money of your own. Who will pay for this

Catholic convent? Not Charles, I can assure you. Jennie *must* go to Roedean. It's a top girls' school and has a reputation for excellence. One day she will thank you for making such a choice."

Appalled at what she had just heard, Jennie sat quietly until the women were gone. It couldn't be true surely, it simply couldn't be true that her father wanted her to be sent away? He loved her. No, it was all Aunt Laura's doing. "*I think you will find you may have to allow it.*" Tears pouring down her face, she rushed into the house and up to her bedroom, passing an astonished Rosa who asked: "Are you all right, Miss Genevieve?" Jennie made no reply, shut her door and threw herself on to the bed, weeping uncontrollably. At last she raised herself up. She had to get away from the house, go somewhere, anywhere, what did it matter so long as no one could find her.

Twenty minutes later she sat dazed and sobbing on Kelly's back while the pony wandered at will, taking the tracks and pathways she knew so well. "*One day she will thank you.*" Thank them! Was Aunt Laura mad? Wiping away the tears with her hand, she found her vision still blurred as Kelly ambled on, across Farthing Field and through the valley before climbing up to the lane where she finally stopped, on a sharp and narrow bend, to graze at the roadside.

Sitting there, yellow blouse tucked inside her jodhpurs, Jennie slowly raised her eyes and stared ahead, wondering vaguely where she was and where she could go. At that moment a cyclist came around the corner, almost crashed into them and, in swerving, overbalanced. The shocked victim picked himself up from the road and shouted angrily.

"You stupid fool. Of all the damned places to stop."

Startled, Jennie looked down and saw Mark Curnow. "I'm sorry. Are you hurt?"

"No," said Mark, picking up his bicycle. "But move on around the corner in case a car comes along." As Jennie eased Kelly to a safer place, he followed, pushing his bike and looking at the wheel to see if it had been damaged. "What on earth did you think you were doing?" Still angry, he glanced up and then the anger turned to consternation as he saw her tear-stained face. "Don't cry. Please don't cry. I'm sorry I shouted. It isn't that bad, really. Nothing's damaged or broken."

Jennie forced a shaky smile and shook her head. "I'm not crying ... I ... I have hay fever." Embarrassed she kept her face turned from him. If only she had brought a handkerchief. Boys hated girls who cried. She'd thought she had found a friend but now he must think her an ass. "I must go. Sorry I ... I'm sorry."

"You *have* been crying," he murmured. "And what's more you've been crying for some time. What's the matter, Jennie?"

He should have shouted in anger, instead his gentle words were her

38

undoing. She gave a shuddering sigh and burst into tears once more. "Oh, Mark. They're sending me away. And I don't want to go."

"Sending you ... where?"

"To a school a long way away from here."

"Ah." Understanding he nodded and felt for her. His father had wanted to send him to a boarding school but finding the fees, on the salary Sir Philip paid, would have meant sacrifices since he was not a man of private means, unlike the former agent who had held sway over a much larger estate. And so Mark journeyed by bus each day to the Boys' Grammar which was academically excellent, and more affordable. He was happy, and could not even contemplate living away from home and Sophie. Trying to find words of comfort for Jennie, he failed. She looked so lost, he thought, taking in the large eyes and long shining hair. Lost and unhappy. "Look," he murmured at last, "I'm on my way home to take Sophie out. Would you like to see her?"

Jennie brightened at once. "The kestrel? Oh, yes."

"Come on then." Pushing his bike, Mark walked on, a dishevelled-looking figure in navy cotton shirt over long corduroy trousers, his roughly blown hair unkempt and in need of a cut. "Scruffy" was how Laura described Frank Curnow's son. "Like a labourer's boy."

The Curnows' large cottage stood one mile from Trevellan, a rambling stone affair divided from the lane by a small green and duck pond. A few mallards were sleeping by the water's edge but moved quickly as Kelly ambled past. Jennie tethered her to the garden gate which was set in a slate wall, and followed Mark through to the rear of the property. He paused suddenly and turned to her.

"She's in her mews. You can come in if you wish, but she'll fly around you. If flapping wings in confined spaces send you into a panic, as it does my mother, then you'd best stay outside."

Jennie shook her head. "I won't panic, I promise."

Something in her steady gaze made him believe her. They walked on through the long vegetable garden and past the chicken run until they came to a large wooden shed. "Dad fixed me up with an inner door so that she can't fly out when we open this one," Mark was saying. He lifted the latch, pulled the door open and they both moved into a small area. When the outer door was shut, he pulled open the inner one, whispering, "It has to be hinged this way otherwise if I pushed it I might slam into her. Whatever you do, Jennie, stay calm. She won't touch you. Flying into people would only mean hurting herself and she won't do that. Ready?"

Jennie swallowed hard and nodded. "Ready."

They entered to see Sophie sitting quietly on one of her two perches. Sunlight streamed in from an open mesh-covered window, giving her light and fresh air on this warm day. At Mark's approach, she stopped preening herself, raised one leg so that the tiny bells rang, then made cheeping sounds of pleasure. He spoke to her in caressing tones, stroking the soft beige and white breast feathers lightly while she stared at him with large dark, mesmerising eyes. "Don't move, Jennie." So saying, he put the leather glove on to his left hand, walked to the other end of the shed, placed a dead vole on the glove and held out his hand. Sophie left her perch, swooped low over Jennie's head and landed on the fist where she tore at the flesh with a hooked bill and soon swallowed it all.

When she had finished, Mark lifted his hand and cast her off. Bells jingling, jesses trailing, she swooped across the shed to the other perch, her brown wings large in the small space, then settled and swivelled her head to look at Jennie curiously. Mark moved towards her; she hopped on to his hand, wings lifting slightly. He caught the jesses between his fingers, placed a small home-made falcon's hood over her head and eyes, then picking up a canvas bag, walked towards the door.

"I only hood her when we're in the lane, just in case a car should go by and cause her to bait," he explained as they walked along. "I'm going to fly her to the lure for exercise. Coming?"

Excited, Jennie nodded, then frowned "What about Kelly? She might be afraid of your hawk."

"Sophie isn't a hawk. I told you, she's a falcon." said Mark.

"Isn't it the same thing?"

Mark shook his head. "Not quite. Hawks have yellow or red eyes, short wings, longer tail feathers and kill with their feet. Falcons have dark, almost black eyes, are long winged and kill with their talons and bills. Hawks mostly like woodland while falcons like open country. I should leave Kelly tethered. Sophie isn't manned to horses yet."

Empty of grazing cattle, Farthing Field proved the perfect place for Mark to swing the lure around with Sophie swooping and diving at it. "If she catches it," he shouted to Jennie, "she's won the game." His skill in keeping Sophie from doing just that left Jennie amazed, given the speed of the kestrel. The lure was soft leather filled with wool and on it was tied a dead mouse. At last Mark let the falcon settle on it and eat. "I bring her here because there aren't any other kestrels around. If there were they'd chase her off for invading their territory. Yet I want her to fly freely, because I hope she'll start hunting for herself one day."

Jennie watched, her heart filling. How could she leave now? She loved Sophie, and Mark had been in her thoughts from the moment he had saved her life. To have to go away the minute she had just found them was something she hardly dared to think about. Surely her mother would prevent this boarding school nonsense?

It was not to be. Shattered at the prospect of losing her daughter, Monique wrote to Charles, asking him to change his mind, and quite believing that he would. Unable to write himself, Charles dictated to a nurse who wrote on his behalf, that because Jennie's name had been down for Roedean since soon after her birth it would be wholly unworthy of them to withdraw her now, when the school staff were doing their utmost to keep up high standards under such trying circumstances. Roedean had been chosen for its excellence and he saw no reason to make changes, even if such changes were possible at this late stage. He stressed also that if Britain was defeated, the south would take the first full brunt of it. "Therefore, Jennie would be safer in the Lake District. Please, my darling, do not fight me on this issue because I will not change my mind this time. It distresses me as much as it distresses you but we must put Jennie's welfare before our own interests."

Monique read the letter in dismay. "Do not fight me on this issue, I will not change my mind this time." He was in hospital because she had fought him last March and she had been wrong. Then as now she had acted emotionally whereas Charles was thinking more clearly, as he always did. It was the very quality she needed in him to balance against her own volatile nature. Even so, she despaired. Not only was she doomed to lose her child she had also lost her opportunity of introducing Jennie to the true faith. The nuns had been willing to take her daughter since she herself was Catholic, but now her hopes were ashes. In any case the convent was too far, requiring two bus journeys and a half-mile walk, twice daily. In the dark months, she would not like Jennie making that journey. As for trying to get her into one of the top girls' schools now evacuated to Cornwall, it was far too late. Charles was right, as Charles was always right. Like it or not, Jennie would be heading to the Lake District in September and Monique's heart would break.

In the last week of August, while the British people held their breath, London burned and young pilots attacked the German squadrons, knowing what the cost would be if they lost air supremacy, Charles Veryan returned home at last. Wildly excited, Jennie ran out of the house and flung her arms about him, unaware of the pain she caused.

Weeping with emotion, Charles ignored the pain and hugged his daughter tightly, recalling the last time he had held her, fighting to keep her by him in the sea. This was a day he had thought never to see. "It's good to be home," he murmured. "It's ... it's so good to be home."

If his manner was a little strained, it was put down to tiredness and pain, worry also during such worrying days. To Jennie, however, it seemed that everyone was smiling through tears, even her stern grandfather. Unaware of the grave danger threatening the country, she was over the moon and felt the world to be safe again because Papa was home at last. After a celebration dinner, Monique tucked her into bed. Scent wafted about Jennie who stared up at her, smiling. "You smell nice, Maman. Papa liked my paintings, didn't he?"

"He said how good you were and that you have an eye for perspective and colour."

"Is he all better now?"

Monique frowned. "Not quite. He has another operation to go through, maybe two."

"I didn't know," said Jennie, crestfallen at the news. "That means he'll go away again. I kissed him goodnight downstairs, but will he come and talk to me before I go to sleep?"

Monique smiled. "Of course. But do not worry him over the school. That is all settled now. Promise?" When Jennie nodded, she kissed her goodnight and moved away, the soft folds of her evening gown drifting about her feet as she left the room.

Jennie lay waiting with eyes wide open and hope in her heart. Her father did love her, that much had become clear this evening. People didn't send away those they loved. She thought of the anguished days of tears and pleading, days when she and her mother would sit painting or chatting alone in the boathouse, while it was explained to her why she must go away to school. Maybe, she thought, there was still a chance of making Papa change his mind, even though she started her first term in less than two weeks' time. She had promised Maman, but this was too important an issue to worry about promises. Thirty minutes passed and, try as she might to stay awake, Jennie's eyelids became too heavy. When Charles finally entered her room he found her fast asleep. Cursing the telephone call which had delayed him, he returned downstairs feeling guilty and depressed that he had let his daughter down.

Awakened suddenly, Jennie opened her eyes, wondered what time it was and walked out on to the landing. Voices floated up from the hallway below; she saw Keynes walking across it with a tray in his hands. Turning, her eyes caught the light shining from her parents' room. The door stood ajar. Since her father had not come to her after all, she moved towards it, knocked lightly then pushed it open. Wearing a white silk nightgown, her mother was seated at the dressing table, brushing her hair. Jennie stood watching, thinking how lovely she looked. Suddenly her father came into view. Already in his pyjama trousers, he was struggling painfully to pull on the jacket. As he turned, Jennie's eyes widened with horror and a gasp escaped her lips.

42

Aware of her suddenly, Charles swung around just in time to see his daughter run from the doorway. "Oh, Christ!" With a determined tug he was into his jacket and rushing from the bedroom. Catching up with Jennie, he held her by the shoulders, feeling her small body stiff and trembling. He knew why but said only, "I'm sorry, darling. I did come to say goodnight but you were asleep. I was called to the telephone soon after you went to bed and couldn't get away. Come on, I'll take you back."

Silently Jennie walked back to her room, climbed into bed and let her father cover her with the blanket once more. She lay there staring up at him in a manner which he found appalling. He stroked her forehead lovingly. "Look, Jennie, you mustn't be afraid of what you saw. I know how ugly the scars are, but more treatment will fix that. I didn't want you to see. You should never walk into anyone's bedroom without knocking. You know that."

"The door was open and I did knock but ..." her voice trailed off.

"Well, we didn't hear you." He kissed her lightly, a tender cherishing kiss though he sensed her recoiling from him. "Now then, you get some sleep. I gather your grandmother's been showing you around the estate. You probably know more about it than I do now. So come with me tomorrow. We'll look at the farms, meet the tenants, say hello to everyone."

When he left, Jennie lay in a state of shock thinking about his terrible disfigurement. Was that what fire did? It was horrifying. For all that she loved her father, and knew he would never have been burned at all had he not pulled her from the flames, she was suddenly afraid to have that tormented flesh close to her.

Anxiously, Monique awaited her husband's return. She too had seen the scars and could readily understand Jennie's shock. But Jennie was a child and a child could be allowed such emotions. A wife could not. How many days and nights had she spent worrying about this moment and wondering how it would be? She longed to lie in Charles's arms again, yet dreaded it also. How pathetic, how cruel, how unspeakably weak she was.

Charles entered the room, his face tense, his eyes heavy. Without looking at Monique, he moved across to the bedside lamps, switching them off and plunging the room into deep darkness before sitting on the edge of the bed in silence.

Monique drew back the heavy curtains, allowing moonlight to flood the room. "Jennie is only a child. She will come to accept ... accept things in time."

"And will you come to accept?" The voice was sharp.

Slowly she walked towards him, her heart filled with love and

43

compassion, yet her senses grateful for the darkness. "No need for such words. I love you. It is all we need, to love each other." She placed a hand upon his shoulder. "And we came so close to losing each other."

He lifted her hand to his cheek then kissed it before pulling her around so that she stood before him. Gently he reached out, feeling her body through the shimmering nightgown before drawing her towards him and laying his head against her. Then, with a sudden movement, he turned away, and fell back on the bed.

Monique had gasped at his touch, had wanted him to kiss and embrace her. Now she felt repulsed. She tried telling herself he was tired, in pain, and had a great deal of re-adjusting to do. And yet there had been anger in his gesture when all she wanted was to hold him close and thank God they were together again. Nothing more, it was far too soon for anything more.

Charles knew her thoughts, but could she read his? Could she know how much he loved and wanted her? Yet, to see Jennie's horrified expression on his wife's face was something he could never bear. Suddenly he wanted to be alone, away from shock or pity. In hospital he had not been a monster. In fact he had thought himself something of a fraud as young fighter pilots with hands and faces burned away came into the hospital almost daily. Seeing their terrible plight had made him grateful that his burns could, at least, be covered. Now all that had changed and, afraid of rejection, he had rejected his wife. Perhaps she was grateful. "*No more babies, Monsieur.*" Remembering the doctor's warning, Charles smiled to himself. How ironic; how bloody ironic.

The night was warm. Monique lay down beside him on the heavy four poster, and pulled a sheet over them. Tense and desolate, she stared at the moonlit window, and heard the distant sea. How soothing a sound it was, even now when her mind was in turmoil. All through the journey Charles had seemed so remote from her, and now this. "You must be so very tired."

He swallowed hard and said nothing.

Monique turned her head away so that he wouldn't see burning tears flowing from beneath the closed eyelids.

Charles lay staring into darkness in growing despair. It was more than the scar which lay so heavily on his mind. Just now he had hurt Monique. Soon she would be devastated and there was nothing he could do about it.

His mind returned to the letter, that terrible letter which he had received only three days before fleeing France. From the postmark it had taken months to reach him and clearly been passed from one Government department to another before finding him in Paris. Having read the contents with shock, he had burned it but not before copying down the name and address of the sender, intending to write back and ward off the threat. He had then placed the address in his wallet and that, along with his jacket, had been lost at sea. Now he lived in dread of a second letter arriving and had given firm instructions to his wife that all mail for him must be forwarded to the hospital at East Grinstead at once. This Monique had arranged, but so far the second act of the drama was yet to unfold. It was like waiting for the executioner's axe to fall. When it did, at least Jennie would be far away and, hopefully, would know little about it.

Thirty minutes passed; he turned towards Monique and reached out to touch her cheek. Realising that she was crying, he raised himself up on his elbow and stared down at her in consternation. At that moment, Monique opened her eyes. They gleamed like dark pools in the moonlight. How beautiful she was and how dearly he loved her. As her hand went up behind his head, he bent and kissed her passionately on the lips.

The Battle of Britain was fought and won. Unable to invade, Germany kept up a massive bombing campaign and summer slipped into an uneasy autumn. In the darkening days of December when wooded lanes were made slippery by fallen leaves and the countryside echoed to the sound of gun shot, Jennie returned home for Christmas. Her journey from Keswick had been very long, ending with Monique and Florence rushing up and down the station platform in the London blackout, searching for her among the other girls and parents. Her excitement at being home was shadowed by the sight of her father. How pale and haggard he looked after his latest operation, she had thought, as he hugged her, staving off her anxious questions with a laugh. "Of course, I'm fine, nothing but an old fraud taking up a hospital bed needed for wounded airmen." Even so, she was worried about him.

Trotting Kelly along the lane towards the Curnows' house, Jennie had never felt so happy or relaxed as she did now. Cold as it was for Cornwall, to her it seemed positively spring-like after Keswick. The sun was shining and already new shoots were pushing through the ground for rarely did frost punish this earth or snow encompass the county where palm trees grew in sheltered areas. Wind alone was the true enemy here, gusting in from the sea and sending washing flying from pegs to fetch up almost a quarter of a mile away. How different it was to the Lake District.

There, rooms which had been fine in September had become iceboxes of late. Longing, in vain, for the comfort of a hot water bottle, she had huddled beneath layers of blankets wearing thick pyjamas and bedsocks to get warm. Each morning, as she thawed out her frozen flannel, she wondered if the Allendale boys were suffering the same at Trevellan. Now she realised there was no comparison. Was it really only three months since she had said goodbye to all she loved, and fetched up in the strange little town among the fells and lakes? For the first three weeks she had cried into her pillow from homesickness, and old nightmares had returned. Shouting out and floundering in her bed as she fell again and again from the lifeboat into the sea, she would be awakened by angry little girls who wanted a good night's sleep. Only one was sympathetic. The most mischievous of all the Lower Threes, and the daughter of a regular army officer, Louise Boyd, her new friend had already got her into a few scrapes. But that was all far away until next January.

Approaching the Curnows' cottages she saw Mark digging the side garden. He paused at her approach and leaned on the handle of his spade, unaware of the mud smear on his forehead. "Ah, so you're back. How was school?"

For all his words Jennie thought he looked surprised and hesitant as she dismounted and tethered Kelly to the gate. Had he forgotten her, as she'd feared he might? Did he resent her visiting him? Suddenly she felt very shy and found herself prattling on about the school. "We're in two hotels. It's better than I thought. Derwent Water is beautiful. We go for long walks when the weather's good. It's a marvellous place to paint. I've seen falcons over the fells. I think they might be buzzards." She stopped talking at last, feeling she sounded foolish and was boring him to death. "How is Sophie?"

By his expression she knew they had reached common ground at last. It came to her then that, without the kestrel, he would have found her presence odd and rather embarrassing.

"I'm about to fly her. They don't start shooting before ten-thirty on the estate. I have an agreement with Sir Philip. He's been very understanding, so has your father. I'll take her to the cove. The gulls are a nuisance but it's safer in the long run. Afternoons are out now because by four it's too dark.

"Do you think she'll remember me?"

"No," said Mark with casual candour. "But she's more used to people in general. I've manned her to being cast off from horseback, so come with me on Kelly. I'm riding Regent."

Later they set off, he on his father's black gelding with Sophie on the gloved fist once more, and Jennie on Kelly. As they reached the path which wound its way over the headland, Jennie looked back and down at the harbour where the morning sun bathed cottages, sea and cliffs. The westerly wind seemed cool up here and puffy white clouds scurried across a pale blue sky. She wondered then just how many times she had

46

painted this very scene and thought how soft the light was after the sharpness of the Lakes.

"Shall we see if she'll fly to you?" Mark was saying. "You've only held her once and that was in the mews. You remember about the jesses? You wouldn't flinch? I don't want her to bait."

Jennie's heart gave a leap. Of course she remembered how to handle the jesses. Assuring him she would not flinch, she allowed him to place a spare glove on her left hand.

Mark removed the hood and cast Sophie off, watching as her brown wings soared into the pale sky. It was some time before she showed any interest in Jennie who persistently held out her gloved hand; at last the kestrel's dark eyes focussed keenly on the pieces of meat held on it. Once she flew towards Jennie then veered away at the last minute. On the second approach it was clear she intended to land.

Jennie's heart was pounding as the falcon swooped towards her. Would Kelly move? Would Sophie bait – attack her even? The wings were closer, the mesmerising eyes and sharp bill a fraction from her face. For one terrible moment, she thought the worst; then Sophie clomped down on the fist, a wing tip brushed Jennie's cheek lightly before folding, and the kestrel settled to her meal. A gasp escaped Jennie's lips. It was a moment she knew would never be forgotten. Kelly moved restlessly; wings opened then closed again as the pony settled. Sophie looked at Jennie for one brief moment then turned to the food once more.

"She came to me," was all Jennie could whisper. "She came to me."

Her radiant expression touched Mark. She was the only one of his friends who had shared this experience with him, the only one who cared and understood. He had missed her these past months.

Walking the labradors at the cove, Laura glanced up at the cliff, pulled her silk scarf close about her head, called the dogs and strode back to the house. There she headed straight for the morning room, and knelt at the stone fireplace to warm her hands before flaming coals. Sunlight streamed through the window, washing the mahogany desk where Charles sat writing a letter. Laura noticed how slowly he wrote and stared at the scar on his hand.

"Is the wrist more flexible now?" she asked.

He nodded, still concentrating on his correspondence. "Getting better all the time."

Removing her scarf, Laura looked up at him, frowning. "You know, Charles, I really think you should have a word with Jennie."

"Hmmm? What about?"

To gain his attention, Laura moved to the desk and leaned on it. "I noticed it in the summer, and thought ... well ... she's lonely. But now, when the first thing Jennie does is to rush back to that boy, then I think it's time you had a word with her."

Charles looked at his sister and realised she was wearing a tweed coat. "Have you been out? What on earth are you talking about?"

Sighing with exasperation, Laura glared at him. "Jennie and Frank Curnow's son. They're always together. It isn't right."

Bewilderment turned to amazement and amazement to amusement. "Good God. Laura, they're children. Mark's a decent lad, so what's the problem? Jennie has no other friend here."

Laura threw herself into an armchair and lit a cigarette. "How can you be so naive? Children do grow up. Mark must be nearing fourteen, and Jennie is more mature than you believe."

Leaning back in his chair, Charles regarded his sister, wondering at her turn of mind. "You've always been against Frank Curnow. Now you're against his son. Why?"

"Nonsense," she said nervously, wondering how much he knew and suspecting it was more than she wished. But she had been young then and green in judgment. Frank had been quite handsome in those days and she infatuated with him to the point of making his life a living hell. A man of integrity and happily married to Mabel, the daughter of a clergyman, he had brushed off her advances with a velvet glove, never referring to her lapse from that day to this. John Willoughby had been a rebound gesture to restore her pride and signal to Frank that he no longer meant a thing to her. Now she was forced back into this house to endure seeing him every day. Was she also to endure watching Jennie humiliate them as she had once humiliated herself? Never.

"Anyway, it's the *kestrel* that Jennie's interested in, not Mark."

"The *kestrel* is only the excuse." Laura walked to the door, then turned. "Don't underestimate little girls, brother dear. They have all the guile of grown women."

Charles smiled wryly. "Speaking from personal experience, are we?"

Laura's eyes narrowed. "Don't speak to me like that. You're no white knight yourself, even if the world seems to think you are. I might have put a dent in the Veryan pride but you, brother dear, nearly drove a coach and horses right through it. Don't worry. Big sister took care of things." With that she left the room.

"*Big sister took care of things.*" The words echoed through Charles's head as he stood up and gazed through the window on to skeletal branches of apple and plum trees. "*Big sister took care of things.*" Damn the woman! Why had she interfered without telling him anything? What had she said, what had she done? Was that why he was in such trouble now?

*

48

The churchbells were silent on Christmas Day and it poured with rain, but nothing could quell Jennie's excitement. Now, as she wore the new dress her mother had made, her brown eyes sparkled at the log fire burning in the large hearth and at the dining room aglow with candles. The dress was blue lawn and reached her ankles. Her first long dress. Cutting into her portion of goose, she stared curiously at the dark-haired RAF officer from the transmitting station who had been invited to share this Christmas dinner with them. She thought Flight Lieutenant Stewart quite good-looking but wondered why he kept staring across the table at her mother. It irritated her a little, but she soon forgot about it as the Christmas pudding was brought in, blue flames flickering as applause greeted its arrival.

In the Grand Chamber later, she sat on an eighteenth-century brocade sofa staring up at the intricate plaster work of the ceiling which had survived in good condition for three hundred years. Before her stood a large Steinway Grand and beside it a Welsh harp. Always used for soirees in the past, its scuffed floor was evidence that the elegant Grand Chamber with its gilded Grinling Gibbons carvings had now become a music room for the Allendale school. Strains of "*Parlez Moi D'Amour*" filled the room, reminding Jennie of the days in Paris when her parents had played it again and again in their apartment. This particular record had been brought here on a previous holiday. Her father had found it in the cupboard beside the radiogram and now he and her mother were dancing to it.

The voice of the female singer sang on as everyone now danced, her grandparents with each other, and Aunt Laura with Flight Lieutenant Stewart. Everyone save her and Clive. He had flatly refused to partner his cousin and stood now, looking bored. As Jennie watched her parents it seemed to her that they were sad. Then she saw her mother's tears and became alarmed.

On the turn, Charles caught a glimpse of his daughter's anxious face, whispered something to his wife who then smiled at Jennie and beckoned to her. Walking on to the floor, Jennie changed places with her mother and let her father sweep her around the room. She had now forgotten about his scars and if he felt any pain at all at having to bend forward, he showed no sign of it as Jennie gazed up at him adoringly.

"Why is Maman crying?"

Charles smiled sadly. "The song brings back memories, that's all. It makes her sad, it makes me sad, yet we play it. Aren't grown ups silly?"

As they waltzed Jennie felt she was on cloud nine. "*Parlez Moi D'Amour*" ... she loved the song, she loved dancing with her father, she wanted it to go on and on. Eventually, Charles drew Monique in and the three danced together – happy – sad – too filled with emotion to speak.

Florence watched them, thinking how perfect a family they were and how happy. Who could ever say now that Charles had not chosen well when he chose Monique? A lump formed in her throat as she thought how different this Christmas might have been, and how lucky they all were.

The following October, Churchill sent two warships to the Far East. *The Repulse* and the *Prince of Wales* set out packed with troops to augment the Singapore garrison. In November, Charles was ordered to the Colony with important despatches for the Governor. Before leaving, he travelled from Whitehall to Cornwall to say goodbye to his family.

Florence was outraged by the cold-heartedness of the Foreign Office. "How could they? How could they do this to a man so recently out of convalescence?"

"I've been back in harness for five months," Charles said. "Time I did my bit for King and country."

Monique was appalled. "The Far East? It is too dangerous. And they ask you to fly. Fly, in wartime, and all that way?"

Charles took her hand and, for one brief moment, allowed the mask to slip before recovering. "Safer surely than running the wolfpack gauntlet at sea? And quicker. Have no fear. B.O.A.C. will get me there in one piece. I have special status. So what few flights there are, I shall be on. All being well the journey out shouldn't take more than a week. I'm not sure how long I shall have to wait before returning, but there's every chance I shall be home in time for Christmas."

Monique knew him well enough to understand his desire not to worry her or his parents. But he was going into danger, terrible danger. The Japanese were slowly over-running the Far East. Supposing Singapore should fall?

As if reading her mind, he said. "Stop worrying. Singapore is probably the safest part of the Far East to be right now. It's impregnable. They're pouring British and Aussie troops into the Colony." But that night he held her in his arms and tried, in vain, to comfort her. Passion flared and their love making was desperate. On the day he left, she went to the station with him; they clung to each other and kissed; he felt her tears against his face and whispered: "Don't cry, darling. If I'm not back by Christmas, I'll make it in time for New Year and that's a promise."

Monique's lips formed a tremulous smile. It was unendurable but he had his orders and, just like everyone else, had to obey them. Had she

50

conceived that elusive son? If not, there might never be another chance, for this could be the last time she set eyes on the man she loved to distraction. The whistle blew, train doors slammed.

Tearing himself from her, Charles jumped on board just as the train started moving. Filled with anguished guilt and a sense of forboding, he leaned out of the window and waved back at his wife, staring until smoke and steam veiled her from his sight at last.

# Chapter Three

Charles was not home in time for Christmas or the New Year. The December attack on Pearl Harbour had closed all routes to the Far East, and he was trapped in Singapore when it fell to the Japanese in February 1942.

Stunned at the news, the family wandered around in a state of shock while Philip kept telephoning Whitehall only to be told again and again that communications with the Colony were cut off. "They don't know a damned thing," he said, slamming down the receiver for the umpteenth time. "Not a damned thing."

Monique was inconsolable. Could God really be so cruel as to let Charles go through all he had endured only to die in some distant British colony at the hands of the Japanese? Her letters to Jennie belied her fears, however, saying that she must not worry unduly for Papa. He would be be home when the war was over. Jennie must remember him in her prayers every night and place her trust in God who had kept them safe so far and would again.

Seven months later, on a warm Sunday afternoon, Jennie thought of that letter as she sat in a deckchair staring on to Portlyn's cricket field. At school, the far off place with the strange name had been meaningless to her, and that her father was there unreal. But during the Easter holidays and now, just starting her summer break, she had been struck by hideous reality. Yesterday Clive had told her in bland tones that her father was probably dead. "I've heard the Japanese are cruel to their prisoners. If he isn't finished already then he soon will be." Appalled at his words she had struck him hard across the face and called him a vicious liar. The look in his eyes was one she would never forget.

"Oh, well played," cried Philip as the spectators clapped.

Cricket! Didn't anybody care? Jennie's eyes and thoughts switched from her father to Mark who was too busy on the scoreboard even to glance in her direction. She willed him to see her sitting there in her favourite cotton dress, shoulder length hair gently curling and, she hoped, shining in the sunlight. Had she not spent over half an hour brushing it before leaving the house?

The match had been arranged by Philip and the Flight Lieutenant. Portlyn's depleted XI was augmented by the middle-aged, the unfit and those in reserved occupations, while Stewart had scratched around other units to find a "boys in blue" team and still leave himself with staff on duty. It was clear enough which side would win, but who cared? Certainly not Florence as she relaxed in her deckchair thinking how peaceful and normal it all seemed; cricket whites against verdant green; the crack of the ball on bat; polite clapping; clinking cups and women's voices from the pavilion – all evocative of better times and a necessary boost to morale. She had been doing a lot of that recently, boosting morale, with her no-nonsense attitude to her own fears and grief whilst dispensing tea and sympathy to those who had lost loved ones.

The Flight Lieutenant was walking to the crease. Jennie noticed that her mother had leaned forward in her chair, eyes intense, a half-smile on her lips. The heavy publican from the Harbour Inn started his run, lifted his right arm and bowled. Stewart's bat struck and a middle-aged Grammar School teacher found himself running breathlessly to the far end of the field as the officer scored four runs. When Monique joined in the clapping, Jennie recalled how the officer had looked at her mother that other Christmas which now seemed so far away. He had that same glint in his eye as he smiled across at Monique before returning to the crease. A chill swept through Jennie. Suddenly she felt threatened by this man.

In the pavilion later, people stood chatting over tea and sandwiches; above the general murmur, Jennie could hear Stewart trying to explain the intricacies of cricket to her mother's uncomprehending mind. Angry with both of them she walked out only to bump into Mark who was just entering.

"Hello," he said cheerfully. "When did you get back?"

"Yesterday," she snapped, pushing past and leaving him staring after her in confusion. Outside once more she stood for a moment looking at the chestnut trees which surrounded the field, her throat tightening with emotion. Papa was dead! Had he been so easily forgotten? Aware that someone was standing close by she turned to see Mark looking down at her anxiously. How tall and sturdy he seemed.

"I'm sorry about your father," he said gently. "Dad told me. But you mustn't worry. He'll be all right, you'll see."

Jennie shook her head. "Clive is convinced he's dead."

The swarthy face darkened with anger. "And he would know, would he? Ignore him, Jennie."

If only she could, but the thought had been with her ever since Clive had said it. Until now she had told no one, fearing to upset her mother. So why had she so easily told Mark, when only a moment ago she had been angry with him for ignoring her? Was it because his presence seemed so reassuring and he was the only one she could confide in? "How's Sophie?"

"She's fine. Come and see her tomorrow, why don't you?" He hovered uncertainly, asked if she would like a cup of tea, and when she shook her head, turned back to the pavilion. After a few moments, Jennie followed, thoughts of Sophie lifting her spirits. Why believe Clive? Why not believe Mark who had never let her down yet?

Laura stirred her tea with rapid movements, a sure sign that she was angered by Stewart's obvious attentions to Monique who was clearly enjoying them. Why she should feel this pang of jealousy over a man so many years her junior, she hardly knew. Perhaps if the woman concerned had not been Monique it would have been more acceptable, but it was Monique and ever since she had arrived in their midst, Laura had felt the coolness of her shadow. Monique shone; everyone adored her; but who glanced twice now at the woman who was once in line for "debutante of the year"? "Look at her," she whispered to Florence beneath the general hum of conversation. "French to her sensuous fingertips. She's acting disgracefully, Mummy. Really, she should remember who she is and where she is. Talk to her, before people start to notice."

Following her daughter's gaze, Florence saw two perfectly innocent people chatting over a cup of tea. "Really, Laura," she whispered. "Must you make such a fuss over nothing?" Smiling for the benefit of observers, she added, "Still, if it bothers you, I'll go over." Crossing to the corner of the room she joined her daughter-in-law and Ian Stewart. "Well now, have you finally managed to make the game of cricket comprehensible to a French woman?"

Laughing, the officer shook his head. "No, Lady Veryan. I'm afraid not. We've been discussing something quite different."

"Really?" Florence turned as Jennie joined them and thought the girl seemed troubled somehow.

"It seems the Government need French-speaking people to act as translators," Monique said.

Stewart smiled. "I was just saying to Mrs Veryan that if she felt like offering her services, she'd be snapped up. My brother's at the War Office and that's how I know about it."

His soft Edinburgh accent was beguiling but Florence raised disapproving eyebrows just the same. "Mrs Veryan already does a great deal of charity work for the war effort and she has a daughter to raise. Her duties are very much centred here without the need to join up."

Rather wishing he had not broached the subject at all, Stewart looked a shade embarrassed, but he had seen Monique wandering around alone without husband or child to care for any longer and knew of her deep unhappiness. "I'm sure there are posts for civilians. But, of course, it would mean Mrs Veryan having to leave here."

"Then it's quite out of the question," said Florence firmly, closing the subject once and for all and noticing, with relief, that people were filing out of the pavilion. "Ah, it seems the match is about to resume. Come along, Jennie. Didn't you have any tea, dear?"

Monique was thoughtful as she followed them. Translate! It sounded interesting and would give her lonely life a focus. Furthermore she would be helping the country she had come to know and love as much as she loved France. She watched as Ian Stewart walked out on to to the field then sat down beside her daughter once more, wondering why she felt suddenly elated. Was it because the Scotsman was attractive and obviously attracted to her? Was it because everyone was certain that Charles was still alive? Or was it because, for the first time since her marriage, someone perceived her to be a person in her own right and not an appendage of the Veryan family. All over the country, women were being called on to serve in the Forces or in factories unless they had children. No baby had come of that last night with Charles and her daughter was more away now than at home, so what was she doing here when more important work called her? Furthermore she rather resented the way her life was organised by her mother-in-law. It was time things changed. Glancing at her daughter, she wondered why Jennie refused to meet her gaze.

"Do you believe Uncle Charles is still alive?"

It was the end of the summer and Laura was ticking off the inventory list as she placed each article of school clothing into neat piles on her son's bed. "Yes, I do."

"Really?" Clive stared out of the window once more. Bitterly disappointed that his father had returned to Buckland Park on leave but had not sent for him as promised, he had spent the past weeks hurt and angry. Now his thoughts turned to the future. He was sixteen, but what were his expectations? Most of his friends were rich while he and his mother had to go cap in hand to his grandfather for everything. Lately he had wondered just where he fitted into Trevellan's well-ordered line if it was no longer so well ordered. "But what if you're wrong? What if Uncle Charles is dead?"

Laura frowned. "Please, Clive. I don't even want to think about it."

"Well, someone must," he said flatly. "Because if he is and Grandpa kicked the bucket tomorrow, it follows that the estate must pass to me as nearest male in line."

For some time Laura remained silent, not only because she found her son's questions heartless and mercenary but because she really had no idea which way things would jump should word come through that Charles was officially dead. "The will isn't tied to the nearest male in line. Until now the Veryans have always produced heirs so that hasn't been necessary. Sadly the title would die out and, as the will stands, the estate would pass to Jennie."

"Jennie!" Clive rounded on his mother. "But that's ludicrous. Grandpa would never let Trevellan go to a girl, for God's sake, and a Frog at that."

"That's enough." Everything her son was saying echoed her own thoughts exactly – now that he had brought them face to face with the issue – but to say such things aloud was foolhardy. "Listen to me, Clive. It is absolutely essential that you keep such opinions to yourself. Do you understand? My parents are good enough to allow us to live here since we have no home of our own. God knows our position is frail enough without your wagging tongue. Do nothing to set your grandfather against you. Meanwhile, we must all pray that my brother will return to us fit and well one day and . . ."

"And if he doesn't, are you saying it's to be our lot to go cap in hand to a French woman and her daughter in order to be allowed to live in a house that has been in our family for generations? This is our *home*, Mother."

Laura started placing the neat piles of clothes into the school trunk and said quietly, "I am saying, go back to Winchester, concentrate on your education and rely on no one. Be independent, Clive. I only wish I could have been. Meanwhile, forget this conversation."

But Clive could not forget it. The matter exercised his thoughts until, restless with anger, he walked to the gun room, took a rifle from the cupboard and strode out of the house without anyone seeing him.

The sunny warmth of morning had not lived up to its promise and the September day had settled into a grey damp chill with a slight autumn mist in the air. Seated astride Kelly, Jennie trotted ahead of Mark into Farthing Field with the kestrel on her gloved fist. Bells jingled, large brown wings lifted slightly, talons gripped the fist for balance until Jennie drew rein. Gently, she removed the crimson hood. The round head swivelled this way and that. "Dear little Sophie. I'm going to miss you so dreadfully. There you go." With that she let the jesses slip through her fingers, watching as the falcon soared higher and higher into a grey sky to hover above the field. As she stared up, Jennie thought of the long warm summer when she and Mark had spent lazy happy days together with Sophie, days which for her had passed all too quickly. In forty-eight hours she would be on her way back to Keswick and they wouldn't meet again until Christmas. Her heart sank at the thought. Christmas was an eternity away. At that moment she saw the kestrel dive to the ground and heard Mark's excited cry.

"She's caught something. She's actually caught something.!"

Jennie looked anxious. "If she can hunt, she'll fly away."

Mark shook his head, delight written across his features. "Manned falcons don't fly off. If they did no one would ever hunt with them. She's probably caught a vole. Look at her, sitting there, proud as an eagle with her first kill. Wasn't she quick though? A peregrine can strike its prey mid-air, killing it instantly."

Jennie shivered, the effects of a cold still with her. "That sounds cruel."

Mark shook his head. "On the contrary, it's far more cruel to shoot game. That's mass slaughter and many of the birds are badly wounded. With a falcon it's one fatal blow and that's that. Nature's precision instrument."

Jennie glanced across at Mark, thinking how manly and attractive he was, especially on horseback. He seemed born to the saddle. "How long can a falcon live?"

"Ten, maybe fifteen years in the wild," said Mark. "In captivity, well, maybe twenty to thirty. It depends."

"That long? What will you do when you get a job and go away?"

Mark frowned. Go away? Until now the thought had not crossed his mind. This was where he belonged, here with Sophie. "I won't. I'll work on the land so that I can look after her. I'm already helping out at Home Farm and earning money." He looked perturbed then said, "No. I couldn't bear to part with Sophie. I couldn't bear that. She's so much part of my life now."

A twinge of jealousy swept over Jennie, but it faded as Sophie swooped across the field and landed on her outstretched hand. "I wish I didn't have to leave. I get so desperately homesick."

Mark wished she didn't have to leave as well, then told himself he was being stupid. Why should it bother him where Jennie was? But it did. How his friends would laugh if they knew. But then they had never met this girl who was not like other girls. There was a mature stillness in her which belied her age so that he had never considered the difference in their years. He enjoyed her company, and took pleasure in explaining things to her, seeing her looking up at him with those wide solemn eyes, eyes that made him feel protective. As Jennie cast the falcon off once more, he realised how pale she was. "You look ill."

"It's this wretched cold," she murmured. Shivering, she conceded defeat. "I'll have to go home anyway. I'm supposed to be helping Maman to pack my things. Shall we meet again tomorrow morning . . . to say goodbye?" Even thinking of it was unbearable.

"Of course," he answered quietly. "I'll be here at nine-thirty."

"Nine-thirty then." Removing the glove and handing it back to Mark she watched as Sophie circled the field, then turned Kelly and rode away until she came to woodland and the old familiar track once more. Everything was still and quiet, the only sound a dull thud as Kelly's hooves trod the muddy path. Jennie hardly noticed, her body craving warmth and hot liquid. Mrs Hodges would offer both and thoughts of the kitchen with its cooking smells and glowing fire in the range were comforting.

A gun shot cracked the air. Kelly started as much as Jennie; it took time to calm the frightened pony. Another shot followed. Birds flew up in alarm and Kelly shied. Suddenly a figure came out of nowhere and stood on the path before her. This time Kelly reared, sending Jennie crashing to the ground. Bruised and shaken, she lay there for a moment then looked up. Clive was standing over her, rifle in one hand, dead rabbit in the other.

"You stupid fool!" she cried.

"Really?" He grinned down at her. "You're the one incapable of controlling your pony."

Struggling slowly and painfully to her feet, Jennie stood still as the world spun around her. The moment passed. She saw Kelly several yards further on, was relieved the pony hadn't bolted and looked up at Clive with blazing eyes. "Thanks a bundle for helping me up. What on earth do you think you're doing? You ought to know better than to fire guns on the pathway and jump out in front of horses. Does Grandpa know you've taken that rifle?"

The grin faded and his eyes glinted like steel. "I've been around guns for most of my life and don't need permission from you on how and when to shoot a bloody rabbit. This is a private path on a private estate."

Jennie was raging but the shock of the fall had still not passed and she just wanted to go home. Saying nothing more to Clive she stumbled past him towards Kelly who, trembling with nerves, moved slightly at her approach. Finally hauling an unwilling and bruised body back into the saddle, she turned to see Clive walking on through the woodland. What on earth had got into her cousin? A row perhaps? This wouldn't be the first time he had fired off at anything moving after losing his temper. She eased Kelly forward once more but after two hundred yards reined to a halt, seeing in her mind's eye Clive walking back the way she had just come – walking towards Farthing Field. Sophie! Turning Kelly at once, she cantered back along the path, fear increasing as her eyes searched for Clive. There was no sign of him. She headed into the wood, finally breaking into the clearing. Clive stood at the edge of the field, his rifle aimed skywards.

"No," screamed Jennie. "It's Sophie!" But even as she cried out her voice was lost in the explosion from Clive's rifle. For one horrifying moment, she watched as Sophie's wings folded and the kestrel plummeted to the ground. There was a deathly silence. Stunned, she just sat there, unable to believe what she had just witnessed. Then, springing into life, she dismounted, raced across to Clive and pounded him with clenched fists. "You've killed her. I warned you but you've killed her..." Breaking off, sobbing, she saw Mark chasing over the field towards the still body of the falcon.

Jennie could not run, her assault on Clive having drained her remaining strength. Staggering to where Mark was kneeling, she stood gazing down in shock. Sophie lay still on the grass, her brown and beige feathers covered in blood. Mark was like stone, while she fell to weeping. "It was Clive. I tried to stop him ... I tried ... but he ... he knew ... he knew it was Sophie." She looked up from the small bloodied falcon and saw how white Mark's face had become. The muscle of his jaw clenched and unclenched and his eyes were dark with hatred. "I tried to warn him," she repeated weakly.

When Mark found his voice it was a strangled whisper. "Would it have made any difference?" There were no more words. The look on his face said everything. Picking up Sophie, he cradled the flopping head gently in his hands. The bells jingled slightly and the jesses hung loose. Standing with the small warm body, he turned away quickly and Jennie knew he wanted to be alone with his grief. When she looked towards the wood, Clive had gone.

In her room later, she glanced at the hideous bruises on her arm but could only see Sophie falling from the sky and the look on Mark's face. His anguish was her anguish. She looked at the wall and saw the painting of Sophie she had completed only recently then fell on to her bed and wept.

"Good God, it was only a kestrel!" cried Clive, unable to understand why everyone was staring at him in such a fashion.

"Only a kestrel?" Florence glared at her grandson, unable to contain her fury as the argument proceeded in the drawing room before dinner. She had heard Jennie rushing into the house sobbing hysterically and gone to the girl's bedroom to find her in a terrible state. Learning what had happened, she decided to wait until the entire family was gathered together so that Clive could have his say, for surely he had made a dreadful mistake? Now, his complete lack of guilt or sorrow was proving too much. It was a tragic thing but Florence had never loved nor even liked her only grandson. There was too much of John Willoughby about him, even to the brown hair and acquisitive grey eyes. She took a glass of sherry from Philip and went on in a quiet voice which was a warning to everyone that her anger was intense: "Sophie was a manned kestrel and meant a lot to Mark. You knew about her. Everyone did. And Jennie called out a warning."

Clive merely shrugged. "Did she? I didn't hear her. It was a mistake, that's all."

Philip glared at his grandson. "You haven't yet explained why you took a rifle without asking my permission. Don't look like that, Clive. You know the rules. No one wanders about shooting on my land without my say-so. Damn it all, you might just as easily have hit Jennie. Has that thought occurred to you?"

No, it had not, but right now Clive rather wished he *had* hit Jennie. Not only was she likely to take what he now perceived as his, she wanted to cause him trouble as well.

Laura placed comforting hands on her son's shoulders. "Clive has clearly made a mistake, but must we keep on at the boy when he only has two more days left at home? Perhaps if you apologised, Clive, we could put this unfortunate incident behind us and enjoy our dinner."

"Very well," he murmured with little grace. "I apologise. Will that satisfy everyone?"

"No," snapped Jennie with hate in her eyes. "Because I know you did it deliberately."

Later that evening, Monique went to her daughter's room and gazed down at the velvet brown eyes staring up from the pillow, sad eyes that tugged at the heart. "You must stop crying, *ma chérie*. I know how much Sophie meant to you and Mark but she is gone now as all wild things go away in the end."

"She didn't go away, Clive killed her, and I hate him. I hate him and wish he was dead."

"Do not be so harsh. I believe Clive is truly sorry. Everyone is so cross with him. He is a sad and unhappy young man."

"I'm not surprised," snapped Jennie. She wiped her eyes with her handkerchief and sniffed. "I was going to meet Mark tomorrow morning to say goodbye to him and to ... but now ..." Her voice choked on a sob and she turned her face away as tears flowed once more. "Poor little Sophie ... I loved her so much."

60

Kissing her gently, Monique murmured, "But soon you will be with Louise Boyd and your other friends and have so much to talk about you will forget in time, or accept it more easily. We shall stay with Maddie overnight. I wonder if she has any more paintings to show us? We shall take her eggs, cheese and some home-made jam. Now then, close your eyes and try to sleep. One cannot change the past."

Jennie lay on her back gazing into darkness for hours. "*One cannot change the past.*" But Sophie's death had changed her future. No longer would she be able to meet Mark as she had. Sophie had brought them together and her death would now part them. To Mark she was just a schoolgirl who liked kestrels, that was all. Her presence beside him now would only cause embarrassment. Clive would never know the true extent of the damage and grief he had wrought. She would never forget or forgive him for this day's work.

Dressed in her navy school gymslip over a white blouse, Jennie stood on the south lawn saying a fond farewell to Portia and Rosalind. Yesterday she had wanted to say goodbye to Mark also and had ridden to his house only to be told by his saddened mother that he was out and would be for the rest of the day. With a sinking heart, she had murmured, "Please tell him how deeply sorry I am ... so very sorry." She had then ridden away and spent the last day of her holidays within Trevellan's stone walls. Now it was almost time to leave. She bent to stroke Portia then saw someone walking along the drive. It was Mark. Heart lifting at his approach, she searched his face for any tell-tale sign of accusation. Was he blaming her for being related to the creature who had killed the thing he loved most in this world?

Mark smiled shyly, thinking how different she looked in her uniform. Even so, seeing her brought it all back, the shock, the grief and the hatred. For a moment there was an awkward pause as they stared at each other and then the false light tones. "Hope you're feeling better?"

"Oh, yes, heaps. I rode to your place yesterday but you were out."

The mask dropped slightly then was raised again. "I know. That's why I came to say goodbye and to give you this." Mark reached into his jacket pocket and produced a small framed photograph. "Dad took it at Easter. Do you remember? I had a copy made for you."

Jennie took the photograph and looked at it. Sophie was on her gloved fist; the kestrel's dark eyes were staring straight into the camera lens. A lump formed in her throat. "If only I'd been quicker, just thought earlier, I could have stopped him. By the time I twigged, it was too late. There's been an almighty row. I think Clive now hates me as much as I hate him." She paused and looked thoughtful. "Wait there. I've something for you." With that she chased back into the house to

61

reappear with the watercolour of Sophie which she handed to him. "Maman had it mounted and framed in St Ives only last week. I've been meaning to show it to you but now I want you to keep it."

Mark took the painting of Sophie on her perch, remembering the day when Jennie had worked on the initial sketch. Now she had painted in the brown and creamy-beige feathers so delicately that he wanted to touch them once more. He gazed lovingly at the soft rounded head, the talons which used to grasp his hand now grasping the perch, the little bells around the leg and that all-seeing eye, and wondered how a girl of Jennie's age could capture Sophie with such surprising vigour. "How can I take this from you?" he murmured thickly. "It's far too good; the best thing you've ever done."

"I want you to have it. I feel it belongs to you anyway."

"Thank you," whispered Mark. His throat ached and he hardly dared say another word for fear of shaming himself by showing emotion. When, at last, he deemed it safe, he went on: "What ... what time are you leaving?"

"Any minute now."

"Well," he murmured, "the next thing you know it'll be Christmas and you'll be home again."

She stared up at him balefully. "But it won't be like it was."

He shook his head, and swallowed hard. "I buried her in the garden. Put her in a box and made a grave beneath the lilac bush. Dad's got his shed back and the perches have been chopped up. I couldn't bear ... I couldn't bear to see them." Voice cracking, he turned away. "Well, I'll say goodbye. Have a good term and thanks again for this."

Walking back across the lawn with the picture under his arm he knew he would hang it on the wall of his bedroom beside the bells and jesses to remind him, not only of Sophie, but of Jennie also who was leaving. "*It won't be like it was.*" One short sentence that said so much. With Sophie gone, Jennie felt she had no reason to see him any more. He would miss her, miss her more than she could ever know. He thought again how his friends would laugh, but they could never be expected to understand those happy, halcyon days he had shared with this girl and his kestrel. Days that would never come again. Clive had destroyed all that with one expert shot. Mark would never forgive him, or lose the hatred he now felt for him.

While most of Britain lay beneath January snows, spring had come early to Cornwall. Daffodils and almond blossom shone in morning sunlight as Monique wandered through the grounds of Trevellan, deep in thought, wondering at the decision she must now make; a decision she had never dreamed would have to be made.

Before his posting in October Ian Stewart had, at her request, given her an address to write to in Whitehall. Within two weeks of sending the letter she was being ushered into a drab London office where a man in civilian clothes wanted to know where she had been born and raised, who her parents were, her relations, and which areas of France she knew well? He asked about her husband's career and wanted to know about the diplomatic receptions she had attended, especially in France. Surprised at such questions, she had been forced to explain, with some embarrassment, that illness had prevented her from attending such occasions. What illness? Blushing to the roots of her hair, she had explained. The interview had ended politely but no position as a translator had been offered, leaving her feeling deflated. Since then she had been called back twice, only to learn that her interviewer was not part of the War Office but in Intelligence, and actively seeking suitable people to send to France where a resistance movement had been formed against German occupational forces. They needed people who could pass as French and who knew France well enough to act as couriers and agents in the field.

She walked on through the orchard remembering how she had listened in stunned disbelief at first. France? Occupied France? He was surely confusing her with someone else? "I am sorry, but I am not the suitable person you require. I have no skills and even less courage. I also have a daughter to think about." He had understood, asked her to give the matter some thought and told her that all she had learned was top secret. She *had* given the matter some thought, in fact for two weeks she had thought of nothing else, then contacted him again and asked: "What exactly is it that you require of me?"

To be in the French Section of the SOE, he had told her. Then he spoke of a long and arduous training period with stringent tests throughout the course. Of those who started this training, few made it through to the end. It took a very special kind of person to be sent to France. Only time would tell if she was that kind of person. He emphasised the danger of the work but spoke of its immense importance when the day came to invade the shores of France and push the Germans back where they belonged.

"But, please, Mrs Veryan, do understand there is no obligation placed upon you because we have had these informal talks. It will take a lot of thought before you decide, and I quite understand if you decide to say no. Your only obligation is to remember that all you have learned is absolutely top secret. Say nothing to anyone, even to your own family."

"*There is no obligation.*" The words kept floating through her mind as she wandered on through the estate and found herself on the woodland path which led to the cove. No obligation! Yet now that the matter had been laid before her she felt there was every obligation. How could he speak of work essential to the liberation of her own country without touching her patriotic heart and stirring her French blood?

She had reached the cove now, the cold wind numbing her as it sent waves crashing down on to rocks with the incoming tide. Feeling the spray on her face, she stood on the steps watching the restless surge of the sea, the woollen cloth of her trousers flapping against bare legs. The sky above was a pale grey-blue, but on the horizon dark clouds were gathering and racing shorewards. Soon they would drive away the sunshine and the day become colder. The roar of the sea and the keenness of the wind touched her turbulent soul; suddenly her whole being cried out to be one of those who would help push the Germans out of her country and back where they belonged. Then she thought of Jennie and felt her spirits sink once more. How could she do this to the child? The dangers of the work were considerable. Oh, if only Ian Stewart had never mentioned the idea of translating in the first place then she would not be in this terrible quandary now. Monique Gravier of St Cloud, daughter of a restaurant owner, working as a secret agent in occupied France? Ludicrous! It was men's work surely? Charles would be appalled; surprised too if he thought his wife could be of some use in this man's world – this man's war. To be of use. Until now that had meant producing a son and heir. She had failed in that but she had a daughter to think about. She must refuse. Of course she must refuse. Surely she must refuse?

The clouds were almost overhead now and the wind even stronger. Her spirit sharpened as the cold air cleared her confused mind. Into it came the memory of Stukers diving on to a straggling column of refugees; of Charles dragging Jennie from the flames and the sound that had never left her – the terrible sound of men dying. Her face twisted with fury and all doubts were overcome. Turning from the cove, she walked back to the house. She had made her decision and, whatever the cost, she knew it to be the right one.


"The First Aid Nursing Yeomanry?" Florence looked up from her embroidery, amazed at Monique's sudden announcement. "Like the VADs, do you mean? But my dear, you're not a nurse."

"I shan't be nursing," said Monique, gazing through the window of the morning room on to the orchard. "It's a voluntary unit that handles all kinds of things, like translating, driving, working in canteens and such like." She did not add that the SOE used this outfit as a useful cover. Enrolled as an officer, she was to report for initial training the following day.

Staring over his copy of *The Times*, Philip frowned. "You've left it a bit late, springing all this on us."

Monique folded her arms and smiled. "I knew you would try to turn me against it. I just want to do my bit to help the war effort. I've been in London quite a lot lately, and seen Maddie risking her life night after night driving ambulances through the most devastating air raids. We're all so safe and out of it down here. If you knew, if you had seen ... well, then you would understand why I feel I have no business being here when I could be of use." They were not making life any easier for her, the fears and doubts having returned soon after telephoning to say she would accept. That had been four weeks ago. Now wheels were turning and she was to report to London in the morning.

Florence frowned. "I thought we had decided long ago that the whole thing was out of the question?"

Monique smiled and headed for the door. "You decided that. I decided nothing."

Laura waited until she left the room then turned to her mother, smiling thinly. "Wants to do her bit indeed! I think we all know what she really wants. Our absent RAF friend seems to have put big ideas into her head. She's out for a good time and I'm sure she'll have no trouble finding it. Poor Charles."

Florence shot her daughter a black look. "That's a churlish and unworthy thing to say. Now that I've had time to digest it, I think we should all feel proud that a French woman is willing to wear a British uniform to help this country. No, I was wrong and Monique is right. She has a skill which is needed and work will be good for her."

"You said yourself that she had work enough here," snapped Laura.

Florence smiled. "Good works and charity all have their place, but there are enough of us to keep things going on that front. No, Laura, let those who can, do. Let those who can't, run the white elephant stall!"

"Thank you, Mummy." Laura thumbed through a copy of *Vogue*, trembling with rage. "At least we shall be here for Jennie. Some of us still retain a sense of responsibility."

"It will take her mind off things," Florence went on. "Monique's had a pretty dreadful time. She's in constant fear over Charles, lost without her daughter, worrying about her friends in Paris and ..."

"Paris!" Laura raised well-plucked eyebrows and flung the magazine down on to the coffee table. "Why should she worry about Paris, for God's sake? While our cities are being razed to the ground, Paris remains untouched and doing very nicely thank you. I hear that night life still flourishes; that the Folies Bergère puts on good shows for the enemy, and restaurants are as busy as ever with all those German mouths to feed. No, darlings, when this war is over, Britain will be a mess while Monique will still have her lovely Paris. One day she'll have Trevellan too. What is so dreadful about that?"

In her bedroom, Monique took a few essential clothes from her drawers and wardrobe, her mind dwelling on what she had been told during her last interview. If caught, she would be alone. The French Section would be unable to help her. Again she had been asked if she was certain about her decision. Again she had replied that she was. Slowly she sank down on to her bed. Now it would begin. First the course, and throughout it the constant assessment of her worth. France! The thrill and the horror of it suddenly overwhelmed her. But France was a long way off. Most failed after the first month of the course. She would surely be one of them. With a discreet knock on the door, Keynes entered with a pressed khaki uniform and a brown leather suitcase. "Lady Veryan asked me to bring this to you, Madam. Would you care to let Rosa help you with the packing?" When Monique said that would not be necessary, he turned as if to leave, then paused and looked back at her gravely. "May I say, on behalf of the staff, how very sorry we shall be to see you go."

Monique looked at him in surprise and a smile lit her lovely face. "Why, thank you, Keynes. That was kind. But I shall be home on leave before you know it."

"We shall all look forward to that, Madam." The butler walked out leaving Monique sitting on the bed, her face twisted with anxiety. Jennie! Supposing she did get through the full training course. What then? Would she be chosen for France? Could she go and leave Jennie? It was her own choice. As they had told her time and time again, "*There is no obligation.*"

Leaning back in her garden chair, Maddie placed plump arms behind her head and listened to the blackbird singing on the rear wall of her Chelsea garden. It had been a warm and busy day, but now in the cool dusk of a September evening she could relax in peace and comfort, thankful she was off duty and praying there would be no air-raids that night. "It was hearing the news from a casual acquaintance that clinched the insult." She glanced at Monique seated beside her wondering why she seemed so detached, almost as though she hadn't heard a word, and wondering also how it was that only a French woman could manage to look good in khaki? "He didn't even have the decency to tell me himself. Weekend leave and Bob's your uncle! Banker's daughter apparently. Ungrateful wretch. I put Bruce on the first rung of the ladder to success. Where would he have been without my patronage, my studio, my gallery or my contacts?"

Monique's mind had been elsewhere but now she dragged it back to the present. "Does it hurt so very much?"

After a pause, Maddie nodded. "Yes. But it's my own fault. I knew what he was and should have been more sensible. But I did love him and we're never sensible at such times. Now I feel shoddy and ... well ... used."

Sad for her friend but not surprised at the news, Monique gazed at the garden which had once been a lovely Arcadia in busy London. Now she found herself staring at rows of vegetables around an Anderson shelter. How many nights had she spent in that musty shelter, listening to the bombs rain down and being deafened by ack-ack guns? "That was a good dinner, Maddie. What do cooks do to camp food, I wonder?"

"God knows. Whatever it is, they spend years training to do it. So then, when are you off to the Land of Song?"

Monique shifted her eyes. "I'm not sure. Three days perhaps. But I must be on that night train, Maddie. There will be little enough time to see Jennie in any case, and no time to stay over in a room this time. Journeys seem to take for ever these days."

Monique had arrived at Maddie's that same afternoon, her training course completed at last. Of the many who'd started she was one of the few who had made it through to the end and been picked for France. She'd never thought it would truly happen. But she had trained until she was physically fit, learned how to use radio transmitters, how to send in Morse code and how to handle explosives and firearms. On a gruelling commando course she had learned the techniques of sabotage, used live ammunition, scaled Scottish mountains and been put through scenarios which tested her courage and endurance to the limit. At the Parachute School she had dropped, in utter terror, from a Whitely bomber, and now the last and most testing part of the training had just finished. In a large house in the New Forest she had learned the fine art of spying and deception. Her quickness of thinking and ability to adapt to any crisis had marked her out as one of the "special" people. Tested again and again on her cover story, she now wore it like a new skin. Monique Veryan was no more. From now on she had a new French identity, a code name, and in two or three days' time would be on stand by for France. The myth of Wales was to allay any awkward questions.

"Why this rush to the Lakes?" Maddie wanted to know. "You'll get leave soon enough and will be nearer to Jennie, in fact."

"I want to see her now." Monique fell quiet, longing to see her

67

daughter yet dreading the moment also. How would she bear up under such circumstances? Would Jennie read the fear in her eyes, or the anguish she was feeling? Whatever happened, she must be convincing for the girl's sake. She would not wear her FANY uniform as she had the last time she'd visited Keswick; she wanted to appear in something bright and cheerful. It might help. "Maddie, I've been thinking about Jennie's future. When she's the right age I would like her to go to a good art school. Would you take her under your wing for me?"

"Of course. No problem, I've masses of room here."

"No ... I mean a little more than that. Should anything happen to me ... oh, I know Florence will raise Jennie well ... but when she's older and studying in London, will you be her guardian and look after her as you know I would look after her? Find the right school, help her and educate her in matters of art?"

Maddie looked bemused. "Of course. But what do you mean, should anything happen to you? What on earth could happen to you in Wales, for heaven's sake?"

"I could be posted anywhere. It is wartime. Who knows what may happen? And with Charles gone ... well ... I would just feel better knowing that Jennie would be in your safe and competent hands."

"You have my promise." Maddie frowned and rose from her deck-chair, a slightly slimmer figure than the pre-war Juno. "But you really mustn't be so pessimistic."

"Where are you going?" asked Monique.

"To get that bottle of malt whisky I've been saving for two years. I reckon you could do with a stiff one. I know I could."

Jennie had been in a state of excitement all day and her heart was in her mouth as she waited outside the hotel which the school had taken over. It had been some time since she had last seen her mother. Her greatest disappointment was not having her around during the Easter and summer holidays. Then last night had come the telephone call from Maddie's house, saying she was on her way.

At long last a woman came into sight, a slight pretty woman wearing a blue suit with a small perky hat. Blue! How lovely to see her out of khaki, although it had to be admitted that the other girls found her mother fascinating with her French accent and her uniform with its smart beret. Jennie ran forward and soon mother and daughter were hugging each other, laughing and crying at the same time.

Monique stroked Jennie's shining face, told her she was looking well and pretty, only to hear the wail: "No, Maman, I'm all spotty and fat."

She smiled. "It is only puppy fat and the spots will go if you drink plenty of water." Her smile faded. "I'm afraid that this time I shan't be able to see your teachers. We have so little time and I want to spend it all with you, *ma chérie*. Now then, where shall we have tea? The same place as before?"

They walked to a small cottage restaurant in the lakeland town and sat chatting over muffins and sponge cake. Asked how her journey had been, Monique replied, "Good," thinking it had been utter hell. The train had been hot and overcrowded with troops. Perhaps it was the blue suit and perky hat that enabled her to get a seat, but she had stayed awake all night in a smoke-filled carriage as the express chugged its way through a blacked out England and had arrived very, very late. Soon she would be making the same journey all over again.

As they drank their tea and ate their muffins, they laughed and chatted, discussed Jennie's school activities, her excursions with the Art Club and progress in class. Jennie wanted to know all about her mother's translating job and whether she had now mastered the typewriter she had been training on for so long.

"You will get home for Christmas, won't you, Maman? They must give you leave for Christmas. So far it's always been during term time, but Christmas is different."

Monique's face shadowed. "I hope so. But I can promise nothing." The crestfallen look on Jennie's face stabbed at her heart. She took her daughter's hand and held it tightly. "I want you to be very adult about this, Genevieve. I have to do as I am told, just as you do. My work is very important and there are certain times when I cannot just leave it. It would help me more than you know to try to understand, because I find it as hard as you do, *ma chérie*..." Her voice began to break, and she swallowed some tea to disguise her emotion. "This really is a beautiful area. I'm glad you go for long walks. I want you to promise me you will paint Derwent Water. Paint it for me. It can be a Christmas present."

As Jennie listened she found her mother's voice falsely bright and tremulous, the smile a shade too brittle. There was something wrong. Something her mother wasn't telling her.

Monique searched in her handbag and produced a piece of paper with something written on it. "Now then, I go to Wales soon but my job may send me anywhere after that. So you must send your letters to this address and they will be posted on to me. It might take time, so do not worry if letters cross... maybe... they will even get lost. If that should happen, you must not think I have forgotten you, *ma chérie*." She thought of the many letters she had handed to the French Section to be posted on to Jennie, boring bland letters saying how much she missed and loved her and hoped they would meet soon. Until now she had written freely, even though her letters had been read before being sent

69

on, but from now on there could be no communication. She wouldn't even know if Jennie was ill.

Jennie looked at the strange address and shook her head. "But I shan't know where you are." She turned to her mother who was looking into her handbag once more, ostensibly searching for a lipstick. Her hands were trembling slightly. There was something wrong. "Has there been word of Papa?"

"No ... no word ... so that is good news." Finding this unbearable, Monique smiled, held up a small mirror and re-touched her lips. "Now tell me more about school life, and the play you've just been in? I would love to have seen it. The Allendale boys put on their play in the village hall. Their parents couldn't go of course but our theatre-starved villagers enjoyed it."

At last Jennie asked about Mark. At Easter and summer she had seen nothing of him. Had Louise not spent three weeks of the holidays at Trevellan, Jennie would have been desolate. Her mother smiled and shrugged. "Mark is almost a young man now, Genevieve. He studies hard and works also. Mr Curnow tells me his son hopes to pass his advanced exams so that he can go on an agricultural course. That takes money and Mark is trying to earn as much as he can during his holidays to help his father."

Jennie felt better after this explanation. At least he was not trying to avoid her.

At last it was time to head back to the school in a hotel close to the station. Dreading the moment to come, Monique tried to sound bright. "I was very surprised to find the waiting room had become a classroom. It must have upset the teacher when I walked through."

"Don't worry," murmured Jennie, feeling already that she was going to cry. "It happens all the time. We're used to it."

When the time came to part, Monique clasped her daughter to her and tried desperately to keep a hold on her emotions. But her anguish was too great as she wondered if she would ever hold Jennie in her arms again?

Feeling her mother's shuddering Jennie knew now that something was very wrong and, fearful, couldn't stop the tears from streaming down her face as she clung to her tightly, crying, "Don't go, Maman, don't leave me!" Her mother looked stricken as she eased away, turned quickly and headed towards the station, wiping her eyes with a handkerchief. Jennie watched her go then waved goodbye as the woman in the neat blue suit and pretty hat raised her hand, blew a kiss then walked around the corner and out of her sight.

Three days later, Monique climbed into a bomber with another agent,

70

wishing her heart would stop pounding. This was it, the moment she had always assumed would never really come. In a few hours she would be hurtling out of this plane into a dark cold void, praying she and her colleague would land safely and be found by the "reception committee" sent to meet them. Dressed in French clothing, even to her make-up and hairstyle, she fiddled nervously with the straps of her parachute; another would drop with her case. On her she had her French identity card, francs, and a lethal pill should she be caught. The last, she told herself, she would never use. The engines turned over; the aircraft shuddered then roared along the runway. Monique crossed herself, murmured a quick prayer and thought with anguish of the child she was leaving. The bomber climbed into the night sky and moved across England towards the Channel and the coast of France.

On a cool April night, Jennie could not sleep and lay tossing in her bed unable to shake off the fearful sense of forboding that kept sweeping through her. Having recovered from a bout of glandular fever, she had returned that day from the sick bay to the room she shared with four other girls. During her illness, her grandmother had written and telephoned but not once had she heard from her mother. It worried and dismayed her. Even the letters had stopped coming weeks ago. Having not seen her at Christmas after all, she had left the painting of Derwent Water, wrapped and ready at Trevellan, should her mother arrive home. But why were there no more letters? Had Maman forgotten her now that she was so very busy in her new life?

Climbing out of bed, she shivered in the cold, pulled back the blackout curtain and looked out on to a bright moonlit night. How beautiful, she thought, gazing up at the millions of stars. How utterly, utterly beautiful.

The moonlight was ideal for the Lysander pilot as he looked down at the Normandy countryside. He was searching for a field and a signal. At last he saw it, tiny pinpricks of lights picking out a small landing strip.

Holding one of the torches, Monique was tense and watchful as the plane made its descent. Her sixth sense warned of danger and her sixth sense had never let her down yet. She hoisted the strap of her sten gun firmly on to her shoulder and, tense as a bird, kept a watchful eye on the woods skirting the field. Beside her stood the agent who had been with her from the first. Together they had shared many dangerous moments, co-ordinated a network of resistance in the area, carried out sabotage raids and despatched coded messages to London, enabling the SOE to evaluate the strength of German troop movements and the locations of

71

potential air targets. Now London was calling him in. A big operation was about to begin and they needed him for the vital information he carried in his head and to take charge of the mission. His importance was incalculable. The Lysander was landing. Was that a movement to her left or a trick of the light? "*Au revoir*, Maurice," she whispered.

Maurice raced out across the field to the plane, waiting with its engines still running. A young woman climbed out. This was her first assignment and Monique knew how she felt as another agent ran forward to lead her to the waiting bicycles hidden in the woods. Maurice was just climbing into the Lysander when gunfire shattered the night. Monique swung to her left and let off a burst from her sten gun, drawing fire from the Lysander to her. As it gathered speed she kept the Germans pinned down by firing round after round. Then the plane soared into the moonlit sky. She saw it briefly, held her breath then let out a sigh of relief as it disappeared. "Go," she cried to the others. "I'll hold them off. Go to the farm ... warn the group. You know what to do. Go. Get her away now..."

Firing off another burst, to give the others time to get clear, she could make out the soldiers in the bright moonlight. About ten of them were heading in her direction. She thrust another magazine into the sten gun, moved deeper into the wood, took up her position behind a fallen tree, and fired again. Soldiers fell. German bullets hit the ground beside her. Still she fired and went on firing, holding the Germans back until the others had made good their escape. When the last magazine had been used up, she tried to move back. The soldiers fired again. A searing pain ripped through her knee and she buckled to the ground. They were moving closer. She tried to drag herself along the ground; another bullet hit her in the shoulder, spinning her around so that she dropped the gun and fell. The soldiers approached and stood over her. One kicked her in the side while another pointed his rifle at her face. Heart pounding, Monique waited for him to fire. She was not to be so lucky. Hauled to her feet, she was half-dragged through the woods before being thrown into a truck and taken to German Headquarters in the local town.

The first aid was basic, her shattered knee agonising, but the Commandant was almost polite as he tried reasoning with her. He wanted the names of agents and plans of future sabotage raids. Co-operation would ensure her wounds would be tended by a surgeon and she would be spared the horrors of Gestapo questioning. Monique said nothing. Maybe the Commandant meant what he said, but she knew he could do nothing to help her now. Her deadly course was set. And so it began. First the journey to a prison cell, then a car drive to Paris for interrogation by the Gestapo at the notorious house in the Avenue Foch.

72

Day in, day out, she faced questions and torture. Pain she thought could not be endured, was endured, just as the Gestapo had to endure her stubborn silence. Poison from her untreated wounds coursed into her bloodstream and, burning with fever, she kept slipping in and out of consciousness to the fury of her inquisitors. One morning, she opened her eyes, glanced around her bare cell and wondered how long it had been. Days? Weeks? Suddenly Charles was standing beside her, smiling down and saying.

"You see, darling. I promised I'd be home for New Year." The blackness closed in once more. When she opened her eyes again, Jennie was walking towards her, the small excited voice echoing. "Get up, get up! We're going to the cove. You can see Derwent Water from there. Get up..."

Suddenly it wasn't Jennie, but the large, loud-mouthed female guard barking an order. "You come now. Up. Get up."

As Monique forced her unwilling body to move, she sensed by the guard's manner that this time would be different. This time, she was not going to that terrible room for questioning. Half-stumbling, half-walking, she was led to a small yard. A man and a woman stood before a line of soldiers. The woman was crying.

So it had come. For all she could scarcely stand, Monique determined to meet death with that same proud defiance which had prevented the Gestapo gaining any information from her. When she faced the soldiers, she saw only Jennie's face. The anguish she felt then was worse than any pain she had endured.

A command rang out across the yard. She heard the click of rifles, crossed herself and prayed that, one day, her daughter would understand.

# Chapter Four

Jennie had risen early to pick roses while the dew was still fresh upon them; their fragrance filled her nostrils as she arranged each one carefully in a vase which stood on a stone window ledge inside Portlyn's thirteenth-century church. June sunlight streaming through stained glass sent a kaleidoscope of colours on to a nave pillar; it washed over the roses and touched the hazel hair which swept back from the small oval face to fall softly at her shoulders.

In this, her "coming out" year, she stood a slim five feet three inches, her small waist shown off to perfection by the cream lawn dress she was wearing. People said she was like her mother, but Jennie knew she did not possess such haunting beauty. Although her eyes were dark in a naturally pale complexion and her lips were well-shaped and full, the resemblance stopped there. At best, she decided, she could pass for attractive and was grateful for it. Others, however, saw a clear-eyed enigmatic face which attracted yet unnerved them a little. Was she shy or did she know something they did not?

She stood back, looked at the flower arrangement critically, then let her eyes swivel to the marble wall tablet beside the window. It was her mother's memorial plaque. With no grave, this and the George Cross medal was all there was. Monique Veryan had taken her place in history among those other famous and courageous secret agents. As always when she looked at the plaque, Jennie felt sick to her stomach, never having got over the shock, the horror, the grief and the immense pride she had felt on learning of Monique's death. Hopes of reconciliation with her father had given some consolation but three years after the war had ended, Charles Veryan had not returned from Singapore. Listed as "missing, presumed dead", he had simply vanished, leaving his family steeped in grief, his fate a matter for anguished concern and his inheritance a matter of growing conjecture.

In spite of all this, Florence had insisted on her grand-daughter going

74

to finishing school and being launched into society in the proper manner. To Jennie it had seemed almost obscene after all the pain and anguish, but heedless of her protests, and certain that Charles and Monique would have wished it, Florence had opened up the house in Kensington Square, taken her grand-daughter to be presented at court, and given her a "coming out" ball at Trevellan. Jennie's photograph had graced the *Tatler* and she had swanned her way through the London Season on the arm of a banker's son. It was almost over; the balls, the parties, Royal Ascot, only Wimbledon yet to come. This week she had slipped away from it all for peace and fresh Cornish breezes, away from the junkets and the banker's son whose love she could not return. As dismayed as the Veryans, he – like they – refused to take no for an answer and lived in hope.

Collecting up the withered flowers from last week, she walked out into warm sunshine and threw the faded blooms on to the graveyard's compost heap. The church clock was striking quarter past nine as she walked along a yew-lined path towards the lychgate. Once through it her heart began to lift; the sun was shining, the air was like wine, cottage gardens were a riot of colour and she was back in the one place she loved and belonged. A black car drove past then pulled up suddenly a hundred yards further on. Recognising Frank Curnow's Wolseley, she frowned. He would offer her a lift when she wanted to walk. The car door opened. She paused, thinking she had made a mistake as a dark-haired man, in a navy fisherman's sweater, unravelled his six-foot frame and smiled as he walked towards her saying.

"I wasn't sure at first but it is, it's little Jennie."

Unsure herself, she could only stare up into those dark blue eyes in utter astonishment. It had been well over three years since they last met when she was only fifteen. While she had continued her education in Brighton and Switzerland, Mark had gone to Nottinghamshire to study agriculture. Their paths had not crossed since the special memorial service for her mother just after the war when he had mumbled awkward words of comfort and returned almost at once to the Midlands. Ever since, he had been in her thoughts constantly and now, here he was when she had thought him miles away. She saw how much he had changed, in looks as well as size. Here was no matinee idol's face, the square jaw and swarthy weather-beaten features fell well short of handsome, but added up to so much more. At last she found her voice. "Mark! What are you doing here? I mean . . . when did you get home? Are you back for good? Have you finished your studies?"

He laughed. "Yes. I came home three days ago. I'm here only to say goodbye though."

Her heart sank. "Goodbye?"

"National Service. Deferred until I finished my studies. I leave tomorrow." His eyes darkened as he thought how impossibly desirable she seemed. Was this really Jennie? "When did you arrive home?"

"Last night," she murmured in dismay. Three days! Mark had been here for three days while she had socialised them away. No one at Trevellan had told her he was home; she might have gone anywhere today and missed him. "How do you plan to spend your last day of freedom?"

"Sailing with Sir Philip." He reached out and took her by the elbow. "I'm on my way up to the house now. Had to go to the village first. Good thing I did, I might have missed you otherwise. Come on. Hop in."

She climbed into the car, thinking how bloody life was. After all this time, they had one day, and it had been snatched from them by her grandfather. All too aware of him beside her, she watched his large hands on the wheel as he steered the car along Church Lane. "How long will you be in the army?"

"Two years."

She turned her face and stared through the window.

Mark was silent as he drove, unable to believe that this young woman with the svelte figure, desirable breasts and fantastic eyes was the same Jennie he had last seen as a plump, grief-stricken schoolgirl. Now that schoolgirl was a debutante, mixing in circles way outside his own. His mother had written to him, describing the coming out ball held at Trevellan, marvelling how the Veryans had managed such an affair since the country was still suffering from post-war shortages and rationing. She had written also of the man Jennie was expected to marry.

"He's the catch of the year, they say. Colin is the eldest son of Sir William Harte-Willis, the famous banker. We're all so happy for her. She is such a lovely girl. We expect an official announcement soon."

"You're having a pretty busy time of it, I hear?"

Sensing an edge to his voice, she smiled wryly. "You're thinking, a bizarre time, and you're right to think it."

He frowned slightly. "Come on. You're enjoying it surely?"

After a pause, she murmured, "Some of it's been fun, but..."

"You feel guilty? Is that it?"

Only Mark could have hit it spot on. "Yes."

He glanced at her anxiously. "That's crazy, Jennie. Your mother wouldn't have wanted you to go through life feeling guilty at being happy." He turned the car through the gateway, eased it along the drive and pulled up outside the door.

She made no attempt to get out. Happy! How could she ever be happy when guilt burned inside her, guilt at thoughts she should not have but which nagged at her just the same? "Maman wanted me to be an artist not a giddy deb. I start at the Slade School of Art in September." She looked thoughtful then turned to him and said, "I think that then my life will really begin. If that sounds ungrateful after all my grandparents have done for me, then it isn't meant to, it's simply that having managed to get into the Slade, I mustn't fail. I must be a success for Maman." Why was she saying all this to him when she had never said it to anyone else? Those other thoughts, however, she could never reveal to a living soul, not even to Mark.

One arm resting on the wheel, he gazed at her, suddenly aware that he wanted to touch those lips with his own and hold her body close to his. It disturbed him; she disturbed him, seeming so achingly vulnerable. "In other words, you feel you have to earn your happiness." His eyes softened. "You always were a grave little thing." He wondered how her ambitions would square with marrying into a famous banking family; the thought was terrible to him suddenly. How could he bear to see her walk into the house and out of his life? "Look here, why not come with us?"

"Sailing?" She shook her head. "You know I can't do that."

He understood her fear, but damn it all, this was the last chance he would have to be with her. By the time he returned she would be the wife of a wealthy man. "Yes, Jennie, you can do that. The only way to conquer fear is to face it. Today's the perfect day to give it a try. Conditions are so calm, we'll just drift along. No harm will come to you. Trust me."

She did; she always had. Hands twisting in nervous indecision, she saw her grandfather emerge from the house, neat in navy blazer and cap. A trick of time had brought her and Mark together for one day. How could she let that day end so soon? And yet ... the sea? She must make a swift decision. "Very well. Wait here. I'll just run up and change."

In her bedroom she put on cream slacks and a blue-striped blouse, tied her hair back into a pony tail then asked herself what on earth she thought she was doing? How could she go through with this when she still had nightmares about drowning? Fear would force her to back off at the last minute and Mark would think her an utter fool. She would not go.

Forty minutes later she was on board the *The Rose*, and melting inwardly as Mark instructed her in sail rigging. She felt his closeness, loved the softness of his deep voice and was calmed by his gentle patience. When his hand brushed hers an erotic charge coursed through her.

"For God's sake, let's move this yacht out of here today, not tomorrow," shouted Philip impatiently. "Jennie, let Mark handle things. He knows what he's doing."

As calm vanished and Jennie stiffened, Mark placed gentle hands on her arms and set her down close to the cabin, whispering, "You'll be fine just there. Relax, and enjoy yourself."

They eased out of harbour on the engine, her grandfather at the wheel as Mark made ready the rust-red sails. When they entered the open sea the mainsail backed until they turned into the wind. Terrified, Jennie clung to the side and watched as Mark tied on, then moved forward to set the foresail. When all was done and they were set on their course, he sat beside her and prised loose her whitened knuckles.

The wind was light, and progress slow with a gentle swell beneath the keel and a tranquil lapping of water against the hull. Slowly Jennie began to relax as Mark pointed out this cove, that village, clifftop or headland. It grew hotter and more hazy. Removing his sweater, he re-set the sails to gain maximum benefit from the wind then settled back, shirt unbuttoned at the top, revealing part of his tanned chest. Jennie was stirred. When he looked at her, their eyes met and held. She knew then just why it was, that of all the men she had met during this crazy year, she could not love one. A sense of longing and happiness flooded over her in one mixed emotion.

Five hours later the happiness had vanished as she helped Mark to stow sails in the undercroft of the boathouse while her grandfather barked orders like a General briefing his troops. "That's it. Make sure they're stored properly and tarpaulin placed over the yacht. God alone knows when I'll be able to take her out again now that you're leaving, Mark."

Leaving! Jennie finished her task and walked slowly back to the car trying to fight down tears that welled up inside her. It was unthinkable that he should be leaving for two whole years when they had just found each other again.

Grim-faced and silent, Mark drove them back to the house where all three stood on the drive for the awkward business of farewells. He looked at Jennie, saw his own despair mirrored in her moistening eyes, then turned politely to her grandfather who was dominating the precious moment.

"Can't tell you how grateful I am, dear boy. Never thought I'd take *The Rose* out again, but thanks to you ... well ... damned grateful. So now you're off to serve King and country? What time do you leave?"

"First thing tomorrow. It's a long way to Yorkshire."

Philip thrust out an ageing hand. "Well, good luck. Hope you get a decent posting. Action is what you need. No point in the whole damned thing unless you see action."

Mark shook the hand, thinking that, at last, he could have his longed for moment alone with Jennie. But as Philip walked into the house, Laura walked out and it was all he could do to keep frustration and anger from showing on his face.

"Ah, there you are." Laura barely glanced at Mark as she headed towards Jennie. "Colin's on the phone, for the third time."

Jennie looked at her in dismay. "Not just yet ... tell him I'll ..."

"You can't keep him waiting. It's a toll call, and very urgent."

Damn him, thought Jennie, her nerves at screaming point. She glanced up at Mark and whispered, "Wait, I shan't be long."

Laura gave a mirthless laugh as her niece entered the house. "Don't you believe it! It's always like this when those two are parted, even for one day. They absolutely adore each other. Colin will be here tomorrow, practically lives here, but that won't stop them chatting away non-stop, oblivious of everything. Still, that's love for you. We're all so very happy about it."

She gave him a disquieting look and sighed in a dismissive manner. "So you're off to the delights of Catterick? No doubt you've many things to do and won't want to hang around. I'll say goodbye to Jennie for you."

Her words brought him down to earth with sickening speed. Whatever wild thoughts had filled his mind, whatever feelings had burned in his body these past hours, Mark knew now that he had been dreaming. What else? It was his ambition to manage an estate; it was Jennie's destiny to own one. Oh, yes, he had been dreaming all right, bloody fool that he was. "Goodbye, Mrs Willoughby."

"Goodbye, Mark." Flinging a cardigan about her shoulders, Laura watched him climb into the car and drive away.

One minute later, Jennie managed to replace the receiver on Colin, and walked quickly out of the house and stood in disbelief. He had gone! There had been so much to say but Mark had not waited to say or hear it. Why? Seeing her aunt strolling towards the south lawn, she rushed after her, demanding to know what had happened.

Laura turned and feigned surprise. "What? Oh, I see. No, Mark couldn't hang about. Said he had too much to do and was going out on the town tonight. I'm to say goodbye to you for him."

Jennie stood numb, her eyes fixed on the tall cypress trees that bordered the lawn. "*Couldn't hang about?*" It wasn't possible. How could she have been so dreadfully mistaken? Had she not seen love and desire in his face? Or had she read only what she wanted to read in those eyes, heard everything she wanted to hear in that voice, and let imagination do the rest? Shattered, she returned to the house and wandered slowly up the stairs to her room. Was this what Colin felt, she wondered, this aching sense of rejection? If so, then she pitied him.

"Look at the strength in that face. I want it lit to show all the jowls and wrinkles." Maddie's own moon-like countenance broke into a wreath of smiles. "Gavin's going from strength to strength. The thing is to keep him focussed on what he does best, instead of all this abstract expressionism he's into."

Looking up at the portrait of an ageing politician which Maddie and her assistant were hanging on the grey walls of the Veryan Gallery in Chelsea, Jennie nodded in agreement. Gavin Ostler, Maddie's latest protégé, was not young, having had his artistic career shattered by war, but he was highly talented and patient enough to allow Jennie, a green student, to share his studio from time to time. She had learned so much from him and prayed that this, his first exhibition, would be huge success.

Yesterday she had finished her second year at the Slade and in the autumn would start her final one. Gazing around at the chaos in the gallery, she watched Maddie, darling, large and generous Maddie, who was mother and friend, and always offered constructive criticism, support and encouragement. Jennie felt she needed it, not sharing the confidence in herself that the school had in her. From general sketching, she had progressed to the Life Class where her true potential manifested itself. As a result, she had been encouraged to think of portrait painting as her field. She studied hard, made plenty of new friends at the school and went home each day to Maddie's frenetic household where artists tended to gravitate, talking and arguing into the late hours. Parties at Cheyne Walk were never planned, they simply happened. Jennie loved it all, but had anyone told her how long two years could feel she would never have believed them. Mark had ever been in her mind, refusing to leave it. He would be home soon. But when? Casual references, dropped into telephone conversations with her grandmother had met with a vague response. Putting from her mind the appalling possibility that he might have found someone else, she saw Maddie approaching and asked if there was anything more she could do to help before packing to return to Cornwall the following day.

"The catalogues have arrived. Be a darling and check them through for me. Make certain there are no errors, last time there were three. Oh, and ask Gavin if he's finished varnishing, then get on to the framers and

80

see how things are going there." Maddie turned away, sighing. "How shall we be ready in time...?"

Jennie turned her attention to the catalogues, taking a glossy one from the top of the pile and checking carefully the printed details against Maddie's list. The telephone on the desk beside her rang. It was Florence, asking what time she was likely to arrive. "I telephoned the house but Mrs Lewis told me you were at the gallery and gave me the number. What are you doing there anyway? I'm sure Maddie has enough staff to cope without you working all the hours God sends, dear."

"Maddie has one full-time and one part-time assistant, that's all." Jennie paused then asked casually, "And how are things there? Anything new happening?"

"No, dear. Everything's the same ... oh, except that Mark Curnow came home yesterday. He's been in the Middle East apparently. I'll send the Riley to meet you at the station. I shall need the Rolls ... I'm attending a Red Cross meeting in Truro."

Weakly, Jennie replaced the receiver. Mark was home! He was there and she was here, fiddling with silly catalogues. If only she could rush for the midnight train instead of waiting for tomorrow. At that moment there was a crash followed by a sharp cry of pain. Swinging round, she saw Maddie sprawled on the floor, her loose cotton dress around her thick thighs, the small painting she had been about to carry to the basement, flung halfway across the room.

Rushing to her side, Jennie helped to raise the shaken woman who was clasping her wrist and wincing with pain. "Blasted heel came off," she murmured. "My fault for not wearing flat shoes. I'll be all right. Just give me a moment to get my wind back."

But Maddie was not all right. The doctor bound her sprained wrist and ordered her to rest. "You've had a shock and you didn't fall lightly. Go home."

"How can I? How the hell can I?" Maddie looked up at Jennie.

"Oh, my dear, would you mind staying for a few more days, a week at the most, just to see me through the exhibition? I can tell you exactly what to do. It's your hands I'll need."

A week! Jennie felt her heart sink with dismay. In a week Mark could be gone. She tried to hide her tears and smiled. "Don't worry, Maddie. Of course I'll stay."

The warm sunny day had changed suddenly. Now the sky was filled with angry clouds and a strong wind whipped foam across deepening waves. Hugging her knees to her chest, Jennie sat on the window seat, staring out anxiously through the boathouse window. On the horizon a fishing trawler wallowed in the swell while in Portlyn's harbour, rough water tossed lobster boats and crabbers from side to side. Seagulls hovered on the strong wind, unable to make headway, just as summer visitors – battling their way along the harbour wall to watch the waves – were forced to turn back.

Six days, six lost days, when she had worked tirelessly at the gallery, helped to host the opening night and looked after Maddie. Now the wrist was much better and that very afternoon Jennie had arrived home, her nerves frayed at the edges, convinced it was all too late. On being told that Mark was sailing with her grandfather, she had offered up a silent prayer of thanks and driven down the hill in the Riley to wait. That was over two hours ago. Eyes drifting to the quay below, she recalled so clearly the hurt of their parting. So why had she raced down the hill? Where was her pride?

Sick with nerves, she glanced at her watch and saw it was twenty-past six. Telling herself *The Rose* was in good hands, she unfolded her legs, left the window seat, smoothed the full skirt of her yellow cotton dress and walked to the old gramophone which had been in the boathouse for years. Searching through the pile of records, she took one from its brown sleeve, placed it on the turntable, changed the needle then wound the handle. The needle hissed on the first groove then a woman's smooth, velvet voice filled the room, singing *Blue Moon*. For a few moments, Jennie danced rhythmically to the song, allowing it to calm her. Then, she glanced through the window once more and stood like stone. *The Rose* was rounding the headland, rust-red sail fluttering as slowly it was lowered. Her heart turned over at the sight of Mark easing the vessel into the inlet towards the mooring below the boathouse, then she was chasing down the stairs. On reaching the bottom, she stopped, counted to three and told herself that for all he meant to her, she meant little to him.

Mark started with surprise as he saw Jennie sauntering towards the jetty, then tossed a line to her to tie up alongside. She grabbed it, and looped it about the capstan. He wondered why she was there and answered her "Welcome home, Mark" with a curt "It's good to be home". His eyes fixed on her small white hands and saw no rings.

Deflated at his coolness and suddenly embarrassed, Jennie hid it by turning to her grandfather and chiding him for being so late. "I've been worried sick about you. The weather's closing in fast."

Philip sighed as Mark helped him out of the yacht and on to the jetty. "Now why should you be worried? Best day's sailing I've had for years, so stop scolding, you've only just got home. Do I get a kiss then?" After she'd planted her lips on his wrinkled cheek, the old man smiled and ambled towards the Riley. "Come on, Jennie, run me back up the hill."

Turning to Mark, she whispered, "I gather he's had you out sailing since you arrived home. You've had no time with your family or friends."

His eyes scanned her face, which had changed from rounded girl to contoured woman, but she was still the same Jennie who had been on his mind day in and day out. "I enjoy sailing. Besides, how can I let him down? He's no one else to go out with these days." Frowning slightly, he ran a hand through his tousled hair and asked: "So what happened? I expected to find you married to Harte-Willis."

She blinked in astonishment. "Did you? Why?"

His smile was hesitant. "Clearly things didn't work out the way everyone thought they would."

"They worked out exactly as *I* thought they would." For all her sharp reply, she was confused. Had his actions been caused by a misunderstanding over her relationship with Colin or lack of interest in her? Unsure what to say, she went on a little nervously, "No, I'm as free as air, Colin was always just a good friend. Nothing more."

"Are you coming or not?" cried Philip with growing impatience.

Jennie turned to her grandfather. "I think I should help Mark put the yacht to bed first."

"He'll get on far better without you getting in the way. Isn't that so, Mark?"

For the first time Mark laughed, an easy gentle laugh that dispelled the bleakness of this meeting. "You heard the man. Go on. I can manage."

"But there's so much I want to know ... two years..." She felt herself blushing and turned away. "You left without saying goodbye. Did you realise that?"

"Yes. It seemed the best thing to do."

"Did it? I see." Her heart sank at his words. Was there someone else in his life? Pride prevented her from asking. "Grandpa won't be sailing tomorrow. He's not well and is supposed to rest. My grandmother's insisting that he does. So you'll be able to be with those you most want to be with for a change." She waited for a brief moment, but when he said nothing, turned swiftly and walked to the car. She had practically thrown herself at the man and he didn't want to know.

Easing the Riley up the steep hill, she told Philip of her grandmother's decision, heard his protests and snapped at him angrily! "Hasn't it occurred to you that Mark would like some time with his own friends and family?"

Philip considered the point momentarily. "Rubbish. He's only too glad to have the opportunity to sail in such a lovely old yacht. How many young men ever get the chance? And if I decide to go out tomorrow then I'll damned well go."

She could have turned on him there and then for his utter selfishness and, at the house, slammed the brake on hard as Keynes emerged to open the door for her grandfather. If Philip saw her thunderous expression, he chose to igore it as he entered the hall where an elderly Rosalind shuffled to greet him.

With a terrible sense of let down Jennie wandered into the drawing room and stood before a photograph of her mother, taken in 1941. She gazed at the lovely face posed in half-profile, the shy smile, the large bright eyes, then looked up. Mounted in a glass frame on the wall above was the silver George Cross medal with its ribbon of blue and beside this the citation explaining why Monique Veryan had received such a high honour. Jennie would never forget the day when the King had presented the medal to her, speaking of outstanding courage and lives saved through self-sacrifice. She had been moved to tears, for who would not be proud of such a mother? Yet proud as she was, there was still that old sense of abandonment which outweighed the pride and filled her with deep guilt for harbouring such wicked feelings.

Maman had known. On that last day in Keswick, as they had hugged each other, she had known. How many times a day did that memory haunt her; the flash of blue and the tearful wave as her mother had turned the corner and walked out of her life for good. There were other memories too, one of a distant cricket match when she had felt a strange sense of forboding. Now she realised just why it was that Flight Lieutenant Stewart had disturbed her so much.

The door opened quietly and Florence entered the room, a stately figure in a blue lace dinner gown, leaning on her walking stick since her hip was troublesome today.

She saw Jennie staring at her mother's photograph yet again and the sight wrenched at her heart. The girl had taken her mother's death very badly. Such lengthy grief was for the old, not the young. At least Jennie had come to terms with the death of her father, unlike Philip who stubbornly refused to accept that Charles was dead and had spent five years writing endless letters to Whitehall and the Red Cross to keep everyone "on their toes", searching for a man who had vanished from the face of the earth. She hated his lack of acceptance but understood it also. Not being able to lay Charles and Monique in the quiet graveyard had left this strange sense of unreality along with the grief. Without a known resting place for them, there could be no rest for anyone. These years of anguish would have been too much to bear had it not been for Jennie; Jennie, who grew more like her mother in looks so that it almost seemed that Monique was still with them; Jennie, who needed all the love and care they could provide for her; Jennie, who was Charles and Monique rolled into one.

"Time you dressed for dinner, my dear." Florence settled herself at her embroidery frame. "Your grandfather's exhausted. I caught him slumped in a chair in his study. I do wish he would heed his doctor's advice."

Jennie's eyes moved to the window. Mark was on the quay. If she hurried she could get back to him before he drove home. But what would she say that he would want to hear? At length she turned and saw her grandmother seated by the tall window, letting the light fall upon her work. What a painting she would make. The whole scene was timeless and still, as timeless and still as Trevellan itself. No matter what happened to people within these walls, the house stood like an old weathered oak and Jennie knew now that she loved it. Moving across to the embroidery frame, she gazed down at the needlework, marvelling as ever at her grandmother's dexterity and remarkable eyesight. Florence had decided that the badly worn Jacobean coverings on some of the chairs would have to be replaced by identical ones and to this end Jennie had reproduced the original designs which were now being worked so carefully and painstakingly that to a casual eye the work resembled tapestry.

"We've been very lucky finding the right colours but I suspect this second batch of pink is a shade lighter." Florence pushed her needle through the fabric and drew it out once more. "What do you think, my dear?"

Mark was on the quay! How could she return to him without arousing suspicion? "It is a fraction lighter," said Jennie forcing her mind back to the issue. "But you'd need a magnifying glass to see it." He was on the quay but soon he would be gone. In a flash she remembered and the memory was a gift from Heaven. "I've forgotten to lock the boathouse door. We don't want people going in there."

Florence looked up in surprise. "Now who would do such a thing?"

"It's not just the door. I was playing a record . . . and forgot about it."

"The turntable will wind down and stop. It doesn't matter. Please, dear, go up and change for dinner." But Jennie was already out of the room, leaving Florence staring open mouthed as she heard the car starting up.

Having stored the sails away, Mark was about to walk home when he noticed the boathouse door stood open. Climbing the steps to close it, he entered the room, saw the record on the player with the needle still down and lifted it to the correct position. Drawn to the window, he stood looking out at heaving seas and was suddenly exhilarated. He loved this place but it had taken the leaving of it to make him realise just how much Cornwall was in his blood. His parents were Cornish, his mother could even speak some of the old language, taught to her by her grandmother. In the Middle East he had wondered how men could live out their lives in hot arid places and barren lands when there was this; and part of this was Jennie who had been in his heart for two very long years. How could he think of one without the other? Just why had she come to the quay this evening when she knew he would have driven her grandfather home? And why had she looked at him in that same way which had been so disastrously misinterpreted two years ago? Whatever her reasons, she had unsettled him. He walked to the gramophone, wound the handle and placed the needle back on the record. The room offered solace and he needed time to reflect.

Stopping the car at the quayside, Jennie stared about her balefully. There was no sign of Mark; she was too late. Sick with disappointment she made her way to the boathouse, then noticed the Curnows' car parked around the corner where Mark had left it that morning. At the bottom of the steps she paused. Jane Froman's voice was drifting down to her. Slowly she climbed the stairs, the strains of *Blue Moon* muffling her soft tread.

He stood with his back to the door staring through the window. Then, as if sensing her presence, turned. They looked at each other and in that moment he knew how much he loved and wanted her. Moving across the floor slowly, he reached out, pulled her into his arms and silently they moved around the floor to the song. He could smell her clean hair and perfume; her body was soft, pliable and light in his arms. The song ended, and the needle hissed on the record. Tilting her face to his, he brought his lips down on hers.

That night she tossed and turned in bed, feeling again his strong body and that burning kiss which had awakened sensations she had never felt before; but then she had never been kissed like that before. He loved her ... he had murmured that in her ear ... he loved her. *Blue Moon*. The song hammered in her brain as did the memory of their slow and sensual dance. God, how long the night was, when all she longed for was morning.

# Chapter Five

It was the sharpest of days, sunny with strong westerly winds driving small white clouds across a cornflower blue sky. On the high peak of Rough Tor, Mark put an arm about Jennie and both stood breathless, staring at the sweep of Bodmin Moor stretching away before them. In the far distance, the wide blue band of the Camel Estuary narrowed to thin ribbon as it snaked inland beyond Padstow to Wadebridge. To the south, dark shapes of disused tin mines stood against the sky, while around St Austell an eerie moonscape of white peaks from the clay industry faded into the green of wild moorland once more.

"Christ, what a day," murmured Mark, still making the mental readjustment between Jordan and England. "What a bloody marvellous day. You can see for ever." His eyes narrowed. "Look, over there."

She followed his outstretched hand and saw hovering wings dark against the sky. "Buzzard?"

He peered, shading his eyes with one hand. "No. Damn it ... no ... it's a peregrine." As he watched, the falcon arched into a breathtaking dive, disappeared from view then flew up again with something in its talons. "That's a peregrine, all right. Did you see that? They can stoop beyond speeds of one hundred miles an hour."

He watched the peregrine fly off then shook his head almost in disbelief. "That was a piece of luck. What are the odds against seeing a British peregrine in the wild these days, I wonder? In the war the army slaughtered them because they threatened carrier pigeons, and game-keepers have always shot them because they take game-birds. God alone knows life's hard enough for the creatures without the shooting gallery."

She saw his jaw working angrily. "It still means a lot to you, I see."

He nodded. "Yes. It means a lot. I've come to know the peregrine very well. They're beautiful and fantastic. To hunt with one is ..."

"Hunting? When? Where?"

Mark settled against a boulder, pulled Jennie down beside him and enfolded his arms about her. His lips brushed her head as he murmured, "Strange how things happen. In Jordan, I was travelling between camps when an eagle swooped over our vehicle. My driver was so shaken we almost crashed. Then I saw jesses trailing from the eagle and heard the bells and realised that the men in the wadi below were falconers. Odd sight. Old world pavilions alongside modern expensive cars. A man came over to apologise." Mark smiled. "He wore arab head-dress and sounded like James Mason. Turned out he was the son of a sheik, distantly related to the Jordanian Royal Family and educated at Eton and Oxford. When he learned of my interest in falconry I was immediately invited to his father's tent for refreshment and to see the falcons. Marvellous family, rich as Croesus. Their houses were small palaces and their kindness and hospitality was boundless. The upshot was that the son introduced me to desert falconry, inviting me to hunt with them." He grinned at the memory. "My fellow officers thought I was a nut case. I didn't care. I was seeing a way of life, something centuries old and still thriving. For a short while I was part of it. I'll never see it again. Here, falconry lies buried in the distant past."

Jennie curled her legs beneath her, leaned back against his chest and smiled up at him, realising that she would always run a close second to any falcon. "You spoke a lot about Jordan on the way here. You said it was beautiful." Seeing his tense expression, she frowned. "You are glad to be home aren't you?"

He stroked her long white throat with his fingers, and murmured, "Where else would I want to be?"

Jennie caught at his hand, entwining her fingers in his. Here in this bleak landscape she had never felt more happy or alive. As she gazed up at him the sun burned hot on her face, then was blotted out by Mark's head as he bent his lips to hers. She melted into him; his kiss became harder and more urgent as his hand slid down to cup her soft breast. At that moment, they heard voices. Jennie pulled away and sat up quickly. Two hikers, a man and a woman, were walking below them. They waved a cheery hello, remarked on the glorious weather and marched on. Jennie waved back sheepishly then turned to Mark who laughed. "Christ, it's worse than Paddington Station." With that he took her hand and led her down off the craggy outcrop and back across the wild stretch of moorland, avoiding bogs and sheep droppings, until they reached the car at last.

They drove south to Mount's Bay. The tide was on the turn but the causeway leading to the castle-crowned Mount was still passable as they hurried across to the island. Climbing up through the steep gardens they stood on the battlements staring out at the wide panorama of the Bay from Penzance to the Lizard.

"This place used to be a monastery," Mark was saying. "The army used it as a look out during the war."

Jennie hardly heard him. She was staring down at the sea so far below. Suddenly she was in the lifeboat again, then falling ... falling! Swaying, she felt arms about her and when the dizziness passed, found herself looking up into Mark's anxious face. It took a moment to recover. "It's all right ... touch of vertigo, that's all."

Mark pulled her down on to a worn step close by the castle, his eyes dark with worry until colour returned to her face once more. "Christ, don't ever frighten me like that again. I love you, Jennie. I love you very much." He looked away. "I'm too damned scared to ask how you feel about me."

She took his hand, whispering, "You've always had my love. I'm just amazed at how long it took for you to learn that."

Her words should have been music to his ears, so why was the melody strangely out of tune? It wasn't the singer, of course, but the song. She was so endearingly naive, so blissfully unaware. "I can't think of life without you, Jennie, but I love you and want you to be happy."

She laughed. "They ask me to marry you, idiot."

Mark looked troubled. "Jennie, I'm jobless, penniless and waiting to get my career started. Managing land is what I'm trained to do and that means living in a tied cottage or house – God only knows where. You weren't born to that and, as my wife, would miss everything you now take for granted. I'm asking you to do more than swap Simpson's for Lyon's Corner House – I'm asking you to live on my limited salary, possibly without domestic help either. It's not like the old days. Take Trevellan, for instance. The agents before Dad's time were men of means, wielded power and lived in that large house which was sold off years ago. Things are hardly likely to be the same for me. Most estates are in deep trouble so salaries won't be up to much ..."

"Is that all?" His serious expression had worried her but now she sighed with relief. "You old-fashioned goose! What on earth does all that matter, so long as we're together?"

Still his eyes were shadowed. "It could matter to your family. They'll be expecting you to land a bigger catch than me. So consider carefully."

It was unbelievable! She just stared at him, then smiled at his Victorian attitude, thinking him a darling for worrying so unnecessarily. "Had wealth been my goal I would have married Colin. God knows he's asked me enough times. But how could I marry him when

89

I've always loved you? Can't you understand that?" People were approaching the steps. She stood up slowly and felt him assisting her. "Besides, there's Trevellan. By right of inheritance it should come to me one day."

He looked at her in dismay, realising then that she had no true understanding. "No, Jennie. Trevellan will go to Clive as the next male in line. So if you're relying on that behind all I've said then it's no use."

"No!" She turned to him swiftly. "You're wrong. You mustn't even think of Clive taking Trevellan."

"If I thought otherwise, then I wouldn't be talking this way. I wouldn't be asking you to be my wife."

Her eyes flashed. "Oh, that's just silly pride talking."

"What's silly about it? Would you look twice at a man who didn't have any?" He put his arm about her shoulder. "Look, darling, it's me and nothing else. And it'll be some time before I'm in a position to support you. But no one in this world can love you more than I do. Remember that."

She touched his face gently. "Don't look so sad. Things will work out. I've got another year at the Slade, so if you're in London working at any of the Land Agents there for that year, then we can be together every day, every evening." She smiled and murmured, "It's all right. Everything's going to be all right. We'll take things easy, and say nothing to anyone until the time is right. It will be, so don't worry."

After an hour they ambled back down through the gardens to the walled harbour. The tide was in, and the small ferry boat battled against a strong swell. Soaked by sea water, they ran laughing back to the car. At six-thirty Mark pulled up outside the house, climbed out and opened the passenger door for Jennie to alight. She stood looking at him, unaware that a curtain had moved at an upstairs window. "Beach tomorrow?"

"Pick you up here at ten." He gazed at her with loving intensity and whispered, "I'll be counting the minutes so don't be late. Goodbye, darling."

She watched as he drove away and felt her heart go with him. Then, walking to the side of the house, she let herself in through the kitchen entrance. The flagstoned corridor felt cool but it was a different story in the kitchen. There a hot and red-faced Mrs Hodges was just putting a sirloin roast in the oven. She turned in time to see Jennie spooning up the remains of a sponge pudding mixture and eating it.

"Ah ah ... stop that." Mrs Hodges shook her head and smiled. "Never change, do you, Miss Genevieve? What's the verdict?"

"Hmmm. Absolutely delicious. Why can't we have ginger pudding more often? It's Grandpa's favourite. I'm starving." Sitting on the edge of the large wooden table, she kicked off one of her sandals and swung her legs casually as she watched the plump hands placing the cloth-bound pudding into a steamer that was already on the range. "We only had time for a quick snack at lunchtime. Mark wanted to show me the moors and the Mount. We had a wonderful, mad, crazy day."

The hands paused momentarily on the steamer lid. "That was nice. Is Mr Harte-Willis coming tomorrow evening or the following day?"

Jennie shook her head. "He isn't coming at all."

"Oh? I was told that he was." Cook saw the stubborn jaw lift slightly. "Such a charming man. Well-connected too, and always ready with a cheeky quip. The things he says to Rosa..." Mrs Hodges frowned, wondering what was going on.

Jennie's eyes were gazing into emptiness. "It was so good being with Mark again. He was a Second Lieutenant, did you know that? And in the desert he became friendly with the son of a sheik. Wasn't that extraordinary? Sort of romantic... deserts, sheiks, and galloping about on horseback with a falcon on his wrist."

A long silence followed this remark then Mrs Hodges spoke in quiet measured tones. "I daresay Mark will be finding a position soon. Then you'll be heading back to art school and this summer will have vanished before it's barely begun."

The eyes became more focused as Jennie watched Mrs Hodges. From childhood she had spent a great deal of time in the kitchen sharing secrets with this ample-bosomed woman who had become a substitute nanny, especially when her parents had died. Jennie needed her again now and her approval was everything. "I love Mark, and he loves me. I want to marry him." When Cook sank slowly into the Windsor chair, unable to mask her shock, the radiance vanished from Jennie's face. "Don't look like that, oh please don't look like that. Tell me you'll be happy for us ... please."

Mrs Hodges stared up at the young woman whose eyes sought comfort and support. There it was again, that lost look which held all the old fears and grief still, reminding her of the times when the child had sobbed in her arms. "Oh, my dear," she murmured, clasping the small hands, "I want your happiness more than anything in this world. You're due for some, Heaven alone knows, but you must know that your grandparents will oppose this."

"Why?" Jennie shook her head in puzzlement. "Mark may not be rich but he's..."

"The son of your grandfather's employee, when all's said and done." Mrs Hodges patted her hands gently "I don't think it will answer, but maybe I'm wrong". She wrinkled her snub nose and smiled. "I hope I am. Still, I think you should take your time over this. Let them get used to the idea before springing anything on them. Say nothing to anyone else. Not yet."

Jennie walked away, her spirits dampened by Cooks' reaction. In the main hallway, she came face to face with Laura who said briskly, "A word with you, my dear. In the morning room if you please."

Apprehensively, Jennie followed her aunt into the room, where Laura placed herself behind the large desk, hands on the top before her, in the manner of a headmistress. Feeling she was back at school and about to admonished Jennie decided to break the illusion by seating herself in an armchair. "Yes?"

The well made-up face below the fading auburn hair was stern. "Jennie, what do you think you're doing? You left very early this morning with no word of where you were going."

"I told Keynes."

"You told him you were going out and that was all. Your grandparents have been very worried. Simple courtesy costs nothing. And look at you. You know how your grandmother and I hate to see women in trousers."

Jennie bit back the retort that Maman had often worn them. She never spoke of her mother; the pain was too intense still. "I could hardly clamber over moorland and climb into ferry boats dressed in a suit now, could I?"

"There's no need for impertinence. Where did you lunch dressed like that?"

Jennie smiled and took some pleasure in revealing that she had eaten a Cornish pasty at Marazion and drunk beer in a pub. Her aunt's expression was everything she expected it to be.

"Have you taken leave of your senses? Supposing any of our friends had seen you behaving like a common shop girl? You are not to go out with Mark Curnow again. Is that understood?"

Stiffening at this, Jennie cast her a defiant look. "No, it is not. In any case, how do you know I was with Mark?"

Laura's eyes narrowed, the thin crowsfeet deepening "I saw you getting out of the car. I watched you together. I thought it absolutely sickening."

Jennie jumped to her feet. "I don't have to stay to listen to this. If I want to go out with Mark, I'll go."

Laura rose slowly, trembling with anger. "My God, when I think of the money squandered on you, and how we sacrificed our clothing coupons for a decent wardrobe to bring you out. And why did we do all this? To give you a chance to marry well. Now go upstairs get ready for dinner, and while you're there you might stop to consider what you're doing to yourself and to your grandparents with this extraordinary behaviour."

At that moment the door opened and Clive entered. "What extraordinary behaviour?" He flung himself into an armchair and grinned. "Sorry. Have I interrupted something?"

Laura's face broke into a surprised smile. "Darling. I had no idea you were back. You're early. What happened to the party you were supposed to be attending this evening?"

"I cried off and zoomed down in the Morgan." He grinned at Jennie, his hard eyes raking her figure. "What's up, Jennie? In the dog house then?"

"Mind your own business." Jennie spun on her heel and walked out of the room. As the door closed behind her she could hear muffled voices through thick mahogany and knew they were discussing her. Laura told her son everything and basked in the false illusion that he confided in her. Foolish woman, thought Jennie, wandering up the stairs deep in thought. Knowing she could deny him nothing, Clive picked his mother's brains then used the information to keep in with his grandfather, showing a surprising knowledge of the estate and all its problems. He drove to Cornwall from London every alternate weekend in order to be a force that could not be ignored when a new will was drawn up. Mark was right. Clive was the "squire in waiting", but his feelings for Trevellan could never match hers.

On the landing she stood for a moment beneath the huge portrait which had been the cause of argument when she had first entered this house as a child. Her great-grandmother stared out like a queen and indeed had been compared with the beautiful Queen Alexandra with her long slender neck, upswept hair, pearl choker and tiny waist encased in a white satin ball gown. Lady Charlotte Veryan had been a famous Victorian beauty and had arrived here with a decent dowry from her father's estate in Somerset. The eyes were blue, like Laura's, the hair auburn, like Laura's, but there the resemblance between the two women ended. In Charlotte's eyes there was compassion.

After soaking in a hot bath, Jennie returned to her room, slipped into a cream chiffon dinner gown, brushed her hair and dabbed cold cream on to her sunburnt face. It stung and she winced. Even powder could do little to take out the lobster red of her once porcelain complexion. Tonight she would lather it in Camomile Lotion and pray she didn't peel before turning a golden tan.

Putting off the moment when she must enter the drawing room and face the inevitable inquisition, she made her way to the Elizabethan east wing and into the Long Gallery which had been closed off during the war years for fear of damage to the tapestries. Now as she walked along its dim oak-panelled interior, her eyes resting on Trevellan's finest treasures, she recalled how they had danced the night away in this gallery during her coming out ball. It was a place more fitted to Pavanes than Foxtrots and she often imagined that the ghosts of long-dead Veryans would gather here, watching and listening. Did the Long Gallery fill with whispers when the living walked out, closing thick oak doors upon it? At the far end she looked up at damage caused by one of the Allendale boys who had left a tap running so that water once seeped through two floors destroying a large portion of oak panelling and part of the barrelled ceiling. The cost of restoration would be immense.

"A bomb would have been easier," Florence had said at the time. "At least we could have claimed war damage."

At last she entered the drawing room, expecting to see hostile eyes turn in her direction. As it was, hardly anyone noticed her arrival since Laura was speaking of matters closer to her heart.

"But you must settle things, Daddy. The estate is too important to leave in the air in this manner."

Philip was standing by the mantel, whisky tumbler in hand, his face tense and white. He looked old, and diminished. "I won't have this, Laura. Charles lives, I know he does."

Glancing at her mother for support, Laura sighed. "Oh, that is nonsense, darling. If Charles were alive then he would be here with us now. I do understand how you feel, but you must consider the welfare of the estate. Should anything happen to you then confusion will follow, to say nothing of crippling death duties."

"Not confusion," murmured Florence with quite firmness. "Should your father die tomorrow, the estate will go to Jennie."

Jennie saw Clive stiffen, then offer his mother a cigarette. She watched as Laura placed it in the tortoise-shell holder and waited for the explosion. When it came it was contained.

"Mummy," said Laura in a thin quiet voice, "you know as well as I do that Jennie is no more capable of running this estate than the dog. I am your first born, so if Daddy is hell-bent on handing it to the distaff side then surely I come first? If not, then it must go to Clive. And it must be handed over now if we're to stand any chance at all of evading death duties."

A long and tense silence followed these remarks while Jennie looked down at her shoes, heart beating quickly, hands clenched tightly in her lap.

Philip poured himself another large Scotch. "What you're asking me to do is to sign a document admitting that my son is dead. It would be like signing his death warrant. Can't you see that? Somehow I know that if I keep faith in his survival, he survives. If I lose that faith, he dies.

Monique lit a candle to him when Singapore fell. Why do you think we still keep it burning after all this time?"

"I really cannot imagine." Laura leaned back in her chair and exhaled smoke into the air. "If he's dead, then he's dead. If he's alive then whatever you write won't suddenly kill him. I'm surprised at you, Daddy, truly I am. This flame nonsense isn't helping you to come to terms with reality either."

"Mother, please," said Clive. He turned to his grandfather and affected his most charming smile. "I quite understand how you feel, Sir. And we must all respect your wishes. Perhaps it would be better if we dropped the subject. It must be very distressing for you and Grandmother. I know it distresses me."

*Oh, well done.* thought Jennie grimly. *You know how to play the game all right.* Seeing the affectionate look her grandfather then gave to Clive, she felt her heart sink. *And you're winning.*

Unlike her husband, Florence was not fooled by Clive's words and knew that the estate would come to grief in his hands. She had no true reason for thinking this, save instinct. On the other hand, was it fair to ask Jennie to take on such a burden? A wealthy husband was her destiny. She turned to her. "I'm told that Colin's been invited here this weekend."

"Not by me," said Jennie quickly.

"But by me," said Clive. "I asked him and he accepted."

"And when he telephoned me, I told him it would not be convenient," said Jennie.

"Jennie! That was a terrible thing to do," said Florence, looking shocked. "Why were you so rude, so cruel?"

"I ... well ... I just didn't feel like having him around, that's all."

Clive had turned almost purple. "You've made me look a damned fool. It's unspeakable behaviour. God knows what he thinks of us now." He lit a cigarette, feeling he would like to strangle his cousin. As an employee at the Harte-Willis Bank in the city he was relying on the son of the owner joining the family.

Keynes entered the room to announce dinner. With a deep sigh of relief, Jennie rose to her feet and followed the others to the dining room. No further mention was made of Colin nor of her day out with Mark. Jennie knew why. Her aunt had already caused enough trouble this evening. Even Laura knew when enough was enough.

After another night of aching longing, the morning dawned humid and still. Jennie stretched in her bed thinking it a perfect day for the beach and relishing the thought of the hours to come.

Mark had the same thought as he entered the kitchen at seven-thirty to see his father already seated at the table and dressed in a grey suit. "You're up early"

Frank Curnow sliced the top off his boiled egg and said, "I'm off to Truro. Sir Philip is thinking of selling that parcel of land over at Manverne. It doesn't yield much and is useless for grazing. Come with me."

Mark buttered some toast as his mother placed a teapot on the table. "Can't. I'm off to the beach with Jennie." When his father asked if he had sought Sir Philip's permission to take his grand-daughter out, Mark just stared at him then laughed. "What? You're kidding surely? This is 1950 not 1850."

"It's merely a matter of good manners, whatever the year," snapped Frank.

Mark frowned. "Jennie's not a child. She can choose her own friends. She does in London."

"But this isn't London. This is Veryan territory and Miss Genevieve is very special. What she does is soon known. You took her out yesterday, didn't you?"

"Yes. What's the problem?"

"Did Sir Philip know, or Lady Veryan?"

At Mark's silence, Mabel Curnow gazed from son to husband anxiously. "Your father's right, Mark." She poured tea into his cup, saying, "When you and Miss Genevieve were children it was a different matter. But now... well, it could lead to misunderstandings. Everyone knows she's going to marry..."

"She isn't, and that's the point." Mark sighed. "Look, you might as well know. We love each other and want to marry."

A stunned silence followed this remark. "Don't be such a bloody fool," said Frank at last. "Have you wealth? Have you land?"

"Oh, Christ, Dad. I'm educated, held a commission and can earn my living. Stop dwelling in the past. We've just come through a war which changed everything."

"The war changed nothing here, not where people's notions are concerned. Miss Genevieve is expected to marry well. You're young and you'll get over it. Cut this off right now, before there's trouble." Frank stood up, his anger and consternation causing him to breathe too quickly so that Mabel feared an asthma attack.

"Sit down, dear. Mark won't do anything stupid. He won't do anything to harm this family. Isn't that right, Mark?"

Anxious at seeing his father's distress, Mark was also confused. "How could my loving Jennie harm this family?"

"Because," said his mother with growing anger, "this is Sir Philip's land, and Sir Philip's house. Your father is Sir Philip's employee. Our livelihood and home are very much in his hands. And whereas he is a decent and honourable man who would not blame your father for your actions, his grandson would. Clive Willoughby is bound to inherit and, as you know from bitter experience, is capable of anything." She sank down on a chair and stared into her son's face, seeing the pain there and wishing she could take it away. "Oh, my dear, you live in cloud cuckooland if you think times have really changed."

Frank recovered his breath at last, made for the hall, picked up his trilby and glanced at Mark who had followed him. "You know, son, I thought you had more pride. Even if people are happy to think of the privileged Miss Veryan stepping down from her pedestal to marry penniless Mark Curnow, what will they think of penniless Mark Curnow for marrying Miss Veryan? There's a word for men like that, several words in fact, and fortune hunter's the least of them. I never want to hear such words used about my son." With that, he walked out of the house and shut the door behind him.

Appalled at the picture his father had unveiled, Mark stood in the hallway still. "Fortune hunter?" he murmured to his mother. "I don't want Jennie's money. I'm not even sure she has any. It's never occurred to me. What does it matter? I wouldn't touch a penny of it or hurt a hair on her head. How could anyone think I would?"

He looked so stricken that Mabel's heart ached for him. "But they will think it, just the same. How can you give Jennie the life she's used to unless . . ."

"The life she's used to! Look at it! Shipwrecked, then sent miles to school, orphaned and raised by grandparents, and now likely to see her inheritance go to Clive which means she'll lose her home too. I don't want to give her the life she's used to. I want her to be happy for once. Now it seems that's to be denied her as well."

"No, Mark, she wouldn't be happy. Oh, she might say one thing now, as young women do when they're in love, but she would soon come to hate her lowered standard of living. And, my dear, she might come to hate you too for trapping her in such a marriage."

Shattered, Mark walked up to his room and stared out across the garden and fields beyond, still trying to come to terms with all that had been said. He had known there would be problems but never such as envisaged by his parents. Feeling his stomach had turned itself into a tight knot, he sank down on his bed and buried his head in his hands.

# Chapter Six

It was humid as Jennie cycled down the hill, the click of pedals and the hum of tyres on tarmac breaking the still silence of the morning. With a towel slung about her neck, she was wearing green shorts and a cap-sleeved blouse over her swimsuit. Something was wrong. Mark had sounded so strange on the telephone. "We need to talk," he said, "meet me at the boathouse in ten minutes." The hill was at its steepest now; she braked from time to time to control her speed, gazed seawards at the ochre haze masking the horizon and felt a sense of dread. What could have happened to change the happiness of yesterday to Mark's discomfort of today?

Mark was already waiting when she arrived at the boathouse. In grim silence he took her bike, placed it in the undercroft then turned and murmured, "Jennie – look, Jennie..."

"Don't", she murmured, placing a small white hand over his mouth. "Don't speak. Let's just enjoy the day." Suddenly she knew what he was going to say and her mind struggled to prevent him saying it. "We have *The Rose*. Grandpa has given his permission. Isn't that wonderful?" Even as the words tumbled out, she wondered where they came from and was alarmed. But it was too late. Mark's dark expression had given way to amazement bordering on disbelief.

"What? Are you sure?"

Jennie forced a small laugh. "Of course. Would I have said it otherwise?" It was done. Having started the lie, she could hardly go back on it. What did it matter? She had forestalled Mark, given him something else to think about instead of the unpleasant words she didn't want to hear. But Mark was still wary. "He knows you're sailing with me alone and doesn't mind?"

"Of course. Why should he mind?" She turned her eyes from his quickly. "Will there be enough wind, do you think?"

Still trying to take in the implications of Sir Philip's generosity, Mark was silent. *The Rose* and the precious grand-daughter had been handed into his care. Such an act spoke volumes surely and did not sit happily with his father's warnings.

He had intended to tell her why they should part, had intended to make her realise that he loved her too much to do anything to hurt her, but suddenly it all seemed such a nonsense in the face of this revelation. Elated, he shrugged and smiled. "If you can remember all I taught you two years ago, I'll ease her out then you'll have to hold her on course until I raise the sails. Will you be able to do that?"

Unconvincingly she nodded. It had worked! Her terrible lie had done the trick and all doubts would be swept away in the hours that followed. Thirty minutes later they were easing *The Rose* out of harbour on the engine. Holiday makers stopped what they were doing to watch the graceful old yacht motoring past. As she cleared the headland Jennie sat at the wheel holding to a course while Mark set the sails. Whatever pangs of guilt she had nurtured now melted away completely. The sea held no terrors; it was strangely calm and the wind practically non-existent. The mainsail fluttered limply until, taking over from Jennie, Mark set *The Rose* on a broad reach. Their progress was slow, the land blurred, hazy and unreal. From somewhere in the haze came the mournful sound of a lighthouse foghorn. Apart from that it was silent; a strange otherworldy silence broken only by the sound of water lapping the hull, a world where Trevellan no longer existed and where she and Mark could drift away for ever in tranquil bliss.

Florence was just about to climb into the Rolls, when Clive walked from the stables to the front of the house. "Ah, so you've been riding," she said. "Your grandfather wondered where you were. He wants a word with you in his study. I'm off to Truro to open a charity fête."

Clive looked bemused. "In his study? But *The Rose* is out."

Florence frowned, the brim of her navy blue straw hat shading her eyes. "Of course it isn't." When Clive insisted he had seen the yacht from the clifftop, she snapped, "Nonsense," then climbed into the car and directed the chauffeur to drive on.

As Clive entered the study Philip looked up from the plan of the estate which he was studying. "Ah, so there you are. I want to discuss this piece of land I'm thinking of selling. Frank Curnow's seeing the agents this morning and..."

Looking utterly bemused, Clive said, "Who is sailing *The Rose* then?"

Philip stared at him blankly for a moment, then leaned over to stroke Rosalind who was stretched out beside his chair. "What are you talking about?" When Clive told him, he said there must be some mistake. "Some other yacht which looks like *The Rose*, that's all."

"Sir," said Clive, "I'm convinced I saw *The Rose*. I'll go down to the jetty and check. If I'm right, then she's been stolen, and in broad daylight too." Within minutes, he had driven to the harbour, found the yacht missing from its berth and spoken to fishermen who told him that Mark Curnow had been on board with Miss Genevieve. Surprised that Mr Clive was asking such questions, they looked at each other knowingly. There was scandal in the air.

Clive drove back to Trevellan seething with rage. Jennie and bloody Mark Curnow! God in heaven, was that why she had ditched the man who could have furthered his banking career? His own father had eased him into a place with the Harte-Willis Bank as a parting shot. With two children from his second marriage, John Willoughby had no further interest in his first born. Now this! Why did it seem that the whole world was against him? Why? What had he ever done to deserve it?

Returning to his grandfather with the news, Clive saw the old man turn pale. It was with a sense of satisfaction that he urged him to sit down. "I can see this is as much a shock for you as it is for me, Sir. Jennie and Mark! Dear God! And taking your yacht without permission. I wouldn't have thought it possible. Would you like some brandy?"

Philip sank into his chair and shook his head. "All I would like is to be alone for a while."

"Of course." Clive walked out, closed the door and stood there smiling. The key to Trevellan's great oak door was almost his.

The red sails picked up more wind as the swell deepened beneath the keel. *The Rose* began to pitch and yaw. Seeing Jennie grip the rail tightly, Mark smiled reassuringly from the wheel. "Take it easy. The currents are strong here, that's all. I'm taking her out further to avoid rocks."

For all his reassurance, Jennie was anxious. They were heading out when instinct told her to head in. She hated pointing into the wind, bucking over the waves with the sea thumping at the bow and sending spray in her face. What had happened to the tranquil other world of two hours earlier?

Having more on his mind than the weather, Mark's face was a study in gravity as he spoke. "This morning, when your grandfather said we could take the yacht, I felt a surge of hope. Since then, I've had time to come down to earth a little."

Jennie shook her head. "Don't. I know there are problems, I'm not a

100

fool. But all problems can be overcome. No one can part us, Mark, no one. When I'm twenty-one I can marry without grandpa's consent."

Mark glanced up at the sail, telling himself she was right, then telling himself she was wrong. It was true that no one could part them if they only had themselves to think about, but unless her grandparents gave their blessing, it would not be like that. A distant rumble of thunder drew his attention to the horizon.

The pale ochre haze which had been with them most of the day was moving inland and deepening in tone. He knew the ominous signs and cursed himself for a fool. *The Rose* carried no radio, so he never put out without checking the shipping forecast first, but this morning everything had happened in a rush. More thunder, this time closer. Sending Jennie forward, he told her how to handle the foresail to help him change course. They were homeward bound but by his estimation the approaching storm would reach them long before they could get back to Portlyn. Even with the engine *The Rose* made poor headway against the strong currents.

Jennie's eyes were wide with alarm. "Go closer to the shore, Mark. I don't want to be out here in a storm."

He shook his head. "We're safer out here if the weather worsens." Seeing her fear, he went on. "Don't worry. The storm will probably pass us, but even if it doesn't, it won't last." He glanced at his watch, and saw it was a quarter to three. The wind began to build with the oncoming front and the swell deepened. Afternoon light faded into dim twilight. "Jennie, I want you to go inside the cabin, put on your life jacket then bring mine out to me." Seeing the look of terror in her eyes, he forced a light laugh. "It's all right, truly it is. Standard procedure, that's all. Do it now, please, darling."

Jennie disappeared briefly then emerged from the cabin, life jacket securely fastened, remembering the last time she had worn one. Mark struggled into his, one hand holding the wheel. "Look, I'm going to set the sails to storm condition. Hold her on this course. Can you do that?"

Frightened out of her life, Jennie took the wheel and watched as Mark reefed in the mainsail. The mournful sound of the lighthouse siren followed them as the front brought stronger winds and larger waves. *The Rose* had a will of her own; her bow turned with the currents and shuddered as it was forced back on course. A large wave crashed down on the bow, the yacht lurched and Jennie over-reacted. They slewed to starboard; the boom swung, hit Mark in the chest and knocked him backwards against the deck rail. Jennie screamed, rushed forward, caught him by the arm and managed to pull him back. At once he raced to the wheel, turned the vessel back on course and shouted, "Don't get broadside to the waves. Keep her on this heading."

101

Shocked, Jennie took the wheel. "I'm sorry ... I'm sorry ..." A flash of lightning made her start. It was followed at once by a loud crack of thunder overhead. Rain cascaded down, cold searing rain, obscuring all view as it swept across the restless ocean. Peering through its stinging touch, she could only just make out the tip of the headland before it disappeared from sight once more. As Mark grabbed the wheel again, he told her to go into the cabin.

"No," she shouted. "I'm staying with you."

"Don't argue. Get inside, I can't worry about you and the yacht. Go on."

As another streak of lightning stabbed the sea close to them, Jennie threw herself into the cabin and cowered there, rigid with terror. Almost at once she was hurled across the small galley as *The Rose* rolled violently. Cupboards swung open and tins crashed down on to her. Bruised and battered, she tried to hang on but, like a rag doll in the teeth of a large dog, was swung mercilessly this way and that. This was madness, she thought, climbing back on to the deck. Mark frowned, grabbed her about the waist and shouted, "Hang on, there's a large wave coming."

Almost at once it struck, crashing down over the deck, trying to draw her back with it into the sea. As he clung to her, so she clung to him. Shattered, soaked and terrified, Jennie lifted her face and saw the rugged cliffs ahead. Closing her eyes, she prepared to die.

The Rolls pulled up outside the front door and Keynes rushed out with a black umbrella to shield Florence as she left the car and walked briskly into the house. "What weather!" she exclaimed. "The traffic lights are out in Truro, the roads are flooding and we had to detour. I expected to be home by four-thirty and it's nearly twenty-past five." Removing her hat, she handed it to Rosa then turned back to Keynes. "Where is Miss Genevieve? She does hate storms so."

Keynes looked a little concerned. "Miss Genevieve went to the beach this morning. Maybe she is in her room. Rosa will ..."

"Don't bother, Rosa." Philip poked his head around the drawing-room door. "That will be all, Keynes, thank you."

Frowning, Florence walked into the room, saw Laura's anxious face then moved around switching on the lamps. "What is it? What's happened?"

"Mark and Jennie took *The Rose* out this morning," said Philip, his voice both angry and fearful. "They haven't returned."

Florence stared at him. "Are you saying that they're out still? In this?" When Philip nodded, she clutched at her throat. "Dear God. We must do something ... warn the coastguard ..."

102

"Clive's been on the cliffs searching," said Philip, "but there's no sign of the yacht, of any yacht. We think they may have put in somewhere."

"But what if they haven't? What if they're in trouble?" Heart racing, Florence glared at Philip accusingly. "How could you allow this to happen?"

"Mummy, they took the yacht without permission," said Laura.

Sinking on to the sofa, Florence rubbed her brow with a trembling hand. "It isn't happening. Please tell me it isn't happening?"

At that moment, Keynes entered with the tea trolley and looked surprised when Philip exploded. "Tea? What I need is a bloody stiff drink."

"Thank you, Keynes." Calmly, Florence dismissed the butler, her voice belying her emotions. When they were alone once more she leapt to her feet. "It's no use. I can't just stay here. Laura, tell Rosa to bring my macintosh and wellingtons. Yours too. We'll go out and see if we can sight them. Philip, you must contact the coastguard at once."

"You're not going anywhere, Mummy," said Laura, pouring tea. "I noticed you were limping when you came home. Why didn't you take your walking stick with you today?"

Florence wasn't listening as she glared at her husband. "Well, don't just stand there – call the coastguard."

Clive entered the room, heard his grandfather on the telephone and said, "I'm not sure that's necessary. I'd bet a thousand pounds that right now those inconsiderate fools are probably having a cream tea somewhere. May I have a Scotch? I think I need one just now."

Philip put down the receiver and walked to the window. "You can pour me a large one too. I think you're right Clive. Mark's behaved abominably but he does know how to handle a boat, I'll give him that much." Taking the whisky from his grandson he said grimly, "Perhaps, though, after this, you could commence looking once more." He stood silent, wishing now that he had fitted a ship's radio in *The Rose*. "Strange how you think you know someone. I always thought Mark so trustworthy."

Laura's mind was on a small yacht struggling in an angry sea, but unwilling to show fear, she found a strange sanctuary in invective. "Give some people an inch and they take a yard. Mark was out all day yesterday with Jennie. What does he think he's playing at? As if we didn't know. Social climber ... that's what he is, nothing but a grovelling social climber. I warned Charles years ago, but he wouldn't listen. Now see where it's all led."

Philip turned to her in surprise. "I had no idea. I didn't dream ... poor Frank. He doesn't know yet. I'll telephone him." He looked at his

103

wife, understanding what she was going through, for wasn't he going through the same thing? Charles, Monique and now Jennie? Could God really be that cruel to them? "Don't worry, my dear. I'm sure everything will be all right. We can only sit and wait. Heaven alone knows, we've had enough practice."

The harbour lights were warm and beckoning as slowly the yacht inched towards Portlyn. The storm, having faded at one point, now seemed to be circling instead and thunder cracked overhead. The sea had been whipped into a fury now and Mark despaired of ever reaching the safety that was so close and yet so far. Fearful of rocks, his concentration was intense as he finally managed to guide *The Rose* through the harbour mouth. In the shelter of the two headlands the yacht stopped bucking like a rodeo horse and was eased back to her mooring. With a deep sigh of relief they tied up quickly and started bailing out but another flash of lightning caused Jennie to insist they both seek cover.

On the steps of the boathouse, her cold wet fingers fumbled among the stones for the key. Finding it in a niche left of the door, she forced it into the lock. Once inside, all her strength left her without warning. She fell against Mark, trembling and weeping uncontrollably, still unable to believe they were alive and home when it had seemed so certain they would die.

He held her close, kissing her face, her neck, her lips and murmuring, "It's all right. It's over, all over." Walking across to the gas fire, he turned it on and reached for the matchbox on the mantle. Striking a Swan Vesta, he placed the flame against the bars. With a slight whoosh, the fire burned into life.

Feeling its warmth, Jennie knelt down, bedraggled, soaked to the skin, her long wet hair hanging straight, dark tendrils clinging to her cheeks. She tried to speak, but no sound would come. Was it only that morning when she had stood on the quay below this room and told Mark that terrible lie? It seemed a century away now. She felt his arms about her and, still shaking, leaned back against him as he murmured, "I'm sorry. Oh, God, I'm so sorry. I should have read the signs, made sure of the weather forecast, should have just stopped and thought instead of..."

"You're not responsible for the weather, and I didn't give you time to think, so it was my fault."

He held her tightly, wishing she would stop trembling so much. What had he once said to her? "The only way to conquer fear is to face it?" How risible that sentiment seemed now. "You were marvellous, Jennie, bloody marvellous."

104

She glanced up at him in surprise. "I was utterly useless and almost sent you overboard."

He grinned. "Yes, but you thought better of it, pulled me back and kept *The Rose* on course. Not bad for someone who is so afraid of the sea." How impossibly young she looked; how close her lips were; how fresh she smelt. He kissed the top of her head. "I'd better get you home before you catch pneumonia. Your family must be worried out of their minds."

"No," she said quickly, looking up at him. "We might be struck by lightning going back up the hill." The fire was warm and she began to relax. How strange his eyes were, intense, dark, and filled with desire. She pulled his head down. His kiss was deep, passionate, almost welding her to him. Then suddenly he pulled away and murmured: "I ... I'll call the house. There's a phone box beside the pub. They'll send someone in a car."

"No." Jennie caught at him as he made to rise. "Don't phone. You mustn't phone." She swallowed hard, stared up at him with frightened eyes and whispered, "You see, they ... they don't know. They need never know. I lied to you, Mark. No one said we could take *The Rose*. I'm sorry ... sorry. You see now why it was all my fault..." Her voice broke off. He was staring at her in stunned disbelief. "I did it because I knew what you were going to say. I love you, Mark, I love you. Oh, I know I've been a fool, but this morning it seemed so easy, so natural. I just thought it would give us a chance to face our problems alone." It almost killed her to see his stricken expression. What had she done? "It's going to be all right. They'll never know."

Despairingly Mark ran a hand through his wet hair. "Jennie ... oh God, Jennie ... of course they'll know. The yacht's taken a terrible pounding." He searched her anxious eyes. Didn't she understand? Didn't she realise what she had done? From this day, he would be despised by the Veryans and mistrusted by his own parents. His father would take the brunt of this folly and have to live with the shame. 'Each man kills the thing he loves...' They could only be together by turning their backs on those they loved, causing pain to them and to each other also. But Jennie had no notion of this, even now. "Stay here," he whispered at last. "The yacht needs bailing out and I must check the rigging."

"No. Not yet, not yet." As Jennie reached out to him again, he caught her in his arms like a lover fearing to part and clinging to the last moment.

For the third time that evening, Clive and Laura climbed into the car to search. Florence watched them go then walked back into the drawing room, unable to accept that this night could see yet another tragedy. She had sworn to herself that she would keep Jennie safe, so how could it be that her precious charge was now in such peril? Taking the yacht without permission and putting Jennie's life at risk was the last thing she would have expected from Mark. Her faith in human nature had been badly jolted.

Walking across to the grand piano she stood looking at the silver-framed photograph of Jennie, demure and virginal in her white Queen Charlotte's Ball gown. The dark eyes stared back innocently. Florence remembered how that same photograph had appeared in the *Tatler*, making all other debutantes look vapid. Was it possible that this vital girl with years before her and so much sadness behind her might never come home again? Tears running down her cheeks, she turned to Monique's photograph. She had failed her daughter-in-law, her grand-daughter and herself, for Jennie was her life and her reason for living.

Impatient in her growing fear, Laura insisted on searching from the clifftops. Buffeted by wind and rain she and Clive peered out on to an ocean still darkened by storm. White foam whipped the waves but there was no sign of a vessel. Back in the car once more, her nerves were at breaking point. She could see nothing through the blinding rain in spite of the windscreen wipers slicing back and forth. "Careful, Clive. Don't drive so close to the edge. I hate this part of the hill, especially the sharp bend. Do be careful." She glanced down at Portlyn below. Lights glowed in cottage windows. "Look at it. You'd think it was midnight instead of quarter to seven." Stiffening, she caught at Clive's arm, causing him to start. "Wait. I thought I saw something. A mast ... a mast at our mooring. No, don't look. Keep your eyes on the road. But I could have sworn ..." She shook her head and sighed. "I could have been mistaken."

At that moment the car turned the bend. Clive glanced across and saw a light streaming out from the boathouse window. "No. You weren't mistaken. *The Rose* is there and so are they." He smiled to himself. Things were looking good, very good indeed.

The storm was easing and drifting inland. Jennie could feel her clothes steaming from the heat of the fire. It was like being wrapped in a large warm towel, calming and comforting. She snuggled closer to Mark, her desire deepening as he fingered her neck then brushed his lips across her throat. Jennie murmured beneath his touch, leaving him to wonder at her sensuality which seemed at odds with her vulnerability. He longed for her and loved her so much that the silent room had become a cocoon, enveloping them both, shielding them from a hostile world. It took a supreme effort of will to pull back from her at last.

106

"Come along, my love. Storm's over and it's time to go home."

At that moment they heard footsteps outside. Even as they turned their heads the door burst open. Clive and Laura stood there.

Filled with apprehension, Jennie paced her bedroom wondering what was going on downstairs. The storm outside had passed but the storm within the house still raged. In the midst of it, she had been sent away from the scene by her grandmother, ordered to take a very hot bath and then to stay in her room.

Clad in a candlewick dressing gown, her hair still damp, Jennie sank on to her bed remembering the appalling moment when Clive, calling her a "common little slut", had moved towards her in a threatening manner, causing Mark to strike him on the jaw. Reeling from the blow, Clive had stared up in startled shock before hurling himself upon Mark. Horrified, she and her aunt finally managed to separate the fighting men. But never would she forget the expression of despairing intensity on Mark's face as he had looked back at her before walking out.

In the car she had turned on her cousin, crying: "It was my fault, you idiot, my fault not his! I lied to him about *The Rose*. And how dare you call me a slut, Clive Willoughby, how dare you? I'm glad Mark punched you in the jaw. You had it coming."

Clive said nothing to this assault, his jaw being too badly bruised from the other, but Laura had attacked her with words so venomous that Jennie still could not get over the shock of them.

Sobbing with relief, her grandmother had hugged her then Laura had spoken, and the eyes which had been so filled with love, filled instead with disbelief then shock and then intense anger. It was a look which finally brought home to Jennie the reality of what she had done. No wonder Mark had stared at her in that heart-rending manner. He had known, whereas she, being she, had acted and thought like a child and now hated herself for it. Where their situation had called for eggshell diplomacy, she had rushed in like a rogue elephant, crushing all hope for family blessings on their future.

Walking to her dressing table, she picked up a comb and tried to sort out her damp tangled hair, recalling how she had stood, trembling with cold, as recriminations and counter-recriminations had heated the drawing-room air. No one seemed in the mood to listen to anything she had to say. They were far too interested in her aunt's version of events. Let things calm down, she told herself, and then she would make them understand. When they did, then surely everything would be all right.

There was a light knock on her door. Pale of face, Florence entered the room walked across to the Queen Anne chair which stood beside

107

the stone fireplace, and sat down. Jennie rushed forward, knelt and took the ageing hands in hers. "Oh, please, Grandma, don't blame Mark. How many times do I have to tell you – I lied. God help me, I lied to him. He would never have taken *The Rose* unless..."

"*The Rose*?" Florence gave Jennie a hard look. "Do you suppose I am concerned about a yacht when my grand-daughter has just been seduced? Have you no shame, no pride, no dignity?"

Eyes flashing with anger, Jennie jumped to her feet. "Mark is a gentleman and has not seduced me. How could you think he would? We love each other."

Florence stared at her grand-daughter in silence for a moment before speaking. "You call it love, to grovel on the floor like animals and..."

"No!" cried Jennie. "Aunt Laura and Clive jumped to the wrong conclusion. Nothing happened in the boathouse, believe me, nothing at all. Mark was about to take me home when..."

"Mark struck Clive. That was unforgivable."

"Clive was threatening me."

"I do not wish to hear any more about this vulgar episode."

"But you must hear it," said Jennie firmly. What she had not been allowed to say downstairs, now came tumbling out: the lie, the storm, and her fear of leaving the boathouse because of the lightning. "Yes, he kissed me. That was all. I love him, Grandma, and we want to marry."

"What?" Florence stood up slowly and leaned heavily on her walking stick. "Oh, Jennie. There are no words to describe the agony which you put us through today, and no words to describe what I feel now. Against my better judgement I obeyed your mother's last wish, to let you study art in London. I see now that was a mistake. Living with Maddie, and the people she mixes with, has taken you away from your roots and confused your sense of identity as well as your sense of priorities. In fact, I believe it has deprived you of any common sense at all."

"You don't understand, Grandma."

"No, dear, it is you who doesn't understand." Florence walked slowly to the window and stood looking out at the evening sky, her back to Jennie. "You rush around telling people you are in love and expect all to be well. Marriage isn't about the kind of romantic nonsense young girls believe in. It's about security and position. When you have those then love grows over the years. Marry a man with no money and no position then see how quickly that love evaporates when it gets lost in bedmaking, cooking and raising screaming infants with no staff to help. What sort of life is that? It certainly isn't the life for you, Jennie. Be grateful you were born a Veryan and look to your own kind for the love you want. It's there, if you wish to seek it."

Jennie sighed with exasperation. "Papa married for love, and was happy with Maman. Why was it all right for him and not for me?"

At this there was a long and painful silence, then Florence turned. "You cannot marry the son of your grandfather's Bailiff. If you did, then your grandfather would cut you off completely. He did it to his own daughter. Make no mistake he'll do it to you. Once cut off, always cut off, as your aunt found to her cost. We love you very much and desire your happiness and well-being above all else. We know also that youthful desires will only make you unhappy if you give in to them."

Jennie sighed. What was the use? Her grandmother was a Victorian. How could she make headway when the generation gap was so wide?

Florence was walking towards the door. "As for Mark, his father found him by the yacht. Quite a mess, I believe."

"And?"

"He came back here to face your grandfather. He's gone now."

"Here! Mark was here and no one told me? Why not? I should have been with him. He won't tell the truth. He won't say how I tricked him into taking *The Rose*. He's too much of a gentleman and you know it. It isn't fair to blame him. He's done nothing wrong."

Florence raised a hand to her brow. "My head is throbbing and I really cannot take any more. I've instructed Rosa to bring you a tray. Then you must go to bed. I don't want you falling ill."

As soon as her grandmother left the room, Jennie changed quickly into a skirt and blouse then put on her dressing gown once more. Even as she was tying the belt there was a soft knock at the door and Rosa entered with her dinner tray. Watching as the maid placed it on the occasional table. Jennie thanked her and asked not to be disturbed again that evening since she was tired and would retire early. "I'll leave the tray outside when I'm finished."

Rosa cast her a disapproving look then left the room, whereupon Jennie raised the silver lid and looked at the lamb cutlets dismally. How could she eat? Yet not to would only arouse suspicion. Forcing food into her mouth as quickly as possible she finished most of the meal then fought back the discomfort of indigestion. Throwing off her dressing gown, she retouched her lipstick and placed the tray outside the door before treading silently down the servants' staircase and out through the side of the house.

Rosa was heading towards the dining room when she saw Keynes at the front door and heard mumbled words. As she watched, the butler took a letter from Mark Curnow, shut the door and was about to head up the stairs. "Is that for Miss Genevieve?" When Keynes said it was, Rosa shook her head. "She's not to be disturbed. He's got a nerve, coming here."

Saying nothing, but thinking plenty, the butler turned and left the letter on the silver salver which always stood on the ancient carved oak chest.

It was almost dark as Jennie stopped the car outside the Curnows' cottage. Mabel Curnow answered the door to her and Jennie could see at once that the woman had been crying. Appalled, she followed her into the sitting room, glanced around for Mark but saw only his father who said tersely: "He's not here. He's gone."

Jennie stared stupidly. "Gone? Gone where?"

"We don't know," Frank answered. He stood awkwardly in the middle of the room, clearly wishing her elsewhere.

"Why? He had no reason to leave. Grandpa wouldn't want that."

"Maybe not," snapped Mabel sitting down on the sofa. "But his father did."

Frank walked towards the inglenook fireplace and lit his pipe before speaking. "I didn't ask him to leave, nor did I wish it. Mark went of his own accord. He had no other choice."

"No. Not after the terrible things you said to him." Mrs Curnow's voice was filled with bitterness. "He's my son too, you know."

"We can talk more reasonably when he returns," said Frank, wishing now that he had not allowed his temper to rule his tongue.

"I don't think he will ever return," whispered Mabel. She turned her face away to hide the tears.

Jennie stared from one to the other in growing dread. "What terrible things did you say to him, Mr Curnow? Did you give him a chance to tell you that I said we had permission to take the yacht? That nothing untoward happened between us?"

Mabel's lips worked in anger. "You know quite well that my son would never say things about a lady. Why couldn't you have left him alone? You can have the pick of anyone. We've waited so long for his return. Now, after one week, he's been forced to leave and I don't imagine he'll be back. You see, Miss Genevieve, what has been said this day will stay with my son for the rest of his life."

Stung by her accusing words, Jennie was at a loss. Without a word to her, Mark had left. Was it possible? "But you must know where he's gone?"

"London, I suppose," Frank said. "He has friends there. I don't know their addresses." His tone implied that even if he had he was in no frame of mind to divulge them to her.

"But when did he leave?" Jennie's voice bordered on the frantic.

"About thirty to forty minutes ago." Frank's shoulders fell. "I think

110

you should return home, Miss Genevieve. Now, before there's more trouble."

Jennie scarcely heard him as she raced out of the cottage to the car.

After a tense and silent dinner, the family filed out of the dining room. It was then that Laura's eyes fell on the letter. No one saw her pick it up. Quickly she made her way to the library and tore open the envelope. Mark's writing was strong, bold and clear; his words direct and un-poetic, yet still able to express strong depths of feeling. Laura remained unmoved as she read things meant only for Jennie's eyes, then with a grimace of distaste, tore the letter into small pieces, placed them in a large Serpentine ashtray and set fire to them with her lighter. She watched as the flames flickered and died, for with them died her long humiliation. Frank was the humiliated one now. With her forefinger she crushed the charred pieces of paper to ashes, realising that she was on top of the game at last. "It's all over for you, Jennie," she murmured. "All over."

With the coming of darkness had come rain once more, driving rain picked up in the glare of headlamps as the Riley sped along narrow country lanes towards Penzance. How could he? Jennie kept asking herself that question over and over again. Mark loved her and yet was leaving her. Why hadn't he stayed and fought instead of skulking away into the night? She would bring him back and make him fight.

Mark climbed into the second-class carriage, placed his battered case on the luggage rack and settled into a corner seat, ignoring the other passengers. Gazing at his own reflection in the window, he recalled the terrible words hurled at him that evening, not only from his father but also from Sir Philip, who had spoken of betrayed trust and disgraceful behaviour. He had no choice but to leave, for leaving was the only way to dissociate his parents from all of this. He thought of Clive nursing a painful jaw. It afforded some grim satisfaction but he knew it was a blow which would cause problems when the arrogant Willoughby took over the estate. Hopefully, by this act of leaving, Clive would not now vent his anger on two innocent middle-aged people who had always served Sir Philip well in the past.

He heard the guard's whistle. Steam escaped from the engine and flowed past his window. Jennie. Anguished, he wondered if she would understand when she read the letter. In it he had said how deeply he loved her but even as he had tried to say goodbye, some other part of his brain had included an address in London where she could reach him should she wish. In London, they could meet, talk things out, be together without anyone in either family knowing. But for how long? She would leave him in the end, under duress maybe, but leave him she would. Family ties and the status quo were the tenets of the landed classes. A parting had to come and his heart would be broken. Maybe it had come already. Including the address had been an unconscious effort to find out. If Jennie did not contact him, then he would hurt her no more by pursuing her. If she did ... well ... there were limits to self-sacrifice and they would face that together, later on.

With a screech of tyres, the Riley came to a halt in the station forecourt. Leaving the car door open, Jennie rushed from the vehicle towards the London platform, her heart in her mouth. She was just in time to see the last London train shunting out of the station into the dark and rainy night.

# Chapter Seven

In the Women's Life Room the atmosphere was as still and silent as the nude model herself. Jennie's shoulders were aching as she stood at her easel, her brush stroking the canvas, the painting emerging slowly from its undertone to full flesh colours. At last the class ended. She stood back, examined her work with a harsh self-critical eye, decided that the muscles and hands needed more of an effort, then cleaned her brushes in spirit.

In too much of a hurry to join her colleagues for coffee and a gossip, she left the Slade and walked out into the October sunshine of busy Gower Street, thinking yet again of the peace and tranquillity of Portlyn. But that part of her life was finished and done with, just as Mark was finished and done with. As the underground train rattled on through dark tunnels she settled back in her seat thinking what a fool she had been to follow so hard on his footsteps, chasing off to London without a word to anyone, fully expecting him to show up at Cheyne Walk declaring that he couldn't live without her. It had been hard to believe that he wouldn't; impossible to understand why he wouldn't; and so she had waited for over three months until the horrible truth finally dawned. He had taken himself out of her life for good. Heart-break and desolation slowly turned to bitterness, not only against Mark but against her own family. She would never return! Never! Her grandmother had sent pleading letters urging reconciliation between them but she had refused to answer until Maddie had turned on her in anger, saying: "What do you think you're playing at? Of course I understand how you feel, but I understand your grandmother's feelings too. She's old and has suffered greatly. You're everything to her, and now you're breaking her heart. I didn't think you had it in you to be so cruel, Jennie."

Brought to her senses by this uncharacteristic outburst, Jennie had relented enough to write back once, but spoke only of her work and

113

progress, saying nothing of the past, or of any desire to visit Trevellan. Yet, as she posted the letter, it came to her then that the love she bore her grandmother outweighed the anger. The old lady had, after all, been deceived by the true culprits, Clive and Aunt Laura.

Arriving at the house in Cheyne Walk, Jennie let herself in through the front door and, as usual, called out Maddie's name. As usual, there was no reply. An appetising smell of fried onions wafted up from the basement kitchen. Mrs Lewis was preparing dinner before going home. When it would be eaten was anyone's guess.

"Is that you, Jennie? You're late. Didn't you get a taxi from the tube station?"

Jennie peered up the stairs and saw Gavin's bearded face staring down. "Yes. Can't I just have a cup of tea first?"

"No, you bloody can't. The light's just right. Get ready and come on up at once."

Groaning to herself, Jennie climbed the stairs to her room, removed her coat and hung it up carefully in the wardrobe before standing for a brief moment at the window to look across the golden ribbon of the Thames. To her left, the power station dominated the skyline; traffic roared across the Albert and Chelsea bridges; on the far side of the river shone the bright green lung of Battersea Park. The view always fascinated her and she thought of Turner living out his last days close to this house, gazing on to the river with its changing light. In his day there had been rural vistas instead of Greater London, but it was the same river and the same sky.

Throwing off her skirt and jumper, she took from the wardrobe the white gown she had worn at Queen Charlotte's Ball two years earlier. Struggling into it she settled the shoulders and skirt, brushed her hair into the loose hairstyle wanted for the portrait and then, taking from her jewel case the necklace which her grandmother had given to her on her "coming out", placed it about her neck and checked her appearance in the full-length mirror. What was wanted, she knew, was a young starry-eyed girl gazing on to a lovely world. That girl had never really existed for the eyes had seen just how unlovely the world could be and that love was not, after all, a wonderful thing but an untrustworthy and destructive one. Lifting her skirt in an ungainly manner, she stomped up the stairs realising that, destructive though it was, love still had a powerful hold on her. Was Mark worth all this emotion, this despair which sometimes turned to dark hatred? Would any man who really loved a woman allow himself to be driven away from her without so much as a fight?

Late-afternoon sun was streaming through the sloping window as she entered the large south-west-facing studio. It had been

114

incorporated into the original nineteenth-century design by the architect responsible for building the house and it was this studio feature which had sold it to Maddie's parents. Lovers of art but failed painters, they had taken under their wing impoverished but talented artists in search of a patron. Maddie had picked up their banner and carried on the tradition.

Gavin was laying out his pallette. His short, rather untidy beard was not for artistic affect but to cover the scar of a war wound. It put ten years on him, thought Jennie, as she took up her position on the chair beside the window so that, angled as it was, the light washed over her. This done, she rearranged the folds of her gown to his liking then put up with the constant instructions as to where her arm should rest, and how she should hold her head. At last Gavin was ready and for fifteen minutes silence fell as he concentrated on his work.

Jennie's eyes took in the studio which was filled with canvasses, easels, a large wooden table covered with tubes of paint, unwashed beakers, the remains of a sandwich and a tray filled with dogends. The aroma of stale cigarette smoke, was only alleviated by the stronger smells of oil paint and white spirit. Suppressing a growing desire to scratch an itch on her forehead, she asked "This is the last sitting, isn't it? May I see it today?"

"Maybe." Gavin looked up and smiled. "Well ... why not?"

"Good," said Jennie, unsure that it was. With Gavin's restless desire for abstract expressionism she wondered what exactly was on that canvas. His exhibition had been a success though and he was now overwhelmed with commissions. "What's all this I hear about you leaving us?"

Gavin looked concerned. "It seems ungrateful, after all Maddie has done, and I'm going to miss you both a great deal, but I've had enough of phizmongering, Jennie. It's time to move on. New York is where the excitement is today – not Paris, not London, but New York. I intend to go there – when I've honoured my commitments here, that is."

Jennie frowned. "Still, it's phizmongering that pays the bills. And you're becoming recognised."

"Not as much as you're going to be. You have a bent for portraiture, whereas I find it a way to earn a crust. This, my old love, is merely *Tatler* on canvas."

Jennie smiled but considered his words since Gavin was not a man to hand out compliments freely. Did she really have a chance to be a professional portraitist, to be independent of everyone, to have something of her own that no one could take from her? "We don't want you to go. Maddie thinks you're throwing away a great talent. You know that, I suppose?" The itch had returned and was driving her mad. "I hope she gets home soon. I'm starving."

Gavin laughed. "Aren't you being a shade optimistic? One thing only is constant in this house: meals come in the right order but you never know when. I'm a great believer in the cheese sandwich." At last he placed his brush and pallette back on the table, wiped his hands with the spirit-soaked rag then stretched. "I've a little more work to do on the gown, but the rest is there. So you may look."

Tentatively, Jennie made her way to the easel then stood silent as the surprise of it all sank in. She gazed at the soft folds of the white gown, the translucent complexion, the large brown eyes, the perfectly painted hand resting on the knee, the whole portrait bathed in a warm light giving it subtlety and life. He was good, there was no doubt about it, he was very good. What was it about those eyes though? What thoughts lay behind them?

"Oh Gavin. I wasn't expecting..." She stopped herself in time. "I'm bowled over by it. But you've been too flattering. It isn't me you've painted, it's Maman."

"I paint what I see, and what's more, I never knew your mother. So then, you think Maddie will like it?"

"She'll love it. Stick to phizmongering, Gavin, the world can't afford to lose you." Jennie frowned as she studied the full-length painting. "Where on earth does Maddie mean to hang it?"

Gavin looked at her with an air of puzzlement. "I understood it was for your grandmother. It's going to Cornwall."

She turned to him in surprise then, crestfallen, walked to the window and looked out. The golden light was fading to dusk; below her, headlights of cars and buses moved slowly along the Embankment. She would never see the painting again. "I wish I had been told."

"Why so down in the mouth?" said Gavin. "I'm flattered to be hung with the masters. Think of it, Jennie. You'll be there, with your ancestors. Doesn't it send a thrill through you to know that future generations will look at it and say: 'How lovely she was. I wonder what she was like?'"

At that moment the distant sound of the front door slamming, coincided with the ringing of the hall telephone. Jennie turned, saying, "There's Maddie now. Sounds like she's alone, thank goodness. Tonight, we eat."

On her way down from the studio, she heard Maddie's voice speaking into the telephone. Jennie entered the bedroom, pulled the curtains and switched on the light. She had just changed back into her skirt and jumper when Maddie rushed up the stairs calling out her name. The

116

door burst open. Breathless and red of face, the large woman stood on the threshold swathed in a purple cape.

"Oh, my dear," she gasped, unwinding the plaid stole which had covered her shoulders. "You'll never guess . . . never . . . oh dear, let me sit down."

"What is it?" asked Jennie, alarmed. "What's happened?"

Collapsing on to a chair, Maddie swallowed and allowed her breath to return. "That was your grandmother on the phone. Now you're not to get excited . . . because it might all come to nothing . . . and just be a hideous mistake . . ."

"What?" said Jennie. "For goodness' sake, tell me."

"Tomorrow morning, we have an appointment at Whitehall. Your grandparents have received a letter from the Foreign Office." Maddie paused and stared at her with wide excited eyes. "Oh, Jennie. Your father may be alive after all."

At ten the following morning, Jennie and Maddie were shown into a small office to be greeted by a sombre middle-aged man in a dark pinstripe suit who introduced himself simply as Caley.

Jennie stood tense, her eyes revealing the sleepless night during which she had tossed and turned afraid to hope if hopes were only to be dashed. Now she could wait no longer and started asking questions before Maddie interceded, saying, "This is Miss Genevieve Veryan, Charles Veryan's daughter."

"Indeed," said Mr Caley shaking her hand, then gesturing to the women to be seated. "I knew your father quite well, Miss Veryan. We were colleagues in London before he went out to the Far East, so this revelation comes as a surprise to me also. As yet, however, we are treating the letter with caution since we know nothing about the sender. His name is Victor Leighton. Does that mean anything to you?"

"Nothing at all," said Maddie. "Please go on."

Mr Caley opened the file on his desk and shuffled through the papers inside, saying, "As you can see, we have a lot of correspondence on your father's disappearance, Miss Veryan. I won't read out the whole letter but will pass on the relevant details. It seems that during the Japanese occupation, this Mr Leighton was at Changi civilian prison with your father. They apparently got to know each other very well and then . . ." He paused and cleared his throat. "Well, suffice it to say that Mr Leighton thought your father had been executed by the guards. After the war the writer went to live in Australia and only returned to Singapore about a year ago. There, he saw a man working in a bookshop and recognised him as Charles Veryan. But here's the rub.

117

On Leighton's approaching him, the man showed no recognition of his old friend and said his name was Williams."

Heart sinking with disappointment, Jennie looked bemused. "I don't understand. Why have we been asked to come here just to hear this?"

Caley glanced back at the letter and started reading from it. "'I returned the following day. The man had his shirt sleeves rolled up and I saw the burn scar. Charles Veryan had such a scar. I asked him again about his identity but was told to leave the shop by the owner. It is my belief that this man is Charles Veryan and has a wife and daughter living in England. I would be glad if this information could be passed on to Mrs Veryan so that she could visit the Colony and check things out for herself. I shall be only too happy to offer her assistance.'" Mr Caley put down the letter and looked at Jennie. "Of course, he had no way of knowing about your mother. We must also take on board the fact that he is very likely mistaken. I wish I could be more positive and helpful myself."

"Indeed, Mr Caley, you have been most helpful," said Maddie, "and it was good of you to see us this morning. May I take the letter?" She caught the warning look in his eye as he said, "Better to leave it on file, I think. I'll just write down the relevant details for you."

"But I want to read it," said Jennie.

Maddie was already rising to her feet. "There's no need for that so long as we have the facts."

Jennie frowned, wondering why Maddie was accepting denial of important information so easily. "But doesn't he say more about my father and speak of their time together in the camp?"

"Jennie, let Mr Caley handle it the way he thinks best." Waiting until he had written out the information on a blank sheet of paper, Maddie took it from him, saying thoughtfully, "You know there's one thing that's always bothered us, and that was the cruelty of it all when surely there were other men available."

Mr Caley frowned. "I'm sorry, but I don't follow you?"

"Sending Charles all that way at such a dangerous time, when he was so recently out of convalescence."

He stared back at her, nonplussed. "No one sent Charles Veryan to Singapore. He asked to be allowed to go."

Florence stood on the platform gazing through a haze of steam and smoke as the express pulled in. She had almost despaired of a reconciliation with Jennie, but now she was returning home and on a wave of such hope for Charles too. It was almost too much. The train had stopped and doors slammed as passengers alighted from their

118

carriages. She felt her heart racing a little and was glad she had dressed in her favourite lavender suit and left her walking stick in the Rolls. Why present herself to Jennie as an old lady when she felt like jumping over the moon? Even Philip's refusal to journey with her could not dampen her joy. Silly stubborn old man. He would sooner turn away from an awkward situation than face it. In his book broken fences would mend themselves, given time. But Jennie was a woman, not a fence.

"Grandma!"

Florence was not a demonstrative person, it went against her up-bringing, but when she heard the small voice over the general din, her anxious, searching eyes widened with joy. Suitcase in one hand, the other holding the strap of her shoulder bag, Jennie was heading towards her, smiling apprehensively. Then, dropping the case to the floor, she reached out and soon the two were embracing, unable to speak as they fought back the tears. "There, there, Jennie. It's all over and in the past." Florence smiled and stroked the soft hair gently, remembering a time when it had been streaked with oil. Her grand-daughter was back again and, God willing, she would soon have her son also.

Relaxing in the Rolls, Jennie spoke of the little she had learned yesterday at the Foreign Office. The shock of Mr Caley's parting words, however, she decided to keep to herself. It was, of course, a silly mistake. Even so, all during the night and the train journey today, she had gone over them again and again in her mind.

"Oh, yes, Miss Veryan," Caley had said emphatically, "it was agreed that the task of taking certain documents out to the Governor was to be assigned to a young unmarried diplomat, given the danger and the amount of air travel with constant changes of aircraft in various countries. But your father became most insistent that he should go and even went over several heads to get his own way. His behaviour was odd, to say the least."

Odd indeed, given that her father had loved his wife and daughter and never wished to be parted from them. Mr Caley's memory was clearly playing tricks. Better to take Maddie's advice and ignore it. She turned to Florence cautiously. "Grandma, we know nothing of this Mr Leighton, so it would be wrong to place too much hope on his letter."

"Hope isn't wrong, Jennie. Without it, your grandfather would have given up years ago. Where is the letter? I'd like to read it."

"They want to keep it on file." said Jennie, wondering whether it had contained information about the treatment her father might have suffered at the hands of the Japanese. How bad had that been? And why had Victor Leighton assumed he had been executed?

119

"Yet you say this man mentioned your father's scar which proves he knew him. So then, we must give him the benefit of the doubt and follow things up."

Jennie agreed. "But how?"

Florence already had the answer, simple in its naivety. "Someone from the family will have to go to Singapore, that's all."

It was almost dark by the time the Rolls turned into the drive. Trevellan stood before them, light from the drawing room falling on to the south lawn. Jennie's emotions were mixed as the car came to a halt outside the ancient oak door. In July she had left at dawn, vowing never to set eyes on the place again. So how would she get through this weekend? Staying in the house would bring her into constant conflict with Aunt Laura whereas wandering about the area would bring back the anguish of memories she was trying to push from her mind. He would be there, in the wind, at the cove and on the clifftops. Wherever she went, each step would be a torment to her.

Keynes greeted them while Rosa took the suitcase from the boot of the car and followed the others into the house. Rosalind hobbled across the floor, tail wagging slowly as she welcomed Jennie and the fuss she was given. Jennie glanced around, but there was no sign of her grandfather. So be it then.

"It's lovely having you back again, Miss Genevieve," said Rosa unconvincingly as she walked up the sweeping staircase with the suitcase. Jennie's return could only herald more trouble and this house had seen enough of it, surely to God. Poor Mr Curnow had even offered his resignation at one time but of course Sir Philip had refused to accept it. Even so, since that awful night Mr Curnow had been a very sad man. The village had fed on the scandal, making her own life a misery every time she had walked down to the shops. Now she would be faced with more questions which she would refuse to answer. It wasn't right. Miss Genevieve had let them all down. She should have known better. She should have stayed away. Opening the bedroom door, Rosa placed the case on the floor then closed the heavy curtains on the gathering darkness. "Shall I unpack for you?"

"No, thank you, Rosa. I'll do it later. The room looks lovely. Are you keeping well?"

"Yes, thank you, Miss Genevieve."

When she was alone at last, Jennie moved to the window opened it and heard the roar of the sea. Cornwall! The air was like wine, the wind soughed through trees and a smell of damp grass wafted upwards. She was home, with its bitter-sweet memories and welcoming arms. But without Mark it was all ashes. Walking across to her dressing table she picked up the photograph of her mother, something left behind in her

120

rush to leave the house that dawn and bitterly regretted since. Had it not been for this and some of Maddie's old snaps, she would by now, almost have forgotten what her mother had looked like. The same went for her father. It was their voices she recalled: her father's clear, unhurried, clipped tones; her mother's soft, sensual accent.

In an effort to bring them back, she crossed to her record player and, as she had done many times since that Christmas, placed a disc on the turntable. As the strains of *"Parlez Moi D'Amour"* filled the room, she closed her eyes. She was small, waltzing in her father's arms and looking up at him. Darling Papa. If only she could focus on him, but no matter how she tried to recall it, the face that had once been so much was now nothing more than a blur. Leaving the record playing on, she stepped out on to the landing and made her way to her parents' old bedroom. On entering her eyes fell on the the small nightlight burning on the Pembroke table, just as her mother had lit the first candle all those years ago. Since then the tradition had been kept up, as though by letting the flame die, the Veryans might snuff out Charles once and for all. Beside the nightlight stood a photograph of her father, a head and shoulders portrait. What a good-looking man he had been, she thought. Suddenly Mr Caley's words jumped back into her mind.

"No one sent your father to Singapore, Miss Veryan. He asked to be allowed to go."


Just before seven o'clock a red Morgan entered the drive, pulled up at the entrance, and an angry-looking Clive climbed out. Barely acknowledging Keynes who was taking his small suitcase from the car, he met his mother in the hallway and snapped: "I hope you realise what hell it was trying to get away? The old boy wasn't at all pleased. I'm up to my ears in work. I'll have to leave before sun-up tomorrow if I'm to get back in time."

Dressed for dinner already, Laura cut an elegant figure in her navy chiffon gown, her fading red hair gently curling about her face. She put a finger to her lips. "Hush, darling, your voice carries so." She kissed him on the cheek. "Yes, thank you, dear, I'm very well and it's good to see you again also. Tomorrow's Saturday in case you had forgotten."

"And I work on Saturdays." Clive glanced about and looked concerned. "I say, it is all nonsense, isn't it? You said it was."

Laura shrugged. "Of course it is. But put a good face on it, darling, you wouldn't want your grandparents to think you didn't care, now would you? Now then, off you go. You've barely fifteen minutes to make yourself presentable. We're meeting early for dinner this evening. Family conference."

121

"Fifteen minutes! God's teeth, I've been driving for hours. I need a long soak in a hot bath before I'm fit for anything."

"You'll be lucky. No family gathering would be complete without our dear Jennie and, it seems, she's taken the last of the hot water."

Clive could not suppress a groan. "Oh Christ, that's all I need. Why the hell did they ask her down?"

"Be tactful this evening," said his mother. "I want no mention of that other crisis to get in the way of this present one."

"And Jennie's taken all the hot water? Bloody hell" Clive turned and thumped up the stairs to his old suite, leaving Laura looking after him with an anxious expression. She heard a door slam in the distance and hoped he would behave himself. Much depended on it.

In an effort to put off facing Laura alone, Jennie had stayed in her room, taking time with her face and hair and putting on the old cream dinner gown she now hated. At last, she walked down the stairs and entered the drawing room. A moment's pause on the threshold told her they were already gathered. Clive's presence was an unwelcome shock.

Florence helped the moment by greeting her grand-daughter with a kiss. "Come along, Jennie my dear. We're all very happy to see you again." Her words fell into an otherwise stony silence.

Ignoring her aunt and Clive, Jennie's eyes were on her grandfather. Would he receive her? In the event, he stood with his back to the fire, whisky tumbler in one hand, and said tersely "Tell us all you've found out, Jennie."

So then, no reprieve, thought Jennie as she took a seat as far from the others as it was possible to be. Her grandfather was as angry with her now as he had been that evening, but he would never refer to it again. That was his way. She might, though, when she had the chance. Her anger was far greater than his. With a supreme effort, and mindful of her grandmother's desperate anxiety, she managed to sound calm enough as she related all that had happened at the Foreign Office, again leaving out the absurd notion that her father had asked to be sent abroad.

As the family listened to her in silence, Laura rose from the sofa, walked over to the grand piano, took a cigarette from the silver box and placed it in the tortoise-shell holder. "Well, it all sounds very fishy to me," she said, reaching for the silver lighter. "Some man who claims to be someone else is considered by a complete stranger to be Charles. It makes no sense. And who is this stranger anyhow? Does he have a name?"

"Leighton," said Jennie. "Victor Leighton." Did her aunt start at this or had it been a trick of the light?

"He certainly knew Charles," said Florence. "Isn't that so?"

122

"Yes," said Jennie, her eyes still bent on Laura who was lighting the cigarette with a trembling hand. Sensing that her aunt was aware of this close scrutiny and disconcerted by it, Jennie took some pleasure in continuing to stare at her.

At last Laura turned to face the others, her face slightly drained. "Well, I've said it a dozen times and I'll say it again. If Charles is alive, then why hasn't he returned to us? I'm sorry but I honestly believe this story to be either a cruel hoax or a genuine mistake. Either way we should forget the whole thing. Oh, I know it's disappointing, crushingly so, but darlings, commonsense must prevail."

"It will" said Florence calmly. "Much as we all desperately long for it to be true, we must keep our heads and check the story out very carefully indeed. The only way to do that is for someone to go to Singapore."

"Clive's the man for that" said Philip. "I'd go myself but..."

"Of course you can't go," said Florence. "Your doctor would have a fit."

Clive had barely recovered from the shock when Philip turned to him, saying, "How soon could you get away?"

When he managed to speak Clive's voice could not disguise his horror. "Well, as you know, Sir, there's nothing I wouldn't do to get Uncle Charles back again but the plain fact is that the bank would never give me leave of absence for so long. I mean ... well ... good Lord, it takes weeks to sail that far, and who could say how long I'd be in Singapore? You must see, that it's quite out of the question."

"Well, of course it is," agreed Laura. "His father went to a great deal of trouble to get him a position at the bank. It would be dreadful to jeopardise his chances now."

"I'll go," said Jennie, brightening at the thought. "Louise Boyd is out there with her parents. I could stay with them." She missed her old school friend greatly, especially when she had needed a familiar shoulder to cry on. "If Papa's alive, I'll bring him home and the Boyds will help, I know they will."

Florence raised her eyebrows. "You can't possibly go. You have your studies for one thing and, for another, I wouldn't allow you to undertake such a long sea voyage unchaperoned."

"I was thinking of flying," said Jennie. "I realise it's very expensive but worth every penny, surely, to get Papa back again? I believe the journey takes about a week. That's not too long."

Florence looked aghast. "No, Jennie. The aeroplane would have to stop in many foreign countries. Anything could happen to a young girl travelling alone."

"Why can't Clive fly?" asked Philip.

123

Looking up from his whisky and soda, Clive stared at his mother for more help and got it. "Clive will not jeopardise his career to go wandering halfway around the world on a wild goose chase." Laura paused and looked thoughtful. "No, if anyone has to go then it must be me. I wouldn't mind a sea voyage. Can one leave the ship in the Canal Zone and go sightseeing still? Only there does seem to be so much trouble in the Empire these days."

Still wondering why Laura had reacted to the name of Leighton, Jennie said: "But a sea voyage would take so long. Who knows what might happen in that time? This Mr Leighton had come from Australia. He didn't say if he was going back. Whoever goes to the Colony must meet him. How can we risk delay?"

Laura shot her a dark look. "I won't fly. I never have and never will. I'll book my passage for just after Christmas. I don't wish to spend that at sea."

Jennie jumped to her feet angrily. "With enthusiasm of that kind, Papa's chances seem to be receding by the minute. I don't understand you, any of you. What has to be done must be done quickly otherwise it might all be too late."

"Jennie's right," said Florence. "I shall go myself, at once. And I shall fly."

"You can't, Mummy," said Laura. "You're, well, you're..."

"Too old?" Florence glared at her. "I'm seventy-one, not ninety. And I want my son back."

"You'll stay right here," said Laura with a deep sigh. "If I must spent Christmas as sea, then so be it." A tense silence fell on the room after this, then Keynes announced dinner.

That night, Jennie was shaken from a deep sleep. Struggling against the sudden glaring light, she peered up from her pillow into a face that was almost frightening in its intensity. "What's the matter?"

"The letter, Jennie. I want you to tell me everything that was in it".

"Letter?" Frowning, Jennie pulled herself up in the bed and flicked the hair from her eyes. "I didn't read it. Neither did Maddie."

"Oh, come now. Of course you read it. I can understand your reluctance to speak out before your grandparents, but you can tell me. Really, Jennie, I'm the only one you can tell."

Jennie shook her head with growing exasperation. "What is all this? I've told you the truth. If you must know, I believe that Mr Caley was just being kind and trying to spare my feelings. I'm not sure I could handle knowing what might have happened to Papa in that camp."

Laura leaned back, closed her eyes, and Jennie thought then that her aunt breathed a sigh of relief. "Well ... yes ... that could be it, I suppose." She moved towards the door then turned back. "Even so, that letter is important to us. I'm not sure the Foreign Office have a right to keep it."

"You know this Victor Leighton, don't you?"

Laura stiffened and turned away. "Goodnight, Jennie." She switched off the light, and closed the bedroom door behind her.

For Jennie, sleep was now as far away as the morning. She lay gazing into the darkness wondering why her aunt was so worried about the letter. What did she know? Could she be trusted, this woman who wanted her son to inherit all this? Jennie tossed and turned, thinking of her father. If he was alive, there were two people in this house who would rather not know it.

She stayed late in bed the following morning, risking hunger rather than face the hated Clive across the breakfast table. Not once but twice he had deliberately set out to destroy her happiness and she would never forgive him. Last night, flushed with wine and brandy, he had, on the pretext of playing the gentleman and opening the drawing-room door for her, whispered as she had passed him: "Still missing our bit of rough, are we? Or have you found some more by now?" The slap she had delivered to his face shocked the others still seated in the room.

On learning he had left the house even as the servants slept, and that breakfast was now cleared away, Jennie took herself to the warmth of the kitchen where Mrs Hodges was genuinely pleased to see her again and happy to produce eggs, toast and freshly made coffee. They sat together at the large wooden table, as Cook chatted on about the exciting news, causing Jennie to wonder how it was that the staff knew everything when no one had actually told them?

"Your grandfather never gave up hope. Never. Even when everyone else had." Mrs Hodges sipped her coffee and stared at Jennie over the brim of her cup. "I pray on my hands and knees that your father is alive and well. When is Mr Clive travelling to Singapore?"

Ah, so they didn't quite know everything. "He isn't. I want to go but my grandparents refuse to let me. They're convinced I'll be kidnapped by white slavers or some such nonsense. So Aunt Laura's going. By sea. Sometime."

Mrs Hodges almost choked on her coffee but said nothing more. The idea of Mrs Willoughby, who never went anywhere, going to Singapore, was beyond all belief. She continued her chores with a heavy heart, knowing full well that when it came to it, Mrs Willoughby would go nowhere. Meanwhile, that poor man, that poor, poor man, was being left to languish.

Wandering out to the paddock Jennie greeted Kelly, then walked along the wooded path towards the cove, deep in thought. She had seen that look on Cook's face and knew she was not alone in smelling a rat.

Yet how could she fight her aunt and grandparents? Reaching the cove, she stood on the steps gazing out to sea. It was a calm, mild day. The tide was at its lowest and the ocean a shimmering whisper in the distance. A seagull soared above and it seemed to Jennie then that she saw Sophie's wings against the sky. Her eyes turned to the clifftop, half-expecting to see a familiar dark figure, but no one stood there. Had he ever returned? No one had spoken of him and she had too much wounded pride to ask.

*Oh, Mark. If only you knew that heartbreak is physically painful. I thought we were as one. I thought we were soulmates. If I couldn't trust you, then I can never trust any man.*

Climbing the steep cliff path, she paused and gazed at the rugged coastline stretching away into haze. A man was approaching from the direction of the village. Something about him seemed vaguely familiar. As he drew nearer she was aware of coming under close scrutiny, and found it offensive. Bidding him a clipped "Good morning" she walked on.

"Miss Veryan?"

Jennie turned in surprise. "Yes?"

For one moment the man just stared at her, unable to say anything. For years now he had blamed himself for Monique's terrible fate and had come on a pilgrimage, walking the ground she once trod, remembering where he had watched and loved her. Then it seemed that she was walking towards him, like a ghost from the past. He had been dumbstruck at first and only the very English "Good morning" had shaken him from his trance.

"You are Jennie," he said. "Jennie Veryan. Of course you won't remember me. You would have been about twelve when I last saw you."

As he spoke she recalled the soft Scottish accent and the good looks that had once held her mother enthralled. "Oh, yes, I remember you. Flight Lieutenant Stewart, isn't it? Of course you won't be that now, if you're still in the RAF?"

He heard the cold tone in her voice and looked at the young woman who was so like her mother. It was unnerving, like pushing back the years and seeing Monique herself again, even to the large brown eyes. Only these eyes were full of anger.

"Yes, I'm still in the service."

"What do I call you? What's your rank?"

"Wing Commander. But I hope you'll call me Ian."

She nodded, still trying to get over the shock of meeting the man who had pointed her mother the way to a horrible death. Well, there he stood, a little older and fuller in the face and figure, but the Stewart of the cricket match just the same. She took in his blazer, the sober tie, the grey flannels, and asked: "What are you doing here?"

"I brought my wife here for a short holiday. We've taken a cottage at St Agnes. I'm just going over old haunts ... you know ... remembering." The smile left his face and the eyes shadowed. "Your mother, your lovely mother. Oh God, Jennie, I'm so sorry and I blame myself. Thought she would get a job interpreting, that's all. I didn't know, you see. The SOE was so hush-hush that hardly anyone did know. She was an incredible woman, a brave and courageous woman. You must be very proud of her. But I shall never forgive myself."

He looked so tormented that the long held bitterness she had always reserved for this man suddenly slipped away from Jennie and she found herself murmuring, "No, please, you mustn't go on feeling like that." She looked out to sea in order to avoid his eyes. "Have you been in touch with my grandparents while you've been here? You see, I only arrived last night."

"No. No, I haven't, and much as I should like to see them again, I doubt they will derive any pleasure out of seeing me."

"I'm sure you're wrong."

"Even so. And what of your father? Did he return safely?" When Jennie shook her head, he murmured, "I'm very sorry."

"Really, you cannot go on being sorry for the war. Anyway there's a chance that my father is still alive." She told him everything then, even to her grandparents' refusal to allow her to travel. "It's so stupid. I'm the only one prepared to fly. I can even stay with army friends when I get there. But they won't have it and won't fly themselves."

Stewart looked thoughtful. "Would you recognise your father now even if you did come face to face with him?"

"He will have changed, of course. But I would know him."

In that small defiantly lifted chin, he saw again the Monique he remembered so well. "Don't give up hope, Jennie. Here's my card. Please do contact me. I'd like to know the outcome and will be thinking of you all." Glancing at his watch, he said awkwardly, "Well, must be getting along. My wife will wonder where I am."

They parted then, he towards the cove and she, deep in thought, towards the village.

No one there had seen either Jennie or Mark since the day they had sailed in *The Rose*. Gossip and speculation had been rife, but the big house had remained cloaked in silence. The maid had spoken to no one and Mrs Curnow was like a mouse, creeping around the village without a smile on her face. Clearly there had been a terrible row. But here was Miss Genevieve, walking about the harbour as large as life, greeting people happily enough. What were they to think? Had she been re-united with her family? If so, where did that leave young Curnow?

For all her outward cheerfulness, the walk brought back painful memories for Jennie. She hardly knew where she was going and let her legs take her where they would. They took her to the boathouse. There was no sign of *The Rose* and she guessed it had gone to the boatyard for its winter overhaul. Yet she saw it in her mind's eye with Mark standing at the bow waiting to throw her a line. The memory tore at her heart. If she had thought she was coming through it she now knew otherwise. Climbing the steps, she found the key in its usual place and entered. The room smelt stale and musty, as though shutting in the scene which had led to so much heartache. She glanced at the hearth, remembering how she had lain in Mark's arms before the warmth of the fire while the storm raged outside. Why was she in here when the memory hurt so much?

Unable to stop herself, she walked to the gramophone, turned the handle and chose a record from the pile on the table. Placing *Blue Moon* on the turntable she sat hunched on the window seat, pain and heartache mingling with a desire to bring back those poignant hours. It was a sweet agony and she allowed the tears to flow freely. When the record finished, she put it back in its brown cover and ran from the room.

She was halfway up the steep lane when a black Rover pulled up beside her and Ian Stewart opened the passenger door. "I'm glad I caught you before leaving. Hop in, I'll give you a lift."

Hoping he wouldn't see that she had been crying, Jennie climbed in, saying, "Thank you. It's quite a haul back up to the house. I wish you would come in and say hello to everyone."

Stewart eased the car up the hill and shook his head. "Best not, under the circumstances. Anyway my wife will be wondering what on earth I've been doing all this time." She was clearly upset. He must do something to help her. "It's just a thought . . . I certainly can't promise anything but if I could get you on an RAF flight to Singapore, would your grandparents let you go then? Transport Command are carrying some Service personnel on a fairly regular basis now, thanks to the Emergency. Most travel by sea and few by plane, but if there was a spare seat, I might just be able to swing it for you. No promises, of course."

Jennie turned to him in surprise. "But I'm a civilian. Why would they let me travel with the RAF?"

He smiled. "Seems to me that if we can't do something to help the daughter of Monique Veryan then we'd be a damned ungrateful country. Add to that the fact that the Foreign Office are interested in this case and you'd be staying in married quarters with an army family, and I'd say the case for you is pretty good. You'd stop at RAF bases en route and be well looked after. It won't be luxurious travel, but we can guarantee to get you there in one piece. Your grandparents would have no objection then, surely?"

The sad brown eyes were sparkling now. "Is it possible?"

"We can but try. Give me your London address and telephone number and I'll contact you. Meanwhile, you must have your passport ready. Oh, and there will, I'm afraid, be innoculations. I'll let you know which ones if things work out. Meanwhile, let's keep our fingers crossed."

Jennie crossed hers and showed him, laughing. "And they'll stay that way until I hear from you."

# Chapter Eight

As the Hastings circled Singapore Island, Jennie stared down at the ships in Keppel Harbour, unable to believe she was here at last. Even now, after days of being bumped and tossed about the skies, it seemed that she might wake up feeling acute disappointment that the moment of being close to her father was nothing but a dream after all. Smiling to herself, she recalled Laura's objections to Stewart's suggestion being quashed by her grandmother, who thought his concern and hard work on their behalf kind and most acceptable.

Gazing at the tankers and cargo vessels in the harbour below, Jennie saw a large passenger liner anchored out in the shimmering roads, while offshore islands stood verdant in a deep blue sea. The Hastings banked to starboard and she caught sight of the city straggling beyond a mass of green where roads wound like ribbons through dense foliage broken occasionally by clearings and dwellings. Suddenly an RAF steward was at her elbow, saying, "We're about to land. Would you fasten your seatbelt please?"

"At last," sighed Jennie's travelling companion, a middle-aged Queen Alexandra nurse, heading for a tour of duty at the military hospital. "I thought it would never end. What a bore flying is after a while. Think of the places we've been to or flown over, yet all we've seen are transit areas. Such a pity my posting was brought forward. I was looking forward to a sea cruise. At least you can be sick in comfort." She placed a gentle hand on Jennie's arm and whispered, "I shall be thinking of you, and praying that everything turns out well."

"Thank you," said Jennie. "You've been extremely kind throughout." a wave of guilt swept over her as she recalled how Maddie had seized on the woman at RAF Lyneham, explaining that Jennie had never flown before and more or less forcing her into the nurse's charge. Maddie had made a good choice for whatever the feelings of the shanghied nurse, she had not failed her duty and, mother-like, had kept

130

an eye out for problems, settling them at once with her no-nonsense attitude.

"Well, my dear, it looks like we're on our way down."

Jennie clenched the seat arm tightly as Changi runway came up to meet her. With a bump, the Hastings landed and the four propellors slowly ceased rotating. Finally she was on the aircraft steps, the fierce heat and humidity of the afternoon pressing down and taking her breath away. By the time she and her companion had walked across the tarmac, towards the RAF buildings, perspiration was pouring down Jennie's face; the bodice of her cotton dress clung like a wet rag to her back and her lungs gasped for fresh air.

In the distance she saw people waiting at the barrier. One, a tall dark-haired woman, was waving excitedly. Jennie's heart soared as she waved back to Louise. Soon they were hugging and laughing with the sheer joy of seeing each other again then Jennie remembered her manners and introduced her companion to the Boyds. As they waited for Jennie's luggage, Colonel Peter Boyd offered the nurse a lift to the Alexandra Hospital. She thanked him, but said she was being met and bade Jennie farewell.

"What a thing, to fly all that way," said Louise as they walked to the car. "I think you're so brave. Tell us all about it?"

Watching as the Colonel placed her cases in the boot of the car, Jennie mentioned the terrifying storm they had flown through, unable to convey in words just what it truly felt like to be tossed about in dark clouds, waiting for the next flash of lightning to strike the plane. Sick bags had been much in evidence. "We couldn't climb above it apparently. I think that was yesterday ... or was it? I'm all mixed up. What day is this?"

"Thursday," said Louise, green eyes gleaming. "As for storms, we have some corkers here."

"Louise," said Ann Boyd, looking at her daughter with distaste. "Such awful slang."

Still chatting, Louise slid on to the rear seat beside Jennie, who thought the car felt like an oven. "We got your letter and I wrote back straight away but you would have arrived here before my letter reached you."

"I received your cable though," said Jennie, recalling how relieved she was to get it. As the car eased its way out of the small terminal area, Jennie leaned forward, saying, "It's very good of you to have me at such short notice, Mrs Boyd."

Ann turned, smiling. She was not unlike Louise but the Colonel's lady had a care-worn face and large sympathetic eyes. Her complexion, like her daughter's, had lost its English rose beauty and turned a

131

jaundiced yellow, a legacy of the climate and a fate which few Anglo-Saxons could avoid. "My dear, we're absolutely delighted to have you with us. You must be extremely tired. Dinner will be early this evening so that you can get to bed. How are Sir Philip and Lady Veryan? I miss our excursions to Trevellan. We always had such fun."

Jennie said they were all well, and felt the warm breeze funnelling through the open window. It did nothing to cool her. They drove past a village with open-fronted Chinese shops set back from the roadside then on through miles of banana and palm trees, broken by small rubber plantations and *kampongs*. In one, Malay children played among *atap* huts while chickens ran about pecking at the hard-trodden red earth. A young woman was washing her long black hair at the village pump, heedless of the men, women and children all about her. With a batik sarong tucked about her waist and her top encased in a pink silk bodice, she was so slim and petite that Jennie felt huge and ungainly by comparison. Her eyelids felt heavy as Louise prattled on about the work she did at a children's home and her forthcoming part in a Gilbert and Sullivan operetta. Then she heard Colonel Boyd's voice calling back to her: "Hot enough for you, Jennie?"

She smiled. "Very. I can't believe it's the last week in November."

"It hits mid-ninety in the shade most days, sometimes higher. But it's the humidity that knocks us out. Cools down a little in the monsoon season, which will soon be upon us."

"I don't recall it cooling down last year," said Ann. "It just became even more humid." She fell quiet, her mind once more on the letter she had received from Lady Veryan only yesterday, in which Florence had thanked her for her kindness and gone on to say how grateful she was that her grand-daughter would be in such good hands. She could, she said, rest secure in the knowledge that young Jennie would be carefully chaperoned by someone who understood the dangers for a girl so far from home. She trusted Jennie would prove a worthy guest and thanked her again. Thinking of it now, Ann Boyd felt that Lady Veryan had just placed a weighty burden on her shoulders. At twenty, they were not girls but women, only women still legally under parental control and usually resenting it very much. And hadn't there been some scandal concerning Jennie and the son of Sir Philip's agent? Louise had only touched on it briefly before closing up like a clam. Then again, supposing this man was not her father after all but a complete stranger? What would happen then?

It was Louise who said openly what they were all thinking. "You must be on tenterhooks, Jennie. We're praying that everything will turn out well. I feel in my bones that it will."

"Thank you," murmured Jennie, "I'll soon know one way or the

132

other." A shudder went through her as she said it. For weeks she had been carried along on a wave of hope and preparations. Then had come the excitement of the journey and meeting Louise again. Now it seemed impossible to believe that, within a day or two, she would know for certain whether her father lived or whether Laura had been right all along to call it a "wild goose chase". If the latter, then how would she handle such devastating disappointment?

They were approaching the city's outskirts and rural *kampongs* gave way to colonial bungalows set back in well-cut lawns and tropical foliage. These, in turn, gave way to busy streets of open-fronted shops, of stalls of mangoes, papaya, betel nuts and dried meats, the Chinese quarter, the Indian and the Malay, the smell of spices mixed with the pungent smell of the harbour and Singapore River. Trishaws weaved their way through busy traffic, Chinese men cooked meals on woks over gas flame along the side of the road and children played beside deep gutters which were carrying away the deluge of an earlier storm. Then the narrow streets became wide avenues where grand colonial buildings stood back among frangipani trees. The smell of blossom wafted through the window and Jennie thought of verbena. Dominating all was the Gothic St Andrew's Cathedral in its stately isolation behind well-kept lawns. Her tiredness had vanished. Suddenly she was excited at the vibrant, exotic city stretching all about her.

They crossed the Singapore River where sampans were locked tightly in the murky waters and a huge bronze lion stood at the bridgehead. The green cricket field of the Padang lay to their left with the harbour beyond; the large Supreme Court stood to their right. Jennie's eyes were everywhere, unwilling to miss a thing; then they were out of the city and heading into leafy suburbs once more. At last, the car turned into a drive bordered with oleander and frangipani trees and pulled up outside a white colonial house. Bouganvillaea climbed the walls; a large fig tree dominated the lawn and at the edge of the garden were banana trees, bamboo and clumps of tiger orchids. It was late-afternoon and the whole colourful scene was bathed in a vivid golden light.

Jennie climbed out of the car and stared about her in wonderment. "Oh, it's beautiful," she gasped. "I've never seen anywhere so beautiful."

A Cantonese woman was heading towards them. She wore loose black trousers and a white cotton tunic. Her greying hair was pulled back in a tight bun and the unlined face softened into a smile as she looked at Jennie.

"This is Ah Kew" said Ann. "She's our amah and an absolute treasure." Another figure appeared, a younger Chinese man in a white

133

tunic who was already taking Jennie's cases from the car. "And this is Chan, our cook boy, steward and batman all in one. He's Ah Kew's nephew. What we would do without either of them I simply dread to think."

The interior of the house was gently cooled by large ceiling fans; the floors were tiled, but where one wall should have been was an open space leading on to the rear garden, giving the room a barn-like appearance. As Jennie's eyes were drawn outwards to lush vegetation and vivid colours, she longed for paints and canvas. A faint tinkling of bells touched on distant memories. Looking up she saw Chinese wind chimes hanging from the lintel. Beyond this the red-tiled terrace was studded with large cactus plants in terracotta pots.

When Ah Kew offered her a glass of fresh lime, Jennie thought she had never tasted such nectar in all her life, but then she hardly remembered being this thirsty in all her life.

"First rule in this climate," Ann was saying, as she sank thankfully into an armchair and lifted her face to the fan so that her short dark hair blew in wisps about her forehead, "always drink plenty. You get dehydrated otherwise and that leads to headaches, and all kinds of problems. Don't forget to take your salt and anti-Malaria tablets, although I must admit to ignoring the salt because then I'd have to drink a gallon a day and well ... my dear ... I would never dare leave the house."

Later, on entering her room, Jennie saw that Ah Kew had already unpacked her things and placed them in wardrobes and drawers with scrupulous neatness. A filigree porcelain Chinese lamp stood beside the single bed and ornate grilles covered the open window. Over the bed was a mosquito net which Ann insisted be used every night if she didn't wish to be eaten to death.

"Ah Kew will run a cool bath for you. Relax and take your time. Oh, never lie naked under a fan. It's very tempting in this heat, but always leads to tummy trouble. We don't dress when we're dining alone. Just wear something cool and simple." She smiled. "My husband won't offend, I hope, if he's in planters?"

Wondering what planters meant, Jennie made her way to the large steaming bathroom then struggled for breath, for here no fan stirred the hot air. Stepping out of her damp clothing she climbed into the tepid water, then lay back, her eyes closing involuntarily from exhaustion. Suddenly she was on the south lawn at Trevellan and peering into bright sunshine. A tall silhouette appeared at the castellated gateway. Then she was laughing and running along the drive, her arms stretched wide to greet her father. Opening her eyes, she sat up quickly, telling herself not to dream of things that might never be.

Thinking what poor company she would make this evening at dinner since all she wanted was twenty-four hours of undisturbed sleep, she put on a white cotton dress, piled her hair into a chignon for coolness and walked into the drawing room. Her nostrils filled at once with the aroma of mosquito coils, their smoke gently curling upwards. The short twilight was over and the night was filled with the sound of a million cicadas. Moths circled the lights and small transparent lizards ran across the drawing-room walls. Unable to prevent it, Jennie shuddered at the sight of them.

"Chit-chats," laughed Louise, as she greeted her friend. "Don't worry about them. They come out each evening and eat up any small insects on the walls. One fell off the other day and was promptly gobbled up by Oliver."

The Boyds' brown Singapore terrier was watching them from the terrace. On hearing his name mentioned he cocked his head to one side and pricked up his ears expectantly.

The night was steaming and Jennie felt as damp as she had before towelling herself dry after her bath. Dabbing at her wet face with a lace handkerchief, she followed Louise on to the terrace where the Boyds were seated in long chairs. Apart from the cicadas and the faint tinkling of chimes swaying in the occasional breeze, all else was silence. The Colonel put down his glass of Tiger beer, stood at their approach and asked Jennie what she would like to drink. He wore no jacket over his shirt and tie. This, Jennie decided must be what was meant by "planters".

With another glass of fresh lime in her hand, she soon found herself laughing as Louise recalled their school days and the escapades that always got them into trouble. Then they fell silent and, as if reading Jennie's thoughts, Louise said, "I expect you'd like to contact this man right away? You did let him know you were coming?"

"Not personally, no," Jennie said. "The Foreign Office thought it best to deal with that. But I have his address and telephone number."

"And you're just dying to ring him, I'm certain of it." Louise turned to her mother. "Why not let her do it now and get it over with?"

Ann glanced at her daughter and frowned. "I think Jennie is very tired and needs a few days to get her bearings before..."

"Nonsense," cut in Louise. "She'll rest a lot easier when her mind is more settled. Don't you think so, Daddy?"

The Colonel looked a little uncomfortable. "Well, er... well, I think that must be for Jennie to decide, don't you?"

Realising now why she and Louise had become instant friends at Roedean, and remembering how marvellous she had been when news

135

of her mother's death had reached her, Jennie nodded with relief. "Yes, I would like that very much."

"Very well." Peter Boyd rose to his feet and lead the way to the telephone saying, "Give me the number and I'll ask the operator to get it for you." When Jennie handed her notebook to him, opened at the relevant page, he picked up the receiver.

Heart beating wildly, stomach churning, Jennie stood beside him gazing at the drawing room, her eyes barely taking in teak furniture, tall brass lamps, and pink silk cushions on the floral-covered sofa.

"Is that the Leighton residence? It is? Good. I would like to speak to Mr Leighton. Name's Boyd. Colonel Boyd." There was a slight pause before he spoke again. "Ah, Mr Leighton? I have someone staying with me from England. She has come in response to a letter you sent to the Foreign Office some time ago, a letter concerning the whereabouts of a Mr Charles Veryan. Yes, that's right. I'll put her on at once."

Trembling quite visibly, Jennie took the receiver from the Colonel's hand and spoke falteringly into it. "Good evening, Mr Leighton."

"I have been awaiting your call, Mrs Veryan" The voice was low and tense.

"I am Miss Genevieve Veryan, Charles Veryan's daughter."

There was a brief pause and Jennie sensed his disappointment at this. "Why did his wife not come herself?"

"My mother is dead, Mr Leighton."

"But will you recognise this man as your father?"

"If he is my father then I shall recognise him."

There was another long pause and Jennie could see again Laura's reaction when the name Leighton had been mentioned in that far off drawing room. "Very well, Miss Veryan. I can manage tomorrow morning at eleven. Raffles Hotel. I'll be in the Lounge."

"That sounds fine. Will my ... will he be with you?"

"Eleven o'clock tomorrow morning, Miss Veryan."

Feeling she had turned white, Jennie replaced the receiver, then tried to smile at the Boyds who were all looking at her expectantly. "He ... he didn't seem to want to elaborate".

"Rum do if you ask me," said Peter. "As I understand it, neither you nor anyone else in your family has ever met this man?"

"No. We only know he was interned with my father."

"Hmm. I'd accompany you but I have a full programme tomorrow and can't take time off."

"Don't worry about a thing, dear," said Ann. "I wouldn't dream of letting Jennie meet this man alone. We shall keep a very protective eye on her. Now come and finish your drink before Chan gets cross at our keeping his dinner waiting."

Dinner was chicken and Chan's cooking was extremely good, but Jennie was too excited and too hot to eat much. From time to time her eyes drifted to the chit-chats scrambling across the walls, but her thoughts were on the mysterious Mr Leighton. Exhausted as she was, sleep did not come to her that night as she lay under the mosquito net, hot and worried. Never had she felt in greater need of Mark. But he was on the other side of the world, in a different hemisphere and with a different woman no doubt. She tossed and turned, trying to put him from her mind, only to have Mr Leighton jump back into it. Who was he? Did he intend to bring her father to Raffles? How could she endure the waiting? And yet she dreaded this coming meeting; dreaded the truth in case it was not the truth she sought.

Ah Kew awakened her the following morning with tea, a plate of pineapple and some other strange fruit which left Jennie baffled. Carefully the amah lifted the mosquito net and folded it back into place. "Ma'am sleep well?"

Having spent so much of the night awake, Jennie had fallen into a drugged sleep and was now trying to claw her way out of it. She glanced at her watch. It was nearly eight o'clock and already the room was baking. When Ah Kew left, Jennie slipped from her bed and walked across to the open window. This was the day, the day she would know. Below her stretched the drive. On its green verge a Malay gardener was cutting the grass with a *parang*, his movements smooth and rhythmic, his head protected by a battered-looking straw hat. An army car stood by the front entrance, the driver waiting beside the open passenger door. At that moment, Colonel Boyd walked from the house. Dressed in tropical uniform, baton beneath his arm, hat firmly on head, he acknowledged the Corporal's salute, climbed into the car and was driven off for another day's work at Fort Canning.

There was a soft knock on her door and Louise entered, still dressed in a cotton nightgown. "No need to get up if you wish to rest. We've hours yet. Did you manage to sleep?"

Jennie fell back on the bed and closed her eyes. "Can't seem to get them open."

Louise was looking doubtful. "You know, perhaps Mummy was right about your needing more time to get settled here before ... well before ..."

"Before meeting Mr Leighton?" Jennie could read her thoughts. "You're afraid I'll go to pieces if the whole thing turns out to be a terrible mistake. But I'd rather know right now than wait one single minute more. Oh, Louise, I'm so scared."

"No need. We'll be with you whichever way things go." Louise

137

averted her eyes and set her voice on a brighter note. "Hope you've brought plenty of simple cotton dresses with you. Can I look?" She rummaged through Jennie's wardrobe and brought out a long blue chiffon evening gown which was two years old. "Oh, it's heavenly. Couture, of course. Lucky you. There'll be dances, both at the Club and the Officers' Mess, so it's as well you've brought something, although my Chinese dressmaker is a marvel and can run up anything you like if you just give her some idea of the style you want. I must show you the girls' home at York Hill where I work, and later you can come to rehearsals for *Pirates*."

Just listening to Louise raised Jennie's spirits. How could the day be so frightening when here was the voice of pedestrian life which would go on no matter what?

Raffles Hotel was a rambling white building, surrounded by lawns and tall fan palms. Famous throughout the world, it faced the sea and seemed to personify Colonial Singapore, as the Houses of Parliament personified Britain.

At five minutes to eleven, a taxi pulled up in the forecourt and out stepped an attractive young woman in a lemon-coloured lawn dress and matching half-moon hat. Her hair was swept into a chignon, her skin was pale and her gloved hands folded over a white clutch bag which matched her sandals. For one moment, Jennie stood staring up at the hotel. Her heart was beating wildly and she felt sick with nerves. Louise touched her arm gently. The touch said "I know what you're going through" but the voice was typically light of heart.

"I came to a party here not so long ago. We dined outside beneath the palms and danced the night away. I drank Singapore Slings and thought of Somerset Maugham. I'm afraid I got tipsy and probably disgraced myself."

"I think I'm going to be sick," whispered Jennie, as Ann Boyd was paying off the taxi. "Supposing this is all a terrible hoax?"

"Why on earth should it be?"

"Oh . . . people will do anything to hurt others, with or without good reason."

"But why would a complete stranger wish to hurt you?"

Why indeed? thought Jennie. But why did she have this awful sense of forboding? Was it because she now suspected that Leighton was not a complete stranger after all?

When Ann joined them, the three women walked through the spacious foyer of the hotel and entered a large comfortable lounge. Jennie's eyes scanned the room for two men who might be waiting for her. All she could see were three single men seated at separate tables,

138

two with their eyes planted firmly on the *Straits Times* and one staring in her direction. Her heart sank as he rose from the table and sauntered slowly towards them, a slim dark-haired figure in a cream lightweight suit. Instinct told her who he was, but he had come alone.

"Miss Veryan?" The voice was softer and a shade more courteous than it had seemed on the telephone; the complexion sallow and the features gaunt. His dark eyes were shrewd and belied the smile that now stretched the thin lips.

Judging him to be in his early-thirties, Jennie nodded. "Yes. You must be Mr Leighton?"

He shook her hand, exchanged pleasantries with the Boyds and allowed an awkward pause to follow, until Ann said diplomatically, "Well now, Mr Leighton, I expect you would prefer to speak with Miss Veryan alone. So my daughter and I shall sit over there, and when you have finished your discussion we shall know."

Victor Leighton led Jennie back to his own table. "You are to be carefully chaperoned, I see." He added when he was safely out of Ann's hearing, "That must be the Colonel's lady wife."

Jennie settled herself into a well-upholstered chair and looked at him curiously. "How did you know who I was?"

He smiled. "My dear Miss Veryan, you are so pale, so very much straight out of England. How could I have missed you?"

When the waiter came, he ordered coffee, then took a packet of cigarettes from his pocket and offered one to Jennie. When she refused, he asked if she minded his smoking then lit one with a silver lighter. Inhaling slowly, he leaned back and studied her as one studies a painting.

"So, you are Charles Veryan's daughter. Not at all what I imagined. Why were you sent? Why not some older member of the family? His sister, for instance?"

Jennie stiffened slightly. "You know her, I believe."

"Ah, coffee. Will you be mother?"

He knew she was fishing and would not be gulled into a swift reply. She looked at him curiously. "I had hoped you would have brought him here. I thought..."

"Don't think, Miss Veryan. Wait. Meanwhile these biscuits look extremely appetising. Try one. I take my coffee black, with no sugar."

Sensing hostility, Jennie poured, then handed the porcelain cup and saucer to him, trying to work out what was going on. He seemed to be deriving some degree of pleasure from this slow torture.

Leighton noticed the trembling hand as he took the cup and saucer and said "Why so nervous, Miss Veryan?"

139

"What do you expect? All I know is what I was told and so far you've not elaborated on that."

"There's little more to tell. You read the letter?"

"No. I was merely told the gist of it. I felt that something was being kept from me."

"In the letter I pointed out that there were things Mrs Veryan should know. I also went into some detail about our time in the camp. Oh, it was not meant to disturb so much as to explain."

"Well, I'm here now so you can tell me surely?"

Smiling, Leighton drew on his cigarette once more and exhaled slowly before answering. "I would have preferred telling it to your father's sister. Why didn't she come? You avoided the question earlier."

"As you did," said Jennie, slowly stirring her cup. "My aunt would have taken the long sea voyage, whereas I was able to come by plane. Where is he?"

"In a bookshop in the Battery Road. He's much changed since I last saw him, but then Changi changed us all. I thought him dead, but here he is in our midst, a shadow of his former self but Charles Veryan as I live and breathe, for all he insists on calling himself by another name."

"Why? If he is my father then why would he hide his identity?"

"Why indeed, Miss Veryan." Leighton finished his cigarette then immediately lit up another. "I have to confess to being as mystified as you over his strange behaviour. But then, he was tortured almost to the point of death." He smiled thinly. "Ah, I keep forgetting, you did not read the letter. Suffice it to say that when men endure such things together they never forget those they endured with. I too was tortured when the guards discovered a radio receiver in the camp. Somehow they learned that your father was a diplomat sent out by the Foreign Office. They thought he had something to do with it, also that he had vital information, therefore..." He paused. "Well ... I won't dwell on that terrible time, but when it seemed he was almost at death's door, they took him out of the camp. We all thought it was to his execution. Such things were common. Dig your grave then stand by it and wait.

"After the war, having no remaining family here, I went to Australia, only returning a year ago to resume my old job in a shipping company. One day I ventured into this bookshop and there he was, seated at a desk and writing. I couldn't believe my eyes."

Jennie stared at him. "And yet you said yourself how much he had changed. You too have been through a terrible experience..."

"Which has robbed me of all reason? Is that what you were going to say, Miss Veryan?"

Feeling her face hot with embarrassment, Jennie stammered, "No . . . no . . . of course I don't think that, but . . . I'm sorry."

"I'm used to far worse things." The tone was icy.

Jennie decided to change tack quickly. "Have you always lived in Singapore?"

"I was born here. My father was a doctor; his field was tropical medicine. He came from Winchester in Hampshire. However, he was killed during the bombing of Singapore and my mother died during internment." He glanced at his watch. "It's getting late. Would you like me to drive you to this bookshop? I have to tell you now that when I persisted earlier, the owner became rather aggressive and asked me to leave since she thought I was upsetting her employee, who now calls himself Williams. But whatever he calls himself, this man, Miss Veryan, is your father."

Ann glanced up from her coffee and saw Jennie heading towards them with Leighton. "You know, Louise," she whispered. "I think that man is Eurasian."

"He's certainly very good-looking" said Louise. "Even so, I find him rather sinister."

Victor Leighton was all smiles as he approached them, saying, "I shall be most happy to drive you to the bookshop but must leave you there since I have to get back to the office. Miss Veryan has promised to telephone me this evening and I am confident she will verify that the man in question is her father."

Jennie was not so confident. Meeting Leighton had done little to put her mind at ease or solve any of the problems which had troubled her. Indeed, as they drove through the busy streets, it seemed ludicrous that her father would willingly choose to remain in Singapore, refuting his identity, when he could be home with his family and taking up his inheritance. In England there had been such hope. Now, faced with the reality as against the dream, she realised, with a sickening finality, that the whole thing was a nonsense. Victor Leighton was a crank. It had all been for nothing after all.

In the Battery Road Leighton stopped his car outside a bookshop with the lettering D.H. WEBB over the doorway, discharged his passengers and drove away with a tense expression on his face.

The door of the bookshop stood wide open and the interior proved to be larger than its street front suggested. Fans whirred over long aisles of shelves which were well stocked with old and new books, classic and modern fiction, biographies, and textbooks on a variety of subjects. On a large table just inside the door were the latest arrivals and it was here that Louise and her mother paused, while Jennie wandered on through

141

the shop, her eyes darting nervously this way and that. A tall grey-haired woman stood before her suddenly.

"Can I be of assistance?"

"I'm ... well, I'm just browsing," answered Jennie.

"Please do." Without a smile to soften her stern features the woman returned to a table where she stacked books preparatory to placing them on the shelves.

Noticing Louise staring across at her expectantly, Jennie shook her head and shrugged, indicating there was no sign of a man. Louise frowned then pointed to the woman and mouthed silently: "Ask her."

Out of the question, thought Jennie. She wanted to observe Mr Williams from a safe distance. Asking this formidable woman his whereabouts could prove disastrous should she prove to be Mrs Williams. Slowly and anxiously Jennie wandered along the shelves, taking out the odd book from time to time, her tension growing so that she was aware of every movement and every breath in that stifling shop. At a slight sound to her left, she turned to see a tall, thin man enter from a back room, walk to a far corner desk and sit down at it. There, in the half-light, the overhead fan rustling paperwork before him, he bent to his work. Tense and still, Jennie observed him for a while then inched her way slowly towards the desk until she turned a corner and was out of the Boyds' line of sight. Close to the desk now, she willed him to look at her, terrified that he would. It was so hot. If only her heart would stop pounding.

The man had removed his linen jacket and it now rested on the back of his chair while he worked with shirtsleeves rolled up to his elbows in a vain effort to be cool. She saw the damp patch of sweat on his back but could not see his arms clearly. Suddenly aware of her presence, he lifted his head and turned pale eyes on her.

Jennie just blinked at him. Her father had been tall and thin, but then her father had been auburn-haired and very good-looking. This man was quite grey and older, much older than he should have been, and yet ... and yet ... there was something familiar about that smile and that turn of the head which now broke through the thick veil of time, raising memories she had thought buried for ever.

"Good afternoon," he said. "Do you require some assistance?"

She opened her mouth to speak but the words were stifled at birth. The room became hotter and darker; she felt ill and reached out for support; there was none. The room disappeared in a long dark tunnel and her body hit something hard.

Shocked back to consciousness by a vicious smell of ammonia, Jennie gazed up to see the gaunt, lean face with the faded blue eyes staring down at her in some alarm. The alarm turned to relief as he

142

handed the smelling salts back to the grey-haired woman who now came into Jennie's sight, murmuring about water. As the man reached out to help her from the floor to a chair, Jennie saw the scar on his arm.

"Mrs Webb is fetching a glass of water. Are you feeling any better now?"

All she could do was nod like an idiot. That voice, that gentle voice. Didn't he know her? But how could he? She knew him, though. For all the suffering etched on those well-loved features, and for all the premature ageing, she knew him.

"It's me, Papa." Her eyes moistened with emotion. "I'm Jennie, and I've come to take you home."

# Chapter Nine

Turning her head towards the open window, Jennie could see the frangipani swaying slightly in the hot afternoon breeze. The fragrance from its large cream flowers wafted into her bedroom while footsteps on the drive below and the sound of water gushing from a hose pipe told her that the *kebun*, having finished gardening, was now cleaning the monsoon drain which surrounded the house.

Since returning from the bookshop she had lain on her bed trying to believe in the unbelievable. He was alive! Her father really was alive! The shock and the joy of it were only blunted by the memory of the disturbed look on his face when she had called him "Papa", for then he had turned and walked away, leaving the grey-haired woman to fluster about with a glass of water. Jennie asked her to call him back, saying he was her father, but her words were received with irritation and disbelief until Ann Boyd had taken Mrs Webb to one side and explained all she knew.

The reaction was surprising. "Really, this is too much. The girl's hysterical, anyone can see that."

"My dear, can you be so sure?" Ann Boyd had whispered in Jennie's ear. "It is quite dark in this corner, and you haven't set eyes on your father for years."

But she had been quite adamant and finally Mrs Webb was forced into recognising that here was a situation she would have to deal with, like it or not. "Well then," she said at last, "we had better talk. But not now. I must go to him. He's a sick man and really shouldn't be troubled in this manner. Perhaps I might contact you later on?"

"I would be most grateful," Ann had said, opening her beige leather handbag. "Here is my card. Please do telephone us. Miss Veryan has come a long way to find her father. I'm afraid the whole thing has been a shock to her."

"To all of us, I think," came the terse reply. "Until later then."

144

All during the journey home her emotions had reeled from joy to despair. Joy that her father was alive when she had quite made up her mind that Leighton had been wrong; despair that there had been no flicker of recognition or even a wish to recognise a daughter in those tired eyes. How foolish she had been, blurting it out like that. No wonder the poor man had taken off like a scared rabbit.

There was a gentle knock on the bedroom door. It opened and Louise poked her head around it, saying brightly, "Feeling better now?" She entered the room, cool and fresh-looking, her lithe figure encased in blue cotton blouse and a dirndl skirt. "We're still waiting for the dragon lady to get in touch."

Jennie sat up and hugged her knees to her chest. "She is a bit of a dragon, isn't she?"

Walking across to the window, Louise stared out silently for a moment. "I always think frangipani smells a little like oranges. Jennie, you don't think you could have been mistaken, do you?"

"No," came the firm answer. "Oh, of course he's changed, but not beyond all belief. And I do have photographs to remind me of how he was. Then there's the scar. But it's more than all of that. I suppose there are things locked away in our childhood memories that surface in adulthood; just something about a person that is of them and them alone. Like a finger print, I suppose." She plucked at the sheet thoughtfully. "Just why Papa chooses to remain here when he should have come home is a mystery I'm hoping Mrs Webb might help to solve. So don't doubt me, please, you mustn't doubt me."

Louise turned and looked at her in grave silence before smiling. "If you're that certain, then why should I have doubts? Anyway you always did have instinct, whereas I have none. Lack of judgement was writ large on my school reports."

Jennie looked at her finger nails; they needed filing. "I've embarrassed your mother dreadfully and..."

"What utter rot," said Louise, turning. "She hasn't had such excitement for ages. It must make a welcome change from coffee mornings, committee meetings, dinner parties and the Wives Club."

"This Mrs Webb seemed very protective of my father. Odd, don't you think?"

"She struck me as being an oddball altogether." Louise crossed to the door. "I'll leave you now. Tea will be ready at four."

Jennie showered quickly, put on a fresh cotton dress then felt ready to face the world once more. She found Louise and her mother at the shaded end of the lawn, watering the tropical lilies which were Ann's special love. Oliver bounded about them attacking the hose on pretence that it was a snake. Tiring of the game at last, he sat on his haunches,

145

scratched himself vigorously, then with a yelp, leapt into the air and chased off towards the rear of the house.

"Ants," laughed Louise. "They're all over the lawn. Oh, not your nice cosy English variety but red things that bite, so be careful. We've just had a telephone call from Mrs Webb..."

At that moment her words were drowned by the roar of Vampire jets flying overhead. When the noise had died away and the squadron had all but disappeared from view, Ann Boyd sighed and shook her head. "Intolerable. Must these new jets fly over us all the time?"

But Jennie was staring at Louise with growing impatience. "Well, what did she say?"

"She wants to meet you tomorrow at Robinson's restaurant."

"Robinson's?"

"Singapore's answer to Harrods," said Ann. "And just around the corner from the bookshop. We'll take you. We always go shopping on Saturdays."

"Oh, drat. I've got a rehearsal," said Louise. "Isn't that typical? I'd hoped you would come to watch but meeting the dragon lady is more important. I'm dying to hear what she has to say. Pop into the theatre afterwards."

At that moment, Ah Kew arrived and announced that tea was ready. They followed her into the house, where Ann felt that another evening in would give Jennie too much time to think and worry. "We're off to an Amahs' Market after dinner. Come with us, Jennie. You'll enjoy it. I need some more everyday glassware."

Singapore at night was every bit as lively as Singapore by day. People wandered about the open shops until the very late hours and the markets drew crowds like moths to a flame. Lamps swung above the confusion of crockery, glassware, records, books, materials and food that was for sale. There was music, noise and bustle as the crowds moved up and down the stalls haggling over prices. Everywhere was life, light and a sense of a city which never slept. Asian children followed their parents, the toddlers in the care of older siblings while babies slept happily on their mother's backs; food stalls did a frenetic trade and delicious smells filled the night air. Swept up in it all, Jennie briefly forgot her fear of what the next day would bring.

But night brought back the anxieties once more and she slept fitfully, her mind excited, her body sweating beneath the mosquito net. Twice she left her bed to stand before the window and gaze out across the lawn now bathed in bright moonlight. The cicadas were still noisy, the night sky filled with stars. She looked up at the Southern Cross and imagined the moment when, in another hemisphere and on her father's arm, she

146

would walk through the ancient oak door of Trevellan once more. What a wonderful home coming that was going to be.

Robinson's huge emporium was filled with Saturday shoppers when the Boyds entered the air-conditioned restaurant. At once, Ann was waving to her many friends, stopping to speak to some as she and her husband, with Jennie in their wake, headed for the far corner where Dorothea Webb was already seated. After a few pleasantries the Boyds left her and Jennie, both feeling it was not their business to pry into the private affairs of the Veryans. Their business was to give support only.

When they were alone at last, sharp hazel eyes studied Jennie from an austere face. Parted to one side, the grey hair hung straight to chin level, giving the woman a look of high intellect. Her navy linen suit was not relieved by jewellery any more than her thin, sallow face was helped by cosmetics.

The waiter came, coffee was ordered and Mrs Webb came to the point bluntly. "So then, Miss Veryan, you have come to the Far East in search of your father. What made you think he would be with me?"

"Would you mind telling me all you know about Mr Williams?" asked Jennie.

The eyes were cautious. "It would surely make more sense if you told me how your father came to be missing."

The coffee arrived; Jennie sipped it black, without sugar, her mind too much on what she was saying to notice the bitter taste. At last she came to the end of her story, showed the photographs she had brought with her and said, "You can see it is the same man. My father has a burn scar which shows on his arm and hand and reaches from shoulder to waist. You know your Mr Williams has such a scar. Why does he call himself that?"

After a long pause: "Because everyone needs an identity."

"I'm sorry, Mrs Webb, I don't understand?"

The face lost some of its austerity and what could almost have passed for a sympathetic smile touched the thin lips. "This might come easier if you called me Dodo and I called you Jennie. What I have to say won't make pleasant hearing."

Jennie's fingers tightened on the cup handle. "Please, go on."

Dodo frowned. "Oh dear. This is all so difficult. He was very upset and confused, poor old thing. I told him I would see you today to find out what was going on. In reality, of course, you're the one who needs to know that. Well, all I can tell you is that the man we know as Leslie Williams was found some years ago, by an army patrol, in a remote *kampong* in Selangore. The patrol was seeking terrorists but instead discovered this tall gangling Englishman. The *Tuan* of the village told

147

them that the man had been found more dead than alive on their outskirts during the war. He was nothing more than a walking skeleton and had almost certainly suffered from beri-beri, dystentry and malaria according to the doctors here. But worse than all this was his complete loss of memory. The Malays cared for him and nursed him back to some semblance of normal health with their own medicines. It couldn't have been easy for them, knowing what would have happened had Japanese soldiers found out. The prison camp was about four miles from the *kampong*. He must have escaped when the guards tried to move the prisoners at the close of the war, nobody knows."

Dodo put down her cup and went on. "Being so remote it was some time before news reached the *kampong* that the war was over. When it did, they were unable, and probably unwilling, to contact the British because of communist terrorists in the area. Then, one day, the patrol arrived. They took him to Kuala Lumpur and from there he was flown here to the military hospital. Identification was impossible. X-rays showed he had been beaten about the head and body, and that broken bones had healed badly, but they still believe his amnesia could be the result of trauma rather than physical injury. He spent nearly two years in a psychiatric clinic but only one flicker of memory returned. Richmond Hill in Surrey. Does that ring a bell?"

Jennie frowned, then light dawned in her eyes. "My grandmother's sister lived on Richmond Hill but I never knew her or the house. I don't recall my father going there during my lifetime."

Dodo sighed and shook her head. "Probably a childhood memory. Just a brief flash, nothing more. In all these years, nothing more. He calls it his brick wall. It must be a terrible thing to come up against every minute of your life. So far and no further. He has no memory of how he came to be at the *kampong* and, I'm afraid my dear, he has no memory of you, or his home and family."

She drank her coffee and smiled. "The nurses all adored him. He reminded them of Leslie Howard they said and so they called him Leslie. My husband's doctor friend is called Williams, and so Leslie adopted it as his own surname. It was something he could remember, you see. Being Leslie Williams, from Richmond, unmarried and an ex-soldier, is a fantasy identity, but it has saved his sanity. No one can live in a vacuum. Our doctor friend decided it was time to let him out into the community and asked if we could help. So Leslie came to stay with us and, eventually, I gave him a job.

"It's a strange thing, but although he had to learn many things which we take for granted, he still knew the names of famous writers and could tell you what they wrote. He knew certain historical events too, and mathematics. But when it comes to ordinary things, concerning his own life, then all remains blank. That's why the doctors think it's a question of trauma rather than brain damage, and with trauma, there's always hope. He's improved so much that I've set him to cataloguing and book-keeping. It's helped me, and helped him enormously. Now he's almost independent and lives much as anyone else does. He drives, plays cricket, likes sailing, and comes to the Tanglin Club on Sundays with us. He never swims though. Never lets anyone see those scars. We keep hoping that being out and about in normal society will do something to jog that stubborn brick wall of his, and send it crashing down. But so far it's stood pretty firm."

Jennie heard all this with a deep sense of relief mixed with anxiety, pity and love. "Amnesia! That explains it all. You've no idea how long we've been searching for him. Well, my grandfather at least. I was convinced he was dead. Oh, Dodo, you can't imagine what it means to know. It's the not knowing that's been so terrible." She longed to go to her father, hug him and say that everything would be all right now that she was here. "Poor Papa. The sooner I get him back to England the better. When he's home and surrounded by family, then his memory is bound to return."

Dodo's mood seemed to change. She opened her handbag, took out a packet of cigarettes and placed one to her lips. Then she removed it, still unlit, and began tapping it on the table somewhat erratically. "I'm afraid you don't understand, my dear. Why should your father return to England, a country he no longer knows, just because you come crashing into his life claiming to be his daughter?"

"Claiming?" Jennie was open-mouthed at this unwarranted attack. "I thought I had surely made everything clear to you? I don't claim to be his daughter, I *am* his daughter."

"You don't seem to have been listening to me," said Dodo impatiently. "He doesn't know you or any of his family. Amnesia is a complex medical problem. Even the experts in this field can only speculate on the chances of his recovery. He may never regain his memory. Taking him away from all that he knows would be cruel. Can't you see that? He has found a kind of contentment here and values our care and friendship. You are a complete stranger to him and can mean nothing."

It seemed to Jennie there was an air of triumph in her words as that old sinking feeling returned. In order to cover her confusion and growing dismay, she drank more coffee while Dodo finally lit her cigarette. The woman was wrong surely? A man with no memory of his past would be only too glad to be back in the bosom of his own family. Even Dodo admitted that no one could live in a complete vacuum. An identity based on fiction was still a vacuum for all that. At home her

149

father would come to know his true identity and learn of his birthright. How could this twilight world compare with the truth? "I know it makes sense to take things slowly, so that he has time to get used to me, but I must see him again as soon as possible so..."

"Not in my bookshop. I don't want him disturbed there."

"Where then?" asked Jennie, fighting down the anger inside her.

Dodo shrugged and inhaled slowly on the cigarette. "You will have to be patient, my dear. The poor man has endured this condition for years. A few days, or even weeks, will make little difference to him now."

"They will to me," snapped Jennie, wondering why Dodo was putting obstacles in her path. Yet, whatever the reason, she needed this woman on her side if things were to go smoothly. As it was, each was becoming irritated with the other. It was time to change course, lighten the atmosphere and win friends. Making a supreme effort to smile, she glanced around the restaurant casually. "I must say I'm glad of the air conditioning. I'd never heard of it before I came here. No wonder Robinson's is so popular."

"It always has been. Everyone meets in this restaurant."

"Have you lived in Singapore long?"

"Since 1933. That's when we started the bookshop." Dodo drew on her cigarette once more then exhaled smoke across the table. "It was a good life in the old days. I fell in love with this city the minute I arrived. I think of home occasionally, but the England of my youth is gone. Now it's all post-war gloom and doom. Rationing, socialism, strikes. I couldn't go back to such a place."

"So you were here when Singapore fell?" If it was an insensitive question, then Jennie was beyond caring. She did not like this woman with the silly name of Dodo, who wanted to keep her father from her and was abusive about her own country. Expats always ended up being harsh about the land of their birth. Louise had told her that only last night, her theory being that they had to convince themselves that leaving home had been a change for the good.

"Yes. I was here when it fell." Dodo's eyes stared into the distance. "I stood at my bedroom window and watched the Japanese army march along the Bukit Timah Road towards the burning city. Even after the air-raids, I still couldn't believe what I was witnessing. Desmond and the cook boy rushed into the garden, dug a huge hole and buried our silverware. Believe it or not, it was still there when we returned after the war. The house was a mess though. Soldiers had lived in it. We were interned, of course."

She stopped speaking. After all, what would a girl like Jennie know or care about the rest of it, such as being ordered to the Padang by the

150

new conquerors where families stood all day without water or food, where babies and children cried beneath the broiling sun; or of heart-rending scenes as men were dragged from their wives and children who then had to walk to their internment camp. Even now she dreamed of those gruelling miles to Changi; the fierce heat; babies and toddlers heavy in their mothers' arms – she herself carried one infant and led another all the way. Keep walking ... keep walking ... The guards shouting, the children crying; then the camp, the ill treatment, the malnutrition, the dysentery and malaria, the old and the young dying first. No, what would a girl from Jennie's background know of death, fear or suffering? What would she know about the anguish of losing those you love?

Dodo lit another cigarette and went on: "Most of our friends lost everything and some went back to England after the war, but we got the house back into shape and restored the poor old bookshop to its former glory. The silver helped pay for restocking. Our amah returned to us, but the cook boy, along with most of his family, had been killed by the Japanese. Their cruelty to the Asian population here was greater even than their cruelty to the Europeans. The island is full of mass graves."

She drew on her cigarette then tapped the table with her fingers in an absentminded fashion. "They say the loss of India has marked the end of the British Empire, but this is where it really began."

Unsure what to say to all this, Jennie wondered about the woman's husband. "What of Mr Webb?" she asked. "Does he help you with the shop?"

Dodo shook her head. "My husband is eight years my senior. At sixty, thanks to internment, he has the body and constitution of a man in his seventies. His health is failing fast. And so I have come to rely on Leslie Williams more and more during this past year and he has been marvellous. Being needed is good for him, and I think he's as happy as he can ever hope to be."

"I'm very grateful for all you've done for my father, Dodo. It can't have been easy. As for a meeting, perhaps if he came to Colonel Boyd's house then..."

"Oh, no. That wouldn't do at all," came the swift reply. "Far better that you should come to our house, then he would be meeting you on familiar ground and I would be there should he need me."

Jennie stiffened at this. Why on earth should Papa need this woman because he was meeting his own daughter? Was he then so weak and without any will of his own? "There is one thing which I find rather surprising. Throughout our discussion you haven't once mentioned my mother."

Dodo smiled thinly. "I felt it might be undiplomatic. After all, since

151

you are the one to come looking for your father it must follow that you need him back more than she does."

The brown eyes hardened. "My mother is dead."

"Oh, I'm sorry." Dodo did not look sorry as she added thoughtfully: "So, he's a free man after all. He'll be relieved on that score. It's been a source of great worry to him that he might have a wife somewhere."

Dumbfounded at her cold-hearted words, Jennie finally found her voice. "Well, relieved or not, I would rather break the news to him myself, if you don't mind."

"Just as you like."

"When?"

Dodo shrugged and stubbed her cigarette out in the ashtray. "I'm not sure. I have to speak to him first. Then I shall let you know when you may see him."

"When I *may* see him?" Jennie counted to ten slowly and tried to contain her anger. "Look, Dodo, I've come a very long way to find my father and now that I have, I intend speaking to him come hell or high water. And I wish to speak to him tomorrow – not the day after or next week but tomorrow."

For a moment, Dodo looked taken aback. "Well, of course you have come a long way. I only have your father's welfare at heart. You must understand that." Seeing the Boyds entering the restaurant, she bent and picked her handbag up from the floor. "All right, tomorrow at my house. I'll collect you at seven. We dine at eight. Afterwards I'll drive you home again. I have the address."

Jennie nodded. Forty minutes it had taken, just forty minutes of civilised discussion to realise that her father was in thrall to a woman who saw his daughter as a threat, to a woman who was married to an ailing man, to a woman whose whole existence was made bearable by being needed by the enigmatic Leslie Williams. Dodo did not mean to let him go. She would fight.

At the Victoria Theatre rehearsals were not going well, and a frantic Louise rushed into the auditorium to whisper breathlessly: "Oh Lord, it's all such chaos. Our leading lady has lost her voice, the scenery isn't finished, half the costumes don't fit and the pirates seem incapable of coming in on the right beat. We'll never be ready for opening night. Never!"

"Everyone on stage, please," boomed a voice.

Louise glanced around and made a face. "The Director's in a foul mood. I must dash. Stay if you like, but I can't say when we'll be finished, or if I'll have time to speak with you. In fact, I'd rather you didn't stay. It'll only make me more nervous."

152

The Boyds and Jennie left.

Victor Leighton rang that evening and said how pleased he was to have been of some real help after all. When Jennie explained about the amnesia, his voice had a strange edge to it. "Is that so? Is that so..."

She thanked him for all he had done and said she hoped they would meet again before she and her father returned to England.

"Oh, we shall. Depend on it, Miss Veryan." With that he had rung off, leaving Jennie standing there feeling that somehow she had just been threatened.

With more rehearsals to occupy Louise throughout Sunday, the Boyds took Jennie first to church and then to their Club for the day. She swam in the pool, enjoyed a curry tiffin and was glad to have the long day fully occupied, but it didn't stop the butterflies in her stomach as the hour for Dodo's arrival approached. In her bedroom, she dressed carefully in the chiffon dinner gown, gave up trying to put cream and powder on her face since it just ran off again, then brushed her hair, leaving it loose. It was hotter worn like this, but she wanted her father to see a daughter, not some sophisticated woman, and unless loss of memory meant loss of all natural instinct for standards of behaviour also, he would surely dress for dinner as he always had. What a strange evening it would be. How would she get through it? Dinner with Papa! Was it real?

At last, clutching her evening bag and an envelope full of photographs, Jennie slipped into the passenger seat of Dodo's old open-topped Morris and they set off into the dark night.

The Bukit Timah and Dunearn Roads were divided by a tree-lined canal. On either side, Jennie could glimpse the odd light shining from houses or the paraffin lamps which lit the *kampong* huts. In a riot of noise and colour they passed a street theatre and saw on the brightly lit stage a Chinese girl in traditional dress dancing before the watching crowd.

Dodo drove a shade too fast and erratically, her conversation consisting of a list of do's and don't's. "Do remember to take things slowly. Let him get used to you, to the fact of you. Do not start prattling on about your family or home. It will be meaningless to him. No sense in embarrassing the poor man. Oh, yes, there's one other thing. I thought it best to tell him about your mother having passed on. Didn't want you getting all emotional on us."

Jennie gasped at this and said thinly, "He should have heard it from me. There's a lot he must hear from me."

"What he wants to know he will ask about all in good time," came the swift reply. "Tonight you just get used to each other." She drove on in silence before making a sudden turn into a drive and jerking the car

153

to an abrupt halt on a steep slope. "Sorry, gears are stiff. I hate changing down."

The Webbs' home was a substantial rambling bungalow. Surrounded by trees, it was lit from end to end and seemed more welcoming than its mistress. They climbed seven steps to be met by an amah before walking on into a large room which ended in a verandah. Two men stood there, drinks in hands and chatting quietly. Both wore white dinner jackets as they stared out across the road to the lights of *atap* huts between banana trees. Bullfrogs from a nearby swamp outdid the chorus of cicadas. Jennie barely heard them, nor did she take in the room's decor. All she saw was the tall, grey-haired man who had now turned in her direction. Placing his drink down on a small table, he walked across to meet her "Jennie, isn't it? I do hope you're feeling better now."

Aware that her father meant to hide behind a reserved formality which said they were strangers, she nodded. "Yes, thank you." Introduced to Desmond Webb, who looked too frail and ill to be anywhere but in bed, she was relieved when he shuffled back into the room to collapse on the sofa, leaving them alone.

Charles looked at his daughter with an air of embarrassment. "Dodo has explained matters. I'm sorry about the other day. I'm sure you understand, it was a shock to me."

Jennie was silent for a moment, afraid that someone would pinch her awake to find that this was only a dream after all. But it was no dream. She really was standing with her father on a verandah in the tropics, waiting for dinner to be served. "No," she murmured at last. "It was my fault, blurting it out like that." She bit back the desire to tell him what she and the family had gone through, and heard him asking what she thought of Singapore. And so she played his little game of making polite conversation while her mind kept screaming: "*This is not how it should be. This is not how it should be at all. Why aren't we embracing? And why am I afraid to call him Papa?*"

They spoke on about the city, the places she should visit and as yet had not, then Jennie picked up the envelope she had placed on the occasional table earlier, saying, "I brought some photographs for you to look at. Snaps taken in Cornwall before you left. I thought you might like to see..." She stopped speaking as he turned away; dismay filled her. "Don't you have any curiosity at all?"

He turned to her once more, and smiling gently, almost apologetically, said, "I was extremely curious about you. Anxious too. Now I see how stupid that was. If God has seen fit to bless me with a daughter, then I consider myself most fortunate that he gave me such a charming and lovely one." He saw the amah approaching. "Ah, but I forget my manners. What would you like to drink, Jennie?"

Unable to fathom his reasoning and angry that he felt the need to resort to flattery in order to put her off, Jennie asked for a fresh lime juice, then stood awkwardly, not knowing what to say. In the distance she could hear a shattering metallic noise as though someone was beating on dustbin lids. "What is it?"

Charles looked out across the Bukit Timah Road, saying, "There's been a death in the *kampong*. The noise is meant to drive away evil spirits."

Dodo joined them at that moment and chatted on about nothing in particular until the amah announced dinner. It was an awkward affair, dominated by Dodo's comments on the day, her opinion of current affairs and her advice to Jennie on places to visit, as though she had come here as a tourist. Throughout, Jennie was aware of her father's eyes on her, then finally he asked if she had any interests.

She noted the word "interests" as opposed to work. Clearly Dodo had explained about Trevellan and his background. "I'm an art student and live in Chelsea with Maddie, my second cousin. She studied art in Paris and has a thriving art gallery." Jennie paused, watching for a reaction.

There was none. Before she could go on, Dodo chipped in with her opinions on art and before she knew it, Jennie found herself fiercely defending Caravaggio.

When the evening ended Charles offered to drive his daughter home but Dodo refused, saying, "I know the way, and you don't."

The golden opportunity to be alone with her father having been snatched from her, Jennie prepared to leave, but before she did so handed out tickets to the show which Louise had given to her earlier. "Please come," she said to everyone, before turning to her father and adding, "I should love it if you did. Wednesday, at the Victoria Theatre. It's on for four nights."

"Gilbert and Sullivan, did you say?" asked Desmond, suddenly taking an interest. "Which one?"

"*Pirates of Penzance*," said Dodo, with an air of irritation. "She's just said so."

Desmond shook his head. "No. You can't beat *The Gondoliers*. Never did think much of *Pirates*."

Charles took her hand firmly in his and said, "Don't worry, Jennie. I'll be there. I shall look forward to it."

"Not again!" Ann Boyd flung the *Straits Times* down on to the

155

breakfast table, saying, "If I have to read one more word about Bertha Hertogh I'll stop taking this newspaper altogether."

Jennie looked up from her scrambled eggs in surprise. "Who is Bertha Hertogh?"

"Our *cause célèbre*," said Louise. "A Dutch girl, born into a Catholic family and and raised by a Malay woman when the Hertoghs and their children were interned by the Japanese. Apparently the little girl was with the Malay woman at the time and remained hidden by her throughout the war. When it was all over the Hertoghs wanted their daughter back but the Malay woman swears that she adopted the girl and therefore has the right to keep her."

Louise drank some tea and went on, "I've simplified a very complex case but the basic substance is that since so many documents were destroyed during the bombing and subsequent invasion, it's difficult to prove who is right: the Malay woman or the Hertoghs. I think that somewhere along the line a misunderstanding occurred. The girl is now fourteen and doesn't want to be parted from the only mother she knows. To complicate matters further, Che Aminah has raised her as a Moslem and given her the name of Nadra. During the court case she was made a ward of court and came to us at the York Hill home. I remember seeing her there earlier in the year, a pretty blonde-haired girl in Malay dress. In the event the Judge, having the girl's interest at heart, finally gave full custody to Che Aminah."

"Which was all wrong," said Ann, buttering her toast. "Those poor Hertoghs were expected to return to Holland without their daughter and knowing that instead of being raised in the Catholic faith, she was now a Moslem. I felt so sorry for them."

"But taking the girl away from the woman she called Mother, and the only life she had known, would have been cruel also," said Louise. "I thought the Judge was right."

"Hardly, dear, since the first thing Aminah did was to marry the girl off to a young Moslem. She's only fourteen, for goodness' sake."

Louise shrugged. "Which by old Moslem law..."

"In Singapore everyone has to act according to British law and that girl is under age. Her father is furious. No one sought his permission for Bertha to marry and he's kicked up a great fuss about it."

Louise folded her napkin and looked at Jennie. "So then the Dutch papers started asking questions. What were the British going to do about this disgraceful situation? So on and so forth. Now we've had another court case and this time the Judge gave custody to the Hertoghs. Che Aminah has appealed and so we await the result of that appeal. If the Hertoghs don't take her back to Holland the Dutch Government will complain to Britain and if they do, then there are

156

fanatical groups of Moslems who see it as an attack on Islam. Either way, the Judge is in the dog house. He simply cannot win."

"And I thought I had problems," said Jennie. "What a thing for the poor girl to go through."

"She's young," said Ann "Once back in Holland she'll come to realise where she truly belongs."

Louise gave her mother a cold look. "Right now she doesn't know where she belongs and must be broken-hearted. They've taken her from Che Aminah, and placed her in a convent. A convent! I mean, how insensitive can you get? We all thought she would return to York Hill – at least that's neutral where religion is concerned. As it is, what started out as a custody case is turning into an Islamic crusade."

Sensing hysteria in her daughter's voice, Ann said: "Oh, nonsense, darling, you're just edgy because of the show tonight. I suggest you and Jennie go and do some shopping to take your mind off things. Order some dresses for the parties. Christmas will be on us before you know it."

Christmas! Jennie stared out at the garden. Would she still be here then? Would it really take that long to persuade her father to return to England? She had already sent a cable to Trevellan and mentioned the amnesia. A letter would follow as soon as she knew more herself.

After a morning's shopping and being measured for dresses, Louise spent the afternoon sick with fright, wondering why she had ever allowed herself to get involved. "I can't remember a single word of any song. I'm dreading it ... simply dreading it."

For Jennie, however, the evening could not come soon enough. She felt in her bones that this meeting would go much better than the last stiff-lipped affair, when they had broken a little of the ice but that was all. As her father had taken her hand and promised to attend this opening night with her, there had been warmth in his eyes a warmth which bordered on affection. With that hope, she had carried the look around with her all day, thinking that maybe things would move more smoothly and quickly than Dodo had said they would. After all, what would a childless woman know of empathy between father and daughter?

The elegant Victoria Memorial Theatre stood opposite the Padang, and was endearingly popular. People now flocked inside the foyer, the buzz of their conversation floating on the hot, steaming night air outside. Excited, Jennie stood with Colonel Boyd and Ann, her eyes searching the entrance for her father's arrival. "He's late," she kept murmuring anxiously. "He's so late."

"We've time yet," said Ann, trying not to sound as anxious as she was beginning to feel. "The curtain doesn't go up for another ten

157

minutes. In any case, he has the tickets. I daresay he's finding it difficult to park the car, that's all." She was looking forward to meeting Charles Veryan and had asked Ah Kew to arrange for a light cold supper to be ready for guests later on.

Slowly the minutes ticked by and finally they were forced to take their seats just as the curtain was rising. Sick to her stomach, Jennie settled herself next to the three empty ones. He had promised to come, promised he would be here, so where was he? At last, it was horribly clear that those three seats would remain empty all night. Jennie tried to concentrate on the stage where Louise was singing with the Major General's daughters and the notes of the leading lady soared with consummate ease across the auditorium. Mabel, it seemed, had found her voice again and it was like a bell. Jennie's eyes drifted to the backdrop and were held there. Here in the heart of Singapore, St Michael's Mount rose from the sea, mocking the ache in her heart as she recalled that day when she and Mark had stood at the top burning with love for each other. How could she have known then that he would reject her? How could she have known last Sunday that her father would reject her also?

Suddenly it was all too much. Tears welled up in her eyes and overflowed down her cheeks. She tried to stop them, tried to control her trembling body, but it was impossible. At that moment she felt Ann's calming hand on her arm, as if to say: "I know, my dear, and I understand your terrible disappointment."

How kind she was, thought Jennie, making a supreme effort to control herself, but how could anyone know what she was really feeling? The three people she loved best in this world had all turned from her for one reason or another and, in each case, they had done it with a lie. Her mother had lied when she said she was going to Wales, just as Mark had lied when he said he loved her. The other night her father had lied too and, like the others, had smiled when he lied, his eyes, like theirs, saying, "Trust me."

# Chapter Ten

The Battery Road was busy as Jennie's taxi picked its way through trishaws and cars to pull up outside Webb's Bookshop. She paid the driver then stood nervously in the blazing noonday sun, telling herself she was doing the right thing. All morning she had waited beside the telephone for her father to ring with an apologetic explanation. She had waited in vain.

Jennie entered the shop and looked about her. There was no sign of her father, and Dodo was too busy with another customer to notice her arrival. She stood quietly for a moment, watching as the woman walked briskly along an aisle to return with some wooden steps which she climbed in order to select a book for the man she was serving. Seizing the moment, Jennie moved to the back of the shop and waited by the desk her father used, praying he would show up before Dodo discovered her presence. Someone was moving about in a room which was screened off by a beaded curtain. Parting it, she peered inside to see a small store which doubled as an office. Her father was kneeling on the floor sorting books from a consignment newly arrived from England. At her sudden appearance he looked up in surprise.

"Jennie!" Rising to his feet, he frowned as he took in the cream dress and the hair now swept back off the face which made his daughter seem older somehow. "Look, my dear, I'm so very sorry about last night. I've been meaning to telephone you to apologise but this lot arrived and I haven't had the chance."

"You promised you would be there." Her voice was like ice.

"I know I did, but Dodo had a slight accident in the shop yesterday. She slipped off the ladder and turned her ankle. Poor thing was in great pain, so much so that by evening it became impossible for her to move without assistance. Desmond couldn't cope alone, and Ah Ling's no spring chicken, so that left me. How could I leave her?"

Jennie stared at him in amazement. Had she not just seen Dodo running around like a schoolgirl? "Did you see her fall?"

"No. I was in here at the time. She told me about it later. Didn't want to make a fuss. That's just like her."

"Did you call a doctor?"

"I wanted to, but Dodo wouldn't hear of it."

"It must have been badly swollen. Did you put a poultice on the ankle?"

"There wasn't any swelling. It's kind of you to be so concerned, but you mustn't worry. There's no serious damage."

"Yes, I know," said Jennie tersely. Telling her father that he had been duped by this woman he admired so much would serve no useful purpose. Dodo had simply not wanted him to go to the theatre and meet his daughter again. Ending her father's thralldom would be harder than she had thought.

Charles looked at his daughter, her voice and expression putting him on his guard. "I'm sorry if you were hurt. It was the last thing I intended."

In spite of herself, Jennie's lip began to tremble and she clenched her fist, willing herself to stay calm. "It's just that it's been six days since we saw each other for the first time in nine years. Six days and we're still like strangers. So, yes, it hurts."

He hardly knew what to say. There were simply no words for this attractive young woman who meant nothing when she should have meant everything. She came from behind that brick wall; how many years had he longed to see beyond it? Now she had come to show him, and he was afraid to look. It was unfair to expect her to understand something he hardly understood himself. There she stood, looking at him with moistening eyes, and suddenly he felt a heel. This was his daughter who had come halfway around the world to find him. It was time to bury Leslie Williams and learn about Charles Veryan. Glancing at his watch, he spoke lightly to hide his inner turmoil. "Good Lord, is that the time? You must be hungry, my dear. How about joining me for tiffin? I know just the place."

"Jennie!" Dodo's voice followed on the rustling bead curtain. "Goodness, how you must have crept in. I didn't see you."

"You were with a customer," said Jennie, turning. She couldn't resist a knowing smile. "I saw how busy you were, bustling here and there, so decided not to interrupt. I'm glad the ankle's better now."

Dodo smiled weakly, trying to contain her anger. "Thank you."

Charles walked to where his cream linen jacket hung from a hook on the wall, and said, "I'm taking my daughter out to the Sea View. Will you be all right, Dodo?"

"I daresay I shall manage perfectly well on my own."

"You're a marvel," said Charles, picking up car keys from the desk. "You won't mind if I take the Morris then?"

"You can hardly walk all the way to Katong."

Her tone of martyrdom flew straight over Jennie's head as elation swept away all the anger and despair she had felt earlier. She watched as her father slipped on the jacket, picked up his Panama and explained a few last-minute points to Dodo, thinking how handsome he still was for all his thinness and added years. And, yes, there truly was a hint of Leslie Howard about him. No wonder the nurses had found him so irresistible.

Soon they were driving away from the city towards the east coast where lines of Malay fishing traps reached, like fingers, into a mirror-calm sea. The hotel stood by the water's edge and here Charles lingered with his daughter, pointing to the green islands and naming them for her benefit, before leading her into the dining room where whirring fans did little to help the steaming temperature. The large room, always popular at weekends, had few people in it now. Quiet as it was, Charles found himself waving to one couple in the far corner and murmured through his smile: "There goes my reputation at the Cricket Club. They'll be calling me a dirty old man. I'll be the talk and the envy of Singapore." At their table, he placed his hat on the chair to his left, wiped his sweating face with a clean white handkerchief, then ordered fresh lime for Jennie and a Tiger beer for himself. His eyes were gentle but his voice seemed nervous as he murmured, "So then, here we are. And you have much to tell me."

Jennie was thoughtful, cautious too as she reached for her handbag. "And suddenly I don't know where to begin. Would you like to see a photograph of your home in Cornwall?" She waited, tense, expecting rejection once more, but he only smiled.

"If it's a decent home, yes. If it's a slum, then no."

"You know already, Dodo told you." Jennie drew from the bag the brown envelope. Taking one of the photographs she handed it to him, saying, "Is this to your liking?"

Staring at the picture of Trevellan, Charles could not conceal his surprise. "Good God. Dodo said something about an estate and an old house. But ... this isn't a joke, is it, Jennie?"

"No, that is the Veryan family seat and we, like the old pile, go back a long way. This is the South Front, taken from the lawn, and this one shows the East Front. That's Portia and the other is her daughter, Rosalind. Portia died of old age some time ago and Roz is no spring chicken any more." She proceeded slowly, picture after picture, the

161

house, the cove, the village and *The Rose*. There was a brief interruption while the waiter took their order, then Jennie produced photographs of the family. First her grandparents, then herself riding Kelly, Laura, Clive, then finally her mother. Staring into his eyes for the slightest flicker of recognition, she found none and felt despondent. She had told herself that pictures of his parents and wife would break through the amnesia little by little. Clearly it would not be that easy.

Holding this last photograph, Charles gazed at it for a long time. "She's ... she was beautiful. What was her name?"

"Monique," Jennie answered huskily. "She was French. You met her in Paris when you were a young diplomat and she was studying at the Ecole des Beaux Arts." She reached out to take the photo from him but he waved her hand away and continued staring at it.

"Christ, it's all so strange," he murmured. "All so bloody strange."

"Well," said Jennie gently, "we've made a beginning. Perhaps you've had enough to take in for one day? There's time, plenty of time so..."

"What was she like?"

"All I know is that I loved her very much." How could she describe the mother who had gone out of her life so long ago? "She was an excellent artist and a strict Roman Catholic. You and all the Veryans are Protestants."

He took this in slowly, still staring at Monique's lovely profile. "Did that cause friction?"

Jennie's brow furrowed as she recalled that conversation in the rose garden. "I'm not sure. Maman wanted to send me to a convent but you wouldn't have it. I went instead to Roedean School which had been evacuated to Keswick. Then you were sent here. When Maman heard that the Colony had fallen, she lit candles for you in the Catholic church at Penmore and one in the bedroom you used to share. We've kept that flame alight all these years for when you return" As she spoke a chill of forboding swept over her. "*When you return.*" But they never returned. They waved goodbye on a sunny afternoon, or crept away on a dark and rainy night, but they never returned. "One thing I do remember was how much you loved each other."

"How did she die?"

Clearly this was no time to burden him with the truth. "An air-raid. She was killed instantly."

An awkward silence followed this then Charles asked if he might keep Monique's picture. She nodded, felt a lump in her throat and watched his sad eyes as be placed it inside a leather wallet.

"And you, Jennie? What of you? Are you happy?"

At that moment the curries appeared and it seemed the signal to lighten the conversation. "Before I came here I'd never tasted curry," said Jennie. "I thought they were very hot."

162

"Not Malay curries." Charles ate slowly, having little appetite. "You didn't answer my question. Are you happy? Because it seems to me that you're not."

Jennie had talked about life at Trevellan a little, and the family; she had described the cove, the old sailing yacht so beloved of her grandfather, but not once had she mentioned Mark. Her father was clearly a perceptive man. "Why should I not be happy? I've found my father after years of believing him to be dead." She put down her fork, swallowed and said, "Look, would it offend you if I called you Papa?"

He smiled. "It sounds extremely Victorian."

"Maman was French."

The smile vanished from Charles's face. He touched his brow, wondering if he could ever explain to his daughter how it felt to live with a barrier blocking off one part of the mind; that it was like trying to recall a dream that evaporates on awakening. "I'm sorry again about last night," he said at last, thinking it was the damndest thing to be out with a lovely young woman who was telling him she was his daughter. Being told it and feeling it to be so were two completely different things. The house, the people, even his dead wife, were all just pictures of scenes and strangers. "Did the show go well?"

"Excellent" said Jennie, trying to put from her mind the memory of St Michael's Mount. "It seems so odd hearing Gilbert and Sullivan out here. *Pirates of Penzance* too. Not the best time ... well ... it made me homesick. Stupid really. I haven't been here five minutes." Coffee came and she chatted on about Louise and the Boyds, but she knew he was only half listening.

"This man who wrote to the Foreign Office ... what was his name?"

Surprised at the question, Jennie glanced at her father. "Victor Leighton. Apparently he was interned with you."

"Leighton." He repeated the name thoughtfully. "What does he look like?"

"Dark-haired; quite good-looking, I suppose. Mrs Boyd thought he was Eurasian, I wouldn't know. But he saw you in the bookshop one day and called you by your real name. Do you remember?"

Charles nodded. "Oh, yes. Odd chap, became bloody aggressive. Dodo practically threw him out. So why would he go to so much trouble for me after being treated like that?" He sipped his black coffee slowly. Here was another shadow from beyond the wall which divided his mind and caused a thousand silent screams. Sometimes he felt like the Man in the Iron Mask, his entire head encased in a dark helmet which was slowly driving him mad. Who, in God's name, was this Victor Leighton?

They left the hotel to find the sky had almost blackened. Trees

163

swayed in a strengthening wind and distant rumbling echoed across a grey sea. "Looks like a Sumatra blowing up," said Charles, hurrying his daughter back to the car and pulling up the hood. They were halfway along the East Coast Road when the storm struck. Gale-force winds from Sumatra brought with them driving torrential rain so that by the time they reached the city, water had filled the monsoon drains and overflowed on to streets which now became shallow rivers. People scurried for cover from the pitiless deluge and shutters went up everywhere.

The Battery Road had almost emptied of pedestrians as the Morris pulled up outside the bookshop. Before Charles and Jennie had made it through the door they were drenched to the skin. For a moment they stood looking at each other as water dripped from them on to the tiled floor, then the ridiculousness of their plight suddenly released all tensions, propelling them both into hysterical laughter.

For Jennie it was marvellous, a moment shared between them as though they were any other father and daughter. "That wasn't rain," she said. "That was a waterfall crashing down on us."

"Thank goodness you're back," cried Dodo, near to panic. "The roof's leaking upstairs. Bring up those buckets. Hurry!"

In a frenzy of activity buckets were rushed up two flights of stairs and stock moved out of harm's way. When she had done all she could to help, Jennie settled in the small rear office and towelled her hair dry. Her clothes were sodden but she felt no chill as she sat back in the chair and thought about her father. What now? Slowly does it, Dodo had said. Well, he had seen his home, his family, and said that she might call him Papa. It was a good start, but all hope of getting him back to England before Christmas had gone. They were into December already. She would write another letter to her grandmother telling her about today, and telling her to rest easy, as she herself could now rest easy. They just needed to be patient, that was all.

The Sumatra passed on, the rain stopped and Jennie left the bookshop, her taxi moving slowly through flooded streets. In some parts of the city murky waters reached halfway up the huge wheels of army lorries surging through the floods, in others the level dropped and she was thankful not to have to wade through it all to reach the house.

After showering and changing she wandered out to the garden and stared at the dripping foliage and flooded lawn. Mynah birds strutted the higher banks, pecking into red rain-sodden earth, while a golden oriole flew across Jennie's path to settle in the fig tree. She looked up at it then found her eyes drawn to the sight of tall cypress trees looming above soft mist which had settled on a distant hilltop. A beacon of light shone through them. To Jennie it seemed hauntingly beautiful, like an island in the sky; somewhere that beckoned and filled her with a strange sense of longing. Held in its spell, she stood gazing until the mist began to evaporate and it was just a house on a hilltop once more. Illusion though it was, Jennie knew it would stay in her mind for the rest of her days.

By the end of the first week in December the Hertogh case dominated the newspapers and all discussions in Singapore. In the English press, the Dutch girl was pictured smiling in the convent while the Malay press showed pictures of the girl weeping.

At the breakfast table Colonel Boyd rustled the newspaper in a fury. "This is all a bit much. What do the press think they're doing? We're given the impression that the girl is happy to be free of her Moslem past, while the Malays think she's being forced to embrace Christianity under duress."

Ann looked up in surprise. "Do the Malays think that? Is that what their press is saying?"

"Didn't I say she should have come back to York Hill until the appeal?" Louise sipped her coffee. "I knew I was right. Why is the Mother Superior allowing press photographers into the convent anyway? Speaking of York Hill, I'm off duty today, Jennie, so shall we take the ferry to Pulau Blakang Mati? They have a good beach there. Unless, of course, you're seeing your father?"

"No, I'm not seeing Papa today." Jennie fell silent, wondering when she would see him again. They had met on several occasions since that day when he had taken her to Katong. Each time they had been at ease with each other until she had mentioned his return to England. Then he had grown quiet before changing the subject completely. When Florence had written to Jennie enclosing a letter for her son, he had not read it in her presence and never referred to it thereafter.

"I don't understand it," she said to Louise, when they were alone half an hour later. "I had thought that, by now, he would be only too eager to see his home and family. But even raising the subject makes him shut up like a clam." She stared out from the terrace to the lawn beyond. The *kebun* was mowing the grass, ignoring Oliver who lay in the shade of the fig tree watching sleepily. "How can you stand this heat, Louise?"

"I can't. You just learn to live with being hot and uncomfortable all day. They call it being acclimatised. Perhaps it's too hot for the island. I don't think I've got the energy to get there." She stretched out on the long chair and stared across to Jennie who was leaning beside a pillar, too restless and worried to relax. "Your father has a lot to come to terms with. We can't imagine what the suffering is like for him."

"In which case you'd think he'd want to put an end to it. He can only do that by returning to England."

"Maybe he's afraid. I would be, arriving in a country I didn't remember to be greeted by strangers who wanted to embrace and kiss me."

"Do you think that's it?"

"Ask him, why don't you. Tell him you're not a child and that he can talk to you with complete candour."

Jennie shook her head. "He would never do that. You haven't met him yet but when you do you'll understand. He's charming, a little old-fashioned and very introspective. He would consider such an intimate conversation offensive."

Louise shrugged. "Then you'll have to be a lot more patient." Her pretty features shadowed. "You may even have to face the likelihood of returning to England without him."

Jennie swung around in dismay. "Don't say that. Don't even think it." And yet, unpalatable as they were, Louise's words had echoed her own fears. Why else was Dodo so much easier to get on with these days? Why had she been happy to let Charles Veryan's daughter into her own house to sketch him on the verandah, paint watercolours of him then take photograph after photograph, to send home? Why, unless she no longer felt threatened?

The wash amah had arrived, a young Malay girl of small stature and exquisite beauty. Her gleaming black hair was drawn back from the delicate face into a long plait; her sarong-clad hips moved with languid grace as she walked along the drive towards the rear of the house.

Jennie came to life suddenly, raced into her bedroom and reappeared with tubes of paints, brushes a small jar of water. and a sketch pad. "I've simply got to get her on canvas, but for now I'll have to make do with sketches and a watercolour. Ah Kew speaks Malay, doesn't she? Will she ask the girl's permission?"

Half an hour later Jennie was seated on a small stool at the rear of the house painting away as the Malay girl knelt over a tub of washing. Ah Kew was cleaning the kitchen floor while Chinese music blared from her personal quarters; Chan was giving a list to the grocer who had just arrived with the daily order; a chameleon sat on the telephone wires, its face to the sun, and a column of ants were working with military precision, to move a dead chit chat along a wall to their nest. Tiring of his position under the fig tree, Oliver now sat watching the operation, ears pricked and alert. Only when Louise mentioned that it was time he was bathed did he turn swiftly and run off to hide. No one could find him for the rest of the morning.

As Jennie worked, she knew she could never leave Singapore without her father. It would mean losing her place at the Slade, but suddenly that was no longer important. Even so she would use it to stab at his conscience. When he realised what a sacrifice she was making, he would surely refuse to let it go on. She would also appeal to his sense of honour and duty over his birthright and the effect on the tenants if he did not return. Clive she would vilify as a walking disaster. Emotional blackmail? So what. A man like her father would put duty before all else. Memory or no memory, he was a Veryan and the heir to a title as well as a large estate. Eventually, he would return.

The Botanic Gardens was hardly the place to begin all this, or to tell her father how his wife had died, but it was time he knew the whole truth. Jennie raised the Chinese parasol to keep the fierce sun from her and paused as a monkey scampered down the trunk of a tree and stood before them in the hope of being offered food. "I kept it from you because you had enough to come to terms with, but I couldn't go on with the lie."

Beside her Charles stopped walking, took off his Panama and wiped the sweat from his face with a handkerchief. "If not an air-raid then how?"

She told him then, told him everything she knew of her mother's part in the Resistance, her courage and terrible death, then stared ahead, frowning. "You once asked me what she was like and I answered in the only way I could, the only way I knew her. But now I realise that I never knew her at all. None of us did. I'm not sure she knew herself. Now she's a famous war heroine, a holder of the George Cross Medal, and Britain is proud of her."

Charles walked on in silence, unable to take in all that Jennie had just told him. His wife, his lovely French wife with the perfect profile, had been tortured and then murdered by the Gestapo. While he had assumed that she had sat in that large old house surrounded by servants with embroidery to amuse her, Monique had been living a very different kind of life. His wife! If only he could feel something other than awe; if only he could feel grief and loss. As it was, learning about her was rather like reading about someone in the newspapers. He cleared his throat. "Thank you, Jennie. Thank you for telling me. It must have been hard for you all this . . . your mother . . . then me . . . it must have been very hard."

"And for your parents," said Jennie quietly. "They've suffered greatly over the years. There's nothing to be done about Maman, but there's something you can do to restore happiness to them. Come home, Papa. Come home now, with me. They're growing old. Time is of the essence to them. Then there's the estate."

They walked on together, he in reflective mood, she in hope, shifting her parasol from time to time then letting the handle rest on her shoulder as she spoke on about Trevellan. More monkeys gambolled across their path and brightly coloured birds flew among the trees.

Charles was silent for some time and then said, "Mr Leighton came to see me yesterday morning," He stopped walking and turned to her. "He said things that make me wonder what sort of man Charles Veryan really is. I'm not sure that I want to know. Better by far to be Leslie Williams, poor old dull as ditchwater Leslie Williams."

Jennie stared up at him anxiously. "What did he say?"

"Nothing specific, just intimated ... things. He doesn't believe I've lost my memory. Says I'm faking. The man's either mistaken about me, or I'm not the fellow that you've led me to believe I was. He's trouble, though, and his altruism nothing but a sham. I still don't know what it is that he holds against me but he had his own reasons for getting someone out here to verify who I was. You came and did just that. It bothers me, so I want you to have no more contact with him."

Jennie stared at him in consternation. "I came here to help you, but if my coming has harmed you in any way, then the sooner you're out of Singapore the better. I'll make arrangements..."

"No. Do nothing yet." Charles glanced at his watch and his attitude changed to one briskly businesslike. "Heavens, is that the time? I'm meeting someone in half an hour. We'll speak of this another day."

"Meeting? You're just putting me off again," said Jennie angrily.

"No. I'm putting you into a taxi. Do as I say, Jennie, there's a dear. Leave matters to me."

They walked out of the gardens. Charles hailed a taxi, placed his daughter in it and said through the open window: "Remember, keep well away from Leighton."

As the vehicle moved off, Jennie looked back at her father in puzzled anxiety. He seemed such a forlorn figure, standing there in his linen suit and Panama hat. He needed someone to look after him, she thought, and who better than his own daughter? "Do nothing," he had said, "have no more contact with Leighton." Well, she had made no promises.

The waiter led Jennie to the gardens of Raffles Hotel where she sat at a table beneath the fan palms and waited. The sun was too hot, but this was where Victor Leighton had suggested meeting when she had telephoned him the night before.

He arrived fifteen minutes later, suit damp and crumpled, hat in his hand as he walked across to her table. "Well, Miss Veryan. What is so urgent that you drag me out of my office at eleven o'clock?" Harrassed,

168

he slumped into a chair, beckoned the waiter and ordered coffee for two.

Jennie was now unsure how to begin. All night she had been troubled by her father's words. Here, in the light of day, she wondered whether he was just being paranoid about the sudden changes and people that were coming into his life. Suddenly, she regretted making that telephone call and tried to measure her words carefully. "I'm sorry. I know it's inconvenient, but there's something I have to know."

"And what is that?"

"You said, at our first meeting, that it had been eight years since you last saw my father before meeting him again in the bookshop, and you admitted how greatly he had changed. So when he denied that he was Charles Veryan, what made you so certain that he was?" She waited, thinking he would mention the scar, but his lips parted, not so much in a smile but in a sneer of triumph.

"The minute he denied it, I was certain."

His words sent a chill through her. When coffee came she ignored it. "My father says you do not believe he is suffering from amnesia. You said things which have distressed him."

"Distressed, is he?" Leighton gave a hollow laugh. "That, Miss Veryan, is the least of his problems. You see, we have a reckoning, Charles Veryan and I." Slowly he poured the coffee, savouring the look of alarm in her eyes.

"I do wish you would stop speaking in riddles, Mr Leighton. If you've something to say, then please say it." She waited, but he just lit a cigarette then stared at her until she wanted to scream. "I presume that something happened during your internment that caused you to feel badly about my father. Whatever it was, I can assure you he has no memory of it. So you're hardly being fair to him."

"Fair! What is fair in this world? My father was an English doctor who married his nurse, a Malay woman. Shock and horror all around. Going native... bad form. Had to resign from the Club at once. I am a product of that union, neither quite English nor Malay. In England...." He broke off and smiled again. "No, don't speak to me of 'fair'."

She heard the bitterness in his voice and saw hot anger in his eyes, but could only guess at the many small humiliations which had turned him into the simmering mass of resentment he was today. "England! You met my father there and my aunt and they upset you in some way? No ... no you met my father in the camp. Please tell me the truth."

Leighton stood up and beckoned the waiter for a bill. "Ask your father. Make *him* tell you the truth."

Resenting his off-handed manner, Jennie snapped. "He can't. He

169

doesn't know. Why do you torment a sick man? It's despicable. I think you owe me an explanation."

The bill came. Glancing at it, Leighton placed money on the waiter's tray then turned to Jennie with an expression of intense anger. "I owe you nothing, Miss Veryan, unlike your father who owes me plenty. He thought his class and background allowed him to take what he wanted without caring who got hurt in the process. Nothing he can do now can ever replace what he took. But I intend to see that he pays for his crime. I have vowed to make him suffer as he made others suffer. I've partially suceeded, I think. As I told you, we still have a reckoning, and it will be paid." Donning his hat, he smiled thinly. "Well, much as I should love to stand here all day discussing your father, I'm afraid I must be about my business, so I'll bid you good morning, Miss Veryan."

He turned and walked across the lawns towards the hotel, leaving Jennie sitting there in dismay.

The last thing Jennie wanted was an evening out with Louise and two young army officers. But Louise was adamant, seeing how upset her friend was. "This Mr Leighton always upsets you. I do wish you'd tell me how. But, since you won't, then I refuse to let you mope around all evening worrying. Nigel and John are taking us to the cinema. You'll find John quite amusing."

Jennie found John a stilted bore and when they returned to the house that evening, was glad that Louise did not invite the men in for coffee. Inside they found Mrs Boyd felt quite differently.

"Really, Louise, I had hoped you'd have been polite enough to ask them in. Nigel adores you and you're so cruel to him."

Louise glanced at Jennie and smiled. "My mother is quite determined to marry me off before I've had any life of my own. Is that why you waited up, Mummy?"

Ann stood up and stifled a yawn. "No ... it wasn't that. I had a message for Jennie and since I'm off early tomorrow – you recall I'm doing the flowers for the Mess – thought I'd make sure she received it now." She turned to Jennie. "Your father telephoned. He wants you to meet him for lunch tomorrow at Robinson's. One o'clock sharp. It's very important, he said."

Jennie's heart took a leap. Important. He had made a decision at last and he had made the only one he could make. Leighton with his antagonism had succeeded where she had failed. Her father had decided to return to England. Thank God.

"We can share a taxi," Louise was saying. "I've a few things to take to back to the theatre."

Ann stifled a yawn. "Oh, Jennie, since you're going into town I should check on that dress you're having made for the Mess Dance on Saturday. Miss Su is very good, but sometimes needs chivvying."

"It ought to be ready," said Jennie happily, thinking to herself that there would be many things to attend to tomorrow.

The girls bade her goodnight and went off to their bedrooms. Ann stood in the room for a moment, smelling the mosquito coils and listening to the chorus of cicadas breaking the stillness of the night. At last, she closed the shutters, drew the grilles across, locked them and putting out the lamps, went to bed.

The following morning, Jennie showered, stepped into a blue lawn dress and fixed her hair into a chignon. She thought of England and the luxury of staying dry after a bath or shower, of breathing clear fresh air, of cold winds, fog, snow, or anything else the Northern Hemisphere could throw at her – just for a few minutes – as a brief change from this steaming jungle heat. England! Soon she would be back there with her father.

Light of step, she walked along the drive then found Louise hauling a small case into the waiting taxi. "Goodness! When you said a few things, I didn't envisage a caseful."

"Bits and pieces I shouldn't have brought away with me, but they got mixed up somehow. Well, it was quite a last night party. I must have been pie-eyed, and then there was Denis and he . . . well anyway I've got shoes, a Victorian bonnet and two shawls, among other things."

Jennie laughed as the taxi made its way towards the city. As it entered St Andrews Road, it was forced to slow down since the route was crowded with Malays and Pakistanis who were moving towards the Supreme Court.

Louise frowned as she stared out of the window. "What on earth . . .? Of course. It's the Appeal today. You remember, the Hertogh case? I'd no idea there would be so much interest."

The taxi driver eased his vehicle through the crowds and pulled up outside the Victoria Theatre. Louise clambered out, still struggling with the case. "Jennie, I'm not sure I like the look of all this. Wait here and we'll go straight home again."

Jennie frowned and shook her head. "I can't. Papa will be waiting." Seeing her friend's worried look, she smiled. "Don't worry. I'll come straight home after seeing him. If Papa's decided to return to England then I'm not going to give him the chance to change his mind."

Still anxious, Louise asked her to wait until she had taken the case into the theatre. She returned quickly, climbed back into the taxi which eased out into the road once more.

It seemed now that the crowds had thickened and were all over the Padang. Star and Crescent banners raised high, they pushed their way

171

through the flame trees bordering the cricket field and were obviously highly agitated. "No, Jennie. I think you should come home with me. Now."

Jennie shook her head. "I promised to meet Papa. Anyway, the crowds will have gone by the time we've finished lunch. Do you think the Malay woman will win?"

Louise shook her head and frowned. "No. That's what bothers me." The taxi moved away and soon they were in the normal bustle of busy Raffles Place. The excitement was over, and the girls relaxed once more as Robinson's came into view.

"Good luck," murmured Louise, as Jennie left the taxi. She raised her hand, adding, "See, I've got my fingers firmly crossed for you. Come straight on home afterwards. I'll be worried otherwise."

Jennie looked at the menu then smiled across to where her father sat opposite. "What exactly is *Nasi Goren*? Louise said I should try it."

"An Indonesian dish with crab, lamb's liver, prawns and so forth, all mixed up in rice. You'll like it, I promise."

Jennie decided to try it and when they had ordered, sat back in her chair regarding him with growing excitement. "Well, come on. Don't keep me in suspense any longer."

He shook his head and avoided her eyes. "I make it a golden rule to eat first and have serious discussions after. When you've been denied food, you learn to appreciate it all the more."

Her smile faded. Although his voice was light enough the words seemed ominous. "All of a sudden I'm not hungry."

"And if you don't eat, you won't know what I have to say, will you? So be a dear, and do as I ask, Jennie."

The dish came, piping hot with stirred omelette covering the rice, the whole topped with crisp brown onions. Delicious as it was, Jennie was too worried to eat and merely toyed with her food.

Charles too ate very little, pushed his plate away and lit up a cigarette before coming to the point. "Why did you see Victor Leighton when I asked you not to?"

It was the last thing she had expected him to say. She felt her face go hot as she fumbled for an answer. "Because he had clearly upset you and I wanted to know why?"

"And did he tell you why?"

"No." That was the hell of it. She had upset her father for nothing, and she had upset him at a crucial time. "He said something about you and he having a reckoning, or some such nonsense. What happened, Papa? What happened to make him hate you? Because he does and he means to harm you."

172

"You said the RAF would fly you out if you wished?" When she nodded, he said, "Then I want you to leave Singapore as soon as they can take you."

Her eyes were wide with shock. "Alone? You can't mean it. I won't leave this place without you."

"You must," Charles said in an urgent whisper. "You only make things worse for me by staying. Have you told him about Trevellan?"

"Of course not. Why?"

Charles sat back and drew on his cigarette. "Because I think his game is blackmail. He thinks I'm a wealthy man. So it's imperative he never learns where the estate is or any of the family."

Jennie leaned forward. "He won't. But what is it between you? What have you done?"

Strumming his fingers on the table, Charles shook his head. "If only I knew. He insinuates but refuses to elucidate. He's a driven man. Is it really possible that I made him that way?"

"Come home to England and then you'll find out. He was there. I believe that he knew you then and Aunt Laura also. England is where the answer lies."

"No," he answered, shaking his head. "The answer is here, in Singapore. But Leighton means to use you to get at me and I don't want you hurt. Go back to England at once. You only make things more difficult for me by staying. And you stay in vain. I intend to remain until I know what's going on."

Her eyes widened. "With that man worrying you the way he does? Surely it makes more sense to put thousands of miles between you?"

"Run away, do you mean?"

"You wouldn't be running away, you'd simply be coming home where you belong, and once there you'd be surrounded by people who love you. Here, you're vulnerable, and open to any accusation a person might make."

"Please, Jennie. No more arguments. Just leave Singapore."

She stared at him in dismay. Her throat ached and she felt stinging tears filling her eyes. "I thought ... I expected that you were going to say ... oh, Papa, don't you care about me at all?"

Stabbing out the cigarette, Charles could not look into those tearful eyes. "That's just it. You've come to mean a great deal to me. You tell me you're my daughter, you call me Papa and I must accept it. But ... I don't know it, Jennie. To me you're a lovely young woman and I find myself ... well, I look forward to seeing you and ..." He stopped speaking.

Jennie looked confused. "But that's how it should be, surely?"

"Christ, no. Don't you understand?"

173

She stared at him blankly for a few seconds then felt that someone had punched her in the solar plexus. He couldn't mean what he was saying. She had misunderstood surely? But as she tried to come to terms with the shock of his words another thought entered her head. It was like the sun coming out from behind a dark cloud.

"God, I'm sorry," he was murmuring. "Sorry if I've shocked you. I shouldn't have said anything. It was unforgivable of me."

Still slightly dazed, Jennie shook her head. "No ... don't you see ... don't you realise? It isn't me. It's Maman. Everyone says I look like her and she would have been about my age when you first met her in Paris." Eyes shining with the excitement of her discovery, Jennie now warmed to her theme. "You don't realise it, but you're remembering, Papa. There's a chink in that wall of yours after all."

Charles just stared at her blankly. It was the last reaction he had expected. Had he not just told his daughter the most shameful, appalling thing? Either she was extraordinarily mature in her thinking and understanding, or still very young and completely naive. Whichever it was he would have to pull himself together and come to terms with this father and daughter relationship. Angry with himself, he wished now he had said nothing. But he had been desperate and telling her, he'd thought, would surely send her scuttling home.

"Are you listening, Papa? When you're back among the family the chink will widen, then crumble altogether one day."

Supposing it did not? The thought haunted Charles. And yet some of Jennie's comments made sense. A chink in the wall. Was it possible? Even so it didn't help things at the moment. There was still Leighton and Jennie would have to leave. "Returning to England will produce no magic formula. It will only bring unhappiness to my parents in the long run. You're asking me to leave a life I know for one which is alien to me. You're asking me to leave friends for strangers. You're asking me to run away from something which ..." His voice trailed off, and he shook his head. "No. And there's an end to it. I asked you here today to tell you to leave Singapore at once. As your father I ask you this, as my daughter I expect you to obey. Isn't that the way it's supposed to go?"

Crushed at this final rejection, Jennie could only stare at him for some time. The lump had returned to her throat. She tried to swallow and then speak, but the lump ached more and her whole body started to tremble.

"Well," she managed to whisper after a few minutes, "far be it for me to keep you from your precious bookshop, and Dodo, and your Godawful boring life. God preserve you from Leighton too. If England is anathema to you, then I must leave you here. I'll think of something to tell your parents. They're going to be broken-hearted of course ..."

174

Unable to finish the sentence she rose from her chair and ran out of the restaurant, tears streaming down her face.

Quickly paying the bill, Charles rushed after his daughter, finally catching up with her at the entrance to the store. He placed a hand on her shoulder, saying, "No, Jennie. Not like this. Don't go from me like this. Try to understand."

Jerking away from him, she snapped, "Oh, I understand only too well. You never had any intention of coming home. You just let me go on hoping, knowing how much it meant. You'd rather spend your life living half in and half out of a community that barely knows you exist. I daresay that suits Dodo very well, but I won't be around to watch you fade away like that."

In a state of high agitation she rushed out into the blazing sunshine of Raffles Place and searched through her tears for a taxi. "Damn it, where are they?" A Malay stopped his trishaw beside her and she was about to step into it when her father pulled her away.

"Look" said Charles waving off the trishaw. "Come back with me and we'll talk. I can't bear to let you go like this."

"Oh? Quite clearly you can." She twisted from him as a taxi drew up at the kerb and two people climbed out. Immediately, Jennie took their place and said to the Chinese driver: "North Bridge Road, please."

As the taxi drove off, she turned to see her father standing on the kerbside staring after her. He looked so shattered and pitiful that, suddenly, all anger fell away from her. But even as she thought of stopping the taxi to return to him, she saw her father disappear into the crowds of shoppers.

It was over! All over! Slumped back on the seat and lost in thought, her eyes saw nothing but her father's face as she had walked away from him. Why had she said such awful things? Never in her wildest dreams had she imagined being so cruel to someone she loved so much. She had failed in her mission. Her grandparents would never understand why, any more than she did, and Laura would smirk and say, "You should have left it to me."

Suddenly realising that she had asked for the North Bridge Road when she had decided not to go Miss Su after all, she was about to tell the driver to change course when the taxi came to an abrupt halt. Peering ahead she saw the road was blocked by a large chanting crowd. The driver backed slightly then stopped, turned to her in alarm, and shouted something in Cantonese. She just stared at him in fear. As he shouted louder, she realised he was ordering her out. She shook her head. "Drive on. Go another way."

It was useless. There was nowhere for the taxi to go. Suddenly the chanting masses became a stream of running figures. People surged on to the road, stopping cars and hauling out their occupants. As Jennie watched in terror, she saw a European couple dragged from their surrounded vehicle. The crowds moved in on them. She heard the screams and buried her head in her hands.

The driver was now hysterical. "You go. You go now." The crowd had turned their attention to the taxi and were closing in on it. Jennie opened the door, saw a clearing and ran for it. Footsteps clamoured behind her. There were shouts and screams, then she felt herself held by one man as another beat his fist down on to her shoulders. Her dress ripped. A woman joined in, screaming in Malay as she pulled at her hair. Then a hard blow on the back of Jennie's head sent her down. She was in pain, dizzy, terrified, and falling – falling amongst the angry baying mob.

# Chapter Eleven

Squadron Leader Guy Lloyd was trying to back his roadster away from the restive crowds by the Sultan Mosque. It proved to be a difficult manoeuvre. One word caught the officer's ear. *Jihad.* It sent a cold chill through him. Holy war? What on earth was going on?

Managing to ease the car away at last, he headed towards the North Bridge Road, relieved to be out of trouble. His relief was short-lived. Suddenly people appeared from every direction, Malays and Pakistanis, shouting and chanting as they forced traffic to a standstill. The mob rushed across in front of him to pull Europeans from a bus. He slammed on his brakes and froze at the sight of innocent passengers going down under flaying fists.

When the crowd turned towards him, he leaped out over the door of the car and, fighting off would-be assailants, started running for his very life. There was a moment's hiatus when it seemed he had outrun them. In that same moment, he saw the girl in a blue dress racing from a taxi with screaming madmen after her. When she went down, he hurled himself on to her attackers, pulled her to her feet then ran on, hauling her after him, and almost pushing her into a side street, until it seemed they had lost their pursuers at last.

Lim Chan Seng had been carving a motif on a teak coffee table when the English couple suddenly burst into his open-fronted carpentry store. The officer was trying to keep a woman on her feet and shouting to him to close up. For one moment Mr Lim blinked in astonishment but when he heard the word "riot", sprang into action and called upon his adolecesent son to help him with shutters and grilles.

Safe at last, Guy Lloyd turned his attention to the girl. She was semi-conscious with blood running down her ashen face from a wound in her forehead. Picking her up and carrying her, he realised vaguely that he was in a carpenter's workshop. A strong smell of camphor and teak oil filled his nostrils as the Chinese owner beckoned him to an

177

upstairs room. There an astonished woman stared at the tall Englishman in the blood-spattered RAF uniform, then rushed to the girl in his arms, speaking in a torrent of Cantonese to her husband who tried to explain the situation to her in the same language.

Moaning slightly, Jennie was set down gently on a sofa while the Chinese woman tutted and shook her head in dismay. Dressed in a floral cotton tunic over loose matching trousers, Mrs Lim was middle-aged with dark hair gently curling around her kind but anxious face. Preparing a tray of antiseptic lotion, cotton wool, a bowl of water and a small pot of Tiger Balm ointment, she gently bathed Jennie's cut forehead before wiping the blood-matted hair at the back of her skull. After this she turned her attention to the badly grazed elbow and forearm, applying the soothing balm gently. Her ministrations were watched by a small girl who sat cross-legged on the floor, her black hair cut short, her fringe almost reaching the large expressionless brown eyes.

From time to time the woman would look up at Guy and shake her head, murmuring, "No good. Head bad, arm bad. Lady need doctor."

Guy knew she was right, but no doctor would come out in a riot. He would have to wait until things had calmed down. God willing, that would be soon.

For all his alarm, Lim Chan Seng showed calm dignity as he introduced his family and said he was glad to offer the shelter and hospitality of his humble home. His English was good since many of his customers were British servicemen and their families. Thanking him for his kindness, Guy counted his blessings that he had stumbled into the right store.

As Jennie slowly regained full consciousness, her eyes took in the kind face of Mrs Lim, then drifted over the room as she tried to recall what had happened. She saw crimson curtains bright oriental ornaments, a silken-fringed shade hanging from a central light, a few pieces of blackwood furniture and, on a shelf in a far corner, a family shrine where a candle glowed.

"How are you feeling?"

Slowly she turned her head and looked up at a tall fair-haired man with a badly bruised face. Blood trickled down his chin from a cut lip. He was dabbing at it with his handkerchief and watching her with a worried frown. She tried to think who he was. Why did she feel so dizzy? And when had a heavy wall fallen on her? Her head hurt badly, so too did her shoulder, arm and wrist. Even so she found herself saying, "I'm quite all right, thank you."

Thinking she sounded as if they had just met at a garden party, Guy smiled. "Sorry if I was rough on you. I really didn't have much choice."

178

She gazed at him in confusion, then slowly her mind began to clear. "You ... it was you ...?" Her voice was weak as memory of the horror returned. "You pulled me away ... you saved me. I'm most grateful to you, Mr ...?"

"Lloyd," he said with a broad grin of relief. "Guy Lloyd. And you are ...?"

For a moment she had to think. "Jennie ... Jennie Veryan."

"Well, Jennie Veryan, you just rest. You know your name and can speak. So then, no great harm done." His voice was light but he still didn't like her colour as he introduced the Lims.

Finished now with Jennie, Mrs Lim turned her attention to the tall fair RAF officer whose khaki drill shirt was splattered in blood. He smiled and waved her away, saying, "Thank you, but it's only a few bruises and the lip's stopped bleeding." She would have none of it, however, and proceeded to dab Tiger Balm on each bruise and the cut lip before going to her kitchen and returning with a tray containing small bowls of steaming hot tea. She set it down just in time. From outside came shouts, a crash, a woman's scream, and everyone started with fear. Mr Lim rushed to the window, glanced out, then closed the shutters quickly, asking: "Why is there rioting?"

Guy Lloyd shrugged. "It seems to have started at the Sultan Mosque. I can't tell you why."

"I can." At Jennie's words, everyone turned to her. She was starting to tremble and wished she could stop. How cold she was suddenly. Her jaw clenched with tension as she tried to speak. "It ... was earlier ... at the Courthouse. I saw them ... the crowds." The trembling grew stronger. "The Hertogh ..." Speech faded as the shaking grew beyond control.

Guy rolled his grey eyes. "God's teeth! Is that what this madness is all about?" Seeing that Jennie was in shock, he held the tea bowl to her lips and helped her to drink.

Jennie was still shaking uncontrollably and tears flowed down her cheeks. How stupid, how embarrassing! What would this kind couple think of a grown English woman acting like a three year old? Still the shaking continued and the tears flowed.

Mrs Lim shook her head and muttered again about a doctor.

Sounding more cheerful than he felt, Guy said. "The police will soon have things sorted out." But the police, mostly Malays, had not been much in evidence so far. It would be up to the Gurkha Riot Squad. If anyone could restore order, then without a doubt it was these loyal and fearless guardians of the Empire.

Jennie stopped shaking and shuddering at last, and was glad of the comforting tea. She looked across to where her rescuer now sat, seeing

179

the weal on his forehead and the bruises on the face and jaw. Had that been the price he had paid for saving her? Supposing he hadn't been around . . .? She shuddered with horror at the thought. As it was she was in this strange room, alive and well, when Heaven alone knew what was happening outside. The sounds of rioting were louder. Everyone became tense and silent. She watched as Guy walked to the window, noticing how lean he was; tall, lean and hard-looking.

Restless, Guy pulled back the shutters a fraction, and saw smoke billowing from burning buildings. Frowning, he turned to his host. "Would you mind if I used your telephone to contact my station?"

Mr Lim said he did not mind. In fact, Mr Lim was only too glad to have someone in authority who might be able to act.

Guy got through to RAF Tengah and explained what had happened. "Things are getting worse. Where on earth are the Gurkhas? People are being killed out here . . . Where? Here, in the city, for Christ's sake. The police don't seem able to contain it . . ."

Jennie's thoughts now fled to her father. He would be worrying about her surely? When Mr Lim said she too might use the telephone she rang the bookshop. Dodo answered, said she was terrified and holed up in the shop with four customers. She wanted to know where Jennie's father was, thinking it bad of him to leave her in the lurch at such a time.

Jennie's heart turned over. "What do you mean, where is he? He should be with you. We left Robinson's ages ago. It's a five-minute walk through to Battery Road."

"Well, I haven't seen him since this morning."

"I don't understand," murmured Jennie. "I took a taxi and he was . . ." Her mind stopped as she thought back. Her father had been walking away from the direction of Battery Road when he had disappeared into the crowd.

"Taxi!" Dodo was saying. "Well, you were lucky. There haven't been any around for hours. We're all trapped here." There was a pause, as though Jennie's words were only now sinking in. "Oh, my dear. Where can he be?"

"I don't know," whispered Jennie in growing alarm. "Dear God, Dodo, pray that he's safe."

Jennie replaced the receiver and turned to Guy. "I lunched with my father, but he hasn't returned to his place of work." And why not? Because she had upset him so much that he was unable to return to the bookshop in his frame of mind. So where had he gone? If only she had mentioned the scene outside the Courthouse then he would have been forewarned of trouble, but she had been too full of her own worries to give it any thought. He might well have walked straight into danger.

180

"Don't worry about him," said Guy "He's probably taking cover."

The words had the ring of comfort and commonsense in them for Jennie. When he was unaware of her scrutiny, she studied him, unable to decide whether he was good-looking or not. His grey eyes had a hard glint in them and the mouth an air of knowing insolence. He was older than she, Jennie decided, by a good ten years. That meant he would be married. She wondered if his family had accompanied him as Colonel Boyd's had. The Boyds! Her mind jolted alert. If they knew of the riot they would be frantic with worry by now. Once again she asked if she might use the telephone.

"Jennie. Thank goodness!" Louise sounded relieved. "We've heard there's been trouble. A big punch up outside the Courthouse apparently. Where are you?"

"Taking shelter. There's serious rioting in the city. I can't get back, but I'm all right. Has my father been in touch?" When Louise said he hadn't, Jennie's heart sank. "If he does, then tell him I'm all right, won't you?"

"Rioting, you say? Just a moment. Daddy's here, waving at me, I think he wants to talk to you."

Colonel Boyd's questions were best answered by Guy, who gladly took the receiver from Jennie. "Good afternoon, Sir. My name's Lloyd. Squadron Leader Lloyd, RAF Tengah. Miss Veryan is safe now but she had a close call. What are they doing about the situation, Sir?"

"I'm not sure," Peter answered. "Just how bad is it?"

Amazed at the question, Guy frowned. "As bad as it could be, Sir. Europeans are being set upon and killed. They damned near killed Miss Veryan."

"Dear God. Is she badly hurt?"

"Well, she's recovering but needs medical attention. From what I've seen so far the mob seem to have the field to themselves. Have the Gurkhas been called out?"

There was a pause. "My understanding is that the Gurkhas had been standing by when trouble seemed to be brewing earlier today, but were withdrawn when the police said they could handle the situation. I daresay they thought that a military presence might inflame the troublemakers even more."

Guy cursed beneath this breath. "Well, Sir, I'd say withdrawing them has achieved just that. If ever a green light was shown to a rampaging mob then that was it. From what I've seen the situation is very serious and from what I'm hearing, it's growing worse by the minute. The army must be brought in."

"Military assistance was offered but refused, I gather. The police seemed confident that it wouldn't be necessary. Of course that was some time ago. I'll get on to HQ and find out what's happening. Meanwhile, stay where you are until I can arrange your safe passage out of there. It may take some time."

Smiling grimly, Guy replied, "Yes, I'm afraid it will, now that things have been allowed to go so far. Thank you, Sir." He gave Peter Boyd the Lims' telephone number, then replaced the receiver, swearing beneath his breath.

As evening fell, mosquito coils burned, and chit-chats scurried along the walls. The sound of rioting grew even louder. Jennie caught Guy's arm in fear. He placed a large, warm hand over hers and she welcomed the comfort it brought.

Fearful as she was, Mrs Lim kept herself busy by preparing the evening meal of fish soup with rice and Chinese dumplings. No one was hungry, but sat at the wooden table forcing the meal down them in an effort to carry on as normal. Jennie alone was exempt, and made to sit very still, her arm in a makeshift sling and a plaster over the gash on her forehead.

Since there was no sleep to be had that night, everyone except the small girl stayed in the sweltering shuttered room, tense and silent as rioters ransacked the city. Then came the sound of gunfire, helicopters and explosions. Guy moved to the shutters once more and opened one the merest crack. "The 7th Cavalry have arrived. Sounds like a war zone out there."

More tea was made and consumed but the Chinese family had grown quiet at the gunfire and explosions, remembering the raids which had heralded the horrors of the Japanese occupation when most of their relations had perished. All they wanted now was to build up their business and live in peace. Singapore was a hotbed of different races, cultures and religions. Mostly they lived in harmony together, but something like this could set race against race. When this madness was over, who could say what legacy of bitterness would remain?

Jennie sipped her tea, thankful for Guy who tried to calm her with general conversation. She knew what he was doing and went along with it. "Where are you from?"

"Brockenhurst. It's a small village in the New Forest." He offered her a cigarette and, when she refused, lit up his own. "And you? Just what are you doing in Singapore, a single English woman living with an army family? Is it work that brings you here? Don't tell me, let me guess. You're a teacher, or just about to be."

Jennie smiled and shook her head. "I'm here on a quest." She explained just as much as she thought he should know, then paused and listened to the noises outside as the army took control. "If anything's happened to my father now, then I'd say that God is having a laugh at my expense."

Guy was anxious for her. There was every chance that a man with amnesia could be in serious trouble. "Don't worry," he said. "He's safe and well, believe me. When do you take him home to England?"

She shrugged. "I don't know. I don't know anything anymore." No, she decided, not handsome. Too stern-looking for that. There was a stiff, almost inhibited manner about the man. Yet he was brave and only hours ago had risked being beaten to a pulp to save her. "Shouldn't you contact your wife? She must be worried sick about you."

"I'm not married," he answered.

Not married! Suddenly her mind filled with memories of Mark's face; the intense blue eyes, curling, dark hair and sensitive, passionate, almost tragic mouth. No one would ever fill the aching void he had left in her heart. Right now though she was glad of Guy Lloyd's protection, assurances and comfort, and couldn't help wondering if, after this awful night, they would ever meet again. It was hardly likely. He was too old for her and she was clearly of little interest to him.

Nearly forty hours after leaving her father outside Robinson's store, Jennie found herself being driven by MPs through sunlit streets made silent now by a curfew. Only then did the full extent of the scale and ferocity of the rioting become apparent. Parts of the city looked like a war zone. Shops had been gutted, cars and buses were burned out shells. The army was everywhere, among them Malay soldiers and policemen who, although Moslem, had done everything in their power to restore order.

Guy was fretting about his car. On the evidence all about him, it was probably burned beyond recognition by now. But he had loved that second-hand MG and had pushed her flat out along the Choa Chu Kang to Tengah, ignoring warnings from the police about excessive speed. Insurance would be out of the question too, he supposed. Acts of God, War, Civil Unrest ... weren't these the things in the small print that were not covered? Bloody idiot rioters! And all over a Dutch girl!

Colonel Boyd was at Fort Canning when the MPs' vehicle pulled up at his house, but Ann and Louise came running to greet them, followed by Chan and an anxious Ah Kew. Jennie climbed out and asked Guy in, but he refused, saying, "Sorry, this is a curfew and I'm under escort." He turned to Ann. "Please convey my thanks to the Colonel. Any news of Mr Veryan?"

Ann's face shadowed and she shook her head. "We've phoned the bookshop several times but he didn't return there or to the house in the

183

Bukit Timah Road. We tried the hospitals, just in case, but things are pretty chaotic. There have been so many casualties that they can't cope and haven't yet sorted out identities." Turning to Jennie, she winced and shook her head. "Oh, my dear. Just look at the state of you. We must get the MO to come and look you over. We certainly can't go to him."

But Jennie could only think about her father and turned to Guy who was now climbing back into the vehicle. "What should I do? How shall I find him? We're all confined because of the curfew."

He looked down at the large pleading eyes and felt he could hardly just leave this girl in the lurch. "I'll get our Medical Officer to check around. He can get hold of facts more quickly than I could. Any distinguishing marks?" He needed such information in case he had to check the mortuaries, but said: "I only ask since you mentioned your father's amnesia. He might be very confused."

Jennie was not fooled however, and her blood ran cold as she said, "A burn scar from shoulder to waist . . ." Her voice cracked. She found it in time to add, "You've been very kind. Thank you, thank you a million times for saving my life."

He looked embarrassed. "I'll be in touch." The vehicle pulled away. Guy did not look back as it turned the corner.

"Wow!" said Louise beside her. "Did I hear you say he had saved your life?"

"You did, and he did." Jennie turned and started walking along the drive. "I should have done as you did and returned home."

"I don't know." The green eyes shone. "Having seen your knight in shining armour, I'm almost sorry I did." Louise's smile faded as she looked at her friend. "Sorry. That was stupid. Oh, Jennie, you look awful and we've all been worried sick. You must have been terrified, you poor old thing. I blame myself for not realising how bad things were. Come and sit down and tell us everything that happened."

Later, they gathered around the wireless to hear the latest news being broadcast to the Colony. A curfew would be in place until further notice and everyone was to stay in their homes. Then the latest casualty figures were given out. Eighteen people dead, mostly Europeans, and nearly one hundred and eighty injured, many of those being in serious condition. Rioting had spread all over the island and was still being brought under control. In isolated areas the danger was acute.

Grilles and shutters remained closed that evening and they sweltered beneath the fans. Ann sighed heavily. "I daresay the Hertoghs and their daughter are well away from Singapore by now. Do they know, I wonder? Oh, it's unbelievable to think that a custody case could end so tragically. Those poor people. Innocent people who had nothing to do with it, now dead or badly injured. Wicked! Wicked! Until this day I liked Singapore, but now ... now I hate it."

Jennie lay back on the sofa looking up at the revolving fan wondering if Guy was a man of his word. She decided he was. In which case, he really would do something to help. Closing her eyes, she relived again that last moment when she had said cruel things to her father and left him standing under the fierce sun in Raffles Place. Maybe she would never now have the chance to say how sorry she was.

The days that followed were heart-stopping ones for Jennie who jumped each time the telephone rang. Guy was subdued as he imparted the news that hospitals and even mortuaries had been checked out but no one of her father's description had been identified. It was as though Charles Veryan had, once again, simply vanished from the planet.

"I can't go through it a second time," Jennie had wept. "It's the not knowing, you see. We had years and years of not knowing."

With her sprained wrist tightly bound and in a sling, the ugly weal on her forehead turning bluish-black in colour, the back of her skull shorn of hair so that the gash there could be examined and treated properly, Jennie sat around the house for three days, the shadows under her eyes speaking of lack of sleep. In the moments when she did drift into uneasy dreams she would awaken with a start, reliving again the horror of her attackers beating her to the ground.

Breakfast was almost over when the telephone rang. Jennie started, and spilt coffee from the cup she was holding on to the tablecloth. The call was for her. In fear and dread, she gazed at the others, took the receiver from Chan and heard Guy's voice speaking from Tengah. He sounded brighter than usual.

"Look here, Jennie. I've just received some information, but don't really know what to make of it. You see this fellow was found wandering during curfew. MPs arrested him, realised he was hurt and drove him at once to BMH."

Jennie frowned. "BMH?"

"The Military Hospital, not too far from you. Anyway, here's the thing, and I don't want you to get your hopes up because..."

"What?" Jennie wanted to scream. "What is it, Guy?"

"Well, this chap had a burn scar rather as you described, so the doctor, remembering our MO's enquiries, telephoned through to Tengah at once. But ... and this is where I have to disappoint you ... the man says his name is not Veryan."

Jennie's hand gripped the receiver until her knuckles turned white. "What ... what did he say his name was?"

There was a pause which seemed endless. "Can't remember. But it's just so damned odd about that scar that I thought you..."

"Williams," Jennie cut in. "Was the name Williams?"

After another agonising pause, Guy murmured, "I believe it was. Why? I don't understand. Jennie? Jennie, did you hear what I said? Are you still there? What made you pick on that name?"

Jennie tried to speak but relief spilled over in unsuppressed emotion. At last she managed a mere whisper: "It's him. Williams ... yes, it's him." Silence followed as tears spilled down her face. "Is he badly hurt?"

"I couldn't say." The utter confusion in Guy's voice belied the positive command he now issued. "Look, I'm not on operational duty for another forty-eight hours and since the curfew's now dusk to dawn, I'll drive over early this afternoon to take you to the hospital. You're in no state to go anywhere alone and it's not safe anyway. We could also call in on the Lims to offer our thanks. It's the least we can do."

"Oh, yes ... that's a marvellous idea."

"Fine. See you later."

Replacing the receiver, Jennie turned a smiling, tear-stained face towards Ann and Louise who were standing beside her anxiously. "Isn't it marvellous? I'd better let Dodo know. She's been utterly frantic. I don't know what condition he's in, but he's alive and ... well ... that's everything."

Ann placed a motherly arm about the emotional girl, saying, "Exactly." She turned as her amah walked in announcing that the *Kebun* had returned. "Thank goodness. The garden's being reclaimed by jungle."

But Ah Kew just stared blankly. "*Kebun* say maybe Ma'am and *Tuan* no want him now."

Still grappling mentally with Jennie's problems, Ann now tried to switch to those of her gardener. "The *kebun* said we wouldn't want him? Why ever not?"

The amah's eyebrows rose in surprise. "*Kebun* Melayu, Ma'am. He sad man. Sad at killings. He say many Melayu feel sad. Melayu good people, not bad."

Ann let her shoulders fall in a long sigh. "I see. Of course. Poor man." She turned to Jennie. "The *kebun* has ten mouths to feed and now he's afraid that, because of the troublemakers, he might be out of a job. Thank goodness Ah Kew can speak Malay." She looked at her amah once more. "I'll come with you, and I want you to explain to Inche Ibrahim that we're very pleased to see him back with us again." She sighed and murmured, "Oh dear, how difficult it's all become."

Soon the familiar sight of the straw-hatted *kebun* pushing the lawn mower sent out a reassuring signal that Singapore was slowly returning to normal.

Later, Louise helped Jennie into her favourite cream lawn dress. This done, she then applied a little make-up before combing the long hair into a French plait to hide the small bald patch covered with a plaster dressing. "There, how's that? I swear no one would ever know."

Jennie sat at the mirror and smiled. "You've missed your vocation. All this nonsense about wanting to be a Studio Manager with the BBC when you could be a make-up artist beats me." She sighed. "How would I have managed without you?" Frowning at the bruise on her forehead that no make-up could hide, she murmured: "I look as though I've been hit by a London bus and I can't wash my filthy hair because of the dressing. Whatever will he think of me?"

"Who? Your father or Guy?" asked Louise with a twinkle in her eye.

Jennie looked down at her fingernails. "Both. It's kind of Guy to come all the way from Tengah just to drive me to BMH. I doubt if the poor man expected to get stuck with my problems as a reward for saving my life."

Louise put down the comb and brushed a few hairs off Jennie's shoulders. "The Chinese say that if you save a life then you become responsible for that life until the end of your days."

"Yes, well, this rescuer is English to his fingertips." She sighed. "Look at me. I wonder how long I'll have to wear this wretched sling? Wouldn't you just know it would be my right hand."

"It might have been your life," came the sober reply.

"Yes," murmured Jennie, feeling again the ice cold horror creeping through her. This was not her first brush with death. "I've been very lucky. Whatever happens to me in the future, I must always remember that."

Guy's borrowed car was a maroon Singer roadster, and as they roared through the suburbs Jennie was glad she had placed a chiffon scarf over her hair in case the breeze revealed the shameful stubble at her crown. Her sleepless eyes were shaded with sunglasses and although she was all too aware of the bruise on her forehead, she noticed Guy made no mention of it when he asked how her arm was. His manner seemed light and held no hint of the trauma both had gone through so very recently. He drove a shade too fast, she thought, braking with her foot every time they reached a corner. Only when the city encroached did he slow to a more sensible pace, then pulled into the forecourt of the large white Alexandra Hospital.

It was fifteen minutes past two as Guy led Jennie towards the men's ward then sat outside while a nursing sister took charge of her.

Shoulder epaulettes revealed the nurse's rank to be that of Major; the stiff veil quivered slightly over the short cape as her manner made it quite clear that she took a dim view of civilians on her ward, when she had enough servicemen from the Malayan jungle to worry about.

"It's only because the General is so full after the riots that he was brought here in the first place. He's clearly been in the wars, probably beaten up by the rioters, but not badly hurt. He does seem traumatised, however, but that's to be expected. Aren't we all after recent events?"

They were walking briskly along a verandah which overlooked lush, tropical gardens. Two wounded soldiers hobbled past, still coming to terms with their crutches, and at a table four men played Mahjong beneath whirling fans. The Sister then turned into a smaller ward containing four beds and walked to the one farthest from the entrance. "Is this man your father?"

Jennie stared down at the almost jaundiced-looking face propped up on two pillows, saw the bruises, the swollen lips and closed eyelids. "Yes," she whispered, afraid to waken the sleeping man. "This man is Charles Veryan, my father." Her eyes brimmed with tears. "That this should happen to him after all he's been through . . . He's suffered from amnesia for years. He was a patient here some time ago, so there must still be notes on him." She looked at the Sister whose expression had changed from one of stern efficiency to sympathy.

"If we have notes, then I'll ask for them. He was in quite an emotional state so we've had to sedate him. I doubt if he'll wake up. Anyhow, you may stay for a short while." With that she took her patient's pulse then turned to Jennie and whispered: "You've been in the wars too, I see. What happened?"

Jennie told her, keeping her voice to a mere whisper.

"How terrifying for you," said the Sister. "I couldn't get a taxi that afternoon and it took me hours to find my way back to the hospital. I was very lucky, but I'll admit I've never been so frightened in my entire life. I'll leave you now. Your father's going to be fine in a few days. All he needs is some tender loving care."

As she turned to leave, Jennie whispered: "Sister, the notes will be under the name of Williams. Leslie Williams, I think."

"Curiouser and curiouser."

When she had gone, Jennie sat quietly holding her father's hand. He opened his eyes once then closed them and slept on. Ten minutes later she got up to leave then saw the eyelids flicker and open. Charles turned his face towards her and frowned. "Jennie?" The voice was barely discernible. A surge of relief swept over her and she sat down again, holding his hand more tightly. "Yes. It's Jennie. Are you in pain, Papa?"

"Thirsty ... head hurts like hell."

Pouring water from a jug into a glass, Jennie held it to the swollen lips then saw how he winced as he sipped. After this he lay back exhausted. She replaced the glass on the wooden locker. "Can you remember what happened? After we left Robinson's, Papa, where did you go?"

Frowning, Charles stared up at her for a while then murmured: "Walked a bit ... somewhere ... just walked. Attacked by thieves. Where am I?"

"The military hospital." She took his hand in hers. "And they weren't thieves you ran into, they were rioters."

But Charles seemed elsewhere as he murmured: "Military. Shouldn't be here ... taking up a bed ... not right ... feel a fraud ... like before with those other poor devils..." He tried to sit up but Jennie prevented him, saying he must lie back and rest. Only then did he really look at her.

"I fell down the stairs," she lied, anticipating the question. "Looks worse than it is."

"Should be more careful." He squeezed her hand, looking troubled. "Nightmares. I get nightmares. They give me something ... but I'm afraid to sleep."

When she asked about the nightmares Charles withdrew into himself once more and said nothing. At that moment the Sister returned and said, "Ah, so you've woken up. How are you feeling, Mr Williams?"

"Veryan," whispered Charles. "The name's Veryan."

The Sister caught Jennie's eye and smiled. Then she took his pulse once more, signalling it was time to leave him in peace. "Mustn't overtire you with your first visit. Your daughter can come again tomorrow."

Kissing her father on the forehead, Jennie left with a sense of deep relief. He was all right. He was going to be all right. And he knew her. He even remembered his name. She was almost walking on air when she returned to Guy. Happy and relieved for her, he drove to the wide Orchard Road where they shopped for Cameron Highland roses for Mrs Lim, brandy for her husband, a doll for the little girl and a fountain pen for the son.

Singapore was still wearing the scars of civil unrest; charred buildings and uncrowded streets seemed a world away from the city of a week since. Guy was grim-faced as his mind started to relive that moment when he had been forced to run for his life. It was about here that he had first seen Jennie and had dragged her into this street; turned again somewhere farther on – ah, yes, into this road where he had seen the open-fronted store. Stopping the car outside the Lims', he had to sit for a moment to recover his composure then, glancing at Jennie, saw how she too was reliving the ordeal.

"I'm an insensitive fool for bringing you here," he said. "I should have come alone."

Jennie shook her head. "No. I would have been very angry had you done that, after all they did for us."

Surprised but delighted to see the English couple again, the Lims stopped work, produced tea and rice cakes, then passed an hour speaking of the riot, the state of the city and how long it would be before Singapore got back to normal. Mr Lim was optimistic.

Such things happened. They had all survived far worse, but he warned them both to be careful since he was hearing stories of people being attacked in isolated areas.

On their way home, Guy glanced at his wrist watch and said: "To cheer you up, there's just time to show you one of the best views in Singapore." With that he headed west, through lush suburbs, then climbed winding Kent Ridge. At the top they left the car and Jennie's eyes were immediately drawn to the panorama stretching before her. Dotted about a turquoise sea were offshore islands, ships and sampans. Farther out were the islands of Indonesia and the hazy land mass of Sumatra.

"Didn't I tell you it was the best view?" Guy was saying. "We call it The Gap. The sunsets are quite something. Unfortunately the curfew puts that out of the question for us. That nearest island is Pulau Blakang Mati. The army have it. Marvellous beach there." He turned to look at her. "You really must see it before returning to England."

She waited, expecting him to suggest they go there together, but he said nothing more. Feeling deflated, Jennie searched for something to say, anything just to break the awkward silence. "How long have you been a fighter pilot?"

"Twelve years."

Twelve years! She blinked, trying to take in the fact that while she had been a child, he was fighting in the skies. What had happened to the age gap that would have yawned so widely between them in those days? What was he ... thirty? How young and very gauche she must seem to him.

Walking her to a small cafe where tables and chairs had been set out overlooking the view, Guy ordered beer for himself and fresh orange for Jennie. He lit a cigarette and looked at her thoughtfully. It was the first time he had really studied that attractive face and those large eyes. Sensual, he thought, and yet very young. Not his type, not really. He liked older women, the kind who could take care of themselves and saw an affair as nothing more than that. Jennie was officer's wife material,

190

but not earthy enough for his taste. A virgin. Definitely a virgin. He avoided them like the plague.

The drinks came and, as they drank, they stared out over the view. Guy drew on his cigarette and frowned. "Hope this doesn't put back my posting."

"Where? When?"

"UK. ETPS at Farnborough."

Jennie sighed. "Why does everyone out here speak in code?"

"Sorry. Empire Test Pilot School. My course starts in February." He smiled. "And the first thing I'm going to do when I get back to England is splash out on a Jaguar XK 120 in British Racing Green."

Jennie remained quiet, thinking of Geoffrey de Havilland dying as his prototype jet blew up over the Thames estuary. "You're going to train as a test pilot? Isn't that a very dangerous occupation?"

He laughed. "It's a damned hard one to get into, I can tell you that much. I've been lucky. Very lucky. And I just don't want anything to mess things up at this stage."

She stared out at the islands, thinking that soon they would say goodbye, never to see each other again. Suddenly the thought saddened her. Until this moment she hadn't realised how much she had come to rely on him. It was his age; his maturity; his knowledge of a world she knew nothing about. When she was a child he had been a man fighting for his country, and a few days ago he had saved her life. She found it a heady cocktail.

"Why did you come to Singapore? Why not your mother?"

The question threw her off balance. "Because she's dead." It sounded so abrupt, so "mind your own business", that instantly she was sorry, found herself apologising then felt forced to explain how her mother had died.

He leaned back in his chair and studied her appraisingly. "Monique Veryan? Of course I've heard of her, who hasn't? I remember seeing her picture in the newspapers. She was a lovely woman, beautiful in fact. So you're her daughter. I can see now that there is a likeness."

Jennie shifted uncomfortably and stared resolutely out to sea. "So I've been told."

"There's that French look about you." Was that what attracted him? French sensuality against English primness?

"My father's family come from Cornwall." Suddenly she found herself talking about Trevellan. When she stopped, she felt his eyes on her and wondered why she had gabbled away like that. Why did he make her feel nervous one minute and comforted the next? "I do hope Papa will be all right. He seemed so vague and was very perturbed at being in a military hospital. I can't imagine why since..." Her voice

191

trailed away into silence as she remembered the whispered complaint. "Not right ... feel a fraud ... just like before with those other poor devils..." Just like before? At the time she had thought it rambling nonsense but now those words suddenly meant everything. Her hand gripped the ice cold glass, her eyes became transfixed. "East Grinstead."

"What?"

"My father remembers East Grinstead. It's where he was treated for burns."

"By MacIndoe? Then he was lucky. That man's a bloody marvel. Some of my friends were his patients." Guy stopped speaking as he suddenly caught her drift. "He remembers? When before he didn't?"

Jennie nodded. "Yes." Excitement caused her hand to tremble so that she had to put down the glass. "Is it possible? Can he be regaining his memory?"

Guy looked at her seriously. "Well, he's had a shock. Another trauma might be the jolt needed to start things going again, or it might just be a blip that could disappear. So don't get your hopes up too much. I'd hate to see you disappointed." As he said it, he realised that he really meant it. She was beginning to get under his skin, and that was the last thing he wanted.

"But it could be a good sign, don't you think?"

Her eyes were pleading for reassurance. Suddenly he longed to be able to give her such reassurance, but all he could do was smile and say: "It could be. Perhaps something good has come out of this bloody madness after all."

Taking comfort in that, she smiled up at him, then suddenly wanted him to hold her and say that everything was going to be all right. As it was, they returned to the car and were soon driving back down the hillside, both cursing the curfew which kept them from watching the sunset together.

# Chapter Twelve

When Ah Kew arrived in her bedroom with the morning tea and usual plate of tropical fruits, Jennie waited until she had drawn back the mosquito net then sat up slowly, her eyes fixed absently on the wall ahead as her thoughts began to click into place. It had been a long wakeful night where her mind had turned on Guy one minute and her father the next, so that when she did sleep she dreamt the two men had become as one.

In a few short hours she would know whether her father had truly regained his memory. Guy had said he would telephone. Not when, just a vague: "I'll telephone you. Keep out of trouble." It sounded ominously final. Yesterday she had been stirred by his presence, physically and emotionally, and now she was beginning to romanticise. Stupid! He hadn't been in the least bit romantic, just friendly, helping her out and showing her a lovely view before returning to Tengah. "I'll telephone you..." Then the Singer had roared away from the Boyds' house.

Slowly she ate the fruit then, leaving her bed, looked out through the window at the familiar sight of Colonel Boyd walking to his staff car. The *kebun* had already arrived and was cutting away at the undergrowth with a *parang*. It looked like being the hottest day yet. What had happened to the much vaunted monsoon? Her wrist was now unbound, felt better, and was more manoeuvrable. She would shower and do her best to towel herself dry without help. Hearing the distant ring of the telephone, Jennie opened her bedroom door slightly and heard Ann's voice. Then the receiver was replaced. Rushing back to her bed she lay there holding her breath, but no one knocked to tell her she was wanted on the phone. Disappointed, her eyes stared up at the fan which whirled in vain to push air around in the stifling heat. Fool, she told herself. He was hardly likely to ring at this hour anyway. After lying there for another ten minutes, Jennie finally headed for the bathroom.

193

When she appeared at the breakfast table, Ann and Louise asked how she had managed alone. In spite of having encountered difficulties, Jennie, who longed for independence once more, answered cheerfully: "Better than I had expected. At last I can say goodbye to the wretched sling."

"Well, don't overdo things," said Ann. She leaned forward, as though about to impart some mysterious news. "Whatever happens today, you must be here by four-thirty."

"Why?" asked Jennie.

"Because you are to receive a telephone call from England, would you believe? That was the operator. I daresay your grandparents have heard about the riots and are worried. According to the operator they're having to take their turn in a very long queue of desperate overseas callers. Four-thirty is the allotted time, so be here."

Jennie frowned. "It never occurred to me to send them a cable, I never thought they'd hear about the riots."

"Well, you've had other things on your mind. I should have thought of it," said Ann. "News of the riots was broadcast on the World Service, so the Home Service would pick it up, along with all the English newspapers." She frowned and sighed. "Oh dear, of course, my husband is driving you to the hospital this afternoon. You wouldn't get back in time. I'm afraid we'll have to put the visit off until tomorrow."

"I'm sure the hospital will waive their stupid visiting hours for once," said Louise. "Daddy can take Jennie this morning instead."

"He has a meeting this morning."

"Then," said Louise, "I'll go with Jennie."

When Ann said an emphatic "no" to the girls going out unchaperoned at such a time, Jennie felt a growing sense of panic. She had to be here for the phone call and she had to see her father before that. Desperation made her incautious. "I have to go, come what may. I promised Papa. Anyway I shan't rest until I know how he is. Yesterday the city was crawling with police and soldiers. They won't allow any trouble to flare up."

"Exactly," said Louise firmly. "It's probably safer now than it ever was."

Ann cast her daughter a dark look. "Louise, you gave your father your word that you would not go out unescorted. I'm sorry, Jennie. I cannot allow it. You must telephone the hospital and ask how your father is."

Jennie tried. How she tried. But the lines were engaged and when she did get through no one could find the doctor who was looking after her father and she was asked to ring back later. By ten-thirty she was in tears and took herself off to her bedroom to despair quietly. The

194

situation was saved by Guy, who telephoned to say that since a flying mission had been brought forward he would not be able to get away that afternoon as he had hoped. Surprised that he had hoped anything of the kind, Jennie explained the difficulty she was having.

"Don't worry about it. I'm on my way," he said.

By eleven-fifteen she found herself back in the roadster, exhilarated by the suddenness of Guy's arrival and feeling now that she must mean something to him after all.

In the busy ward, Jennie explained to a nurse why she had come early and was promptly told to wait since the doctor wished to have a word with her. She turned to Guy in alarm. He took her hand and gave it a slight squeeze.

The army doctor appeared at last. Harassed and overworked, he lost no time in coming to the point. "We were going to telephone you but it's been so chaotic. I'm sorry but we've had to move your father. He became extremely disturbed, screaming out and wandering in his sleep. The other patients were becoming upset and so, looking at his old notes, we discovered the psychiatric clinic where he was treated initially. Two hours ago we transferred him there. I'll give you the address."

The clinic was a rambling white single-storey building set back in lush gardens on the East Coast Road. There, Jennie found she was expected as a grey-haired man in a dark lightweight suit shook her hand then bade her and Guy take a seat in his office.

"Someone telephoned from BMH and told me you were coming. I'm glad you found us all right. My name's Fraser, by the way. I treated your father before. He remembers me well enough so that's a good start." He sat down at a large desk and smiled. Leaning forward anxiously in her chair, Jennie said, "Yesterday he said something that made me think he was beginning to remember from much further back. Am I right?"

Dr Fraser played with a paper clip as he spoke. "There has been a breakthrough, yes. Whether it's partial or full recall is too early to say. Either way he's going to need help with his rehabilitation." He paused and stared at her as though trying to weigh his words carefully. "You see, when your father developed amnesia it was as though nature had taken pity on him, wiping from his brain the thoughts it couldn't contain. As a result of some dreadful trauma, the mind simply shut down. Rather like a safety valve. Now, as a result of another trauma, something in his brain has released the blocked off memory."

Jennie's heart was thumping and she turned to Guy, almost afraid to believe what she so wanted to. "Go on."

"There is a problem, however. You see, with the normal good

195

memories of home and family, will also come the horrors from which his mind recoiled. Many who suffered physically and mentally during internment have learned to live with that horror, even though they still suffer from it. Your father, however, has not. Nature cut it out of his mind along with everything else. Consequently, the shock for him now is tremendous and he's very confused. Even under sedation he's been having terrible nightmares, only these nightmares are real, are memories in fact, and these memories are bombarding him in one go. That's why I'm glad he's been returned to me, because I can help him through this time as I helped him before. No doubt you'd like to see him." He got to his feet and walked to the doorway. "He's not sedated now. I want him up and about, I want him talking openly and not trying to shut things away in his mind. He breaks down from time to time but that's nature's way of release, so it's a good thing and you mustn't let it alarm you. Recovery won't happen overnight so don't expect too much. His memories are patchy at the moment and he tires easily, so I would ask you to stay no longer than fifteen minutes at the most. He's taken a liking to the orchids I grow. It's a hobby of mine. He finds it calming. So that's where you'll find him, Miss Veryan." He pointed ahead. "Straight along the passage and through to the verandah."

Guy stayed seated in the office and lit a cigarette, reflecting on how Jennie would react if things did not work out the way she thought they would. How vulnerable was Monique Veryan's daughter? Did she have her mother's courage? She certainly had her looks. Yes, she certainly had those all right. Was that what drew him to her? Or was it the glamour of the famous mother and the mystery of the lost heir? Either way, she needed his help, so here he was.

Jennie found her father at the far end of a verandah, watering exotic orchids and examining each one with interest. He turned at her approach, frowned a little, then smiled. "At least I'm dressed today. Dodo brought my things to the hospital yesterday evening."

"I went there first. Didn't realise..." Jennie stepped towards him. "Oh, Papa. Is it true? How much can you remember? The family? The house in Cornwall?"

Placing the watering can down on the floor, Charles smiled nervously then took his daughter by the hand. "I remember a little girl with a pony, a little girl who also loved a kestrel. I remember my parents and Laura..." He stopped speaking and turned his eyes from hers. "And I remember your dear mother." He felt Jennie squeeze his hand at this. "Small scenes pop into my mind then ... well ... there's no continuity. I'm told that will all come back."

Shattered at how tired and ill he looked, Jennie glanced at the orchids and forced a smile for his sake. "They're exquisite. Do you know all their names?"

"Not all." He smiled and looked pensive. "How uncomplicated and serene some lives can be. I think I should like to be an orchid grower." Patting the cushion on a wicker chair, he bade her sit then settled himself down on another and stared out across the lush gardens. "Dr Fraser has spoken to you?" When Jennie nodded, he seemed relieved. "It's a funny thing. I thought, that at this point, I would be over the moon. Instead ... it's rather like emerging from under a dark blanket into daylight, but the day is cloudy and the sun barely breaks through."

But brick by brick the wall was coming down, thought Jennie, as she sat listening to her father speaking of half-remembered things. Then he would lapse into silence, leaving her wondering at the horrors in his mind. She said nothing of the riot, or of events since, knowing that just being there with him was all he wanted or needed at this juncture. Then it was time to leave. As they got up, Jennie longed to put her arms about him and say that everything would be all right. But in Robinson's he had made it plain that such a natural gesture was out of the question. She must wait until his mind had really cleared and she was his daughter again. As though reading her thoughts, Charles looked perturbed. "There is one awful memory I'm not proud to recall. I said things to you that day ... things that now I'm dreadfully ashamed of and which you must forget."

Looking up at him, she smiled. "I can't honestly remember what was said that day now." Seeing the nurse hovering on the threshold, she added, "And I'm overstaying my welcome. I'll telephone Dodo and let her know you're here. Oh, yes, that reminds me. I'm to receive an overseas call this afternoon. I'm sure it's from Grandma. I'll let you know what she has to say."

And so she left him there, tending the orchids, a wan shadow of the man she had lunched with at Robinson's that day.

On the journey home, Guy suddenly turned the car off the East Coast Road towards the sea, then stopped outside a brick-built bungalow which stretched along the shore road, was well set back among trees and looked directly on to the narrow beach. Once well run, it now had the worn look of a place rarely used or loved and was in desperate need of re-decorating.

Climbing from the car, Guy opened the passenger door. Curious, Jennie stepped out. He led her along the drive, then stood with arms folded, staring at a hammock slung between trees, and smiled. "It's where I come to unwind. When I have enough leave, that is. Since the riots, of course, the place has been out of bounds. We shouldn't even be here. The house belongs to friends of mine. I met the Pattersons when my squadron was in Kuala Lumpur. They own a large rubber plantation up country but used to come to Singapore whenever possible. Since the Emergency, they refuse to leave in case of terrorists. He has armed guards up there now. So he offered me a key to this place, thinking it better to have the house lived in occasionally which keeps the amah and *kebun* up to scratch. It also affords me the luxury of getting away from the Mess once in a while." Guy grinned. "Here I can live like a slob, entertain my friends and generally relax. I'm eternally grateful to the Pattersons."

At that moment the Chinese amah emerged from the rear of the house. With a surprised look on her face, she walked over to where they stood. "*Tuan* stay for tiffin?"

Guy shook his head, and said they were not staying, then asked how she and her children were getting on.

She said they were all well, then looked perturbed. "Here not good, *Tuan*. Bad Melayu." With that she turned and walked slowly back into the house.

Guy's expression darkened. "Someone must have been attacked out here just after the riots. I shouldn't have brought you, but I so wanted you to see it." Before returning to the car he walked her to the thin strip of beach where they stood looking out at the green islands. He pointed to the Malay fishing traps. "*Kelongs*, they're called. At night lanterns from them attract the fish. It's such a beautiful spot ... damned shame everything's ruined."

"It won't last. You'll be back." She wondered why he had brought her here. Was it for the same reason any man takes a woman to a lonely place? Hardly his style, surely? Certainly not hers. But no, he was just standing beside her, hands in his trouser pockets, seemingly unaware that she was beside him even.

Guy, however, was very much aware and asked himself why he was becoming more and more involved with this girl, acting as protector when he wanted to make love to her. Yesterday he had decided not to see her again. Then he had made that fateful call this morning and here he was. "You must be very relieved about your father. Poor devil. What memories are going through his head now, I wonder?"

"And will he ever come to terms with them?" She turned to him, her eyes large and moistening as emotion took a hold once more. "Oh, Guy. This has been an awful time. I would have gone crazy without your help."

It was too much. He looked down at the upturned face and suddenly pulled her to him, feeling her soft pliable body against his own. Slowly he brought his mouth down on hers and almost smothered her in a long, lingering kiss. At first she seemed to resist, then he felt her relax and return the kiss. Releasing her at last, he murmured throatily, "Come on. This was not what I had in mind when I brought you here."

I rather think it was, thought Jennie, shocked at her physical reaction to his embrace. Trying to recover her composure, she followed him back to the car, wondering how she could have let herself go in such a manner with such a man. The last time she had been kissed was at the boathouse, a loving, cherishing kiss; unlike this one which had been hard, urgent, almost demanding.

Why had she allowed it? And yet, deep down, had she not wanted it? Was she falling in love with this man? Throughout the journey home, she, like he, could find no words to say and so they remained silent.

"It's a miracle," Ann Boyd said as she hugged Jennie. "Oh, my dear, I can't tell you how happy we are. I'm quite sure it will be a full and permanent recovery. He's clearly in very good hands. And to think that shortly you'll be able to tell your grandparents yourself. You'll be talking to them on the other side of the world. Isn't it beyond all belief?"

The afternoon seemed exceptionally long and, as four-thirty approached, the tension mounted. Jennie sat on the sofa, hands twisting in her lap, her eyes travelling towards the carriage clock which stood on the bureau. "It's almost time. What will it be in England now?"

Ann looked thoughtful as she did rapid mental calculations. "Well, we're about seven hours ahead, so your grandparents have probably just finished their breakfast."

Jennie tried to imagine the scene. It would just be getting light now for these were the shortest days. The fire would already be lit in the morning room and study, and Mark's father would have arrived with his files and accounts ready to go through the problems of the estate with her grandfather. What of Mark? Would he deem it safe to go home for Christmas now that she was so far away? It hurt even to think of it but, as she did, Jennie felt again the warmth of Guy's kiss. Had it finally happened? Had someone come into her life who could make her forget Mark and take away the pain of these long dark months? The telephone rang. Jennie jumped to her feet, heart thumping against her ribs.

Ann walked coolly to the instrument, picked up the receiver and said, "Thank you." Smiling, she beckoned to Jennie. "An overseas call for you."

"Jennie? Jennie? Is that you, dear?" Florence's voice was distant amidst the static interference on the line. "Are you there, Jennie? I can't hear you."

"I'm here, Grandma. Is everything all right at home?"

There was a decent pause before the voice found its way back across the high frequency radio signals. "We are all well. Are you? And your father? We've heard about the riots, darling. We've been so worried."

"We're fine and the troubles are over. I have good news. Papa is beginning to get his memory back."

Another long pause, the transmission seemed to be breaking up. "What? Jennie, what did you say about your father's memory?"

Before Jennie could answer, Laura's voice cut in across the miles. "Your grandmother's having difficulty hearing, Jennie. What was that you just told her?"

Jennie repeated her words to Laura, then heard more static and distant voices coming and going across the ether.

"Marvellous news," shouted Laura. "Does this mean you're bringing him home now?"

"As soon as he's well enough, yes."

There was another long pause, then Laura's voice again. "Jennie, have you spoken to this Mr Leighton? You didn't say in your letter."

Surprised at the question, Jennie shouted back: "Yes, I have spoken to him."

"What has he said?"

"Horrid things. I don't like that man at all, and neither does Papa." She waited for her aunt's response with curiosity, but there was none. "Can I speak to Grandma again, please?"

Laura ignored the request. "You are well, though? Is it very hot out there? It's raining here, but quite mild."

Jennie grew anxious. Laura was wasting precious moments. "Let me speak to Grandma, please. She is well, isn't she, and Grandpa?"

"They're both absolutely fine and thrilled at the news."

"I want to speak to them." But, at that moment, the operator's voice cut in telling them their time was up. "Goodbye," shouted Jennie. "Tell them I'll write."

The call was over, usurped by Laura. Angrily Jennie replaced the receiver and could almost hear her disappointed grandmother's words of admonishment at her daughter's strange behaviour. Strange maybe, but calculated all the same. Just what was it that must not reach the ears of the family?

The following morning, Jennie telephoned the clinic only to be told that her father was to receive no visitors until further notice. Everything was going along as expected but Dr Fraser wanted his patient left in peace for a few days.

Feverish activity had taken hold on the usually calm Boyd household. Chairs and tables were being moved around and from the kitchen came the sound of clinking china as Chan and Ah Kew prepared for many guests.

With a pained expression, Louise explained in hushed tones: "Coffee morning. Mummy's wearing her Colonel's Lady hat today. Very soon the house will be swarming with officers' wives who will chatter on about the Hertoghs, the riots, and amahs, in that order. If we don't make our getaway now then it'll be too late. Let's do some Christmas shopping."

"But you promised your father you wouldn't go out unescorted." said Jennie.

Louise sighed with frustration. "I could scream with boredom. God, how I should love to come back to London with you. You can keep the tropics, the heat, the insects and the very smell of Singapore. Just give me back my life."

At that moment the sound of aircraft overhead sent Jennie chasing out into the garden. Flying in strict formation, the Vampire jets streaked low over the houses. Jennie looked up wondering which plane was piloted by Guy and whether he had any notion that he was flying over the spot where she stood? Then the squadron was gone leaving her with a sudden sense of loss. She turned and stared vaguely at the *kebun* who was hosing down the terrace and monsoon drain. The fierce sun dried it almost immediately.

Louise walked across the lawn, her smiles belying anxiety. Guy Lloyd, she thought, could well hurt Jennie, and she had been hurt enough already.

Jennie was again looking skywards. "He said he would telephone when he returns."

Bending to stroke Oliver, Louise murmured, "Be careful. He's a good bit older than you and, I'd say, has been around a bit." Even as she spoke she knew that his extra years and experience were, in themselves, an added attraction and she could readily see why. Next to Guy, Nigel was as drippy as a leaking tap. But Second Lieutenant Nigel Crombie was young and relatively inexperienced with women. Squadron Leader Lloyd was a very different kettle of fish. Right now Jennie was vulnerable. If she was looking for a rock to lean on, then Louise feared she had picked on the wrong man.

Jennie saw the squadron return, but Guy did not telephone. Dismayed she waited; saw the squadron go out again and return once more; and waited again. She waited in vain. Finally allowing Louise to drag her back into the city to collect their dresses, she wondered why she was bothering. Even if the curfew was lifted in time for Christmas parties, she had no desire to go to any of them without Guy. It was that kiss, she told herself. He had been checking her out only to find she was not to his taste after all. Just as well, she told herself, trying to mask the hurt. She needed more complications in her life like she needed a hole in the head. Her main task was to take her father home. That was her only reason for being here. Even so, her mind dwelt on Guy. He had been so marvellous, and then had to go and spoil it all with that kiss which had clearly meant nothing to him. Now she felt a little shoddy. How dare he take such insolent advantage of her and then decide it meant nothing!

When she was allowed to visit her father again she found that his memory was fully restored, but with the restoration had come grief for the loss of Monique. The longlost years behind the brick wall now seemed never to have existed and he had wept as though his wife had died yesterday. Doctor Fraser's decision to keep all visitors away was in order to give his patient the grieving time he needed. But now, at last, Charles felt the need to talk about those days. As she listened, Jennie held his hand, felt again that painful lump in her throat and wished with all her heart that she could take his pain and anguish from him.

Tea was brought to them by a Chinese helper and, in that moment, Charles studied his daughter carefully. "I see your bruise has gone. Now don't give me that nonsense about falling downstairs because Dodo told me all about the attack on you. I'm deeply grateful to the man who saved my daughter and should very much like to meet him."

Jennie stirred her tea and looked out across the gardens. A humming bird hovered at an oleander flower and golden orioles flew between the trees. "That's all in the past, Papa. I don't really want to talk about it."

"Ah, now there old Fraser would disagree with you. Talking, he maintains, is nature's way of release."

And so Jennie obliged him by talking, not about the attack or Guy, but about the telephone call from England and how excited everyone was about his recovery. "Doctor Fraser says you'll be out just before Christmas but he'll want to see you three times a week after that, so I don't see us getting away before mid-January. Do you mind flying, Papa, because otherwise I'll be dreadfully late starting the next term? I've a lot to catch up on as it is."

Charles said nothing to this, his mind on Monique. How could he sleep in that same bedroom, or walk about the house and grounds of Trevellan without seeing her, without feeling she was watching him, haunting him? His mind still dwelt on that lovely tear-stained face as his train had pulled away. If he had not left her, she would still be alive. Would he ever come to terms with that? After forty minutes it was time for Jennie to leave. Charles walked with her to the front of the clinic where Louise and her mother were waiting beside the ordered taxi. Jennie introduced him to them with a light laugh.

"They insist on guarding me." The laughter faded and her eyes became serious. "Quite honestly I don't know how I could have managed out here without them. They've made all this possible."

Charles thanked the Boyds and said how sorry he was that the rules kept him to one visitor. "Perhaps you would all allow me to take you to dinner one evening? There's so much to say ... I don't know where to begin."

Jennie kissed him goodbye and followed the others down the steps to the taxi. Suddenly a thought occurred to her and she turned. "Papa, do you remember why you came to Singapore in the first place?"

The smile left Charles's face and he became guarded. "I was sent with important documents for the Governor. Bad timing. Rotten luck."

So much for Caley of the F.O., thought Jennie, climbing into the taxi where Louise was staring at her with bright eyes.

"Jennie, he's an absolute poppet. I've often wondered what he would be like."

"A charming man," said Ann. "Such a gentleman."

As the taxi moved away, Jennie leaned out, waved goodbye to her father, then relaxed back in her seat. Suddenly, for the first time in years she felt an inner peace that even Guy Lloyd's desertion could not destroy. Her father had been restored to her, and everything would be all right once they were home. She had always thought of him as a rock. He would be again and Trevellan would pass into safe hands. If only her mother had lived to see it. She closed her eyes and smiled. Home. Soon they would arrive back home and the small flame could be extinguished at last.

Robinson's was packed with last-minute shoppers as Jennie stood with Ann Boyd at the jewellery counter contemplating whether or not she could afford the plain gold cuff links she wanted to buy for her father's present. There were clinic fees to pay and she would need money to buy air tickets. Her grandfather was making financial arrangements through his bank but all that took time. As Ann moved across to another glass case to stare wistfully at jewels she could never hope to wear, Jennie's attention wavered between the selection of cuff links laid before her. If only she could make up her mind. If only Louise hadn't crept off to another department to buy her presents in secret. She sighed, aware of the assistant waiting patiently.

"You'll have them engraved, of course."

Starting at the voice in her ear, Jennie turned and found herself looking up into Guy's quizzical eyes. The shock took her breath away momentarily; she felt her face burning and prayed it wasn't lobster red. "Yes. That was my intention." The voice was sharp to cover her nervousness.

"Who's the lucky man?"

"My father," she said coldly.

His eyes raked her body, taking in the firmness of her breasts against the soft lawn dress. "I thought, perhaps, someone back in England?"

At that moment Ann returned to the counter, saw Guy and beamed a bright smile at him. "Ah, Squadron Leader, how very nice to see you again. Isn't this a crush? The riots put everything back and now everyone's shopping at the last minute. How are you?"

"Busy. We've had more missions than usual. And you?"

"As you say, busy. I've hardly seen my husband these past days. We're having a few guests on Christmas Day and would be delighted if you could join us."

Jennie stood rigid, her eyes everywhere but on Guy.

"How very kind," he said with impeccable politeness. "I should love to join you but, unfortunately, I'm already committed to serving Christmas Dinner in the Airmen's Mess. Tradition."

Jennie felt like dying on the spot. It might be true but she sensed he was glad of the excuse anyway. He was not just rejecting the invitation, he was rejecting her. Her humiliation was now complete. She glanced at the assistant, apologised for keeping him waiting and, turning her back on Guy, decided to take the gold cuff links. When the transaction was completed, she looked up just in time to see him saying goodbye to Ann. Then he moved away and was lost among the crowds.

In the gathering twilight, Charles Veryan stood on the verandah of the Cricket Club staring out across the Padang. Harbour lights flickered on and were reflected in the water; there was a distant roar of traffic and birds settled among the flame trees bordering the field. It was better out here. In the Long Bar he had been stifled, not only by oppressive heat, but by the extraordinary interest in his recovery. How his colleagues had found out he never knew, but they had gathered around him with their beers and whiskies, drunk to his continuing good health, then turned their attention to other matters while he slipped away for a quiet moment in the purple dusk.

Christmas was two days gone, the New Year not yet arrived and the curfew lifted at last. He had been out of the clinic now for a week and was already seeking solitude away from friends, from Dodo and even from Jennie. Gladly he sank on to a long chair with a gin and tonic, the quinine in the tonic keeping his Malaria attacks at bay, and pulled from his pocket the letter he had received from Laura that very morning. Voices wafted across to him from the Long Bar and fans whirling in the overpowering heat and humidity were unable to bring relief. Holding the letter to a light he read it for the fourth time that day. Laura had oozed warmth and happiness at his recovery, but then had come a sudden change of tone:

However, now that you have your memory back and the knowledge that has returned with it, you alone can say whether your arrival home will bring shame on our proud family name. How do I know what you now know? My dear, Mr Leighton came to see me at that time. Our interview ended badly. That he, of all people, should be the one to restore you to us is, you must agree, an ironic twist of fate. We all long to see you again, but do remember our standing in the community and how much store our parents have always set on it. If, by returning, you damage that standing in any way then, my dear, it would be kinder to everyone if you remained in Singapore with your secret and allowed Clive to inherit the estate.

Laura had then tempered these harsh words with softer ones but Charles had been shaken by the letter. Now he was angered by it. She lived in another world, he thought wryly. They all did back on that windswept peninsula. To speak of harming a proud family name when he was still coming to terms with the nightmare of all he had been through, was too ludicrous to take in at this moment. He had seen horrors beyond belief but that was something his sister would never understand. She, like they, knew nothing and lived in a cocoon – a time warp.

He thought of his father, that doughty old knight of the shire who had never given up hope for his son. Then his mind drifted back to the Elizabethan house with its huge hearth fires, the gales, the mournful sound of fog horns, the bright sunlit days when white horses tipped the waves, his parents, Jennie and ... Monique. He longed to return, but dreaded it also. As it was, the choice had been taken from him for between Monique's ghost and Laura's admonishment, it seemed he was condemned to a life of exile.

Replacing the letter in his pocket, he drank the gin and tonic down quickly. Leighton! Christ, how he hated and feared that man. But, he must face him as Scrooge had faced the ghost of Christmas Yet to Come.

"Jennie." Guy Lloyd's voice surprised her at such an early hour. Still in her nightgown, she stood in the hallway holding the telephone receiver and watching as Ah Kew moved silently between the kitchen and dining room. An appetising smell of coffee and toast filled the house. "Look, I'm ringing now because I'm off on another mission soon. It's been very hectic lately and I've been more or less confined to the station even when I'm not flying. I couldn't make your party so now I'm hoping you can make mine. Saturday, at the Pattersons' place."

Completely taken aback, Jennie tried to collect her thoughts. She

205

had seen nothing of Guy since that day in Robinsons and now this. What was she to make of the man?

"Saturday, you say?"

"I'm hoping to get a crowd together. Say you'll come, otherwise I'll know you're still angry with me? That silence of yours was utterly deafening, Jennie. The longest car journey of my life."

She gasped in amazement. "What? I did have other things on my mind as it happened." How dare he think she found him so important? On the other hand, this was not the moment to stand on false pride, this was the moment she had been waiting for. He probably had been very busy and since there was nothing really between them, meeting at a crowded party might be the best way. After all, time was running out. Soon he would go his way and she would go hers.

"Jennie? Jennie, wake up. Are you still there?"

Starting, she said, "Yes ... yes ... I'm here. Saturday, did you say? That's only two days away. Just let me check in the diary. There's so much going on at the Mess these days, and the Club." She placed the receiver down on the table, stared at the blank wall for a minute then picked up the phone once more. "Saturday is fine." It was not. There was a Christmas dance at the Mess and she was expected to go with the Boyds.

"Good. How is your father?"

"Completely well and ready to go home. Now I'll have to find out where to get documents and so forth. Will he need innoculations, do you think?"

"I'll say. They take exception to Cholera in Tunbridge Wells. Look, I can help you with all this, tell you how to go about it and arrange for his passport. So if I collect you at around four o'clock on Saturday, you can come early, help me with the preparations while I go through the arrangements with you. Four o'clock at your place, all right?"

"Four o'clock then." Replacing the receiver, Jennie sank into a chair weakly. Where was her pride? She should have said no and let him go from her life. And yet he had saved that very life and still wanted to help her. She was being stupid, childish even. Of course he had been busy and should be given the benefit of the doubt. The Pattersons' old bungalow though ... on the other hand, what could happen at a party?

Mindful of all that Guy had said would be needed, Jennie began working on the passport application form which Colonel Boyd had produced for her. It needed her father's signature. Telephoning the Webbs' house, where she had been assured he was resting, she was told he was back at the bookshop. On telephoning the bookshop she was told he was not available by a curt Dodo. She tried several times, and always the same reply. He had just gone out, or was busy in the stock room and Dodo couldn't leave a customer. In every case Jennie asked if he would ring her, in every case the answer was, "Of course", but no call came. Jennie became anxious. She had not seen her father since Christmas Day when she had had lunch with him at the house in the Bukit Timah Road. What was going on?

The monsoon had broken at last and it was pouring with rain when she left the taxi in the Battery Road and entered the bookshop. Folding down the Chinese umbrella, she left it in a corner to drip away on the tiled flooring while she searched around for her father. There was no sign of Dodo, thank goodness, no sign of anyone in fact. Then Charles appeared from the back room, saw her and looked visibly uncomfortable. At once she knew that something was very wrong. Dodo entered on his heels, saw Jennie and forced a smile.

"My dear, how delightful to see you. Are you very wet?"

"No," said Jennie coldly. "Just confused." As her father returned to his old desk and started fiddling with paperwork she walked across to him. "Papa, why haven't you returned my calls? What is it? Have I angered you in some way?"

Head still bent to his work, Charles murmured, "My dear child, how could you think such a thing? I'm sorry if I didn't call back. I'm working again as you can see. I get tired quickly, I'm afraid." Slowly, he looked up and his eyes were troubled.

"I'd never want to do anything to hurt you, Jennie. Always remember that."

She looked down at him, frowning. "How could you possibly hurt me, Papa? I've come with the application form for your passport. All you have to do is sign it. The next step is the needle, I'm sorry to say, but without the innoculations you can't have the medical forms necessary to..."

"Jennie." Charles rose slowly to his feet like a tired, crushed man. "Come into the back room. I have something to tell you."

Feeling cold suddenly, cold and desperately afraid, Jennie followed him into the office where she sat on a wooden chair staring up at him with large, intense eyes.

He lit a cigarette and inhaled deeply, as he tried to find the right words. There were none. In the end he could not avoid the plain, awful truth. "Jennie, my dear, I won't be returning with you to England after all."

Stunned, she just sat there, trying to take in his words. "Don't be silly, Papa," she murmured, smiling nervously. "Of course you will. It's all right now. Everything's all right now. If you need more time, then I'll wait ... I'll wait until you feel ready."

207

"No, that time will never come. You must go home without me. I did try to tell you once before. It must be this way."

Jennie stared up at him in blank astonishment, then emotion took over from the cold shock. "But that was different. That was when you had no memory of me or of your family and that man was taking advantage of you. Everything's changed. So why?" When he made no answer, her brow furrowed. "You don't want to come home do you? It's Dodo, isn't it? I always knew she had a hold on you. Oh, I can see plainly how she's been reminding you of all she has done and why you can't leave her in the lurch. And you're too much of a gentleman to fight your own corner."

"Stop it, Jennie, you're speaking wildly. Dodo has nothing to do with it. She has been very supportive throughout. You just don't understand."

"Then make me understand," cried Jennie, jumping to her feet in anger. "You're going to break their hearts, just as you're breaking mine, so tell me why?"

Charles was silent for a long time, then, stubbing out the cigarette in a glass ashtray, he murmured: "I can't." Turning, he rushed through the curtain into the shop, his parting words barely audible: "I can't."

When Jennie finally left the back room she found herself face to face with Dodo. There was no sign of her father anywhere.

"What's this? Have you upset him?" asked Dodo angrily.

Jennie glared at her. "The other day he spoke about England and his home. He was anxious to return. Now ... quite suddenly he's had a change of heart. Why?"

Dodo looked at her in surprise, then frowned. "When did he tell you this?"

"Just this very minute. Where is he?"

"Gone! He stumbled past me and is God knows where by now." Dodo looked thoughtful. "He had a letter which seemed to upset him rather. Then yesterday that awful man was here again, the one who worried him before, only this time your father went off with him. When he returned, he looked ... well ... shocked is the only word I could use to describe him. Since then he's said hardly a word and refused to eat a thing."

"Leighton?" Jennie stared out at the tropical downpour as she recalled that twisted smile. "*We have a reckoning ...*" Saying goodbye she picked up her umbrella and walked out into the pouring rain, determined on her course of action. The shadow of Victor Leighton had stretched across them for quite long enough.

That evening she telephoned him and heard his exasperated sigh. It sounded false. "My dear Miss Veryan, I can't possibly see you

208

tomorrow. It's Saturday and I've too much on, I'm afraid." Then, after a moment's pause: "I have to visit my nephew in the morning. By the time I get back I'll be up to my eyes in other matters."

"Mr Leighton, I don't care if you're opening Parliament, you've said something to my father which has affected him very deeply. We do need to talk."

Leighton sighed, then said in a weary tone, "Very well. Meet me at the Cold Storage in Orchard Road at ten-forty-five. Goodbye, Miss Veryan."

At dinner that same evening Jennie kept quiet about her father's strange behaviour and her forthcoming meeting with Victor Leighton. Least said, soonest mended. Whatever was wrong, it would not be discussed with anyone unless it became necessary. It was bad enough speaking of Guy's party which caused raised eyebrows all around.

Ann cut into her chicken then laid her knife and fork down and looked at Jennie anxiously. "My dear, I hate to be a wet blanket, but this party is in some old bungalow, you say? It would be quite a different thing if he were taking you out to a restaurant, or even to the Officers' Mess, but a private house? Well, you do see the difference it makes. And I have to say that, charming as he is, Squadron Leader Lloyd is far too old for you. Oh, we're all very much in his debt, of course we are, but he must be thirty at least. I would prefer that you came to the Mess with us."

Jennie smiled politely. "It's only a party. I won't be alone with him. He's coming here to fetch me and promises to bring me home afterwards. After all he's done for me, it seemed churlish, and rather silly, to refuse."

Ann glanced at her husband for support but he was too busy eating to notice. "It's just that you're not yet twenty-one and, in a sense, I suppose we must consider ourselves *in loco parentis* while you're here, under our roof. It's what your grandmother would expect of us, surely?"

"Oh, Mummy, don't be so old-fashioned," said Louise impatiently. "Jennie's been 'out' for two years. She's quite used to parties and sorting out the type who should be on the list and the type who should not." But even as she spoke, Louise had her doubts. Had she been invited also they would not be having this conversation. As it was, Guy had slipped up rather badly by not thinking the thing through. Had he thought anything through? Did he know, as she did, how much Jennie was beginning to rely on him and care about him? Did he know the heartache she had already been through? Of course not. And yet he seemed caring in many ways and, after all, had risked his own life to save Jennie's.

\*

209

The following morning found Jennie in fighting mood as her taxi drove along the wide tree-lined Orchard Road. She had expected constant rain from now on, but the sun shone and a hot breeze brushed her face from the open window. The Boyds' barometer had registered eighty-eight degrees in the shade at nine o'clock. It had climbed steadily since then. Leaving the taxi at the Cold Storage, she stood in front of the large white building feeling the scorching sun beating down on her and toying with the temptation to wait for Leighton inside, in the cool of the air conditioning. On the other hand, if she did that she might miss him and he seemed to be in no mood to hang around waiting for her. She remained where she was, wondering how long she could stand there before fainting while shoppers moved in and out of the store, the only place where they could buy fresh milk, safe ice cream, and other groceries that reminded them of home.

Within three minutes of Jennie's arrival, a black saloon pulled up and Leighton put his head out of the window as he reached across and opened the passenger door. "Climb in, please, Miss Veryan. I haven't much time."

Jennie froze. Meeting him was one thing, getting into a car with him was another. "I thought we were going to talk here," she said as she approached. "It won't take so long surely to tell me why you're preventing my father from returning home?"

He laughed thinly. "Is that what I'm doing? Well, well. Look, do get in. I don't want to disappoint my nephew. We can talk on the way, but right now I simply must move on."

There seemed nothing for it but to obey and so she settled herself beside the man she had come to loathe and asked how far he intended to drive.

"Not far. Just out past Bukit Panjang on the Woodlands Road."

That meant nothing to her. "And while we journey there, can you tell me what I need to know?"

Leighton stared ahead impassively as he drove through the busy Saturday morning traffic. "I've bought my nephew a Meccano set. Do you think that's suitable for an eleven year old? It's his Christmas present, but I couldn't get over on Christmas Day. Being an orphanage, they had their own party so I don't think I was missed."

"Orphanage?"

Leighton nodded. "He was raised by my parents, but then my father was killed when the hospital he was working in was bombed. Anyway, just before the Japanese invaded I tried to get my mother and the boy away. It was difficult, almost impossible in that last-minute chaos. Somehow I got them on board a ship to Australia and watched as they sailed away. Later, I learned they had been bombed by Japanese planes

210

and sunk. I thought the boy and his grandmother were dead. I went on believing that throughout the war and long afterwards. I even went to Australia to start a new life. But that didn't work out so I returned."

"It was only then that I learned how both had survived the sinking, were found on an island by a Japanese patrol boat and taken into internment. My mother lasted just three more days in the camp and so it fell to the other women to look after Jamie. When the war ended one of these women took him home to live with her, but she was old and not well enough to raise a child alone. Since my mother had given her some information about me she contacted my old employer. But they had lost touch with me so the child ended up in an orphanage. When I returned, and made contact with my old shipping company again, they told me what had happened. Since then I try to visit the boy every Saturday. He looks forward to it. So you can see why I can't keep him waiting today."

Jennie smiled. "Of course you can't." Suddenly, the ogre had turned into a caring man. "Poor little boy. But are you just going to leave him in an orphanage? Don't you have plans to raise him yourself?"

Leighton smiled. "I'm hardly in a position to raise a child."

Feeling she would like to buy the boy a present also, Jennie persuaded Leighton to stop briefly in Bukit Panjang village where, on finding most of the toys too young for an eleven year old boy, she settled on a large jigsaw puzzle.

They journeyed on through countryside, past *kampongs*, and then turned into a tree-lined drive, stopping at the closed gates to a large compound. As they waited for someone to come forward and open the gates, Jennie looked through the tall chain-linked fence and saw a cluster of buildings in the distance. The children, all dressed in blue, sat under a large *atap* roof writing at their desks while a European woman pointed to a blackboard. Beyond the collection of single-storey buildings stood a white church. Well-tended lawns and shrubs ended in a wild tangle of lalang, bamboo and banana trees.

"The place is run by missionaries." said Leighton. "They do their best, but there are almost two hundred children here, mostly war orphans. As you can see, the races are mixed. It is not exclusively European."

A man approached the gates, opened them and waved the car through. Beside what appeared to be the main building, Leighton brought the vehicle to a halt and they both got out. He glanced at his watch. "Lessons finish at eleven-fifteen on Saturdays."

A plump woman walked towards them, her face wreathed in smiles. "Good morning, Mr Leighton. I'm so glad you're here. Jamie's been excited all morning." She glanced at the large wrapped box. "He's dying to see what you've brought him."

Leighton turned to Jennie, saying, "This is Mrs Singleton, who helps to run the place. Now then, where is my errant nephew?"

"On his way over," said Mrs Singleton.

Jennie followed the woman's outstretched hand, and saw a thin colt-like figure chasing across from the class. He slowed a little at seeing her then approached his uncle breathlessly. Fairer-skinned than Leighton, with light brown hair and hazel-green eyes, the thin face was shining with excitement as Leighton handed him the parcel.

The boy practically fell on it, tearing off the brown paper, his eyes widening as he saw the Meccano set which he fingered lovingly.

"Jamie, you haven't said hello to the lady. This is Jennie and she has come all the way from England."

"Hello, Jamie," said Jennie, handing over her wrapped gift. "Did you have a nice Christmas?"

"Yes, thank you," said the boy quietly, as he scrutinised her face. "Is it true that in England rivers turn so hard you can walk on them? Have you walked on a river? Do you have a toboggan? What does snow feel like?"

Jennie laughed, remembering Keswick. "Yes. I've walked on frozen water and tobboganed across the snow."

Leighton stood watching thoughtfully. "Jamie, this isn't what I taught you. Where are your manners? Introduce yourself to Jennie as a young gentleman should."

Jamie had already turned his attention back to the much-wanted Meccano set, but now his eyes shadowed slightly as, with some embarrassment, he tried to recollect. Then, placing both presents on the ground, he put out his right hand to Jennie and intoned solemnly: "How do you do? My name is James Veryan."

212

# Chapter Thirteen

Charles sat in a wicker chair on the verandah of Dodo's bungalow, unable to meet his daughter's gaze. Waves of despair flooded over him as he leaned forward, hands dropping between his long legs, fingers entwined, flexing and unflexing. "I told you to stay away from that bloody man. I told you to go back to England. You should have gone, Jennie."

"So that I would never learn the truth?" Her tone was bitter as she turned from her father and stared out across the Bukit Timah Road to the *kampong* beyond. A Tamil woman was washing clothes beside the water pump while children played about her in the clearing. "You left your wife and daughter to come halfway around the world to be with your mistress and illegitimate son. Yes, I can see why you wanted me to go."

Charles shook his head and murmured, "You don't understand. It wasn't like that at all. God knows what that man has said to you. I should have called his blackmailing bluff and told you myself but when I tried, I just couldn't do it."

Still trembling from shock and rage, Jennie was breathing too quickly as thought tumbled over thought. It was all quite clear and all quite sordid. She had loved him, spent years in anguish for him and remembered him as a perfect being – a rock. It had been an illusion. Perfection did not exist and her father, far from being a rock, was nothing but a man of straw.

Knowing his daughter's thoughts, Charles got up, walked into the airy drawing room and headed for the drinks table. Pouring himself a very large Scotch, he took a swig and thanked God he had been alone when Jennie had suddenly appeared in such an emotional state. He drank more, then headed back to the verandah, wishing he had died in that camp after all.

Jennie turned and watched as he sank back into his chair then her

213

thoughts returned to that awful moment. One look at the small solemn face had told her that Jamie, at least, believed in every word he had said. "What a cruel thing to do to him," she had said to Leighton as they had driven away from the orphanage. "You have a very juvenile sense of humour."

He had merely laughed and retorted: "Miss Veryan, you come from a feather-bedded background that knows nothing of the real world, nothing of sex and lust. And, I fear, you know nothing about your father. Ask him to tell you how he destroyed my sister, how instead of becoming a doctor she returned to Singapore from London pregnant, wearing a wedding ring and calling herself Mrs Veryan. My parents knew the truth, of course, but kept up the charade for pride's sake. Not long after Jamie was born, my sister died. She was beautiful and highly educated. Then she met your father and he destroyed her. I mean to make him pay for it."

She had stared at him in utter disbelief then said that her father could not possibly be to blame. His sister had lied.

"Ask him. Ask him to tell you how my sister died."

Angrily she had snapped, "Drop me off in the Bukit Timah Road, at the five and a half mile."

In a sudden torrential downpour, Leighton had stopped his car on the Dunearn Road, leaving her to dodge traffic in order to cross the canal to the Bukit Timah side. She finally arrived at the Webbs' house soaked, angry and bemused. Relieved to find her father there and alone, she explained all that Leighton had said, expecting a quick denial. But the expression on his face told her it was all true. The rain had stopped now; water droplets fell from her lank straight hair on to her face and shoulders and her soaked dress clung to her body. Unaware of all this, she was still trembling with the shock of her discovery.

Devastated, Charles looked at her with anguished eyes. Of all the suffering Leighton had caused, this destruction of Jennie's love had been the cruellest blow of all and the one he had come to fear most. "For Christ's sake," he said at last. "Let's go inside."

Jennie kept her eyes turned from him however and made no effort to move. She was seeing clearly, for the first time, how cleverly she had been duped for surely today had been a carefully planned affair, even to rehearsing Jamie's devastating little speech? Leighton knew that upsetting her father would have her demanding a meeting. He knew everything she was thinking, every move she would make. It shocked her to think that such a man could read her so well. The Tamil woman had finished washing now and was walking away from the pump with the basket of wet clothing.

Charles sighed and ran a despairing hand through his grey hair. "It

214

happened in London, just prior to my Paris posting. You see ... well ... things were difficult. Your mother had been unwell and ...."

"Ah, yes, the miscarriages," snapped Jennie. "Maddie told me what Maman went through trying to give you a son. I remember how ill she was on the road to St Nazaire."

Feeling the ground cut from beneath him, Charles looked into his glass and tried to continue with his story. "It meant that I had to attend diplomatic receptions alone for most of the time. After yet another one, a colleague persuaded me to go on with him to a party, and that's how I met Serena Leighton. She was a medical student and the most beautiful woman I had ever seen. I was completely knocked for six. She told me that her father specialised in tropical diseases and lived in Singapore. I also learned that she had a twin brother. Not that he resembles her in looks or character. I never met him then, even though he was in London at the same time. The fact is, Jennie, I simply fell in love with Serena."

"And stopped loving Maman? Just like that? How could you?"

"Believe me when I tell you that I never stopped loving your mother, Jennie. It is possible to love two people at the same time, in different ways."

He spoke of the affair which lasted for five months, of the flat he rented under a different name, of the false identity he had given to Serena who had no idea he was married. "How could I risk losing her by telling her the truth? When I look back, I see now that I didn't so much love her as covet her."

Jennie listened in cold silence. Was this her father, this man deceiving his wife and lying to a young woman then ending an affair by letter when he was posted to Paris? "And that was when you told her that you had a wife and a child at home?"

"Yes," he murmured, lighting up a cigarette and inhaling deeply. "Coward's way out, but I couldn't bring myself to look her in the eye and say what must be said. She didn't tell me she was pregnant, and once I'd left the flat she had no way of getting in touch with me." He looked at his daughter. "She trusted me implicitly, you see. Learn from that, Jennie. Never trust a man implicitly. I then told myself that it would be all right, that a woman with her looks and intelligence would never want for a man's love and that she deserved more than to be the mistress of a married man. I thought I would get over her, but I was wrong. Much as I loved your mother, I still could not get Serena out of my mind.

"Then, when France was about to fall, I received a letter from Singapore. God knows where it had been, because it had taken nearly four months to reach my home in Paris. The F.O. sent it on. It was from

215

Victor Leighton telling me that his sister had given birth to my son and was extremely ill. It seems he had spent his time in London finding out what he could about me. Serena's son, he said, was the child of a wealthy land owner and I was not to forget that any more than I was to forget my position as a career diplomat. For his silence, he wanted the boy named my heir and demanded a hefty sum of money as a mark of good-will, along with a legal document recognising the child officially. Of course it was out of the question, all of it. The letter I destroyed, the address I kept in my wallet, meaning to write back and explain that I would do what I could for Serena and the child. But when the *Lancastria* went down, the wallet went with it. I knew then that it was only a matter of time before Leighton carried out his threat and I lived in fear of the day. How was I to face your mother then? I was relieved when you went to Keswick. I wanted you far away, just in case. But nothing happened. The war, I suppose. Letters could easily be lost."

Charles walked back inside the house and refilled his glass. When he turned, Jennie was standing on the threshold, her expression a mixture of despair and contempt. Only the whisky gave him the courage to go on. Leaning against the table, eyes staring into the glass tumbler rather than at his daughter's face, he said, "I had no way of knowing whether Serena lived, or how my son fared. The only thing I did know was that things were getting worse in the Far East. And the threat was getting closer to Singapore. I'm afraid I did not share the belief that this Colony was impregnable. So, when the chance came to play courier, I jumped at it. Here, at last, was my chance to make things right for her and the baby and send them both to safety in Australia."

"Instead, you found her grave?"

Charles shook his head. "No. I found no one in my circles who had even heard of Doctor Leighton. It was a chaotic time. The island was filling up with refugees from Malaya, troops were pouring in and everyone had more than enough work to cope with without answering my constant queries. I even checked the hospitals, but drew a blank. I now know that Doctor Leighton had retired long since, only returning to one of the Indian hospitals to help out during the bombing. And that's where he was killed. Having a Malay wife didn't help his social position and, it seems, he kept himself very much to himself. Hence, few Europeans knew of him. Singapore came under attack and ... well ... you know the rest." He gave a wry smile. "I ended up in the same prison as Victor Leighton. How's that for bloody irony? When he found out who I was, he half near killed me until others intervened. He told me Serena was dead. He also told me that while he was in London trying to find out about me, his search led him to Kensington Square where your aunt was living at the time.

216

"Laura, it seems, heard his demands, money for silence, told him I had left the country and threatened to report him to the police, saying blackmail was a very serious offence in Britain and that he would be imprisoned or deported. She even called him a half-caste. He was young then and reading for a degree. Clearly he took her seriously and didn't go near her again. Perhaps he just returned to Singapore, I don't really know. But he was here when Serena died and is, quite naturally, filled with a burning hatred for the very name of Veryan."

Charles drained his glass, placed it down on the table then sank wearily on to the sofa. Hunched forward, eyes bright, teeth clenched as he went on: "Somehow a radio receiver had been secretly built at Changi. Messages were picked up from India and that's how we learned which ships had been sunk. Among them was the one my son was on. I had never seen him and now he was dead." He fell silent for a while, his eyes reliving the horror. "The guards found the receiver, tore the place apart looking for more then tortured those they thought responsible. Leighton told them I was involved, and also for good measure that I was a diplomat with important information." He shuddered, teeth clenched even tighter. "I only learned that the other day. He enjoyed telling me."

Jennie looked away from him and her voice was pitiless. "You don't have a monopoly on suffering, Papa, and you brought yours upon yourself by what you did. When I think how Maman grieved for you, how desolate she was, how she would cycle miles to the Catholic church every day to make sure a candle burned for you when all the time you had really left her for another woman ... then I feel *her* suffering and not yours. She would be alive now but for you. So would Serena. God, why are men so cruel? You have the lives of two women on your conscience. You say you loved them both, but still they're dead. What does that make you?"

He sat in stunned silence, then murmured, "Oh Christ, Jennie, don't say such things. You can't hate me more than I hate myself. I'm heartsick at what happened. But I'm not the first man to have an extra-marital affair or an illegitimate son. Had Serena told me of her condition, and had it been peacetime, then I could have made arrangements for the baby's welfare. But it wasn't peacetime and the war changed everything."

Jennie's eyes burned with anger. "You left your wife and daughter for a woman who had given you a son. Had you not left, Maman would never have got involved with the SOE. She would be alive today and you would be with her, at home in Cornwall. It wasn't just the war that changed our lives, Papa, it was *you*."

At this twist of the knife, Charles clasped his fingers tightly and

217

stared up at his daughter. She stood at the threshold still, but the sun had come out, the bright light behind her masking her expression.

"What do you intend to do about Jamie?" she asked coldly.

Charles turned his gaze to the ceiling and swallowed hard before answering: "I can't return to England without him and yet I can't return with him. Your mother is a famous war heroine, so how would it look for the longlost husband of Monique Veryan to return to the fold with an illegitimate son? Oh, I've thought of boarding schools, but it still wouldn't work. In England, Jamie would soon come to learn that he was nothing but the product of, what others would term, a shameful liaison. Leighton would follow us to England to pursue his vendetta and his claims for Jamie. That man can cause real trouble, Jennie. He has the means. I'm afraid there's more to this than I intend to tell you. Suffice it to say that the newspapers would have a field day. I couldn't do that to my parents, to the name of Veryan or to our tenants. Your aunt made me see that only recently."

"Did she?" said Jennie, raising her fine eyebrows slightly. "Did she really? Well, she has her own reasons for keeping you out here. I think you know what they are." Her throat began to ache and she tried to fight back the tears. "So then, now that you've decided to let everyone down, me, your parents, and your future tenants, what exactly are your plans for Jamie? He's suffered too in his short life. You can't just leave him in that orphanage."

"I don't intend to. I'll tell him I'm his father, and legally give him the name of Veryan. We shall stay here in Singapore for the rest of our days. I will never give Leighton money or make Jamie my heir. But we shall both be a very long way from Portlyn and therefore can harm no one. Leighton can bay to the moon if he likes. Who will listen or even care, if Charles Veryan isn't in England?"

"And what exactly am I supposed to say to your parents?" The tears had brimmed over and were streaking down her face. She felt physically ill. "They're over the moon because soon they'll have their son back again, their son who has returned from the dead. I came a very long way to take you home." Anger was rising now to mingle with the despair. "So what am I to tell them, Papa?"

"Don't," he murmured thickly. "Great God, if you only knew how much I long to return. But which will hurt them most, my staying or my returning? As I've already said, there's more to this than you know; more than I can tell you. So there it is. I can't take Jamie with me and I can't abandon him either."

"Why not?" cried Jennie, bitterly. "You could abandon me."

Tears pouring down her face, she rushed from the house and down the drive, then found herself standing on the edge of the busy road, searching through blurred eyes for a sign of a passing taxi. She could hear her father calling her name as he followed. A taxi was heading towards her. She hailed it and had just climbed in as Charles reached the spot.

"Jennie, don't go like this," he shouted through the open window.

"Drive on," cried Jennie. The Chinese driver wanted to know her destination. Jennie tried to think. Not the Boyds'. She was in too much of a state to go there. Where did she know? "Raffles Place. Robinson's."

"Not like this, Jennie, please. Don't go!"

The taxi moved off. Jennie turned her head to see her father standing there staring after her. Soon his diminishing figure had disappeared completely and she told herself that she would never see him again. With trembling hands, she searched her bag for a handkerchief. No, she would never see her father again.

At the Pattersons' old bungalow, Guy Lloyd sat on the verandah, *Straits Times* in one hand, glass of cold Tiger beer in the other. It was very hot, but after the drenching downpour he felt the humidity had dropped a little. Not so his anger and humiliation. He wasn't used to being "stood up" by any woman, much less a mere slip of a thing like Jennie. And all this in full view of Colonel and Mrs Boyd who had invited him into the house and then waited in an awkward and embarrassed silence as time had slowly ticked by. He had waited for forty-five minutes then made his excuses and left, foot pressing down on the accelerator as he sped along the East Coast Road, disappointment overtaken by sheer fury.

Now, in the brief twilight, the amah was on her way home and he had only himself for company. The party was off. It had never been on really. Unable to find anyone who wasn't already doing something this Saturday, he had decided to forget the whole thing, knowing that by the time he returned from his mission it would be too late to arrange anything. This fact he had not mentioned to the Boyds. Explaining that time had not been on his side and had simply run out was not in his nature. Why should he explain? It was Jennie who had the explaining to do. Had she been at the house, waiting for him, he would had told her how things stood and taken her out to dinner instead. As it was, to hell with her.

In no mood for isolation now that tranquility had deserted him, Guy toyed with the idea of returning to Tengah. A few drinks with the squadron would restore his usual sang-froid, he told himself. He showered, dressed, and was about to lock up when he heard a car entering the drive. Opening the front door, he stared in amazement.

219

Jennie climbed out of the taxi then looked at him uncertainly. "For a moment I thought the place was deserted," she said. "No lights. No people."

"No party," said Guy coldly. "You'd have known that had you kept our date."

Jennie was tense, trembling with the effort to stay calm and wondering whether to send the taxi on its way or not. She wanted Guy's comfort and affection but he looked so angry. "I'm sorry. I shouldn't have come." With that, she made as if to climb back into the passenger seat, but Guy caught her by the arm, leaving the driver nonplussed for all his impassive expression.

It was only then that Guy saw the state of her, the unkempt hair, creased dress and red puffy eyes. Turning, he paid off the taxi driver. The vehicle backed out along the drive, then reached the road and moved away. Anger turning to concern, he looked at her. "What's the matter? Why have you been crying? Is it your father? Has he had a set-back?"

"No ... yes ..." The words came out as a strangled cry at the back of her throat. "Yes. There's a set-back."

"Oh, I see. Jennie, I'm so sorry." His heart sank for her as he placed an arm about the quivering shoulders and murmured gently: "Come on. You look as though you could do with a drink."

Jennie was still unsure why she had come here. She had wandered about Robinson's in her wet dress, her mind anywhere but on shopping. All she had known then was that she needed Guy, then slowly she recalled that they had been due to meet that afternoon. There was something about a party ... Unsure she could face a party, she had nevertheless let down the one person she needed the most. Rocked by her father's desertion after the other desertions, she needed to feel loved, to feel safe, for the world was a cold and lonely place where all that she cared about or hoped for was systematically smashed to pieces. She wanted to pour out her feelings to him, to have him hold her close and say that everything would be all right, but one look at his bemused face told her that, having treated him so badly, this was no time to fall on his shoulder demanding sympathy.

"Could we just walk a little?" she asked.

The short twilight had turned to darkness as they ambled through palm trees to the shore. Lights from *kelong* lamps reflected in the still water; mosquitoes were everywhere and the steaming night was already filled with the sound of bullfrogs and cicadas. Sensing she was deeply troubled, Guy placed a casual but comforting arm about her as they walked along in silence. A new moon was rising and soon millions of stars would scatter a jet black sky.

Her mind and emotions in a turmoil, Jennie found she could say nothing and was glad of Guy's silence. The last thing she wanted right now was to speak of the father who had chosen to put his son before his daughter, and family honour before all else. Looking across the water to the islands where *kampong* lights reached out into the darkness, she realised then that she could share his shameful secret with no one, not even her own family.

A dog barked from one of the houses along the shore. The moon vanished behind cloud and trees swayed slightly. What had promised to be a beautiful night was changing. A flash of lightning lit the horizon. The dog barked louder, then came the sound of not-too-distant thunder.

"Time to make our way back," murmured Guy. What was going on? Why was he walking along a beach at night with this young and distraught woman when all he wanted was to have some fun? It had been a hell of a week and he wanted to unwind. Her presence troubled him; it troubled him also that she didn't wish to speak of her father. What on earth could have happened? Another flash of lightning; a louder clap of thunder; wind swaying the trees, and things crowding in on him. "Damn, it's going to pour. Come on!" The storm caught them before they reached the bungalow. Within seconds they were drenched to the skin but since Jennie's dress had barely dried from the earlier deluge, she hardly noticed. Guy led her into a large comfortable sitting room where blackwood furniture stood among chintz-covered armchairs and a sofa. He switched on table lamps, and closed the shutters to keep out the rain. The fan whirled slowly above them; the heat was stifling; thunder cracked over their heads. Jennie leaned back slightly against the side of the table, pushing a hand through her dripping hair. The clinging dress emphasised her breasts and slender hips. Finding her erotically disturbing, Guy walked to the drinks table, poured two large brandies then handed a glass to her. "Here. Drink this. You need it."

She frowned as she took the glass. "I don't normally..."

"Come on. Drink it and tell me about your father's set-back."

His words were fatal. Emotion welled up inside her once more. "I can't ... I can't. Oh, Guy ... it was awful ... I don't know what to do..." Her voice broke. She took a swallow then shuddered as the fiery liquid coursed through her. The second swallow was larger, the fire not so fierce. It stopped her shaking and soon she found it strangely relaxing. Without even realising it she drank more. Guy refilled her glass, and she drank. His hands reached out to her wet hair, twisting a tendril between his fingers before letting them slide down to the back of her neck. Her body quivered beneath his touch. She moved closer to him; their arms went about each other and she leaned against the wet

221

shirt, feeling his heart beating. How disturbingly exquisite was the nearness of him, and the heat from his breath as he drew her face closer to his and brought his lips down on to hers. Dazed and lost in his deep kiss, she felt his hand caressing her breast before letting it slide to her back where, fumbling for the zip, he caught it and pulled slowly. The dress eased from her shoulders, then fell to the floor. She should stop him but felt powerless. A mellow warmth rushed over her and targeted her loins. She felt a little dizzy.

"Come on," he murmured. "Get out of these wet things." His hand unhooked her bra then cupped one breast as he kissed it lightly.

A tremulous shock went through her and she clasped her hands about his head, murmuring, "Love me. Say you love me?"

"I love you," he groaned, pulling her down with him to the carpeted floor. His lips brushed hers once more in a hot burning kiss as his hands caressed her body and stripped off the rest of her clothes.

Jennie felt strange and wished the room would stop spinning. She had no will anymore and, feverish with desire, gave herself up to him, murmuring incoherently.

# Part Two

# Chapter Fourteen

It was exceptionally warm for March. Under a cloudless pale blue sky, primroses and celandines scattered embankments and woodlands. Exhilarated by the weather, Guy longed to push his new drophead Jaguar XK 120 to its limits but in the narrow Cornish lanes any kind of speed was impossible. He glanced at Jennie, snug in her thick woollen coat, blue silk scarf about her head to protect her from the wind. Her face was turned from him as she leaned back against the seat. He wondered what was going through her mind.

"Is it too windy for you?" he asked. "Would you like the hood up?"

She turned her head slightly and shook it slowly from side to side. "No. The sun's marvellous. The fresh air helps."

"Feeling all right?"

"Yes, but I do wish you wouldn't drive so fast."

"I was barely doing fifty." With an irritated sigh he eased off the accelerator, asking himself yet again how he could have allowed it all to happen. Why hadn't he stuck to his principles and stayed away from virgins? As it was, she had come at him from the sun and shot him down in flames with the news that she was pregnant. There had been fear in her eyes, fear that he didn't love her. He had taken her in his arms, telling her that he did, unsure as he said it was it was true. It was his own fault. Too many years with older women who knew how to take care of themselves had left him complacent. Jennie had come to him in a vulnerable state of distress and he had given her brandy. Why hadn't he realised she was the worse for drink instead of assuming that she wanted what he wanted? He never had been a one for adolescent games, it was all or nothing at all as far as he was concerned. Jennie Veryan, of all people!

He glanced at her again, remembering how she had cried in his arms, vehement that she was pregnant when it was far too early for any doctor to confirm it. He could have insisted on waiting before tying the knot, but had word of her condition got out then, between the Boyds and the Veryans, his whole future might have come unstuck. Conduct unbecoming an officer and gentleman might well have got him struck of the ETPS course. In any case, Jennie had come to mean more to him with each passing day. From the moment he dragged her from the rioters her life had become entwined with his. The Chinese would have nodded wisely and said, "Of course."

The road ahead was empty of traffic; he pressed his foot down on the accelerator once more. Husband and father to be ... Christ! Had anyone told him that last Christmas, he would have laughed. How quickly things had moved: special licence, the Boyds' arranging everything, including the reception. Had they guessed in spite of Jennie's deception? He told himself at the time that things could have been worse. If he had to get a woman in the family way then at least it was someone he cared about, someone whose father would one day inherit a title and an estate which would go to Jennie eventually. Useful when the time came for him to retire from flying. Only on the wedding day did he learn that Colonel Boyd would be giving the bride away, and not Charles Veryan. Why was still a mystery since Jennie refused to speak of her father. On asking when he would finally meet his father-in-law, she had shocked him by snapping back: "Never!"

Never? He was all at sea. Had Charles Veryan decided to remain in Singapore? Was that it? If it was then would Jennie inherit on her grandfather's death or would the house and estate go to this male cousin of hers instead? Why the hell wouldn't she confide in him? Not much further to go now. He felt a twinge of anxiety at meeting Sir Philip and Lady Veryan for the first time. They could hardly be delighted that their beloved grand-daughter had wed in such haste and in a far off country. They were probably even less delighted that instead of marrying into the landed gentry, she had "thrown herself away" on an underpaid pilot. He was in deep trouble before he had even met them and they didn't yet know she was pregnant. Right now a dog fight over the Kent coast would be positively cosy in comparison to what lay ahead.

Jennie was watching the tall hedgerows flashing past, her thoughts on her father so far away. Two days after that awful confession, he had come looking for her and in the privacy of the Boyds' garden had begged his daughter to see reason, to understand, to forgive. She had tried, but nowhere in her heart was there room for forgiveness. Understanding, yes, since men would be men and Guy was living proof of that, but if their desires led to disaster, then forgiveness was impossible. She hardly knew whether she loved or hated her father, so how could she forgive? Later, having missed her period and realising that the

226

strange nausea which had plagued her for three weeks was not a tropical bug after all, she had panicked, told a shocked Guy what she suspected, then wept with relief in his arms when he said he loved her and that they would marry before leaving Singapore. Marriage! Such a thing had been a long way from her thoughts until that moment. It hadn't helped matters when, being under twenty-one, she had been forced to swallow her pride and go to her father to gain his consent.

"But I've never met him," he had answered. "How can I give my consent?"

"He's the man who saved my life. The RAF officer who drove me to the hospital and clinic when there was still danger after the riots. How could you refuse?"

"You haven't known him long. How can you be sure that you love him? Well, are you?"

Mark's face swam into Jennie's mind and she hesitated. "Yes. Why else should I want to marry him?" Pregnant, after her very first time, and the horror of it was that she hardly remembered anything save that it had hurt. Had she been drunk?

"But why this sudden rush?"

For one moment she had toyed with the notion of telling him the plain truth. How ironic! Would he play the outraged father and berate her for having no morals? If so, she would remind him of his own. "Because he's about to be posted back to England and as his wife I would automatically go with him. We're flying, you see. He starts his course in February. All I require is your formal consent. Nothing more."

"Nothing more?" The hurt in his eyes had been plain to see. "Shan't I be able to give my daughter away?"

"You already have, Papa," she had answered coldly. "You already have."

And so she had married Guy Lloyd in a Register Office without her father being present, much to everyone's bewilderment for surely the reason for this hasty wedding was so that Charles Veryan, who would not return to England for some time, could give his daughter away in marriage before Guy left the Colony taking Jennie with him? Only Louise knew the truth of it. Colonel Boyd had sadly, but dutifully, stepped into Charles Veryan's shoes after Jennie had said that her father was too unwell to attend the ceremony. Everyone had felt so sorry for her. Such a quiet little ceremony too, with only ten guests, four of those being from Guy's squadron, looking on in amusement that the one man they had deemed a rogue bachelor for the rest of his days, was suddenly marrying this young woman in such haste. "Randy" Lloyd had clearly been caught! Oh, yes, she had sensed what they were thinking, but had taken her marriage vows wearing a cream silk outfit, matching hat, and trying to push Mark's face from her mind. The Boyds, having failed to persuade her to wait until she had gone through a formal engagement and then have the wedding in England, which her grandparents would want and expect, had finally caved in when Charles had given his consent. After this, they went into overdrive, insisting on making all arrangements and holding the reception in their own home. As cables were dispatched to England, the wedding night had been spent at Raffles. The following day, she and Guy had embarked on the long flight home to find a surprised and anxious Maddie waiting for them at RAF Lyneham, almost as though she had never left.

One last memory would always remain with her. It was of a thin little boy staring through a tall chain-linked fence. She had returned to the orphanage on the day before her wedding, returned to Jamie who remembered the lady from England. This time she had brought him a football, several books and a penknife. They had spoken of London and he had wanted to know about the King and Queen and whether she ever had tea with them. She answered his questions as best she could then bade him an affectionate farewell. Poor little Jamie was going to have to come to terms with some startling facts pretty soon. Would her half-brother accept his father or resent him? As she had waved good-bye, her heart went out to the boy who had been in a camp or institution for most of his life and must remain hidden away in shame, far from his father's country, because the rules had been broken.

Once back in England, Guy had said it would surely be better for her to remain in London until he was through the course at the Test Pilots' School. "There's nowhere for us to live at Farnborough, and besides you need to finish your art studies if you want that Diploma."

Even though his words made sound commonsense, she had felt a little hurt that he should be content to see her only at weekends. As a temporary measure, she moved back in with Maddie who could see at once how it was and thought she had been a fool. "It isn't so much the moral thing, it's the sheer stupidity in this day and age not to take precautions. Don't you know anything? As for Guy, he should be thoroughly ashamed!"

Within a week of resuming her studies it almost seemed that the whole Singapore episode had been but a dream. Only Guy and the baby made her realise how all too real it had been. Now she was taking him home to Trevellan. Guy at Trevellan! Guy belonged to Singapore and Mark to Trevellan. Everything was on its head suddenly. "Grandpa has offered us the use of the house in Kensington Square until we can find a place of our own." She smiled to herself, thinking of the unsuspecting Clive being asked to move out to accommodate the newly weds. It was a delicious thought.

"That's very good of your grandfather," said Guy in surprise. "Kensington Square, eh?" Cheered at this news, he changed gears as they entered Portlyn and climbed the steep hill towards the house.

Jennie's stomach started churning. This was the moment she had long dreaded, the moment she had not been able to face on returning to England. Instead she had written letters and telephoned, thankful not to have to look her grandmother in the eye with her lies.

It was almost three-thirty as they drove through the castellated gateway and drew up outside the main entrance to the house. Guy looked about him in growing amazement. "Great God! It's bloody fantastic." Was it possible that Charles Veryan could turn his back on all this? If so, it was even more of a tragedy than he had hitherto realised.

Keynes, Rosa and Mrs Hodges were lined up in the hallway to greet the newly weds and offer their congratulations as Jennie introduced them to Guy. "Her Ladyship is on the terrace, Madam," said Keynes as he took the suitcases inside. "Shall I prepare tea for you?"

"We'll wait, thank you, Keynes," said Jennie. "We had a good lunch in Truro. I'll take my husband out to meet Grandmother immediately." She watched as he walked up the stairs with the cases, thinking how strange it was not to hear him refer to her as Miss Genevieve any more. Madam! It sounded odd and not so comforting. Keynes, Rosa and Mrs Hodges were more than servants to her, they were like family. But, in their book, the old familiarity would have to end now. She had left the house as one person and returned as another. Everything seemed so unreal suddenly. Guy in this house seemed unreal.

Having moved from the terrace to a more sheltered place beside the old orangery, Florence was dozing in her favourite garden chair, feet on a stool, head back against a blue cushion, warm sun on her face. Jennie approached silently, looked down at the closed crepy eyelids, and thought how far away the autumn seemed now – a lifetime away.

The eyes opened suddenly and Florence stared up at her granddaughter. Saying nothing, she reached out her arms and Jennie entered them. They hugged each other in silence, each thinking how this moment should have been. "He just needs more time, Grandma, more time to rehabilitate. Be glad he's well." Jennie hesitated nervously. "Look, I've brought my husband to meet you at last."

Pulling herself up to a more erect position, Florence eyed the tall man like an art connoisseur eyeing a painting to check its authenticity. This one had no provenance that she knew of, yet he was a senior officer, his manners were good and his face not unpleasing. He was older too. That was good usually. Older men meant stability and Jennie needed that. But what kind of man meets a girl one minute then marries her the next without any of her kin being present? How dare he take it on himself to behave in such a way. Why had Charles allowed it? Oh, she could understand Jennie's desire for her father to give her away but Charles should never have given his consent in the first place. What did anyone know of this man? His daughter should have been engaged for six months, and married here with half the county attending the wedding. But then Charles was no longer himself and could not be blamed. Jennie knew better, though, and had behaved extremely badly. It made no sense when only six months ago she had been broken-hearted over the Curnow boy.

"Lady Veryan," said Guy, taking her outstretched hand. "It's good to meet you at last. If I've kept Jennie away then I'm extremely sorry, but since our return to England such a short while ago, I've been on an intensive course and Jennie has been continuing her art studies."

Florence smiled politely. "You have your lives to lead. I wouldn't dream of expecting you both to rush about like wet hens at our beck and call."

"It's my fault," said Jennie, recognising the cool tones. "I couldn't take time off from the Slade. They've been extremely considerate about my late start into the term as it is."

How could she add that all journeys made her feel queasy, that even travelling on a bus was a nightmare at times? The shrewd eyes staring up at her made Jennie feel uncomfortable. Had her grandmother guessed?

Florence stood up slowly and leaned on her cane. "It's getting chilly. Come. We'll go in. You must both be longing for tea and a rest after your journey. It takes for ever driving to and from London. Your grandfather will join us shortly. He's resting in his room. Doctor's orders."

"He's ill?"

Florence paused at Jennie's anxious question and turned to her with sad eyes. "He seems to have lost the will to be anything else these days. It was such a blow to us, you understand. We thought your father was coming home, then your letter came and ... well, he's very down. Still, Charles is alive and well and we're all greatly relieved, so your journey achieved that much at any rate. You must tell me everything and show me those photographs."

Laura was already in the drawing room as they entered. She stood by the window, fading auburn hair glinting in the light, cigarette in its tortoise-shell holder, oatmeal tweed dress decorated with a pink silk scarf as though she had deliberately posed for this scene.

230

Introductions were made, Guy was studied as once Ian Stewart had been studied, then Philip entered, kissed his grand-daughter lightly on the cheek and shook hands with Guy. In the awkward silence that followed, Jennie was shaken by her grandfather's ashen complexion. *Poor man, poor devastated man.* How long he had hoped, how long he had waited, and for what? She wished her father could see the look on the old man's face. Then perhaps he would realise the true harm he had done.

As tea was brought in, Florence wasted no time in coming to the subject which taxed her mind without mercy. "So your father needs more medical care? But why could he not receive it here? Harley Street has to be better than Singapore any day."

"Papa trusts Doctor Fraser, who has known him for a long time. He's a very good man and ... well ... it's better that Papa rehabilitates with him than with a stranger."

Philip gave her a stern look. "I don't understand. You told us he was better and that his memory had returned. So what's the problem? What is all this rehabilitation nonsense?" Leaning forward in his chair, he stared at Jennie with that familiar penetrating gaze. "He does want to come home? Jennie, he does mean to return to us?"

"Of course," she murmured, not meeting those eyes. "It's all my fault. I assumed too much too quickly. I didn't understand the medical facts. Apparently his recovery will be a complex matter and Doctor Fraser feels that confusion could set in if he isn't completely well before coming back to England." She looked at her hands. What utter non-sense. Who in their right mind would believe it? Yet the truth would finish off her grandfather and shatter her grandmother. This way, they could absorb things slowly, until their son wrote and told them himself. The last thing her father had asked of her was to keep his secret. "Tell them anything you like, but not the truth. That's my task. Promise me, Jennie, if not for my sake then for theirs?" She had given him her pledge, and would never break it.

"But how long will this rehabilitation take?" Florence was pouring Lapsang Souchong from the Georgian silver teapot. She handed a cup to Jennie who took it, frowning.

"I've really no idea. Doctor Fraser said it could be months, maybe more than a year." At the look on their faces she hurried on: "But he's in good hands, and the Webbs look after him magnificently so set your minds at rest. I'll show you the photographs and you can see for yourself." Putting down the tea which she hoped no one would notice she was unable to drink, she pulled from her handbag a bunch of photographs and charcoal sketches and handed them to Florence.

231

"I've made some watercolour sketches also, in order to work on a portrait of him later. They're in my case."

Shocked at how much her son had aged, Florence touched one of the pictures lovingly. "How thin he is, poor darling. How terribly he must have suffered." She gazed at the photographs one after the other then the sketches, and in silence passed them on to Philip who was too moved to say a word.

"Goodness, he looks like an old man," was Laura's swift verdict. When she had finished looking at them she turned to Jennie. "Now for the wedding pictures. I simply can't wait to see what you wore, my dear. After all, you couldn't have had much time to prepare for the greatest event of your life."

Ignoring the barbed words, Jennie glanced anxiously at her husband, who met her eyes, knowing that this moment would be the trickiest of all. "I sorted out a few photographs. The Boyds were simply marvellous, weren't they, Guy." Tensing, she watched as her grandparents and Laura stared at pictures of herself and Guy and informal groups of people at the reception.

"But where is your father?" asked Florence. "I don't see him in any of the photographs."

Already prepared for this one, Jennie rose to her feet, wandered over to her grandmother and glanced at the photos, tut-tutting. "Oh, how stupid of me. I've brought the ones I intended to leave behind. I'm sorry. I grabbed them in such a rush that I didn't have time to check. Never mind. Next time I come you'll see them, I promise." It was all becoming too much of a strain. She longed to be away from the lies and the questioning eyes. "I'll fetch the watercolour sketches. They're in my room."

Laura laughed. "Your room? Have you forgotten you're married now, my dear? I've put you both in the Chinese Room. It hasn't been used for years but you should find it suitable for a short visit."

Jennie had always hated the Chinese Room and Laura knew it.

Leaving Guy to the tender mercies of Veryan curiosity, she walked up the stairs then paused outside the room her parents once shared. No one was ever put in there. It had become a shrine. She hated shrines. They were for the dead, not the living, and certainly not for those who betrayed people who loved them. Slowly she opened the door on the room that was trapped in time. The flame her mother had started still burned. Her poor mother. Her poor darling betrayed mother. Anger flushed over her suddenly and her fingers reached out to the candle. Yet, for all she wanted to snuff it out, she couldn't do it. The flame began to burn her hand as it hovered indecisively. She lowered her arm, walked out and shut the door on grief and bitterness.

In the Chinese Room, Rosa had already unpacked both cases and hung everything away in the large ivory-inlaid wardrobe and drawers. Jennie gazed dismally at the silk wall covering of oriental birds and trees, finding it all rather depressing. The nineteenth-century bed was far too short for Guy's long legs and she knew how much he would hate the large porcelain wash bowl and jug that stood on a table in the corner. Wearily, she lay on the gold satin counterpane, gazed up at the ceiling, and thought of a mellow evening when the plane had taken off from Changi and she had gazed down on Singapore where her father would remain in his self-imposed exile. Suddenly she had felt such pity and love for him that the memory of her ugly words filled her with terrible guilt and grief. After all he had suffered, how could she have said such hateful things? She had left him hurt and tormented and it was too late to say how sorry she was. Yet now she had seen despair and anxiety on the faces of her grandparents and knowing, as they did not, that all their hopes were dashed, her heart had hardened once more. So much hurt and anguish caused to everyone because her father had a roving eye. And now she was expected to lie for him since she didn't know how to tell her grandparents the truth without breaking their hearts. She must hope her father could manage it better.

Ten minutes later, there was a quiet knock on the door. It opened and in walked Laura.

"Ah, resting, I see." She smiled but her eyes remained watchful. "I thought how pale you were and noticed you didn't touch your tea. I went quite off tea and coffee when I was expecting Clive." She glanced around as if finding the room distasteful. "When is it due?"

Jennie sighed. Trust Laura to know. "November." Another lie.

"A honeymoon baby! My word you must be fertile. How quickly things happen in your life, my dear, hurried wedding, instant baby." The false smile left Laura's face. "You went to bring back your father. Instead you return with a man you've only known for five minutes and already you're in the family way. You do seem to have made a dog's breakfast of things, don't you? I said you should have left everything to me."

Jennie's eyes flashed. "You didn't seem so eager to go to Singapore, as I recall."

Laura ignored the remark and sat down on the bed. "What happened to your father during internment? Was he ... well ... was he very badly treated? Is that why he lost his memory?"

"Dodo told me he was tortured, put into a small cage each day with five other men, taken out every morning and beaten until his flesh was raw and ... I can't imagine how he survived. It went on and on

233

apparently. I don't want to talk about that any more and I don't want my grandparents to know."

"Perhaps, then, you can tell me about Leighton?"

"He's the reason why Papa was tortured. I don't want to talk about him either."

Laura sat down on the bed, openly curious. "Nonsense. You must talk to me about everything. I'm the only one you *can* talk to."

"No, Aunt Laura, you talk to me," snapped Jennie. "Tell me why you wrote that letter to Papa, when you must have known he was in no state to cope with it?"

The blue eyes glinted dangerously. "He told you, did he? Well, you know perfectly well why I wrote as I did. You must know ... after all, you've been with Charles and spoken to Mr Leighton. So tell me what I want to know."

Why the hell should she? "Didn't Papa answer your letter then? Didn't he tell you?" Jennie fell silent. Laura knew only that Serena had been pregnant and Leighton wanted to blackmail the family. "I don't know what it is you want me to say."

Laura's lips tightened. "All I seek is clarification of the situation as it is now."

Smiling, Jennie lay back on the bed, her hands behind her head, and said: "But I explained everything downstairs. I thought I had made the situation quite clear?"

Furious, Laura stood up and marched to the door. There she turned. "Clive was right. You really *are* a little slut, aren't you?" With that she slammed the door shut, then stood in the corridor wondering how much Jennie really did know. Had Charles found his half-caste woman after all this time, and was there a child? It must be the case, for why else would he take her letter to heart and stay in Singapore? But would he tell his own daughter all this? Knowing Charles, it was hardly likely. He would choose instead to fob her off with this nonsense about rehabilitation. On the other hand, Jennie seemed to know what the letter meant, and then there was Leighton ... Had he told her and piled on the threats once more? If so, then Jennie was lying to them all as well as Charles. Oh God, how infuriating it was, not knowing. What exactly had been going on and what did Charles really mean to do? She should have gone to Singapore herself.

Slut! Jennie heard the word reverberating in her brain. She had let Guy strip off her clothes and ... that was the trouble ... she simply didn't remember what happened after that save for the sharp pain. On their honeymoon night, although she had worried about the baby, he had told her not to be such an idiot and wasted little time in attempting arousal before driving into her until he was satisfied. When it was over,

234

she lay flat and unfulfilled. Was that it then? Was that really all there was to this great thing called love making? Or was Guy angry over this marriage, perhaps believing himself to be the victim of a lie? Yet he had said he loved her and could be very tender at times. Now that the baby was a certainty and her doctor had cautioned against it, their sex life had come to a grinding halt which had not pleased him. Not that they saw much of each other since most weekends he had to work, the course being exceptionally intense. Or so he said. Sometimes she wondered if he simply did not like having to go to Maddie's house and mingle among a crowd of people he had nothing in common with, especially Gavin whom he thought a little mad and "probably a queer". If that was it, then things must change for the better when they moved to Kensington Square. She told herself that he loved her and that she loved him. It must be so, for now they were man and wife and that was that. How would things have been, she wondered, if instead of going to the Pattersons' place that evening she had returned to the Boyds' house?

Rest being out of the question, Jennie returned to the drawing room with her watercolour sketches, then looked at Guy who was obviously very uncomfortable. "Let's take a walk to the cove before it gets dark."

"Why not show Guy the boathouse?" said Laura in waspish tones.

Thankful for his rescue, Guy shot to his feet at once and soon they were heading across the grounds to the old woodland path.

Mark pulled his car to a stop outside his parents' house. He had just come from the General Hospital in Truro where his mother was recovering from an operation. Still unsure what this operation was all about, his question had been answered in a whisper: "Women's problems." Finding the door locked, he glanced at his watch. Six-fifteen. His father was probably still at the big house. Might as well stretch his legs for a bit.

It was good to be back, good to have restored relations with his parents after so long. Last Christmas he had stayed away, and hurt them both deeply. But his mother's illness and subsequent operation had changed everything. He wandered towards the clifftops, thinking that these last six months had been the worst he had ever known. In London he had waited daily for Jennie to contact him but he had waited in vain. Never in his heart had he expected her to take him at his word. When he had written that letter and rushed from the scene it had seemed the right and proper thing to do. Now he regretted it bitterly. What he'd thought of as strength and decency, she had seen as weakness and betrayal. Finally, he had broken his own resolve by going to her, only to be told, at the house in Cheyne Walk, that Jennie had left for Singapore just three days earlier. That was the first he had heard of her father's return from the dead. Three days! After all those weeks of waiting he had missed her by three bloody days.

Christ, what an idiot he had been! What else was there in life for him but Jennie? He loved her and should have run off with her. Singapore! So far away? In London at least they shared the same city. Now he felt empty and desolate. How long did she mean to stay? No point in asking his parents; to them Jennie's name was taboo. Turning, he found himself walking towards the cove, remembering those days when Sophie had stood on his gloved fist and Jennie beside him. How could he have known then the deep hurt she would cause? She knew where he could be reached, but had put family first and stuck to the status quo. He walked on, and reaching the clifftop, gazed out to sea. The wind was stronger and the ocean almost grey in the fading light of day. Cornwall! After London it was marvellous. How much he would miss it all should he accept the position recently offered him. It was all he had studied for and encompassed everything he wanted in career terms. But it was far from Cornwall . . . far from all he loved. This was her home, where she belonged and where she would be. She would never be where he was going. If he accepted the position he might never see her again.

At last he came to the cove. Looking down from the clifftop he saw that the tide was well out. A dog appeared on the steps below. Mark recognised Rosalind, remembering the time when she had almost caused Jennie to drown. Expecting the hated Laura Willoughby to follow, he watched then froze. Jennie! It truly was Jennie walking down the steps in casual slacks and short jacket, her hair tossing in the wind as she picked up a piece of driftwood and threw it for Rosalind, who just waddled towards it. Heart pounding, Mark started for the downward path then stopped as another figure emerged at the steps. The fair-haired man strode across the beach towards Jennie. She smiled up at him as he put his arm around her, said something and laughed. Backs turned to Mark, they walked on across the wet, rocky sand.

Feeling as though he had been punched in the stomach, Mark stood watching then turned and walked away.

Jennie was thinking how long the dusk lasted in England and how different the light was here to the vibrant tones of Singapore – a soft-toned watercolour to a vivid oil painting. She was also thinking how strange it was to be here at the cove with Guy. From the moment they had started along the woodland path she knew it to be all wrong. Not Guy. Not here. He didn't belong here for this place belonged to another. Suddenly, she felt a tingle at the back of her neck and had the strangest feeling that Mark was there, gazing down at her. Quickly she turned and looked across at the clifftop. There was no one. Why did she still look for him when he no longer gave her a second thought? She was married, a mother-to-be, and must bury this old love. Could she though? In far off Singapore she had thought she could. Now she felt that only time would bury it for her. As for Guy, the feeling she had for him could not compare with the feeling she had for Mark. Was it possible to care about two people at the same time, as her father had said it was? If so, he might have added how painful such a dilemma could be. But, unlike her father, she had not chosen this way. Fate had chosen it for her.

Frank Curnow was inside the cottage and pottering about the kitchen when Mark returned. He greeted his son with some surprise. "Ah, there you are. Didn't you bring your own key?"

"Yes," murmured Mark, still unable to take in what he had seen. "I took a walk."

"How did you find your mother?" Frank looked anxious. His son was ashen-faced. "She is all right, isn't she? There hasn't been..."

"No, no. Mum's fine. I thought she looked very pale and much thinner, but the nurse told me she was doing well enough."

Frank sighed with relief. "Well, that's a blessing. I'm going to the hospital this evening." He filled the kettle and placed it on the gas stove. "They reckon she'll be there for another seven days at least. Anyway, thank God it isn't what we thought it might be. Are you staying the night?"

Mark shook his head. "No, I have to get back. Too much work. Jennie's returned from Singapore then? Have you seen her father yet?"

"Sadly, he didn't return with her. Don't ask me why. They're all pretty shattered about it. How did you know Jennie was back?" There was a hint of disapproval in his voice.

"I've just seen her at the cove." Mark paused, then steeled himself to ask: "Who's the fellow with her?"

Frank could not meet his son's eyes. "Her husband. Funny business. Met him in Singapore. Hardly had they met than they married. All I know, all anyone knows, is that he's a fighter pilot." His son had gone through a great deal of pain for nothing it would seem. Well, at least this would bring him to his senses.

Mark tried to digest his father's words slowly. Married! He felt physically ill at the shock. All those years, those words, those feelings, and she had married? Oh God, it couldn't be. Why? Why had she pushed him aside so quickly, and not for the well-connected banker or land-owner, but a pilot! He sank into a chair. It was a rebound gesture, of course it was. A stupid way of showing how well she could get on

237

without the man who swore he loved her then left her on that rainswept evening. But on the rebound or not, she was married now and lost to him.

As Frank prepared a greasy fry up, he asked Mark to tell him about the position he had been offered.

"It's a large estate," murmured Mark trying to get his thoughts back together. "Eighteen thousand acres. Visitors to the big house as well. I'd be assisting the agent at first, learning the ropes so to speak. He's getting on, though."

"It sounds a good position but a damned long way to go. We'll hardly see you. I've never understood why you wanted estate management. You'd earn far more in business." Later, as they walked out into the darkness towards Mark's car, Frank asked: "Well, have you made up your mind to accept?"

Mark opened the car door, then nodded. "Oh, yes," he said bitterly. "I've made up my mind all right."

# Chapter Fifteen

In the last week of September Florence telephoned Jennie. "Now look, my dear, I realise Guy is taking leave when the time comes, but I really don't like to think of you alone in that house. I want you to come here."

Jennie blinked but said calmly, "I'm not alone. Mrs Hale is here. Anyway I'm booked in at the hospital and Guy will be here when the baby's due."

"Mrs Hale is as deaf as a post," snapped Florence. "And she's no spring chicken either. With Guy at Farnborough, I cannot have you depending on an ageing housekeeper if you go into labour early. I'm coming to collect you. Don't worry, dear, I'll get you back to London in time for the birth, then I'll stay with you for a while."

Jennie's hand tightened on the receiver. "No ... no ... you mustn't. I'm fine, really, and I've six weeks to go yet."

Brooking no argument, Florence turned up at Kensington Square, expressed surprise at Jennie's size, stayed one night then bundled her grand-daughter into the Rolls and set off for Cornwall. The game was up, thought Jennie, almost with relief. This was one lie she no longer had to maintain.

Alexander Philip Veryan Lloyd was born at Trevellan six days later and weighed in at 8lbs 10oz, thus confirming what some had suspected in the first place. As his lusty lungs produced a cry that could be heard all over the south wing, Florence's anger at being gulled was rapidly overtaken by deep relief that Jennie had come safely through a long and difficult labour.

The morning after the birth, Jennie lay in her old bed, aware of her grandmother entering the room to gaze yet again at her first great-grandchild sleeping in his broderie anglaise-covered crib. The nurse had just finished bathing Alexander and the sweetness of baby powder filled the room.

Only when the nurse had left, did Florence speak. "You might have

239

been more honest with me, instead of letting me find out from the doctor that you only had days, not weeks. Thank goodness I called him in to look you over, otherwise we'd have been in a pretty patch. I hope it's a happy marriage, Jennie. I see now it was a necessary one." She turned from the crib and, looking at her grand-daughter, saw the pale face and large dark-shadowed eyes set against the white pillow. Instantly her heart melted and she recalled the terrible long night which, thank God, had ended. "Still, that's all by the by now. He's a beautiful child, and so like your father when he was born." She walked across to Jennie and patted her hand gently. "Now you're to rest quietly and not get out of that bed. Doctor's orders."

Rose entered with a breakfast tray and waited, smiling, while Florence eased Jennie to a sitting position and plumped up her pillows. "Tea!" murmured Jennie, her throat parched, her body feeling battered and bruised, her head a little light. "Wonderful. For nine months I couldn't touch the stuff."

Placing the tray on the bed, Rosa wandered across to the crib and gazed down, murmuring, "He's 'andsome lad and no mistake. My sister's little maids all looked like wrinkled prunes."

Jennie sipped her tea as though it were a life-giving force and swore to herself that she would never go through that hell again. Alexander would be her only child. When Rosa had left the room, she asked if Guy had been informed.

Florence nodded. "I telephoned the Officers' Mess then Guy rang us. He says he won't be able to get here today, he's committed to testing, but in another twenty-four hours, if all goes well."

Jennie's eyes were rivetted on the older woman's face for any give-away signs. "Did he sound pleased?"

"My dear, he's over the moon." Florence bent her head to the crib once more to avoid the close scrutiny. If anything, Guy had sounded rather short and muttered some nonsense about its being too early surely? That had angered her. "I'm not a doddering old fool so don't treat me like one," she had snapped. "Your son was born at full-term, and because of the difficult birth, Jennie's blood pressure is very high. If it doesn't start going down soon she'll have to go to hospital. I think you should make an effort to get here as soon as possible." She had then replaced the telephone before Guy could say another word. He may have saved Jennie's life, but he had behaved extremely badly. As for Jennie, the very thought that she could . . . well! The shock had been great. She should never have allowed her to go to Singapore in the first place.

"What exactly did he say?" Jennie wanted to know.

240

Florence kept her head bowed to the crib. "Oh, thrilled to bits. He said there would be drinks all round in the Mess."

"But he can't get away just yet." Jennie put down her cup and lay back against the pillow in reflective mood. So then, what had happened to the special leave Guy had promised to take at this time? She turned her head to the window and suddenly burst into tears.

The nurse entered the room at that moment and smiled sympathetically. "Post-natal blues? Most of my mothers feel that way for a bit. It's natural and passes."

It was noon the following day when Guy stopped the Jaguar outside the main gate. With eyes closed he tried to get a grip on his thoughts and emotions. He was a father! Dear God, a father. It wasn't real. Soon he would be entering the house, and climbing the stairs to his wife's room where she would be sitting up in bed looking serene and beautiful with a baby in her arms. The room would be full of females and all would search his eyes for the required reaction when he entered. He had to make sure it was there.

Starting the engine once more, he eased the car through the gate and pulled up outside the main entrance, grateful now to Florence for insisting that his wife be safe in this house during such a time. It had let him off the hook. He could carry on with his hard and complex training, and just wait for the telephone call. No anxious driving through the night with a woman in labour beside him, no wandering up and down hospital corridors – no sense, in fact, of being a father at all. And that, perhaps, was the problem. Florence had, by her actions, made it abundantly clear to him that this baby was a Veryan, not a Lloyd. His part in its creation was purely biological so far as Jennie's family were concerned.

Laura met him in the hallway, the cardigan of her blue cashmere twin set flung about her shoulders. "Jennie is sleeping. I shouldn't waken her yet. Come and have a drink. My father had a bad night, I'm afraid, and is resting in the morning room. I don't wish to disturb him."

With a sense of relief that his wife had not been rushed to hospital, Guy followed her to the drawing room where his eyes went instantly to Monique's photograph and the silver George Cross medal. It was impossible to avoid either and, not for the first time, he found himself wondering what his feelings would have been had the mother been here instead of the aunt. Monique Veryan had been a stunner in his book and, had she survived, he might have found life here very difficult indeed. After all, who ever heard of a man falling for his mother-in-law? His eyes drifted to the portrait of Jennie hanging on the wall. He knew little about art and was called a Philistine by his wife, but Gavin

241

had created a painting that any man would be proud to own and say to his children: "That was your mother, when she was quite young." Yet it graced the walls of this house instead of theirs. That said it all surely? Suddenly he felt like a stranger who had wandered in by mistake.

"Scotch, isn't it? Water not soda?" Laura was speaking to him from the drinks table.

"You've a good memory." Guy walked to the hearth and stood before the blazing logs. It dawned on him then that maybe Laura had planned this moment since he knew from Jennie that come hell or high water the drawing-room fire was never lit until mid-afternoon. It wasn't even necessary. The weather was mild.

Laura handed him the whisky then sat down on the sofa holding a dry sherry, saying, "I'm afraid Jennie has had a rough old night. Babies like to be fed at the most inconvenient times. The nurse is marvellous. She'll stay until a nanny is found. We favour Norland, but you may have opinions of your own on that score."

He blinked. Nannies? Babies? What had happened to his carefree life and why was Laura staring at him in that disconcerting manner?

"Lady Veryan said that Jennie had a difficult time."

"Yes. I'm afraid she did, rather. It seemed at one stage that the doctor was going to send her to hospital for a ceasarian. In the end he managed a forceps delivery. Poor Jennie! Forceps in the wrong hands can leave a baby brain-damaged. Our doctor is good, but a little out of date. Things could have got very nasty. As it is, Alex is fine in all departments. Jennie isn't, I'm afraid. You know about the high blood pressure, of course?" She sipped her sherry and leaned back on the sofa. "Frankly, I think she should have been delivered in a hospital."

"And so she would have been. I had everything arranged."

Laura smiled with amusement. "But, Guy, you made all the arrangements for November. And look what happened. Although how she could have gone to full-term with anything larger than Alexander is a mystery to me."

"Come on, no need to play games."

Her smile vanished. "It isn't much of a game, is it, Guy? Do you love her? No, truly. Did you really intend to marry my neice?"

"If I said yes, would you believe me?"

"No. She isn't your type."

Guy smiled, but said nothing.

"What age are you, if it isn't a rude question?"

"Thirty-one."

"Really? You seem older somehow, but that would be the war, I suppose. I'm told you were quite an ace, shooting down twelve enemy planes in your Hurricane and being decorated for it." She placed a cigarette in her holder. At once he jumped to his feet and lit it for her. "Any young woman would be rather bowled over by such a hero. Clearly Jennie was." She inhaled then leaned back, smiling up at him. "Poor Guy. What a mess it all is for you."

Sitting back in his chair once more, he lit his own cigarette then placed the lighter back in his pocket. "I don't know what you mean."

Laura's eyes narrowed. "Oh, come now. Wife too young, easily seduced, now a baby. A mess for you and a mess for Jennie, coming on top of everything else." She paused and drew on the cigarette once more. "I suppose you've already gathered that since my brother shows a marked reluctance to return home, Trevellan could well go to my son, Clive? You two still haven't met. Clive was the one forced out of the London house to accommodate you and Jennie."

"Ah ... yes, that was rather unfortunate," murmured Guy, feeling wrongfooted.

Laura stood up, took his glass and refilled it, saying, "I do hope you weren't led into thinking you were marrying an heiress? That would have been the last straw."

Stung by this acid remark, Guy's patience snapped. "That was a bloody thing to say. Bloody and completely wrong."

She handed him the glass, still smiling. "Then I'm sorry. Perhaps you didn't need this second drink after all. You have my word we shall not speak of it again." Returning to the sofa she sat down. "Is what you do very dangerous?"

"What I do," said Guy tersely, "is classified." He drank quickly, his irritation with this woman now hard to control. "Damn it, how long must I wait to see my wife and son? Should I have booked an appointment perhaps?"

"Patience. You'll need a lot of it where Jennie's concerned. Tell me something, Guy. Charles was not at your wedding, was he?" When he shook his head, she sighed a little and nodded hers. "I thought as much. I know the reason why he isn't coming home so we don't need to skirt around each other on that one. You see, I've always known. What a pity it all is." She paused, hoping he would open up and confirm to her what Jennie refused to admit she even knew. When he remained silent, her anger was hard to contain. "Well, frankly I think it's a cruel nonsense to keep the truth from my parents. They'll have to learn it soon enough. Not all of it, of course, but they'll have to know that Charles is never going to return. You can see why, can't you? So much depends on it. I would like you to persuade Jennie of that then perhaps we can escape crippling death duties when my father dies."

Guy felt his heart sinking. Charles never to return? Did Laura really believe that or was it wishful thinking on her part? Either way she must deem him stupid if she thought he would persuade Jennie to act against her own interests. He stared down into his glass feeling depressed, but said nothing.

Taking his silence for doubt, Laura decided to change tack. "I see you understand these things. You struck me from the first as being an intelligent man who knows what is right. My father will never hand the estate to Jennie. Therefore, I've asked Charles to write to his father, giving up all claims in favour of his nephew now. The handover should be soon since, I believe, it must be done seven years before my father's death. As you know, he is not a well man. But I'd rather the blow was softened for my parents before that letter arrives and Jennie is the only one who can do that." She paused and smiled. "You do see, don't you?"

He could see only too well, but still had no idea why Charles Veryan had fallen out with his daughter and remained in Singapore. Jennie refused to discuss the issue and he had grown tired of asking. By saying nothing to Laura now he thought she might produce the answer to this mystery but the door opened at that moment and Keynes entered, saying that Mrs Lloyd was now ready to receive visitors.

Visitors! Guy put down his drink and followed the butler up the stairs to his wife's bedroom. Jennie, as he had supposed, was sitting up, but far from serene and beautiful, looked frail with dark shadows under her eyes and seemed to be disappearing into the bed. Trying to mask his shock, he approached and kissed her gently on the mouth. "Well done, darling. Well done."

The nurse walked towards him holding a small cream bundle. He looked down at the tiny scrap of humanity wrapped in a lace knit shawl, small fist in mouth and looking up at him with the brightest blue eyes. His son! It was hard to take in. Strange sucking noises came from that rosebud mouth. There was a sweet smell of baby powder. Asked if he wished to hold his baby, Guy looked as though he had been asked to jump without a parachute.

"He won't break," said the nurse.

"It'll wake him up or something."

"He's already wide awake," said Jennie. "Don't you think he's beautiful?"

Guy nodded then turned and walked back to the bed where he sat down on the chair beside Jennie. She looked so ill and exhausted that he suddenly felt a love for her which, until now, he was not sure he possessed. Taking her hand in his, he stroked it gently. "I'm glad you've agreed to call him Alexander."

She smiled. "Do you expect him to conquer worlds for you?"

"Why not? He's my son after all." My son! How odd it sounded

244

when it was difficult to accept that the small bundle with sandy hair and bright blue eyes was anything other than a stranger to him. But for a pretty Dutch girl being returned to her parents, little Alexander would not now exist. So much for planning one's life. What was the point if a man's fate turned on events which had nothing to do with him in the first place? His son! He watched as the nurse placed the baby back into the crib and then left the room. "Alexander." He repeated the name as if trying to fix it in his mind as belonging to someone other than his brother. "He was the hope of the family, the one who would take over the law business after my father's death. Unfortunately, he was torpedoed early in the war. Mother never got over it. It did something to her mind."

As he spoke, Jennie remembered the cold autocratic widow who, apart from a housekeeper, lived alone in a large Victorian house in the New Forest. Remote from her younger son in every way, Mrs Lloyd had made it plain enough that she regarded Jennie as an interloping stranger. It was also made plain that she had never stopped mourning for her first born and heedless of Guy's feelings had talked ceaselessly about Alexander throughout. Angered and hurt, Jennie had decided that her mother-in-law was quite "ga-ga" and had not returned to Brockenhurst since. Afraid that giving this name to her son might only evoke unpleasant memories, she had finally given in to Guy's wish then added "Philip" to keep her own family happy.

"How long will you be remaining here?" asked Guy.

Jennie held his hand tightly. "Until the doctor says I'm fit enough to leave. Blood pressure isn't going any higher so I'm spared the hospital at least." She looked at him with soft eyes. "I feel so tired and woozy that it's nice to be looked after and waited on. But it's a long way for you to travel, so you mustn't think you have to keep driving down here. Oh, that's another thing. Grandmother's insisting on a nanny. Can you afford that?"

Guy shrugged. "If you're not well enough to cope then we shall need someone who can."

Jennie smiled and shook her head. "It's Grandma, sticking to the only way she knows. I never had a nanny. Maman raised me herself." She stared at him with searching eyes. "What are we going to do? We're a family now and need to live together all the time, not just at weekends. We need a home of our own, Guy."

He became guarded, and patted her hand. "And we shall have one. But there's no point in uprooting you and baby from London until I'm settled. Wait until the course is finished." To his surprise and dismay, Jennie suddenly burst into tears.

Reaching under the pillow for a damp handkerchief, she held it to her eyes. "Sorry," she sniffed, "I keep doing this ... crying when I should be happy. I don't know what's wrong with me. I feel horrible, look horrible, and have this awful dread every time they bring the baby anywhere near me. I'm afraid of my own baby, isn't that terrible? I'm afraid to hold him, afraid when he cries. That's all wrong, isn't it? Mothers shouldn't feel that way."

"Oh, you'd be surprised how many do," said the nurse as she re-entered the room. "That too passes with time." She looked at Guy and signalled with her eyes. "Time now for this young mother to rest."

He left and took luncheon with the rest of the family in the dining room, noticing that only Philip was affable. He wondered why. Later he accompanied the old man on a stroll through the wooded valley and, seizing the moment, touched on the question of accommodation. "I feel it's so wrong that we should be living in your London home, Sir, but I want to do what is right for Jennie. When I leave Farnborough I'll be posted to Boscombe Down. Accommodation is limited there. I don't think Jennie would like to live in some little rented cottage where she knows no one. So, if it is possible to stay on at Kensington Square, I should be most grateful and, of course, insist upon paying rent."

Philip, who had been kept in the dark by Florence and Laura on the truth about Alexander's sudden arrival, and hadn't for one moment thought to count the months himself, now turned to Guy and said: "Of course you may stay on, old boy. And forget the rent. You can put that towards a house of your own one day." He was proud to have one of "the few" as a son-in-law. Guy had fought for his country and the Empire, had saved Jennie's life and was brave enough to be a test pilot. He was the right sort. Older than Jennie too, and she needed a steadying influence. He wanted no more scandals around the Veryan name, especially now that Monique had made it so illustrious.

"That's kind of you, Sir," Guy was saying. "But I really should pay rent."

"Nonesense. Use the place for as long as you wish. After all, I pay a housekeeper to look after it. We rarely get up to London these days and Clive's resettled himself in a mews flat." He stopped to catch his breath. "How's the course going?"

"Mind boggling," said Guy, kicking up last year's fallen leaves and listening to the sound of the stream that flowed down to the cove. "We fly anything and everything from piston engines to jet fighters and bombers. There are lectures galore, hours spent studying aerodynamics, long reports to write up and constant checks to see that we're up to scratch. I love it, but won't pretend it isn't a strain."

"And Boscombe Down? How long will you be there?"

Guy considered this for a moment. "That depends on whether I stay in the Service or not. If I do, I'm bound to wind up at a desk sooner or later. I want to fly."

"You'd resign your commission?" Philip stopped walking and frowned. "Where would you go? De Havilland's, Hawker's ... where?"

"When the time is right, I'd try for Hadleigh's. An old colleague of mine is now their Chief Test Pilot. He's already asked me to think about joining their team one day." Guy turned to the old man. "So you can see why there's little stability in my life at present. It doesn't matter for me, but I do want Jennie and Alex to be secure."

"Then stay at Kensington Square, my boy. I mean to hand the estate over to Charles when he returns. Until then, the London house is in my gift."

Guy thanked him but as they walked on thought again of Laura's words. Was this kind old man being allowed to live on false hope? That was iniquitous. If Jennie knew that her father was not going to return then she should say so. On the other hand there was Alexander to think about. The grandson of the heir could hardly be ignored, whatever Laura thought. Had Jennie been playing for time? Was she that shrewd? It dawned on him then that he really knew very little about the woman he had married.

On the morning of Christmas Eve, Jennie stood at her easel in the Grand Chamber, while Florence sat with the light from the window falling on to her face. The painting had been started a week earlier, a calming thing for Jennie as her blood pressure had finally dropped to normal and she had been given a clean bill of health at last. But this close to Christmas, it seemed better to stay put rather than upset Alex's routine by journeying back and forth to London. She had spent only one Christmas away from Trevellan since arriving here during the war, and it simply had not occurred to her to be anywhere else. During her long convalescence she had painted daily, but this was her first attempt at portraiture since leaving the Slade with her Diploma, and Florence had agreed to be guinea pig. After a shaky start, things were now going well and her confidence had grown with each stroke of the brush.

Florence sighed a little and moved her shoulders. "I don't understand it. I simply do not understand it. I thought your father would be home for Christmas, truly I did. He must be well by now, but when he bothers to write at all he says nothing about his health or when we can expect him. I think there's something wrong, something he's keeping from us. I sense it in his letters. Have you any idea what it might be?"

Jennie's hand tightened on the brush and she stopped painting. Should she now break her silence? Was this the time? But she had made that promise and must leave it to her father. Supposing she said one

247

thing and he another? How would that look? Besides, she hardly relished being the one to strike such a blow. "I did say it might take months. He has a lot to come to terms with. It can't be easy for him." Why wasn't he telling them the truth? He had said he would. Now that the rage had gone, she had written to him apologising for her behaviour, but words once uttered and actions once committed could never be taken back, even though she longed for it with all her heart. Poor Papa. Between Japanese ill treatment, his sister's letter and his daughter's rejection, he had stood no chance. Two weeks ago she'd received his congratulations on Alexander's birth but the letter seemed remote and formal. There was no hint of an acceptance of her apology, no word of his relationship with Jamie, and no word either of a change of heart over returning home.

"They'll be here by tea-time," said Florence, changing the subject. "I do hope we shan't miss the carol service from King's College. I don't want everyone chattering away over that. I wonder what you'll think of Clive's fiancee?"

Clive coming for Christmas! It was an appalling prospect, since she had banked on his spending it with his prospective in-laws. The brush moved on the canvas again, capturing the lock of grey hair about the temple. "What do *you* think of her?"

After a pause: "I didn't see enough of Fenella to gain much of an impression when they came here in August."

Jennie smiled. "That's Veryan for 'don't like her'. Why not?"

Easing her body into a slight stretch, Florence murmured: "Oh, I don't know. I suppose it's because she just isn't one of us."

"Oh, Grandma, that's snobbish and old-fashioned."

"No. Just realistic. She's a grocer's daughter. Oh, I grant you a very wealthy grocer, with a chain of shops, but a grocer when all is said and done, so what would she know about the ways of a country house and the responsibilities that go with owning an estate?"

Jennie's lips tightened. "You think she'll need to know such things, do you?" When Florence made no reply, her anxiety increased. Clive! She hated him as much as ever. Yesterday was the first she had heard of his imminent arrival. "What does Grandpa think of her?"

"Your grandfather's a silly old fool. His brain's going soft, I'm sure of it."

"You mean he likes her. And Aunt Laura?"

Florence looked anxious. "Your aunt hopes this wedding won't take place."

Jennie looked up in surprise "But they're officially engaged now. *The Times* carried the announcement and they had that huge party." It was a party she had neither wished to attend nor been able to. Alexander had been a shade too obvious at the time. She put down her brush and stood back to examine the half-completed work with a critical eye. "That's it for today."

"Thank heaven for that." Florence got to her feet and rubbed her aching back before picking up the walking stick and making her way across the room towards Jennie. "Am I to be allowed to see this masterpiece today?"

"No," said Jennie. "Not until it's completed."

"Well, make it snappy or you'll be propping up a corpse in that chair." Florence headed for the door. "Sitting is very tiring, but at least I've enjoyed our chats. We never seem to have the time otherwise. Now then, I must see Keynes and Mrs Hodges and check on all the arrangements."

When her grandmother had gone, Jennie cleaned her brushes and left everything in good order, unlike Gavin who always left his studio in chaos. As she made her way to the small bedroom which had now become a temporary nursery, Alexander's hungry cry could be heard shattering the peace of the old house. Nanny Davies was walking up and down the room with the baby resting on her shoulder as Jennie entered. Norland-trained and in her mid- forties, the nanny was busty, capable, and would brook no nonsense from baby or mother. At first, it seemed they would never get on but these past two weeks had made Jennie change her mind. For all her "no-nonsense" approach, the woman was kind and had a sense of humour so that Jennie felt she would have no qualms about leaving her precious son in the care of such a person.

Having breast fed Alex for five weeks, Jennie had now put her son on the bottle which Laura had urged her to do from the beginning, saying she would never get her figure back otherwise. Since her son was more important than her figure, Jennie had only stopped when Alex needed more than she could give. Slowly, she was getting back to her old self. It was just as well, she thought now, as she sat with Alex in her arms, easing the teat of the bottle into his mouth. Guy would have been embarrassed at the sight of a child suckling from its mother, and during his second visit she had taken herself off to the privacy of the nursery.

The fact that Guy had not come more than twice had only served to focus her thoughts on Mark and, as her health improved, she spent her days walking to the cove and across the cliffs always hoping, always looking, always wondering what she would say or do should he suddenly appear. Then had come the day she knew had to come sooner or later. She could not for ever keep away from the Curnows and avoid Frank when he was around the house so much. The ice had to be broken between them, and so she had called on Mabel to enquire about

249

her health and finally, casually, with heart pounding against her ribs, asked: "How is Mark these days, and where is he? Will he be home for Christmas?"

Mabel had given her a long, hard look and then delivered the terrible blow. "Mark is to be married soon. He's spending Christmas with her family. We haven't seen him since April and so we know nothing about her."

Even the memory of that terrible moment made her feel physically ill. At the time she must have turned pale for Mabel had become concerned, wanting to telephone for a car to come from the big house to take her home. She had finally managed to walk away with some small measure of dignity, but once back at the house had rushed up to her room and wept until she could weep no more. That had been over three weeks ago. Since then she had forced herself to come to terms with the inevitable, concentrating on her baby, her painting and her future plans. And the worst of it was, that she still had no idea where Mark had gone. Alexander had stopped feeding and was gazing up at her with a little smile. She murmured to him; he kicked his legs then hooked his tiny fingers about hers. Loving such precious moments with her child, she insisted on them even now that Nanny could give him his bottle. Turning Alex over, she laid him across her lap and patted his back very lightly until he gave the loudest burp. "Good boy."

Later, when she had handed him back to Nanny Davies, she prepared for Guy's arrival. The last thing he would want to see was the mumsy creature she had happily become. After a long relaxing bath, she returned to the Chinese Room where she lay on the bed, reading Louise's Christmas card and letter once more. Louise was thrilled about the baby then said that her father had been promoted which meant a posting to Hong Kong. She, however, was not going with them:

Much as I should love to see the Colony, I really have to make a start on my future career. I've already written to the BBC and hope to get an interview. So then, I'll be home in April. Any chance of staying with you until I find a flat?

By the way, I went to the bookshop yesterday. Everything there is just the same. Dodo didn't recognise me but your father did. We talked for some time. He said he was very happy about his grandson and hopes to have a photo soon. But, oh, Jennie, I thought he looked so very sad. I still don't know why you left him out here, but that's your affair. I'm just so very sorry.

I do hope you and Guy are happy. Once again we're all so pleased

250

about your baby – and a boy too. Can't wait to see him, and you.
Until April then.
All my love,
Louise.

At ten to three, while Florence and Philip were taking their afternoon rest, Clive and Fenella arrived. Both were the worse for wear after an all-night party in London yet, even in a state of acute hang-over, Fenella sent Jennie's heart to her shoes. Dressed in a tailored green suit, her long slim skirt covering the equally long slim legs, she strode with confidence into the hall, gloved hand on the mink stole about her shoulders, an elegant hat over her short brunette hair. Her bright lipstick was rather startling on such a pale face, and the blue eye shadow too harsh for the grey eyes which were fixed on Jennie.

Groomed, thought Jennie. Not pretty, not even attractive with that bland expression and a shade too much make-up, but beautifully turned out. She walked forward to greet Clive's future bride and the two shook hands. Fenella then removed her black gloves to reveal long scarlet nails which drew attention to her fingers as much as the rings which adorned them.

Laura was waiting in the library, a tense expression on her face, as Fenella went through the usual show of kissing her on the cheek without making contact, before throwing herself down into Philip's favourite chair, crossing her shapely legs and declaring: "That was, without doubt, the worst journey I've ever endured. Fog, traffic – oh, and an accident somewhere near Honiton. I thought we'd never get here."

"What time did you set off?" asked Jennie.

Fenella turned to her as if trying to recall who she was. "Oh, about ten. We stopped for lunch. Hair of the dog, you know. Do you have an asprin? I've got this damned headache. I think I should like to lie down for a while."

"What a good idea," snapped Laura. "Drink plenty of water. Too much alchohol does dehydrate one so."

Glancing at her aunt's cold expression, Jennie saved the moment. "Come on, I'll show you your room."

Unconcerned at Laura's little outburst, Fenella followed Jennie up the stairs, pausing briefly to admire the tall Christmas tree which dominated the hall. "It really is quite beautiful."

"We've had it for a week now. It always goes up in time for the estate party."

"Estate party? Really? How quaint and Dickensian. I didn't know such things still happened." Fenella started up the stairs once more.

251

"You've just had a baby, I believe, and you're married to a test pilot?" When Jennie said "yes" to both questions, Fenella brightened considerably. "I've never met a test pilot. Is he here yet?"

Pausing slightly, Jennie shook her head. "No. You said the fog was bad. How bad?"

"Thick as soup in some parts," came the tactless reply. She stood looking at Jennie quizzically. "You live apart from him, I understand?"

Trust Clive. "It isn't what you think. I'll explain some other time." Jennie opened the door to her old room, saying, "Here we are. I hope you'll be comfortable. I always was."

Fenella sauntered in and glanced at the antique furniture. "Rather heavy, isn't it? I'd have all this out and a modern suite put in. My parents live in Cowes. Daddy's a keen yachtsman. I thought our house was big enough but Trevellan ... well ... it takes my breath away." She shivered and walked to the fireplace, bending to warm her hands at the glowing coals. "Ours, of course, has good central heating, four bathrooms, and an indoor swimming pool. It was built to Daddy's design."

"Well, central heating is something we hope to install when the estate can afford it."

"Afford?" The dark pencilled eyebrows rose in surprise.

"Yes," said Jennie, lightly. "The upkeep of a place like this is incredibly expensive." She glanced through the window and saw mist drifting about the tall trees bordering the south lawn. "But I love Trevellan, for all its problems and antiquated plumbing. At the moment it needs a great deal of restoration work. The roof to start with, and a host of other things: dry rot, rising damp, woodworm ... you name it, we've got it."

Fenella stared, unsure whether this was a joke or not, then repeated that her head ached like mad and that she would die if someone didn't bring her an asprin soon. Jennie fetched the tablets and a glass of water then left the woman in peace.

In the Chinese Room she changed from the twin set and skirt into a blue wool dress then stood in front of the full-length mirror wondering why she had bothered. The dress, bought solely because her others still did not fit, no longer seemed as slimming and sophisticated as she had thought it did. Against Fenella, she looked a poor dumpy thing tied up in a sack. What had happened to her French flair for dressing? Why had all things French suddenly deserted her? Running her fingers through the shoulder-length hair, she decided to put it back into a French plait, buff up the make-up and put on the double row of pearls which Florence had given to her on her twenty-first birthday. The pearls were an heirloom, and Laura had been furious, saying that all of her mother's jewellery should, by rights, go to her and not a grand-

252

daughter. This little outburst had upset Florence, much to Jennie's dismay, and the birthday party had been spoilt. Now it seemed there would be three Willoughby magpies to take what they could so why not wear the pearls as a cautionary tale to the greedy? Anyway, she needed all the help she could get right now.

Guy arrived as "Carols from Kings" finished. Jennie ran to greet him in the hallway, relieved he had made it in one piece. She knew the way he drove the Jaguar and often wondered if he had forgotten he was still on the ground.

He kissed her lightly on the lips, and watched as Keynes took his things up the stairs. "Bloody awful journey. Peasouper for most of the way. Sorry I couldn't make it yesterday, as I'd hoped, but there was so much paperwork to finish. Christ, I could do with a stiff drink."

Jennie put an affectionate arm about him. "Alex is about to be put down for the night. Wouldn't you like to see him first?"

Feeling suitably chastised, he followed her up to the nursery in time to watch Alex being bathed and dressed in a winceyette gown, then walked with Jennie to their own room. Inside, he pulled her close to him, kissed her roughly on the mouth then pulled away awkwardly, almost guiltily.

Feeling the sting of rejection, Jennie tried not to show it. "Clive and Fenella are in the drawing room," she said brightly. "They're both suffering from gigantic hangovers. Even so they'll be waiting for you to join them. Meanwhile I must feed Alex."

"Oh, Christ, I couldn't face any of your family alone. Ask Nanny to feed the baby. It's her job, isn't it?"

"But I love feeding and cuddling him. He'll miss me if I don't."

"Jennie, you have nothing to do all day but play mother. It's a hellish long way to drive only to play second fiddle."

Second fiddle? Was he jealous of his own little son? Was that why he had only been here twice since the birth? Shocked at the thought, Jennie decided he was more likely just tired after the bad journey and that she was being selfish. "All right, Nanny can feed him. I'll get Keynes to bring up a drinks tray, then you can relax before you bathe and change for dinner."

Guy let his shoulders sag, then fell back on the bed, too weary to be bothered taking his shoes off first. "No ... no. I didn't mean to snap. Go and feed our son. Whatever the routine, I'll fit around it. But I would like that drink."

She turned at the door and looked back at him. He thought her beautiful then, radiant almost. The last time he had seen her she was fatter of face and figure, not at all the slip of a thing he had saved from a mob. But now, in the soft light of the bedroom, she was slim and glowing once more. He wanted to hold her, kiss her naked body, smell her perfumed flesh and clean shining hair. He would have to be patient. He smiled, his eyes softening.

Jennie saw the look on his face and felt loved once more.

Throughout Christmas she tried to hang on to that feeling as Fenella dominated the household. Clive could not take his eyes off his fiancee and hung on her every word, fascinated by her worldliness and sophistication. It seemed she knew every nightclub in London, rubbed shoulders with the "international set" and name dropped at every opportunity, something the Veryans found vulgar.

"It was in Monte that I met Clive. He had just lost heavily at the gaming tables and I was in the nick of time to prevent him shooting himself. Then we made a real night of it, ending up tearing around hairpin bends at four in the morning to crash in on a party that the Viscomte de Valois was giving. Don't you remember, Clive?" She laughed loudly, and went on and on, oblivious of cold stares from Laura.

Guy also was unable to keep his eyes off Fenella and she knew it, thriving on all this male attention, even twisting staid old Philip around her little finger. Jennie watched in silent fury, thought of Mark spending Christmas with his new love and somehow felt doubly betrayed. But her true dislike of the woman started on Christmas morning when the family attended church, filling their private pews and drawing much interest. Being the cause of this interest Fenella played it up to the hilt, as though already adapting to the role she thought would one day be hers. After the service, Philip, Clive and even Guy stood in attendance on her while the men of Portlyn could not take their eyes off the tall, sophisticated woman in their midst.

O Come All Ye Faithful, thought Jennie. Damned cheek!

After Christmas dinner, they took coffee and brandy in the drawing room where Florence suggested that Jennie play the piano for them. "You used to play so well."

Surprised at the sudden request, Jennie smiled, feeling staid, boring, plain and lumpy against Fenella's firebird. "No, Grandma. I've always played badly."

"Too right," said Clive, re-filling his brandy glass. "Anyway it's time to dance. Come on, everyone, upstairs to the Grand Chamber."

Fenella jumped to her feet and started pulling Guy to his, laughing a shade too loudly. "And I insist on having the first dance with you."

"But there's no fire lit up there," said Florence.

"Yes, there is," said Clive, heading for the door. "I asked Rosa to light one late this afternoon and to keep it going."

"Did you indeed?" Florence raised her eyebrows. How dare he give orders to her staff? "Well, we mustn't let Rosa's extra work on Christmas Day go to waste, must we? But Jennie's painting my portrait in there. I don't want any harm to come to it."

Fenella looked surprised. "Jennie is painting your portrait? What fun. Are you any good, Jennie?"

"She studied art at the Slade," said Florence, using her stick to help her stiff body out of the chair. "Of course she's good."

"Don't worry," said Clive sarcastically, "we won't go within ten feet of the great masterpiece. Come on, everyone. Let's party."

Inside the elegant room, Philip made his way to the sofa and sank down on it, brandy balloon in one hand, cigar in the other, both against doctor's orders but this was Christmas. Having said nothing of his heartaching disappointment that Charles was not here among them as he had fully expected he would be, the old man glanced about him wondering when they had last used this room for dancing. Not since the war. They'd both been here then, Charles and Monique, waltzing away so happily. Then those brutes in Whitehall had sent his only son to Singapore. He would like to shoot the lot and stand their heads on London Bridge.

As Clive made for the radiogram and started searching through the records kept in a walnut cabinet, Fenella made straight for the painting. Jennie headed her off, saying that she would prefer that no one saw it until was completed.

Smiling with amusement, Fenella's eyebrows arched. "Why ever not? If you're that good, what's so secret about it?"

Her attitude set the hair rising on the back of Jennie's neck but her voice remained calm as she answered: "Even Grandma hasn't been allowed to peek. Not until it's finished. Sorry."

Feeling suitably snubbed, Fenella scoffed, "Goodness, what a fuss over nothing. Come along, Guy, let's dance."

Guy glanced at Jennie, thought how attractive she looked in her long turquoise gown, then allowed himself to be dragged on to the floor. As he danced with Fenella he was all too aware that she was flirting with him, but stayed the course, even when she leant her head against his shoulder. Drunk, he told himself. She'd drunk too much and was becoming a bore. Later, when he danced Jennie around the floor to a foxtrot, he seemed bemused. "Why are you against anyone looking at the painting? Is there a problem with it?"

"It's going very well, as a matter of fact," she said quietly. "But I don't like people making judgements on half-finished work. In any case, Fenella isn't really interested, she just wants to make fun of me.

255

And whereas I welcome constructive criticism from the well-informed, I don't need it from someone who knows nothing about the subject."

He grinned infuriatingly. "Sounds more like bitchiness to me."

"I didn't think you would understand," she retorted.

Another record was put on. Sensing he had angered her, Guy pulled Jennie closer to him and moved around the room slowly to *As Time Goes By*. "Did you see *Casablanca*?" She looked vague then shook her head. To Guy it was yet another reminder that ten years stood between them, ten years going on twenty suddenly. He found himself looking towards Fenella who was closer in age to him and did not have the Veryan stuffiness.

Sensing his thoughts, Jennie wanted to stamp on his foot. Instead she drew his attention back to her by saying, "Maddie's going to come down later to see the portrait. If she thinks I'm good enough, she'll try to put some work my way. So it's very important to me that the painting should be as perfect as I can possibly make it. I'm nervous about it, Guy."

He looked surprised and grinned. "Nervous? Good God! It's not that important, surely?"

Jennie looked up at him sharply. "Not important! It's everything to me. What am I if I can't be a painter?"

"My wife. That's all you're meant to be, surely?" He frowned, remembering those occasions when he had sat with Jennie and Maddie and all their arty friends. How they had gone on about painters and writers he had never heard of even. Jennie was of that world, setting her apart from him and making him feel inferior when, before, he had felt himself her superior and protector. Independent women were fine, and he had always felt safer with them, but independence in his wife was another thing. That threatened his role.

Wife! Jennie's anger was rising. He wanted her to be a shadow without an existence of her own, just like all those other wives who lived through their husbands, sitting at home, waiting, waiting. What was the use in arguing about it? He would never understand that painting was to her what flying was to him.

"Change partners for a waltz." Clive's voice shattered the atmosphere as he reached for Laura.

Before Jennie could work out what was happening, Fenella had pulled Guy away from her, the record started and a female singer closed up the years singing, *Parlez Moi D'amour*.

As she heard the music, Jennie stood frozen in time while the dancers moved around her. Then she stepped to one side, seeing not her husband with Fenella but her mother waltzing with her father. Her mother was smiling through her tears, her father was tall and

256

handsome, then they looked towards her and beckoned. For one split second she started moving towards them then checked herself as they suddenly became Guy and Fenella once more. On and on went the song until she could bear the heartache no longer and slipped from the room.

When the dance had finished, Clive approached Guy and said: "You've put up a bit of a black, old boy. Your wife's just left in a foul temper."

Fenella feigned surprise. "Oh, I am sorry, Guy. I'd no idea that my dancing with you would cause trouble."

Embarrassed and angry, he excused himself and left the room to find Jennie seated on the top stair dabbing at her eyes with a lace handkerchief. "Christ! Wasn't that rather childish? Grow up, Jennie, for God's sake."

Starting at his voice behind her, Jennie turned a tear-stained face up to his angry eyes. "Oh, Guy. Please go back and enjoy the dance. I'll follow later."

"How the hell can I after that juvenile display of jealousy?"

She frowned in puzzlement for a moment, then said, "What? No ... no ... you're mistaken ... you don't understand."

"I understand all right. I'll leave you to your little tantrum. If you get over it, come back to the party. If not, go to bed." As he returned to the Grand Chamber, Florence left it and slowly approached her distraught grand-daughter with deep concern.

"I know ... I know," she murmured. "Clive didn't realise, of course. He doesn't remember as we do." She frowned. "Guy looked very put out. I believe he misunderstood. Did you explain to him?"

Jennie dried her eyes and tried to pull herself together. "He didn't give me the chance." She rose slowly, holding the taffeta skirt of her long gown. "I must look dreadful."

"You look just fine," said Florence. "Quick splash of cold water and a touch of face powder will do wonders. But you know, my dear, it's we old folks who live on memories and drive everybody mad with them. You have all your life ahead, so be happy, otherwise people will turn away from you. Now, you must make your peace with Guy. It *is* Christmas after all, and no one in my house is allowed to cry at Christmas."

Jennie nodded and sniffed. "How did the record get among the others? It was in my bedroom."

"I expect Rosa moved it when she prepared the room for Fenella." She sighed. "Well, it's way past my bedtime. I'll just go back and bid them all goodnight."

Jennie kissed her grandmother on the cheek. "Goodnight then.

257

Sorry for my outburst. I can see how it looked. Stupid of me. But it's been a lovely Christmas, Grandma.''

Florence smiled and nodded. "Alexander's first. Did you see the way he looked at the tree? What a little darling he is.''

In her room Jennie sat in front of the dressing-table mirror, touched up her make-up and thought how quick Guy had been to judge her juvenile and jealous. Such thoughts must have been in his head for some time otherwise he would never have uttered them aloud at this first outburst of real anger. She put more lipstick on, telling herself that it was understandable. How could he have known after all? And what did he see when he came here? Fussing grandmother and nanny; his wife being mollycoddled in the Veryan bosom and living a life of luxury in this lovely old house instead of being in their home. Such a wife would be jealous, for such a wife could not be loved. A cold shudder swept over her. Jennie stared at her reflection, knowing she could not handle rejection yet again. Then she recalled his words: "juvenile display of jealousy." Even so, that was a bit much! How dare he?

The door opened and Guy walked in. "Now look, Jennie . . ."

"No, you look," she said, stiffening at his tone. "You can dance with the Whore of Babylon for all I care, but don't you *ever* speak to me like that again, Guy Lloyd. I'm not jealous and I'm not juvenile. I'm a woman who would prefer to sleep alone tonight, thank you very much." She left the stool, walked to the bed, picked up his pillow and hurled it at him, saying: "Here. You'll find blankets and sheets in the large cupboard one floor up. There are spare rooms on that floor also. Plenty of them. It's the servants' quarters."

Shocked at her outburst, Guy just stood there, too nonplussed to speak. Then he picked up the pillow, threw it back on to the bed and walked out.

Jennie sank on to the bed, trembling. Why, oh why, had she done that? What on earth was the matter with her?

In the drawing room, Guy sat alone by the dying fire, remembering what Florence had told him a short while ago. What a hellish boor he must seem. But how could he have been expected to know? Jennie kept so much locked up inside her that not since that time at the Pattersons' bungalow had she shown so much emotion. It was as though something in her had died and only flickered back into life when that record had been played. And what had he said to help her through that moment? Pouring himself another brandy, he raised the glass. "Well, here's to you, you stupid bastard."

Twenty minutes later he returned to the bedroom to find Jennie seated beside the hearth in her silk nightgown. The firelight glowed on her face and he could see she had been crying. "I was about to tell you earlier how sorry I was and that I understood what had really upset you, but then I came under fire and decided on a strategic withdrawal."

Jennie rose from the chair and walked to the bed. "I'm sorry too, for letting my temper get the better of me. But it hurt, Guy. You must have thought that of me or you wouldn't have said it."

He sat down on the bed, pulled her down beside him and slid an arm about her. "What I do think is that the sooner we're away from here, the better. You're well again now, and I want you back." He cupped her face in his hand and turned it to his. Her tense body began to yield to him as his hands smoothed over her breasts, feeling them soft beneath the nightgown. He gripped it in his hand and said: "For God's sake Jennie, take this bloody thing off."

# Chapter Sixteen

Jennie stood by the window of the large south-facing bedroom, which had now become her studio, and looked out on to Kensington Square. In the mellow sunshine of a September afternoon an elderly woman was feeding sparrows in the central gardens, the trees about her just touched by the first hint of autumn. Below Jennie's window, pyracantha berries sent a splash of bright red across the walls of the house.

The Veryans had owned this three-storied dwelling since 1830 and, save for Laura's insistence on modern beds, new brocade curtains, and a soft sofa with large cushions, the furniture was of the late-eighteenth and early-nineteenth centuries. Jennie loved the well-proportioned rooms, the fine arts and antiques, as much as she loved the peace and quiet to be had here, just a stone's throw from busy Kensington High Street. It was useful for her painting career and for entertaining her many friends, yet still she felt lonely, isolated from Guy and normal family life. That elusive place of their own seemed more elusive than ever and she and Guy seemed to be growing further apart as his weekends home became ever more infrequent. She had tried to pretend it wasn't happening but Louise had made her face up to it.

She had arrived at Southampton in late-March when the country was still mourning the death of the King and claimed at once that she had quite forgotten how pink and podgy the English were. Her animated chatter filled the house as she had set off for an interview with the BBC Appointments Officer, only to return sullen-faced, bemoaning the fact that, instead of working on programmes at Broadcasting House, she was being sent to the television studios in Shepherds Bush. "Television! Not the real BBC at all. Who on earth watches? And it's out in the boondocks, just a poor relation of the real thing." She had, nevertheless, accepted the position offered and before leaving to share a flat with friends in Holland Park had sat up late with Jennie, reminiscing about Roedean, Singapore, and the riots.

"Do you really love Guy?" she had asked, quite suddenly.

"What makes you ask that?"

Louise had shrugged. "Oh, I see things, sense things, like a wide distance between you, a distance that shouldn't be there at this time in your marriage. There's none of the usual affectionate banter between man and wife, almost as though you're both on your best behaviour when you're together. Perhaps it's because of my presence, or perhaps it's because of this strange weekend-only marriage. But do you understand what I mean?"

Jennie had understood only too well. "Things will improve when we have our own house. I know I married him in a panic, but I've come to realise how much I do care for him and I know he cares for me. It's his work . . . he's so busy. When he has a home to come back to each night instead of Messing, then he'll change. I'm sure of it."

Yet even as she spoke she knew that she could never love Guy in the way she had loved Mark. That love was still with her as a distant and unattainable dream which, being just a dream could not really harm her marriage. Now she asked herself if the dream would have faded had the marriage been working? She wanted it to work so much, but Guy was not making it easy. Did he love her? That was the question Louise had not dared to ask. Never in a casual moment did he place his arm about her and, when making love, he was rarely sensitive to her feelings, being too much a man in a hurry. Was that love or merely lust? Even those moments were now few and far between. Absence, she now realised, did not make the heart grow fonder. It only produced an independence of spirit which lessened the need for each other. She had needed to feel loved but was slowly learning to live without that need. Work filled the void and she was lucky to have it. Again Maddie had come through for her.

"Your portrait of Aunt Flo was very good, good enough for you to accept a commission, I think. It's the daughter of a friend of mine, only ten years old but she'll sit quietly, I'm sure of it."

The girl had not sat quietly but fidgeted and sighed with boredom until Jennie had felt utter despair. Only by bringing the child into her confidence and explaining, with the utmost patience, that they were making a painting together and showing her each process, even to the point of letting the girl add a few brush strokes herself, did the situation improve. The result was a portrait of a bright, blue-eyed child with an incandescent face that summed up the vitality and mischievousness of her character.

The mother was delighted and, by word of mouth, more commissions followed. To Jennie's horror they were all to be portraits of children. Maddie rescued her in the end by producing the debutante daughter of another friend.

"*Tatler* on canvas, Jennie," Gavin had laughed. "You have been warned."

But she had been only too glad to have the work and was enough of a realist to know that, for all her talent, it was Maddie who was getting the commissions that her Slade contempories would have died for. Without her second cousin, she too would be just another artist struggling to make a name. Now, as she inspected the portrait, she felt pleased with it. Just a few finishing touches then it would be ready for varnishing.

Turning to the window, she wondered if Guy would telephone? At four o'clock on a Friday afternoon it would be useful to know whether she could expect him home or not.

At that moment, Nanny Davies moved into her sight, pushing a large black pram. A small teddy bear suddenly flew from it to the ground. Nanny bent to pick it up and Jennie smiled. At eleven months, her son was highly active, curious and demanding. The teddy routine was a wearisome part of the daily walk and Nanny had clearly had enough of it. She placed the toy in a small basket and walked on. Alexander's howls of rage could be heard across Kensington.

There had been two weddings that summer. The first was that of her old suitor and now close friend, Colin Harte-Willis, to the pretty but vacuous Arabella Meacham, a baronet's daughter who had befriended Jennie at the many dances they had attended during that dizzy "coming out" year which now seemed so very long ago. Fond of them both, Jennie was glad that Colin had found his soulmate at last. Between their Knightsbridge flat and his parents' country estate, the couple would no doubt ride to hounds, raise two perfect children, four labradors, and live in blissful contentment.

The wedding which followed Colin's was not such a welcome affair.

So that his daughter's marriage would not interfere with his preparations for Cowes Week, Cedric Lytton had given Fenella away to Clive Willoughby on a chilly day at the beginning of July when most of the guests longed to be at Wimbledon. It stayed fine for the wedding photographs outside the church but poured down later, turning the fine lawns of the Lyttons' rambling home into a quagmire and causing everyone to huddle inside the large marquee for the rest of the day.

Somewhat surprised at having received an invitation at all, Jennie and Guy had only attended to please Florence who had telephoned them with a *cri de coeur*.

"But you must go, if only to even up the odds at the church. There'll be hundreds of her people, and so few of ours. Your aunt will be absolutely furious if she's forced to sit next to John Willoughby, as I expect she will be, so I'll need some moral support, Jennie. Your grandfather's not well enough to go, and I don't want to be left sitting on a chair in a corner all by myself. Then there's that wretched ferry crossing to the Isle of Wight. Why they couldn't get married at St Margaret's, Westminster, and have the reception at The Ritz, like normal people, I'll never understand."

"Why must you go at all?"

At this her grandmother had sounded indignant. "If I don't it will be seen as a snub. They might accept your grandfather's ill health but not mine as well. They'll think we don't approve."

"But you don't."

"Of course we don't. But it's a *fait accompli* now. So why make matters worse?"

And so they had accepted the invitation and Jennie had shivered the day through in her tight-waisted, full-skirted, dark blue grosgrain dress, watched her own husband eyeing the bride admiringly, listened to a witless, *risqué* speech given by Clive's best man, and finally waved the couple off for their Monte Carlo honeymoon with great relief. As the Daimler pulled away and confetti lay everywhere, Florence, who had spent most of the afternoon seated on a chair surrounded by strangers and looking marvellous in powder blue, said quietly: "Well, that's that. Sad about the weather though."

Jennie had smiled. "'Happy the bride the sun shines on'." She glanced about her then whispered: "And Fenella's just tied herself to Clive."

"Now that was uncalled for, my dear," murmured Florence as they returned to the marquee. "Although I do have to say that things are not off to a good start. It seems that John Willoughby gave the happy couple a Royal Doulton dinner service while, not to be puffed by a man living in a mansion, the Lyttons have given them a rather substantial six-bedroomed house in Dorking complete with indoor swimming pool. Goodness! Clearly we should have been grocers instead of land-owners." She sat down in her chair once more and sipped the remains of her champagne. "Battle lines have been drawn." The pale eyes twinkled mischievously. Florence was having a very good day.

Jennie saw Guy enter the marquee at that point. For a moment he stood searching the crowd for her, found Laura instead and another glass of champagne. "What did Aunt Laura give them?"

"Six crystal sherry glasses. And they were lucky to get those, I might add." Florence glanced about her and lowered her voice to the merest of whispers. "Apart from disliking Fenella she looks down on the Lyttons too, which is a shame since, now that I've met them, I think

263

they're quite charming. That's more than can be said of their one and only, however. Spoilt to death, that's the trouble there. And a tippler into the bargain."

Smiling now at the memory of that day, Jennie's thoughts turned to another wedding, one which no one spoke of and she dare not ask about. Where was Mark now? What was his wife like? Could he really love another when he had looked at her with such intense emotion? Would this dull ache in her heart never vanish?

Nanny had entered the house now and was manoeuvring the large pram along the hall to its resting place in the old, and now redundant, butler's pantry. Jennie rushed down the stairs and picked up her heavy son from the pram. "Hello, darling. Have you been a good boy then?"

"Couldn't you hear him?" said Nanny tersely. "There are times when I hardly know where to look. Isn't that so, Master Alex?"

Alex laughed with glee, pulled at Jennie's hair then demanded his teddy bear from the basket. Jennie gave it to him, just as the telephone rang. Nanny answered, then handed the receiver to Jennie. "It's the Squadron Leader, for you. I'll take Alex up to the nursery."

"Fine. I'll be there to play with him in a minute." Jennie took the receiver, pushed down her anger at being taken for granted and asked Guy calmly whether or not he intended to come home for the weekend.

"It's the Farnborough Air Show. I want to see Keith putting the Hadleigh jet through its paces."

Jennie frowned. "Farnborough? You didn't mention it to me last week."

"Didn't I? Could have sworn I did."

"No, Guy, that must have been someone else," she said tartly.

After a moment's pause, he said: "You ought to join me, you know." She blinked in surprise. "At Farnborough?"

"Yes, at Farnborough. Oh, forget it. It's not your kind of thing."

It wasn't. The idea of standing among thick crowds at a noisy airshow was not her kind of thing at all, but she hated the assumption that it wouldn't be. "How would I know? I've never been given the chance to find out."

There was another pause. "All right. I'm giving you the chance. Come tomorrow. Kay will be there and you'd be company for each other." He waited for the penny to drop then sighed. "Kay Chatham. Keith's wife. I've spoken about them before. Keith and I were in the same fighter squadron during the war. He's the Chief Test Pilot for Hadleigh's."

"Keith Chatham! Yes, of course I remember." Knowing she was about to be accused, yet again, of not listening, she fended off the accusation with one of her own. "I seem to recall asking you to invite them both for dinner. But you never have."

"They have two young children, and London's a long way from Stannington. A dinner invitation would be out. You'd need to invite the whole family for a weekend. Anyway, come tomorrow and you can ask Kay yourself. She'll be pleased to meet you."

Jennie was thoughtful, realising that since he hoped to be on Keith Chatham's team one day, he needed the support of his wife now. "Of course I'll come." She must, otherwise she risked becoming, what her mother once became, the absent wife. She knew from bitter experience where that could lead.

"Good." Guy sounded surprised. "You'll adore Kay and have a marvellous time, that I promise."

When, at last, Jennie replaced the receiver she stared ahead thoughtfully and felt a warm glow. Apart from the odd occasion at the Mess, this was the first time Guy had tried to draw her into his world. Perhaps he did really love her after all.

The following morning, she travelled by train to Farnborough where Guy met her at the station and drove her to the airfield. She had never seen him so animated, his eyes sparkling as he showed her around, speaking knowledgably about the aircraft on show and the technology on display in the exhibition tents. He was a different man, a man who was happy, relaxed and totally at home in his own environment. Small wonder, she thought, he had not adapted well to hers. Bemused, Jennie followed him here, there and everywhere and tried, with difficulty, to take in everything he told her. She had not known what to expect, certainly nothing on this scale. All week the aircraft industry had shown off its newest and latest to would-be purchasers but today that part of it was over, the weather was bright, clear and sunny, and thousands had crowded to Farnborough. The sound of the tannoy echoed across the vast area as she was introduced to Kay and Keith Chatham. Both were in their mid-thirties, he shorter than Guy with kind, smiling eyes and receding hair; she slim with brown hair softly curling about her attractive face. Capable, was Jennie's first impression of her, kind, capable and unflappable.

Keith couldn't stay long. He had to prepare his aircraft for the flying programme. It seemed it had been touch and go whether the aircraft would fly today or not. "We had a few problems, but they're ironed out now." He smiled kindly at Jennie. "Have a good time. Kay will look after you, she's an old hand at this." He and Guy walked away leaving the two women alone.

As they waited for the flying display to start, Jennie listened to Kay chatting on about her children, the unlovely village of Stannington close by the Hadleigh factory, and the two farm cottages knocked into one to make an acceptable home for them. "The builders took for ever. But it's habitable now. You really must come down for a weekend."

Jennie said she would love to and invited Kay and her family to Kensington Square.

"I do miss London," said Kay. "There's nothing to do in the village. Guy tells me you paint? Portraits, I believe. He's very proud of you." Seeing the look of surprise on Jennie's face she smiled and went on, "He says he wants nothing to hinder your career. Most men wouldn't give two hoots about their wife's ambitions. You've a rare beast there, Jennie."

Jennie just looked at her.

Guy joined them as Keith put the Hadleigh jet through its programme. The aircraft rolled and soared above the crowds, flew low across the runway then did an inverted return run which sent Jennie's heart to her mouth. She glanced at Kay and saw her tense face turn ashen beneath a hand which shaded anxious eyes from the sun; the other hand stayed clenched at her side. When the display finished, Kay visibly relaxed, smiled and said: "Well. How was that for showing off?"

As the programme continued, and the noise and thrills seemed less of a shock, Jennie began to enjoy herself. Guy joined them once more, and the earlier tension having passed, the conversation was relaxed and happy. "We're so lucky with this weather," said Jennie. "It really is a beautiful day." The clear blue sky seemed empty now save for a thin white trail. At that moment there were two loud bangs. Alarmed, she turned to Guy. "What was that?"

"Sonic booms," he said, not taking his eyes off the aircraft high above. "John Derry has just flown through the sound barrier."

"The sound barrier?" murmured Jennie, wondering why it made a noise but not daring to voice her ignorance. She turned her eyes skywards once more to see the De Havilland jet descending. Flying low past the excited spectators, it then climbed again.

Suddenly, the aircraft exploded. Wreckage hurtled outwards then downwards, straight into the thick of the crowd.

For one horrifying moment on that beautiful day the world seemed to stop.

The Farnborough disaster dominated the news that night. John Derry and his observer had been killed, as well as twenty-six people in the crowd. Many others had been badly injured. After the news had finished, Jennie switched off the wireless, unable to clear from her mind the horror and the clanging of bells as fire engines raced on to the runway and ambulances tried to remove the dead and injured from the

266

crowd. To her surprise, after the runway was cleared, the flying display continued, taking attention away from the appalling accident and leaving Jennie wondering at the courage of these test pilots. Severely shaken, she had stood with Kay until the show finished when Guy drove her home in grim-faced silence.

Now she looked at him and said: "I want you to give up test flying."

He was standing with his back to her, staring through the window as dusk fell over the quiet square. "That's a rather pointless thing to say. Testing aircraft is what I do."

"It's too dangerous."

He turned then, saw the fear in her eyes and cursed himself for having persuaded her to go along to the show on this day of all days. Sick at heart, he walked to the drinks table and poured himself a large neat Scotch, wondering at the perversity of fate. He had been through a war, lost many friends and was no stranger to disaster. But today had been different. It was peacetime, and a day so beautiful, with thousands enjoying themselves, that sudden death seemed an obscenity. On this day, of all days.

"We don't know what happened yet," he said quietly. "When we do, it won't happen again."

"No," said Jennie, looking up at him. "Because another test pilot will risk his life finding out. Please, for my sake, accept some other post in the RAF – anything. But don't resign your commission to go to Hadleigh's."

"Christ," he said, running a hand through his hair. "Do you have any idea of the work and training that I've been through? At thirty I was damned lucky to get on the course in the first place. It's what I've always wanted."

"But you're a family man now. A family man shouldn't have such a dangerous occupation."

"Most test pilots are family men. And most live to a ripe old age." Placing the whisky tumbler down on the table, Guy walked across to her, took her hands in his and said in measured tones: "Jennie, I can't be what you want me to be. Flying is my life. Don't ask me to wither away behind a desk because I won't."

"I just want you to be safe."

"And who on this planet is safe, for God's sake? You? On the day you had a quiet lunch with your father at Robinson's and were damned near killed by a mob? The golfer struck by lightning last Sunday? Those poor devils who decided to have a day out at an airshow? Who is ever safe?"

"That's different. But you want to put your life at risk all the time and I'm afraid for you."

267

Guy smiled. "I'm afraid for you, every time you drive your car. You're a terrible driver, you know. Look, Jennie, we're not 'gung ho' types. We're highly trained, careful and cautious. Of course there's always an element of risk, but think how many test runs are made without mishap. When there is an accident it becomes big news. How many people die in their cars without making news at all? Don't try to change me. As I said before, I can't be what you want me to be."

Jennie's eyes shone with tears as she stared down at the Wilton carpet, remembering Kay's face during Keith's display. She had wondered then where she drew her courage from. It seemed the wives also had to be highly trained. Looking up at him she murmured in a choked voice: "And I can't be what you want me to be."

That night she wanted him to hold her close but he lay staring into the darkness, lost in a world where she could never belong. Small wonder he felt so alone, she thought. He needed her support, had wanted to draw her into the life he knew and loved, yet in the face of disaster she had folded her wings and collapsed like Sophie. So much for the daughter of Monique Veryan. If she only had a quarter of her mother's courage then perhaps Guy would be holding her in his arms instead of lying there like a board beside her. He must think her a whingeing idiot. Restless, she switched on the bedside lamp and sat up.

Blinking through the sudden glare, Guy turned to her and sighed. "Do try to settle, for God's sake."

"How can I?" She pushed back her hair and looked down at him. "I was wrong to speak as I did. Of course I'll stand by you. If and when you go to Hadleigh's, we'll buy a place in Hertfordshire and start living the way any normal married couple live."

Looking serious, Guy reached for a cigarette, thought better of it and said, "We'll see." With that he settled down in the bed once more.

Dismayed at his reaction, Jennie switched off the lamp then lay back, feeling the chill of rejection. In the grey light of dawn she turned to look at her husband. He seemed to be sleeping soundly.

Guy was not sleeping, however. He would go to Hadleigh's, he told himself, but Jennie would not move with him. Better by far to leave her in this well-appointed house painting portraits than have her pottering about Stannington, terrified every time she knew he was flying and asking too many questions concerning his whereabouts. Besides, he too had seen the expression on Kay's face when Keith had flown. He never wanted anyone to see it on Jennie's.

"Look out!"

At Jamie's warning shout, Charles turned quickly to where his son was pointing. Behind them a large grey submarine was cruising along the Johore Straits towards the Woodlands Naval Base. At once he eased the tiller to starboard; the mainsail swung across and Jamie leapt into action with the jib sail. As the submarine sailed past, leaving them bobbing precariously in its wake, Charles breathed a sigh of relief and then laughed with his son. The wake fanned out, catching other yachts, before the water settled into flat calm once more.

"Wow!" Jamie's eyes were almost popping out of his head. "Crikey! I'd love to see inside a sub. Angus went to the naval base last week. He was shown over an aircraft carrier. His father knows someone who works there." He frowned. "I wish I'd been asked to join him. After all, he is supposed to be my best friend."

"I expect the visit was restricted," said Charles, wishing with all his heart that instead of this small boat in the Straits, they were in *The Rose* together and the shoreline was that of Cornwall, instead of Singapore's east coast. These moments with his thirteen-year-old son were very precious to him. Their relationship was now a good one, unhampered, thank God, by interference from Leighton who seemed to have gone to ground. Shy at first, Jamie had taken time adapting to his father, for after the camp and years of living a strictly disciplined institutional life, he had found the world beyond that a strange place. But now he was glad to be like the other boys at his school and to have a family of his own. He knew nothing of the truth, of course, only that his mother had died when he was born, that he and his father had been separated by war and then reunited when Charles's lost memory had returned. So far as his father was concerned, there was no reason to tell him anything else. Charles' one great fear, however, was that Jamie might learn the truth from Leighton.

After her initial surprise at being told of Jamie's existence, Dodo had not reeled in horror but said quite calmly that the boy must live with his father under her roof and that she would keep the dark secret to herself. "There are far worse things, as we both know."

What a brick she was, thought Charles now, wishing his own family and the people of Portlyn would take such a philanthropic view of his infidelity. Portlyn! With Coronation fever gripping the Colony, England was very much in the news right now. Dear God, how much he longed to go home and announce to everyone: "Here is my son, James. I love him as dearly as I love my daughter and I want you to accept him as I have." Matters were not helped by Jennie's constant letters accusing him of reneging on his promise, and, instead, telling his parents half-truths and excuses, anything to put off the evil day. She was, she said, quite sure they now realised, even if they refused to admit it to themselves, that their son did not intend to return to them after all.

269

"You are cruel and cowardly, Papa, to go on crucifying them in this way. Please, please put an end to it."

Yes, he was a coward, he thought as the yacht drifted slowly beneath the unrelenting sun, because it took courage to hurt those you loved for their own sakes. How many times had he tried to write that letter and then abandoned it? Jennie had his measure all right, darling Jennie whom he had hurt so deeply and who knew how to hurt in return. That some strange man should give her away in marriage to another strange man he had never even met, was something he could never forget or forgive.

They were sailing past the small beach at Changi now. He gazed at the shore, aware how close he was to the place that still filled him with cold horror. Even now he woke up screaming, and could only sleep when drugged. That was the trouble with Singapore. Everywhere he looked the past haunted him; even here in this innocent yacht race, for boats from this club had once joined many others fleeing the burning city, hoping to reach safety in Sumatra or one of the islands. They had no way of knowing that Japanese warships were waiting for them. The little armada had been blown out of the water. England, he thought, only in England could he perhaps forget.

"Wake up, Father," called Jamie. "You're taking us into the shallows." He grinned. "Did you know that last week a hammerhead shark followed the yacht race along here? It was spotted from an aircraft. So don't go aground, please."

Charles pushed on the tiller and smiled at his son. "Hammerhead, you say?" Just looking at the boy, so happy and well-adjusted, made him realise why he could never return to England.

The next day, he and Jamie went to the British cemetery where the long-sought grave had been found. As Jamie placed lilies in the vase, Charles stared down at the inscription on the marble tombstone:

Serena Anne Veryan,
Beloved wife of Charles.
Born 1917. Died 1940.

Even here, in this quiet graveyard, the lie was maintained.

Jamie arranged the lilies and then stood up. Thin and still colt-like, his mid-brown hair and light complexion told the world that he was English to his fingertips – as English as Jamie thought he truly was. Suddenly he caught sight of a man in a cream suit standing farther off, looking at them from under the trees. The Panama was pulled down, shading his face, but Jamie recognised him at once. "Uncle Victor!" he shouted. But the figure vanished into the trees, leaving the boy frowning in confusion. "It *was* him, I'm sure it was. Why didn't he speak to me, and why did he stop visiting me?"

Charles was staring towards the trees, fear coursing through him. He placed a hand on Jamie's shoulder and said, "Come along, it's getting late and you've still got that homework to do before school tomorrow. Aunt Dodo will only go on at you if it isn't done before dinner."

As they walked away, he looked back over his shoulder. Had Leighton been visiting Serena's grave, or following them? If the latter, then why? Was it a silent threat to remind Charles he was under surveillance? That any attempt to leave the island would not go unnoticed? Whatever it was, it set the hairs rising at the back of his neck.

That night he awoke sweating, remembering that moment when the guards had dragged him to a cell and beaten him almost to a pulp. They poured water down his throat, almost drowning him; they kept him in a small cage, and each day beat him mercilessly. And all this at the behest of Leighton. Not only would he like to kill his Japanese tormentors, he now had a very strong urge to kill Leighton.

# Chapter Seventeen

In January 1954, Guy resigned his commission and joined the staff of Hadleigh's as Keith Chatham's number two. Although relieved to get the post he wanted, he felt the loss of Service life more deeply than he had expected since, from the age of eighteen, the RAF had been his family. Now, suddenly finding himself a civilian among civilians, he was lost, restless, edgy and unsettled. Understanding this, Jennie agreed to his request for more time to adjust, putting homebuying on the back boiler for the time being and even helping him to move into the tiny gamekeeper's cottage he had, surprisingly, managed to find for himself.

Thinking how self-sacrificing Guy was to his wife's needs, Kay took him under her wing, inviting him to dinner often, and finding a farm labourer's widow to clean, cook and launder for him. It was quite wrong of Jennie, she thought, to behave like this just because people paid her to paint their portraits. Wives should support their husbands, not the other way around.

Unaware that Guy was giving this impression of her, Jennie saw little of him once he moved to Stannington, accepting that he often flew at weekends and also had a lot of paperwork to catch up with when the office was peaceful. Left alone so much, she was glad to have plenty of work. There were commissions and Maddie needed help at the gallery. As if this wasn't enough, Jennie was constantly urged to start building up a collection. Unsure she was ready for such an undertaking, she would look at her sketches and watercolours of Singapore life, telling herself that the paintings from these would form an important part of any such collection. One of these sketches she had already tried to work on. The task upset her so much she had finally abandoned it. But it was time to make a fresh start on that portrait of her father.

First she had to complete the full-length painting of Guy in his flying gear which had been hanging around her studio for ages. Getting him

272

to stand still long enough had been a *tour de force* in itself, but on a blustery weekend in April she signed the portrait in black paint and put down the brush at last.

Guy was pleased and flattered, but had no idea whether the painting was good or bad. He seemed happy, drank more than usual and made rough love to her before falling asleep exhausted, leaving her feeling used once more. On the Sunday evening he climbed into the Jaguar, roared off around the square and returned to his world, leaving Jennie to hers. She stood at the window and watched him go with mixed feelings. Not once had he mentioned the word "house". She began to realise that he never would, that this was how it would always be, how he wanted it to be. In that moment, she realised something else. It no longer mattered. She had come to value her independence, having had so much of it. Did it mean that she no longer loved Guy? The answer should have been plain, but was not. For some reason, she had no feelings about him one way or the other and no passion left in her.

In May, Jennie finished the portrait of her father and took it, and Alex to Trevellan. As luck would have it she chose the best week of the year so far. Wild flowers filled fields and hedgerows, trees were bursting into bright green leaf; the sea was dotted with sailing vessels fresh from their winter yards, and early holidaymakers wandered about, enjoying the warm sunshine.

Overjoyed to see her again, Florence made a great fuss of Alex, then waited as, with mounting trepidation, Jennie produced the half-portrait of Charles. Moved to silence, Florence and Philip looked at the strong brushwork, the deeply etched lines about the haunted face, the wiry grey hair. So quiet were they it seemed they hated it.

"Well, Jennie," said Florence at last. "I really don't know what I was expecting but this . . . well . . . this is simply one of the best things you've ever done. And from sketches too. I love it, love it. We must hang it in the drawing room."

Laura blinked. "We already have Gavin's portrait in there so where exactly is this one to go? I don't think Opie or Lely quite blend with Ostler and Lloyd, do you?"

"Then I shall move the Opie," said Florence.

"Mummy!" Laura looked as though she had been struck. "You can't mean it. You want Opie to take second place to Jennie?"

For once in her life, Jennie agreed with her aunt, but Florence was obdurate. Her son was more important than some distant ancestor of her husband's, no matter whose hand had been on the brush. It was only Jennie who managed to persuade the old lady to put her painting in the morning room and leave Cornwall's hero in his rightful pride of place.

"It's a good thing you didn't come last week," said Mrs Hodges as she offered Alex the large gingerbread man she had made for him. The kitchen was warm and the smell of baked scones made Jennie feel hungry. "The weather was terrible. I felt quite sorry for Mark Curnow. Hasn't been here for ages and when he does it rains cats and dogs."

Jennie's heart did a somersault. "Mark is here?"

Realising that she had put her foot in it, Mrs Hodges shook her head and turned quickly to the oven. "Oh, no ... he left a few days ago."

Trying not to show her bitter disappointment, Jennie hoped she sounded casual as she braved the question she had wanted to ask for years. "Where exactly is he now?"

Before Mrs Hodges could answer, Rosa and Keynes entered the kitchen and the subject was dropped at once as they made a fuss of little Alex who was quite full of himself and had managed to get gingerbread all around his mouth and chin.

But as Jennie played with her son at the cove and helped him to build sandcastles, her mind was in turmoil. A few days! She had missed him by a few days. God, how cruel life was. Yet how could she have faced him or endured meeting his wife?

The weather began to change, the warm sunshine giving way to Cornwall's soft drizzle and mist. Jennie began to change too. Her sudden aversion to tea, coffee and alchohol were familiar signs. She needed no others to tell her she was pregnant. The realisation appalled her. Guy, who had taken precious little interest in Alex, no more wanted a second baby than he wanted his wife and son around him every day. To go through all that again for a child not wanted by its father, was too much. Feeling nauseous, she left Trevellan the minute she learned that Clive and Fenella were due to arrive, much to Laura's relief and her grandparents' surprise.

When the pregnancy was confirmed her doctor voiced anxiety. "At the moment your blood pressure is normal. We'll monitor it regularly. If it starts rising, then I'm afraid you will have to stay in hospital, possibly for the duration of your pregnancy."

Jennie reeled at the thought.

Three months passed and she remained as fit as a fiddle. Even the morning sickness was easing a little. Having slowly become used to the idea of the baby, she now wanted it very much but dreaded the prospect of telling Guy, knowing the atmosphere would be impossible afterwards. "Don't be feeble, Jennie," she told herself. "Screw your courage to the sticking place and get on with it."

"Must you spread your things all over the bathroom?" complained Guy one Sunday evening. "Nylons, talcum powder, make-up and God knows what ... where the hell am I supposed to find room to shave?"

274

"Why don't you buy an electric shaver?" said Jennie, picking up Alex's toys which had been scattered about the drawing room floor. She could hear Guy in the hall, pushing things into his canvas bag ready to return to Stannington after dinner.

"I don't want a bloody electric razor, I just want some room."

"Well," said Jennie, "when you have the bathroom to yourself all week you do tend to spread." This, she thought, was the time. If he wanted to sulk then he had a week to do it in without bothering her. Later, in the large dining room, she looked at Guy across the polished Hepplewhite table and said: "You don't say anything, but you must be sick and tired of living in that little cottage all alone?"

Looking up from his roast beef and Yorkshire pudding, Guy shook his head. "On the contrary, I'm coping very well."

"It's just that . . . well, I really do think it's time we thought about a house of our own."

Silent at this, he finished his dinner, leaned back and lit a cigarette. "Why? Damn it Jennie, we're living in Kensington Square rent free. Why look a gift horse in the mouth? Your grandfather isn't champing at the bit, is he?"

"No. And I like living here, but it isn't our house. Any woman, any mother, feels a desire . . ."

"Yes, but you like to fuss about with your paints and you have your studio here. Some of your stuff's pretty good. You'd miss your hobby if you lived out in the sticks, believe me." Sublimely unaware of the anger in her eyes, he went on, "Let things stay as they are. It suits me, and it suits you."

"I know it suits you," she snapped. "I also appreciate how you like to feel free to come and go, using this house as a London Club, but you're not free, Guy, you're married and have a child." She paused and then said: "I think you should understand just how things truly stand. First there's Papa. You probably already know that he won't be returning from Singapore. Ever." Seeing his grim expression, she started telling him everything she had vowed to keep to herself. "Grandpa will have to act soon if he wants to avoid crippling death duties. He may pass the estate to Clive."

The grey eyes turned to steel. "But why? We have a son who is in direct line of inheritance. The old boy must hand the estate to you so that it can go to Alex." He looked bemused. "Jennie, I can't bring myself to believe that your father is giving up his birthright simply because he's had a bit on the side. What's unusual in that? Pretty common practice among the upper classes, I always thought. And even if he wants to be a martyr, that's no reason why the estate shouldn't go to you. It must."

275

"There's no must about it." She smiled wryly. "I'm here, Aunt Laura is there, and so is Clive more often than not. Grandpa may do anything he likes. And if it all goes to Clive then he'll have us out of here in two shakes of a lamb's tail." She stopped speaking and summoned up the words she found so hard to utter. "I desperately need to feel secure. I mean ... supposing we had another baby?"

Angry at the revelations about her father, and alarmed at the prospect of having to buy a house, Guy glared at her. "Another baby? Christ, no! Alex is more than a handful, and anyway I don't wish to see my wife blown up like a balloon again. And look what happened to you the last time. Do you really want all that again? Why the hell do you think I insist on precautions?"

Stunned by his words, she just sat there while he left the table walked into the hall and pulled on his leather jacket. "I'm about to leave," he called out. When she didn't answer, he poked his head around the door and thought how small she seemed at that large table, with his full-length portrait behind her. "I said, I'm about to leave. Aren't you going to say goodbye?"

"Goodbye," she snapped, keeping her eyes averted from him.

For a moment he seemed taken aback, but then sighed. "Oh, Lord. Sulking, are we? Well, I've no time for discussing houses. I'm late as it is." With that he walked out and slammed the front door.

Jennie sat like stone as the car kicked into life and roared it's way around the square. How long she remained at the table, she hardly knew. Suddenly she felt very cold and, leaving the dining room, climbed the stairs to her bedroom. There she pulled on her dressing gown and sank on to the bed in utter despair. "Precautions, dear Guy, do not always work." "*Blown up like a balloon*". How would she ever forget such a phrase? She placed her hands on her stomach, convinced now that she carried a girl, so convinced that she had already given the baby a name: Tara. Tara Monique Veryan Lloyd, loved and wanted by her mother but not by her father evidently. Damn him! He would never touch her again. Never! He didn't want to know about the child? Very well. He wouldn't, until it became blatantly obvious, since blatantly obvious was the only way he was ever going to realise what many other men would have known even without having to be told. "*Blown up like a balloon*". To Guy, then, a pregnant woman was an ugly woman and something of a joke. In that moment, she hated him.

Guy did not drive to Stannington. Instead he made his way to a road close to Ealing Common, climbed from the car, walked towards a grey brick Edwardian house and let himself in with his own key. A door opened and a woman stepped into the well-lit hall. Wearing a

276

close-fitting dress, she was fortyish, well-endowed and sensuous-looking. Her plain features were well made-up, the bottle blonde hair curling about her face which creased into a surprised smile. "Christ almighty," she said in a throaty voice. "You're early this evening." The smile faded as she saw Guy's expression. "I'll open that bottle of best malt. You look as though you need it."

Later, as they lay naked in each other's arms, Guy wondered what he would do without Zoë. He had known her before ever setting eyes on Jennie, and picked up their old relationship after returning from Singapore. And what a relationship! They had no secrets from each other; she was his confidante, his friend and uninhibited lover. With Jennie he felt strangely repressed: with Zoë he was free and very much at home. Divorced long ago and wishing to remain free, she owned a boutique, enjoyed life to the full, was warm, loving and dependable. A touch too common to grace the Officers' Mess, she was, nevertheless good solid earthenware to Jennie's fine porcelain. Guy needed both to keep his life in balance.

He stroked the large white breasts, noticing the freckles on them, but his mind was no longer on sex; it was on Charles Veryan, all sackcloth and ashes, poor sod, for having had an affair. The boy complicated matters, of course, as he knew to his own cost, but for Charles to give up an estate like Trevellan because of some wild fling in his youth was madness surely? What crime had he committed? Perhaps he was unhinged after all he had endured for no sane man would condemn himself to such an exile. A twinge of guilt shot through Guy as he recalled something of his angry words to Jennie early that evening. But her constant harping on a house threatened his freedom to be with Zoë, and that had made him want to strike out at his wife. Still, a bit harsh perhaps, not the thing, not the thing at all...

He glanced at the woman who lay so silent beside him, knowing he could never give her up. How tactful she was, not asking questions when it was blatantly obvious he had come from a marital row. But Zoë was too good a sort to discuss Jennie, and no more did he, for it went without saying that his wife must be treated with respect.

On a grey August day, Guy's descent in the jet fighter was smoother than the flight had been. As he touched down on Hadleigh's newly extended runway and brought the H-14 Panther to a stop, he could see Keith and the rest of the design team walking towards him across the tarmac. Climbing out of the cockpit, Guy stepped down the ladder, as disappointed as everyone else that this latest prototype was now causing problems after successful initial test trials at Boscombe Down.

He turned to Keith whose face was glum. "It's that damned

277

vibration again." They chatted on quietly about the problems which the team had heard as the test proceeded, then walked to the office where the inevitable inquest would now take place. Reports would be written out and the test tape played and replayed again and again. Guy glanced at his watch and knew he hadn't a prayer of getting home this Friday evening. That was bad. Jennie was hardly speaking to him as it was, spending most weekends incarcerated in her studio and pleading a migraine at nights. When he had tried remonstrating with her she had hurled a cup at him, narrowly missing his head. Hell hath no fury like a woman at the receiving end of misplaced words. If only he could take them back. Even so, she was over-reacting surely? In every way she seemed strange these days. What on earth was the matter with the woman?

Halfway through the meeting a call came through for Guy. He left the room and took it in his own office. "Lloyd speaking." His frown changed to a broad grin. "You have? Bloody marvellous. How much? Ah, well ... it'll be worth it. I'll bring her down tomorrow. No, she doesn't know. I want to surprise her. Thanks. See you around eleven then." He replaced the receiver, a happier man. Tomorrow would put a smile on Jennie's face.


Alex pointed to the picture of Peter Rabbit and drew in his breath as he murmured the words with Jennie: "'... not to go into Mr MacGregor's garden...'" Curled up on the sofa beside his mother, he turned the pages of the small book which he now knew so well.

Jennie smiled and tried to continue reading. It was the hour of the day she loved best, the time always reserved for Alex no matter how busy she was. When work was slack she took him out and enjoyed playing with him but today had been hectic. "Leave the pages alone, darling. I'm trying to read the story. Do you know that word?"

Alex screwed up his podgy pink face then shouted: "Peter."

"Clever boy," said Jennie as Nanny opened the door and entered the drawing room. At that same moment the telephone rang. Jennie sighed and picked up the receiver to hear Guy's voice. He sounded strange, excited.

"Jennie, we have a serious problem here, so I shan't make it tonight, but tomorrow I'll be with you early and am bringing you back to Stannington. No, don't speak, I've no time to talk. There's a meeting on. I want you to wear warm slacks and a thick sweater."

"In August? Whatever for? And why ...?"

"Don't interrupt. Wear warm clothes and bring your best bib and tucker too. We're dining with Kay and Keith. I've a surprise for you, and ... well ... can't say any more. Jennie, if I've upset you, then I'm sorry."

With that he rang off, leaving Jennie holding the receiver with a stupified expression on her face. What on earth was she to make of the man? Surprise? At Stannington? Best bib and tucker? Had he really not noticed her bulging stomach and plumper face? True she had worn her painter's smock during his visits and made it plain enough that she wanted to be left alone in bed, but even so, well into her fourth month, she might have expected her own husband to have noticed something.

Later, still bemused, she searched through wardrobes and drawers until she found a mohair sweater and a pair of slacks made for her during her last pregnancy. Intended for country walking, they had proved invaluable for lounging about the house. Time to bring them out once more. Clearly he was thinking she would get cold in the car with the hood down. She sank down on to the bed, remembering those last words. *"If I've upset you, then I'm sorry."* Suddenly her mind swung into focus. A house! Guy had found a house and wanted her to see it before reaching a conclusion. Where though? And what kind of house?

The shock of it took her breath away. But was it so unbelievable? This was clearly his way of saying he loved her, this boyish action which spoke louder than any words he was capable of uttering. Even so, it was not the way to go about a matter so important to both of them. Another thought took hold. Supposing he had reached a decision without her?

When he arrived the following morning, something in his manner, his excitement and sense of intrigue, melted the freeze in her emotions and touched a loving core within her. How could she go on being angry when he was like this? Swallowing her pride, she prepared to be surprised.

Waving goodbye to Nanny and Alex, they climbed into the open topped Jaguar and set off for Stannington. When they were close to the sprawling village, Guy told her to close her eyes and placed a hand over them. "No cheating now."

"I won't," she replied, trying to imagine what she would see when she opened them once more. Would it be a thatched cottage, a Victorian villa or what? Please God, not one of those modern boxes newly built on the outskirts. No, Guy wouldn't do that to himself. Problems were crowding in on her now. How could she continue with her career so far from London? Did it matter? Guy had clearly thought about their marriage and how he had treated her. Now he wanted to put things right, not with soft words, that wasn't his way, but with practical deeds. How she responded was crucial. Their future together depended upon it and she would have two children to think about. This last stretch of the journey seemed so long. If only she could open her eyes...

279

At last the car came to a halt. "Right. You may look."

Jennie removed her hands, glanced about her and blinked in astonishment.

"Well," he said. "What do you think?"

"I think it's a Tiger Moth."

"Well done."

For a moment she couldn't take it in. They were on the airfield with the bi-plane some two hundred yards away. A man stood beside it, holding a leather jacket. He waved. Guy waved back.

"Why are we here, Guy? Why are we looking at a Tiger Moth?"

"Because it's mine. Well, half mine. Tim Dorcas over there owns the other half. He found it was up for sale last month, rang me and we've been negotiating for it since. It's been worked on and is in tip-top shape."

Dismayed and confused, Jennie's mind was reeling with questions. "But what are you going to do with it?"

He laughed. "Fly it, of course. Out you get. Come and meet Tim. You'll remember him. Boscombe Down. Battle of Britain Reception a couple of years back? He's still in the Service."

Still in a daze, she walked with Guy to where Tim stood. Wearing a fleeced leather flying jacket, he was carrying another over his arm. Having said how good it was to see her again, he pointed to the aeroplane. "Isn't she beautiful? Flies like a bird too." He held out the jacket. "Here. Hope it doesn't swamp you too much but they don't make them your size."

Jennie just stared at it stupidly. "For me? Why?"

"Because it's bloody cold up there, that's why." Guy was pulling on his own flying jacket which he had thrown into the back of the car, and now handed Jennie a leather helmet and goggles.

Her eyes opened in horror. "You ... you want me to go up in that?"

"You'll love it," laughed Guy. "Wait and see. Conditions are perfect. Clear as a diamond."

Suddenly finding herself engulfed in the jacket, Jennie tried to resist the helmet and goggles but Guy was getting impatient. "For heaven's sake, don't keep saying you're scared. Listen to her, Tim. Tell her she's an ass."

Seeing the fear on Jennie's face, Tim looked worried and thought Guy rather insensitive. "If she doesn't want to go then it's all right. We'll go up together and she can watch."

"She wants to go up, all right," said Guy. "She's surprised, that's all." His eyes said: "Don't embarrass me."

Feeling she was on trial, Jennie thought of the baby and wished now she had spoken out. This was hardly the time to break the news.

Anyway, what harm could a simple flight do? She was making a fool of herself. Had her mother not parachuted from a bomber into Occupied France?

Guy ushered her to the front cockpit, strapped her in and said: "There you are, Mrs Biggles. Nothing to be worried about. You'll have the experience of your life, I guarantee it."

Finding herself staring at the nose and propellor, Jennie shouted back in alarm: "But why am I in the front? You're driving." Behind her, Guy had already started the engine, the propellor was ticking over and Tim pulled the chocs away. Then the Tiger Moth was moving along the grass. "Guy," she shouted over the engine, "how can you see if you're behind me?"

"What?" The noise drowned his voice as it drowned hers. Guy turned into the wind and the aircraft made its run, gathering speed until they lifted off the ground.

Jennie clutched the side, her knuckles whitening, then closed her eyes. When she opened them again, the ground was disappearing below her. Ahead was the sky and the whirling propellor, huge double wings, struts and criss-crossing wires. Cold wind rushed into her face, the sun dazzled, then Guy banked to starboard. Fearing she would fall out, she grabbed the sides even more tightly. The plane bumped on the thermals; she looked down and saw the patchwork of fields dotted with villages. In the distance, a large town; off to her right a busy main road with cars and a bus; a shimmering river; churches and more villages. Her fear was melting away with the wonder of it all. How lovely England was. This was real flying; this was fun.

For ten minutes they sailed the skies over Hertfordshire, then she heard Guy shout: "Hang on." The nose came up, she gripped the sides for dear life, the sun blinded her, then to her utter horror she was looking up at the ground before the plane straightened out, leaving her stomach somewhere below. The shock of the "loop" set her heart hammering against her ribcage.

"Don't ... don't do that!" But her shout was carried away on wind and engine as Guy pulled the stick back again and she found herself upside down, utterly disorientated, dizzy and nauseous as the plane straightened out once more.

"Enjoy it?" he shouted.

"Don't ... please ... don't do that again." Jennie shook her head from side to side, hoping Guy would understand. It seemed he did. After that it was a straightforward run back to the airfield and a smooth landing.

Weak with relief, she let him help her out of the aircraft and was

281

never so glad to feel her feet touch the ground. He was laughing down at her.

"Gave you a bit of a shock, did it? I know. But I wanted you to see what she could do. Second time wasn't so bad though, was it? You soon get used to it." He stopped laughing and frowned. "Are you all right? You look a bit groggy."

Tim approached and asked how she had enjoyed the flight. She smiled and said, "Marvellous." But as they stood talking, Jennie began to feel a strange sensation in the pit of her stomach and thought she might faint. She leaned against Guy for support, to Tim's eyes seeming the loving and happy wife. Slowly the awful moment passed and she was able to watch as Tim climbed into the Tiger Moth, took off and flew out of their sight. How quiet it was on the airfield suddenly. The only sound breaking the stillness came from a skylark high above.

"Bloody fantastic!" Guy said. "Glad you enjoyed it."

Jennie smiled. "I did, until the aerobatic display." Something strange was happening to her head. It hurt so much she thought it might explode.

"Ah, but that's the thrill of it all, looping and rolling. Come on. Let's go to the pub before lunch."

At that moment, Jennie felt a sharp pain above her groin and shook her head in alarm. "I think we'd better get back to the cottage."

By the time they arrived, the pain had gone. She took two asprins for her headache and searched kitchen cupboards for whatever he had that she could turn into lunch. Cheese, bread and pickles seemed to be it. As she worked in the tiny kitchen, she watched him through the window pulling up straggling bushes and plants from overgrown and long-neglected flower beds. They needed a house and he had bought a Tiger Moth. Their minds and desires were oceans apart. Today he was on top of the world, completely unaware that he had just made it blatantly obvious to her that an aeroplane was more important to him than a home life with his wife and child. He hurt without realising he was hurting, then looked surprised and agitated when she tried to tell him that he had. Today she had not told him. It would be cruel when he had so wanted her to share his joy in flying.

Suddenly another sharp pain seared her body. Dropping the bread-knife, she clutched her stomach and tried to move towards the open door.

Guy was enjoying his first taste of gardening, pulling out the old, planning to plant the new. Hollyhocks would be good. He remembered those from the house in Brockenhurst when he was a child. Hollyhocks and a few vegetables perhaps. Gardening, he had just discovered, was an excellent form of relaxation. Thinking he heard Jennie calling, he stopped working and listened. It was Jennie all right, but something about her voice alarmed him. Within a second he was running towards the cottage.

Through a cloud of pain, hushed voices, hands lifting, overhead lights flashing past, Jennie succumbed to the anaesthetic. When she opened her eyes hours later she was looking into the pretty young face of a nurse. The baby? Her baby? When she tried to ask, no sound came from her throat. The nurse finished taking her pulse, then gave Jennie some water to sip.

"Baby?" The hoarse whisper was almost inaudible.

The nurse shook her head sympathetically. "I'm sorry."

With a silent scream, Jennie turned her face to the bare white wall in disbelief. Dead? Oh God! Tears rolled down her face. The nurse tried to calm her, but how did you calm a mother who had just lost her baby? Soon, however, Jennie lapsed back into her drugged sleep.

The next time she opened her eyes she saw Guy looking down at her. "She's gone." Her voice was still weak and hoarse and tears wet her cheeks. "It *was* a girl, wasn't it?"

Guy nodded, then took her hand and squeezed it gently, his face tortured with anxiety and confusion. "Why didn't you tell me? Four months, the doctor said, four months, and you said nothing."

She stared at him coldly. "I tried ... tried ..." It hurt to talk and she felt so weak.

For a moment he stood there, desolate and helpless, remembering the blood, her agony, and how frantic he had been waiting for the ambulance, and then that race to the hospital with bells clanging. What did she mean, she had tried? Had he known about the baby he would never have taken her up in the Moth, let alone have executed those "loops". Never in a million years. She should have told him. Why hadn't she told him? Why was she so damned mysterious?

Driving from Hertford to Stannington, he could still hear the doctor's voice. "She's very poorly. As you know she haemorrhaged badly and there are complications with her blood pressure. In her distressed condition I think it best that she remains quiet now for at least another forty-eight hours. I can't say how long we shall keep her in." Guy had listened thinking: I did this. I killed our child. Oh, why the hell had Jennie not told him. He loved her so much and now had hurt her badly.

Jennie's recovery was slow, not helped by high blood pressure. But this time it fell more quickly and, after nearly four weeks, she left the hospital, pale, thin and, unbeknown to anyone, slipping into a deep trough of depression which lacking, as he did, any understanding of the

283

condition, drove Guy to distraction. Physical mishaps he could handle, but emotional and mental suffering was alien to him. Guilty as he felt and comforting as he tried to be, his patience finally wore out.

"It's been three months now. For God's sake, snap out of it. So you had a miscarriage. It's not the end of the world. You can always have another baby, if you really want one. I understand that you're disappointed, but this is ridiculous."

She heard him in stunned rage. Disappointed? She was grieving and he used the word "disappointed"? When she hurled a large ashtray at him, he ducked then left the house, wondering whether his wife would ever stop bursting into tears.

In the early hours, Jennie would wake, wander down to the kitchen and make tea, raging at Guy one minute, the whole world the next, then blaming herself in the end. If only the anguish would go, but still it caused that fearful ache which anger alone could help to dispel. She knew it was wrong to feel so badly about Guy as she did, but there was no way she could sleep in the same bed with him, or even bear to let him touch her. Why blame him? After all, she had allowed herself to be bullied into flying when she should have simply said "no". All he had wanted to do that day was make her understand why flying was his life, to see the world as he saw it. There was love in that, surely? So why did she feel this awful anger, and wake up with a terrible forboding each morning? Why did this heavy darkness oppress her? And why did she keep bursting into tears, in the shops or just out walking? Was she going mad?

Slowly the depression began to disappear and she finally crawled out of that deep and dark hole in the winter of 1955, wondering how impossible she had been to everyone and feeling that life was worth living again.

Maddie, who along with Louise had tried to help her through the crisis, now came into her own. "You did many sketches of Alex in your more positive moments, so now that you have plenty of material to work on, paint a portrait of your own son, Jennie." She knew, as Jennie did, that it was too soon to take on commissions once more. Working on the painting of Alex and building the collection would be the best therapy yet.

Relieved at first, Guy then became alarmed at the sudden change in his wife. Her flushed face, bright eyes and restless energy, along with her great zeal for work and a desire to sit up late with her art colleagues, all seemed abnormal to him. It was as though Jennie wanted no time to think. No time to just "be". Gavin and Maddie were invariably at the house whenever he came home, and the talk was of art, art, art. He felt like a third sock, in a world which he found alien, a world where he

284

could only be an ignorant onlooker. And so he spent less time in that world, and more at the house in Ealing.

Then, something happened which brought Jennie's mind crashing from its crazy whirling height to earthly reality.

Sir Philip Veryan died during one of the worst summer storms to hit the Cornish coast for years. Not that he heard it. The stroke had been massive and death almost instantaneous, so that when Keynes walked into the study on a July evening to find the baronet sprawled on the floor, there was nothing to be done.

Three days later the funeral cortège passed villagers lining the lane from Trevellan to the church, the men raising their hats or holding caps, the women tearful, having drawn their curtains as a token of respect. As the old man was laid to rest in the Veryan plot, everyone knew it was the end of an era and most dreaded what might follow since Sir Charles, now the Tenth Baronet, had not returned from Singapore after all.

Devastated with grief, Florence carried herself through the ordeal with quiet dignity, moving among the many friends who had gathered to say goodbye to her husband. After the wake, she announced to the family that the solicitor would be arriving the following morning to disclose the contents of the will, then walked out of the drawing room.

Jennie watched her leave, and decided to give her grandmother a quiet moment to herself. Standing beside the piano, she looked through the long window to see lengthening shadows reaching across the south lawn. Aware that Guy was standing beside her, she murmured: "Do you know, I've never been to a funeral before. It's supposed to rain, isn't it? It always does in films." She bit back the tears. "It should rain. There's something terrible about being lowered into the ground on such a lovely day as this." She glanced at her mother's photograph thinking that at least there was a grave this time, somewhere to plant flowers, knowing that you were close to the loved one. There was comfort in that. No comfort, though, in the knowledge that the poor man had died without ever seeing his son again. Anguished at the thought, she turned. "I'd better find Grandma. She shouldn't be left alone too long, not today."

Florence was standing on the terrace, a frail figure in widow's weeds, leaning on her walking stick, alone with her thoughts. She turned at Jennie's approach.

"Maddie told me you were out here," said Jennie softly. "You shouldn't be. It's getting chilly."

"Nonsense. It's a beautiful evening and I need fresh air after ... after..." The stoic expression crumpled at last and she turned to face her grand-daughter. "Oh, Jennie. Oh, my dear, how can I go on without him?"

Placing her arms about the weeping woman, Jennie tried to give comfort where there could be none. Later, when her grandmother had managed to compose herself once more, she said: "I sent a cable to Papa."

Florence stiffened. "Why? A letter would have sufficed, for all he cares." She walked on, towards the rose garden, the fragrance of the blooms strong in the evening air, her mind seeking comfort in ordinary things. "We've been troubled with black spot this year, so the roses look a bit straggly. Philip was so worried..." As the voice broke, she turned and moved across rougher ground, heedless of the pain in her hip. "He had been busy that last day but seemed well enough. We had dinner, and talked about *The Rose*. I was for selling the yacht since no one has sailed it in years. But he wouldn't have it. Stubborn to the last. Then he left the table, saying he had work to do and that Keynes could take his coffee and brandy to the study. How could I have known, when he walked through the door, that I would never see him alive again?" She paused, frowning. "It isn't right. Such an occasion should be marked, surely? Perhaps it was, by the dreadful storm." She stared ahead vacantly and murmured, "I keep wondering if he cried out for help. It haunts me that I didn't hear."

Jennie placed a comforting arm about the old lady. "No, Grandma. The doctor said it was instantaneous. He wouldn't have known anything about it. So you can rest easy."

Florence looked at her for reassurance, then nodded. As they walked on, she said: "He changed his will, you know. His refusal to discuss the issue with me leads me to think he has left the estate to Clive. I could be wrong. I hope and pray that I am."

Sick to her stomach at this news, Jennie said only, "I see."

"Do you? Well, I don't. Not when your father is still alive." Her eyes fixed on Jennie; hurt, angry eyes. "Why did he do such a thing to us though? We were patient. Oh, how patient we were. Still believing, still hoping. His letters kept reassuring us with excuses, his health, Dodo's business and so on. A few weeks ago we received another letter. In it he made it plain that he must give up all thought of returning to England since Mr Webb was on his last legs and that this Dodo woman could not cope. Since she had been so wonderful to him, he felt compelled to stay and run her business for her. He no longer felt he was the right person to take on Trevellan and asked that the estate be passed to you, Jennie, so that Alexander would one day inherit. He said he hoped we would understand and forgive him for having to make such a painful choice."

So then, he had done it at last. Years too late, of course. Eyes averted, Jennie stood like a rock, unable to speak.

"Why, Jennie? Why after all these years did he do that to us? I believe it killed your grandfather. He started acting very strangely after that. Then, one day, he burst into the morning room saying he had been betrayed and deceived, went up to your parent's old bedroom, and extinguished the flame. All he would say to me was, 'It's over. All over. I have no son.' He never spoke about it after that. The next day he sent for Mr Longwood and I knew then that he was changing the will."

After a thoughtful silence Jennie asked, "Did you show Aunt Laura the letter?"

"Of course."

Jennie's lips tightened in anger. It was all quite clear now why her grandfather had flown into that sudden rage. Having read the letter and her brother's wish for his daughter to inherit, Laura would have fought like a lioness for her own cub, even if it meant shattering the frail old man. There was only one blessing, left. Whatever Laura had said to her father, had clearly been kept from her mother. Even Laura wouldn't dare to go that far.

Florence continued walking. "Everything's been shattered to pieces. I've lost my husband and son all in one go. And now..." She turned to Jennie, her lips trembling. "And now I have this terrible foreboding for Trevellan."

"Oh God, it isn't right!" cried Jennie in despair. "It just isn't right. Clive doesn't love Trevellan as I do. He doesn't understand it or care about it. I doubt if he even knows the names of our tenants."

"I told Philip all that. I told him also that Clive is a man of excess who will destroy the estate. But I don't think he listened. He was so consumed with anger. That last evening together, chatting about *The Rose*, was the only normal evening we had enjoyed for a long time." Her lips twisted. "Normal!"

Wondering if Laura's revelations had triggered the stroke, Jennie took her grandmother by the arm. "Come. It's getting too chilly for you to be out here now."

Florence nodded. "You will be here for the reading of the will, won't you? Only Guy said something about leaving first thing in the morning."

"He has to leave, but I'll stay a few days before returning home." Home! This was home surely? Jennie glanced about her sadly. Had she lost it? Would this be the last time she could come to the place of her childhood?

Glad to get away from the mourners Guy had been in the kitchen

287

garden when Fenella, having followed him all over the place, came upon him once more and suggested they walk to the cove together. Against his better judgement he agreed. Unsuitably dressed for such a location, she now stood beside him on the steps looking out to sea, her high-heeled court shoes and long straight black skirt completely at odds with the rough ground which was still damp after yesterday's rain. The sun had set behind a thin bank of cloud, leaving the sea grey in the fading light.

"Disappointing," said Fenella at the lack of pink and purple clouds. "Disappointing all round. We were forced to return from Cannes just to attend the funeral. Laura telephoned our hotel with the news that the will had been changed in Clive's favour." She smiled to herself, remembering how she had prevaricated over marrying Clive until he told her what his mother had told him: that Charles Veryan would remain out of the country and he would inherit. "So, of course, we had to be here. Jennie's going to be pretty miffed, don't you think? Especially after the miscarriage. You'll have to buy her a diamond necklace, Guy, otherwise life won't be worth living."

Guy heard her in dismay, then anger. Clive! Jennie had warned him, but he hadn't believed her. God, it was intolerably unfair when his own son should be the true beneficiary. All because of Charles Veryan's misplaced sense of honour. The man truly was mad: mad for betraying a woman like Monique in the first place, and mad for wanting to be a martyr over it. Perhaps this mental scourging helped his guilty conscience but in the end it was Alexander who would pay the price.

"Clive has a good position with the Harte-Willis Bank, doesn't he? So how will he find time to run an estate like this."

Fenella shrugged. "I don't suppose there's much to it and he'll have that Curnow fellow to run things."

"Thank God for Frank then."

A smile played across Fenella's lips. "Thank God things are turning out the way they are. It certainly would be impossible for Jennie to work with that man, not after the awful scandal..." Her words produced a reaction at last. Guy had practically ignored her today, and she was not used to being ignored.

"What on earth are you talking about?"

The bright red lips parted in feigned surprise. "Oh, you didn't know? There now, I'm speaking out of turn. Sorry. Forget I said anything at all. I'd hate to be the cause of trouble."

"You won't be." The voice was terse. Almost dismissive.

Miffed at the tone, Fenella wanted to shake him badly. "I thought you knew. Everyone else around here seems to so far as I can tell.

Curnow's son and Jennie were found in the boathouse in ... well ...
let's forget the Latin term and just say, a very compromising situation.
Shock, horror all round. Our local Romeo was sent packing while
Juliet ... well ... she went to Singapore and found someone else. Sorry,
but there it is.'' She observed his grim countenance with a degree of
satisfaction. "Stuck up lot, the Veryans. 'My dear, she's trade.' If they
feel that way about me then imagine what they thought of Mark, poor
chap. It must have been hell for Frank Curnow. So you can understand
how he feels about Jennie now. She threw herself at his son when she
should have known better and Mark, having been sent packing for
getting above his station, didn't return home until last year." She
paused and then delivered the *coup de grâce*. "In May. Now I come to
think of it, Jennie was here then. She bolted like a scared rabbit when
she knew we were on our way. I've often wondered why."

Fenella turned to him, smiling triumphantly, but the smile froze as
she saw the anger in his eyes. She had gone too far. Turning quickly she
said, "We should be getting back. The light's fading and I hate this
woodland path." She started hobbling along the track, aware that he
was following.

"A woman of your age shouldn't listen to malicious gossip, or repeat
it," said Guy. "It does you no credit, Fenella, and, I have to say, lacks
class."

She stopped, turned and glared at him. "How dare you say such a
thing? Don't take it out on me because your wife has put herself about a
bit."

Not trusting himself to say anything else, Guy walked on past her
towards the house. Shattered by her remarks, he entered the kitchen
garden once more and stood in the fading light for some time, phrases
going around and around inside his head. "In the boathouse ... a
compromising situation..." Jennie? Was it possible that he had not
been her first after all, that she had caught him on the rebound and
played him like a fisherman plays a fish until she had finally hauled in
the line? Jennie? Yet she had been a virgin on that first night, he could
swear to that. And whatever had happened before their marriage, she
had been faithful to him ever since. May! Just why had Jennie chosen to
come here for that week of all weeks? Coincidence? But the more the
thought twisted and turned inside his head, the darker that thought
became. It was no coincidence. She had known that Mark would be
here. Convinced of that now, he walked on as another suspicion took
hold, a suspicion so terrible that he felt sickened by it. He had always
assumed that he knew his wife. Now he realised he didn't know her at
all.

Storming back to the house, he packed his case and left, refusing to answer Jennie who wanted to know why he had suddenly changed his mind. Looking at her was bad enough. To speak would have choked him.

# Chapter Eighteen

Surrounded by family, Jennie had never felt so alone. Unable to account for Guy's inexplicable behaviour she wondered if Laura had said something to upset him. He'd once told her that, in this place, he felt like an appendage of the Veryan family instead of a person in his own right. Would that, however, have accounted for the dark expression on his face as he had walked out?

Seated at the head of the dining table, Robert Longwood, the family solicitor, placed his hands on the document that lay before him and let his eyes fall on no one in particular as he spoke. "This is a very sad occasion for me since Sir Philip was a good friend and, during our salad days, an excellent sailing companion. I shall now miss him dreadfully. His greatest sadness in these last years was the continued absence of his son and heir. Because of this, Sir Philip decided to draw up another will." He read out the formal text and various bequests to staff, Frank Curnow and Maddie. Then he came to the family.

"'To my dearest wife, Florence Charlotte, the right to live in the house known as Trevellan until her death, supported by dividends from stocks and shares which are to be held in her name. To my daughter, Laura Mary, the sum of two thousand pounds and the use of the dower cottage until her death. To my great-grandson, Alexander Philip, a trust fund to cover his education at Winchester and Cambridge and the rest invested until he is twenty-five years of age.'" He paused dramatically. "And now we come to the estate and house itself."

Jennie sat bemused since her name had not been mentioned. She glanced across at Clive who had visibly straightened in his chair and was fiddling nervously with his tie.

"'To my grandson, Clive John Willoughby, a five-year interest in the estate, to run it under the terms of the will and the auspices of the trustees. To enjoy revenues from the estate without touching capital assets unless agreed by the trustees. This five-year period to end on 1

291

August 1960 when full title shall then pass to Clive John Willoughby. Should my son Charles Philip return within that time, the house and estate revert to him, as the sole heir.'"

Robert Longwood removed his spectacles and glanced at the astonished faces all about him.

It was Clive who broke the long silence. "What does it mean? I don't understand."

Raising surprised eyebrows, the solicitor explained: "Simply, that if Sir Charles returns within a period of five years, the estate goes to him. Meanwhile, it is yours to look after, rather like a steward, until the five years are up and you become sole owner."

Clive turned red to his eartips. "It's monstrous! Bloody monstrous. Whoever heard of such a will? I'm the owner and yet I'm not? Oh, yes, and who are these trustees, may I ask?"

"Your grandfather appointed me one," said Robert Longwood, "and left it to my discretion to appoint a co-trustee. To this end I should like to ask Mrs Lloyd if she would agree to undertake such a responsibility?"

Jennie was still trying to take everything in. How plainly her grandfather had shown his bitterness towards her for deceiving him. It hurt more deeply than she could have thought possible. Five years! A stay of execution! Her grandmother had wielded some influence after all. And now here was Mr Longwood offering a chance for her to keep a wary eye on Clive and have a say in the running of Trevellan. God bless him for that. For five years she could watch over this house that she loved. She gave Clive a long and hard look then turned to the solicitor and smiled.

"Thank you, Mr Longwood. I should be only too happy to undertake the responsibility of trustee."

Clive banged the table in anger. "This is iniquitous. That my future as the owner of this estate should rest on a whim of my uncle must be considered an insult. I shall contest the will."

"Be quiet, dear," hissed Laura, through clenched teeth. "Everything is all right."

Fenella turned angry eyes on her mother-in-law. "No, it isn't. Of course the will must be contested. Is Clive the squire here or not? Am I the mistress of Trevellan or not? Are we to take up residence here or not?" She turned to Robert Longwood. "Forgive us if we seem a little at sea, but you surely realise how untenable this extraordinary document makes our position here?"

The solicitor smiled appeasingly. "Of course you may live in your properties, but as caretaker-owners until they become yours by right in five years. There are no grounds for contesting the will but if you..."

"Thank you, Robert," said Florence, standing and thus signalling the end of all argument. "You will stay for luncheon, I hope."

The solicitor turned to her and nodded. "Thank you. Afterwards I should like to discuss estate finances while those concerned are here. There will be death duties of course. I'm afraid they could be quite considerable."

As everyone made their way to the drawing room for sherry, Laura grabbed her son's arm and hissed, "Now you just calm down. I won't have you creating a scene. I agree the will is monstrous. I was led to believe that everything went to you without conditions. But it doesn't matter in the long run because your uncle is not going to return. Trust me in this. Put a good face on it, do nothing to upset the trustees, and all should be plain sailing. In five short years you will have full title."

"Five years!" Clive glared at his mother. "Anything can happen in five bloody years."

"Oh, do grow up, Clive." Laura smiled for the benefit of those watching and murmured under her breath, "You're the head of the house now, so come and be nice to everyone. Think of your grandmother and how she must be feeling."

Clive's eyes narrowed. "Did she ever once consider how *I* might be feeling? She's behind all this, I'm damned sure of it. And to add insult to injury, I'm expected to defer to Jennie every time I want something done or changed. Grandfather didn't leave her a single penny because he didn't consider her worthy of it, yet old Longwood's given her power she should never have."

"In which case you'd better not antagonise her." Laura set her lips into another false smile and walked into the drawing room where Keynes was serving sherry to everyone.

"Christ, no," shouted Clive in a booming voice. "Give me a large Scotch."

Florence sought out Jennie, who was standing alone beside the piano, as far from the others as she could possibly be. "My dear, I'm so sorry, so very sorry. It was utterly cruel of him to leave you out like that. I hadn't expected it. Do try to understand he wasn't himself. He just wasn't himself."

"It isn't that," murmured Jennie. "What hurts is that he went to his grave hating me, when I've always loved him." She glanced sideways at Clive, anger rising once more. "And my son has paid for that hatred."

From across the room, Laura's voice rose above the discreet murmurings. "Yes, well, had my father listened to me years ago, there would be no death duties to worry about now."

Jennie looked at her grandmother thoughtfully. "Whatever happened to Maman's watercolours? For years I thought Maddie had

293

them, but she tells me they're still here, somewhere. I'd like to take them back to London with me before they're classified as estate property. They belong to me, if nothing else does."

Florence dragged her mind away from other problems. Mrs Hodges had barely stopped crying since Philip's death. Would luncheon be on time? Should she go to the kitchens and check?

"Watercolours ... Now let me see. I believe they were put in the tallboy in the master bedroom to keep from fading. I wanted to have some of them mounted and framed years ago, but Laura said it would only upset everyone, especially you. I don't know, though. I think she was wrong. I would still like a picture or two, my dear. Your mother was so talented."

"Leave it to me," said Jennie. "I'll sort through them and bring you the ones I think you'd like best."

After a strained luncheon, Jennie joined Clive and Mr Longwood in the library where Frank Curnow was seated at the desk, glancing at a sheaf of paperwork laid out before him. He spoke of the estate, which was in fairly good shape, and of the house, which was not and needed restoration. He gave detailed accounts of revenues received and taxes paid. Finally he gave a guess at the estate's worth and an estimate of death duties to be paid.

Gasping at the amount, Clive lit a cigarette then settled back in his grandfather's leather chair, crossing his long legs. "Well, what's to be done? Sell a farm or two, I suppose. The Pentocks hold the largest acreage. What are land prices anyway?"

Surprised at his naivety, Frank Curnow shook his head. "Tenant farmers have rights these days. Besides," he pointed to dusty leather-bound ledgers high on the bookshelves, "if you read those historic documents, you will see that the Pentocks have farmed this land for almost two hundred years. One could say they've more than paid for the farm they still have to rent."

Miffed at Frank's tone and deeming it a shade impertinent, Clive snapped: "Then we'll give them first refusal. At today's prices, of course."

Frank looked astonished. "They could never afford it."

"Rubbish," snapped Clive. "All farmers plead poverty, but I've yet to come across a poor one. Well, if we can't sell the farms, how the devil do we raise money for this Government theft they like to call death duties?"

Frank spoke of free land which the Council wanted to purchase for housing, then added that it wouldn't fetch enough to satisfy the tax man. The discussion then turned to the family art collection. Jennie was heavy of heart at the thought of what must be done, but it was inevitable. "I'll arrange for a valuation of each painting." She said, "Maddie can help me there." Her mind went to the portrait of Sir Ralph Veryan who, having fought for the King during the Civil War, had gone into exile leaving Trevellan confiscated by the Parliamentarians. He returned after the Restoration. The only other Veryan to go into exile was her own father.

"The paintings were valued about six years ago," Frank was saying. "Some are so valuable that the insurance premiums proved too costly and were allowed to lapse."

Jennie just blinked in astonishment. "All this time, they were uninsured? Supposing there had been a fire, or a robbery?"

"Exactly," said Mr Longwood. "An offer to give one, or two if necessary, to the Nation in lieu of death duties could well be the best solution."

"And that way they would stay in the country." Brightening at this, Jennie nodded. "Maybe the Royal Academy would be interested in the Reynolds?"

"I don't care who gets what so long as they pay up," said Clive, getting to his feet. "Well, if that's all, I'd like to get back to London. We shan't have the tax man breathing down our necks just yet, so we'll have time to consider further options. Keep in touch, Curnow, and you, Robert. I'll return the weekend after next."

Jennie watched as he headed to the door, thinking how sad it was that this house with its art and rich store of literature should go a couple of Philistines who would one day auction them to the highest bidder. Fenella would probably sell off most of the antique furniture as well, replacing it with something modern and quite out of keeping with a country house.

When Robert Longwood left, Jennie found herself alone with Mark's father. In tense silence, Frank replaced papers in his file and cleared the desk. She watched him for a while, longing to ask him about Mark, but his silence and stern expression told her that he knew her thoughts and still deemed the subject taboo.

"We've never talked, Mr Curnow, never cleared the air. So I want you to know now how deeply sorry I am for the heartache caused to you and Mrs Curnow and hope we can put it all in the past. Clive will not lean on you as I shall. I think you know he can be difficult. But, for the moment, this is my father's house and my father's estate. It will need guarding very carefully from now on, but I shall support any decision you make during the next five years."

Frank's eyes softened and, suddenly, he felt sympathy for this woman his son had loved. "I admired your father and was extremely sorry that he chose to remain in Singapore. I care about Trevellan very much. It's been a large part of my life. I'm glad I can count on your support."

As she left him in the library, still shuffling through his papers, Jennie's shoulders sagged with relief. What could go wrong with such a man at the helm? Frank Curnow was as solid as the granite cliffs themselves.

After tea, she walked into her parents' old bedroom and found fifteen of her mother's watercolours in the Georgian tallboy. Some had been mounted and all were carefully wrapped in tissue. As she spread them out on the bed, Jennie's mind flew back to those sunlit summer days when she and her mother had sat painting together. Slowly she looked at each picture, remembering this scene and that one, until the memory became too painful and she placed the whole lot, still carefully wrapped, between two large pieces of cardboard and tied it with string. She had just finished doing this when the door, which had been left ajar, opened wide.

Pale in her black linen suit, Laura's eyes went straight to the package. "What on earth are you doing?"

"Taking Maman's paintings to be framed and hung. They've been locked away far too long." She stared up at her aunt for a moment, then said in a thin voice, "What exactly did you tell Grandpa?"

Laura's expression of surprise turned to one of defiance as she realised there was little point or dignity in denials. "The truth, of course."

"And what is the truth?"

Laura sighed and folded her arms. "Don't come the innocent with me. You've been trying it since you were ten years of age, but I know Genevieve Veryan and her duplicity. You didn't spend that amount of time in Singapore without learning about your father and his half-caste..."

"Eurasian is the correct word," snapped Jennie. "What exactly did you tell Grandpa?"

"That your father had chosen to live in Singapore with a half-caste Malay woman and their bastard, rather than return to his family and birthright. That this sordid little affair started before the war, which meant that he was unfaithful to your poor mother. I said also that it seemed an extraordinary coincidence that he should have been sent out there during the war but that, as a result, he had found this woman again and, mindful of our family name, chose to remain there rather than dishonour it." She smiled. "I also told him that you knew and had colluded in this deceit for your own ends. Well, it's true, isn't it?"

Jennie listened in growing rage, then exploded: "No wonder

296

Grandpa had a stroke.'' Seeing her aunt's shocked expression, she went on to tell the true story.

Laura stood like a rock until she had finished, then said coldly. "You knew what he had done to you and your mother, yet you kept your silence? I wonder why? Could it be that you hoped your grandfather would die before finding out?" Her mouth twisted into an ugly smile. "You see, my dear, I've always had your measure. You're as devious as ever."

"Devious!" Jennie jumped to her feet, causing Laura to step back in alarm. "And what is it when you reveal such a thing to a sick old man? No, that's called something else. Lady Macbeth would have had more pity. Now your father is dead and your son has benefitted from that death. What does that make you?"

Shocked at the implication, Laura could only gasp, "How dare you ... how dare you ..." before storming out and walking down the stairs to the drawing room. Shaking with anger she stood alone, yet felt that she was being watched just the same. It was always so when she was in here. Those bright clear eyes staring out from Monique's photograph seemed to follow her wherever she moved, making her remember past words with a sense of guilt. But why should she feel guilty? Was it her fault that Monique had joined the SOE or that Charles had indulged in an affair with a woman of mixed blood? So why should she feel guilty? Yet she did. Like her daughter, Monique had that same enigmatic look which seemed to say: "I know what you've been doing."

Swivelling her eyes away from the photograph, Laura let them rest on the silver George Cross with its blue ribbon. It was all too much. Wondering now, for the first time, if she really had helped to cause the death of her own father, she walked across to the drinks table and poured herself a very large brandy.

The train to London was slow, the journey seemingly endless. Jennie glanced at her watch and thought she would be lucky to get home before eight that night. Being a Friday she wondered if Guy would be there already. Relaxing back against the padded head rest of the first class compartment, she glanced out through rain-splashed windows at the Wiltshire countryside drifting past. He would be there surely, on this weekend of all weekends, if only to learn the contents of the will? Why, though, had he rushed away on the evening of the funeral in such silent anger? Whatever the reason, he would tell her when she arrived home. Her eyes kindled at the thought of holding Alex once more, and smelling the sweetness which still clung to the back of his neck. It would be a long time before she left him again.

At that moment a memory leapt into her brain. How on earth could she have forgotten the commission accepted so lightly four weeks ago, when Arabella's sister, Viscountess Belmore, had asked Jennie to paint a portrait of her two children at their family seat close to York? Bereavement had sent the whole thing flying from her mind. But the awful fact remained that on Sunday evening she was booked on a sleeper which would speed her many miles away from the little son she had missed so deeply. What on earth had possessed her to accept the commission in the first place? She must have been out of her mind. Looking back now, she began to wonder if she truly had been a little off balance? Yorkshire! Children too? Madness! On the other hand Arabella and Colin were very close friends and had sung her praises to everyone, gaining her more commissions. To have refused the Viscountess would have lacked grace and embarrassed Arabella. Maddie had been the first to agree. "You're well enough now to take it on, and you should. Such a chance is not to be sneezed at, Jennie. It will set you on the road to becoming a society portrait painter. Your fees will rocket." That had been then. Right now all she wanted was to have more time with her son.

When her taxi turned into Kensington Square, Jennie peered anxiously through the window but no Jaguar stood outside the house. Greeted by Nanny, she was told that Alex had fallen asleep waiting up for her, and that the Squadron Leader had telephoned to say he wouldn't be home that weekend owing to pressure of work.

"He's just too busy. Having to take time off for the funeral has put him back." Nanny Davies let her face soften. "You look very tired. Would you like me to cook something for you? I don't mind, really I don't."

"That's kind of you, but I'm not hungry. I'll just look in on Alex." Too busy? Really? Angrily, Jennie walked up to the nursery, recalling again that dark look on Guy's face as he had left her on the evening of the funeral. She opened the door quietly and entered. Alex was sprawled across his bed in the usual untidy fashion, arms spread out, face angelic in sleep, hair like spun gold curling on the crumpled sheets. Jennie moved him gently, pulled a light blanket over him then kissed her son, dreading to break the news to him that she was going away again. It would mean tears. At four years of age, he sought her attention more and more. Why, oh why, had she accepted?

Later, in the basement kitchen, Jennie cooked herself an omelette, drank two cups of tea then washed her dishes. Mrs Hale, who had seen this house through two world wars, had now retired to Eastbourne and Jennie missed their cosy chats beside the old cooking range. Now there was only the daily, an efficient woman who was younger, aloof, did not get on well with Nanny, preferred to drink her morning coffee alone, and left on the stroke of noon.

Angry at the thought of Trevellan's future, and wondering how long it would be before Clive turned her out of this house, Jennie went to the drawing room, sat at the walnut desk and penned a long letter to her father. She explained the will then told him why the house and estate were now in the uncertain hands of Clive. She spared him nothing: not the circumstances of his father's death nor his rage against a son who had stabbed him in the back. She spoke of Laura's part in the affair and the hatred against a grand-daughter whose only crime was to have kept her pledge to her father. "Did you really think your letter would resolve matters and undo the harm you have done? Your sister made sure it would not." She sealed the envelope and posted the letter that same night before her heart had time to soften.

By morning it had, but it was too late. Why was she so cruel to a man whose mind and body could never be the same again and who was afraid to return to people he could no longer talk to and duties he could no longer cope with?

Guy did not telephone. Having forgotten to tell him she was going away she tried to contact him at his office and at the cottage, but received no answer from either place. Meanwhile there was a canvas to prepare, sketch books, paints and brushes to sort out and pack into her special case, then she must address her thoughts to the vexed question of what to wear. Country clothes obviously, and perhaps a dinner gown or two.

Late on Sunday afternoon, when her bed was covered in clothes waiting to be packed, the telephone rang. Thinking it was Guy, she raced to the bedside table and picked up the receiver.

"Jennie? Hello there, it's Kay."

Crushing her disappointment, Jennie made her voice light. "Kay, how nice to hear from you. How is everyone?"

"We're all fine. And you?"

"I'm just packing. I leave for York tonight. I'm to paint a portrait of two children and absolutely dreading it."

"Oh ... sorry. I won't keep you then. Only I hadn't heard from you and just wanted to check that Guy had passed on my message. Not that it matters now that you're going away."

"Message?"

"You didn't get it?" Kay sighed. "Isn't that just like a man? I was at the factory on Friday and just caught Guy about to drive home to you. He promised he would tell you the minute he got into the house. Typical. If they're not talking about aircraft or flying, they just go to sleep."

299

Drive home? Guy had told Kay he was driving home? Jennie's heart began to beat too rapidly. "What was the message, Kay?"

"I'll be in town tomorrow. I just hoped we could get together for lunch somewhere. Clearly not, since you're heading north. Never mind. We'll make it some other time."

"What a shame. I'd have liked that very much." Why was her voice shaking? Why couldn't she sound normal? She tried to form the required words. "We've just had a family bereavement so, what with one thing and another, I daresay Guy forgot the message."

"Oh, I'm so very sorry. What must you think of me chatting on like this when you've . . . well . . . look, I won't hold you up any longer. I'll be in touch again. Have a safe journey, and I'm sure the painting will turn out just fine."

Mind spinning, hands clammy with sweat, Jennie replaced the receiver, sank weakly on to the bed and closed her eyes as she tried to take in the implications of Kay's words. Guy had not been at Hadleigh's or at the cottage. Where then? Boscombe Down perhaps? But then Kay would have known about it through Keith. And at the end of all this was the unmistakable and damning evidence of that little chat as Guy had left Hadleigh's on Friday evening – to drive home. An accident? He carried identification and she would have been told by now.

She walked over to the window and stared out at the central gardens. There had been no accident. Guy had lied to her and lied to Kay. How many times had he lied before? Her mind flew back to those many weekends without him and his refusal to be drawn on his work, saying it was classified information. Two little words which had shut her up and formed a cloak for him to hide beneath. God, what an idiot she had been. *"Never trust a man implicitly"*. She should have heeded her father's words.

Stomach churning, hardly knowing what she was doing, Jennie went on with her packing. Alex entered, insisted on helping and chattered on as he put things into her suitcase that she neither wanted or needed. Realising suddenly that he was all she had left in the world, she hugged him to her. "I'm sorry, darling, but Mummy has to leave you again. You'll be a good boy for Nanny now, won't you?"

The chubby arms clasped her neck and, aware that his mother was unhappy, Alex planted a wet kiss on her cheek. "Don't cry, Mummy. Will you bring me back a present?"

"Of course, darling." With a supreme effort she let him go, then straightening up, tried to collect herself. "Now then, what else do I need, Alex? You come to the studio and help me sort out the paints."

Late that night, when she was on the point of leaving, with the taxi waiting outside the house, the telephone rang again. As the driver put her luggage into the vehicle, she ran back into the hall and grabbed the receiver.

"Jennie!" Guy sounded terse. "Just thought I'd ring to find out what happened? Has Trevellan gone to Clive?"

"It has," she snapped. "Was that your only reason for phoning? No explanation for your strange behaviour in Cornwall? No message for me from Kay perhaps?"

"Message?" After a pause. "Damn. You've spoken to Kay then? I clean forgot. I've been..."

"Caught out? Can't stop to discuss your sordid life, I have a taxi waiting."

"What? Where are you going?"

"If you had been here this weekend, as you told Kay you would be, then you would have known where I was going. Who is she, Guy?"

"I don't need this from you of all people," he snapped.

She blinked in surprise. "What on earth do you mean by that?"

"This is hardly the time to discuss it."

"Whether it is or isn't, I'm fast running out of it." By now Jennie could scarcely control her rage. "Don't bother coming home next weekend, or any other weekend come to that. Go to your fancy woman instead. Meanwhile I've a night train to catch." With that she slammed down the receiver, picked up the nearest object to hand and hurled it across the hall. The valuable Meissen shepherd shattered into fifteen pieces.

For one moment, Jennie stared at the appalling result of her vandalism then looked up and saw an anxious Nanny Davies standing on the stairs. Had she heard everything? "I ... er ... I caught it with my handbag. Oh dear ... what a shame. Look, my taxi's waiting and is clocking up a huge fare. Would you be a dear, Nanny, and..." She gestured wildly towards the mess then rushed out of the house.

In her sleeper, Jennie lay watching lights and shadows as the train rattled and shook its way through the night. She turned over, pulled the blanket about her then threw it off again. With a thunderous noise another express rushed past. How was it possible to sleep? Even without the noise and motion her mind would not rest. Kay's innocent words had lit the blue touch paper. Now she remembered some of Guy's.

"*I can't be what you want me to be.*" He had said more in that sentence than she'd ever realised. What had she wanted him to be? A faithful husband; someone to love and who loved her, who would come home to her each evening and share her life as she so wanted to share his? On that awful evening of the Farnborough disaster he had told her that he could be none of these things, and she had misunderstood.

301

What he had really meant was "don't tie me to a desk or one woman". How long had it been going on? As far back as that holiday two years ago, when they had driven through the Loire Valley together and had seemed happy in each other's company? He had wanted her then and led her to believe that their marriage was going to work after all. Now she knew it had only been the sun and wine. Desolate, she lay back thinking that maybe she had driven him to this after losing the baby. But then, he had driven her to feel as she did. And, when all was said and done, she had not been unfaithful to him.

When she stepped out of the train early the following morning, Jennie was red-eyed, tired and slightly disorientated as she tried to sort out her luggage with the porter. A fair-haired woman in grey slacks and yellow twin set came forward along the platform to meet her.

"You're Jennie. I doubt if you'll remember me, but we met at Arabella's coming out." She extended a hand. "Lavinia Collingham. It's so good of you to come all this way. We can't go to London just now, and when we can the children will be back at school. Did you manage to sleep? I never can on trains."

Before she could gather her wits, Jennie found herself speeding along wooded country lanes in a mud-spattered Land Rover with two springer spaniels panting down her neck as she listened to the Viscountess who, even at this ungodly hour, was as bright as a shiny button. When they entered the Capability Brown parkland and finally came upon a grand Palladian palace, Jennie's eyes widened in surprise. She had expected a country house but this made Trevellan look like a lodge.

"I know," said Lavinia, anticipating the reaction. "It's a barn of a place. When the Earl decided to hand Belmore over to Robert to avoid death duties I was pretty shattered, I don't mind admitting. We had our own lovely house and were very happy. Taking this on changed our lives completely. It's not a home, it's a business. We hide away in a small flat in the west wing. The rest of the house is open to the public. They'll be arriving in droves by eleven, so we have to make an early start. July and August are our busiest months." She stopped the Land Rover outside a large flight of steps which led to the main entrance. "Still, I think you'll be impressed with our art collection. Arabella has spoken very highly of your work. I'm so glad you could come all this way to us. I've been looking forward to having you here."

After settling in her strangely plain and small bedroom, Jennie joined her hosts in their private apartments for a breakfast of kedgeree, then met the children who regarded her with deep hostility for spoiling their holidays. Both had been told by their nanny that they must sit very still for long periods and not upset the painter who would get cross with them. If the painter got cross with them, then they would be punished by not having one of the labrador puppies from Home Farm after all.

Blissfully ignorant of all this, Jennie turned to the eldest child, and thought at once of Alice in Wonderland. Lady Lucille was nine years of age with long straight fair hair held off her face with a band which matched the colour of her clear blue eyes. Her younger brother Andrew screwed up his face and proclaimed that his tummy hurt and he felt sick.

Showing no visible signs of having even heard her offspring, Lavinia asked, "We did discuss size, didn't we?"

Seizing the moment of parental inattention, the children ran out of the room as quickly as possible. Watching them go, Jennie smiled. "Yes, we agreed on half-length, which would be thirty inches by twenty-five."

Lavinia nodded, glanced at her husband who was completely engrossed in *The Times*, and said, "Half-length, Robert." The paper came down, the prematurely grey head nodded, then the paper went up again. Lavinia smiled and carried on. "Now they'll sit for as long as you wish, or I'll want to know why. You're to stand no nonsense."

"Well, twenty minutes is the longest for a child. They won't concentrate after that. Mornings would be best, when they're fresh. What they wear is important. I would like to have a say in that if you don't mind? As for how long it will take, it depends on so many things. Light for one. It must always come from the same source, of course, so that means twenty minutes each morning. I can work without the children later, but I'll need about three, possibly four sittings. The painting must dry before varnishing, so you'll have to put up with me for a week, I think."

A whole week before she could see Alex again!

"Delighted." Lavinia beamed and pushed her hair back. "Come and go as you please. Now you're to work in the music room because that has the best light. You'll find an easel and worktable in there, as you requested. Andrew must dominate the portrait. He will be the Earl one day. Don't let little Miss Bossy Boots get the upper hand. She's very good at it."

Jennie laughed. "Experience has taught me to spend time getting to know the children first, letting them handle the paints, bringing them into the whole process, so that they don't dread the thing but find it fun."

Lavinia stared at her in surprise. "Oh, they won't find it fun. They can be very difficult at times. But Nanny will be in the room with you to make sure they behave."

Jennie's heart sank but she said nothing more, resolving to work things out in her own way as time went on. She wanted happy relaxed children for a happy relaxed portrait, not two sullen-faced statues. That same morning she let the children help her to get things ready then, giving them old tubes of oil paints, showed them how to mix colours and let them loose on an old canvas which she kept for this very purpose.

When Lavinia walked in, she had never seen her offspring so quiet and absorbed as they worked away in smocks which Jennie had thoughtfully provided. Andrew had managed to smear a mixture of Yellow Ochre and Alazarin Red on his brow; his older sister favoured Prussian Blue on her nose and smock. They looked supremely happy. Jennie meanwhile had made copious notes on her sketch pad, examining the shape of their heads, noses and eyes. They had good faces and clear skin. She saw the points to bring out and the ones to diffuse slightly; and with Gainsborough's two little daughters in mind would pose her young subjects in a similar manner. Left alone, later on, she made her second preparation by laying on to a white canvas a base of diluted Raw Umber.

At five o'clock, when the house had closed to the public, Lavinia took Jennie on a tour. With the children pulling her by the hand, she passed along corded off rooms through one door then another, up flights of stairs into bed chambers, then down again to see one of the finest private collections of art in the country. Belmore was a treasure house of such breathtaking splendour that were she to spend three months there, Jennie knew she still would not have time to take it all in.

The following morning, she laid out her pallette and, when the children entered the music room, stood them where light from a tall window fell on to the small bodies, taller girl with right arm about her younger brother whose head leaned back slightly against her shoulder. Totally absorbed as she outlined their figures in pale Raw Umber, Jennie was unaware of their tense silence or of their eyes darting to her from time to time, wondering why she was saying nothing to them.

Having been given little time to think yesterday, she had lain awake all night trying to come to terms with the fact that her marriage was at an end. She would no longer be wife to a man who was unfaithful to her. Perhaps it was her fault that he had turned to another woman? All those "headaches" when, after the loss of Tara she had not wanted him near her. Yet she could have loved him, if they had not been so many miles from each other in thoughts and emotions.

"Are you angry with us, Jennie?"

Startled at Lucille's question, Jennie looked up from her work. "Of course not. Why on earth should I be? You're both perfect models."

"You look very angry," said Andrew, moving from his position. "Don't you like us any more?"

Horrified to realise that her thoughts had manifested themselves in her expression, Jennie forced a smile. "Of course I do. You mustn't mind how I look when I'm working. That's just concentration. You have to concentrate very hard when you want to do something well." She continued with her work, now placing a base green on the faces, necks, arms and hands, ready to absorb the flesh tones.

"It's sunny outside," Andrew sighed, fidgeting as he looked through the window. "Can we go and play now?"

Jennie glanced at her watch. The twenty minutes had stretched to thirty-five. Appalled, she put down her brush, stood back and said, "You've both been extremely good to stand for so long. Time to call it a day." Stretching and easing out her aching back, she said, "In fact, a brisk walk would do me the world of good."

"We'll take you to see our birds if you like?" said Lucille.

"Yes, the birds, the birds!" shouted Andrew in growing excitement. "You must see the birds." With that he took her hand and pulled her towards the door.

"Very well," said Jennie, holding back. "Give me a chance to clean my brushes then we'll tell Nanny where we're going."

It was hot and humid as she walked with the children through sun-drenched grounds, past the deer park, alongside the lake with its stone Palladian bridge and temples, and on through woodland where visitors rambled and picnicked. The children's constant chatter gave her little time for thought, and just now she didn't want to think. They had reached the boundary of the park and meadows lay beyond the fence to her right.

"Goodness," she laughed. "How far is this aviary?"

Lucille laughed, and pointed to a cluster of low wooden buildings ahead. Around the field stood a small crowd of people. "Silly, it isn't an aviary, it's a mews."

Jennie stopped walking. A mews!

The peregrine swooped low over the people as it tried to catch the swinging lure; the ringing of tiny bells sent flashes of memory stabbing into Jennie's brain. Farthing Field; incandescent wings hovering over the cove; Sophie on her perch in the old shed, and folding her wings and plummeting to earth. After all these years, it still haunted her. She approached in awe and stood in the crowd with the children beside her. Mark had once called falcons "nature's precision instrument". Looking at this creature now, Jennie had to agree that he was right.

"We've got a hospital too," Lucille explained. "It started about two years ago. Any wild bird of prey found in distress is brought here until it's well again, then set free back into the wild. We've a few owls."

At the end of the display, the peregrine was allowed to catch the lure and eat it. Muffin, one of the springer spaniels, lay down beside the falcon, and watched as it devoured the flesh. "The dogs are used to flush out game," Lucille was explaining, "and also find the falcon when it settles. Sometimes that can be in long grass, so then they sit beside it until the falconer arrives. Muffin and the peregrine are old friends." At last the peregrine was urged back on to the gloved hand, an ornate little hood was placed over its head and the falconer walked with it back to the mews, telling the crowd when the next display would begin.

"That will be with the eagle." Lucille shuddered. "I'm afraid of the eagle."

In the mews, peregrines and lanner falcons sat on perches, watching the people who were watching them, but the golden eagle had an aviary to himself. "I'm not afraid," Andrew was saying. "I want to hold a bird, but I can't until I'm older."

"I've held a kestrel," said Jennie, as they started back on their return journey. "But that was a long time ago when I was just a little girl." She glanced at her watch. "What time does Nanny expect you for luncheon?"

"Half-past twelve."

"Goodness, it's twenty past now, you'd better run on and let me take this at my own pace."

"You're sure you won't get lost?" asked Lucille, looking a little anxious at abandoning her responsibility.

"Look," cried Andrew suddenly. "There he is now. I'm going to ask if I can hold the peregrine on my birthday. I'll be seven then and quite big enough." Before anyone could stop him, he raced off across the parkland, ignoring his sister's command for him to return at once.

Frowning, Jennie looked over to where Andrew was running then saw a Land-Rover heading towards the mews. It stopped as the little boy drew closer and a dark-haired man, wearing a casual shirt and sports jacket, leaned out and spoke to the child.

"I'll get him back, Jennie," said Lucille, racing after her brother. "Then we'll go straight on."

But Jennie scarcely heard her as she watched the tall man climb out of the Land-Rover and bend to the little boy. Lucille had approached him now and was running off with her brother towards the mansion.

Sun gleaming on his dark hair, the man straightened up and was about to get back into his vehicle when he paused, turned his head in Jennie's direction and stared at her.

# Chapter Nineteen

Frozen to the spot, she could only watch as Mark slung his jacket over shoulder and crossed the park to where she stood. Then he was before her, the craggy face as tanned as ever, the deep blue eyes gazing in sheer disbelief.

"Jennie!" His voice was a shocked whisper. "What on earth...?"

She tried to speak; her voice failed her, so she tried again. "I...I... what are you doing here?" Was it possible? Oh, if only her heart would settle down. He had filled out a little, it made made him seem sturdier than ever. The face too had matured and changed. Gone was the carefree expression of earlier years. Now the eyes were heavy, the mouth tense.

Placing a firm hand on her arm, Mark led her towards the lake. For a moment they stood by the willows gazing at each other and, now that the initial shock had passed, remembering the pain and the rejection. Mark's voice was guarded as he answered her question. "I help to manage this place. And you?" His eyes rolled a little as it dawned on him. "Of course. Harte-Willis married Lady Belmore's sister and you're all good friends. I should have realised."

She heard his sharp tone and stood, hands clasped, small washing movements revealing her utter confusion. "I came here to work on a portrait of the children. I'd no idea you were here," she whispered.

"If you had then you wouldn't have come, is that it?" Jaw tensing, Mark stared out across the lake in silence then his tone changed. "I'm glad that marriage hasn't prevented you from doing what you always wanted. I was very glad to hear that your father is alive and well. Sorry though that he didn't return to Trevellan. Odd business that. I'm sorry your grandfather died but I'm even sorrier that Clive now has Trevellan." He watched a swan gliding across the water and told himself that the past was dead and that it would be foolish to touch on things too painful to remember. "Any children?"

Jennie nodded. "A son. He's four now." Why were they speaking in this unreal manner? She wanted to scream at him for leaving her as he had. But he had a wife and she had her pride.

A son, he thought. It should have been his son. Why did it hurt so much after all this time? He turned and looked at her, his eyes taking in the sunkissed hair which he longed to touch and the face which had matured from girl to woman, the face he had once covered with his kisses.

"And you?" she was asking.

"And me?" Her words had struck a chord of anger that surfaced rapidly, knocking off the protective mask. "Why the hell should you care? I never thought we would part, not after all we were to each other. In spite of everything that was against us, I just never really thought you would walk away from me."

She heard him with disbelief. "Walk away from you? It makes my head spin to think how quickly you rushed out of my life when things got tough."

His mouth twisted, his eyes looked strained. "Is that what you think? Even after my explanation? I had to get away, to calm the anger, to give you a chance to make a choice between me and the life you were born into. You made it. Strange choice – someone you'd only known for five minutes – but you made it."

Jennie was baffled. "What choice? You left me no choice."

The blue eyes darkened with rage. "This is getting us nowhere. And it's in the past anyway. I must go." He turned abruptly then paused and looked back at her. With a deep sigh, he let go of the rage and murmured: "Dear God, this is bloody ridiculous. Surely we've been too much to each other to carry on like this? Our lives have changed, so let's just accept that. As two mature beings, we can enjoy a civilised dinner together at least." Before she could answer he went on. "Meet me on the main steps outside the house at seven. Please, Jennie, just be there." With that he walked away, leaving her open-mouthed.

"I'm not so sure . . ." Her voice drifted away as she watched him walk back to the Land-Rover. Dinner? Just like that? The nerve of the man! How dare he cast her to one side then try to pretend they could now be friends? And how could she go? Mark was married. What excuse would he give to his wife? No, she wouldn't do to Mrs Curnow what another woman had done to her.

By the time she had reached the house, however, her ruffled feathers had settled once more and a smile softened her face. Dinner with Mark? It was all so unreal. How often had she thought of him, dreamed of him, felt his imaginary arms about her, his absent lips warm on hers?

Yet, now that they had met again, here she was wondering whether she should cold shoulder him or not. How prosaic real life was.

Prosaic or not, that night she found herself dressing carefully in a favourite ballet-length sea green silk dress, sweeping her hair into a chignon, and arriving on the top step of the main entrance at exactly ten past seven on a beautiful mellow evening, still wondering if she was making a big mistake. Was Mark any different from other men? What excuse had he given to his wife to explain away the fact that he was taking out an old flame?

Wearing a dark grey suit, he was standing beside an open-topped green MG. She had never seen him dressed so formally. At her approach he looked relieved, smiling, and climbing the steps to escort her to the car. In that moment Jennie knew that standing on false pride would have been the biggest mistake of her life. This was fate surely? In the past fate had not been good to her. Maybe this was by way of atonement. Just one evening, one quiet tranquil evening with the man she still loved, was all she asked.

And what an evening, with the countryside bathed in a soft golden light. They drove for half an hour in silence, then came to a seventeenth-century coaching inn on the outskirts of York. There, among oak beams and soft lamps, they sat at a corner table, each unwilling to be the first to break out of hiding, their cover being a discussion of the inn and menu.

Mark recommended the Chateaubriand then gazed across the flickering candle, thinking how lovely she looked with those large eyes staring out from an incandescent face. It was his fate, he realised now, to love her as much as ever while she clearly regarded him as an old flame who had somehow let her down.

As he ordered, Jennie watched him carefully, wondering what they could talk about that would not end in a scene. Why was she so nervous? The waiter left, Mark bent his eyes on her once more and she wondered how he could look at her like that yet be in love with his wife. What was she like, this woman who shared his bed, this woman who had taken her place? How happy was their marriage?

As if wary of treading on quicksand, Mark drew the conversation to Singapore and the search for her father. She told him, leaving out the true reason for his continued absence, saying only that Charles was unwell and preferred to remain where he felt secure. After this there was a long and awkward pause then Mark came to the matter he had been avoiding. "And so you returned with a husband instead of a father?"

"Yes," murmured Jennie, looking down at her sherry glass. "It happened strangely. I was caught up in a riot. He dragged me away and saved my life." She kept her eyes averted as she sipped the sherry and

309

explained what had happened on that terrible day. Afterwards she looked across at his tense face and said: "I was unhappy and desperate at the time. He was there for me and I began to lean on him. Then he was posted home ... and ... we married quickly in order to return together."

Frowning, Mark sipped his whisky and soda, as though trying to take this in. "Ironic, isn't it? After all that happened you're not married to a land-owner or a banker, you're just an officer's wife living in married quarters."

Refusing to rise to the bait, she shrugged. "Not quite. We live in the London house and Guy comes home at weekends. He resigned his commission and is now a test pilot at Hadleigh's."

Test pilot! Mark swallowed more whiskey; a test pilot who played knight in shining armour. He hated the man already. What was Mark Curnow against such glamour and derring do? Yet this man had saved Jennie's life. The alternative was too appalling even to think about. Instead of being jealous he should be grateful to Sir Galahad. "I saw him," he murmured, the bitterness now gone from his voice. "Saw you both together at the cove one day. You had just returned from Singapore."

Jennie's hand relaxed on the glass. "You were there," she whispered. "I knew it ... sensed it ... sensed you were on the clifftop watching me. But when I looked, there was no one." There it was again, that special something between them that said they were soul-mates. How then had it all gone so dreadfully wrong?

When the dinner was served and the wine waiter had poured claret, Mark raised his glass and said in a choked voice: "Here's to our meeting again and to your continuing happiness, Jennie."

Guy flew into Jennie's mind, Guy lying with another woman. As they touched glasses, she said: "Here's to our meeting." Her eyes softened and her voice dropped to a tearful whisper. "Oh, Mark, it is good to see you once more."

He lowered his gaze as he murmured, "You have no idea ... no idea at all just how much it means to me."

She looked away from the burning candle and the face beyond it, the face she loved so much. "And your wife? What excuse did you ...."

"None." He looked into his glass. "Not necessary, you see. It didn't work out. Rebounds rarely do. She looked like you. I wanted her to be you. Bloody stupid and cruel of me. I made her miserable, I made us both miserable."

Jennie looked at him sharply. The pit of her stomach was doing strange things. "You use the past tense. Does that mean you've separated?"

His shoulders fell. "Jennie, we were never married. Three weeks before the great day, we called the whole thing off."

She stared at him stupidly. "What?"

"I don't want to talk about it. Let's just say it was a Godawful time. I thought she would help me to get over you. Then I realised that no one could help me to get over you. Forget about it. I didn't bring you here to embarrass you."

"But . . ." She was trying to make sense of it all. "If you felt that way, why did you leave me?"

"Leave you?" He frowned in disbelief. "How can you say such a thing. I explained everything in that bloody letter. Oh, Jennie, I still had hopes for us in those days. You knew I was in London, you had my address. It seemed only a matter of time before you contacted me. Christ, I even hung around Gower Street, and Cheyne Walk, just hoping for a glimpse of you." He smiled weakly. "Love makes grown men regress to fourth-form behaviour. Then, when I felt you had been given enough leeway, I decided to make my move, even though I had promised you it was something I would never do. I was too late. You had just left for Singapore. I waited for your return. Then . . . well then I saw you from the clifftop that day and saw also that you had not returned alone." He paused sipped his wine and shrugged. "And so I came here. Nothing else left to do."

Jennie was still trying to take everything in. Mark not married? Mark still in love with her? Mark looking for her in London? Suddenly, like a giddy schoolgirl, she felt an upsurge of joy, then came down to earth with a bump. It was all too late. She was married, and worse than that, married to a man who did not love her.

"I told myself I was young," Mark was saying. "That I could put this whole unhappy part of my life well behind me. I would get over you. Most people have to get over an early love sooner or later. After that, there were other women, and then Penny came along. But you know the rest. So now I help to run a very large estate, a famous stately home and a falcon centre. It's enough to keep me from thinking, wouldn't you say? Your meal is getting cold."

She watched bemused as he poured more wine into her glass. "But if you felt that way, why did you let them chase you away from me in the first place? You say you hoped I'd contact you, but how could I when you ran off without a word?"

"Without a word?" He looked angry suddenly. "Christ almighty, Jennie, my letter was full of words, too many perhaps because clearly you didn't bother to read them all." Aware suddenly that the couple at the next table were now looking at them, he lowered his voice. "Have you forgotten?"

311

Jennie's mind flew back across the years to the storm, and that brief moment of happiness in the boathouse before the world crashed in on their love. She recalled every single moment of that night. "There was no letter."

He felt crushed as well as angry. "I gave a letter to Keynes to give to you, just before I drove to the station. Now do you remember? It was the letter of a callow youth making a supreme sacrifice for love, only with a get out clause, giving you my address in London should you decide love was more important than the wealth and position everyone else wanted for you. Clearly you did not. Chased away? No one chased me away, Jennie. I went because of anger and pride and the strain my parents were going through. Had you come to me in London we could have talked things over and maybe we would have found a way together. But you didn't come to me."

Tears stung her eyes. "I would have done, but I received no letter, that night or any other. I chased after you, did you know that? But I reached the station just as your train was pulling out. Even your parents didn't know where you had gone, or if they did, they certainly weren't going to tell me. I swore I'd never forgive you." She paused and forced a shaky smile. "But here I am, you see."

Her words and tears devastated him, but all he could do to comfort her in that public place was to hand her his clean handkerchief and watch in dismay. "Don't, please darling, don't cry. I can't bear to see you unhappy." He watched as she dabbed at her eyes, then frowned. "So what the hell happened to the letter? Keynes is the last person to shirk his duties."

Jennie thought back, remembering how she had crept from the house. Unable to deliver the letter to her personally, Keynes would have placed it on the chest in the hall. Had she missed it in her state of mind or had someone else taken it? Two people only were capable of such a thing. She let out a sigh of despair and murmured "I can only think that my aunt or Clive found it and opened it. It was never passed on to me."

Appalled, he just stared at her as she twisted the handkerchief in her fingers, then tried to visualise someone else reading words meant only for the woman he loved. It made him feel sick, nakedly exposed and intensely angry. "You never read it! You never knew! Christ, Jennie, it's an outrage. Someone's head should roll. I'd happily wield the axe myself."

"I'll help you," she said bitterly.

"What a young fool I was. I should have fought tooth and nail for you but I thought I was doing the decent thing, being the gentleman and all that." He grimaced. "Look where it got me. I wouldn't make that mistake a second time." He paused then, letting the anger fade, reached across the table and took her hand in his. "Anyway, it's now in the past, and you're an old married woman with a son. So we'll have coffee and liqueurs and put the whole Godawful business behind us."

They drove back through the warm still evening and Mark brought the car to a stop beside the flight of steps. For a moment he sat without moving, his large hands gripping the wheel tightly as he told himself that he must be fair to Jennie and remember she had a husband. But she was too close and he loved her to distraction. Turning, he saw her face pale in the bright moonlight and let his hand reach out to rest lightly on her cheek. Her skin felt like velvet to his touch.

A small electric shock quivered through Jennie as his hand slid down to her neck and his face came closer. Suddenly he crushed her to him, she placed her hands about his head and their lips met, pressing down with a passion that brought with it a million memories. Melting into his embrace, she was lost. Her head told her to be sensible, her body was telling her something completely different.

Reluctantly, he released her at last then, grim-faced, helped her from the car. She felt a little weak and shaken as she stood on the steps looking up at him. Something should be said, but what was there left to say?

It was Mark who broke the silence. He took her by the shoulders and said firmly, "Darling, I'm not trying to come between you and Guy, but it seems to me that I don't have to. I know you as I know my own soul. You're very unhappy. I sensed it earlier and now you've told me for certain. Maybe fate has given us a second chance to straighten out our lives. Think about it, Jennie."

She looked up at him like a lost child looks at an adult wanting to help it. Unsure, yet almost relieved. "Yes ... no ... I don't know." Her mind was in such a whirl.

"Tomorrow." said Mark. "We'll meet again tomorrow. Only earlier, around five. I'll show you York, then we'll drive out into the country and ..." He stopped speaking as she ran up the steps and approached the house. The huge front door opened and in the light a butler emerged to let her in. Mark stood there for some time feeling the bottom had just dropped out of his world, then returned to the MG. Suddenly the door opened once more and Jennie reappeared. She rushed back down the steps and stood by the car, smiling.

"Very well then. Here at five tomorrow." With that she ran back up the steps, leaving Mark on cloud nine.

After a night of joy, despair and doubt, she felt strangely different in the morning. Nothing was certain but suddenly all things were possible

313

and she was walking on air. Even the children thought her exceptionally happy as she got on with the portrait. It was raining and they couldn't go out, so sat still while Jennie talked to them as she worked.

In the afternoon the sun came out. She took a relaxing walk through the gardens and then joined Lord and Lady Belmore in the library for tea.

Having established that she had enjoyed her evening out, and that the portrait was going well, Lavinia poured from a silver teapot, handed the cup and saucer to Jennie and said: "I'm afraid I completely forgot to mention that we have to attend a charity ball this evening. Will you be all right here alone? I'll have the maid bring you something on a tray if you like and . . ."

"Oh please don't worry," said Jennie brightly. "I'm being taken on a tour of York anyway." Suddenly feeling foolishly mysterious she added "Mr Curnow is taking me. He's the son of our agent at Trevellan. We've known each other since childhood, so it was a very pleasant surprise finding him here." Did her voice sound as normal as she hoped? "His father will want to know everything when I next visit Trevellan."

Lavinia looked interested as well as surprised. "Mr Curnow? How extraordinary. We both think very highly of him, isn't that so, Robert? I suppose you know he's written a book on falconry and is now working on another. The first book did well, considering the subject matter, and on the strength of it Mr Curnow's been asked to participate in a television programme. He's incredibly knowledgeable and his great crusade is to preserve the British peregrine from extinction. He's responsible for the falconry centre here. It's very popular and brings the visitors in. My children talk about him all the time. He's so good with them. Please, do help yourself to cake." She sighed and sipped her tea. "I hope we don't lose him to fame and fortune. We can ill afford to. Although he's Captain Mulholland's assistant, it's Mark Curnow who has turned this place around, putting us from the red into the black after so many dark years. Death duties almost wiped us out when Robert's grandfather died, which is why the family don't intend to be caught out like that again. Captain Mulholland has been the agent here for many years but he's an old die hard. It was very necessary to bring in someone who understood today's problems. Mark Curnow proved to be just that man."

Jennie smiled. "Yes." She glanced at the plate Lavinia waved in her direction and helped herself to cake.

The River Ouse shone in the wash of another golden evening. Arms about each other, Jennie and Mark ambled slowly along its banks,

314

totally at ease now in each other's company. Earlier, they had walked around the ancient walls of York and Jennie then admitted how much she loved Mark still. Now, beside the riverbank, they kissed once more and she spoke of her unhappy marriage and desire for a divorce. She said nothing of Guy's affair with another woman, or of his coldness to her. Five years of marriage coming to an end was a sad enough thing. No need to make it worse.

They dined in an old country hotel close to the river and, in the hushed and slightly reverential atmosphere, discussed the possibility of a future together. Jennie could see no reason why Guy would not want to be free. "We're incompatible, that's all. There are ways of getting a divorce without kicking up a lot of scandal. I'm certain he won't stand in my way."

But Mark was not so sure. If Jennie had been his wife, then no power on earth would force him to give her up. There would be a struggle ahead. The last thing he wanted was for Jennie to get hurt, but if there was even the most slender of chances to get her back again, then he would fight. He could only pray that Jennie would stand fast.

When they turned in through the rear entrance to Belmore, Mark drove away from the big house, past the stables and into a small yard. "This is my home," he said. "The flat above the coach house. Coffee?"

He led her up the stone steps to the oak door. It was a warm, sensuous night when the scent of honeysuckle, freshly cut grass and warm earth all mixed together in a heady concoction. She looked up at the clear starlit sky, her senses reeling with it all.

He opened the door, switched on the light and stood back to let her enter. She let her eyes wander across a large room. White-painted walls were covered with paintings and photographs, mostly of falcons. Books filled the many shelves and magazines cluttered every available surface. An old leather sofa, shabby after seventy years of wear and tear, stood against one wall while an oak desk filled the area beneath the window.

"The flat, Madam, consists of one bedroom, a bathroom with ancient shower, one small and impossible kitchen and this elegant drawing room. Please note the Grinling Gibbons carvings, and of course the marble Adam fireplace." As he spoke, Mark swept a pile of magazines off the sofa and asked her to sit down while he prepared coffee. "You see, I'm being very good and not falling on you as you thought I would."

Jennie laughed lightly and glanced at the old black iron grate with its wooden surround, thirties clock and clutter of letters and notebooks. From the kitchen came the sound of cups and saucers, then the aroma of percolating coffee.

"How did you come to fetch up here?" she called out.

Mark re-appeared and leaned against the door frame. "Jordan. If I hadn't gone there, I wouldn't be here. The fellow I told you about, the one who showed me desert falconry, is an school chum of Lord Belmore. He recommended me and so here I am."

"The sheik's son?" She turned to him and smiled. "I gather the falconry centre was all your idea?"

"More or less. Lord Belmore likes falconry. Which was one of the reasons I was chosen to come here. The centre started by accident really. A mews for his peregrines, an injured owl or two, a kestrel in distress, and suddenly the whole thing turned into what you see today. The large falcons were all bred in captivity by people who no longer want them. They contacted us. We took them in.

"That's what the centre is for, teaching people about raptors, making them understand a species under threat of extinction. Now it's one of the big draws to the place so I must be doing something right. Mulholland's a tricky old boy. Doesn't trust anything new and so we've had our differences. But he's getting on now and should be retiring soon."

"I've been hearing things," she said, "Something about a book and now a television programme? I'm impressed."

Mark looked a shade embarrassed. "Coffee's ready. No, you stay there. I'll bring it in." He let his eyes feast on her for a moment longer thinking how lovely she was in that amber chiffon dress with the sunkissed hair loose about her face, then disappeared once more into the kitchen.

Left alone, Jennie looked about her once more. It was then that she saw it. To the right of the desk hung her painting of Sophie and beside it trailed the jesses and tiny bells. The sight clutched at her heart. In all these years, he had not let go of the picture, the pain or the love. It said everything about Mark. Turning away she saw a record player in the corner of the room and, wandering across to it, searched through a pile of records, seeking one in particular. It wasn't there. Her heart fell in disappointment. She found a Frank Sinatra song instead and opened the lid of the player. Mark had left a disc on the turntable. Swivelling her head to read the song title, she smiled and switched on *Blue Moon*.

Mark entered with the coffee at that moment and placed the tray down on the table. Eyes dark and intense, heart burning with love for her, he walked across the room, pulled her close to him, and slowly they moved to the song which caused the years to slip away, so that it seemed they were back in the boathouse.

When they stopped dancing; she lifted her face and his mouth pressed down on hers, the kiss deep, long, and becoming more urgent.

Bending her back slightly, his lips slid to her throat, his hand to her left breast, which he caressed gently. She quivered beneath his touch then let him carry her into the bedroom, lay her on the bed and slowly undress her. Each caress, each touch of his hand, sent a new shock wave through her so that without any will to stop him, she lay looking into his eyes, seeing the desire burning in them.

His lips brushed her naked breasts, then moved down slowly as, passion increasing, their bodies entwined, came together and moved in unison until Jennie shuddered at the exquisite moment when they seemed to melt into one being.

Afterwards they lay in each other's arms, not letting outside thoughts or problems destroy this moment. Mark watched her tenderly, kissed and stroked her face, and was filled with the wonder of her. He thought then that he had never felt such happiness or contentment.

She lay in the crook of his arm, the warmth of his strong muscular body against hers, and wanted this moment to last for ever. Their love making had been so right, something she had never experienced before. This sexual at oneness was a bonus, she knew that. For even had she not been swept to the peak of ecstasy, she could never love anyone the way she loved Mark. If they sat in armchairs just staring at each other she would love him still. As it was, their bodies matched their kindred spirits. How right could any two people be together?

Suddenly a disturbing thought broke into her tranquility. A week ago, no more, she had been attending her grandfather's funeral.

"Now what are you thinking?" asked Mark, stroking her hair gently. He kissed her again, she turned to him, and once more they were engulfed in the heat of desire.

In the dawn light Mark opened his eyes, leaned up on one elbow and gazed down at the face of the sleeping woman beside him. He had never felt so at peace with the world. Love for her flooded over him, dragging him from that living death of cold despair he had known for so long. He had found life again, and it was wonderful. Bending, he kissed her eyelids gently. They fluttered and opened. Jennie gazed up at him sleepily.

"Hello there," she murmured, stretching like a contented cat then snuggling into his arms once more. "What time is it?"

His lips brushed her hair. "Forget the time."

"I would but the maid won't. She'll bring my tea at eight o'clock on the dot." Glancing at her watch, she saw it was six-thirty. "Oh my Lord..." Her head fell back into the crook of his arm. "I must go."

But he couldn't bear to let her go, so they stayed locked in each

317

other's arms, silent, wanting this moment to last for ever, afraid that once it ended they would never find it again. At last she tore herself from his arms and slipped into the bathroom. A short while later he found her bathed and dressed, sprawling on the sitting-room floor in her chiffon dress, searching beneath the sofa for her court shoes. Having found one, she reached for the other. Mark smiled, then his face shadowed as clouds of uncertainty gathered.

Clutching the newly retrieved shoe, Jennie looked up at him, saw his troubled expression and said: "I won't return to that sterile marriage. I'll seek a separation and then a divorce."

How sweetly naive she was, he thought as he helped her to her feet. "You'll need grounds. I can't imagine he'll agree to give them to you. I can't imagine he would want to lose you."

Holding on to him as she struggled into her shoes, her face was troubled. "He must agree ... he must. There are ways, aren't there?" Her eyes met his, searching for reassurance. "There are ways?" But even as she spoke she knew the way was long. Even if Guy did agree, it was still a long drawn out process. "In America they handle these things so much better." She put her arms about his neck and whispered, "It's going to be all right. Whatever happens, my darling, it's going to be all right."

He led her out into morning sunshine towards the MG, saying: "I'll get off early. We'll meet and make plans." What plans? Their future happiness lay in the hands of one man, a complete stranger to him. He drove her back to the house in silence, filled suddenly with a terrible forboding.

Back in her room, Jennie undressed, climbed into bed and found herself smiling like a schoolgirl after a naughty escapade. Elated and feeling she could fly on wings of happiness, she looked through the window at the morning sunshine. It was going to be another hot day.

At the same moment, Guy stood watching as the Panther was rolled out. The sleek silver fuselage of the aircraft gleamed in the August sunshine; he thrilled at the sight. Having been with the project, nursing it along from design board to runway, it now seemed that all the work had paid off and problems with vibration were a thing of the past. In test flight after test flight the aircraft had proved itself a trustworthy performer.

He climbed the ladder into the cockpit, went through the drill checking everything, then started up the engine. Sleepless nights, wondering what would happen when he came face to face with Jennie once more, now told on his face. The world he had thought so happily sewn up was ripping apart at the seams. Having cuckolded him, Jennie

318

now knew his own, long kept, secret. They were two of a kind it seemed. But it was only now, when their marriage was well and truly on the rocks, that he realised just how much she meant to him. How was that for bloody irony? He could no more lose Jennie than he could lose Zoë. Somehow the situation would have to be retrieved.

Right now though, he needed all his concentration. Pushing her from his mind, he adjusted his helmet and oxygen mask, peered out at the mechanic, waved the chocks away and began to ease the Panther along the perimeter track to Hadleigh's number two Runway.

The sun was climbing. Soon it would dry up the heavy dew in the fields and turn cool, clear morning to hot, hazy day. By then, he would have finished this test run and be back in his stuffy office with a mound of paperwork and Mrs Horton, his marvellous secretary. He turned the aircraft into the wind.

Over the whine of the engine, a voice from the tower. He was clear for take-off. One last check through the instruments, then it was full throttle, accelerating along the runway, his voice informing the recorder of each move as the plane lifted into a steady climb. Stannington disappeared into the distance amid a patchwork quilt of fields. Twenty thousand feet, thirty thousand. He straightened out and prepared for more tests at supersonic speed.

As Guy crashed through the sound barrier, the bang was heard for miles. In her kitchen, Kay looked through the window, saw a jet stream high above then turned her attention to her children's breakfast.

After thirty minutes of tests, Guy turned for home once more, his voice still informing tower and recorder of each manoeuvre and the aircraft's reaction. He had descended to eighteen thousand feet when he felt a slight vibration. Cursing, he saw lights flashing on the instrument panel. The machine shuddered violently. Fighting to gain control, Guy informed the tower. Ten thousand feet. The vibration grew stronger, more violent, until the aircraft was bucking all over the sky. Afraid it would break up, he was about to eject then dismissed the idea. There was the village to think about. Three thousand feet. He managed to get the wheels down but still couldn't control the aircraft. He could see the runway below him; fire engines were racing along the perimeter track: he was coming in too fast. Cutting off the fuel supply, he braced. The Panther touched down halfway along the runway. The speed was too much; tyres began to burn. Overshooting the runway, the aircraft cut through a thick hedge, then slewed around as a burning wheel collapsed. It raced on. A high embankment lay dead ahead. Guy put his arms up to his face as the Panther crashed head on.

# Chapter Twenty

"That's it," said Jennie, smiling at the children who were fidgeting with boredom after their third and final sitting. "Off you go for your morning ride."

Like corks let out of a bottle, Lucille and Andrew ran from the music room shouting noisily, leaving Jennie filling in the background of the picture. Two more days would see her task completed and she would leave Belmore. Leave Belmore! Leave Mark! Desolation swept through her at the very thought. Having found him again, how could she leave him, leave love, leave life? There was little Alex however. Her heart ached for the child. If only she could go home, scoop him up in her arms and bring her son back here. Then she would have everything. Stupid! Who in this world has everything?

She walked to the window and saw the children heading out on their ponies with Lavinia riding beside them on her chestnut gelding; a quiet moment, before the visitors arrived, when they could call the place their own. What was she going to do? At six-thirty this morning the world had seemed so sweet. Now the reality of what lay ahead began to weigh heavily on her. Mark had known and tried to tell her, but she being she hadn't listened. Divorce! Even if Guy agreed, it would take so long. If he refused, then ...? She pushed the thought away. He knew that she knew he was being unfaithful. He would not refuse.

Glancing up at the sky, she saw clouds drifting towards the house. What had promised to be a lovely day was changing. Deciding to take her daily walk while the weather held good, she wandered through the herb garden, feeling the warm sun on her head, the smell of herbs in her nostrils and her feet scarcely touching the ground. What was the matter with her? One moment down, the next up in the air. She was a grown woman, not a giddy schoolgirl. But the dread had left her and it felt marvellous. When she reached the front of the house, a coach load of visitors were arriving and a small queue had formed on the twelve wide steps which led to the entrance. She moved through the chattering people who had cameras slung about their necks and realised they were American. It was then that she caught sight of the Land-Rover heading away from the gate lodge which served as an estate office.

Mark saw her, changed course and drove slowly to where she stood. There he stopped and for one long moment, oblivious of the curious looks from people on the steps, their eyes met and held.

"Five o'clock, darling," he murmured.

"Five o'clock." Jennie watched as the Land-Rover moved away. Five o'clock! How long the hours would seem until then.

Mark glanced in his rear-view mirror and saw the woman in a cream shirtwaister dress receding from him. A cold chill coursed through his body, as it seemed then that she was receding from his life. She waved. He waved back, then turned the corner and Jennie was gone from his sight.

An hour later, engrossed in her work once more, Jennie became aware of the butler hovering on the threshold to the music room. "A telephone call for you, Madam," he said. "It sounds very urgent, so I've had it put through to the study."

Jennie caught her breath. Alex! She dropped the brush on the table and almost ran from the room and along the corridor towards the study, wild thoughts flashing through her mind. An accident? Illness? Yet only last evening Nanny Davies had told her that he was fine and not pining for her in the least. An accident then? Suddenly finding herself at the study desk with the receiver in her hand, she clenched her fist and said calmly: "Hello. This is Mrs Lloyd."

It wasn't Nanny's voice, but Kay's. Heart thumping, Jennie listened, turned white, lost the use of her legs and sank on to the chair, feeling faint.

After that she hardly knew what was going on. Lavinia moved into over-drive, getting Jennie to the station just in time for the next train to London. The guard was blowing his whistle as they rushed on to the platform. Unimpeded by luggage, Jennie jumped into the first available carriage; a porter rushed forward and slammed shut the door as the train pulled away. Breathless, she just managed to lean out of the window and wave goodbye before falling into a corner seat, feeling weak and ill.

Still shattered at the news, she stared out through smoke and steam, remembering how the de Havilland jet had broken up and recalling her last angry words to Guy. Had the accident been unavoidable or the result of pilot error? If the latter, then those last words might have been preying on his mind when ... She couldn't bear to think of it. *Mea culpa ... mea culpa.*

It was early-evening by the time she arrived at Hertford station where the Chathams were waiting. As Kay rushed forward and placed a comforting arm about her, Jennie stared at Keith with frightened eyes, convinced that her worst nightmare had come true.

"He's going to live, Jennie, he's going to live." Keith's eyes were moist. "He's in a very bad way, but he's going to survive."

The relief and sudden release from a day of immense tension sent her into floods of tears. All during the long journey she had thought he must be dead. Now her sense of guilt was remorseless. While she had been with Mark, thinking only of him, her husband had come within an inch of his life and was now critically ill.

At the hospital, she was met by a middle-aged surgeon who frowned as he informed her that her husband had suffered concussion, a broken pelvis and a fractured spine. Having undergone surgery he was now encased in plaster from the neck down and it was too soon to be sure whether there would be paralysis or not.

Slowly, Jennie took it all in and into her mind came a memory of her father pulling on his pyjama jacket. The horror of that moment had never left her. "Was he ... was he burned?"

"No." The surgeon saw her shoulders relax and smiled understandingly. "Thank God for that anyway. Initial testing for possible paralysis has proved promising, but it's early days. Later, he will be transferred to a specialist orthopaedic unit. He's going to be in that plaster for many weeks, I'm afraid. And afterwards there will be months of careful nursing to get him moving again. He will be unable to do the things we all take for granted. You must be prepared for this. He's going to need you very badly." He glanced at his watch. "He came round from the anaesthetic half an hour ago and is barely with us yet, but you may see him for a few minutes, just to let him know you're here."

In a daze she followed a Staff Nurse to a quiet room where Guy lay in bed, wired to a drip with a blanket frame over his entombed body, so that all she could see was his neck collar and badly bruised face. The shock of seeing him like that was hidden behind a weak smile as she moved towards him and took his hand gently into hers. "We should send for Mrs Lim and her little pot of Tiger Balm."

He smiled weakly at the memory, his eyes swivelling towards her, "What a bloody mess. Two years work up the spout..." The voice faded away to the back of the throat and his eyes started to close.

She sighed and blinked back the tears. He had given her the fright of her life and all he could think about was the aircraft. In silence she sat there while he slept and, again, remembered their last harsh words before she had left for York. He had no idea she had been there; even Kay had found the telephone number through Nanny Davies.

When the nurse entered the room she looked from her patient to his wife and wondered which one needed her ministrations the most. "I'm afraid you must leave now," she whispered. "He needs to rest, and so do you by the look of it."

Jennie spent that night with the Chathams and heard from Keith of the miracle he had witnessed that morning. "I told him to eject but he stayed with the aircraft to steer it away from the village. I was in the tower, listening ... watching. The plane seem to fall out of the sky. I thought it would explode, but the fire engines were on it almost immediately. Guy was brought out unconscious. I thought he was dead. It was a miracle, Jennie, believe me." He sighed, still shaken by the events of the day. "And because he stayed with the aircraft, and has lived to tell the tale, we'll be able to hear from him what really went wrong. When he's well enough, of course." Thinking that sounded a little harsh, he smiled at Jennie. "Sorry. I didn't mean ... well ... anyway, you're married to one hell of a man, Jennie and we're all very proud of him, and praying for him."

Later, as she sat in the pretty but small dining room, toying with the cold chicken and salad Kay had managed to produce after a day of shock and waiting at the hospital, Jennie suddenly started shaking as fear and tension found release. The next thing she knew she was in floods of tears once more, apologising profusely for her behaviour and being taken up to bed by an understanding Kay who gave her hot milk and sleeping tablets.

Jennie lay back on her pillows thinking now of Mark. With an explosion of clarity, she knew that the dream was ended. Guy would survive, thank God, but his body was broken and he would need her. All thoughts of leaving him had vanished. Whatever her feelings for Mark, whatever her anger at Guy, this brush with death had put things into perspective. She closed her eyes thinking how bloody life was, how fate always did have the last laugh. Only that morning it had seemed so simple. Leave Guy who did not love her and go to Mark who did. Simple! How long ago that happy morning seemed now. The Chinese were right after all. As Guy had become responsible for her, she would now be responsible for him. They were tied, in this strange bond. Love or pity, call it what you will, she felt it for him still. He had missed death by a hair's breadth but could be left disabled for life; a cruel blow to a man in his thirties, a man who had to fly just to live, a man whose career as a test pilot was over. Yes, she pitied him desperately. Life would not be easy from now on for Guy would rage against dependence upon her, and his dependence would be total since she would be the bread winner

323

in the future. The future! A future without Mark! It stretched ahead of her in one bleak vision. The sleeping pills began to take effect; Mark's face swam into her mind, then she slept the sleep of the dead.

The next morning, she clawed her way back to the world, trying to remember whether or not she had telephoned the news through to Lavinia the night before as she had promised. Slowly her mind cleared. Yes, she had, and also asked her to tell Mark why she had been unable to say goodbye. Goodbye! She covered her face with her hands and felt that no other word in the English language held so much anguish within it.

After a sleepless night, Mark was in the estate office by seven-thirty getting through a mound of work to keep his mind from thinking the unthinkable. Yesterday evening he had waited by the steps in vain, then Lucille had come into sight walking one of the spaniels. From her he learned that Jennie had returned to London. At first he had thought the child mistaken, yet Lucille insisted that Jennie had left very suddenly, before she and Andrew were given a chance to say goodbye. "We don't know why. The painting isn't finished yet."

His feeling of dismay and disbelief had turned to anxiety. What could cause her to rush away without a word, without finishing the painting even? The child? Had her son been taken ill? Yet surely she would have left a message for him? The only other possibility was one he refused even to think about. No, she wouldn't turn her back on him again, not now, not after all they had been to each other.

The secretary arrived, bringing with her the morning paper, which he seized on as he did every morning. "Thanks, Pat. We'll have a coffee then go over those accounts. After that I'm on the farm rounds to see how the harvest is progressing. The yield is up this year, thank God. Will you arrange a staff meeting for tomorrow at six o'clock. Mulholland's ill, so I'll be taking it."

Pat smiled as she put the kettle on a small gas stove. "He's always ill these days. Too old. My husband says it's time the old boy retired and gave you a free hand."

Mark smiled, his mind still on Jennie as he opened the *Daily Express* and glanced at the headline: "Test Pilot in Jet Crash". He frowned, read through the article and felt as though someone had punched him in the solar plexus. When Pat had made the coffee and turned to give him his beaker, he was no longer there.

In his flat, Mark read the article again and again, trying to take it all in. He glanced at the sofa, remembering how, only yesterday morning, Jennie had been struggling to find her shoes beneath it. He could feel her now in his arms, the sweet softness of her, the joy and the love of her. But she had fled to Guy's bedside. Of course she had. What else could she do? But he knew what it meant. In cold dismay, Mark leaned forward, dropped the newspaper on the floor and placed his head in his hands.

Two days later, Jennie returned to Kensington Square where she swept Alex into her arms, hugging and kissing him while Maddie, Nanny Davies and the daily help were anxious to hear news of Guy's progress. Glad to have Alex chattering on to keep her from thinking too much, she said to Maddie: "All my things are still in Yorkshire. Lady Belmore's sending on the luggage but the painting isn't quite finished. I shall have to go back and complete it ... sometime." Go back! When? How? And how could she face Mark with the news that the only way she could survive as a loyal wife to a disabled husband would be for them to make a pact never to see each other again?

"You'll have enough on your plate here," said Maddie. "I'll see what I can arrange." Her full face was puffy, her eyes red-rimmed from lack of sleep and crying.

The telephone calls were coming in thick and fast, Fenella offering unconvincing platitudes, then Florence and Laura, both anxious, with Florence insisting that they journey to London to be with her at this time and go with her to the hospital. As diplomatically as she could, Jennie explained that Guy could have no visitors except her and that, since she was at Hertford so much, there was little point in their coming at the moment. The last thing she wanted now was a house full of well-meaning people.

When Lavinia finally got through it was to say that they had read about the accident and seen the devastating picture of the crash. "It's a miracle, an absolute miracle that he survived. Don't worry about the painting, my dear. We close the house at the end of September then have a week in London before the shooting really gets under way. I'll bring it to you then. No hurry as far as we're concerned. We can collect it in January. Your luggage and painting equipment is on its way to you. I've had a thought. Would it help if I send Lucille's dress?"

"Yes, it would help tremendously. And thank you for being so marvellous. Everyone's been so marvellous..." Choked, Jennie replaced the receiver, thinking that now she never would see Mark, never be able truly to explain that, no matter how much they might love each other, she could not turn her back on a crippled husband, a man who had once saved her life and now needed her to help to make something of his.

When Maddie had left, Alex crept into the drawing room, climbed on to the sofa beside his mother and held out the well-worn Beatrix

Potter book, demanding that she read *Peter Rabbit*. She kissed his golden head and started reading until Nanny took him for his afternoon walk. Then she lay back against the large soft cushions wondering why Mark had not called. Slowly her eyes closed and she fell into a light, dream-ridden sleep. The telephone rang. Starting, Jennie leapt up to answer it. Her shoulders fell when she heard Louise's anxious voice, giving comfort and offering help. Darling Louise.

Later she wandered across to the window and stared out at the square, wishing she had taken Alex into Kensington Gardens herself instead of letting Nanny boss her into resting. The house seemed so large and empty suddenly. If only she could rest. If only she could take more sleeping pills and just go out like a light for eight solid hours: to forget what might have been and what, instead, was going to be. Oh, Mark ... Mark. What's the matter with you? Why don't you call me?

The telephone rang again. She paused before picking up the receiver, knowing for certain that this time it was Mark.

"Jennie!" His voice was thick and hoarse. "I read it in the paper. I tried to get through earlier but the line was engaged. How is he?"

"You *read* it? Lavinia didn't tell you then?" She thought of him waiting for her, wondering at her behaviour and being so dreadfully hurt. Then she spoke of Guy's appalling injuries. "He's going to be dependent ... unable to do anything for himself ... I don't know for how long. Oh, Mark, he may be paralysed. They don't know for sure yet." She paused. "You understand what it means?"

There was a long silence. "I've a horrible feeling that I do."

"He could have been killed!" Tears streamed down her face and she could hardly speak. "You must try to understand that ... that what we had hoped for, can never be. Not now."

There was a long pause, as Mark struggled with his emotions. "Of course I understand. But, darling, you mustn't think so far ahead. He could recover, become fully independent once more."

"And pigs might fly! And even if he did, how could I then suddenly ask him for a divorce? Don't you see? It's no use, Mark ... no use ..." She sank to her knees and thought her heart would break. "Please, darling, we have to forget what happened between us. Forget our plans ..."

"No. Don't shut me out of your life again. I'll come to London, to be near you. I have to be near you." He sounded stricken. "God, if you love me ..."

"If you love me," she cried, "then please help me because I can't bear it otherwise." Unable to endure it a moment longer, she slammed down the receiver. Within thirty seconds it rang again. She stood weeping, begging it to stop. When it did, she fell back on to the sofa, biting into

326

her hand as tears fell. Ten minutes later it rang again. Fleeing down to the kitchen, she started preparing the evening meal. Still it rang, the incessant clamour reaching her from the hall, until her nerves were at screaming point. Each ring, she knew, was a cry from Mark. In the end she could stand it no longer and rushed up the stairs deciding that he was right. Of course they must see each other still. Who would know? Just as she reached the telephone, the ringing stopped. She stood waiting, trembling, willing it to ring again, telling herself that if it did, she would find a way ... any way to be with him in some clandestine arrangement. If it did not ring, then that was it. She would let fate decide as fate always did. It was the longest silence of her life. Abandoning the dinner preparations, she went up to her room, threw herself on to the bed and collapsed in convulsive sobs.

Guy was lucky. There was no paralysis and, after eight weeks in a London hospital, he returned to Kensington Square, dependent on crutches and Jennie, and raging inwardly that he was no longer a man but something to be pitied. The worst of patients, his body was strong, his willpower even stronger, and his insistence on getting back to full strength and into the cockpit as quickly as possible was mind-boggling, even to Keith who understood his feelings.

As Jennie ignored his frequent outbursts of temper and carried on calmly, dressing and undressing him, helping him with his exercises each day and checking on him each night as he lay on his special hard bed in the guest room, he would look at her grimly. She knew about his infidelity yet said nothing and was being so bloody decent and understanding that he wanted to scream at her. Martyrdom to the bloody end. God, how he hated it all.

Accepting his mood swings as frustration in a man so active and in such pain, Jennie tried to curb his insistence on wanting to run before he could walk. She drove him to the hospital each day for physiotherapy, waited about for ages, then drove him home again and tried to work on her paintings late into the night. She thanked God for Nanny Davies, who would brook no nonsense from child or man and was of immense help to her at this time.

Later, Guy took slow walks around the square, always alone and always ending in the privacy of a telephone booth where he kept in touch with Zoë. But the more he phoned, the more guilty he felt.

One morning, as Jennie put on his socks and shoes, he caught at her hand and held it tightly. "If I've been bloody to you, then I'm sorry. You've been a brick to put up with it all." He had been wrong about her surely? If she loved another, then how could she do what she had done

327

for him? His hand moved to her blouse and cupped her right breast. "I do love you, Jennie."

She stiffened and stood up quickly. She no longer wanted physical contact with him. For all that she cared, she no longer wanted him to come out of that spare room. Her heart and body belonged to Mark now. "What time are they all arriving?"

Aware of her reaction, Guy's face shadowed. "About eleven." Slowly and very painfully, he rose to his feet and made for the dining room. "You realise that this is a very unusual procedure? They're only being forced to come to me because I can't go to them. And it was at my suggestion so don't go thinking they're heartless. The sooner they find out what happened, the sooner they can get to work. And they'll find out a lot quicker if I can fill in the missing details."

When Keith arrived with Sir Robert Hadleigh, the Chief Engineer and the Designer of the Panther, she left them in the dining room seated around the table with fresh coffee, listening to the test recording. It was highly classified, she knew that, and not wishing to hear, was yet unable to move away from the hallway. She could hear Guy's voice, quiet, efficient and undramatic. Then it changed, grew louder, alarmed, faint then loud again, becoming urgent and rising until that final devastating shout. After that was silence. For a moment she stood trembling, then rushed up to her room, wondering what could be going through Guy's thoughts and emotions at this moment.

Still shaking, she sat for a while then drew from her dressing-table drawer the letter her father had sent in answer to her angry one. He was greatly saddened by his father's death and devastated at his refusal to hand Trevellan to her. But the strange five-year clause changed nothing.

Jamie is now happy and well-adjusted. To remain that way, he must stay here and not learn the truth. I cannot return. It grieves me deeply that my father found out the way he did and died hating me. That he blamed you also was iniquitous. He has done you a great wrong, darling. We both have.

As Guy progressed, the house began to fill with visitors, including Ian Stewart, who was staying at the RAF Club in Piccadilly and thought he would "just pop in" to see how they both were, after the appalling accident. Having been to dinner several times before, he was a welcome guest. Guy liked him and Jennie would never forget his kindness in getting her to Singapore in the first place. He asked after Charles and said: "You know, I've learned a great deal about the effects of the war on men returning from Japanese internment. Some are so traumatised that they're afraid to face the world, afraid of people, and need the constant support of one person – a wife, a friend – and then become totally reliant on that person. You once told me that your father has such a friend in Singapore. Be glad for him, Jennie. Because he needs her and ... you must understand ... will never leave her."

Jennie thought of those words, "I cannot return", and knew that Ian was right. It was more than Leighton, Jamie or the scandal. Even though he didn't realise the truth, it was his own fear that kept her father where he was.

After a quiet dinner, Jennie went down to the kitchen to make coffee, leaving Guy and Ian to talk. Climbing back up the stairs with the heavy tray, she entered the drawing room quietly to find both men standing with their backs to her, looking at her mother's photograph on the small walnut table.

"It was all my fault," Ian was saying. "I've never forgiven myself. She truly was a lovely woman in every way. And I'll admit to you now that I was in love with her."

Jennie stood quiet, remembering the cricket match so long ago.

"I understand," Guy murmured. "I would have fallen in love with her myself. Maybe I am a little. I think it was the mystique of Monique Veryan that drew me to Jennie in the first place."

"They certainly look alike."

Guy shook his head. "A little. But they're not alike. Brandy? I don't because of the painkillers, but that's no reason why you shouldn't."

Feeling crushed, Jennie placed the tray on a side table. The men turned and smiled, unaware that she had been listening. "I'll have a brandy too," she said tersely. "A large one."

On a cold, dank Sunday afternoon in early-January, Clive and Fenella showed up without warning. They found Guy, looking surprisingly well and Jennie positively wan to the point of fading completely. Both had enjoyed a long and rather liquid lunch and Clive sank unsteadily to the sofa then stared around as though unsure of his surroundings. He had put on weight, looked flacid of face and discontented.

Wearing a navy wool suit, with a pencil slim skirt and nipped in jacket, Fenella cast an appraising eye over the drawing room, taking in the Hepplewhite furniture, the paintings and ornaments, then settled beside Clive, crossing her long shapely legs. Ignoring Alex, who was staring at her curiously, she turned to Guy and smiled. "You certainly look a lot better than I had expected."

"I feel a lot better," said Guy, wishing to God they hadn't come and bending stiffly as he offered her a cigarette from a silver box. One telephone call was all the interest they had shown so far, so why were they here now? "In fact, I'm almost fit enough to go back. Alex, put your things away and take them up to the nursery, there's a good little chap."

Fenella's thin eyebrows arched as she looked up at Guy. "Go back? To flying, do you mean?"

"Of course." Guy offered Clive a cigarette then settled himself down in his chair once more.

Worn out from the long weeks of careful nursing, Jennie listened to this piece of nonsense and moved to help her son who was struggling to pick up his toys and dropping them across the room as he staggered to the door. "Guy has therapy only three times a week now instead of daily. So he's improving, slowly."

Fenella smiled, her full attention on Guy. "We've been so worried about you."

Liar! thought Jennie. Why were they here? In her heart she knew why but pushed the appalling thought away. "Well now, since I haven't been able to visit Trevellan, perhaps you can tell me what news there is on the valuation front? I've heard nothing."

Clive drew on his cigarette and stared at her strangely. "The Reynolds is already in Christie's catalogue. It goes for auction in two weeks' time. I've a copy for you."

"Christies?" Jennie gaped at him open-mouthed. "I thought ... the Royal Academy. Didn't they want it?"

"If they do, they'll have to bid for it. The reserve that Christie's set is – well, very impressive." Seeing her expression, he shrugged and smiled. "Bob Longwood discussed it with me. We knew you had too much on your plate to be bothered with such a matter, so we went ahead. Mother agrees."

Jennie's heart sank. "Your mother is not a trustee. As for Mr Longwood, he's a very good solicitor but knows nothing about art. Burlington House is the natural home for that painting. In future please consult me as well as Mr Longwood. It's bad enough losing the painting in the first place, but I had thought that at least I could look at Emma Veryan whenever I wished. Now it could go out of the country. We're not just losing a work of art, we're losing an ancestor. I hear we're selling a hundred acres too?"

"Come now, Jennie," murmured Fenella. "Clive thought he was doing the right thing. He was only trying to help." She smiled, stubbed out her cigarette in an ashtray then stood up. "This is certainly a lovely house. I would dearly love to see over it. Would you mind very much?"

Yes, she would, and Jennie's first inclination was to refuse. But in the end she led an eagle-eyed Fenella from room to room on a double quick tour, saying: "Of course, it's pretty draughty. No central heating."

"But marvellous for entertaining. And such character too."

Jennie's eyes flickered. For months she had lived in dread of having to move. To face such an upheaval just now would be too shattering for words. "I expect you would like some tea?" She paused in the hallway, praying they weren't stopping.

"Marvellous," murmured Fenella looking surprised as Jennie then walked down to the kitchen. "What's this? No maid?"

"I'm afraid not," said Jennie, heading for the door. "Just a weekday domestic and, of course, Nanny."

Fenella returned to the drawing room, and warmed her hands by the blazing fire. "It's a cold house all right. We must install central heating. Jennie's making tea."

Clive turned his pallid face to her. "Rather have a brandy."

Ignoring him, Fenella's attention was on Guy, thinking how different was this hero to her own idiot husband. She wondered what he was like in bed then asked herself what on earth he saw in dull as old ditchwater Jennie? If only she could get him alone. "There now, Jennie didn't show me her studio, and she promised." She put on her "little girl look", which seemed incongruous on a woman of such maturity and sophistication. "Would you, Guy? Please?"

Knowing how protective Jennie was about her work, he shook his head. "Better leave it until she returns."

"Oh, but there won't be time and I do want to see what she's working on," said Fenella. "She won't mind."

"She did once before," groaned Clive. "Do you want to put poor Guy in the bloody dog house again?"

Fenella bit her lip and smiled. "Oh, yes, I'd quite forgotten. Shouldn't like to get you into trouble, you poor dear."

Resenting the implication that Jennie wore the trousers, Guy got slowly to his feet. "What utter rubbish. If you want to see Jennie's work, you shall see it. It's damned good, and I'm proud to show it to anyone."

Stiffly and slowly he led the way up to the studio, still angry with Fenella for the remarks she had made about Jennie after the funeral. Life had been hard for his wife since the accident. Knowing he had been unfaithful, she had nevertheless nursed him tirelessly. Today, he had thought her pale and tired-looking and was anxious for her health. Yet here he was taking this bitchy woman into Jennie's personal domain simply because she had goaded him into it. Would he never learn?

Glancing at the paintings grouped around the room, some on the floor leaning against the wall, some laid on a table and one on an easel, Fenella headed straight for the portrait of the Collingham children and opened her eyes in astonishment. "Oh, it's lovely. Such soft colours, and look at the skin – like a peach. That portrait of you in the dining room is really good. I have to admit I was surprised. You must be very relieved, Guy. Now that you can't work, she'll be able to bring money into the household."

Clive, who had not dared to leave his wife alone with Guy, now winced and darted a black look at her. Never noted for her diplomacy, Fenella's tongue was growing ever sharper and causing him much embarrassment these days. He knew all too well that she cut an unpopular figure in Portlyn and Trevellan, and not once had she visited the tenants' wives, even though his grandmother had asked Fenella to accompany her on several occasions. He glanced at the portrait of Andrew and Lucille. "Who are they?"

"Viscount Belmore's children," said Guy. "She was working on this portrait when I had my crash, so she had to leave it in Yorkshire to be brought down later. It's completed now. I like it, but I've no idea what's good in art and what isn't."

"Belmore?" Clive looked thoughtful. "Yorkshire!" A tiny bell rang through the alcoholic haze. "Belmore ... of course. Knew it meant something." He scratched his chin slowly. "Funny that." A slow smile spread across his face. "By God..." He glanced at Fenella knowingly and the smile became a broad grin. Guy saw the look and asked if they knew the family.

Clive shook his head. "No, they're Jennie's bunch. Wouldn't mind being invited for the shooting though. Quite a place that." His thoughts flashed to the boathouse and his own bruised jaw. He could almost feel the pain now. "Belmore, eh! I'll bet Jennie had a good time." He started laughing, and being slightly drunk the laughter fed upon itself so that Guy became irritated to the point of snapping: "What is it? What's so funny?"

Clive's laughter faded into a mere grin. "Ah, well, you couldn't know this, of course, but her ex-lover now manages Belmore. Curnow's son, Mark. We had quite a scandal over that one. Now what has our Jennie been up to, I wonder?" He sniffed with satisfaction at this little act of revenge perpetrated on both Jennie and this hero who had his wife's full attention. "Come on, you poor old bugger. Time for tea." With a laugh that rang through the house he walked out of the studio.

When Jennie entered the drawing room with the tea trolley there was a silence she could have cut with a knife. Fenella, seeing Guy's terrible expression, suddenly remembered an important appointment, made profuse apologies and dragged her husband to the door. As Guy showed them out, Jennie stood mystified, looking at the freshly made tea, thinly cut sandwiches and Dundee cake.

"How rude!" she exclaimed when Guy returned in grim silence to the room. She glanced at him, then saw the anger in his eyes. "What is it? What's happened?" When he still said nothing she went on: "Are we being turned out?"

In silence, Guy walked across to the window and stared out at the cold darkening evening. It was snowing lightly but the flakes were not settling. Still deeply shaken, he looked at the skeletal trees, lights in windows, a few cars moving past the house, and said: "I'm going to Stannington tomorrow."

"Stannington? Are you mad? It's too far for you to drive. You're not ready for that yet."

"I want no arguments, Jennie," he snapped. "I'm going and that's it."

Dumbfounded, she poured his tea, wondering what had happened to bring this on. "Have you heard from Keith? Is that it? Only you didn't tell me." Had he been let go as he feared he would be? "What is it, Guy?"

He turned, suppressed a great desire to strike her, then walked into the study, made a telephone call out of her hearing and slammed out of the house. Jennie rushed to the front door and saw him climbing painfully into the Jaguar.

"Guy ... where are you going?" she called. "Come back." The car kicked into life, and moved off. With screeching tyres it turned the corner and disappeared out of sight.

Dumbfounded, Jennie walked back inside. What had happened? Where had he gone? Why had he gone? Clive had upset him, but how, and why was he taking it out on her? In the drawing room she stood looking down at the tea trolley, the sandwiches and cake, and two full cups still untouched. This was only the third time he had driven the car since the accident and even then it had been just local. Where on earth had he gone? Worried sick, she waited up for his return.

Guy drove westward, his mind reeling with pictures he wished would go away. Belmore! Had she been forced away from bloody Mark Curnow to hold his hand? Had all that loving nursing been nothing more than pity after all? Pity! He was a pitiful cuckold. Well, thank God he had another home and another woman. At the house in Ealing he stopped the car. The front door opened and light fell on the garden path.

Just after midnight, Jennie heard his key in the lock, raised her head off the sofa cushion and waited for him to enter the drawing room. The light was full on, the door open so he could see she was still up. When she heard his footsteps on the stairs Jennie rushed into the hall and called out: "Where the devil have you been all this time?"

He turned and was about to accuse her with stinging words when a

sense of self-preservation came over him. If he asked about her infidelity, she would demand to know about his. Then this little house of
cards would collapse about him. It was the last thing he wanted,
especially now, when he hoped to get back to Hadleigh's. Much as he
hated even to think of Jennie with another man, these past months had
proved it was over surely? And, now that his rage was over too,
softened by Zoë's attentions, he had to remind himself how Jennie had
worn herself out looking after him. "I went to a pub, then drove
about."

"But why?" She was looking at him in disbelief. "What did they say
that upset you so much?"

He shrugged. "Maybe I over-reacted. Anyway, I'm very tired now
and want to make an early start tomorrow." With that he went upstairs
and closed his bedroom door.

After a sleepless night Jennie found him still hell-bent on going to
Stannington and, unable to understand or stop him, insisted on driving. "Two and a half hours is too long. You'll tire." Heedless of his
angry protests, she got into the Jaguar and sat tight behind the wheel.
"Unless you want to cause a scene in the square then this is the only way
you're going anywhere. I've had enough of your nonsense."

"Christ, you're worse than a mother hen," he shouted, glaring at her.
But since she refused to budge, he was forced to give way. "All right
then, but when we get within six miles of the place you let me drive."

She agreed and they set off on a snow-threatened cold morning, at a
pace which set his nerves screaming with impatience.

At the Hadleigh factory, Guy was greeted warmly by a surprised Keith
and soon joined by the rest of the team. Jennie watched as they swept
him off and wondered if they could guess at the pain he was in. Then she
drove out to Kay's home to say hello, before purchasing a few provisions at the village stores and making her way to the cottage. She
found the place spotless thanks to Mrs Mottram, who eschewed all
modern household aids in favour of "good old-fashioned elbow
grease" and who had used this time to give the cottage an overhaul
from top to bottom.

She was putting the provisions away in the kitchen larder when she
heard a car pull up. Opening the front door she saw Kay beckoning her
out to the small lane, saying: "Can't manage it by myself. It belonged to
a friend of ours who hasn't needed it for years."

Bemused, Jennie watched as Kay walked back to her estate wagon,
opened the back and started pulling at a bedboard. She walked forward
and said, "How very kind, but he won't need it. We're returning home
tonight."

Kay turned and frowned. "Are you sure? Odd. Keith rang, saying you'd need this and would I deliver it pronto?" She shrugged. "Well, now that I've gone to this trouble you might as well have it. I'll help you."

Negotiating the board up the narrow winding stairs prompted the question of how beds and wardrobes were ever brought up in the first place. "In Cornish cottages," said Jennie, breathlessly, "they have little trap doors for the coffins because they couldn't get them up or down the staircase. Here they must have hauled everything up through the window."

After the board had been placed beneath the mattress, they walked down to the small sitting room where Jennie put a match to the prepared fire and, since the cottage was like ice, they sat in their coats drinking coffee. When Kay then rushed off to Hertford for a dental checkup, Jennie stood at the stone kitchen sink washing and peeling potatoes to make a warming shepherd's pie before their long cold journey home. By one o'clock, it was ready for the oven. As she cleaned cabbage, she saw snowflakes falling and hoped they started back before they became snow-bound. By three o'clock Guy had still not returned. She paced the cottage, anxious for him. He would be in great pain and desperate for rest by now. Today there had been no time for his exercises. They were crucial. Without her to chivvy him into doing them daily his back would never have strengthened the way it had. He had jumped the gun by coming here today, yet she understood his frustration and wondered what had been said yesterday to bring it to such a head. Whatever it was, he was foolish to allow his fears to push him to this brink. Clive or Fenella? Which one had made him feel a useless cripple?

She made herself some tea, then sat down by the fire thinking of Mark. He had not telephoned again and she still fought down her desire to contact him. How was he feeling? Like her ... stumbling from day to day? In a sense, she was the lucky one. She was needed; her days were full, her mind for ever on the next thing that had to be done as well as keeping up with her own commissions. For all the heartache, she had managed to get through this terrible time but nothing could still her longing to lie in Mark's arms once more and have him whisper that he loved her. Did he though? She had hurt him, not once but twice. Could love withstand that amount of pain before turning to hate? How could he, a bachelor, understand that she could love him to distraction yet still care and feel responsible for her husband?

Keith dropped Guy off at five o'clock, saying that he hoped they would dine with them the following evening. Jennie had been about to explain that they were leaving when, to her complete surprise Guy said,

335

"Thanks, old boy. I'd love to. Unfortunately Jennie's off home tomorrow."

Keith frowned. "Sorry to hear that, Jennie. Kay will be disappointed. Can't tell you how marvellous it is that Guy's returning to the fold. Fabulous news. Well, cheerio. Have a good journey back tomorrow."

Aware that Jennie was waiting for an explanation, Guy closed the front door then eased himself slowly on to a fireside chair. "Well, that went better than I could have hoped." He took a bottle of pain killers from his pocket, swallowed a pill, then said, "Had a long chat with Sir Robert. I'm now back in harness."

Jennie blinked. "In harness? In cloud cukooland, you mean! Have you lost your mind? You're scarely out of convalescence. The doctor said..."

"The doctor said I was fit enough, so long as I keep up the exercises."

"I hardly think he meant fit enough to start flying again. Did you make that clear to Keith?"

He placed a hand to his brow and sighed. "Please, Jennie. Not now. I'm weary to the bone. Until the new Panther's ready I'll be testing Hadleigh's latest executive aircraft. There'll be no G force to worry about. It's a turbo prop six-seater."

She was bemused. "I thought this little trip was just to see that your position was assured? Now that it is, you must come home and wait a few more weeks. I assumed that was the plan." When Guy said nothing she shook her head in desperation. "You must be crazy. Only a few days ago I was still putting your shoes and socks on for you."

"Getting back to work will make my back more flexible than hanging around at home." He stared into the fire, pale-faced and utterly exhausted. "And I've decided to start tomorrow so there's an end to all argument." As Jennie set the table, in grim silence, he watched her and wondered. Suspicions were not facts and he had no way of knowing what had passed between her and Mark Curnow during that week in Yorkshire. He would rather not know. But it left that other, darker suspicion rising to the surface once more. The painkiller was kicking in now, but did little to help his mental torment. With such a terrible shadow hanging over him, how was it possible to live in the same house with her? Time to go back to the old way. It was best in the long run. He would miss little Alex, that was the hell of it, for during these past months he had come to know and love the boy. Would he miss Jennie? Right now he was too confused to feel anything, apart from a slight fellow feeling for Othello. What was his wife, saint or strumpet?

Jennie brought in the shepherd's pie and they sat at the table, eyes on

336

their plates rather than on each other. No longer hungry, she toyed with her food then asked, "And how will you manage here all alone?"

"Oh, I'll be fine." he said.

"You're putting your recovery in jeopardy."

He leaned forward and sighed. "Jennie, I am recovered. I need to become independent again. Please try to understand." They ate in tense silence. When the meal was over, Guy said quietly: "I'll drive you to the station tomorrow. You won't mind returning by train, will you?"

Too angry to speak, Jennie cleared away the dishes then stood with her hands in the kitchen sink, staring out into darkness. Dismissed! Go home, Jennie, I don't need or want you any more. She had given up the man she loved to be with her husband because he would need her. Now she was surplus to requirements. Of course she was glad he had a place at Hadleigh's still, of course she was glad he could get his life together once more, it was what she had prayed for, but this . . . this cold-hearted dismissal was something else.

When she returned to the sitting room, Guy was settled beside the fireplace once more, drawing on a cigarette. Flames licked about the coals, the smoke billowing back into the room as the wind got up outside. Wearily she sank into the armchair opposite, thinking how stubborn he was. And yet that same stubborness and willpower had got him through to this day, a day that had once seemed too far away to reach.

"Look," he said, "I'm grateful for all you've done, but we both have work get on with, and lives to lead. It's time to get back to normal."

"Normal? What is that exactly?"

"Please, Jennie, I'm in no mood for talking."

"That's just it, we never do talk. For instance, we never talked about that weekend after Grandpa's funeral."

Aware of the anger in her tone, he was ready for the question, and had been for months. "Ah, yes. You had a taxi waiting, I recall. Something about a message from Kay followed by a strange accusation. If you must know, I had a call from Brockenhurst to say that Mother was ill. Another of her turns. So, I went to Hampshire instead."

Jennie just stared, unsure whether to believe him or not. Had she been so terribly wrong all this time, or had years of practice turned him into a consummate liar?

As if reading her mind, he said quietly: "Don't look for demons where there aren't any."

All certainty now scattered to the wind, she stood to her feet and headed for the stairs, murmuring, "I must make your bed. I'll sleep on the couch tonight."

Halfway up she heard him say: "And what of Belmore, Jennie? Not once have you spoken of your visit there. Why don't we talk about that?"

Her heart stopped. He knew something; it was in his tone. How did he know: Alarmed for Mark and any scandal which could hurt him, she turned to Guy, unsmiling. "You can drive me to the station as early as you like. The sooner I get back to Alex the better."

Her silence confirmed his fears. For a moment he could not speak, or even look at her. "Very well," he snapped. "I intend to be in the office by eight o'clock and . . ." He stopped. Jennie had gone.

For a while, Guy sat looking into the fire, trying to fight down an anger which made him sick to his stomach. Nothing had been said, yet everything had.

# Chapter Twenty-One

After a nerve-wracking fifteen minutes, the gavel finally came down on a price far in excess of the reserve put on the Reynolds portrait. Much to everyone's relief, death duties could now be paid in full.

As Jennie, Maddie and Robert Longwood left Christie's and walked out into a rain-swept King Street each had one thought. It was voiced by Jennie. "Will it stay in the country?"

"I doubt it," said Maddie, still fuming about the whole thing. "As trustees you could have over-ruled Clive on this, surely?"

Robert Longwood was slipping his black coat on over a dark pin-stripe suit. "We can only do that when the estate is threatened in any way. I did make overtures to the necessary Government departments but everything seemed to take so long. Mr Willoughby's patience ran out. The R.A. never had the chance to accept or refuse. You must understand that Mr Willoughby has the right to do many things." He straightened his homburg and hailed a taxi. "Such as turning his mother out of Trevellan."

"What?" Jennie climbed into the taxi and settled back, staring at Robert who pulled down the seat opposite.

"Simpson's, please." Turning back to the women, Robert smiled. "Then I must go to Jackson's and arm myself with tea. My wife will never forgive me if I don't. You didn't know that Mrs Willoughby took up residence in the dower cottage three weeks ago?"

Staggered, Jennie shook her head. "That cottage hasn't been lived in for years. Do you know it, Maddie? As a child I always thought it rather creepy, tucked away behind the church among all those trees. It has out-of-date plumbing and is in a very rundown state. I've heard nothing from Mr Curnow about renovations though."

"That's because Mr Willoughby said the estate couldn't afford it and has requested his mother to pay for all that herself."

Jennie exchanged glances with Maddie then leaned back and gazed

339

out at a sea of black umbrellas, thinking that if Clive could do such a thing to his own mother, then what would he do to others?

She found out five days later. The letter was from Mr Longwood, informing her that she had one month to vacate the house in Kensington Square since Clive wished to take up residence without further delay. Her heart sank. It was no surprise, of course, especially after that unexpected visit from Clive and Fenella just over a week ago. But one month? She went to the telephone and gave the exchange operator the Dorking number. Fenella answered and laughed at what she considered an idiotic request.

"More time? Good Lord, Jennie, we've been extremely generous as it is. But for Guy's accident, you would have been out of there last September. No, my dear, you've lived grace and favour style for far too long. The house is ours. In one month you must vacate it."

Cold-hearted bitch, thought Jennie, slamming down the receiver. When she finally managed to get through to Guy, he was in his office, going over the details for his first flight since the crash and had no time for anything else.

"Oh, Christ!" he snapped. "Trust that bloody cousin of yours. What the hell does he want with three houses? Well, it's impossible for me to help you. You'll have to find somewhere with a low rent. Don't rush. Make the bastard wait."

"Clive won't wait. I warned you years ago that this would happen. Now, in one month's time, we shall be homeless. We need to look at property together with a view to buying."

"Buying? Are you mad? How the hell can I pay rent here, a mortgage on a London home and Nanny's salary at the same time? And how the hell can I suddenly take time off to go househunting after all these months away? Sorry, Jennie, I'll have to leave it to you. Find something to rent, just for now."

Angrily he replaced the receiver. Losing the house was more of a blow than he had expected. He dreaded the indignity of having to explain to everyone why they had been forced to move, but he dreaded more any complications in his tidy life. For now the sudden rush was working for him, but how long could he go on stalling for time?

Walking from the telephone, Jennie rubbed her brow anxiously. She hadn't expected help and wasn't going to get it either. On the other hand she understood the pressure Guy was under. Even so, she felt alone and horribly vulnerable. Supposing she hadn't found somewhere by the end of the month, would Clive send in the bailiffs? The answer should be: Of course not. But this was Clive who would enjoy humiliating her as much as he enjoyed taking Kensington Square from her. After wearing her heels down, wandering London looking for

340

something suitable, she began to despair until Maddie waved her proverbial wand. "Why on earth didn't you tell me sooner that Clive was turning you out? You can have Gavin's studio. Now that's he's decamped to New York it's just sitting there until I find another protégé. At the moment that's you, and you've better things to do than waste hours househunting."

Without the need to look for a place with a suitable studio, the field widened. Time was not on her side, however, and Jennie finally settled for a terraced house in Flood Street which was close to Maddie's place but needed decorating and was in a bad state of repair. Exhausted with her search and mindful of commissions to honour, she took it for one year. Guy raged at the rent, Nanny at the state of the place, and Jennie at the landlord's agent to put matters right. He did! While a decorator repapered and painted, Jennie scoured the Portobello Road for antique furniture which Maddie restored. Jennie moved her own few pieces out from Kensington Square, including Guy's special bed, then purchased comfortable armchairs and a sofa for the small drawing room, and three new single divans for the bedrooms.

When it was done, she surveyed the house and decided that a tatty unloved dwelling had become a comfortable home after all. Even Guy grudgingly gave her credit but still thought she could have found something cheaper. Having used her own fee money to pay for most of the furniture, she found his constant pleas of poverty rather grating. Test pilots were well paid, she said. He snapped that insurance premiums on his life were excessive in a high-risk occupation. She retorted that Tiger Moths didn't come cheap either. Their life resumed its old course. Back to normal? Not quite, thought Jennie. Having weathered the crisis, she suddenly felt a sense of independence she had never before known. She could manage her own affairs. It felt good.

For all the chill of a rainswept April evening it was very hot, stuffy and crowded inside the Veryan Gallery where Jennie's first collection was being shown. Stomach churning, she stood in a far corner wondering why she had allowed Maddie to put her in this embarrassing position. Seeing her work on public display in this manner only made her the more critical of it. It was all going to be a terrible failure and she would look a fool. Once she had advised Gavin to stick to phizmongering. She should have taken her own advice.

Swathed in black chiffon, hair now fading from auburn to grey and swept back in an untidy chignon, Maddie had flung a crimson silk stole about her shoulders and looked like a large prima donna as she spoke to the invited guests. There was no need to launch Jennie any more, the Collingham portrait had done that after Lavinia had thrown a party at

Eaton Square for her friends to view the painting. This exhibition was to show that portraiture was not Jennie's sole forte, although many were on view, including the full-length one of Guy. But here also were landscapes, seascapes, studies of London life, and of Singapore; the *kebun* bending to his work in scorching sun, the Malay wash amah, Ah Kew in her white tunic and black trousers, and soft lantern light on Asian faces at an evening market. Among all this much-admired work, one painting stood out alone and was receiving much attention. It was a small study in soft muted oils of the tops of cypress trees shooting clear from a mist-shrouded hill; through the mist a beacon of light – strong, beckoning, and touching everyone who stood before the painting. It was like somewhere they thought they knew, and yet had never ventured.

Glancing at her watch, Jennie bit her bottom lip and frowned. Guy was late. For all their aloofness to each other, he had promised to be here to give her moral support. For the past three years she had worked tirelessly in Gavin's old studio to get the collection together. Surely he would want to see the end result now they were framed and lit to perfection?

Maddie was moving in her direction, beaming like a Cheshire cat. "People are saying marvellous things, so why are you skulking in this corner? Come out and be introduced."

They were mostly Maddie's people so far. Jennie made a brave attempt to chat casually and hide her nerves until her own friends starting drifting in. When they did she moved to greet them, made certain they had a glass of champagne then left them to wander. From the corner of her eye she saw Maddie talking to an art critic and, afraid of being called to join them, turned away. At that moment the door opened and a blast of cold air rushed into the room, bearing with it Louise on the arm of her latest manfriend. Seeing Jennie, she rushed towards her.

"I'm sorry to be this late but I had to finish a script and . . . oh, by the way this is Kevin. He's ex-St Martin's and one of our best set designers. Kevin, this is my oldest and dearest friend, Genevieve Lloyd – Jennie."

Jennie greeted Kevin who was dark-haired, sported a short beard, wore horn-rimmed spectacles and a green corduroy jacket. He looked like a revolutionary plotting the overthrow of Monarchy and Government. These days, Louise always had someone like this on her arm and the Boyd's despaired! A waiter approached with a tray filled with glasses of champagne. Louise took two, handing one to Kevin and gazing about her appraisingly. "Jennie, how marvellous they all look. Until now I've only seen your work scattered about the studio."

At that moment the art critic joined them and looked at Jennie quizzically. "So then, you're the one responsible for all this? I have to say now there are paintings here that no artist would be ashamed of producing." He paused and frowned slightly. "Excuse me for asking, but are you the daughter of Monique Veryan by any chance? My editor reckons you are."

Jennie said she was, and as they chatted, wondered if she would go through the rest of her life being the daughter of Monique Veryan rather than a person in her own right. Even her own husband would have preferred the mother, it would seem. As the critic moved away to look at the rest of the paintings, Louise moved in again, whispering: "Strange he should say that. I wasn't going to bring it up here but might as well now. You see, we're working on an idea for a series of programmes about British agents with the French Resistance, and want to use your mother's story in one of them. Would you have any objections?"

Taken aback at the suggestion, Jennie frowned. "I'm not sure ... I don't know ... it's so odd. No, I suppose I don't mind so long as it's handled well, not embellished or fictionalised."

"It won't be. It's more of a documentary which uses actors with a 'voice over' narration. David's one of the best producers we have. He's spot on about accuracy and very sensitive."

Thoughtful and silent, Jennie glanced through the window to see if Guy was anywhere in sight. There was no one save for a solitary figure huddled in a duffel coat beneath a street lamp on the far side of the deserted road. He was staring across towards the lights of the gallery. It was still raining heavily. Jennie felt sudden pity for him, wondering if he had been stood up by some girl. "When is the programme to be?"

"Autumn," said Louise, eyes sparkling. "A series of six episodes, each one devoted to a different agent." She helped herself to the offered canapes. "David would like to talk to you about it, and Kevin is to do the set designs for the entire series. There's going to be a lot of location work, and ..." She stopped speaking suddenly, wishing the ground would open up and swallow her. "Oh, Jennie. Please forgive me. That was so awful. We television folk wear clogs instead of slippers, I'm afraid. Whatever must you think of me?" When Jennie said she quite understood and was interested, Louise still felt an insensitive idiot. "You're sure it won't upset you? The idea of such a programme?"

"No," said Jennie quickly, not wanting to think about her mother for fear of becoming emotional. She wished Monique could be here now, to see her daughter's work and feel that her wishes had been realised. "I'd like your opinion of the Singapore paintings," she said, in an effort to change the subject. "The one of Ah Kew is not for sale. I'm

343

giving it to your parents. When the exhibition's over, you may take it home with you."

Having already seen the portrait in the studio, and knowing what Jennie could command for her paintings, Louise stared at her openmouthed. "Jennie! Oh, but how wonderful. They'll be over the moon. I'm expecting them home in a couple of months. It's very kind of you."

By nine o'clock the room was filled with people and getting even warmer. Wondering what was keeping Guy, Jennie moved towards the door. The young man was still there, standing beneath the street lamp and staring across at the gallery. Suddenly, he made as if to cross over to her, then turned instead and walked away at a brisk pace. She watched until he rounded the corner then realised, with sudden clarity of thought, that he hadn't been waiting for anyone. He had been standing there all this time just watching them. Why? Why would anyone stand for so long in pouring rain just staring at an art gallery? Who could it have been?

At ten o'clock the last guest had gone. Compliments ringing in their ears, Maddie and Jennie slumped on to gilt chairs and kicked off their high-heeled court shoes wearily. "Well," said Maddie rubbing her stockinged feet, "that was, I think, an unqualified success. You must be very happy."

Jennie hardly took in her words. Guy had not attended this, her first and probably only exhibition. People had come from far and wide, people she knew and people she didn't know. Only her husband had deemed it unnecessary to show up. Mark would have, she thought. He would have been standing beside her, his gentle presence calming and reassuring. Three years since she'd seen him! How achingly long they were, in spite of everything. He was never out of her thoughts and in them she saw him slipping away from her. There was nothing she could do about it. Mark had found a life beyond Belmore. Now famous as an author and authority on birds of prey, he had a series of wild-life programmes on television which had proved very popular. How often had she seen him on that small screen and how many times had her hand reached for the telephone to contact him again, only to have it freeze on the receiver? She had hurt him dreadfully and could offer him nothing but more hurt, especially now that Guy's suspicions had been aroused.

"You don't seem as bowled over as I thought you would be?"

Aware of Maddie's voice once more, Jennie came out of her desolation and blinked. "Yes ... yes, I'm bowled over. Completely. I expected people to drink the champagne and mouth the usual platitudes. I don't think I envisaged anyone actually buying."

Maddie laughed. "You are a funny thing. Of those for sale, quite a

344

number have been taken already and the exhibition has three more days to run." She gazed around the empty gallery, her face shadowing. "All evening I kept thinking of your mother and wishing she could have been here to see her hopes and dreams for you come true. She would have been so proud." She frowned and asked what had happened to Guy.

"He didn't come."

Maddie's eyes clouded. Jennie said little about her marriage but clearly it was a disaster. "Oh, my dear, how very disappointing for you." She placed a motherly hand on Jennie's arm and squeezed gently. "Still, art never was his thing. Well..." She heaved her bulk from the chair and got wearily to her feet.

"We've been invited to the Brittens' for a late supper. Quite a number of people going, I understand." She sighed. "Frankly I could just fall asleep where I'm standing."

Jennie stood up suddenly. "Well, I couldn't. I couldn't sleep for another week. I'm ready for a good night out. I feel like boozing until I'm pie-eyed."

It was almost two-thirty when the taxi dropped Jennie outside her house. A little light-headed, she entered the drawing room and stood before a long-dead fire, looking at the white envelope set against the carriage clock on the mantle. Her name was on it, written in Nanny's hand. Tearing it open she read the message:

The Squadron Leader rang to say he had to deliver an aircraft to Boscombe Down this morning. Unfortunately, the light plane he was to return in developed a fault and he didn't get a lift back to Stannington in time to make it to your exhibition.

I hope it went well.
Nanny

It sounded plausible enough, but then his excuses always did. Had he spent this evening, of all evenings, with "the other one"? Could he really be that cruel? How could she even think such a thing? Jennie suppressed a giggle. This was only Wednesday and "the other" always shared him at weekends.

On Friday morning Jennie was chatting casually to a sitter, in spite of feeling at her lowest. Yesterday evening she had picked up her copy of *Shire* magazine and seen in it a picture of Mark at a race meeting. Hanging on to his arm and gazing up at him adoringly was Angela Styles, a glamorous television announcer who was always in the news.

345

Try as she might, Jennie couldn't push the picture from her mind. Had Mark not looked into her eyes and said that he would never get over her? Someone like Angela Styles could help him to do just that.

The telephone rang. She picked it up and heard Maddie's anxious and apologetic voice. "Oh, my dear, something simply dreadful has happened. It isn't Anthea's fault, it's mine. She hasn't been with the gallery for very long and I shouldn't have left her to cope alone. Unfortunately, she has sold a painting you placed in the exhibition on loan."

Jennie's hand gripped the receiver. "Which painting?"

"The one you loved the best, darling."

She sank on to a chair in dismay. Her evocative mist-shrouded hill was lost forever. She would never capture it again, never. Maddie's voice chatted on, saying it was the first time that such a mistake had happened. She was furious and Anthea was in tears.

"It's still there, though, in the exhibition? Only, I was wondering if . . ."

"No, Jennie," said Maddie, reading her mind. "A legal transaction is a legal transaction. What would happen to my reputation otherwise? Of course, had it been on loan by someone else then it would be different and I would have egg all over my face. But as it is, please, darling, do try to understand. Anthea tells me that the buyer is collecting the picture around six-thirty. We'll exhibit it for as long as we can. Sorry about it, my dear, I do know you loved it so . . . we all did."

There were a few people wandering through the gallery when Jennie arrived at five minutes to six. A tall, willowy girl approached and stared at her with tearful, lugubrious eyes. "I'm so sorry . . . I feel so dreadful," she whispered.

"It's all right, Anthea," murmured Jennie, feeling sorry for the young History of Art graduate. She had only been with them for two weeks after Maddie's faithful assistant of many years had left through ill health. "What happened exactly?"

"He was in a hurry . . . and there was someone else I was attending to at the time and, well . . . I got into a state, checked in the catalogue and confused the title with another. He's paid for the wrong painting. Miss Veryan is furious and says there's nothing to be done about it."

Jennie placed a comforting hand on Anthea's arm and smiled. "There isn't. But worse things have happened. Don't worry about it any more." Deeply saddened, she turned and walked to the painting she would never see again, wondering who had bought it. Who would look at it and feel what she had felt? When it was removed, she had a sudden sense of loss, as though a part of herself was going with it. For a while she just stood there looking at the empty space on the wall, then

346

wandered on about the rooms, listening to the hushed whispers of visitors, her ears straining to hear comments, favourable or otherwise.

At the desk she drew before her the book listing the names of buyers, and started searching through it to spot the error, intending to rectify it for reasons of provenance. She was still searching when she heard the sound of a taxi engine outside, and knew that this was the buyer come to take her beloved painting away. Slowly she looked up.

The glass door opened and in walked Mark.

Raincoat slung over his arm, large bulging briefcase in the other hand, he found himself face to face with Jennie and stood like a statue for one moment. Somehow it was the last thing he had expected. Only that morning he had wandered through the rooms, pausing for a long time at each picture, astounded at the strength and vigour of her work. One painting had drawn him again and again and he had seen in it Jennie's unhappiness and a longing which echoed his own. He knew then that no one else should have something that so obviously was meant to be his. How long had he stayed, hoping against hope that she would suddenly appear? When she did not, his disappointment was keen but he had to get to the Television Centre and could wait no longer. And now, here she was, looking soft and lovely in brown velvet which matched her liquid eyes, and he could hardly believe it was happening.

"Hello, Jennie," he murmured at last.

Still recovering from the shock, she smiled weakly. "Hello, Mark."

He moved towards her, his eyes searching hers for a reaction. "I read about your exhibition and since I was in London..." He paused, aware that the assistant he had spoken to that morning was already walking towards him with the wrapped painting. "For God's sake, Jennie," he whispered, "let's go somewhere quiet to talk. Grant me that much at least?"

Still slightly off balance, she could only nod. Then, seeing Anthea's approach, smiled and raised her voice to a more business like level. "Ah, is that the gentleman's painting?"

Anthea said it was, handing the package to Mark who placed it under his arm and turned to Jennie. "Well, it's been nice meeting you again. What a good thing I caught you, since you were just about to leave. Look, I have a taxi waiting to take me to the station. Can I offer you a lift anywhere?"

Picking up his cue like a well-trained actress, Jennie nodded. "Thank you, that's most kind. Would it be out of your way to drop me off in Flood Street?" Slipping on her cream woollen coat, she turned to Anthea, smiling. "We're old friends. Isn't that extraordinary?" She lowered her voice to a whisper. "Stop worrying because everything's

347

turned out fine. By the way, I want you to tear up his cheque. Do it now, Anthea. Now."

Anthea saw them both climb into the taxi then watched as it pulled away. At that moment a Jaguar turned into the road and pulled up outside the gallery. Although she had only seen him once before, she recognised the man as he walked in and looked around him.

"I'm not too late, am I?" asked Guy. "Raced to get here before it closed. It is the last day, isn't it?"

"Oh, no, Squadron Leader, that's tomorrow. I'm afraid you've only just missed your wife. She's on her way home."

Guy let out a sigh and frowned. "Damn! Still, she wasn't expecting me, so give her time to get home then I'd be glad if you could telephone her and ask her to come back." With that he wandered along the rows of paintings, staying only a short while before each, until he came to the Malay wash amah. Thinking how well Jennie had captured the girl's fine-boned beauty, his mind travelled back to those extraordinary days in Singapore. He wished he could have them again. Things were better then. Life was better then. He heard Anthea's clicking heels and turned to see her furrowed brow as she told him that Jennie had not arrived home yet. He glanced at his watch. "I've been here over ten minutes. Was she walking?"

"Oh, no. She was given a lift by a friend." At his questioning look Anthea found herself prattling on nervously about the mix up. "Anyway since it was a friend who bought it she's clearly able to sort the matter out. I was asked to tear up the cheque so it looks as though she'll have the painting back again. I'm so relieved."

"So am I. Which friend of ours bought it? Do you know the name?"

"I can soon find out for you." She walked to the desk and searched the records book. "Curnow." Smiling, she looked up. "Of course. I knew I'd seen him before. Expert on falcons, has a television series. Shall I ring your wife again?"

Guy's face darkened as he made for the door. "Don't bother."

As the taxi eased its way through the London rush hour traffic, Mark gave the driver new instructions then turned to Jennie beside him. "It's just a bistro, but it's quiet and we can talk there." He took her hand in his and, with so much to say, could say nothing more.

The cloudy evening was cool against the warmth of Marcel's where the smell of French cuisine filled the air. It was early still, the small restaurant practically empty. Removing their coats, the waiter showed them to a quiet corner table, and lit the candle that stood in a wine bottle.

Eyes brilliant in the flame, Jennie gazed at Mark, thinking: And suddenly three years has just fallen away. "I thought you had a train to catch?" she said.

"Which I'm happy to miss," he replied, ordering drinks from the hovering waiter who then handed them menus. "I'll catch the late one instead." Looking at her in the candlelight, he thought her pale, thinner too, and a little tired. For all she was smiling, he saw only sadness in those eyes and felt an aching tenderness for her. "How is he?" he said at last. "Not paralysed. I was greatly relieved to hear that."

Jennie shook her head. "No, thank God. Even so it took months for him to recover. His back will never be the same. He walks stiffly and is in constant pain. No one is supposed to know that because he's test flying again, would you believe?"

"Then he's mad as well as lucky." The deep blue eyes darkened. "Bloody lucky to have you for a wife. I hope he appreciates you?"

"Don't." She reached out and touched his hand. He caught it and covered it with his other. "We have so little time together, let's not waste it. Tell me about your life since we ... well ... tell me what's been happening. Now that you're a famous man, are you still at Belmore?"

He smiled. "Mullholland retired, which gave me his position and my head. Now I'm busier than ever. The rest is just a flash in the pan bonus. But something good is coming out of it all. People are listening and beginning to understand and care. And that's what it's all about, not fame or money."

"You must come to London quite a bit?"

He shook his head. "Most of the programmes go out from the Bristol studios. I'm here today for a dubbing session. Otherwise, I only come up to visit my publisher. That's why I was so desperate to see you." He squeezed her hand gently. "Oh, darling, it's been a very long three years." Pausing, he smiled tenderly. "But look what you've achieved in that time. I can remember an anxious eighteen-year-old girl desperate to succeed in art for her mother's sake. Well, darling, you can rest easy. I expected your paintings to be good, but I hadn't realised ..."

"What made you pick that particular painting?"

He was silent for a while, too afraid to say: *Because it was like looking into your soul.* She might think that to be pretentious nonsense, even though it happened to be true. Instead he murmured. "Strangely titled for something so evocative, I thought."

She smiled. "It's true title is A Distant Light, not the title you were given. Evocative you say? Yes ... it is ... even though I never knew what it was that I was trying to capture ... something lost, elusive ... I don't know."

"Don't you?" He had known at once.

She said nothing about the mix up, realising that there was only one

349

other person in the world who should have that painting and now, because of a silly mistake, he had. It came to her then that fate had caused this, not Anthea. It had been meant to happen.

Mark was searching her face. "Don't tell me you're happy because I won't believe it."

She sipped her sherry and looked down at the menu. "What does it matter any more? I made the only choice I could have made."

"But that was over three bloody years ago. Christ, the man's back in harness now. I see you live in London while he's in Hertfordshire still? Nothing seems to have changed."

"One thing has changed. Since the accident we have separate bedrooms. That's how I want it and it doesn't matter that much to him because he has someone else. Difficult to prove, but I'm pretty sure there's another woman. Either way, our marriage is dead." She smiled wryly. "It expired quietly. Like you read on old gravestones . . . 'Died of a Decline'."

"Then bury it."

"How?" She pushed a hand through her hair. "Ask him outright for a divorce? Change the locks, keep him out? I've thought of it time and again but can't bring myself to do any of these things. Not after all that he's been through. Oh, I get so angry with him at times but then he'll say or do something which is kind and thoughtful, and I think of his pain and his terrible fear of being thrown on the scrap heap if his body fails him. In those moments, I know I can't do anything to hurt him. I just can't." Her voice choked on a sob and she couldn't stop the tears.

He face tightened. "It seems to me that you do love him still."

She shook her head. "Love, pity . . . I don't know."

"Pity!" Mark leaned forward. "No man wants to be pitied. If your love for me ever turns to pity, then for God's sake let me know." He looked at the menu and snapped: "Perhaps we should order. The Lamb Provençal is pretty good."

She dried her tears then said, "I wish you could understand. My love for you is as strong as it ever was and certainly won't die of a decline. But I'm married and there it is. Anyway, there's something else. Guy once asked me about the time I spent at Belmore. His words were innocent enough but I sensed that he knew something, or thought he did. We have to be careful. You're famous now and your work is important. I don't want any hint of scandal to hurt you."

"Scandal! Christ, Jennie, what do I care about all that?"

"Well, I care," she whispered. "I love you too much to see all you have achieved shattered to pieces because of me." She gazed at him searchingly. "Or am I being a little ridiculous perhaps? After all, three years is a very long time. Tell me about Angela Styles."

Aware of the sudden sharpness in her tone, Mark shrugged. "She's beautiful, she's witty, she isn't you. End of story."

Eyes widening, she laughed. "Well, thank you, Mark. But I think I know what you mean." There was a long silence, and then she asked: "I thought that you and she ... well, you're a passionate man and three years without making love is a very long time. Believe me, I know."

"Angela is just a friend among many friends. But I'm no monk, if that's what you mean."

Jennie sighed. "Hmm. I might as well be a nun. Men are allowed complete sexual freedom but we women must tighten our chastity belts and smile."

"For men most relationships mean very little." He looked serious. "But what I feel for you is true love, and even though you wanted me to kill it, it won't die. It will never die." He squeezed her hand hard. "Don't go from my life again, darling. Give me some hope. I can't bear it otherwise."

Neither could she. There must be a way ... somehow they must find a way. She could go to York; they could rent a cottage, and be together. Why not? Who would know? She wanted to say goodbye to Mark at the station, but he insisted on seeing her safely home. In the taxi they kissed, and she cried in his arms, finally tearing herself from him when the vehicle stopped outside her house. Then she stood, watching until it moved out of her sight, taking all that she loved with it. Yes, she thought, they could meet on rare occasions, in dark corners or hotel bedrooms, always hiding, always in secret, but at the end of each clandestine encounter would come the anguish of parting. Then, one day, what had been a perfect love would become a strained and squalid little affair which would end unhappily with bitter rancour. No! The only way was through divorce. But there must be no hint of infidelity on her part if she was ever to get Guy to agree. It was all a matter of timing.

Letting herself in through the front door, she stood in the hallway and listened to music floating down from the drawing room. Friday! Dear God, she had forgotten it was Friday. Stomach churning, she walked up the red-carpeted stairs to find Guy seated beside the dying fire.

He switched off the radio and turned to her angrily. "Where the bloody hell have you been?"

She could only stand there, staring like an idiot. "Out with a friend. I didn't know you were coming home. You didn't say."

"I didn't think I had to make an appointment." He clasped his hands, then cracked his whitened knuckles. "I went to the gallery. Felt bad about missing the opening night so drove like a bat out of hell to get

351

there in time. The girl told me you had just left ... with a friend. Tell me about this friend."

Her heart sank at his menacing tone. Anthea, in all innocence, would have told him Mark's name. And if Guy knew the truth about Belmore it could only be through Clive, who would delight in causing mischief for her. Pulse racing, she tried to sound casual. "Oh, you wouldn't know him. He's Frank Curnow's son. He bought a painting. I happened to be there when he collected it. We grew up together and hadn't seen each other for so long that it seemed churlish to refuse his invitation to dinner."

How guileless she sounded, he thought. What a little actress she was. He wanted to shake her suddenly, throw her on the floor and take her by force just to remind her that she belonged to him. Standing up, he advanced towards her, shouting: "Don't treat me like a complete bloody fool." Suddenly a figure appeared in the doorway, shocking him from his rage.

Nanny Davies stood in her dressing gown, holding a glass of milk. Slowly it dawned on her that she had walked into another marital row, presumably because the Squadron Leader wanted Alex to go to boarding school in September and his wife did not. "I couldn't sleep," she murmured, embarrassed. "I came down to get some milk, then heard ... well ... I'm sorry."

"It's all right, Nanny," said Jennie, trembling with shock. She moved towards her quickly, trying to force a smile. "We were talking rather loudly, sorry." Glancing back at Guy's angry face, she added, "But it's all said now and I'm very tired after a long day. Goodnight, Guy."

Still shaking with rage, he stood in the middle of the room listening to the women murmuring to each other on the stairs, then sat down once more. His back was hurting after the long car journey and pain killers had done little to ease the discomfort. Slowly the rage died away and he thought, with a sickening shock, how close he had come to striking Jennie. Mark Curnow! How long must he live in that man's shadow?

For the first time in their married life, Jennie decided to lock her bedroom door. His face, that terrible look on his face! Would he really have struck her? Still trembling, she sat on her bed staring at the door, realising now that she was afraid of her husband. She had never seen him like this before. Did his rage mean that he still felt a spark of something for her after all? Perhaps it did. Why else would he have rushed to the gallery as he had? Oh God, of all nights, why had fate picked this one to bring Mark back into her life?

Unable to face Guy, she left the house early the next morning and after working in the studio went to the gallery and spent the rest of the

352

day there. When she returned at six o'clock that evening, it was to learn that Guy had taken Alex to the Zoo, then left for Stannington at four. The Zoo trip surprised her, the disappearing act did not. She knew quite well that if she rang the cottage, there would be no reply.

# Chapter Twenty-Two

"Alex, leave my paints alone." Jennie put down her brush and sighed with exasperation. It was not the best day for Nanny to visit her sister. Bored with the school summer holidays already, her son had abandoned his own tubes of paint for her top quality ones and was now squeezing them on to a canvas then swirling them into a multi-coloured vortex.

"Padre Wilson says heaven is filled with bright colours where Jesus is waiting and when we die we're drawn up into the colours."

"I see," said Jennie, wishing Padre Wilson could see the result of his words. Clutching a spirit-soaked rag and wiping her son's messy fingers with it, she forced a smile. "So this is heaven you've painted, a kind of Jackson Pollock heaven?"

"No," he snapped, looking up at her with hard blue eyes as sudden resentment flared. "I don't believe in heaven. This is the Panther crashing and Daddy's in it." Ah, now his mother looked shocked. Good. He had meant to shock, to get his own back on her for allowing his father to send him to boarding school. He was to start in September, leaving his mother and Nanny and all his present school friends, including his best friend, Graham Sturgess. He wouldn't know anyone and was afraid. "It's Daddy and he's crashing and . . ."

"Stop it, Alex." Jennie stared at him in disbelief. "How can you say anything so horrible? Don't you love him?"

"No. He doesn't love me. He wants to send me away. Why don't you stop him, why don't you?"

Jennie wiped the paint off his hands then led him to the bathroom and made him wash them very well. "The school in Hampshire is very good. You've seen it, and met the Headmaster and your Housemaster. There are lovely grounds to play games in and some of the boys there will go on to Winchester with you later on. I know, darling, I know how you feel, but once you get used to it you'll like it."

354

"I like my school here." He splashed his hands into the water, sending small jets flying in all directions.

"But you must go to a good preparatory school before you can go to Winchester College." How many times had she told him this, and how many times had she seen the fear in his eyes and thought of him crying into his pillow at night as, once, she had cried into hers? But she, at least, had been eleven. Alex was not yet eight. It seemed so horribly cruel. Guy might be right but he didn't feel the anguish that she felt over losing her baby to the strict unloving life of boarding school. Now she knew what her mother had gone through.

As they left the bathroom, they heard the front door slam. Maddie came running up the stairs, purple cloak about her, hair falling from it's chignon. She stood on the landing and stared at Jennie breathlessly. "Something ... something very funny is going on." She paused, swallowed and gasped: "Come downstairs, I'll tell you."

"May I watch *The Lone Ranger* on your television, Aunt Maddie?"

Momentarily distracted, Maddie looked down at the child and nodded. "The what? All right ... don't get too close. You'll ruin your eyes and ... worse still ... become radio active. Ask Mrs Lewis to switch it on for you." She glanced at Jennie. "I've heard terrible things about television sets. God knows why I ever bought one. I never watch the wretched thing. It sits there in that study, like a cold empty grate. Mrs Lewis loves it, of course."

In the drawing room she fell into a armchair, a puzzled frown bringing furrows to the otherwise smooth plump face. "You would tell me if you were planning to sell a painting from Trevellan? You would consult me first, wouldn't you, Jennie?"

"Of course. Why?"

"Well, I've just come from an auction at Heppenstall's. A Sisley came under the hammer, a Sisley which I know was at Trevellan."

Jennie stared at her then shrugged. "You're mistaken surely?"

"If by that you mean that one Seine bridge looks much like another then you're very wrong. I thought at first it might be one of his different perspectives of the same bridge, but ..." She shook her head. "No. I know that painting as well as I know the back of my hand. It has hung in the morning room for as long as I can remember. So then, if yours is genuine and this one was sold as genuine then ... oh, Jennie, when did you last go home?"

"It must be ... four months perhaps? I just haven't had time since. But Clive wouldn't sell anything without the trustees' permission. He couldn't."

"Couldn't he? Wouldn't he? Don't you believe it!" With that, Maddie got to her feet and walked across the room to the telephone. "I thought I should check with you first. Well, now we'll find out what's what."

Heppenstall's knew Maddie well enough to give her the provenance of the painting. "I see," she murmured into the mouthpiece. "Well, thank you, Mr Troy, but I have to tell you now that nothing may be sold from the Trevellan Estate without permission of the trustees. Certainly one has not given her permission, so it is – to all intents and purposes – an illegal sale. Yes ... yes ... of course you acted in good faith and we can do nothing about it now. All I'm saying is, please bear this in mind in future."

Jennie had turned pale. "Mr Longwood wouldn't do anything without consulting me. Well, he can't. Oh Maddie, how many other auction houses have acted in good faith on Clive's say-so? I've been so lax. But surely Grandma or Aunt Laura would know if a painting went missing suddenly? It's all very odd. I'll take Alex and Nanny and catch the first train to Penzance tomorrow."

"Why not go to Kensington Square and confront Clive face to face?"

"No. I need to see for myself what's missing and how we stand legally before going any further." Jennie bit her lip thoughtfully. "Only three weeks ago he was swanning around the Med on some gin palace of a yacht. Friends of hers, of course. Now this. If he's finding it difficult to live up to her lifestyle, then the estate could be in real trouble."

That evening she telephoned Florence, deciding only to say she was arriving the following morning and to give the time of the train's arrival at Penzance. Her grandmother sounded agitated. "Thank goodness you're coming. I didn't realise you knew. I only found out myself this morning. Oh, Jennie, it's so terrible. I'm at my wit's end."

"I know, I know," said Jennie, trying to calm the old lady. "Don't worry about it so much."

"What do you mean, don't worry? Poor Frank."

Confused, Jennie frowned. "What are you talking about?"

"Frank Curnow! It's dreadful. Get here as fast as you can."


Alex sat in the corner seat of the train, forehead to the window pane as he watched the Devon countryside rushing past. He was counting bridges and humming to himself, wearing a grey jacket over short grey trousers, his fair hair as untidy as his tie. Beside him, Nanny Davies was reading a book, glad to have the chance of a few days beside the sea and hating the thought of leaving this household in September. She knew that Mrs Lloyd wanted her to stay, but the Squadron Leader could see no use for a nanny now that his son was almost eight and going to boarding school. It would break her heart to say goodbye. It always did. She would keep in touch though, as she had kept in touch with all her babies, some now quite grown up, even with children of their own.

Jennie sat opposite her son, the usual frisson of excitement she always experienced when journeying home to Cornwall now overshadowed by acute anxiety. Her grandmother had said nothing more about Frank Curnow, preferring to wait until she could tell Jennie face to face. As a result, she had spent a restless night worrying. Now, as the train rushed south-west through glorious rolling hills and tantalising views of the distant hazy sea, she wondered how many more times she would make such a journey since in just over one year's time Clive would have full title and the right to lock her out of Trevellan for good. It didn't seem possible. Trevellan was her home, she belonged there, felt secure there and loved every stone and window pane of the house. She knew, instinctively, that the house wanted her, not Clive. He would have a fight on his hands if he tried to lock her out while her grandmother was still alive.

Florence was seated in the Rolls when Jennie and Alex climbed in. There were hugs and kisses; the chauffeur placed suitcases in the boot, Nanny sat beside him at the front while Alex climbed into a corner seat, nose pressed to the window once more. Slowly the stately old Phantom III eased away from the forecourt and out into the road.

Jennie turned to her grandmother and thought how frail she looked, frail and unhappy. "What's this about? You were so mysterious on the phone. I've been awake most of the night."

Florence placed a kid-gloved hand on Jennie's arm and murmured so that Alex couldn't hear: "Frank has resigned. Left us. Can you imagine? After all these years, he has left us because of Clive. Oh, he says it's ill health, and it's true he's not a well man, but I know it was Clive."

Dismayed at this news, Jennie looked at her. Without Frank they were in deep trouble. "He can't resign! He promised me he would stay, come what may."

"He's at his wit's end, poor man. My dear, you have no idea how things have been these past months. Your grandfather must be spinning in his grave. At first Clive was careful, leaving the handling of everything to Frank yet showing a keen interest in the estate, and I decided I'd been over harsh in my judgment of him. Fenella even enjoyed playing 'lady of the manor' for a while. Didn't care much for charity work though. Not the type to roll up her sleeves and get her hands dirty. Sees herself as Princess Margaret rather than the wife of a country squire."

Florence sighed and continued, "But the novelty has now worn off, and they treat the place like a country club, arriving in noisy convoy

357

with their friends, spending weekends partying, playing loud music and drinking far too much. There are glass stains on the furniture and such noise... I've found it all most distressing. How can he afford to live like this? Having spent a great deal on repairing the tennis courts, he now wants to build a large swimming pool. I ask you! Rather ostentatious don't you think? He's done nothing to the house and money that should be spent on repairs is being squandered in this manner instead. It's been the cause of much friction between Clive and Frank. Even so, I couldn't believe it when yesterday Frank told me he had resigned. I spent most of the day trying to get him to change his mind. But to no avail. So now we're to lose our manager and old friend. I was about to telephone you when you rang me." She frowned and looked thoughtful. "Why did you ring me? I've forgotten."

Jennie told her and, to her surprise, Florence did not seem in the least bit taken aback. "Did you know?"

Florence shook her head. "You must be mistaken, my dear. There's nothing missing. I know my eyesight isn't what it was, but your aunt would know if anything was amiss."

"Yes," murmured Jennie. "She would certainly know." But what would she do about it? "Did you tell her we were coming?"

"Of course. She lives at the house when Clive and his wife aren't around. The dower cottage is so lonely for her. How could he do such a thing to his own mother?" She tapped her handbag with irritation. "Though it's what he's doing to our good name that bothers me more. I've heard things. The villagers neither like nor respect Clive and Fenella, and our tenants feel threatened."

Alex became more excited as they neared Portlyn and on arrival at the house wanted to go straight to the cove. Jennie promised to take him later, and, as Nanny took her charge up to his room, she and her grandmother entered the morning room to find Laura seated at the desk, writing a letter. She looked up and smiled thinly, her eyes narrowing. "Ah. You've arrived. I really don't see why. If Frank won't stay for your grandmother, he certainly won't stay for you."

Florence settled into her own armchair, put her walking stick against the arm, then removed her gloves and hat and placed them on the small table beside her. "Jennie's here for a few days' holiday. Alex will love it."

Jennie's eyes went to the wall. The Impressionist painting was there all right, but it was a different bridge and a different hand, the hand of a student. She knew the picture well, it had hung in her parents' bedroom for years, but who went in there now save Clive and Fenella? Her cousin had merely replaced one picture with another. She turned to her grandmother and smiled. "Even after all this time, I still expect Rosalind to come waddling in to meet me."

"She lived to a good age," said Florence. "Sad to be without dogs though. But Fenella doesn't like them any more than she likes horses. And Clive does as he's told these days."

"Rosalind is irreplaceable anyway," said Laura.

"Like the Sisley," snapped Jennie.

"What?" Casting a wary glance at Jennie, Laura then turned to look at the picture.

"That's right," said Jennie. "It's gone. I'm surprised you didn't spot the switch, Aunt."

Face draining of colour, Laura shot to her feet and, instead of going to the painting as would have been natural, stared instead through the window on to the orchard. "I hadn't noticed," she said unconvincingly. "I expect Clive has taken it to the London house."

"He's sold it." Jennie was watching her aunt closely. "Maddie was at Heppenstall's when it came under the hammer. It fetched a good price, I might add. Maddie had the provenance checked. It's our Sisley all right."

Laura kept her face turned to the window. "Clive wouldn't do such a thing. I know he wouldn't."

"But he has. And tried to cheat with this replacement. Heppenstall's are furious. What he's done is illegal. He must put that money back into the estate, otherwise we take him to court."

Florence looked shocked. "We will do no such thing! I will not have our family squabbles aired in public. In any case, the painting was mine as it happens. A Silver Wedding gift to me from your grandfather, Jennie. I might want to kill Clive, but I won't prosecute him." She stared at the student's work, remembering that party so long ago when Philip had made her walk in here with a blindfold on, so eager was he to surprise her with a work by her favourite artist. The memory evoked, and the loss of that precious gift of love, sent tears to the old woman's eyes and her mouth began to quiver.

Seeing nothing of this, Laura breathed a sigh of relief. "I'm sure Clive has a perfectly good explanation."

"I'd like to hear it." said Jennie. "Meanwhile I'm going to go through that inventory with a fine tooth comb to see that nothing else is missing." She walked to the door. "If there is, then it becomes a matter for the trustees. So keep your fingers crossed, Aunt Laura. I know how much you hate scandal."

With a face like thunder, Laura watched the door close then turned to her mother. "And what is that supposed to mean, I wonder?"

"Oh, Laura, you knew all the time. You're too sharp not to have

359

known. Is Clive so worthy of your love?" Florence grasped her walking stick and stood slowly to her feet. "My lovely Sisley. Your son is a thief and a liar. Face up to that fact."

Ten minutes later, Jennie was reclining on the bed in the Chinese Room, leafing through the inventory she had brought with her. Looking up as her grandmother entered the room, she saw how upset the old lady was and climbed off the bed, saying, "I'm so sorry, Grandma. It must be a terrible blow for you. I know you don't wish to prosecute, but threat of court action might prevent him trying such a thing again. I've only had a cursory look so far, but there are two lithographs missing from the library. You don't know where they could be, I suppose? No?" Jennie sighed, almost afraid to go on.

"Oh, my dear, you've really upset your aunt now." Florence moved slowly to a chair, easing herself on to it. "She's gone off in a huff, refusing to stay for luncheon. Clive's behaviour grieves her as much as it grieves me. But it's Fenella we should really blame. She's a bad influence, that one. Not one of us, you see. I did tell you this years ago and was called a snob for my pains. Now perhaps you can understand what I mean. She's new money with no background, and no sense of duty or worth. Between her lack of breeding and Clive's lack of backbone, they will lick the plate clean. I hope I never live to see it." She stopped speaking and gazed into the distance for a moment. "When Singapore was granted self-government, I thought . . . I hoped that this would be the miracle for which I have prayed these many long years. But it was not to be. Your father wants to stay on, with that Dodo woman." Her voice dropped to a bitter murmur. "I shall never forgive him, never."

She sat for another moment then rose and headed slowly towards the door. "I don't think this sunshine will last, my dear. So if I were you I'd take Alex to the cove now. I'll tell Mrs Hodges to keep luncheon back for half an hour, it's only cold chicken and salad."

Twenty minutes later, Jennie sat on the steps, watching her son racing across the cove and peering into rock pools just as she had done in her childhood. It was low tide, the wind was strengthening and the sky beginning to cloud over. She wondered if Mark knew of his father's resignation. After that last meeting she had telephoned to warn him of Guy's reaction, urging him, pleading with him, to do nothing to make her husband even more suspicious and jealous. "Please wait until things have calmed down again. For my sake, Mark." After much argument, he agreed, then told her he had been invited to America to lecture in four different institutes in four different states. His under manager would hold the fort at Belmore for a month. It was a providential move at a dangerous time, thought Jennie, since Guy not only came home every weekend but sometimes, in a vain attempt to catch her out, turned up suddenly mid-week also. She had left a message with his secretary, and half expected him to come racing to Cornwall, convinced that Mark was here.

Florence had been right about the weather changing. By early-afternoon, Jennie found herself battling against wind and sheeting rain as she cycled off to the Curnows' house. There, Mabel took her drenched raincoat, murmuring how sad it was about the weather and how disappointing it must be for Alex. In the small and cluttered sitting room, Frank was clearing out his files.

"Ah, Mrs Lloyd," he said, as Mabel went off to make tea. "I was about to write, but I'm glad you've come instead. Please, do sit down. This is terrible weather to be out in."

She sat down, staring at Mark's father with large anxious eyes. How changed he was suddenly. How ill and gaunt-looking. It was all the harder to ask what she had come to ask. "Please do reconsider, Mr Curnow. I know how difficult my cousin can be but he knows nothing, and without you I really do fear for Trevellan. Clive won't want you to resign. It will shake him. And, after this, you may well find him easier to get along with."

Frank looked bemused as he settled himself in the armchair opposite Jennie. "I didn't resign. I was fired. I received formal notice the day before yesterday." He paused and looked visibly moved. "No one knows this except you. I kept it from Lady Veryan because she doesn't need any more problems."

"How dare he!" Jennie was still trying to take in her cousin's high-handedness. "I want you to stay and so will Mr Longwood. I'm seeing him this afternoon."

Frank shook his head as his wife entered the room with the tea tray. "What would be the point? I couldn't go on. Had I been a younger man, perhaps ... but as things are..."

"He's just not well enough," said Mabel. "Not well enough to cope with Mr Willoughby."

How crushed they both look, thought Jennie in growing desperation. "I gather there was some disagreement that sparked things off?" She took the cup and saucer from Mabel, remembering the days of her childhood when she had sat in this house with Mark. If only he would walk in now.

"It was a build up of many things," Frank was saying as he walked to the desk and took from the drawer a buff-coloured folder. "The house has been surveyed as you asked. Here is the report. I'm sorry to say your fears were well-founded. There are serious problems which should

361

have been addressed during your grandfather's day but were not. The roof needs repairing. There's damp in the attics and old servants' quarters, right down through the nursery. In a few years it will have reached the main bedrooms. The Long Gallery, as you know, was damaged during the war when the schoolboys left taps running and flooded the place. It was never put right. Rot has set in. Woodwork needs replacing ... I could go on all night. Anyway, when I tried to discuss this with Mr Willoughby he was very short-tempered and said that he had never asked for a survey and that I was to stop listening to you and remember who was in charge." He handed the folder to Jennie and sat down again.

"We've had so many arguments ... mostly over cottage maintenance and rents. He wanted the Wakerleys evicted. As you know, Mr Wakerley had an accident when driving the tractor. He's getting on in years anyway, and couldn't continue working. Your grandfather said they could remain in the cottage rent-free for the rest of their lives, but Mr Willoughby has reneged on that promise and now wants to sell the place over their heads. Things really came to a head when I learned of a field survey being carried out about which I knew nothing. When I asked Mr Willoughby, he told me to mind my own business and get out of his hair. It was the last straw. So we parted. Then I received the letter."

She listened to all this in cold anger. "What on earth does he think he's doing? Who will manage the estate?"

"He will, or so he tells me. How he can do this from London remains to be seen." Frank looked embarrassed. "When your grandfather died, the accounts balanced and there was a restoration fund, not enough but growing. But since then our outgoings have far exceeded our income. These past months have been the worst. The tennis court cost a great deal and work is about to start on the swimming pool. To pay for this, Mr Willoughby has dipped into the restoration fund, but if we don't start on the fabric of the house soon then we risk having even more expense in the long run. Either that or a ruin. Bills are beginning to mount up, but he refuses to settle them. There's this one from the field surveyors." He handed her an invoice, "And I've an estimate for land drainage."

"Land drainage?" Jennie frowned and looked at the estimate. "The Long Meadow? Well, I know it's a quagmire in winter, but we keep livestock out of it then. In summer though it's good rich pasture. The milk yield goes up."

"So you don't know why he wants such a survey carried out?"

Jennie shook her head. "Perhaps Mr Longwood knows. He'll be at the house for tea. I would be very grateful if you could come along at

362

four-thirty to show him these estimates and reports. Also, you could explain to him about the unsettled accounts. Meanwhile, I should like to go through the work that needs doing to the house and the costs involved. Would you be so kind?"

How could he refuse her? Trevellan had been his life for so long. Now, to see his careful work going for nothing was unbearable. If there was any hope for this estate, it lay with the little girl who used to fly a kestrel with his son. Eight years ago he had almost hated her, but now ... now he felt very differently.

"Of course. Let's get to work."

Forty minutes later, Jennie walked to the gate with Mabel and said: "I still can't believe this is happening."

Mabel turned to her. "Frank is very ill." Her moist eyes said the word her voice could not utter, the word only spoken of in hushed whispers. "He doesn't know how ill, but I do. They're going to treat him at Truro, but ... well, between us two, I've been told it's only a matter of a few months."

Appalled at these words, Jennie put her arms about the woman who might well have become her mother-in-law. "I hadn't realised ... I'm so sorry ... so very sorry. Does Mark know this yet?"

Mabel shook her head. "I didn't want want to alarm him." She turned. "I'd best get back to Frank. We were going to Truro this afternoon, to look for a small flat there. Of course, we'll do that tomorrow now."

Jennie shook her head quickly. "There's no reason why you shouldn't stay on here. You must."

Smiling through her tears, Mabel touched Jennie's hand ruefully. "Quitting the job means quitting this cottage. Anyway, it was all in the letter. It's a tied house. In any case, we both have our pride. How could we live here after this? Frank is anxious to get settled as soon as possible. Anxious for me, you see. Neither I nor the doctor have told him, but I think he knows."

When Jennie left the Curnows to cycle back, the rain had eased a little; a shaft of sunlight stabbed down through thinning clouds and sent a silver ribbon across the sea. She stood for a moment watching it, depressed beyond belief to think of Trevellan without Frank Curnow, of Portlyn without Mark's parents living along the lane. It was going, all slipping away. One day, when Florence had gone too, she would never return to the place she loved and Alex would not play at the cove or have the chance to know Trevellan or to feel about it as she felt about it.

By the time she reached the house, the sun had burst through the clouds and a rainbow arced over Portlyn. She found everyone in the library where Laura, having thought better of being away from any discussion which concerned her son, was now pouring Lapsang Souchong into Royal Worcester cups.

As Mr Longwood ate thinly cut sandwiches the conversation was kept light, touching on the weather, the state of the gardens and Florence's attempts to bring in new hybrid roses. "There's so much to do. Poor Ben does Trojan work, but it's all getting away from him. We do what we can, and his grandson comes in some weekends, but more help is needed."

When tea was finished, Mr Longwood leaned back in Philip's old leather chair and, fingertips touching, came to the matter at last. "Well now. This problem of the missing painting and lithographs. I shall write to Mr Willoughby explaining that it goes against the terms of the will and that any monies realised by such a sale must be classed as estate capital and returned to estate funds."

"He will, of course, refuse to return anything," said Jennie tersely, ignoring her aunt's black look.

"In which case, the trustees will take him to court." Mr Longwood frowned. "I don't believe he would want things to go that far."

Jennie smiled thinly, thinking that by the time the courts got around to Clive he would have full title anyway. Her eyes drifted around the library suddenly taking in the valuable leatherbound first editions and land records that went back for three hundred years. They included the fate of Royalist Veryans during and after the Civil War. In this one room was part of England's social history. Such documents should be preserved, not left to gather dust. Fenella would hate the dust. Who knew whether she might not already have had some of the thick volumes destroyed? Who knew which valuable first editions had already been sold? For years there had been talk of cataloguing the contents of this library, but no one had ever got around to doing it. Now it was too late. What a fool she had been, thinking only of the paintings when there were other treasures of great worth in this ancient house.

Laura was glaring at Mr Longwood. "Well, of course they won't go that far. Clive will return the money. I shall speak very firmly to him."

Jennie smiled grimly. "Clive's well beyond your reach now, Aunt, and has more things lined up to worry us into the grave. Do you know why he's looking into land drainage, for example? No?" When Mr Longwood shrugged in bemusement also, she frowned. "Then what exactly is he up to? He sacked Mr Curnow, by the way, and ill as he is, that poor man is having to move out of his home." She stirred her tea, feeling sick to her stomach, aware of the stunned silence her words had produced. "He will be here quite shortly to go over matters with Mr Longwood and myself. Meanwhile, I must finish my tour with the inventory. Perhaps, when Mr Curnow arrives, you could send Rosa to let me know."

At dinner that evening she turned to Florence and spoke of the discussion with Frank and Robert, saying, "We've decided to waste no more time and give the builders the go ahead to undertake renovations. We've also agreed that, in order to raise revenues for this work, we must sell the London house which is far too expensive for the estate to maintain now."

Laura glared at her. "Sell? Oh, come now, you're only doing this to score off Clive for turning you out of a house which is rightfully his."

Jennie had expected this but remained calm. "I would it were that simple. No, Aunt. I'm selling one house to save another. There's no other way. It makes me sad because I loved it so, but Kensington Square is an expensive place to keep up. On top of everything Clive dips into estate funds to keep a new staff of three there. Maintaining that house is draining this one. It can't go on."

"Jennie's absolutely right," said Florence. "Anyway what on earth does Clive want with three houses? And since poor Frank will no longer be with us..." Her voice cracked. "Jennie must now make these decisions instead."

Laura glared at her niece, wondering when the girl had changed into this formidable woman. "I rather thought that was Clive's job since he is the owner, or soon will be." But in her heart she knew that Clive had shown himself to be unworthy of the trust that she and her father had placed in him. He would do nothing to get this historic old house into good shape. She feared also that his land drainage scheme meant that he wanted to build in the Long Meadow. Was it his intention to sell off the land piece by piece until the estate dwindled to nothing? Was that why he had driven poor Frank away? Frank! Once she had thought herself in love with him. Perhaps she still was and always had been. John Willoughby was just an unfortunate episode. Quietly, Laura began to despair of what that episode had brought about.

Later that evening, having gone through the inventory and found that no more paintings were missing, Jennie then asked herself what she thought she was doing. What was the point of this fruitless exercise? Soon they would all belong to Clive and he would sell them off if and when he chose. She might just as well give up now. So why couldn't she? Why this compulsion to complete her task and watch over something she would have to let go of sooner than she cared to think about?

Florence found her in the library, seated at the desk looking through a leatherbound book. "Ah, so here you are. Your aunt has gone home in a very black mood." She walked to the desk and peered over Jennie's shoulder. It was getting dark, and the table lamp shone on pages she recognised and had not seen for years. "One of the first editions given to me by my father for my coming out. Or was it my twenty-first birthday? Do you know, I really can't remember."

Jennie looked up at her. "Your first editions? If they're yours then they're not part of the estate, surely? They're yours to do with as you wish."

Shrugging, Florence nodded. "Yes, I suppose they are. So was the Sisley but it's gone now just the same." She touched the book. "Look how the pages are yellowing. Isn't it sad? I suppose they'd be quite valuable now." She walked along the shelves, touching the volumes and murmuring: "I never could get on with Tolstoy. All those Russian names."

Jennie gave a wry smile. "Thank God Fenella and Clive have as little interest in literature as they have in art, otherwise these might have disappeared also."

"In which case you'd better take them back to London with you before they find out." Seeing Jennie's astonished expression, she smiled. "Why not? They're mine to give. But, just in case Clive gets difficult after my death, I'll put it in writing and lodge it with my will." She sighed and shook her head. "Who would have thought things would reach this sorry pass? But then, old houses reflect their times. And times do not favour the likes of us any more. Landowners, farm labourers, the English village and even the Empire are all disappearing. It's so wrong and short-sighted. When we give up our responsibilites we create chaos. Your father gave up his and now look at the result." She walked slowly back to the desk and patted Jennie on the shoulder. "So take the books, my dear, and save something while there's still something left to save."

Three days later, Jennie and Alex waved goodbye to Florence from the open window of the Rolls as it moved along the drive and out through the gateway. Sadly, Jennie leaned back against the padded upholstery as the car eased its way slowly down the steep and winding hill, through the village and up past the dizzy drop where, over the wall, she could just see the boathouse. It was a poignant moment.

"We will be coming back soon, won't we?" Alex wanted to know. "Because I promised Sturgess."

Jennie smiled and glanced at Nanny. "A promise is a promise and we shall all be back for our summer holidays. You tell Sturgess that."

About five miles out of Portlyn, she vaguely noticed a hitch-hiker on the far side of the road, his attempt at thumbing a lift meeting with no response from the oncoming traffic. Feeling sleepy, she closed her eyes, failing to see the green MG roadster which passed them, then pulled in to where the hitch-hiker stood.

Mark grinned at the young man. "Where are you heading?"

"Portlyn," came the reply.

"Fine. Hop in."

The hitch-hiker took off his canvas knapsack, and climbed into the passenger seat. "Thanks for stopping. I've been standing there for over half an hour. I'm not taking you out of your way, I hope?"

Mark shook his head, and glanced briefly at his passenger who had brown hair, hazel eyes, and seemed in need of a good shave. He looked about nineteen. "Student?"

"Medical," came the reply.

"Touring Cornwall during your vacation?" When the man said he was, Mark went on: "You're not taking me out of my way. Portlyn's where I'm heading anyway. There isn't a YMCA around here, I'm afraid, but if you're looking for a cheap bed and breakfast then I can recommend Mrs Martin in the High Street."

"Thanks. I slept on a beach last night, hence the stubble and stink. Sorry." After a pause he asked, "Is there a large old house at Portlyn?"

Surprised at the question, Mark frowned. "Portlyn, no. There's only Trevellan, on the hill outside the village. But it isn't open to the public. Why do you ask?"

"Just interest. I'd heard about it. Saw a picture somewhere, looks like a small castle."

"Sounds like Trevellan all right. You can just see the house from the lane on the far side of the village." Mark's mind was on other things as he set the young man down outside Mrs Martin's house and drove off to do what he could to help his parents at this terrible time.

The hitch-hiker watched as the car drove away, then wandered off up the steep hill. By the time he reached the top, he was warm enough to remove his woollen sweater. He had reached the castellated wall now and could see the upper part of the house. Walking on, he came to the gateway, stepped a few paces inside the grounds and gazed along the drive towards the south front.

How long Jamie Veryan stood there he hardly knew. But the very fact that he was there at all seemed unreal.

Slowly, he set his feet crunching on the gravelled driveway and moved towards his father's house.

# Chapter Twenty-Three

Clive stood looking out at the gathering dusk. All around Kensington Square lights were appearing in windows and street lamps flickered on. Still slightly tanned, he had grown fatter, his face even more flaccid, the eyes smaller and mouth discontented with anxiety; anxiety over another failed business deal, over a profligate wife who wanted more than he could afford to give, and over his childless marriage. Fenella showed as little interest in motherhood as she did in him and lay like carved stone in bed so that any spark of desire he felt was soon quenched. Whereas there were other women to take care of that problem, they could not give him the heir he desperately needed.

He knew people thought he cared little about Trevellan. They were wrong. He cared a great deal and always had, but times had changed and estates could no longer survive on the profits of farming alone. Wealth was generated by business and it was business that would keep Trevellan afloat. Sell the land and use the money to invest. So far he had been unlucky, lacking the Midas touch perhaps, but his luck would change, given time. If only he could be allowed that time. But here was bloody Jennie, haranguing him for selling a painting and sacking his agent. It was too much. Turning, he glared at his cousin.

"Frank is out of date. He had to go."

Sitting on the sofa in the room she had loved, Jennie stared at him coldly. "Frank always kept things under strict control. Now we're in the red. I know how much the Sisley fetched. It was quite a sum which; being capital, you may not touch. I have Mr Longwood's formal letter asking for that money to be returned to the estate accounts at once."

Clive smiled wryly, and poured himself a large Scotch. "Sorry! You'll just have to whistle for it. Every penny has been invested in a business deal which will help Trevellan far more than a picture hanging on its wall." He said nothing of the money also used to pay off large debts acquired from unlucky nights at the Casino, bad investments on

368

the Stock Market and mounting bills from his tailor, shoemaker and gunsmith.

Jennie felt ill at the news. "I know you're a fool, but you couldn't be that much of a fool!" She took a despairing breath and pointed to the large buff-coloured envelope she was holding. "I have here details of the renovations and estimated costs. Now you tell me that the money for the Sisley has simply disappeared?"

Unwinding herself from the sofa where she had been reclining with her white Persian cat, Fenella stood up and brushed a few hairs off her black faille dress. "Oh, really, Jennie, this is Clive's business not yours, and we do have an engagement this evening." The cat stretched lazily, and settled back against the brocade cushion.

Feeling a rage she hadn't known she possessed, Jennie looked up and said: "Perhaps it will wipe that silly smirk off your face when I tell you that we are now forced to sell this house."

Clive paled. "Over my dead body." He gulped down the Scotch and gave a nervous laugh. "Come now, things aren't that bad."

"Of course they're not," snapped Fenella. She glared at Jennie then allowed the merest smile to lift the corners of her bright red mouth. "Jennie's just paying off old scores, isn't that so, my dear? In any case, you haven't the power to sell what is ours."

Jennie gave her the sweetest of smiles. "There is no alternative, and yes, we do have the power. It's Mr Longwood who is adamant about the sale."

"Look, Jennie," snapped Clive, pouring another large whisky, "I've had Mother on my back over Frank and the Sisley ever since you went to Trevellan. Give me a break, for God's sake. You'll get the money back, don't worry. I just need time. And speaking of time..." He glanced at his watch. "It's well past nine and there's a thin line between Fenella's need to make a late entrance, and sheer bloody rudeness. So if that is all..."

"You'll be receiving Mr Longwood's letter setting out everything the trustees have agreed," said Jennie, remaining cool and calm. "It will explain your legal position if you fail to return that money." She stood up and placed the envelope on the table. "I thought it more courteous to tell you in person about the sale of the house. The contents will have to be auctioned off, of course. I have a copy of the inventory and will contact the auctioneers in due course." She turned to go, then paused. "How will you manage the estate from London, Clive?"

He gave her a thunderous look. "I do know how to handle accounts and taxes, Jennie. A firm of land agents will collect rents."

"And land drainage? Are you planning to sell land?"

"No, it was just an idea that won't amount to anything."

369

"A pretty expensive idea," said Jennie. "Financially and emotionally, given that it was the last straw for poor Frank. You know he's dying? Your mother must have told you that. Well, goodnight. Enjoy your party."

Clive's grip on the whisky tumbler tightened as Fenella showed his cousin to the front door. For all his swagger, Jennie's visit had punctured a large hole in his confidence. Selling up here lock, stock and barrel would do little to boost his reputation as a man with assets. Appearances were everything. Being seen to have money unlocked many doors, and since a gentleman's word was still his bond he had made much of the opportunity and borrowed heavily. A court case would destroy him. One year was all he needed to get on top of things, just one little year, and then, if all else failed, he could sell up here and pay off some of his debts at least. Now, thanks to his bloody cousin, the money for this house would go out of his control and be used up even as his creditors were hammering on the door. Roll on next August. Returning to the window he stared out at the square once more, the women's voices wafting up to him from the hall downstairs. It was quite dark now. He felt a little sick and would cry off the party.

Fenella opened the front door, handed Jennie her cream woollen jacket and watched coldly as she slipped it on over her summer dress. "You can fool Clive, but you can't fool me. I know what this is really all about." With a slight smile of triumph she leaned back against the wall and folded her arms. "He told you, of course. Told you everything that was said. No doubt you had a fierce row and are now blaming me for your failed marriage. Well, my dear Jennie, it was doomed from the start – a girl like you with a man like that. Ludicrous! Goodnight."

Already having moved out on to the step, Jennie turned quickly at these words but the door shut firmly in her face. She stood for a moment then walked to her Morris Traveller. "He told you of course." Unexplained incidents crowded her mind; Guy's early departure from Cornwall after the funeral and his equally swift return to Stannington after the accident. Both had occurred after Fenella had been on the scene.

It was Friday and Guy was home. Jennie found him as she had left him, seated beside his son, helping Alex to construct a Spitfire out of plywood. The kitchen table was covered with tools, paper and glue, and Alex, dressed in pyjamas and check dressing gown, was happily chatting away to the father whom, only a week ago, he had seemingly hated. He turned as his mother entered the kitchen and shouted excitedly: "We've finished. Look."

Jennie looked down at the model and smiled, happy to see father and son sharing something together. "Goodness! You have been working hard. I'm surprised Nanny hasn't whisked you off to bed by now."

"Special dispensation," said Guy. "This is no kit. All home made from a well-drawn up design. It took many man hours, isn't that so, Alex? How did it go tonight?"

"I've had better evenings."

"I should have gone with you."

Jennie shook her head. "No. It's more important that you spend some time with Alex."

When the model aircraft was finished to perfection Alex picked it up, held it high, and, making the sound of a fighter diving, ran around the kitchen utterly lost in his new world. Thrilled and excited, he took it up to bed with him and laid it on his dressing table lovingly so that he could look at it in the moonlight. When Jennie kissed him goodnight, he said, "Daddy's taking me to Stannington to see the Panther."

She looked surprised. "Oh? When?"

"Tomorrow. Wish you were coming. Why aren't you?"

Tomorrow! She could hardly tell him she had not been invited. "I have work to do. So you have a lovely time, and keep close to your father."

"Dad's flying the Panther at Farnborough this year."

Jennie's hand tightened on the blanket. "Are you sure?"

"Yes, and I'm going to see it tomorrow."

"I know. Isn't it exciting?" She kissed him once more then stroked his head gently, wondering how she would ever be able to part from him in September. "Well, darling, you've got a big day ahead so get some sleep. Goodnight." She left the bedroom, shutting the door behind her.

When she returned to the kitchen she found Guy removing the detritus of model-making from the wooden table, his slow movements making it clear to her that his back was troublesome again. After all this time, he still had severe pain to contend with and stiffness after sitting. It worried her to see him slowing down like this and she wondered how long he could go on.

"So you're taking him to Stannington tomorrow?"

Guy nodded. "I've been promising him a trip for ages. Now Farnborough is almost on us and you know what the build up's like. Weekdays are out. Tomorrow's the only time. I'll let him look over the hangars and the aircraft, then take him to Kay and Keith's for lunch. We'll be back by six."

She smiled. "He's over the moon about it." Filling a kettle with water, she placed it on the gas stove and paused with her fingers on a match. "He seems to think you're going to fly at Farnborough. In the display too?" When Guy nodded, she struck the match and lit the gas, her eyes fearful, her mind recalling what she so desperately wanted to forget. "But Keith always..."

"Keith is no longer Chief Test Pilot for Hadleigh's. I am."

She turned quickly, her eyes wide open in surprise as Guy spoke of Keith's failing eyesight. "Nothing terrible. Just age, that's all. He's now Hadleigh's right-hand man and has a seat on the Board. At least he has something else to go to. We're not all so lucky."

There it was again, that look that said he feared the future. "And so you are Chief Test Pilot?" The strained look vanished and a large grin took its place, so that she could only be happy for him. "Congratulations, Guy. That's marvellous."

Moved by her smile, he suddenly wanted to reach out for her, hold her, kiss her. So why couldn't he? Because she would draw away? Because he had frightened her that night? Because it was now much too late to be anything other than polite to each other? Or because the dark thought that had been with him for so long still held him back? Yet it was over, thanks to his increased watchfulness, his constant telephoning, and his regular appearances at home, Jennie was safely back in the fold. Keeping her there was the next problem. Time to dangle the carrot.

"We've been in this place for over three years when we only meant to stay for one. I've never liked it and neither have you. Since Mother died I've had a hard time selling her house. Too big and old-fashioned for today's market. I hope that when I do, it'll be enough to buy a place outright. I don't want to take on a mortgage at this age. I'm think of London, of course, for your sake. You can't paint society portraits in the country."

Was she hearing aright? The kettle started to boil over quenching the gas jet with a loud hiss. Switching off, she poured boiling water into the teapot, then realised she had forgotten to put the tea in it first. At a time when they had never been more apart he was talking of buying a house. Why? Was it fear? Fear of being almost forty; fear of failing health; fear of having nothing to go to when the flying had to stop, as one day it would? Unlike Keith who had fallen on his feet, Guy would have no warm family nest and, in all probability, no career either. He needed a house. Somewhere to call his own.

He frowned. "You're very quiet. I thought you might have been pleased. Damn it, you've gone on about buying for long enough."

She thought of Mark. How could she be excited now at the prospect of a house with Guy? "Property prices have gone up rather since we first married. And I have to have a place large enough to include studio space. I've played on Maddie's kind hospitality for too long."

He nodded. "Fair enough. You're wrong about prices. They've remained pretty stable."

"Not in London." She produced cups and saucers then poured out the tea which they drank in thoughtful silence for a while until she told him of her meeting with Clive. "We'll never see the money even if we did take him to court. The Dorking house is peanuts against the sum required."

Guy raised an eyebrow at this. "He's out of luck there anyway. Fenella once told me the house was in her name. Lytton had Clive's measure right from the start. Are you serious about taking him to court?"

She shook her head. "Warning shot over the bow, that's all. Grandma won't prosecute. The Sisley was hers."

Guy stood up and stretched his aching back. "I enjoyed my evening with Alex. It's the first time we've ever really chatted away. We discussed the new school. I think he's happier about it now." He looked concerned. "I know how you feel about Farnborough and why you've stayed away, but Alex is looking forward to it. Please bring him, Jennie. It would break his heart if you didn't."

What option had he left her? "Of course I'll bring him." She met his eyes then he turned away and she heard his slow footsteps on the stairs. Her hand clenched tightly about the cup. Farnborough! She would stand watching, as Kay had stood watching, and try not to show her fear. But before that day came, she would have to face another which she dreaded just as much.

The television series on the Resistance started at the beginning of September. Maddie came to Jennie at Flood Street to watch, and sat in deathly silence, her hands clenched about the arm of the chair until she finally succumbed to the habit she had broken years since and reached for a cigarette. Afraid to watch at first, Jennie found herself strangely distanced from the events on the small screen. Was that really her mother, that actress controlling agents, sabotaging strategic targets, sending coded messages, lighting a small fire to signal an arms drop to an aircraft in the night sky? Was it really her mother, shooting at German soldiers, being captured, held in cells and tortured for weeks before finally being led before a firing squad? Who were the people who knew her, spoke of her ... this woman with a secret life ... this brave, strong and courageous woman, so loved and admired? Impassive throughout, Jennie wondered why she felt nothing when Maddie was shaking with sobs. Only later did the true horror of it all finally sink in and she too found release in tears. Until now all she had really known was what she had read or been told and that had been horrific enough.

But now, having seen the cells, and watched the interrogation, feeling the terror that only an SS officer knew how to instil so skillfully, she had nightmare after nightmare and woke up shouting as she had in childhood. Then she would lie in bed weeping for the mother she had loved so much.

The series brought Monique Veryan back into the public eye once more and the people of Portlyn were proud to say, "She lived here among us."

Guy's flying display at Farnborough was heart-stopping, and Alex's first day at school heartbreaking. Fighting down the urge to hug and kiss him as he said a stiff and self-conscious goodbye, Jennie watched as he went off with his Housemaster, Matron and a host of new boys into his new world. The house in Flood Street was so horribly empty all of a sudden. No Alex, no Nanny Davies and no Guy at all since he was on a tour of the Middle East, seeking orders for the Panther. Only at Cheyne Walk did life seem normal, and busy days at the studio were capped by long nights chatting to Maddie's assorted collection of friends, or talking to Mark on the telephone, their sweet words of love humming along the telephone wire from York to London. Afterwards she would lie thinking of him, longing for him, and wondering how they could on like this.

On a misty day in October, Florence rang with the news that Frank Curnow had passed away at noon in Truro's General Hospital. When Guy arrived home the following evening, Jennie met him in the hall, saying, "Even though it was expected, I still find it hard to believe. Aunt Laura rang back to say that the funeral is on Tuesday. Frank wanted to be laid to rest in Portlyn, so Laura and Grandma insist on holding the wake at Trevellan."

Strangely subdued, Guy removed his sheepskin jacket then followed her into the drawing room, glad to see she had lit a fire. "Are you going?"

"I must. Especially since Grandma's asked Clive to stay away."

Guy frowned. "Tuesday, you say? I have a meeting then to discuss the forthcoming trip to Canada." He poured himself a Scotch and soda and sank into an armchair, his eyes not meeting hers. "So we can't go."

Jennie stood, staring into the fire. A piece of coal shifted, causing sparks to fly upwards. "It doesn't matter. You didn't know Frank that well. I'll go alone."

After a long silence, he said in a tense voice, "Curnow's son will be there, of course?"

Stiffening, Jennie kept her gaze on the flames. "Mark? I should think so." She tried to sound nonchalant, but had thought of little else all day.

He smiled thinly. "And Tuesday can't come quick enough for you. Is that it?"

She gave him a level stare. "What is that supposed to mean?"

"Oh, don't play games, Jennie. We both know what we're talking about."

"I don't. So tell me." Settling herself on the sofa she tried to keep calm. How quiet the room was. Only the sound of flames cracking in the hearth broke the dreadful silence.

"Well," said Guy, "let's see. There was the boathouse of course. Even though that was before we met, it altered my perception of you. Then there was Belmore. But the worst betrayal of all was trying to pretend that Mark's child was mine. No wonder you were so silent about your pregnancy. It also goes a long way to explaining why you went to pieces afterwards. It was his baby you lost, and yet you made me bear the guilt for that loss. Christ! When I think of it..."

Stunned, Jennie just sat there until the overwhelming injustice of his accusation sank in. Then a slow-burning rage ignited somewhere inside her. When she spoke it was in a voice that was dangerously quiet. "I cannot believe I heard all that. She was yours, Guy. *Yours*. But you didn't want her, didn't want to know about her!" Her voice rose with the rage. "Just how long have you nursed this terrible thought, and who put such a lie into your head?"

Surprised at her anger when he had expected guilty fear, he turned from her. "It was at your grandfather's funeral that I learned you had been at Trevellan the spring of the previous year ... at the same time as Mark ... at the same time that you conceived."

"I was never there with Mark. Ask anyone at Trevellan if you like. It was your baby and you know why I lost her." Memories of that awful time spilled over into tears. "How could you ... how could you? Dear God..."

Devastated, he watched her. Anger he could cope with, tears left him helpless. Was she lying? He wanted her to be lying, otherwise he had killed their marriage for nothing.

At last, Jennie managed to control her emotions. "So then, who put all this nonsense into your head? The accused has a right to know the accuser." At his silence she suddenly recalled Fenella's words: "He told you then..."

"All these years ... all these years ... you've lived with that thought and never once given me the chance to tell you how wrong you were? That you didn't think I was even worth that chance is very hard to live with, Guy. Too hard. We cannot go on together after this. I think it best that we separate and start divorce proceedings."

Wrong-footed, but refusing to wear his guilt like a brand, Guy bounced the ball back into Jennie's court. "Now tell me about Belmore, and don't say that Mark wasn't there, because I know he was."

She looked into the fire, her rage slowly abating, leaving her strangely tranquil. "Did I ever say he wasn't? Frankly, I no longer care what you know or think you know any more. Yes, he was there. I'd no idea he would be when I accepted the commission, but I haven't seen him since we had dinner together that evening in London. Can you say the same about your fancy woman?"

He made no answer, aware that he had pushed her too far. Divorce! He *had* killed his marriage. Now he could cheerfully kill Fenella. Realising that Jennie would soon be in Cornwall with Mark, he felt a sense of panic and, moving to the sofa, sat down and took her hand in his. "Look, I'm sorry . . . sorry if I got it all wrong."

Tranquility shattered, she snatched her hand away. "It's too late, Guy. Much too late. I've played second fiddle for years. And I've had enough."

Sighing with despair, he stood up and walked back to the drinks table, saying: "Strange, because I've always felt that *I* was the one playing second fiddle. Jennie, I do love you. In spite of everything, I do love you. Don't go to the funeral."

She heard him without emotion. "I must go. Even someone as insensitive as you can surely see that?"

"I'll ask you one more time: please do not go." At her silence, he turned angrily. "Tell me one thing. If the baby was mine, then why in God's name did you keep it a secret from me?"

She turned to him with bitter eyes. "Because you didn't want it. You said, and I quote: 'I don't wish to see my wife blown up like a balloon.'" With that, Jennie stormed out and rushed up to her bedroom where she locked the door and flung herself on to her bed.

A few moments later she heard a gentle knocking and Guy's soft voice. "Oh, come on, Jennie. I'm sorry. Sorry for everything. Look . . . don't hide away in there, that's no answer. If I've been wrong then all I can say is I'm sorry. But we have to talk this out . . ."

"Talk?" She lay back on her bed. "When did you ever want to talk? Go away. Go back to your fancy woman. Go to hell!"

She tensed as he tried the door handle, then heard his footsteps descending the stairs once more. She got off the bed walked to her dressing table and gazed absently at a list of properties for sale. Not that it mattered any more. It was too late, years too late; years during which Guy had let a thought eat away at him like a cancer. Her mind drifted to Belmore. Yes, she had lain with Mark and had never known such happiness before or since. Adulteress she might be but she felt no guilt now. How could there be guilt where there was love? How could there be guilt when Guy had kept another woman all these years and felt only contempt for his wife?

Awake all night, she rose at dawn, pulled her blue velvet dressing gown about her and stepped out on to the landing. The door to Guy's bedroom stood open. Peering inside, she saw that his bed had not been slept in. Drained of any emotion, she moved downstairs, looked in all the other rooms, then made her way to the kitchen. She was alone. Thank God. Shivering in the cold autumn morning, she made a pot of tea and sat drinking her first cup of the day. It was warm and comforting. Not so the house. She would leave it and find herself a comfortable flat where loneliness might not seem so terrible. After all, she had money of her own now and a career. Divorce Guy! It had finally come, and suddenly all pity and love for him had vanished. Divorce! How would that affect little Alex who had so recently watched his hero father putting the Panther through it's thrilling paces over the heads of crowds at Farnborough? The price of freedom was high if it meant hurting the son she loved.

# Chapter Twenty-Four

Wind and rain lashed inwards from the sea, strong gusts tearing through Trevellan's grounds, destroying the fading roses, sending small branches crashing from trees. In the kitchen garden, Ben was battling to save the autumn plants when a strong gust hit the large greenhouse, smashing panes and leaving dangerous shards of glass everywhere. Groaning and muttering to himself, the sixty-five-year-old gardener looked at the mess then at his watch and decided that if he stayed to clear things up he would be too late to bid farewell to his old employer; a man he, like everyone on the estate, had respected and now mourned. There was talk, terrible talk, but how true it was that Mr Clive had given the agent the push was anyone's guess. No one knew for sure, but in Portlyn everyone had something to say about it. Now that Mr Curnow was dead, Mr Clive was not just unpopular, he was hated.

Inside the church, Jennie sat between her grandmother and aunt in the Veryan pew and waited in tense silence. She had arrived late last night and lain awake listening to the gale, worrying about the tarpaulin-covered roof and the scaffolding which had scarred the old house for the past two months. Rising at dawn, she had gone to the warm kitchen, had a cup of tea with Mrs Hodges who was in need of comforting, inspected the workmen's progress and helped Rosa and Keynes with the wake preparations. She needed to be busy, to have no time to think of the moment when she would meet Mark again. That moment was almost upon her. She glanced around at the familiar faces from estate and village. The church was crowded, not a space left in any of the pews, and people standing at the rear. Tension mounting, she glanced at her mother's memorial tablet and at the chrysanthemums on the window beside it, then let her eyes wander to the alabaster effigy which stood close to the altar. Sir Hugh Veryan, who had built Trevellan, lay with his wife beside him, hands set in prayer, sixteenth-century clothing so carefully carved that Jennie had always felt it likely that a slight movement would send the folds of the woman's gown slipping over the edge. Seeing them now gave her a strong sense of knowing who she was and where she belonged. It was everywhere she looked, portraits of ancestors, graves of ancestors, things brought to the house by ancestors. Family. Trevellan meant family and home. Here she had always felt at peace, here she felt strong.

Suddenly there were footsteps at the rear of the church. The Rector spoke the first words of the funeral service and pallbearers carried the wreath-covered coffin along the nave. Jennie glanced around and saw an ashen-faced Mark walking behind, his arm supporting his grieving mother. As the coffin was laid on a bier, Mark settled his mother and himself into a pew opposite Jennie.

*How ill you look, my darling*, she thought. *How heavy and sad. I want to hold you and comfort you, but all I must show on my face is correct sympathy.* At the graveside, her eyes held his for a brief moment, and said all she could not say aloud.

The dining room was filled with people and a general low hum of conversation rose and fell as Mabel and her son walked among old friends. A cold buffet was laid out on the table and Keynes and Rosa served sherry.

Mabel murmured, for the umpteenth time, that her husband's parting was a "blessed release", then told Jennie of the flat in Truro which was comfortable and convenient to shops and family. As she listened, Jennie could see Mark chatting to a group of people. *Look at me, why don't you? Damn you, look at me.* It was too warm. Rosa had lit a log fire to cheer people on such a gloomy day. But with the press of bodies, Jennie could hardly breathe and moved to the threshold to find that people had spilled into the hallway. She glanced back into the room. At that moment Mark turned and met her gaze. A silent message passed between them. Slipping into the hall, Jennie moved quietly and unnoticed among those gathered there, opened the front door and stepped out into the cold damp day.

The gale had faded to a cool stiff wind, the rain too had eased although threatening clouds still hung overhead. Arms hugged about her in a vain attempt to keep out the cold, Jennie ambled along the drive towards the rose gardens and gazed at the sad sight of broken stems and scattered petals. All that remained of summer had been destroyed within minutes. Everything was dying and soon it would be winter.

Would he come to her? Or had she misunderstood that look? Why should he come? He was filled with grief and anger, thinking it in her power to have prevented his father's curt dismissal from office and house. What must his feelings be now to see a large "For Sale" notice outside his own home? Clive had put the house on the market two days after the Curnows had moved out.

"Why keep an agent's house when we no longer require an agent?" had been his sharp reply to her angry enquiry. "Ask old poker-faced Longwood. For once he actually agreed with me."

"Hiding from me or the mourners?"

Starting slightly, she turned to see Mark staring down at her, his eyes still heavy with grief. "Oh, my dear . . . I'm so sorry, so very sorry."

His mouth tightened, and he nodded. "At least Clive had the sensitivity to stay away. Just as well. I might have throttled him at the graveside." He stared at her pale face, made paler by the black dress softly folding about her slender figure, relieved only by a single row of pearls. She was trembling. Taking off his jacket, he flung it about her shoulders and kept his arm there. "You'll catch your death. Keep it on." As she looked up at him, he saw dark shadows beneath her eyes and felt a surge of anger. Like the roses all about him she was fading and it frightened him. "He's crushing you, crushing the life out of you."

Shyly, unsure of anything anymore, she put a hand to her face realising now how terrible she must look. Sleepless nights and mourning black did little to become her. "It isn't just Guy, it's all that has been happening here. I tried to persuade your father to stay, but he wanted to go. He was too ill to fight Clive."

"Clive!" Mark's face darkened. "He's destroyed everything I ever loved. He made my father's last months unbearable. I want the bastard to pay for that."

She turned away; his pain was her pain, his anger her anger. They walked on, past the stable block, the old coach house and laundry, reaching the kitchen garden just as the rain started. Jennie headed straight for the large greenhouse. As she entered, her feet crunched on glass from the broken window pane.

"Careful," said Mark, catching her arm and holding her back. "There's glass everywhere." He swung her around to face him, gazed with deep intensity at the sad eyes, then gathered her into his arms.

She leaned her head against his breast and felt the pounding heart beneath his crisp white shirt. "Can you forgive me? Forgive me for putting Guy first and pushing you away?"

"No," he murmured, brushing her hair with his lips. "No, I can't forgive you." He pulled her closer, kissing her eyes, her cheeks, and finally her lips. She yielded to his kiss and clung to him. Rain lashed the glass above, cascading down through the broken panes, but lost in each other they barely noticed. Finally letting her go, he saw the tears, produced a clean handkerchief from his trouser pocket and wiped her face gently with it.

She sniffed and her lips curved into a tremulous smile. "Sorry. Anyway, people are supposed to cry at funerals, aren't they? Oh, Mark, I've been such a fool. I know now just how much of a fool. I've told Guy that I want a divorce."

"He jumped for joy, of course," came the flat reply. Mark pulled her back from the broken glass and battering rain. "You're cold. We'd better return to the house. Careful." Leading her through the shards of glass, he looked up at the missing pane and frowned. "Ben must fix this soon or the whole roof could go."

They ran back through the rain until they reached the main entrance; the large oak door stood half-open before them. Here Jennie paused and turned to him, rain-soaked hair clinging in tendrils to her face. "We had a stand up row, Mark. I told him I wanted a divorce and he left. I think it's all over. I think I'm alone. I think I would like a large brandy."

He stared at her for some moments, afraid to let his heart soar at the news, for how many times had his hopes been dashed. "How long are you staying?"

"Until the day after tomorrow. It's almost half term and I must fetch my son from school. And you?"

"One more day. I'm driving Mother to her cousin in Exeter tomorrow afternoon. Oh, Christ, Jennie, have you really done it?"

She smiled. "Yes. Now that the first step has been taken, talk of divorce will be easier."

They walked into the now deserted hallway and came face to face with Laura who appeared from the dining room and glared at them coldly. "I've been looking for you everywhere, Mark. Your mother is ready to leave. And, Jennie, don't you think you should be circulating?"

She nodded. "We'll be along directly."

"You might dry your hair first, and tidy yourself up," said Laura as she walked back into the dining room.

Mark winked at Jennie and smiled. "I love the way you look. Oh, darling, so much to say and only one more day to say it in. I'll come tomorrow morning. You can show me the repair work while we talk. That should keep your aunt from nosing around."

"What the hell do I care about her? If she hadn't connived to put her son where he is now, then we shouldn't be in the mess we're in. You don't know, Mark, you just don't know..."

"Yes, I do," he answered quietly. "I'd like to check the books and find out how much Clive really knows about managing an estate."

A sigh of relief escaped her; he felt the warmth of its release touch his face. With supreme willpower, he turned and walked back into the dining room.

At ten the following morning, Mark arrived back at the house and followed Keynes to the library. Inside he found Jennie seated at the large desk, her small white hands leafing through an open ledger. She looked up and said, for the butler's benefit: "Good morning. You can see I've made a start."

Keynes hovered at the door. "Will you take coffee in here later, Madam, or in the morning room?"

Fending off his suspicious look, she said, "Well, we've a lot of work to get through, so I think here would be best." When the old butler had left, she glanced at Mark's amused face and laughed. "My God, I do believe we're causing another scandal. I thought I should look busy, but the fact is I haven't a clue what it is I'm looking at."

"Not that anyway," said Mark, standing behind her and letting his arm fall over her shoulder. "It's three years out of date, or hadn't you noticed?" Their hands met, fingers entwined; an electric charge quivered through them. She reached up and touched his face with loving tenderness. He bent and covered her mouth with his. When he made to move away she caught his hand once more.

"I haven't slept," she murmured. "I spent the night wondering, worrying, trying to work out how to go about things. There's another woman, but he won't admit it."

Mark sat on the desk and looked down at her. "Get evidence of the man's infidelity. Have him followed. Then find a good divorce solicitor who'll tell you the next step."

"Spy on him?" She shook her head quickly. "I can never forget that once he risked his life to save mine, or put from my mind that he's no longer the fit man he pretends to be and is fearful that everything could fall apart for him."

"Christ, you make him sound like an old wounded guard dog."

Jennie smiled weakly. "They're the most dangerous. He knows about you through Fenella and Clive. We had a fearful row but I've succeeded, I think, in clearing your name and discrediting the innuendoes and outright lies. Even so, we have to be very careful. I don't want you dragged into it otherwise everything you care about could be taken from you."

He gazed at her. "Everything I care about has already been taken from me."

The door opened and a second before Keynes entered with the coffee tray, Mark moved from Jennie and opened a folder. When the butler

382

had left, he took a cursory glance around the room, slipped off his dark jacket and said "I'd better keep my mind on other things. So then, to work."

By eleven-thirty, Mark had discovered that his father's once meticulously kept records had been abandoned to chaos. "It's impossible," he said at last. "There are no records of revenues, yields, or transactions. Few accounts have been settled and there are final demands from all kinds of people. What the hell is he doing? If he's handed everything over to Lyle and Church to deal with, they should make sure that copies of their records and accounts are sent here to keep these books straight. I hope Clive remembers that tax will be levied on revenues and that a percentage of those revenues must be put back into the estate."

Fumbling through the mounting bills, he picked up a third and final demand for payment. "This is serious. They threaten to take him to court if payment isn't made by the end of October. What's it for anyway, this field survey?"

"Land drainage. But Clive abandoned it in the summer."

"Not according to this." He held up another letter. "This is from the firm dealing with land drainage and is dated two weeks ago. It seems they expect to hear further from him with regard to the project. What project?"

"Let me see that." She read the letter twice, while Mark started rummaging through cupboards for a plan he felt sure would be there. In the end he found it, well hidden away on the topmost shelf, and spread it across the desk top. Bewildered, Jennie frowned. "What's all this?"

"I hope you're right and it was just an idea that isn't likely to take off," said Mark, bending to look at the layout. "I thought at first it was a housing estate, but it isn't. It's a goddamned caravan site, a vast bloody caravan site to run from Pentock Edge through Long Meadow and the valley, then on past the cricket field to spread out again on the hill above. It will be seen from every aspect, in all its hideousness, and for this Clive is willing to give up five hundred acres of valuable pasture. What isn't clear is whether the council have given him permission or not. Although, judging by what's happening all over this county, I should think it more than likely."

Mark rolled up the plan and replaced it in the cupboard, saying angrily, "It's so utterly senseless, reducing farm and livestock income for the vagaries of summer campers. One rainy season is all you need to send you further into the red. Reducing acreage means reducing labourers; reducing labourers mean empty cottages, empty cottages bring in no rent and are sold. You see where I'm leading? Within six to ten years, the estate will be totally broken up and parcelled off to different buyers."

She listened to him in growing horror, then shook her head. "No, he can't mean to do this. When I asked him about land drainage he told me it was just an idea that came to nothing."

Mark smiled wryly. "And you believed him? My father was certain that Clive saw no future in keeping the estate as it is now. Well, it's true that estates like this are running into trouble. But there are other ways to resolve the problem, through careful husbandry and ..." He stopped as he saw the dismay on her face and could have kicked himself. "Cheer up. Things may not be so bad as all that." He picked up the telephone and got through to Robert Longwood on Jennie's behalf. After explaining how he had found matters, he listened for some time, then, frowning, replaced the receiver. "It seems that Longwood has already checked with Lyle and Church and found that large sums have been removed from estate accounts by Clive. He's written to him but received no reply."

Jennie looked alarmed. "Clive's using that money to further his business interests and if they fail ... oh, Mark ... if they fail?"

"As trustees you must put a stop to it. Don't let the bastard frighten you off, Jennie."

Feeling weak, she sat looking at him. "We can only put a halt to his activities for a short while. And he knows it. Next summer he'll be able to do as he pleases. I have a horrible feeling that within a few years, Trevellan itself will go under the hammer." She paused and swallowed hard, trying to force back the tears. "And I think it will kill me ..." Her voice cracked, her eyes filled and she felt his arms enfolding her trembling body.

"Things are probably not that bad," he murmured unconvincingly. "Come on, darling, it's time to walk away from all this for a while. We have but half a day left together and I'm taking you to lunch."

She dabbed at her eyes with a lace handkerchief and smiled. "Yes please, somewhere quiet, expensive and near a stream which is clear and flowing. I need to shake off ... this ... this grime."

They fell quiet, aware that soon they must part and go their separate ways once more. Mark tried not to think of it as he pulled on his jacket, kissed her tenderly and murmured, "Jennie, my love, my dearest, my angel, I want the rest of this day to be one you'll never forget."

Having pushed with all her might, Jennie could push no longer. Pausing, red-faced and breathless, she started at Mark's voice.

"Don't stop, for God's sake."

Wearily she stretched out her arms, set the weight of her slim body

384

against the rear of the car and started pushing once more. Frank Curnow's old Wolseley had broken down just a half-mile short of the garage outside Portlyn.

"Come on," shouted Mark, hand on wheel as he pushed from the side. "Almost there. Keep going. One small mercy anyway. It could have happened at the bottom of the hill."

Englishmen! Jennie grimaced as she pushed, thinking what a strange end it was to a romantic, tranquil idyll. They had dined in a woodland setting at the Old Mill Restaurant, then wandered beside the mill race, lost in each other and the beauty of the autumn colours lifting in warm sunshine. Now this! Peering around the car she saw, with an overwhelming sense of relief, the small wayside garage ahead.

John Small rubbed his greasy hands on an even greasier black rag and advanced towards them as they pushed the car into his small forecourt. "Broken down then, Mr Curnow? Sorry about your father." He looked at the car. "Fuel pump again, I shouldn't wonder, It's done some mileage, this old Wolseley. What is it now, over twelve years old? Your father was having a lot of trouble with it. Earlier in the summer he spoke of buying a new one but . . ." John Small shrugged and shook his head sadly.

Breathless, Mark removed his jacket from inside the car and flung it over one shoulder. "I didn't know." It seemed strangely upsetting that his father should have been thinking of buying a new car only a short while ago. Upsetting too that he had been having trouble with this one. Grief flooded over him once more. He turned to Jennie and tried to force a smile. "Sorry about this. You look quite done in and your face is dirty."

Still trying to catch her breath, she was about to touch her face then saw the mixture of dust and exhaust that had blackened her hands. "Where?"

"Here." Mark tilted her chin gently and wiped the dirt from her cheek and forehead with a clean handkerchief, whispering, "Where would you be if I didn't carry one?" He wiped his own hands then threw the handkerchief into the boot of the car as John Small emerged from under the engine hood.

"It's the fuel pump all right. Give me an hour or so. I'm just finishing another job at the moment."

Mark glanced at his watch, nodded and turned to Jennie. "Well, if you can push a car half a mile then walking a full mile should be a doddle. Again, darling, I'm sorry about all this."

"Why?" She smiled. "You did say you wanted this to be a day I'd never forget."

For a moment they stared at each other then the stupidity of the

385

whole thing suddenly sent bubbles of laughter to the surface, shocking John Small who thought it indecent to be merry at such a time. They set off towards Portlyn while Mark spoke of selling the car. The laughter that had broken through his grief now faded as he thought again of his loss. Soon he would lose Jennie too. Divorce! Unless she resorted to having Guy followed, she hadn't a prayer. Jennie might be unhappy, but she was not vindictive and since she was what she was, he could see no light at the end of this long, dark tunnel. They had reached the hill and looked down on the harbour, bathed now in mellow sunshine.

Descending into the High Street both became aware of the occasional movement at cottage windows.

"Curtains are twitching," murmured Mark, one hand thrust into his trouser pocket, the other holding the jacket still slung over one shoulder. "Nothing has changed, yet everything has."

At the harbour they paused among late holidaymakers to watch the fishermen mending nets or preparing their boats. Caps were doffed to "Miss Genevieve" and sympathetic glances headed Mark's way, but as the couple walked on, the weathered faces turned towards each other and shrewd eyes spoke of old memories and thoughts best left unsaid. Aware of all this, Jennie ignored it. Nothing – not even wandering over cobbled stones in court shoes and a navy linen suit – could mar this wonderful moment when it seemed that the years had suddenly been stripped away. She was twenty again and Mark had just returned from the Middle East. She looked up at him, unable to mask her feelings. He read them in her eyes and without speaking they turned back up the hill then made their way to the boathouse.

There the dream ended as Jennie said: "Clive sold *The Rose* and the boathouse. Did you know?"

Mark's jaw tensed. "No, I didn't. I wish I had, I'd have bought both myself."

"Why? What would be the point? You're never here."

He shook his head and smiled. "Women are supposed to be the romantic ones. It isn't true. Men are the true romantics while you're all so bloody practical."

She gave him a thoughtful look. "It will always be our place, no matter who owns it." As he put his arm about her she cuddled into him, lifted her face and felt his warm lips on hers. They wandered up and across the cliff path, then paused to look back. The late-evening sun slanted across the harbour way below them. Beyond stretched the spectacular coastline rising from a deep turquoise sea; the light so diamond sharp it was possible to make out every headland for miles. The tide was in as they reached the cove. Jennie took off her court shoes and was paddling about the edge of the waves in her stockinged feet.

"Do you remember the day we first met? I was caught by the tide and you hauled me out. I thought you were a gypsy at first, all brown and tawny. Not a bit like the grandson of a clergyman."

"And I thought you were some little urchin from London," said Mark. He led her by the arm towards the steps then looked up, as he always did, searching for brown wings hovering high above. All he saw were seagulls wheeling and circling the sky. "I love this place," he murmured. "I can't bear to think that I shall never come here again."

"Don't, Mark." She placed a hand on his arm, unable to bear the thought either. "Whether we come back here or not, we will be together. It has to be, and will be."

Mark said nothing as they ambled back along the woodland path, arms locked about each other. His darling, gentle Jennie would have to toughen up considerably before they could ever be together. They passed the paddock where Laura's chestnut mare was grazing peacefully and both remembered the days when Kelly had grazed with her. In the kitchen garden they found Ben watching critically as a glazier replaced the greenhouse glass; the sun was low in the sky, burnishing crimson Virginia Creeper that covered the walls; a small bonfire sent a column of sweet wood smoke curling upwards into the mellow air.

By the old coach house Jennie stopped. "I've often thought this would make a perfect place for a summer school for artists. Replace these huge doors with windows and you have a spacious studio with light coming from the south for most of the day. Ten students at a time, I think, sleeping in newly decorated rooms in the east wing. Visiting tutors, of course."

Mark smiled. "You'll have to have your summer school somewhere else."

Brought back to earth with a bump, Jennie sighed and folded her arms. "Well, what are we without our dreams? The Portlyn school to rival Newlyn and St Ives. Why not?"

Their steps were slower and dragging as they came round to the east front. The terrible anguish of parting was almost on them. At the entrance, they stopped and gazed at each other.

"Stay, Mark," urged Jennie. "Stay to dinner ... oh, of course, your mother ... your dear mother. You're driving her to Exeter. But I can't ... I can't let you go ... not yet."

He looked down into her moist beseeching eyes and knew he had to be strong. Feeling anything but, he swallowed hard. "You forget, I've a broken down car to collect. John Small will close up at six."

"That's no problem. Our chauffeur will run you up the hill in the Rolls and you can drive back down again in the Wolseley. I'd take you myself but Aunt Laura has the other car."

At that moment, a dark-suited figure appeared in the doorway and stood barring their way. Jennie turned quickly, unable to disguise her astonishment and devastation. "What on earth are you doing here?"

Unsmiling, Clive put a hand to his ear. "What was that? What am I doing here? In my own house?" He turned his attention to Mark. "More to the point is what you're doing here. The funeral was yesterday."

"Must you be so offensive?" snapped Jennie.

"And must you be so obvious?" Clive retorted. "Don't you have a husband somewhere, Jennie? As for you, Curnow, yesterday was yesterday, special dispensation and all that, so I kept away. Today, however, I am back and find you on my property. Why? Snooping perhaps? Poking your nose into my affairs?" His face darkened with rage. "If you so much as set foot on my land again, I'll have you prosecuted for trespass. Do you understand?"

Eyes flashing with anger, Jennie stepped forward to face up to her cousin. "How dare you speak to him like that? How dare you? And how pathetic, coming all this way just to prove a point. You are childish in the extreme, Clive."

"It's all right," murmured Mark, trying to keep a hold on his own seething fury. "I have to go anyway. Don't waste words or emotions on such a man."

Outraged by this remark, Clive lunged forward but Jennie intervened, only to be roughly pushed aside. Moving in to defend her, Mark grabbed Clive by his shirt, muttered an oath then delivered a strong punch to the flaccid jaw, sending the new squire reeling. He lay on the porch, head spinning, blood pouring from his lip. Mark stood over him and was about to drag him to his feet to punch him down again when Jennie stopped him.

"No, Mark. No ... please, please." He looked at her strangely then turned and strode along the drive. She ran after him. "Stop ... don't go like this. Oh, Mark ... please."

He paused, shoulders heaving as he tried to control his rage. "I wanted to kill him ... I wanted to kill him." He walked on until reaching the entrance where he leaned back against the stone archway and closed his eyes. "Christ, I didn't know I hated him so much. I wanted to smash his face to pulp." When he managed to calm down, he murmured: "Oh God, I'm sorry. As if things aren't bad enough for you, I have to go and make them worse."

"He had it coming." Only twice before had she seen such fury in her gentle giant – when Mark picked up the corpse of Sophie all those years ago, and when he struck Clive in the boathouse. "Only Clive can drive a man to the point of murder. You struck that blow for both of us."

Anxiously she reached up to his sweating face and stroked it gently. "It's over. You said it yourself, don't waste emotion on such a man."

"You can't stay there tonight," said Mark. "Not now. Come home with me. Even if it means a journey to Exeter."

She shook her head, knowing how his mother and others would react to that. If she and Mark had any hope at all, there must be no gossip about them. "I shall return to London on the next train. It's the best way, and you know it. In any case, your mother is griefstricken and I've kept you from her far too long."

"I'll drive you to the station. Meanwhile I'll walk off my anger. Go back to your room and pack. Stay out of Clive's way. I'll be at the front door in forty minutes." With that he strode through the gateway and out into the lane.

Jennie watched him go; sick at heart that these last precious moments had been ruined and cut short by Clive's unlooked for return. When she returned to the house, it was to see her cousin standing on the doorstep, blood-soaked handkerchief at his lip. She stared at him with contempt. "I should have thought that once was enough, but then some people never learn."

He glared at her. "The bastard." It hurt to talk. He wondered if he would have a large bruise on his jaw to proclaim to the world that he had been in a fight. "I'll prosecute him, depend on it. He'll be sorry we met this day."

"Well, you certainly must be." Jennie smiled and walked past him to the staircase. "I'm off to pack. You'll be pleased to know I'm leaving for London as soon as possible."

"Amen to that."

She paused as she headed into the main hall. "By the way, Clive. I'd say nothing about this. You don't want to be the butt of local humour, do you?"

Amazed at his own forbearance, Clive watched in silent fury as she climbed the stairway, then he walked into the drawing room and poured himself a large neat Scotch.


They drove in silence along dark country lanes, Mark's grim face set, Jennie biting her trembling lip in a vain attempt to stop the flowing tears. When they reached the station, he brought the car to a halt then sat rigid, hands gripping the wheel, unable to speak or look at her. He knew she was crying and dreaded to see it. If he did, he might break down himself. Then he felt her soft small hand fold over his whitening knuckles, and the next moment he was crushing her to him, kissing the tears, rubbing his hands through her hair and thinking he would die if

389

he let her go. His lips brushed her face and sought her mouth; his kiss long, hard and lingering as though they were melting into each other. "I can't let you go," he murmured at last. "I can't."

For one brief moment Jennie thought of throwing all care to the wind. They could start their lives together right now. But the moment passed as commonsense returned. This was no fairy tale, this was real life, and tomorrow Alex would be waiting for her to take him home again. "I *will* ask Guy for that divorce. I *will* be free of him. It *will* happen. Trust me, darling, it *will* happen."

They climbed out of the car; Mark took a suitcase from the boot and walked with her on to the platform. There were people everywhere and those who saw the tearful woman with the equally unhappy-looking man turned away with a sense of sadness for parting lovers. They were early for the London train and waiting, dreading to part, was the most agonising thing of all. At last the train arrived; he helped her into the first class carriage, placed her case on the luggage rack and nodded at the two middle-aged women seated in the corner seats. Then he was standing on the platform and she leaning out of the window holding his hand, unable to speak. Somewhere through the steam and smoke, the guard blew his whistle and the train shuddered forward.

"Goodbye, my darling," cried Jennie, still clinging to his hand, as he walked along beside her. Tears streamed down her face as she said haltingly: "I'll ring you, my love. I'll ring ... and let you know the verdict."

He already knew the verdict. It would be a death sentence on their future.

As the train gathered speed, Jennie looked back at the receding figure, knowing she would never forget the look on that beloved face.


In the hallway at Trevellan Clive was answering the telephone with some difficulty owing to a swollen lip and bruised jaw. His lower molar had worked loose as well. "Guy? No, Jennie's not here. Would you like to know where she is?" He gave a curt laugh. "Making an idiot of herself with young Curnow, that's where. I told you all about him, remember? Anyway, after causing quite a scene here this evening, he's now taken her to the station for a loving farewell. Can't you just imagine it? All that's missing is the bloody Rachmaninov!"

Slamming down the receiver Clive finished yet another whisky. He was quite alone. Fenella had stayed in London, his mother had no idea he was even here, and his grandmother, to avoid being alone with him, had taken herself off to her room where Keynes was now serving her dinner. He wondered if he would be able to eat his. Bloody Curnow, bloody Jennie! Well, that timely little telephone call would be the best revenge he could have. Serve the silly bitch right when she faced her furious husband. She had it coming. And being cited as co-respondent in a divorce case would ruin Mark.

# Chapter Twenty-Five

To Jennie's heart-sinking surprise, Guy was home when her taxi pulled up at the house that night. He appeared in the hallway, unsmiling, and took her case without a word, then answered her question tersely. "The reason I'm here is because I leave for Canada on Friday morning and need to pack. The trip's been brought forward and extended." He walked back into the drawing room then turned to her. "I phoned to let you know, but you had already left."

Jennie's heart turned a somersault as she removed her coat and flung it over the back of the sofa. "Did you speak to Grandma?"

After a short silence: "No, but I had a strange conversation with Clive, though."

Inwardly she groaned but kept her voice light. "Have you eaten?"

He nodded, then stood with his back to the unlit fire, the steel grey eyes searching hers for reassurance. Not finding it he knew now that Clive had been speaking the truth. Damn Mark Curnow to hell! Jennie had lied to him after all. But she was his wife and their lives, good or bad, were entwined by fate and no faceless rival was going to change that. Look at her, guilt written all over her face. How could she do this to him? Trying to keep the lid on his simmering fury, he said sharply: "You look as though you need a drink, Jennie."

She sat down, shook her head and shivered. It was cold in the room. Why hadn't he bothered to light the fire? What had Clive said to him? He would see her shivering and think she was afraid. Fear meant guilt. Why hadn't he lit the fire?

"It seems I missed a merry old time. Clive said that Mark had caused trouble. What was Clive doing there anyway? You told me he wouldn't be?"

"He turned up this afternoon."

"I see. Why was Mark at Trevellan today when the funeral was yesterday? I understood that his parents had moved to Truro."

"His car broke down outside Portlyn." Something very strange had happened to her voice. "I was in the village when he appeared. We walked about together, then I invited him to the house for tea. He had an hour or two to kill until the car could be fixed. Then Clive appeared, was hideously rude and ... Mark punched him on the jaw." She huddled forward and found herself chatting on. "On the eve of the funeral there was a terrible gale. I was worried about the scaffolding and the tarpaulin ... the gardens are a mess. Everyone came, all the tenants and villagers..."

"Stop it, for God's sake." Guy glared at her. "I can't believe you've put me through an evening of hell just to chatter on about a funeral. Mark took you to the station this evening when you could have gone in the Rolls. Why did he do that?"

She leapt to her feet and screamed at him: "For Heaven's sake, why the third degree? He gave me a lift, that's all. I had thought you might be about to apologise to me for the other evening, but no ... here you go again with the same stupid accusations."

"And here you go again with the same stupid lies."

She stared at him bitterly. "Give me a divorce. This is no marriage. You've always wanted your freedom, so take it and be done with the whole damn' thing."

He let out a long breath and said in an ice thin voice: "So that you can run off with Mark? No, Jennie. There'll be no divorce, and no scandal. You're my wife and will continue to be my wife."

The manner of his reply, his coolness under fire, took Jennie by surprise. She had known he would be difficult, but his cold deliberate words had a horrible finality about them. "But why? You don't love me, you've never loved me. Yet, when you have the chance to be free, you won't take it."

Guy moved to the drinks table and poured himself another large brandy, the fourth that evening. "No. You're wrong as it happens. I do love you. And somehow I don't want to be free thinking of you with him. I knew it would happen if you went to Trevellan again. I asked you not to go. But you wouldn't listen. Now you arrive home and the first thing you do is ask for a divorce. The answer is no." He gulped down the brandy, slammed the glass down on the table and said, "Now, according to our tradition, this is where I slam out of the door and drive back to Stannington. Tonight I have a mind to stay however."

Jennie backed away in growing fear. "Do as you please, I'm going to Maddie's."

He caught her arm as she headed for the door. "You'll do no such thing. Rushing all over London and discussing our marital problems is a little tacky, don't you think?"

393

She turned on him with blazing eyes. "You accuse me of being tacky when you climb into bed with that whore and tell her every damned thing about us! Take your filthy hands off and go to her ... go on ... now, why don't you?"

She gasped as Guy's arm came spinning round, struck her full on the face and sent her crashing to the floor. A searing pain shot through her head; she was starring at the carpet just half an inch from her eyes. Dazed and shocked, she lay there unable to move, then felt his arms about her.

Horrified at his action, Guy picked her up and settled her back in an armchair. Why had he allowed her to goad him like that? Drunk! He was drunk! For the first time in his life he had lost control and it frightened him. "Christ ... oh, Christ, I'm sorry." He touched the ugly red mark on her face and saw that her eyes weren't focussing properly. "Jennie. Look at me ... look at me." He staggered to the drinks table, poured her a brandy and tried to make her drink it. She murmured incoherently, and pushed his arm away. The liquid spilt on to the floor. He waited until her eyes returned to normal, those eyes that were looking up at him in fear. "Christ ... but ... you push a man too far, Jennie. I never thought it would come to this." With that he walked from the room, and out into the night. Too drunk to drive anywhere, he hailed a taxi and asked the driver to take him to Ealing.

Jennie heard him go and felt as if she were falling off a cliff. She had been in the house barely fifteen minutes and her future had been decided. What had happened to the long speech she had rehearsed on the train, the speech that would win him to her side? Why had she let him seize the initiative and then failed to stand her ground? Why had she ever pitied him and thought he needed her? He needed one women only and she didn't live in this house. God, if she had only kept her wits about her she could have grabbed another taxi and followed him. Proof. She needed proof. Now she would get it, come hell or high water.

In the morning, she had a large painful weal on her cheek that would take some explaining. Still shocked, she stayed inside her locked and bolted home, wondering what she could do. What did women do when they were trapped in a relationship with a man who could hit out when the mood took him? Drink had governed his actions last night, but it could happen again. When Guy phoned at eight o'clock to ask for her forgiveness, she said bitterly, "How can I forgive you? I ask for freedom and you insist on keeping me chained. In the end I shall grow to hate you. Is that what you want? Think about it while you're away."

"You don't exactly send me off with a song in my heart." After an awkward pause, "When do you fetch Alex?"

"This afternoon. Quite how I disguise the ugly bruise on my cheek is a problem I've yet to work out."

"Don't tell Alex," said Guy. "For God's sake, Jennie, spare him our troubles."

"My God, you think little of me! As if I would do anything to hurt our child."

"Tell him I'm sorry I won't be around for his half term."

"I will. Oh, by the way, you went off without your case. I found it on your bed. You'd better fetch it while I'm collecting Alex. That way we shan't have to see each other." She was about to put the receiver down when she recalled how that other rancorous call had ended in near tragedy. This had been a far worse incident and would surely prey on his mind. Fear gripped her suddenly. "Guy. You take care now. Don't try impressing the buyers too much."

"I won't." He hung up.

In her letter to Mark later, she said nothing of Guy's violence, writing only of his refusal to even consider divorce which placed the ball in her court. As she wrote she told herself that when Mark returned to Belmore the letter would be there waiting for him. Then she thought of the despair on his face when he read it, and tore the sheet of paper into tiny pieces.

Dinner was over, and the amah had retired to her quarters. Bull frogs, cicadas and the ever-increasing amount of traffic in the Bukit Timah Road could do little to puncture Charles's thoughts.

Three days earlier he had received a letter from Laura. How many years had it been since her last one? Now she had written telling him of the television series which had held a nation enthralled and included his wife's part as a British agent with the Resistance. How they had all wept with grief, horror and pride as they watched. "You have no idea, Charles, just how courageous your wife was or what she endured." She felt he would wish to be told that, once again, his wife's name, along with those other brave secret agents', was on everyone's lips. "I know how proud you must be."

And he knew that rubbing salt in the wound like this was an extra insurance against any notion he might have of returning to England. As he thought of Monique, grief for her took hold once more. Thankful that he had not seen the programme, he sipped his gin and tonic and looked out at the *kampong* lights opposite, grateful that Dodo, seated beside him in a rattan chair, was silent. She knew about Monique and the letter and, having lost Desmond four months earlier, understood what grief was. The telephone rang, shattering thought and emotion.

Putting down his drink, Charles rose and walked into the drawing room.

From where she sat, Dodo could hear his voice, along with anyone on their way to Bukit Timah. "Thank you, Operator. Jennie? Is that you? What's the matter, darling, what is it?" Anxious, Dodo stood up and moved into the room, strands of grey hair wafting about her head from the breeze of the overhead fan. At the look on his face she became alarmed.

Hand at his brow, Charles heard his daughter's emotional voice speaking of disasters and her plea for him to return home. "You must, Papa, before it's too late and Trevellan is ruined. Only you can stop Clive having full title. Give whatever excuse you like to Dodo and Jamie but come home and take back the estate."

Her pleas tore at his emotions. That she had lost the estate was bad enough, that his father had died hating him was even worse, now here she was crying for help. If only he could think. But there was Jamie, and Dodo, and that damned letter. "Frank is dead? I'm so sorry. What? Oh, darling, that's terrible. No ... I can't. Desmond died a short while ago and I couldn't just leave ... and Jamie is in London. Jennie, he's in London and doesn't know the truth. I'm worried about that television programme. If I returned the local paper would pick it up, linking me to your mother and ... just now that would ensure it getting into the nationals. Oh, darling, you know what the press are like. How could I risk Jamie finding out like that? No ... please, Jennie, do try to understand ... Jennie? Are you there?"

He turned to Dodo ashen-faced, wondering how he could live away from her without having those terrible panic attacks that had assailed him for so long. He was no longer fit for the world his daughter felt he belonged in. With Dodo he felt safe. "She's either put the phone down on me or we were cut off." He walked back to the verandah and leaned on the wall, murmuring, "Oh, Christ, everything's in a terrible mess. She wants me to go home and claim back the estate before it's too late."

Dodo stared at him in growing fear. The very thought of his leaving her was impossible to contemplate after all this time. She must take control, as she always took control. "I heard something of what you said. You're right about the press. Jamie would learn the truth the hard way and turn on you. How could you even think of risking that?"

"But I feel so damned responsible. Four hundred years the Veryans have lived in that house, and owned that land. And now, because of me, it could be the end. I don't know whether I can save the estate, but successful or not, it would all be at the expense of my son."

"You cannot lose your son, nor will the estate be lost. Jennie exaggerates, she always did a little. I don't blame her. In her shoes, I too would be doing everything in my power to get you to return before the year is up. I think you can expect many such calls in the next few months."

"Supposing she isn't exaggerating? I ought to be there. I ought to go even if only for a few months and then hand Trevellan to Jennie. Perhaps if I explained to Jamie by letter..."

"Even then would you still be capable of undertaking such a journey, of leaving this... this haven for a world which is now quite alien to you? As for Jamie, you must never tell him. It would be too cruel. And... not just to him but to me, because I know that if you go away you will never return." Dodo allowed a tear to flow. Charles was very susceptible to a woman's tears. "Don't leave me, not now. I need you as much as you need me. I couldn't cope, my dear, and would be so terribly alone... so desolate. If you go away, I don't know how I could go on. Please, Charles, think of me and of Jamie."

Charles was thinking of his son, thinking how strange Jamie had been before leaving for England: staying out with friends, not looking his father in the eye and even avoiding him wherever possible. At the docks he had not acknowledged their waves, staring down briefly from the deck before turning to be lost among the other passengers. Devastated, Charles had taken comfort in Dodo's words.

"He's upset at leaving you and refuses to show it, that's all."

When his first letters arrived addressed to Dodo only, she had smiled. "The silly boy thinks he's being diplomatic. After all, I suppose some would say our position is a little scandalous now that Desmond is in the nursing home."

When Desmond died, Jamie had sent condolences to Dodo but no word to his father. "Stop worrying about him, Charles. Jamie's letters are filled with the things he's doing, the people he's met. He's just a little slapdash about writing, that's all. At his age it's a wonder he bothers to write at all. Be happy for him, Charles, and stop looking for shadows when Jamie's in the sun."

Torn between two families and two hemispheres, Charles looked out across the Bukit Timah Road and thought of Jennie, who was not in the sun.

Her last hope having failed, Jennie decided that she would never bother with her father again. Never! But despair and growing bitterness had to be concealed while Alex enjoyed his first break away from boarding school and wanted her to take him here, there and everywhere. He was fascinated by her blue-black bruise and laughed when she told him she had walked into an open cupboard door. On the fourth day of his holiday he went out with friends, leaving her to work on a new portrait.

Having covered her fading bruise with heavy make-up, Jennie hoped her sitter, a socialite and gossip, would notice nothing as she made her initial sketches. By noon, she was relieved to be showing her client through the door and watched as she climbed into a waiting taxi. It was then that Jennie noticed the young man hovering close by the house. A shade suspicious, she glanced at him, taking in the mid-brown hair, light tweed jacket with leather patches at the elbows and green tie flapping in the autumn breeze. He had about him a general air of being rather shabby and lost. She turned to enter the house.

"Jennie?"

Looking back she saw he had moved forward and was now standing with one hand on the wrought iron railing. "You won't remember me," he was saying, "but I remember you. We met years ago. I was in an orphanage. You brought me presents."

For a moment she just stared at him while a vision of a thin boy looking at her through a large chain-linked fence swam into her mind. Staggering back in shock, she tried to speak. "Jamie!" It came out as a mere whisper. "You're Jamie?"

"Yes." He looked unsure of his reception.

She seemed rooted to the spot, then suddenly her mind swung into action as she vaguely remembered that her father had said something about Jamie's being in London and that he knew nothing of his true background. In which case, what was he doing on her doorstep? How had he found her and why? A thousand questions came to her tongue but, suddenly aware that this strange reunion was taking place in the public way of Cheyne Walk, she stretched out a beckoning hand. "You'd better come inside."

As he followed her into the house she was only too thankful that Maddie was at the gallery. Had Monique's closest friend ever become aware of how Charles had treated his wife, she would never have forgiven him.

Jamie stood in Maddie's comfortable but untidy drawing room, and looked at sofas and armchairs draped in colourful Spanish shawls, at walls covered with sketches and paintings, at art books scattered on tables, and canvases propped against walls. He liked the room. It seemed lived in and filled with interest.

Offering him a seat, Jennie's mind was still trying to accept the fact of Jamie's actually being here, sitting in that armchair and smiling at her. She smiled back at him, thinking that this good-looking young man was the unwitting cause of her mother's death, her father's self-imposed exile and Trevellan's demise. But how lost he seemed, how nervous and shy. There was something else in those eyes, however, something she couldn't quite pin down. Why was he here? What to say? How to start?

"How long had you been standing out there?"

"About half an hour," he answered in a low voice. "I was still trying to make up my mind whether I should ring the doorbell or not when out you came. I recognised you at once."

She looked surprised. "From your childhood? I'm amazed you remembered me. I must have changed considerably as well."

He shook his head, his face solemn. "No. You haven't changed. And I've never forgotten you."

She took this in, feeling strangely moved. "And how long have you been in England?"

"Just over a year." He hunched forward, hands clasped between his knees, putting her in mind of the way her father used to sit. "I'm studying medicine at UCH."

"But ... but how did you find me? You only know me as Jennie."

He gave her an odd look. "Your name is Genevieve Lloyd, née Veryan, and you are my half-sister. I tried the house in Kensington Square last February and was told to go to Flood Street. But the woman there told me you were at the Veryan Gallery showing your collection of paintings. I went along and thought I saw you through the windows, but wasn't sure. It seemed to be an invitation only affair so I went home."

Jennie's mouth dropped open. "So it was you, standing there in the pouring rain ..." She stopped, and frowned. "You know who I am, you know about Kensington Square. I don't understand, Jamie. Only the other day, Papa told me you didn't know. He's been in touch with you since, is that it?" Her hopes started to rise. If her father had deemed it necessary to tell Jamie the truth at last, then it must be to pave the way for his return. Thank God! Her relief changed to doubt when she saw his eyes darken and heard the bitter note in his voice.

"Father didn't tell me. It was Uncle Victor. I hadn't seen him for years, not to talk to at least. But just before I was due to leave for England I found him waiting for me outside the bookshop where I'd been helping out. Apparently he had been in K.L. with his firm. He took me to the Adelphi Hotel for tea and told me everything."

Jamie fell silent remembering that appalling afternoon and how, at first, he had refused to believe a word of his uncle's dark tale. But the man's graphic account of everything had finally convinced him. So shocked had he been that he left the hotel hating his father. Now he remembered the hurt bewilderment on that gaunt face as they journeyed to the docks on their last day. Looking down from the ship's rail, Jamie had seen Charles waving up at him. Instead of waving back he had turned and walked away, vowing never to return, never to see his father again. Yet now the vision of that forlorn figure in a cream linen suit, staring up so anxiously, would haunt him all his days. Perhaps he should have told him that he knew and given the man a chance to put his side of the story. But those doubts had long since fled. He was a world away from it all now.

Jennie looked anxious. "Leighton!" she said at last. "The last man on God's earth you should have heard it from. And how well he times everything. You were eighteen, about to embark on a long voyage to a country you didn't know. It was the cruellest of times to tell you. And it was meant to hurt. That is his way, you see."

Jamie shook his head. "My uncle doesn't know I've left the country. He didn't ask, so I didn't tell him I was coming to university. I was too shocked even to think of it."

She sighed with relief. At least Leighton would not follow to stir up trouble here. "Well, that's a blessing anyway. What did Papa say when you wrote and told him?"

"I haven't told him. He doesn't know that I know and that's how I want it to remain. I never want to see the man again."

"Oh, come now, that's quite unfair." Jennie gave him a hard look. "You have no idea of the cruel vengeance your uncle exacted from my father because of what happened, and you have no idea of what Papa gave up to stay with you, or how that decision has affected my entire family." Letting her shoulders sag, she thought how he had come to her, his half-sister, the only living relative he knew in this country which must seem so alien to him. "I'm glad you remembered me," she added softly.

"You knew who I was," said Jamie, "yet still you came to say goodbye. I've thought about that ever since Uncle Victor told me. You didn't know the first time you came, so it must have come as a shock to you when he asked me to tell you my name."

"Yes," she answered quietly. "And I was very cruel to Papa and said things that should never have been said. But I'm older now and understand much better." She smiled and sighed. "It's good that you've come to me. I'm probably the one person in the world you can talk to about all this, but I doubt you want to talk on an empty stomach. Students, I know from experience, are a hungry lot. Come down to the kitchen. I'll rustle up an omelette and chips. How did you know I was here by the way? This is my cousin's house. I only borrow her studio. I'm a portrait painter."

"Are you?" He followed her down the stairs then sat at the large pine table watching as she started peeling potatoes and washing lettuce. "I went to Flood Street, and was told where you'd be. I've been there several times since the evening of your exhibition, but no one ever answered the doorbell. I thought you might have moved."

"I only have a domestic in the mornings," said Jennie, slicing the potatoes into chips then placing them in a sizzling pan of oil. She asked Jamie about her father and his own upbringing. He told her then said: "Mr Webb died earlier in the year."

"Yes, I was sorry to hear that." Why was she sorry? She hardly knew the man and was surprised he had lasted so long. Creaking gate! His demise was another reason why her father was staying away. Desmond, Dodo and Jamie. Together they weighted the scales against her. "You know, Jamie, we've all tried to make Papa come home, but he stayed because of you and..."

"He stayed because he knew that my uncle would reveal some unpalatable facts about him had he returned. I think the chips are done."

Jennie turned to see blue smoke curling upwards from the sizzling pan, and switched off the gas in time to avoid a fire. Aware of the bitterness in his voice, she sighed. "Papa went to Singapore in the first place to look for you and your mother. After the war, and after he regained his memory, he took you from that orphanage and gave up his birthright here to raise you. Haven't you been loved, educated, given everything he could possibly give? What more could he do for you, Jamie? And think of this. To raise his son, he abandoned his daughter. So I want no bleeding heart stuff from you, thank you very much." She put an omelette and chips on to a plate, passed it to him and quickly made a salad. "And since you've a mind to feel sorry for yourself, think of things this way. If my father hadn't fallen in love with your mother, you wouldn't be sitting here now about to enjoy a plate of greasy chips."

His look of astonishment collapsed into a broad grin. "They're not greasy." He tried one. "They're just right."

They ate quietly and she asked him about his studies, his friends and life at university. "Have you been out of London at all?"

He nodded. "Cornwall." Having devoured the meal in a few moments, he placed his knife and fork together on the plate, put his napkin on the table and stared across the table at her. "During the summer, I hitched my way to Portlyn."

"What?" Jennie almost dropped her own knife and fork.

He nodded. "I went to Trevellan. I was there a week and..."

"Wait ... wait ... what are you talking about?"

"I slept at the village and went to the manor house every day."

Dumbstruck, she could only stare until finally managing to croak: "What are you telling me?"

"Lovely place." he said nonchalantly. "Mrs Hodges gave me some wonderful meals in that old kitchen. I liked my grandmother but the other one, Aunt Laura, was a first-rate bitch." The expression on Jennie's face was almost funny, he thought.

She gave him a hard look. He was teasing her and she found it irritating to say the least. "I've just come from Trevellan and no one has said anything to me about you. Come on, Jamie, stop playing silly games."

The smile vanished from his face. "It wasn't a game. I wanted to see the house and family I wasn't supposed to know existed, and now I have."

She could only stare at him in horror. "You really were there? You met them? Oh, Jamie, you didn't ... well, you didn't ...?"

"Tell them who I was? No, but I thought about it." If he had ever entertained doubts about his place in the scheme of things, her expression now confirmed who and what he was. In England James Veryan was a walking disaster, able to send shock waves reverberating outwards for a very long way. In England he was a bastard, an embarrassment to be hidden away from a dynastic family. In the gardens of Trevellan and here in this London house, he had been forced to come to terms with a reality that life in Singapore had kept from him.

"You don't have to worry," he said tersely. "God knows what I had in mind originally. Perhaps to confront them, to laugh at the shock on their snooty faces, stir things up a bit, you know the sort of thing." The hard edge to his voice began to soften. "In the end, I asked for a job and was given one helping Ben in the grounds. It meant I could be there, even if only as a jobbing gardener. It gave me a chance to see my father's house and his family. I suppose, too, it gave me some quirky satisfaction, wondering what they would think if they knew that their little black sheep was wandering about the place and village, eating in their kitchen, chatting to the servants. It's amazing the things one can find out in such a short time."

"I hope you enjoyed yourself," she whispered, trying to picture him working side by side with Ben, being ordered about by Laura, fussed over by Florence and plied with food by Mrs Hodges. Only the horror of her grandmother's finding out stopped it from being funny. Her face took on a puzzled expression. "But your uncle couldn't have told you about the house or estate. He didn't know where it was."

"It was written on the back of the photographs I found in my father's chest of drawers. You see, after Uncle had told me everything, I wanted to know more about where I came from, and so I turned over Father's things until I found out. On the picture of the house were the words: 'Trevellan, Portlyn, Cornwall'."

She sighed as she remembered. "I wrote it in a vain attempt to jog Papa's memory. Unfortunately, it took a riot to do that. You also mentioned going to Kensington Square? There were no photographs of that house."

Jamie smiled. "There didn't need to be. That address is engraved on Uncle Victor's heart. So too is the name of the indomitable Mrs Willoughby. Having met her I can quite understand why. The woman I saw at the Kensington house, though, was probably the other Mrs Willoughby whose husband now owns the estate. The villagers don't think much of her or of him. They seemed to be upset about a man called Curnow at the time. I gather he was the estate manager and had left. Some say after a fearful row."

"Nothing like the local pub for giving away all the family's closely guarded secrets. All this will be put right if Papa comes home, and he won't do that unless you write and tell him that you know everything and that it is all right." She poured hot water into a bowl, started washing the dishes then flung a teacloth at him, saying, "All hands to the pump. No amahs here and Mrs Lewis has the day off."

As Jamie started drying the plates she waited for his reaction to her earlier words, but he remained silent. At last she turned to him and said: "You know, your uncle is a deeply vindictive man. He was hell-bent on blackmail at first, and when that didn't work turned his attention to destroying Papa instead." She told him all that had passed in the camp and of her father's terrible torture. "Leighton was responsible for the things that happened to Papa. So, in that sense, he's every bit as bad as the Japanese. Be sure of one thing, Jamie, your uncle didn't tell you the truth out of a sense of duty. His idea was to turn you against your own father. He used me for the same purpose. It seems we came up trumps for the man. We were both wrong."

Jamie gave her a strange look, placed a plate down on the table and stood for a moment, deep in thought. "Jennie, I want you to leave this to me. If you write it won't help at all. I want your promise on this. Will you give it?"

She wiped her hands, remembering how her father had once made her promise. "Only if you make a promise in return: that you *will* write. You have no idea what it will mean to him if you say you know and that it doesn't matter. Do I have such a promise?"

"Yes," he said quietly. "Only, you see, it *does* matter."

Concerned at his tone, she placed a hand on his shoulder. "Don't let bitterness get the better of you, Jamie. Doctors have to know about people as well as their bodies. Make your peace with Papa as soon as possible. He loves you dearly."

Jamie left the house that afternoon on a happier note than when he

403

entered it. He had found a sister and she had, for a few hours, helped him with his burden although she could not lift the hatred from his heart.

In a small stone cottage beside a stream, some eight miles from York, Jennie and Mark lay on the floor gazing at the log fire burning in the hearth. For all that it had not stopped raining these had been three idyllic days.

Mark was resting back against the armchair base and Jennie lay snug against him, remembering his rage when she had telephoned with the news that Guy would not even discuss divorce. To stop him throwing all caution to the wind and heading to London to be with her, she had come to him instead. The cottage she had found advertised in *The Lady* and rented sight unseen.

"I wish to God he would stay in Canada," Mark was saying, his hand stroking her face gently. "But when he does return..."

Jennie put a hand to his mouth. "We'll cross that bridge when we come to it." She didn't want to waste the last moments of these three days, worrying about Guy; three idyllic days wandering the isolated countryside, making passionate love and forgetting the cares of the world; three idyllic days when she had felt loved, cherished and beautiful. Something she had never felt with Guy. She spoke of her father and Jamie, feeling an immense relief to be able to speak of it to someone who was sympathetic.

"Even if Jamie does write, it won't change a thing. I've come to understand that now. Papa feels safe out there. Odd really, you'd think he'd want to be a million miles away ... but he needs Dodo. Had he returned to England after the war as so many others did, he would never have come to depend on her so much, but now it's too late. He needs her and is afraid to be without her, afraid to be away from a world he's come to know. At first I assumed his trauma would end. Now I know it will be with him for the rest of his days."

"The poor devil," murmured Mark. "One can't imagine what hellish suffering he has endured. This Leighton sounds evil."

Now, as they relaxed before the fire, she reached up to him and, as his face bent to hers, tried to push from her mind the sense of deep forboding that kept overwhelming her. Memory, she told herself, memory of that last time when she and Mark had lain together and Guy ... *Stop it, you fool. He'll be all right ... he'll be all right!*

Mark kissed her deeply, his hands caressing her so that she quivered beneath his touch. In the throes of passion she gave herself up to him once more and forgot Guy at last.

*

404

When she returned to London it was to find a letter from Canada waiting for her.

... and having thought about things, have decided to allow you to divorce me. I do this not because you have grounds, although I suppose these things can be manufactured, I do it because I love you too much to see that look in your eyes ever again. That you should end up hating me for simply being your husband is something I cannot live with. When I return to England I shall remain at Stannington, until Christmas when I would like to be home with my son. I hope you will agree to that, for his sake...

Hardly allowing herself to believe in his sudden change of heart, Jennie read the letter for the fifth time then telephoned Mark with the good news.

When he managed to speak, his voice was strained. "Strangely enough, this is the worst moment. Rather like being hauled up a cliff face by rescuers, terrified that, just before you reach safety, the rope might snap. He's got us hanging on that rope."

"At least there is a rope ... a chance ... hold on to the thought, my love."

Two days later the telephone rang. When Jennie heard Guy's voice she felt a shudder of deep relief. He was home. He was safe, thank God. Guy sounded downcast as he said, "I'll agree to stay out of your life as much as you like but, for this last Christmas, I want a family occasion: Christmas tree, presents, everything normal for Alex."

She thought how difficult that would be, but agreed for the sake of their son. "Was the trip a success?"

"Very much so. But I'm dog-tired and ready for a break. In the New Year I'm off to Australia, to promote the Panther." He paused. "I'm glad about Christmas. I've missed you, Jennie. I know you won't believe that, but I have." After a long and awkward silence. "So then, for Christmas it's Pax?"

"Pax," said Jennie.

"I've been an ass," he said, "and now that I'm going to lose you I realise how much I must have hurt you, without ever knowing that I was. You're wrong to think there's anyone else. That was a one-off thing and over years ago."

Before she could reply, she heard the click as Guy replaced his receiver.

No one knew why the ceiling suddenly collapsed in Jamie's room, but the students who shared the rundown Victorian house with him said

405

what a lucky devil he was to have been lifting his elbow in the local at the time. Having surveyed the appalling scene Jamie was forced to agree with them as he rummaged through the debris for his belongings. His landlord blamed the London traffic; Jamie and his colleagues blamed the rising damp.

"The thing is, Jennie, that I've nowhere to live or study until the landlord gets the ceiling fixed. We get chucked out of Hall in the second year, which is why I'm in digs."

Jennie listened to the frantic voice on the other end of the telephone and smiled. "Then you must come to me. I'll drive over and we can bring your things back here."

And so, on a cold November morning, having retrieved his worldly goods from the shambles and piled them all into Jennie's Morris Traveller, Jamie was set up in her spare bedroom. Once there, he took command of a bookshelf, a small sturdy table and two chairs, a brand new radio and electric fire, an oriental rug and two lamps. Jennie had thought of everything. He had his own door key and could come and go as he liked. Jamie did like. He liked Jennie and he liked living in Chelsea very much, even though he missed his friends and had to travel a long way every day.

Before Jennie could open her mouth, he introduced himself to Maddie as simply 'Jamie', a friend of Mrs Webb's from Singapore. Maddie accepted this without question, leaving Jennie weighed down with guilt at denying Jamie his identity. It was wrong and cruel, but he told her it would be worse for him to have everyone knowing who he was. "Believe me, I would rather be a friend of a friend. That way I can hold up my head. If anyone wants my surname then it will have to be Leighton."

"Singapore? Where Grandpa lives?" Alex had asked, when confronted with this strange man on arriving home for the Christmas holidays. "Do you know Grandpa? What does your father do? My father's a test pilot. He can fly anything. He flew the Panther at Farnborough. Where is Singapore? Is it far away? Is it as far as the Isle of Wight? My friend lives on the Isle of Wight..."

As Jamie had listened to the non-stop chatter, it dawned on him that this boisterous little lad, so full of questions and excited at the prospect of Christmas, could never be told that he was talking to his uncle.

Jennie sat in her drawing room opening the pile of Christmas cards that had come through her letterbox that evening. When she came to the overseas envelope in her father's handwriting her heart leaped. He had written once since her frantic cry for help but had only repeated why he could not come. Jennie had not replied. The next letter her father received must come from Jamie. Let father and son work their problems out in their own way. She had given her promise to Jamie on this and he trusted her.

She opened the envelope, took out the card and letter and began reading. Eyes almost popping out of her head, she leaped from her chair and rushed upstairs, shouting, "Jamie ... Jamie ..." Opening the door she saw him look up in astonishment from his desk and said breathlessly: "They're married!" She waved the card at him. "Papa and Dodo have married."

Jamie merely shrugged. "Somehow I always thought of them as married. Not sharing a bed, of course, they're far too old for that ... but just an old married couple."

"They're not as old as they look, Jamie." She sat down by the desk and frowned. "Dodo, though. I suppose it all comes down to the dependency thing, and since they live together it's tidier to be man and wife." But even as she spoke, she simply could not imagine that stern-faced, grey-haired woman taking her mother's place. So Dodo had got her man at last. It was the final act that said he would remain out there until the end of his days. Jennie hated the thought of his dying one day and being buried in eastern red earth instead of the Veryan plot at Portlyn, but it was time to draw the curtain on Singapore, just as one day she would draw it on Trevellan. She turned to Jamie. "Have you written as you promised?"

He twisted his fountain pen in his fingers. "Well ... not just yet. I've been so busy and it's a letter that needs careful thinking about. Give me time, Jennie."

She gave him a dark look. "Jamie, he must be devastated at your long silence. You have sent a Christmas card, I hope?"

He nodded. Jennie was doing her big sister act again. He quite liked it really. It made him feel like family. "And I'll send him another, congratulating them both. In it will be the letter, I promise."

When Jennie left the room, he sat there thinking of the life he had enjoyed with his father. They had been good days, happy days, but that was before Uncle Victor had handed him a letter and put that hideous picture into his mind. It blotted out everything else, including promises.

"Perfect," said Guy, watching as Kay turned this way and that in exaggerated mannequin style, showing off the donkey brown suede coat he had brought from Canada for Jennie's Christmas present.

"I'm a size twelve and so is she," said Kay. "A detachable warm lining, too. Autumn, spring and winter ... she can wear it for all occasions. It's a marvellous present, Guy. She'll be thrilled." She picked up the high and slim leather boots, recalling the trouble she had gone through to learn from Jennie that she was a size four, B fitting. Too small for her to try on. "They're so elegant, Guy. Not like the clumpy things people walk around in here."

Placing the coat and boots back into their boxes, Guy returned to his cottage where he wrapped them carefully in Christmas paper, wrote on the gift tags and placed them in the wardrobe. He knew she would not buy him a present this year, and would hardly expect one from him either, so when she saw this it must surely help to soften her heart. It must because, for all his words, he would never let Jennie go out of his life into the arms of Mark Curnow. Taking a smaller package from his dressing-table drawer, he wrapped that also and placed it, unmarked, on the topmost shelf of the wardrobe.

The following morning he felt good as he made his way to the Hadleigh factory. Orders for the Panther had exceeded all expectations, his hard work had paid off and he was looking forward to a rest. His secretary was waiting anxiously in his office. Keith needed to see him urgently. He hoped and prayed it wasn't anything important. Work had mounted during his absence and he had a lot to get through if he was to leave early.

In the afternoon, Jennie shopped with her son and shared his sense of wonder at the West End Christmas lights. Having counted his pocket money and finding he could just afford to buy his father a Nat King Cole record, Alex then dragged Jennie into Hamley's crowded store and stared goggle-eyed at the toys. "Jamie's already helped me to choose something for you, Mummy, so can you help me to choose something for Jamie? Can I have a dartboard? I'm good at darts."

Jennie's mood was swinging from fear that her happy little boy could be made unhappy, to relief bordering on sheer joy that, whatever the future held, at least she and Guy would part well and give Alex all the love they could together. The anger was over. The acceptance at hand. If this was to be her last Christmas with Guy, then she wanted it to be a good one for everyone's sake.

At last, weary and weighed down with parcels, Jennie hailed a taxi and took her son home. The curtains were not closed and the tree lights shone through the window.

"Jamie's home," she said, paying the driver and gathering her packages. As she approached the door it opened and Jamie stood back to let her in. Alex started talking at once about the mechanical toys he had seen in Hamley's and was flushed with excitement as Jennie asked him to take some of the packages up the stairs and put them on her bed. "No peeking." She turned to Jamie and laughed as she pulled off her coat which he took without smiling. "You should have seen him in

Hamley's. He walked through each department pointing and saying: 'I'll have that, that, and that...'"

"Jennie, you have a visitor. He came about fifteen minutes ago. I showed him into the drawing room and gave him tea."

"Thank you, Jamie." For all her calm words, Jennie's heart was pounding as she approached the drawing room. Mark! It was Mark, she just knew it. He could be in London for a programme ... for anything. Dangerous, though, with Guy about to arrive home. What did he think he was doing? Her hand paused on the handle. "Jamie, could you give me a few moments alone? And keep Alex amused for a while."

He nodded solemnly. "Of course. We'll be in the kitchen."

Steeling herself, she opened the door and entered. Keith Chatham rose from his chair and she, fighting down bitter disappointment, walked towards him, all smiles. "What a lovely surprise. It's been so long since we saw each other. I'm sorry I wasn't here when you came. What are you doing in London?" He looked strange in spectacles and his hair had receded even more, she noticed.

"Jennie." Keith was not smiling and was clearly struggling to find the words to go on.

An ice-cold hand slithered down her back. She turned and gazed into the fire, her voice falsely bright, desperate to put off the moment. "How are Kay and the children?"

"Jennie, I've come from Stannington with some news."

She raised her head and stared at his pale face. "It's Guy."

Keith walked to the drinks table, poured brandy into a glass and bade her sit down. She did as he asked and took the brandy without realising what she was doing. And so she sat there, cold as a statue, unable fully to grasp Keith's words. How kind he was, she thought, how quietly spoken and considerate. How chilly the room was, yet the fire burned so brightly and the tree lights shone.

"He had to go to Boscombe Down, there was a problem that came up suddenly, so I arranged for him to go in the Company's own small aircraft. I knew how tired he was. His back was playing up as well. I told him he was in luck this time and could just sit back and let Tom Hadleigh's pilot take the strain. He grinned, I remember, and said if there was one thing he hated it was not being in control. Anyway, a flight plan was filed and off they went. Contact was lost after twenty minutes. That was at ten-fifty this morning. The wreckage of the plane was found in a field not far from Devizes. He would have died instantly, Jennie. Both Guy and the pilot, neither would have suffered."

He lit a cigarette. "It's all so bloody ironic. Why that way when he's risked his life time and again ..." His voice cracked. "We went through

409

the war together. How many times did he cheat death then! To have it happen this way is such a pitiful waste." Putting his cigarette down in the ashtray, he walked across to Jennie who had not moved. Her face held a deathly pallor. Afraid she might faint, he urged her to sip some of the brandy.

Having left Alex with lemonade and cake in the kitchen, Jamie was on his way up to his room when he thought he heard a strangled cry from the drawing room. He stopped, then heard sobbing. The sombre visitor had brought Jennie bad news. The thought of what it might be sent him rushing back to Alex. The boy had barely stopped talking about his father and was excited at the prospect of his return. Jamie could only hope and pray that Guy did.

In a daze, Jennie sipped the brandy and felt a fiery glow burn her throat. At once the years fell away and she was back in the Patterson's bungalow. First brandy, first night of love, the night when Alexander's life had begun, the night when her life had changed. Nine years plus one week ago, Guy had pulled her from a deadly mob. Nine years plus one week ago.

# Chapter Twenty-Six

For Jennie the days that followed Guy's death blurred one into another as family and friends gathered about her to offer help and comfort. Alex had moved from disbelief to sobbing his heart out and, in spite of efforts by Kay, Florence and even Louise to take him away from the scene for Christmas, refused to leave his mother. It was Jamie who was able to help him the most and who brought him through; Jamie who could have spent a better Christmas with friends but instead stood by Jennie and took on the task of keeping the household on an even keel.

Letters of condolence arrived with the Christmas cards. The letter from Mark, Jennie read alone in her bedroom:

> What can I say to you, my love, what words to ease your grief? I long to be with you, to comfort and help you, but I know there is no place for me at such a time. God willing, there will be...

Jennie could not read on. Her eyes filled up once more and she threw herself on to her bed in shuddering sobs. She had wanted to be free, but not like this ... dear God, not like this. Was she being punished for loving another? Yet she had cared for Guy, and only now that he was dead did she realise how much she had cared. He had been going to release her because he hadn't wanted her to hate him. Hate him? Anguished, she thought how much she must have hurt him and felt now that she had been wrong all these years. Almost his last words to her had been to deny infidelity. Something she could not.

Keith knew Guy's wishes. They were laid out in a letter, placed in his hands some years ago. "Just in case," Guy had said. "Better you than Jennie. Hopefully you'll never need to read the blasted thing."

In the large church at Stannington, he gave a moving eulogy before Guy's RAF colleagues, the staff of Hadleigh's and Jennie's family and friends. For her it was harrowing moment to hear how liked and respected her husband had been, to realise how many people had travelled from far and wide to be here this day. It served to heighten her sense of guilt and grief.

The service ended and the pallbearers carried the coffin along the aisle ready for its journey to the crematorium. Following, Jennie's attention was suddenly drawn to a woman standing beside the font at the rear of the church. She stood alone, black hat covering blonde hair, short veil partly concealing her face and, by the act of trying to be inconspicuous, making herself the more so. For a moment Jennie paused, glanced at her, then walked on behind the coffin and out to the waiting hearse.

Later, in the hotel where the wake was being held, Jennie cast her eyes over the small groups of people who chatted quietly among themselves, but there was no sign of the strange woman who had stood within a hair's breadth of her lover's widow to bid him farewell. Walking among the guests Jennie thanked them for coming, her mind in total confusion. Guy had said it was over and had been for years. Yet 'the other one' had come to the funeral. Strange that she should be so much older than expected, plain too; quite middle-aged and plain. So what had Guy seen in her? It had to be more than sex surely, much more? Whatever it was, one thing was blatantly clear. This plain, middle-aged woman had managed to penetrate the extraordinary repressiveness of the man where she, his younger and better-looking wife, had failed so miserably. Guy had always made her feel inadequate. Now she knew that she was.

Sipping dry sherry, Florence settled back in her chair and gazed about her to see how many people she could recognise. Clive, she decided, had already drunk too much, having first fortified himself with whisky at the hotel bar. He should eat something from the cold buffet or Fenella should take him out before he made a fool of himself. Laura was monopolising that nice Ian Stewart who was an Air Commodore now. Strange how he kept moving in and out of their lives. Widowed apparently. Just like poor darling Jennie. Dreadful. Such a terrible shock. Not that she had ever really known Guy. How could she? He rarely visited Trevellan. But her heart went out to her grand-daughter. Then there was poor little Alex, so young to be fatherless. Who was that man with the child? He seemed familiar somehow...

Clive was not in the best of moods as he moved, a shade unsteadily, from group to group. He supposed he ought to feel sympathy for Jennie, but since his London house and its contents had just been sold, leaving him without a penny from the sale, he loathed her and wouldn't have been here at all but for the sake of keeping up appearances. With the Harte-Willis Bank mourning the loss of one of its senior staff, the promotion escalator was on the move and, since Jennie would certainly have invited Colin and his wife, it did no harm to be on familiar terms with the son and heir of the boss. Anyway, he had liked Guy, good egg and all that, bloody good pilot. Christ, what an awful week! Consolidated Minerals was still under-backed. If things didn't pick up soon his own heavy investment in the company would be lost. Goodbye Sisley money! Why did everything he touched blow up in his face? Time to move in on young Harte-Willis. Shaking Colin and Arabella by the hand, he thanked them both for coming.

"Means a great deal to Jennie. Dreadful blow. Sad loss, not only to Jennie but to the country. Britain needs its heroes..."

Later when Arabella said how sad it was for little Alex, Clive turned and saw the boy who was standing between Maddie and the strange young man. He would have to go over to the child, if only for the look of the thing. Still, poor little devil. Of all times for it to happen ... Christmas. He knew what it was like to lose a father, except that the father he had lost was still alive. Walking over to Alex, he smiled, said something which he thought sounded comforting, then turned to Maddie and the young man. "I take it this gentleman is your latest protégé?"

Surprised that Clive should put himself out to talk to her at all, Maddie shook her head. "Hardly! Jamie means to be a doctor. He's from Singapore. The son of one of your uncle's friends. His ceiling fell down, so he's lodging with Jennie at the moment."

Jamie had been keeping his head down rather and had only come because Alex had wailed in despair when he said he wouldn't and Jennie had persuaded him to change his mind, saying she no longer cared if he was recognised or not. What did it matter any more? It mattered to him though. He extended his hand. "James Leighton."

Clive shook it, saying: "Clive Willoughby." Was it his imagination or did the hand clench a little more tightly about his?

As she walked to the buffet table, Laura was still thinking of her encounter with Ian Stewart who grew better-looking with age. Placing salmon, potato and green salad on a plate to give to her mother, her eyes fell on the young man talking to Clive, and widened in surprise. Returning to Florence, she handed the plate to her and frowned. "Who is that young man with Alex? He's so like the student who helped Ben in the summer. Rather an arrogant fellow, I thought."

"Did you, dear?" Florence hated eating buffet-style and tried to juggle napkin, plate, roll and butter and knife and fork, until Laura was forced to come to her aid. "I found him quite charming myself."

Seeing her son heading unsteadily across the room towards them,

413

Laura pointed to a chair beside her and snapped: "I think you'd better sit down and eat something. Who was that man you were talking to?"

Clive sank into a soft upholstered chair and let out a sigh of relief. "Oh, some boring medical student, lodging with Jennie. Something to do with a ceiling ... couldn't get the hang of it."

Florence tutted impatiently. "Presumably he has a name?"

"Hmmm? Oh ... Maddie calls him Jamie."

Laura frowned. "But that was the name of our student. And the more I look at him the more certain I am it's one and the same fellow. How extraordinary. And he knows Jennie, you say? How?"

Clive sniffed in a bored fashion. "Oh, I don't know. Comes from Singapore. Friend of Uncle Charles apparently." He looked thoughtful. "What was that name? Leighton ... James Leighton."

Laura's face drained of colour. She murmured something about getting food to soak up the contents of Clive's stomach, stumbled to the long buffet table and stood there for some time with her back to everyone. After composing herself, she turned to see her mother chatting happily to Ian Stewart who had sat himself down beside her. Attracting Clive's attention, Laura beckoned him to the table and whispered angrily: "Don't you remember anything you're told? Don't you take anything in? Leighton, you say? Leighton! Think Clive, think. Uncle Charles? The Eurasian woman? The baby? Leighton?" She saw the expression on her son's face and smiled. "Ah, is that a flicker of life I see? The baby was called James."

In the act of helping himself to potato salad, Clive's hand froze on the serving spoon which hovered mid-air. "You don't mean ...?" He stared at his mother, jaw partly open in stunned disbelief. "Christ, no. It couldn't be."

Laura sighed. "Oh, well done, Clive, you've twigged at last. Of course it's him. He's the right age, he comes from Singapore, and his mother's name was Leighton. What I'd like to know is why Jennie, of all people, has suddenly taken him under her wing?"

Clive was staring across at Jamie through porcine eyes. "So, the family skeleton is out of the cupboard and rattling around London? Why is he here? What does he want? Christ, if this gets out..."

"Keep your voice down," snapped Laura, rather wishing she had kept her thoughts to herself. "I've no idea what he wants. As for why he's here, well, for the moment we must take it that he's here to study medicine, even though he managed to spend a week at Trevellan studying us." Seeing his shocked expression: "Oh, yes, your uncle's little secret has had a quiet laugh at our expense. God, when I think of his impertinence! How dare he?" She was breathing more rapidly now as thought tumbled after thought. "There's only one answer and we both know what it is – my brother means to return in order to take back the estate then make Jamie his heir." She glanced at her son and frowned. "You're looking rather green about the gills, dear. Are you all right?"

Dropping the spoon, Clive murmured something about feeling sick and moved quickly out of the room.

At first light on a raw cold morning, Keith climbed into the Tiger Moth and, with Tim Dorcas at the controls, took off. At two hundred feet, he carried out Guy's wishes by scattering his ashes across the airfield.

Watching with Kay beside her, Jennie could only feel cold horror. Some thought it the best way, Guy had thought it the best way, but she hated it. "It's as though he never existed at all. No grave, no memorial even. He didn't want it."

Kay placed a comforting arm about her shoulders. "I know, I know. As to a memorial ... well ... Keith has a suggestion to put to you. But you must feel free to say no if you would rather not do it."

The Tiger Moth was landing now and had drawn to a stop. Jennie turned a tearful face to Kay and said: "You've both been so wonderful to me during this awful time. Keith knew I couldn't do this ... so he did it for me, and it must have been very hard for him."

"He was worried that later you might regret it," said Kay. "For all he was our dearest friend, Guy wasn't ours, he was yours."

Jennie shook her head and said in a strange, distant voice: "No, Kay. He was never mine."

A week later, Jennie stood in the impressive marble foyer of the Hadleigh Aircraft Corporation building where, with due ceremony, she unveiled the full-length portrait of Guy which had once graced their dining room. At first she had hesitated at the thought of losing the painting, even though she had two half-portraits of him, but the more she thought about it, the more she felt that this was his fitting memorial and that here, of all places, was where Guy would want the portrait to be.

A bitter east wind blew across London Airport and flurries of snow settled on Jennie and Maddie as they made their way down the steps of the Vickers Viscount. Gasping at the shock encounter with her native land, after Rome, Maddie knew now how right she had been to insist on taking Jennie away for two weeks to friends who had made them so welcome. Some had counselled against this, saying that it only put off the inevitable, but Jennie had been so low, so strange and distant, that once Alex was back at school it seemed the only thing to do. Two weeks of sightseeing and art galleries, Maddie hoped, would help banish the

415

sorrow, momentarily, and give Jennie strength to face what every widow had to face.

"Come to my house, why don't you?" she said, driving towards Chelsea.

Jennie shook her head. "I'll go home, unpack and ... well, there are things yet to be done. I've been putting them off for far too long." She glanced at Maddie and smiled. "Even at this time of year, Rome was lovely and it did help. Thank you, my dear, for everything."

As Maddie drove away, Jennie stood looking at her front door, the door she dreaded opening. Inside, she put down her suitcase, took off her coat then saw four piles of letters on the hall table. So many? From upstairs came the hum of a vacuum cleaner; the rooms smelt of beeswax polish. Everything looked so clean, so utterly tidy, that only the blazing fire in the hearth brought life to the place. Engulfed in desolation, she stood there with her memories; memories of two people hurting each other when deep down they had cared. The vacuuming stopped and the daily poked her head around the door.

"I'm sorry, I didn't know you was back." Mrs Nolan stood awkwardly, trying to find the right words. "Did you have a nice time?" was hardly appropriate under the circumstances. "Was it warm in Rome? Only it's been rotten 'ere. Keeps threatening to snow."

"Yes. It was warmer in Rome. Thank you for lighting the fire. The place looks ... looks lovely."

"I know it's almost lunchtime but I expect you could do with a coffee?" When Jennie said that would be very welcome, Mrs Nolan turned to leave then paused on the threshold. "If there's any extra thing I can do ... I mean ... you know ... with sorting stuff out and that, then please do ask."

Sorting stuff out. The detritus of a life. "That's very kind of you, and I may well need someone to help. Goodness knows when I'll manage to get around to it ..." Too choked to say more, she waited until Mrs Nolan had gone to the kitchen then picked up the piles of letters and took them into the drawing room. "Sorting out" had yet to be done at the cottage as well. Kay had already cleaned out perishables, the rest awaited Jennie. She dreaded the day. How empty the house was. If only Jamie were still here, she thought. But his landlord's studied inactivity in getting the ceiling fixed earlier had moved into overdrive and Jamie had returned to his lodgings the day before she left for Rome. The letter on top of the pile had arrived that very morning from him. It was a chatty chronicle about his own world and ended with a request that she should contact him on her return so that he could meet her one evening.

You need company and I don't like to think of you spending

416

evenings alone. Anyway, I miss you, big sister, and would like to take you out for a drink. I may fail my exams but I'm an expert on pubs. So get in touch. Hope Alex has settled back at school all right. Perhaps I'll see him at half term.
Jamie

Dear, sweet-natured Jamie, she thought. Not Leighton's man at all, but very much her father's. If only she and he had shared the same mother.

Mrs Nolan bustled back into the room. "I forgot to mention it but someone called 'ere one day. Wouldn't give 'is name. I told 'im you was abroad."

"Oh?" Jennie hoped her voice sound casual. "What did he look like?"

"Good-looking. Tall, quite dark. I seen 'im before somewhere."

Mark! Mark had come looking for her. She should have told him she was going away, but everything had happened so quickly. What was the matter with her, hurting him like that? Quickly she searched through the rest of the letters, many from friends, many looking horribly official, until she came to the one she was certain would be there. Tearing open the envelope, she read his anguished words. Why was she not answering his calls or his letters? He knew she needed time but her silence only caused him to despair that he was to blame in some way.

... I know it is hard for you just now but don't, my love, go on tormenting me in this way...

She sank back in her chair and closed her eyes. Mark! If only this terrible time was over, if only her heart would lift from this trough of despair so that she could go to him with inner peace. But for all that Mark meant to her, Guy still had the power to stab at her conscience from beyond the grave. Rousing herself, she moved to the telephone, picked up the receiver and was about to place a call to Belmore when she checked herself. No, not yet. She wouldn't know what to say, or how to explain her feelings. Better surely to write? Replacing the receiver, she walked to her writing desk and penned a letter explaining that she had been in Rome, had just returned, and asking him to give her more time, time to sort out her emotions, time to come to terms with things. Realising what his thoughts might be, she set them right by telling him that Guy had not been flying the plane and that the accident was the result of engine failure.

So you see, my darling, it would have happened anyway. He had

417

flown the Panther in Canada and seemed in good spirits when he returned, saying he would discuss the divorce. There was no bitterness, just acceptance. Somehow that makes it all the harder now. I need more time, my love, it's still too soon. Please understand.

A letter from Florence inviting her and Alex to Trevellan at half term was followed by a curt note from Clive informing her that he knew of his grandmother's request, but that since he and his wife would be in residence to check on the builders who, in his opinion, were taken an unconscionable amount of time in completing their task, it would be better if she stayed away.

"Swine!" she cried, hurling his letter into the fire. It would be hard for Alex coming back to this house so filled with sad memories for him. After the funeral he had gone to his friend's home for a few days where he had slowly adapted to being back with others of his own age in an environment which was not heavy with sorrow. Then had come the awful day when she had driven him back to school and, on taking his tuck box and other belongings from the car, had noticed several boys staring curiously. Alex had looked dismayed, and aware that everyone knew, dreaded how it would be. The Headmaster had uttered sympathetic words and an assurance that he and the Housemaster would keep a wary eye on Alex, and so she'd watched with heartaching anguish as the small boy in his grey suit walked into the school and out of her loving reach.

Clive still could not believe it. On his third double Scotch, he sat in his London Club reading the appalling news in the *Financial Times*. Why did God hate him so much? When Consolidated Minerals had failed, he had tried desperately to find a way back from such a loss. Only four days ago his chance arrived. "Can't go wrong, old boy," a business friend had said when speaking of a company going under. "It hasn't a prayer. The takeover bid has been made by the giant Transmore conglomerate which is desperate to swallow it up. Right now shares are low. After the takeover, they'll rocket. You sell immediately, make a quick killing, and no money has to change hands at all. Go all out for it, but keep it under your hat."

And so he had bought a great many shares, sat back and waited. At the eleventh hour, Transmore pulled out of the deal, the takeover collapsed and he was now holding shares that were practically worthless. The business friend was very sorry. "One of those things, old boy. It was a shock to us. You won't be the only one to have got your fingers burned."

No, thought Clive, as he gazed at the silent room with its old leather

418

armchairs and aroma of cigar smoke. But I'll bet I'm the only one who couldn't afford to put them in the bloody fire. How the hell could he find the money to pay off such a debt? The London house had been sold and the money put into Trevellan's restoration. Now he had Longwood breathing down his neck asking dodgy questions about estate accounts which he was using up pretty quickly. Jennie's doing, of course. That woman really was a millstone around his neck. Then there was Jamie, his presence hanging over everything like the Sword of Damocles. So far, thank God, there had been no sign of Uncle Charles. That threat seemed to be diminishing.

He drank more whisky and addressed his mind to the problem of raising enough to pay for the shares before he found himself in serious trouble. He needed to borrow quickly, which would mean using the Dorking house as collateral. Unfortunately, Fenella was rather fond of her home and entertained there on a lavish scale which had not helped his finances. She would never agree. There was only one thing for it: Jennie. Every nerve in his body screamed out against it, but he would have to go cap in hand to her to save his skin.

Leaning back in his chair, Jamie felt a warm contentment creeping over him. "Jennie, that was a feast to remember. I can't recall when I last had roast beef and Yorkshire pudding. We live on fry ups mostly and will all have coronaries before we're twenty-five."

Jennie smiled, thinking that the kitchen was more of a haven than the dining room for brother and sister just enjoying a quiet dinner together. She was glad of his company; cooking for him had given her something ordinary and familiar to do and he had repaid her with stories of student escapades and medical ignorance, causing her to laugh for the first time in weeks. But in between the jokes and the laughter, she could sense that her half-brother was a deeply troubled soul still. It was in his eyes, those haunted eyes. She longed to help, but this was something Jamie would have to come to terms with in his own way just as she had. And so no mention was made of their father, or Guy, or anything that would invoke sadness on what had been a pleasant evening which both had found beneficial. Yet still she wondered if he had written that all-important letter.

Switching on the coffee percolator, she heard the telephone ringing. Climbing the stairs into the hallway, she picked up the receiver and listened to Clive's hysterical voice.

"Jennie, you've got to help me. I'm in serious trouble, and need to borrow money at once. A good deal of money. So I want permission from you and Longwood to raise a loan on the house."

"The house?" As he explained the mess he was in, Jennie paled.

"Clive, you must be mad. There is no way we can allow you to put Trevellan up as security. How could you even think we would?"

"Christ, it's only temporary. I'll be able to pay it back. There's the Van Dyck to start with, but I need the money now, not weeks later. I can raise a loan against the house at once. I don't want my own bank to know about it so I'm using another, but they will want to see the Deeds and that's where you and Longwood could sign a written statement, explaining everything and giving your agreement as trustees."

She could hardly believe she was hearing all this. "Clive, you must be tight. In fact you sound it. Go home and sleep it off."

"Sleep it off?" he screamed in rage. "Jennie ... listen to me ... I could go to prison ... God, I need your help."

"I can't possibly help you to lose Trevellan. Sorry, Clive."

"Then damn you to hell!" The receiver was slammed down, causing Jennie to jump.

She walked away and suddenly felt very cold. Prison? What on earth had Clive done that he would happily use Trevellan to secure a loan and risk seeing the bank foreclose on him? It was unbelievable. She and Jamie discussed it over their coffee and had just finished when they heard a loud banging on the front door. Jennie's heart jumped. "No, I'll go, Jamie. If he sees you it will only make matters worse." Alarmed at the din echoing through the house, she walked to the front door, paused for a moment then opened it. Clive stumbled into the hall, reeking of whisky and mumbling incoherently. She wondered how he had managed to drive.

"Clive, you're even more drunk than I thought you were."

"No, Jennie ... no more pushing me around. You ... you must agree ... need your help." He leaned against the wall and placed a hand to his brow. "Christ, it's your fault I'm in a mess ... your bloody fault ... I'll go to prison."

Jennie took a deep breath and said: "You'd better come into the drawing room and sit down. I'll bring you some strong coffee." She took his arm but he threw it off, causing her to stagger back in alarm. "On second thoughts, I think you'd better leave. Come back when you're sober."

"Oh no, Miss high and bloody mighty Frog ... you're not gonna push me around ... whore ... bloody whore!" Clive poked a menacing forefinger just inches from her face, saying things she couldn't imagine any one individual saying to another. Frightened, she backed along the hallway, aware that he was out of control. "Go home, Clive. Whatever it is that's wrong we can discuss it in the morning."

"Now ... discuss it now ..."

"Leave, Clive, or I'll call the police."

They were shouting above each other now, and still Clive advanced abusing, threatening. The kitchen stairs were behind her. She heard Jamie rushing up them. At that moment Clive struck her on the face; she fell to one side, then Jamie was there, tackling the heavier man. In a haze she watched them struggle, but Jamie was on the edge of the stairway. Suddenly Clive brought his fist into Jamie's stomach. Jamie bent forward then staggered back as the fist thudded into his jaw. Jennie watched with horror as her brother fell back, arms flailing the air. She heard the sound of his body crashing down the stairs and, screaming, ran down to help him. Jamie lay still, blood gushing from his temple, his eyes closed. Frantic, Jennie felt his neck for a pulse as Clive stood glaring down at her, shouting: "Him ... you two ... plotting against me ... bastard!"

"He's dead," screamed Jennie, looking up at Clive in horror. "You've killed him."

He staggered back and blinked stupidly, the shock of her words beginning to sober him up. "I didn't mean ... he got in the way ... oh God!" With that he rushed out of the door, got into his car then sped off, tyres screeching along Flood Street.

When the ambulance came, Jamie had regained consciousness but his speech was slurred and one leg was thought to be broken.

Jennie's relief was unbounded. He had been so still and she hadn't been able to find a pulse. Frantic, she rode with him to the hospital casualty unit then waited until the doctor came to tell her that the leg was indeed broken and that he had suffered a concussion. "It isn't serious. He was lucky. You say he's a medical student and tripped down the stairs? Seems to me he's been in a fight. Students!"

It was early-morning when she arrived back at the house. Cold, she lay on the sofa and pulled the cushions over her, worrying about Jamie and Trevellan. Clive was a man in serious trouble and now the house itself was in jeopardy. At the moment she could stop him from using it as collateral but later ...? The telephone rang. It was Clive calling from a telephone booth. Sobered up, and clearly alarmed, he wanted to know if Jamie really was dead.

She paused long enough to frighten him to death, then said: "You were lucky. Just! He's in hospital. They've had to operate."

"Alive?" Clive's voice choked on a sob. "Thank God ... oh, thank God. I didn't mean ... I can't remember a bloody thing except that I was shouting a lot."

"The doctor felt I should inform the police, but it's really up to Jamie to decide whether to prosecute or not. When he's come round from the anaesthetic."

"Anaesthetic? Operation?" After a lengthy silence, Clive murmured despairingly, "He will prosecute. You can be sure of it. This is the chance he's been waiting for. Now everything will come out ... about your father and his half-caste, the whole bloody works. I'll go down for GBH and the papers will have a field day." The line went dead.

She replaced the receiver, wondering where on earth he had been calling from at four o'clock on a cold frosty morning. He ought to go home before the police picked him up.

That evening she walked along the men's orthopaedic ward, placed grapes and books on Jamie's bedside locker and smiled down at the pale face resting against the pillows. "I see your friends got here before me," she said, indicating his plastered leg which was already covered in signatures.

Still a little woozy from the effects of drugs and anaesthetic, Jamie smiled. "Have you any idea what hell it is to be a medical student in hospital?"

She saw the ugly weal on his temple and thought how close a call he had received. What words would she have found to tell her father if the worst had happened? Sitting down, she took his hand and gave it a gentle squeeze. "I feel responsible. I shouldn't have opened the door to him. He was too drunk. He telephoned in the early hours, shattered at what he'd done and anxious about you. He'd been wandering about London all night. You could prosecute. He deserves it. But I don't see it helping anyone in the end." She sat back. "How long before you can leave here?"

"They've X-rayed my skull, just to be on the safe side. If everything's all right, then it's just a case of mastering the crutches, I suppose. The plaster won't come off for six weeks."

"Six weeks! How will you manage? You'll have to come to me."

But Jamie shook his head. "You've enough on your plate. Anyway, you're at the studio most of the time so I'd still be alone. Better to be with my friends. We're in the same year, so they can keep me up to date and fill me in on lectures I've missed."

How cheerful he seemed, she thought. Yet what hope had he of passing this year's exams? It was all so bitterly unfair. "Papa will have to be told, Jamie." When he said it was better not to worry him, something in his voice confirmed what she already suspected. "You haven't been in touch with him, have you?"

Jamie stared straight ahead and said nothing. Only when she persisted, did he answer. "No. Why pretend everything's peachy between us when it isn't and never will be?"

Dismayed at his words, she said, "But you promised. I kept my word to you. Even when I wrote and told Papa about Guy, I didn't mention

422

your name." She took his hand once more to gain his attention. "This can't go on. Give him the chance to make his peace with you."

"How can I?" His eyes flashed with anger. "How can you expect me to, knowing the way my mother died?"

So that was it.

"You must not think like that. Childbirth was more dangerous then than it is today." Why was he staring at her like that? "Even had they been married, she still would have died."

The haunted eyes held hers. "I thought you knew. But he didn't tell you, did he? Jennie, my mother killed herself."

Jennie sat motionless, her mind rejecting the shocking words. "No, Jamie, she died..."

"Uncle Victor found her." Jamie sounded tired and a little hoarse, not just from the drugs and the effects of the anaesthetic, but as if carrying this knowledge around in his head had taken a toll on his strength. "He had to break down the door of the bathroom. My mother was lying in a bath full of blood. She had cut her wrists. She had been dead for over an hour. Imagine it, Jennie, the horror." He fell silent, trying to compose himself before he went on: "I was two months old at the time."

Appalled, Jennie listened as he spoke of Serena's despair and deep depression; of his grandfather's anger that the brilliant daughter he had loved so much should have disgraced herself and the family and thrown away her chance to be a first-class doctor. "My birth was a complicated affair and she was ill for some time afterwards. Then came the depression... oh, not just the usual post-natal blues, you understand, but real despair. She left a letter saying how meaningless her life was without the man she loved and that I was to bear the name of Veryan even though my Birth Certificate said I was James Leighton. Father later changed it legally. I have the letter. It's in the drawer of the desk in my room. I'd hate anyone to find it there. Will you bring it to me?" His lips twisted bitterly. "Read it. Then you'll see for yourself." He stopped speaking, his eyes distant. "'Remember your mother!' That's what Uncle said when he gave me the letter. 'Remember your mother!'"

"And hate your father?" Jennie took his hand again. "Oh, Jamie, that's evil. Leighton's evil. You'll be destroyed if you carry hatred through your life as he's carried it through his."

"But I shall carry that picture in my mind for life." Jamie twisted his head slowly and stared away from her. "So how can I betray my mother by forgiving my father?"

Jennie sat still and thoughtful, remembering words said so long ago in a far off country. "He has the means ... there's more to all this than you know." Her father had been referring to the letter which named him. She thought of him tending the orchids at the clinic. "Amnesia caused by severe trauma," the doctor had said, but what exactly had her father's mind blocked out: the memory of torture or the memory of the woman he loved dying by her own hand? Leighton would have planted that picture in her father's head at Changi prison. It had been passed on to poor Jamie and now to her, like some deadly virus with no antidote.

"You mustn't hate Papa," she said weakly. "Your mother would not have wanted that. She loved him, remember. He's suffered so cruelly. Don't make him suffer any more." Still badly shaken, she got to her feet. "I'll find that letter for you, don't worry." She turned to leave, then stopped and said: "Do you know where your uncle is now?"

"Hong Kong. He said we would never meet again."

Jennie smiled wryly. "Why would you? He's achieved his goal."

Jamie caught her hand. "Don't read the letter, burn it."

She smiled. "You look very tired. Sleep now. I'll return tomorrow." With that, she walked out of the ward.

The following morning, Jennie took from her handbag the letter she had found in Jamie's sparse, uncomfortable room and unfolded it. The paper was soft, yellowish, and had mould spots caused by Singapore's humidity. Such a delicate thing to hold so strong and anguished a message. Poor woman, thought Jennie, poor tragic, shamed woman with all that beauty ending in ugly death. 'Burn it,' Jamie had said. Walking to the fire she held it to the flame then threw it in, watching until it was consumed. Would that the picture in her head could be as easily destroyed.

Hyde Park was covered with a fresh fall of snow which dazzled in the bright morning sunshine and muffled the distant sound of London's traffic. A thin layer of ice covered the Serpentine and ducks scurried about the paths as nannies helped their small charges to scatter pieces of bread, One mallard almost came to grief beneath Jennie's boot as she ambled along, distanced from anything outside her own thoughts. The mallard squawked and found sanctuary beneath a park bench.

She walked a great deal these days, unable to find rest. Her mind was filled with ugly images: ashes being scattered from the sky; a woman lying in a bath of her own blood; her own mother being tortured and shot; men drowning in a burning sea – images that would not go away. And so she walked and walked and walked, thinking that if she could walk far enough for long enough, then exhaustion itself would drive them from her mind. It must, or she would go mad.

Staring at the frozen lake, sparkling in wintry sunshine, she had lost all sense of time and only vaguely recalled leaving a cold house that morning to deliver a painting. Mrs Nolan was ill with influenza; no fire had been lit and no housework done. The house would be unutterably cold. What of it? Poor Jamie, poor lost and haunted Jamie. Now she had been forced to break her promise to him by writing to their father explaining what Jamie knew; how Leighton had given him the suicide note and how Clive had put him in hospital. He had to know. How he and Jamie resolved their differences was now out of her hands.

She pulled her coat about her, the warm-lined suede coat which Guy had brought from Canada for her Christmas present. Yesterday, Kay had helped her with the painful task of clearing his things from the cottage, found the wrapped parcels in the wardrobe and handed them to her. The card had said simply: "To Jennie, my darling wife whom I shall always love."

She had collapsed in tears on Kay's shoulder, and Kay had said: "You know, he loved you very much and was worried because things had been a little strained between you both of late. And so he was making plans to take you away to the Canaries in February. A second honeymoon, he called it."

Finding this rather difficult to take in at the time Jennie had gone on with the terrible business of tidying up a life now finished when she discovered another, much smaller, package on the top shelf of the wardrobe among a collection of collar cases. This had no card attached. Thinking it would be for Alex she placed it in a suitcase, added Guy's bank statements, bills and other important documents, then returned home, leaving the cottage ready and vacant for letting once more.

Last night she had gone through the paperwork and found an August receipt for the purchase of a Renault Dauphine. A mistake surely? They had never owned such a car. Later, she unwrapped the small package and found herself holding a velvet jewel case from Garrard. Inside was a small diamond brooch in a silver setting. She had never liked brooches and Guy knew it. How long had she sat there holding it in her hand? The diamonds sparkled and seemed to jeer. For the wife a coat, for the mistress a new car and precious jewels. This was the gift she had not been meant to see.

Heart thumping with anger, she had searched through the paper-work for some clue as to the identity of her rival. But there was nothing. With the exception of the car receipt, Guy had covered his tracks very well. As for the brooch, well, how could he have known he would be called to fly to Boscombe just before taking his leave? Furious, she had put the coat and boots away, swearing to herself that she would never wear them. Then, that very morning, had taken one look at the snow and said: "Why not?" What did the other woman matter any more?

Guy was gone; the coat and boots remained. She was cold; the coat and the boots were warm.

She stopped walking, her mind finally unlocking. He had lied! Right up to the end he had lied, even about the divorce. The present and loving message, the trip to the Canaries, the brooch and the car, all blindingly clear that Guy had intended to keep her chained to him and have his mistress as well. She felt his hold on her slip at last.

The Canadian coat had a warm hood. Pulling it up against the cold wind, she turned and started back towards Park Lane. A dog bounded across her path churning up the virgin snow in an effort to retrieve a ball. Children threw snowballs, their shouts disturbing the strange silence of the scene. In the distance a tall man was walking towards her, hands thrust into the pockets of his sheepskin jacket. There was something about his size and gait, something so wonderfully familiar.

Mark, having been in despair these past weeks, now decided it was the moment for action. He had done the decent thing and given Jennie the time she obviously needed. He had done the decent thing once before and lost her. It was a mistake he would not make again. Travelling from York overnight, his train had finally arrived three hours late because of the weather. Having then taken a taxi to Jennie's house, and finding the place empty, he had gone to Maddie's. She had offered him coffee and said how worried she was over Jennie. "She's very strange, very distant. Doesn't paint, doesn't do anything but walk, walk and walk. This morning she had to go to Curzon Street with a painting. Goodness knows when she'll be back." When he asked where she walked, Maddie had shrugged. "Parks mostly. Hyde Park today probably. Wait here, then phone her house later. No sense in wandering all over the place."

But Mark had not waited; he had waited long enough already and heading for Hyde Park had walked about looking for her. Almost on the brink of giving up, he had changed course and then seen the woman in the brown suede coat. The hood hid her face, but there was something about the walk, and that slight shrug of the shoulders, he had always loved. How bright the snow was on this brittle, beautiful day. Mark moved quickly towards Jennie who was just standing there. When he reached her at last, he fought down the desire to wrap his arms about her and instead placed his hands on her gloved ones firmly. Emotion made words impossible. He saw how ill she looked with purple shadows beneath eyes that seemed vague, almost as though she were sleepwalking. Shocked, he cursed himself for not coming sooner, and overwhelmed with love for her, cherished the small gloved hand that now lay in his.

To Jennie it seemed she must be dreaming. How tired she was

suddenly. Emotionally and physically tired. Her shoulders fell, her tightly coiled body began to unwind. Now she could rest at last. His arms enfolded her, and she leaned against him, loving the strength of him, the smell of him, the feel of his warm breath on her upturned face. Her hood slipped back. He kissed her on the lips, pulled her hood up again to keep her from the cold, then walked with his arm around her out of the park.

# Chapter Twenty-Seven

As always, spring had come early to Cornwall. Forsythia shone in pale sunlight and daffodils swayed in strong westerly winds before bowing beneath sudden showers. Riding Laura's chestnut mare, with Alex on the black pony Florence had bought for him, Jennie felt she could look to the future with hope for the first time in years. If only Mark could be here instead of preparing Belmore for its spring opening. Her thoughts returned to the memory of that moment when he had found her, taken her home, lit a fire then sat with her on the sofa and held her close. Cradled in his arms she had let go at last and, in an emotional torrent of words and tears, had unleashed her thoughts. When the words stopped, she had fallen into a deep sleep while Mark watched over her. Whenever she opened her eyes he was always there, then she would sleep again feeling safe, cosseted, cherished. After fifty-two hours, she returned to the world where he had been waiting for her.

He had taken her to the hospital where Jamie, struggling with crutches, was worried that her absence had been because of the things he had said. Then, as Jamie had lost his balance, Mark rushed forward to help him and it was at that, moment both men felt certain they had met before. On learning who Mark was, Jamie recalled the driver who had once given him a lift, and thought it a strange world indeed. With Mark's help he struggled with the crutches once more, only for both to wind up collapsed in chairs, utterly defeated and laughing.

For eight days, Mark had stayed with her, eight wonderful days when they planned their future and this time knew they had one. He wanted her to return to Belmore with him then, but half term was on them and Florence had phoned to say that Clive was not going to Trevellan after all. She wanted Jennie and Alex there with her and Jennie decided it was the best course, so soon after his father's death. Reassurance and all things familiar would help Alex far more than seeing his mother with a strange man. Mark understood and left for

York, taking her heart with him. Now she looked at her fair-haired son and thought how smart he was in his hacking jacket, jodhpurs and black riding hat. At first Alex had hated being placed on the pony but now he had settled happily, was quick to learn and would probably make a good horseman one day. But how like his father he was. Every time she looked at him she saw Guy. They paused on the clifftop overlooking the cove. The wind sent clouds scurrying across the sun so that the light was constantly changing. Here Jennie told Alex how she and the famous Mark Curnow he had seen on television had once flown a kestrel called Sophie, from these very cliffs.

"The falcon man, do you mean?" Alex's eyes shone. "You knew him? You never told me. Wait till they hear at school. No one there knows anyone who's been on television."

Smiling at his reaction, she said: "We're still very good friends and have been since childhood. Only he lives a long way away now. But when I last saw him he said how much he was looking forward to meeting you. He'll tell you all about the falcons. Would you like that?"

Relieved at his excited reaction, Jennie led him back across the pastures and came to the lane where the Curnows' house stood. Sold as a holiday home, it was empty and sad-looking. Jennie told him of Mark's childhood spent here, and pointed out the shed where Sophie had been kept. Alex wanted to go in, but Jennie had to stop him. "It doesn't belong to the estate any more so that would be trespassing." There were quite a few cottages that no longer belonged to the estate, she thought grimly. What would be left when Clive had full title?

They rode back to Trevellan, both sad that they must journey to London in the morning and the day after that to the school. But this time, she thought, would not be so harrowing, for slowly Alex had changed from a shattered, bewildered little boy to one who was coming to terms with the fact that he would never see his father again. Even so, she dreaded his leaving her. She would miss him dreadfully, as she missed Mark. The scurrying clouds had been overtaken by dark thick ones now, and by the time they reached the stable yard, hailstones were falling, clattering on to rooftops and battering the earth.

It was Mrs Hodges who discovered that Alex was feverish. Watching her bake, he had been happily licking cake mixture from the bowl when suddenly he sank on to the Windsor chair, looking very seedy.

"Measles!" said the doctor, as Alex lay in bed in Jennie's old room.

When she telephoned the school it was to hear a distraught Headmaster saying that eight of his boys had gone down with it and Alex made the ninth. Jennie sat with her son for most of the time, making sure he remained in bed, keeping his room darkened and trying to keep

429

down the roaring temperatures. Soon the fever had gone and only the spots remained.

Work on the house was progressing well. The attics had been cleared and most of the contents scattered in various rooms. Jennie spent this extra time, sorting through old things: toys, unwanted chairs, and trunks smelling of mothballs and filled with clothes. Most were of the twenties and thirties, some in exquisite materials, and one, a cream party dress, of such delicate georgette that she thought it might fall apart in her hands. It had belonged to Florence at the turn of the century. "Oh, please, Grandma, promise me you won't get rid of a thing? They're all so fantastic. They'll be useful in my work as well. We just don't see these materials now."

On the day the doctor declared that Alex was almost well enough to get up up, Jennie entered the morning room with the good news to see a puzzled look on her grandmother's face. "Maddie rang just now," said Florence. "It's all very strange but she's on her way here. I'm sending the car to pick her up from Penzance later."

"Maddie? Why?" When Florence said she didn't know, Jennie began to worry. This was very un-Maddie-like behaviour especially when she was preparing for an exhibition at the Veryan Gallery. Something was wrong. Very wrong. Anxious, she walked out into the hall once more, only to be cornered by Laura just returning from a week's visit to friends in Bath.

"Ah, at last," she whispered as Rosa took her things up to the room she used when Clive and Fenella were not in the house. "Now I want the truth. Is Jamie my brother's child?"

"He is," said Jennie, thinking how aged Laura looked. The hair was quite grey now, the bright blue eyes faded to a shadow of their former glory, the porcelain complexion the same but the skin so rice-paper delicate that lines had appeared all over the once lovely face. Women of sixty had lines, of course they did, but these were lines of discontent and made her look almost ugly. The tall, slim figure could now only be described as thin. It seemed to be a Veryan trait.

Laura let out a deep breath. "I thought so. What's his game? What does he want? There are things you have to tell me."

Jennie folded her arms and gave her aunt a hard look. "Yes, there are. I can tell you that Jamie is here to study medicine, was almost killed by Clive and was rushed to hospital with concussion and a broken leg. I can't tell you what he's said to the Police, or whether he intends to press charges, because I haven't seen him lately. I can tell you that Clive attacked me in a drunken rage because I wouldn't give permission for him to borrow against this house. I can tell you also that your son is in deep financial trouble and that one day Trevellan will be taken by the bank."

Laura listened in appalled silence then whispered vehemently: "I don't believe you. How dare you make up such terrible lies? You'd say anything to hurt Clive. But have a care, my girl, lest he sue you for slander."

Jennie smiled as she watched her aunt climbing the stairs. "Well, you did ask."

After a cold start the afternoon had brightened up and Jennie, restless and thinking of Mark, painted at the cove then returned and settled herself in a garden chair on the south lawn, lifting her face to the sunshine. Maddie should be here soon. She would wait and learn what disaster had brought her all this way.

It must have been almost four when she heard the soft crunch of car wheels on gravel. Opening her eyes she saw the Rolls just entering the long drive. It had cleared the gate but instead of coming onwards, stopped. Frowning, Jennie sat up, wondering if the vehicle had broken down. A door opened and in a flash of bright blue cape Maddie emerged, then turned back to the car as if to collect something. Someone else was getting out, a tall thin man in a dark grey suit. He stood, hands on his waist, staring about him and then caught sight of her.

Jennie stood up slowly, blinked in astonishment and clutched at her throat. A strange sound emanated from it. At last the sound released itself. "Papa! Papa!"

Slowly she moved forward, then quickened her pace until she was running along the drive, her arms stretched wide, her face radiant with joy.

As Charles opened his arms to Jennie, she flung herself into them and laughter mixed with tears as they hugged and kissed. She hung on to him and slowly they walked to the house together. Suddenly he stopped and stared about him, murmuring, "A moment, darling, just a moment to see it, to take it all in. I've dreamed of it for so long that I'm almost afraid to believe I'm home at last."

She gave him his moment, so many questions filling her mind. How much older he looked, poor darling, the Singapore complexion at odds with the pale blue eyes and thinning grey hair. When he turned to her at last, she steeled herself to ask the question. "Are you home for good, Papa?"

He nodded. "For good. Dodo's following – selling up and moving back to England. I took the earliest flight out as soon as I received your letter." He watched as Maddie walked on ahead discreetly, then looked

431

at his daughter with a bleak expression. "I'm scared. You don't know how damned scared. I've had panic attacks ever since I left Singapore. Bloody stupid. Must get a grip on myself."

"It isn't stupid. It's understandable. What about Jamie?"

Charles looked troubled. "I've seen him. We talked for a long time. It was hard . . . very hard. He was so bitter. But the last time I left him, we embraced. It isn't over, but we've made a start. Time alone will do the rest, God willing."

As they neared the house she found herself thinking: *He wouldn't come for me, he wouldn't come for his parents or for Trevellan, he came for Jamie.* The thought hurt, but at least he was home. He had made that quantum leap and broken from his chains at last. That was everything. She saw tears of emotion in his eyes and put her arm about him. "It's all over now, Papa. The letter is burned and Leighton has washed his hands of us at long last."

"I wanted to kill the swine," he hissed, almost beneath his breath. "I truly think I would have done had I set eyes on him again. There, in the street, in full view of everyone, I would have drawn strength from all my hatred and killed him with my bare hands."

Alarmed at the look in his eyes, Jennie wondered at the forces which had driven her gentle father to such a hatred. "Then it's as well you never met again and never will." As they walked on, she said, "You're home now, and all that is behind you." A thought occurred to her suddenly. "Does Maddie know who Jamie is? Have you told her?" When he said no, she breathed a sigh of relief. "Grandma doesn't know a thing either. For their sakes and for Jamie's I think we should keep it that way. So don't unburden your soul to them. That won't help now."

At the house, Charles paused, unable to walk in and face any of the staff just yet. He had to make his peace with his mother first. Would she forgive him? Would she receive him?

Florence had just awoken from her afternoon rest when Jennie entered the morning room, which was now used for most of the day. The eyes flickered into life when her grand-daughter knelt by her chair and spoke so gently to her. As she listened, a strange look crept over her face, a look that said: *I must be misunderstanding you. I'm afraid of what you're saying. Do not fill a silly old woman with false hope.*

"Did you hear me, Grandma? Papa is here. He's come home at last." Jennie felt the trembling hand in hers, and stroked the long fingers gently. "Yes." She smiled and nodded. "Maddie's brought him home. Isn't that wonderful news?"

The door opened. Florence turned her gaze from Jennie to the tall thin man standing there. For one moment she froze with disbelief and confusion, then her lips trembled and her arms reached out to him.

432

As Charles moved towards his mother, Jennie walked out, closing the door quietly behind her.

"My dear," said Maddie, alone with Jennie in her bedroom, "it was the most unbelievable thing. He just telephoned, out of the blue, saying he was in London and could I put him up for a night or two? Well . . . when I recovered from the shock I told him to come at once. He's been with me for two days. Keeps going out . . . doesn't tell me where though. Very mysterious. But then, everything about Charles is mysterious. He asked me to say nothing to anyone until he was ready. He only had a lightweight suit on, so I rushed to Harrods and bought him a sheepskin jacket and some thick sweaters before he caught pneumonia."

"Aunt Laura's out riding." Jennie smiled. "She doesn't know yet." Oh, to witness the moment when she did!

Mysteriously, word had already spread among the staff and an excited Keynes made certain the welcome would be fitting. When he had greeted an emotional Rosa and Mrs Hodges, and the happy yet dignified butler, Charles said in strained tones how glad he was to see them all again and how wonderful it was to be home. As he spoke he thought how old they had all become, then asked himself what they must be thinking about him.

Tea was served in the library where Charles gazed into a log fire, almost mesmerised by the flames after eighteen long years in the tropics. Florence sat in a leather armchair, still trembling with emotion. Charles was home. Her son had returned at last. She thought she might wake up to find it was just another cruel dream, but she *was* awake and he really was home. Why? Why now when Philip was dead and the estate in such a mess? Why now, after all the shattered hopes and dreams and grief?

Maddie had been thinking along the same lines. "What made you come back after all these years, Charles?"

He glanced into Jennie's deep eyes, then settled back in Philip's old armchair, saying: "I know there are many questions I should answer but you must trust me when I tell you that what I did, I did because I thought it was for the best. It . . . it was difficult. Things have changed however. I'm now married to Dodo and have finally persuaded her to come back to England. I've put matters in hand to help her with the move. She won't have to cope alone. The bookshop already has a buyer, a larger bookseller who has been interested for years. The house went on the market just before I left. Dodo must decide what furniture she wants shipped home and what she wants to sell."

Florence considered his words then said, "But, my dear, she won't need to ship any furniture at all, surely? I think we can safely say we have rather a lot of it."

The question was greeted with a long silence, leaving everyone mystified. Jennie broke it at last. "Aunt Laura should be here soon. I thought she might go to the dower cottage, so I've asked Rosa to pop a note through her door." She smiled wryly. "I wish I could see the look on her face when she reads it. What joy!" She finished her tea, and stood up. "Come and meet your grandson, Papa. You have had measles, I take it?"

Charles rose to his feet and smiled thinly. "Jennie, my dear, I can safely say I've had everything." He followed her up the staircase, waves of memories flooding over him. At the door to his and Monique's room he paused for a moment, then moved on to where his grandson was resting, all measly against a large white pillow, jigsaw spread out before him on his bed.

Alex stared at the tall thin man who had just been introduced to him as his grandfather and thought he was very, very old. "From Singapore? Jamie comes from Singapore. He's my friend. He says it's hot there and that it's a long way away."

"It is." Suddenly realising he had walked into a tangled web of his own spinning, Charles wondered how he could ever put things right. How long before he could tell Alex that Jamie was his uncle? Did he have to wait until the child was grown up? He had tried that with Jamie and the result had been disastrous.

Later, as they strolled in the grounds, Charles shivered inside the sheepskin jacket and Jennie feared he would catch a chill. But he wanted to walk about, feel the air of Cornwall on his face once more, and remember.

"Promises!" said Jennie. "You and Jamie both made me keep promises. I kept yours and paid the price. I didn't keep Jamie's and must pay the price again by losing his friendship and trust. But how could I keep his secret? You had to know. Leighton spared him nothing, not even that which you spared me."

Charles stopped walking and saw the hideous picture in his mind once more. "That was the one thing I couldn't tell you and the thing I dreaded Jamie's learning the most." He turned to his daughter and placed an arm about her shoulder. "You're wrong to think he feels badly about you. That isn't the impression I received. In fact, I think it's almost a relief to him that someone stepped in as mediator. He would never have said anything otherwise and I would never have known."

They walked on together through the gathering dusk, finally returning to the south lawn. Jennie stared at the house and said, "Will Dodo like living here, do you think? It's not exactly her style."

434

"She won't have to live here," said Charles. "Much as I love this place, I'm no longer the right person to own it."

She looked up at him, feeling cold suddenly. "I thought you had returned to do just that, to take back your birthright? You don't mean to let Clive go on, surely?"

Charles stopped and breathed in the salt air. Everything looked just the same. Timeless Trevellan, sleeping on a hill. "If not Clive, then who? Jamie? It would keep the name of Veryan going. But no. Too many awkward questions, shocked neighbourhood and all that. Besides, he wants to be a doctor and what would he know about land-ownership? So then, how about it, Jennie? Are you willing to take it on?"

She found herself staring at him stupidly. Was it happening? Had he really said what she thought he had said?

He frowned and looked down at her. "You do want it, don't you? You do want Trevellan?"

Too filled with emotion to speak, she put her arms about his lean body while tears filled her eyes. Everything was blurred. A sea mist was drifting inland. It swirled through the woods and across the south lawn where it slowly enveloped the tall cypress trees so that only the tops stood clear. Someone turned on the drawing-room light. It shone through the mist, beckoning, enfolding.

"Oh, yes, Papa. I want Trevellan, and I feel it wants me."

Later that night, she awoke, wondering what was wrong. The first thing she remembered was Laura's stunned expression when she had walked into the drawing room to see her brother standing there, staring at the George Cross medal. It was a look Jennie would never forget. Neither would she forget the look her father had given Laura. After dinner, Charles had told everyone his plans for the estate, saying that the sooner he handed it to his daughter the better. "We can't afford any more death duties. I only hope I'm good for another seven years yet." Florence had almost cried with relief, while Laura had rattled her coffee cup and said how unfair Charles was being to Clive. Yet something in her voice told Jennie that the fight had gone out of her. Maybe she was, even, a little relieved?

What was it that had awoken her? Jennie listened carefully and thought she heard music. Somewhere in the dead of night there was music. Stepping out of her room, she followed the sound and saw light streaming out of the half-open door of the Grand Chamber. The music was louder now; the strains of *"Parlez Moi D'Amour"* floated out to her. Pushing the door gently, she looked around it to see her father sitting on the sofa with Monique's photograph in his hand. Lost in his memories, Charles Veryan was quite unaware of his daughter's presence. And so she left him there and quietly made her way back to bed.

Earlier that same evening, in a large mock-Tudor house near Dorking, a telephone rang. A maid walked into the study, answered it then moved to the large drawing room where her mistress was greeting dinner guests. Sighing, Fenella slipped into the study, picked up the receiver, frowned then beckoned to Clive who was hovering just outside talking to friends. "Your mother," she whispered. "Sounds hysterical, but when did she ever sound anything else?"

Clive took the receiver from her and then moved it away from his ear as Laura's voice rattled away like a machine gun. "Hold on, Mother, you're not making sense. Calm down. What did you say about Uncle Charles?"

Looking across at him from the cluster of well-heeled guests, Fenella saw her husband pull at his black tie, sway a little, close his eyes and lean back against the wall. His pallor was so ghastly that, thinking he was about to have a heart attack, she rushed back into the study asking if he was all right.

Clive was speaking still. "What? Christ, no ... he can't ... he can't ... he'll ruin me if he does. You don't know ... you don't know." Suddenly his hand lost all strength, the receiver fell back on its rest, cutting off Laura mid-sentence. With a stupified expression, Clive collapsed on to a chair and finally managed to gasp: "Uncle Charles has returned. He's claimed back the estate and means to make it over to Jennie."

Open-mouthed with shock, Fenella finally found her voice, keeping it to a whisper. "But he can't. He can't do that to us. We'll fight him in the courts. We have a legal right." She looked puzzled. "What was all that about him ruining you?"

As he told her she heard with growing horror of interest piling on interest, borrowing from Peter to pay Paul, and worst of all, managing to flannel his way into borrowing against a house that was no longer his to sell. He needed help. Her help, her father's help. She glared down at him with contempt and whispered: "You stupid fool of a man. How in God's name did I ever get mixed up with you? We had position, now we have none. We had three houses, now we have only this and that poky little flat in Maida Vale. We had wealth and now you tell me we are up to our ears in debt, a debt you cannot pay back. Why don't you ask your own father for help?"

At a shout from one of the guests, Fenella put her head out of the door, assumed a fixed smile and waved. "Coming, darlings. Do have another drink." As a maid passed her with a tray of champagne cocktails, she turned back to Clive. "I suggest you get down to

Cornwall first thing tomorrow and sort this mess out. Meanwhile, we have guests. So pull yourself together and help me to entertain them."

Clinging to his arm, she inched him back to the party, whispering, "I don't understand. You said he was out there for good. What brought him back?"

Clive straightened his tie and thought of that moment when he had knocked Jamie down the stairs. One blow struck in a drunken rage had resonated around the world and brought about his own downfall.


On a hot August day Sir Charles Veryan, Tenth Baronet, gave his daughter in marriage to Mark Curnow. Church bells pealed out over Portlyn as Jennie and Mark stood for their wedding photographs with most of the villagers looking on. They crowded the churchyard, glad that their own local hero was marrying Miss Genevieve. Rumours had abounded for months, ever since Sir Charles had returned so unexpectedly. No one knew what to believe at first but now it was true. The estate had passed to his daughter and, with Mark Curnow beside her, things would be as they used to be. Willoughby had been ousted, thank God. What a day. It boded well for the estate; it boded well for Portlyn. There would be some elbow lifting at the Harbour Inn that evening.

Dodo had never seen anything like it, but ever since she had arrived in the country just six weeks earlier, there had been no time to draw breath. People kept calling her Lady Veryan and half the time she thought they were addressing Charles's mother. Now she watched as the photographer clicked away and saw how stunning Jennie looked in her wide-brimmed hat which matched exactly the white lace ballet-length dress with its underskirt of pink. A magnolia bride, she thought, recalling the swooning girl in the bookshop and that first meeting over coffee in Robinsons's when each had taken a dislike to the other. It all seemed such a short time ago yet what changes she had faced since then: Jamie's sudden arrival in their midst; Singapore's independence; Desmond dying; her own marriage to Charles and the swift decision to return to England which she had been unable to prevent, such was Charles's state of mind. Now Jennie was her daughter-in-law. It was all so strange. What a place. What a house. What would poor old Desmond have made of it all?

Lavinia Collingham sighed as she threw confetti and watched Mark and Jennie driving away from the church. Turning to her sister, who was Jennie's matron of honour, she murmured: "Charles Veryan isn't just gaining a son, he's gaining the best estate manager we ever had. Oh, Arabella, how can this be happening to me?"

At the marquee on the south lawn, bride and groom prepared to greet their guests and, in that brief moment, Mark lifted Jennie's face to his and kissed her. He had never believed this day would come. "You look utterly beautiful. Happy, darling?"

Jennie nodded. "I've never been so happy in all my life."

At that moment Arabella arrived, then Florence, Charles and Dodo, the kissing and congratulations had begun, champagne was being offered to the guests and Mark and Jennie addressed their minds to duty.

Later, as he listened to his father-in-law's hesitant speech, Mark thought of these past hectic months when he and Jennie had written reams of letters, spoken on the telephone for hours and chased up and down the country to spend time with each other. They had talked and worried, but in the end he had known he would come home to Trevellan. How could he not? And was there anywhere he would rather be? Having got Belmore into shape, he could leave it in safe hands with his under manager and accept this new challenge. And challenge was the word. But he and Jennie would meet it together.

Wedding cake cut and speeches over, the guests wandered about the marquee and grounds while Charles looked at his radiant daughter and took her hand. "I heard from my mother that once you and Mark were in trouble for being in love. Now I know why you were unhappy when we first met in Singapore. You wouldn't speak of it then, but I knew there was something. I hope you have many years of happiness to make up for the years of loss."

As Jennie moved across to Louise, who had married her Kevin and was now heavily pregnant, Florence approached Charles, leaning heavily on her walking stick. "I still think it extraordinarily mean-spirited of Laura to go away at a time like this. Just because Jennie is marrying a Curnow. Clive and Fenella were not invited, which was wrong of Jennie, I think, but they wouldn't have shown up anyway." She sat down on a gilt chair, sipped more champagne and surveyed the scene. They were all there again, that nice Ian Stewart, the Chathams from Stannington, Lord and Lady Belmore, the Harte-Willises and a host of Jennie's old friends, all laughing, chatting and growing very merry on the fast-flowing champagne. Even so, she had a feeling that things were being kept from her. What had happened to Clive? No one mentioned him these days.

No one dare! In order to keep his son-in-law from the shame of fraud and bankruptcy, Lytton had met most of Clive's huge debts with the proviso that every penny of it was to be paid back if it took Clive a lifetime. The house in Dorking had been the first casualty, his marriage the second. Fenella had left him for an American shoe millionaire and now sought a divorce. Word of his financial misdealings had filtered through to the bank and Clive had sought a lesser position with a smaller one at a much reduced salary. He now lived in a mews flat thinking of what might have been and cursing Jamie, Charles, Jennie and that bloody Mark Curnow who had, it seemed, managed to have the last laugh after all.

As the Rolls pulled away from the house, bearing Mark and Jennie to the station on the first leg of their journey to Tuscany, Jamie, Alex and Louise stood smiling at their handiwork. Tin cans and a bunch of balloons trailed behind the dignified Phantom III as it made its way along lanes lined with villagers and holidaymakers, down the hill and out of Portlyn.

# Epilogue

A dark-haired toddler was chasing a springer spaniel across the south lawn. Jennie scooped up her daughter, cuddled her then handed her to Nanny before walking to the large studio she had built in the coach block. The summer school students were working on a life study with one of the visiting tutors Maddie had found to help with this project. A fount of knowledge and a source of contacts, she was excited about the summer school and had offered to help finance the scheme along with Jennie, who used her own fees from 'phizmongering', which she still did from time to time, as well as teaching art here. After four years the school was paying for itself, had become well-known and was always so fully booked that Jennie had to keep a waiting list. The trick was not to clash with paying visitors to the house.

In order to fund renovations, which had proved more costly than estimated, and feed money back into the estate, which was far into the red, Mark had persuaded the Veryans to open the house for three days a week during summer months. Opposition from Florence and Laura had finally been overcome and now groups of people walked through the historic house where Cromwell had slept, Royalty had visited and Monique Veryan had once lived. With a guide they strolled into the Great Hall, to stare at the family's crested dinner service set out on the long dining table, wandered through the Long Gallery, admiring the tapestries and paintings, then moved into the Drawing Room where their eyes fell on Monique's photograph and the George Cross, before turning to the portrait of her daughter, a young woman in a white ball gown who was the present owner of the house. Then it was up the stairs to the Grand Chamber with its ornate ceiling and the Green Drawing Room with its gilded Grinling Gibbons carvings and French eighteenth-century furniture. All over the house were delicate, skilled watercolours by Monique Veryan, and before these, visitors lingered the longest. After the guided tour they would wander the grounds, still being brought back into shape after years of neglect, until they came upon a notice by a woodland pathway leading to the sea, which said: PRIVATE.

Florence had seen many changes in the place over the years, but these past five had been different from anything since the schoolboys burst in on them during the war. Yet she remained unfazed by it all, having ceased to be amazed at anything since her longlost son had returned without warning and her grand-daughter had married the son of her former agent. What were a few visitors and an art centre, compared with all that? At least by focussing on the house, Mark and Jennie kept it in good repair. The estate accounts were in the black once more and everyone could breathe a sigh of relief. Now Trevellan would go on from Jennie to Alex, and, hopefully, to his children. Laura had made her displeasure at such changes known by remaining in the dower cottage and out of everyone's way.

The Falconry Centre was intended to be only half the size of the one at Belmore, since raptors were expensive to feed. Mark had reckoned without his fame, however, and soon the casualties were coming in to the local man who knew how to handle injured owls or abandoned kestrels and could not turn away any creature in distress. People flocked to see the birds of prey, enjoyed lectures about them, and demonstrations of their flights to the lure. Mark had never been busier or happier and, after the first couple of bad seasons, the centre was now cost-effective with television outside broadcasts being transmitted from it which, in turn, brought more people flocking to Portlyn since the falcons and owls could be seen every day of the week, unlike the house. Eschewing commercialism, the harbour remained unchanged, and fisherman, moaning about the Bretons stealing their lobsters and crabs, took their boats out each day while the cottage tea shop and Harbour Inn did a flourishing trade.

Mark's happiness was complete when Jennie, after two miscarriages, finally managed to give him a daughter. Helen Monique Veryan Curnow was blessed with deep violet eyes and a mass of dark curly hair. A Curnow to her fingertips, she was spoilt by Florence, Mabel and Mark alike. His relationship with his stepson was a good one, probably because he treated the boy as a friend and was always ready with a sympathetic ear, as now, when Alex was anxious over starting his first term at Winchester College tomorrow. The subject had not been pushed aside but discussed openly and intelligently so that Alex began to relax, feeling there was a solid background behind him no matter what he might come up against at school.

Jennie meanwhile had dragged Charles and Dodo from their house near St Ives and set them to work in the library doing what they did

441

best, cataloguing books, old manuscripts, and restoring the ancient ledgers giving details of the estate in the seventeenth and eighteenth centuries. It would take years but Dodo was back in her element, which didn't surprise Florence who'd had her marked down as a blue stocking from the first moment they had met and still did not understand why her son had married such a dowdy creature.

And so, after five years of gruelling hard work, a slightly shabby historic country house with a 'lived in' look which visitors liked, was able to look the future in the eye without land or labourers being lost.

Jennie walked out of the studio into the golden light of a September evening. House martins swooped and cut through the still evening air. Inland the harvest was in, while the pastures were rich with damp, sweet-smelling grass. In the distance she could hear the sound of the sea and thought of Alex, all packed and ready for a new life. She and Mark would drive him to Winchester in the morning. How she would miss him. He was so nervous, poor boy, that Mark had taken him riding earlier and both were probably now in the mews so that Alex could say goodbye to the falcons. Turning towards it, she thought of the letter received from Jamie saying he would be staying with his father at St Ives for the weekend and hoped they could all get together. Of course they would. It was a pity he would miss Alex but as a Junior Doctor, Jamie's days off were limited. Florence still thought he was the son of Dodo's friend.

Jennie had only covered a short distance towards the field where the centre stood when she saw her son and husband riding towards her, a hooded peregrine on Mark's gloved fist, the springer spaniel bounding along beside them.

"I was just coming to find you," she said.

Mark grinned down at her. "I promised Alex he could fly Esmerelda before leaving for Winchester. Shall we try Farthing Field?"

The wooded path smelt fresh and earthy, the trees and bushes tinged with gold in the mellow evening sunlight and Farthing Field a peaceful pasture still. Jennie wondered how it would have looked had Clive been given his head and covered the whole place with hideous caravans or sold the land to developers.

Mark handed Esmerelda over to Alex then removed the little hood. The peregrine swivelled her head, black eyes staring, beak parting as she lifted her wings.

Jennie was a little anxious, knowing that Alex was nervous of the falcons. He loved to watch them but had never touched one. No one had forced him to try, they'd just waited until he asked, and if he never had then that was all right too. Today Alex had asked.

Mark gave quiet instructions to his stepson, explaining how to hold

442

the jesses and untie the knot with his teeth. Then he walked into the centre of Farthing Field and prepared the lure. At his command, Alex let slip the jesses and the peregrine was off, soaring and swooping, tiny bells ringing in the warm air. At last the falcon settled on the lure, the spaniel moved forward and settled down beside her. When she had eaten her prey, Mark picked up Esmerelda and settled her back on Alex's glove. The boy caught the jesses securely then walked the pony back across the field. The mount became restive suddenly, the falcon baited. Alarmed by the beating wings, Alex was also afraid she would hurt herself as she tugged at the jesses. Before he knew it he had let them slip through his fingers and Esmerelda was off. She hovered above them for a brief moment then veered seaward.

Alex watched in horror. "She's gone. I'm sorry ... I'm sorry."

Mark cantered on to the cove with the spaniel running before him. Alex urged the pony forward and Jennie ran behind. By the time she caught up with them, the peregrine was soaring higher and higher as gulls gathered to mob the predator. Mark had dismounted and was heading up the cliff. She saw him reach the top then, standing against the light, stretch out his arm.

Mortified, Alex kept saying: "I'm sorry ... I'm sorry I let her go. I let Esmerelda go. Will she come back ... will she?"

Jennie smiled. "Sophie always did. In any case, Esmerelda's used to free flight. She can be very naughty at times, staying up long after we want her down. We just have to be patient. See how high she's gone to shake off the gulls?"

How still the falcon was against the pink-tinged mackerel sky. The gulls tired, thought they had chased off the predator, and flew away. Still the peregrine hovered. Jennie looked at Mark waiting on the clifftop with outstretched arm and thought she could be ten years old again. Suddenly she felt so at peace with the world, so happy with Mark, her children, and her life at Trevellan. It was good to see the estate picking up. It was good to see her father almost daily. It was good to see the wings of a falcon above the cove once more.

Esmerelda stooped, homed in on Mark, swerved and made a perfect landing on his wrist. "I told you she would come back." Jennie smiled at her anxious son, then gazed out to sea, feeling the cool breeze blowing through her hair. Once she had thought she would never return. But, like the falcon, she had. They all had, all who belonged to Trevellan – all that is, except one.

You have been reading a novel published by Piatkus Books. We hope you have enjoyed it and that you would like to read more of our titles. Please ask for them in your local library or bookshop.

If you would like to be put on our mailing list to receive details of new publications, please send a large stamped addressed envelope (UK only) to:

Piatkus Books: 5 Windmill Street
London W1P 1HF

PIATKUS
The sign of a good book